A NOVEL

JAY TYVON

tyvonbooks

tyvonbooks
P.O. Box 4419
Dublin, GA 31040
www.jaytyvon.com

The poem "Plain and Simple" appears courtesy of Mye Janan and Big J Publishing.

ISBN-13: 978-0-9790123-0-3
ISBN-10: 0-9790123-0-9
LCCN: 2006909810

Cover design: www.mariondesigns.com

First Edition: February 2008

Manufactured and Printed in the United States of America

For information regarding distribution and bulk order discounts, please contact Tyvon Books at: info@jaytyvon.com

Dedications

I dedicate this book to three very important ladies—the matriarchs of my life,
each having uniquely labored in love on my behalf.

To my *Grandmother* …in loving memory,
for her inspiration and faith.
In her pain, she taught us the meaning of standing in the will of God—
unconditionally. We're missing you.

To my *Mother*,
for all her silent prayers.
We thank you for the life you vested in us
…the nurturing, the time, and the love.
We appreciate and love you for it.

To my *Wife* …and my life,
for her relentless enthusiasm to follow God above all else.
…Her energy tends to be contagious.
For the push, every now and then, to keep me moving in the right direction.
(Though you may beg to differ—smile.)
All that you do—hasn't gone unnoticed.
Love, *Cletus*

He who does not love does not know God, for God is love.
(1 John 4:8 NKJV)

Prologue

Plain & Simple

Nothing is plain and simple anymore.
I thought that with age the "understanding" would be clearer.
It's clear, yes clear, clear as the mud that has formed beneath my feet from my tears.
Funny enough, even the tears were unclear.
I've cried and I still cry when I'm happy, when I'm sad and even confused.

I thought with time the understanding would be certain.
I'm certain, real certain.
Certain that I'm probably more confused today than before.
Well, it's because the feelings that I thought I could keep at bay have become my wants.
They've become my needs—not my maintenance.
It has never been less plain or simple.

I'm at a place in life where I want to be selfish,
And I have to remind myself not to respond to your sweetness.
Not to respond to your warming touch.
Not to harbor the happiness that you bring.
Not to let myself express more than you do to me.

Not to squelch the fervor that you approach "us" with.
It's as if I'm waiting on the real you to unveil—the tart lemony you.
It's as if I had forgotten that there are things other than the sun that warm.
It's as if I worry that there is no happiness left in the coffer for tomorrow.
It's as if I think that my feelings will scare you far, far away.
There's nothing less plain or simple today.

If someone had told me that unadulterated feelings would come to me again,
Well, I would have scoffed, laughed, and told them it was unlikely.
You see I am woman with lots of testosterone and very few needs.
But I need you.
I've left my first sense.
No, I've left all my senses except the ones that you bring to life.

There's no one else in my life although it seems that way to you.
There's no other fire burning, no other caress.
There's no other person desired the way I yearn for you.
I wish things were plain or simple.
I can't sleep through the night without first hearing you wish me pleasant dreams.
I can't get through the day without your charter into the slaving hours.

It's not plain what you bring to my life.
It's not simple because years, people and time will add variables.
Variability isn't something that my heart is ready to embrace again.
The clock has struck twelve before and off into the sunset went my dreams.
I want to believe that this time things will be different.

So I lie beside you and listen as the minutes go by.
I want to tell you that I'll be with you forever,
But your forever may not include me.
I want to tell you that I'm not afraid of commitment,
But, I'm really afraid to commit.

I want to listen and help you fix things broken in your life;
Help you heal when you get bruised.
I want to make each moment a memorable one,
All of these thoughts because in the morning I'll have to leave
But I hope to return to your arms, to your charms.

It seems so plain and simple for you.
You seem to be able to satisfy me and stay unattached
Care for me without caring too much

Make love to me without loving me
But this is just what I think and I'll not ask.

It would be much more plain and simple
More simple, if being with you meant you'd be here, not there
More plain if being with you could involve less of my heart.
Somehow we understand that what we have isn't simple or plain,
But it's good.
It's good for you—good for me.
Simply, plainly—just good;
Good enough for right here and right now.

-Mye Janan

It's with a yawning sigh that she—a figure of blurred emotions removes the reading glasses from her jaded face. Sliding comfortably underneath quilted covers, the thought-spent woman places a satin bookmark once used as a wedding announcement between these familiar, often-read pages. She soon closes the jacketless hardbound edition of Contemporary African-American poetry having meditated on the passage and it's uncanny resemblance to her own life, then tosses the book next to a Vaio laptop which has vicariously taken permanent residence amid the seldom-occupied vacancy on her queen-sized bed. It's soon after turning down the lights—and scooching her petite frame into its favorite nighttime position that she drifts into a sound slumber. "…*Goodnight Justin.*" She incoherently mumbles in her sleep now deeply committed to a dream.

one

The Morning After

A half sleep—half-inebriated Justin Vaughn stumbles out of the warm cozy confines of his down linen bed and onto the cold boundaries of a marble-inspired granite bathroom. After shrugging off the affects of the inverse climate, he leans across his Corian basin—intently gazing into the oval shaped vanity that lies just above. With eyes stretched wide—he examines the aftermath of the night before.

"*Damn.* I'm too old for this shit!"

The image would reveal the blood stained eyes of a man who had spent the greater part of the night, out partying amongst friends—a few drinks, a little smoke, only to return home to share an intimate encounter with unfamiliar bedfellows.

For Justin, yesterday was a damn good day—reason for celebration. Things were finally coming together, his years of sacrificial labor were beginning to pay off. On the horizon, a promotion—and even better, one of relocating consequence. Not that he wasn't happy where he was—for he epitomizes the personality of the city for which he was born—Atlanta, GA—the ATL.

With his new assignment he heads northwest to the "Windy City"—the Chi, Chicago, IL. Home of the original pimp—Don "Magic" Juan, his long fantasized idol. Here Justin will have a chance to break new ground—conquer uncharted territories. It would represent a fresh start to a seemingly exasperated career. Sho' Nuff Entertainment—a division of Arista Records and run by Chicago native, CEO and founder Rico Pittman, now had the go ahead from its parent company Arista to form a parallel organization to explore and develop new talent in the mid west. It would be Justin's responsibility to find and cultivate such talent in his new role as A&R Director.

Now awake, he takes a step back unveiling the reflected image of his full upper torso. In recognition of his latest accomplishments he gives himself some overdue acclamation.

"It's about damn time. I'm runnin' shit—head nigga in charge." he mumbles.

Taking his left hand across his face, he discovers his apparent need for a shave. Already naked, he steps into the lavish all-glass shower stall. As the steamy water cascades off his fatigued body it washes away any residue of unprotected sex left behind from his early morning exploits. He reflects on the previous night's festivities—especially the private ones. Smiling to himself, he quietly utters, "It's official—I'm the shit!"

His latest conquest was Tonya Campbell. Tonya was a local up and coming poet, whom he had been introduced to about two weeks prior at an area showcase for undiscovered talent. She would become his most prevailing folly. At the age of 28, and being a veteran of the underground circuit, she knew of Justin and his position at Sho' Nuff. She requested to meet him in hopes of igniting her slow smoldering calling. Unaware of what she was inviting herself into, Tonya committed willingly within Justin's cycle of never-ending drama.

Stepping back out of the shower while reaching for a razor inside the medicine cabinet concealed behind the vanity, Justin bumps one of several miscellaneous hygiene products causing a chain reaction of descending personal items. In his sink topples a bottle of half-used tetracycline. A painful reminder of repercussions once served for sexual escapades carelessly rendered.

"Shit! …Betta hang on ta these after last night. Hell yeah! Y'all know how I get down!" He remarks as though he's quite proud of his repugnant accomplishments. Picking up the bottle, he reads "October 11, 2004" and immediately replies, "Skank bitch!" referring to the woman from whom he had contracted the STD. Yet this was the life for which he led—far removed from the young man whom so eloquently graced the Leon County Civic Center stage some ten years ago in Tallahassee, on his way to receiving a BA in Arts & Science from FAMU, Florida A& M University.

Deferred dreams had stolen his innocence and shaken his pride. Years of obscure mediocrity had inadvertently taken his incentive. His failures renown—his successes removed. Contentment sets in as the dream fades. Simple pleasures become idols and idols become Gods. For Justin, women were the addiction, as the lasciviousness of sex became its release. Yet this is exactly what his life has been so drastically reduced to—finding significance through the fulfillment of his dick's every desire. It's in his continuous need of attaining affirmation that Justin loses himself. *Love* as defined by Justin, would be while in the middle of climaxing—having the capacity to utter such erroneous propaganda in the ear of the woman who has innate ability to make him feel—just that gooood! Love to Justin—is lust—nothing more, nothing less. His entire life is a facade, and as good as it may appear on the outside, the inside reeks of loneliness—echoing the years of disappointment and pain. His silent screams represent a childhood lost—and the beguiled memories of a father that never allowed a boy to be a boy. And with bitterness still in his heart, he continues the legacy as seen through the life of his very seed.

As Justin leaves the bathroom, he is drawn to the projection over in the far corner of the ceiling—7:42am, and now sensing the urgency to get dressed to be out of the house by 8:00am. While moving toward the closet, he notices a piece of paper lying amidst the wrinkled sheets that drape across his soiled bed. It's a note from Tonya—who has apparently let herself out at some point before Justin awoke. Upon further examination, he recognizes the scent of Sand & Sable— Tonya's favorite fragrance dispersed across the small memo. Its contents—all of two words—"CALL ME". Justin sarcastically smirks while simultaneously balling up the note and tossing it in the nearest wastebasket. For it would be an abomination of his character to do such a thing. He was not about to send out any perceivable mixed signals of an advancing relationship. What had happened the night before was nothing more than your everyday, garden variety, run of the mill—SEX! Two people just enjoying each other's company. That's it—that's all!

To Justin commitment meant allowing compromise into his life. He tried that once. And all he was left with was a summons of child support and an ensuing custody battle. That experience in itself left a bad enough taste in his mouth to never repeat. It would also cause an adjustment in lifestyle—an interruption in plan. For he had worked long and hard in building this persona for himself: Mr. Justin Vaughn—man about town and ladies love, a local celebrity in certain circles. What's funny—to the average Joe, a catch like Tonya Campbell would be the ultimate blessing from the skies above. A pedestal piece that any man would love to love. A thick caramel-coated hazel eyed beauty enswathed in long naturally wavy sandy brown hair and infused with the ethnicity of India—easily making her a ten. Her temperament added also to the attraction—one of peace and compassion. But Justin, who has been linked to supermodels and other notable personalities, kept a slew of pretty horses in and around his stable. Tonya would only signify just another notch on the old belt. A prime choice cut of sirloin ready to be tasted.

Finally inside of his nearly room-sized closet, Justin detects the faint distant sound of music vibrating from the floor below, acknowledging the either early departure or late arrival of his younger brother Jerome. As Justin recognizes the tune playing beneath his feet, he nods—bobbing his head back and forth, obliterating the words of the latest Destiny Child track "Girl".

"*Yyeeaahh*—that's that shit. ...*Gurrrl*—I can tell you've been crying, and you're needing someone to talk to—*Gurrrl*..."

While attempting to sing, he flips through his vast array of designer clothing—stopping upon his choosing of a baby blue fleece Sean John sweatsuit, which is quickly yanked from its hanger to surmise his suspicion of a light workload today at the office.

"That's cool. Ain't shit goin' on this morning...I ain't gotta meet with nobody!" He ponders that thought as he questions the validity of his own statement. He then grabs a pair of baby blue and white Reeboks amongst the numerous pairs of tennis shoes that litter his closet floor.

Once dressed, Justin performs a quick inventory of personal effects. "Wallet—good, keys—good, cell phone—good. Damn—I almost forgot...," as he trots over to the other side of the bed, grabbing a Targus leather carrying case equipped with a Dell notebook that is inseparable to his duties at the office. "8:10am," a last second glance at the projected time above his head. "Shit! Let me take my ass on," as he walks out the bedroom door realizing that he may easily be late considering the usual morning rush hour traffic on I-285. On his descent down the staircase, he's greeted by Jerome on his way up the stairs toward his room.

"What up?"

"What's up man?"

"Shit!"

"Just gettin' in?"

"Yeah—we finished BeeGee's shit last night."

"Word! I know dat shit's hot?"

"Hell yeah! …His shit gonna blow up the South!"

"Word! …Was Rico out there?"

"Hell, ya know he was—probably til about two, you know how he is—got to be overseein' shit. Nigga don't trust a nigga for shit."

"Good. That'll give me a few extra minutes. I know that nigga ain't gonna bring his ass up in there by no nine o' clock."

"Hell nah."

"Al-ight then—let me bounce."

"Alright."

The two brothers share a two-story 2800 square feet brick home quietly nestled in the West Atlanta suburbs located off Cascade Road. Vaulted ceilings and hardwoods throughout, highlight this impressive structure, with two huge master bedrooms situated in a loft setting overlooking the living room—further enhanced by the 16 foot massive stone constructed fireplace. Words could not begin to describe the beauty of this exquisitely designed domicile. Even the basement boasts of a state of the art 48-track digital recording studio constructed for the likings of baby brother Jerome, who has been the most recent influential force behind the Sho' Nuff sound. With the success of Rico's latest artist lineup, Jerome has been thrust into the limelight for his production talents becoming one of the most sought-after producers in the industry.

Their bond is close—two men living one dream, from humble beginnings haven arisen through adversity. Yet they couldn't be more different in personality and moral principles—living together, working together, but that's where the similarity ends. Jerome—a man of few words, is consumed by his passion for music. A perfectionist of his craft, he has little time or regard for the social bureaucratic aspects of the industry. He would much rather stay behind the scenes conceptualizing beats and experimenting with new sounds. His persona is one of quiet—yet measured rule. A chronic thinker of calculated actions who never jumps into anything without careful evaluation. A standard he follows in everything—whether business or pleasure. While Justin on the other hand, selfish and shallow-minded at times, only entered the profession merely by mistake. Yeah Justin loves music, but he also loves the perks even more—the clout, the women, and of course—the money! For Justin has always put his mouth where the money's at—and one must, to understand his profession. Seen by his peers as a natural born bull-shitter and pathological liar, he uses manipulation to get what he wants—easily gaining access into the naïve mind. A simple twist of the truth goes a long way in his business, as it takes that to be the best. And without a doubt—Justin is at the top of his game. He's very cunning with words and smooth with the tongue. In a world where there are so few fish—and so many fishermen, his bait has to be better than the rest. Therefore, what he dangles has to be the shit! With so few exceptional artists on the market and every Tom, Dick, and Harry company vying for the same talent, it's his job to stand above the crowd—putting the perception that there is no better record label than Sho' Nuff Entertainment—as his livelihood depends on it.

two

21 Peachtree Plaza

Sitting under a stop light at the corner of Cascade and Childress, Justin, while admiring the interior detail of his new 2005 Dub Edition Chrysler 300C, flip flops between Hot 107.9 and V103 morning shows on the Infinity stereo system. He rolls the windows down—leans his left arm out of the opening while his right hand remains on the steering wheel. Justin, now sporting a pair of non-prescription "Transitions" eyewear, gazes from behind the smoke tint generated by the bright early morning sun. He's in peep mode—trying to see everything he can see, while in the process—being seen himself. It's become a morning ritual ever since he and Jerome moved into the area. The Cascade District reaps of affluence—with a higher concentration of sophisticated, educated, and largely single independent fine ass black women—Justin's specialty! And so every morning—in right about this same spot, spontaneously the stereo seems to get a little louder, the windows come down as the shades go on, and the ride tends to slow down in this high traffic region of his daily journey.

On this morning, as he gets good into his usual campaign—his cell phone rings. And resonating from its speaker is a weak rendition of Africa Bambataa and SoulSonic Force's "Planet Rock," reflecting the generation of his musical origin. Swiveling open the receiver after the second ring—he answers.

"What up?"

"Hey—whatcha doin'?" replies a female voice.

"On my way to work. What's up?"

"How did it go last night?"

"What do you mean how do it go? You know how it went…I tapped that ass!" Justin replies with confident swagger.

The voice on the other end bursts into hysterical laughter retorting, "Boy—you stupid!"

And Justin, imitating his favorite Chris Tucker character, Smokey, from the movie *Friday* blurts, "And you know dis!" Both continue to laugh. Justin realizing his upcoming approach on to the habitually congested 285 expressway, cuts the conversation short. "*Hey—whatcha doin' later?*"

"Nuthin'—why?"

"I'll come thru—cool?"

"*Yeeaahh*," she replies softly. For that was music to her ears. A visit from the man she has secretly loved for years—just made her day. "Bye Boo." She finishes her part of the conversation.

"Holla." Justin then hangs up the phone.

The female voice on the other end of the conversation was none other than Jackie Hewitt, Justin's best friend and #1 fan. For years Jackie had been diligently by his side—long before his rise into the public spotlight. During those early days when he considered himself "po', broke, and lonely—busted and disgusted"—and always seemingly on life's short end, she was there feeding him, supporting him in whatever capacity she could—even at the sacrifice of her own marriage. She is Justin's rock—the wind beneath his wings—that ride or die chick who's always been down for whatever. They've been through the cycle of being friends—and then lovers—and back around as friends more than a time or two. For Justin she represents the only stable, cordially maintained female relationship to have graced his life. When he needs someone to talk to—it's her number he dials, any day or hour. She's always there. Yet he remains blind to the actual depth of her romantic feelings for him. What Justin sees as loyalty is actually unconditional love. A love strong enough to bear watching Justin go through his countless sexual encounters, with all the play by play accounts, while still having the ability to smile despite her own personal agony.

And yet, even in this relationship, Justin manages to let his true shallow colors shine gloriously through. For as good of a woman that Jackie is, she doesn't meet the physical standards of his reputation. Therefore, she will always remain in the backdrop of his life—never the leading lady. Though still very attractive, the years have added pounds to her already curvaceous figure. Now at about 180 lbs., this tall red big-boned woman has fallen completely off of Justin's sexual radar. His interest in her is only as an appreciative and devoted friend.

As he passes the Old National Highway exit, Justin sees that traffic will quickly be coming to a stand still. Taking a glimpse downward at the clock on the analog display that reads 8:42am, he realizes that he's definitely going to be late for work. He then relaxes his tense disposition muttering under his breath.

"Fuck it—oh well!" He pauses and says, "Damn I hate to hear this nigga's mouth."

He then proceeds to reach for his cell. This time, he connects one of those hands-free headsets to the side of the phone. Using voice-activated dialing, he says, "Teresha".

His phone automatically dials the number—he hears her phone ringing. She picks up.

"Hello?"

"What up?"

"*Heeey!*" as she recognizes his voice.

"How's everything?"

"We're doing fine. How 'bout you? You're hard to catch these days."

"I'm cool—you know how shit is right about now—its hectic! I ain't even had time ta think."

"By the way—congratulations on your promotion. I heard about it through the grapevine—you've earned it!"

"Appreciate. That's what I wanted to talk to you about—Justice. What are we goin' to do 'bout him? I'll be in the Chi."

"I know—but I don't know what to say. He worships you! You're an important part of his life. He'll miss you."

"And what 'bout you?" he advertently flips the statement.

"Stop!" as she blushes in the background. "This ain't about me. It's about our son—and his feelings."

"That's what I wanted to ask you…let him come with me. He's thirteen now—he needs a man to become a man," repeating one his father's classic proverbs.

There's silence. She's the first to speak.

"You know I can't do that. I can't let you do that. Look at your lifestyle! When would you have time for a child? You said it yourself… You don't even have time to think."

"I can do this. I'll work it out!"

"Justin you're full of it. I don't want my son stuck somewhere in some far away city with nobody while *yo* ass is off doin' whatever! I can't do it. *Hell no!*" Her tone becomes angered as she reflects on the many broken promises and fabricated stories she experienced during their life together.

"But baby it's not goin' to be like that—you'll see!"

"Justin, who do you think you're talking to? I know you! And it ain't gonna happen. I said *NO!* …End of conversation!"

He hears nothing but a dial tone. She's obviously hung up on him. Devastated by her response—he flings the headset to the floor.

"Stupid bitch. FUCK you!"

Quite shaken by the conversation, he nearly misses his turn onto 75N. His slow simmering anger turns to a quick boil. Heated, he begins to blurt out his frustrations.

"Fuck her—I'm tired of her shit! She can't play me like that! I got a lawyer—fuck that! TAKE custody from her ass! She ain't gonna *play* me like this! …Who in the *FUCK* does she think she is? …That's *MY* son! Ain't no other mutha fucka gonna raise *MY* kid! I'll kill her mutha fuckin' ass. …Fuck wit me! …That's my goddamn son!"

Justin, who's by now visibly upset, is swerving out of his lane causing other vehicles to avoid hitting him. A horn beeps from his left side. Justin leans out and shouts, "Fuck you!" as the car passes.

Here's a side of him that few have seen—stored anger and hostility that has haunted him for most of his adult life. The years of abuse that he and his brother experienced during their childhood has taken its toll on Justin. The animosity he feels toward his estranged father has begun to spew outwardly and openly to those closest to him. He begins to sob, realizing that he's way out of control.

Upon exiting the expressway, Justin collects himself knowing that he is only a few blocks away from work. This latest conversation reinforces his decision not to attempt a reconciliation of the relationship—not even for the sake of his son. He and Teresha went a long way back, but from day one they seemed to find ways to bump heads, both stubborn, strong-minded individuals—unwilling to grant concessions. In Teresha, Justin met his match. He can't control her like other women—and that's what pisses him off. When it comes to her it doesn't take much to get the spark started. She is the constant thorn in his side. Once upon a time—he loved her—and yet the relationship didn't work. Thus it changed the way he looks at all women—as nothing more than *bitches* and *hoes*.

Within minutes, he pulls in front of this colossal, fifty plus story office centerplex housing some of the most prominent businesses in the country—21 Peachtree Plaza, home of Sho' Nuff Entertainment. As Justin enters the underground parking facility, he must travel some three levels below to finally find an open park. With one last look at the clock—at 9:21am, he wastes no time getting to an elevator. On his way up, he tries to remember if he's seen a black chromed-out H2 parked anywhere signifying the arrival of his boss—Rico Pittman. The elevator stops on the twenty-sixth floor and once the stainless steel doors open, Justin steps around the corner where the offices rest directly adjacent to his position. "The House of Glass" as it's affectionately known, represents the solid glass walls and doorway that compose the front entrance of Sho' Nuff. Stretching from the ceiling to the floor, anyone who passes by can clearly view all activity within the main lobby. Clean lines and contemporary furnishings punctuate the interior décor. To understand the internal design is to know CEO and founder, Rico Pittman—smooth, clean, and minimal.

He greets the girls at the front desk, while making his way to his office. "Hey ladies."

"Hey Mr. Vaughn." Two voices speak in perfect unison.

"Y'all al-ight?"

"Yes Mr. Vaughn." Again—the two speaking on one accord.

Smiling, Justin asks, "Have y'all seen Rico today?"

One of the girls responds, "No sir—he hasn't made it in yet."

Walking away, he thanks the ladies for their cooperation and leaves one tidbit of parting wisdom. "Oh by the way ladies, just call me Justin."

The two giggle amongst themselves as Justin continues down the hall. After grabbing a cup of decaf, he enters his office—a modest space with a few pictures and no real color palette. Laying his bag on the desk, he first checks for any messages, then unzips the leather carrying case—unpacking its contents. Taking a second to unwind, he stares out the window exposing the beautiful Atlanta skyline. And like his morning mocha, it's meditation to his soul—a small piece of tranquility. Justin, caught in the moment, loses himself. His door suddenly swings open.

"Wake yo ass up nigga!" It's Dee, other wise known as Demetrius McPhail, a recent addition to the Sho' Nuff A&R family as a transferee from Connecticut by way of Def Jam Soul. "Where the fuck you been?" he asked, harping on the fact that Justin is a few minutes late as usual. To know Dee is to either love him or hate him, his silly antics have already become legendary with the office associates. Quickly, he has gained Justin's trust and comradeship—in and out of the office.

"So when we headed for the Chi?"

Justin, checking over the itinerary answers, "Monday, we're takin' a flight out from Hartsfield-Jackson International to Chicago Midway on Airtran."

"*Airtran.* Y'all niggas down here are cheap man! …Ain't this the home of Delta? Y'all niggas can't get a discount or sumthin'? Where's dat nigga Rico?" Dee playfully runs off at the mouth—as he would any other time.

"Chill nigga—it's all good! Jus leaves us a lil' sumptin' to play with," brags Justin.

"Oh, it's like that?"

"*Yeah*—it's like that!"

By this time Shantel, Justin's assistant, slips through the doorway. Both turn in acknowledgment of her entrance. Dee speaks.

"What's up Shantel—Shante'—Ashanti' or whatever the hell you call yourself. …Po' ass need ta find her an identity—and stick to it." Both men laugh. Once again, Dee speaks after further examining Shantel's very slender figure.

"Homegirl sufferin' from that disease—NoAssAtol!" Their laughter gets louder.

Shantel, now fed up with Dee's sarcasm comes back with, "Shut da hell up—ig'nant ass!"

Dee quickly rebuttals, "Grow you sum ass—*beeeotch!*"

Disgusted, Shantel walks away.

After a couple more minutes of idle discussion, Shantel buzzes Justin.

"Rico's here and he wants to talk to you—*NOW!*"

"Al-ight," Justin reluctantly answers. Dee takes it as his cue to leave.

Justin analytically rambles through the possibilities of reasons why Rico would so urgently want to see him. He comes up empty as he approaches Rico's door—three offices across the hall. Justin lightly taps on the door. Rico invites him in.

"What up Riq—I heard you wanted to see me?" In one motion Justin has found his way to the first of three ergonomic leather and chrome executive chairs that line the front of Rico's desk. To be in Rico's office for any first time visitor would be 1200 square feet of "shock and awe," laced with exotic artwork, at least four plasma monitors—leather and chrome everything, a 250 gallon aquarium, walls lined with platinum and gold plaques, and a who's who of framed photos and other accolades gathered over the years in a special display called "the wall of fame." Imposing—yet quite inspiring!

Rico, a medium complexioned young black entrepreneur in his late twenties—maybe thirty at the most, stands about 5' 8"—and no more than 160lbs. Always well-dressed, he keeps a clean cut with just a tinge of facial hair, with his upper body covered with tattoos—looking like a thug turned prince—your typical ghetto superstar. He's a self-made man who happens to be young, gifted, and black—the same ole' story seen across the board with the rise of Hip Hop in today's society. Rico, who's not one for mincing words—gets straight to the point.

"Y'all takin' Tae (Shantel) wit cha to Chicago."

"Al-ight. Can I ask why?" Justin answers with stuttered inquiry.

"First—because I said so. Second—because I know she'll keep y'all niggas straight! This ain't no pleasure trip—this is all 'bout business. We gotta get *dem* girls signed. ...I need you to close the deal next week."

"Riq, you know I got it!" Changing the subject, Justin brings up the night before. "Rome told me 'bout the session last night. Said BeeGee gonna take the South."

"Yeah—we hope so. If we keep a nigga out of jail."

Justin smirks. Rico continues to talk.

"Your boy Dee—you need to talk to him. Tell him to calm his little ass down. I spoke to Tae—I ain't havin' it! Either he calms the fuck down or I'm puttin' his ass out on some sexual harassment bullshit! We ain't catchin' no lawsuit on his petty shit. I mean that Jay! I ain't havin' it—betta talk to him."

Justin, feeling the pressure of that last demand, simply tells Rico "I got it," then commences to walk out of his office. Knowing the tone of Rico's voice, it meant that the conversation was over.

Headed back to his office, Justin passes Shantel in the hallway, who doesn't make eye contact—obviously feeling the guilt behind telling Rico of Dee's actions. He wanting to desperately say something makes a rare concession—bites his tongue and walks away shaking his head. There's this love/hate thing going on between he and Shantel. Under normal conditions, the two get along quite well. In fact, they make a great team. But Shantel doesn't really fit in with that *it* crowd while Justin does. She wants to—but doesn't know how. Therefore, she can't run in the same circles as Justin. Yet, she's intelligent, crafty, and organized as she envies Justin's social status—although sometimes to the point of being vindictive. Other times, the two appear to be the best of friends. In keeping the peace, Justin decides to let this latest incident go.

He makes a short detour en route to his office to find Dee. And as suspected, he's up front in the main lobby—fraternizing with the girls at the desk. The group shares a laugh as Justin interrupts.

"Hey man—come holla at me for a minute."

"What up?" Dee, now looking concerned, follows Justin back to his office.

"Man, leave Tae alone—stop fuckin' wit her."

"*What?* I was just teasin' her lil' bony ass."

"Jus don't fuck wit her."

"What? That's from Riq or sumthin'?"

"Jus leave her alone." Justin repeats his plea once more.

"*What's up?* She snitched?"

"Nigga, you heard me! Jus do it!" Justin remarks with a slight grin on face—refusing to concede any more information. They then wander off on some other tangent, changing the course of their discussion.

As initially forecast, the day ends fairly uneventfully. Justin has opted to hangout at the office a little later than usual to avoid the afternoon rush hour. It's now 6:30pm, as he puts away his various things, he abruptly plops back down at his desk—grabbing the phone and dialing "404-419-2727". The line rings—but no ones answers, so he hangs up once the machine picks up—leaving no message. Ready to go, he turns off all lights, secures the premises and heads home.

three

Movin' In Circles

It's late Thursday evening and Justin chooses to make it an early night. In lieu of events the day before, he figures tonight he'll catch up on some much needed rest. Having slipped his mind, he's totally forgotten about Jackie, who sits in her Marietta apartment alone and waiting. Tonight she relives an all too familiar occurrence—hollow promises. For Jackie, who believes in fairy-tales, has patiently waited for the day that she and Justin can finally put all the pieces together. To him, she's given everything—her mind, body, and heart, along with the very spirit to which she has breath—answering his every beckoning call, no matter the sacrifice to her own life. And yet once again she sits all alone—under romantic ambiance, she waits. Finally after the last candle has burned to an ember, she removes a plate from the microwave, placing the untouched cuisine into the refrigerator. With a deep sigh—she prepares for bed.

Across town the two brothers have gathered in their basement studio—critiquing Jerome's latest roster of fresh beats. It has always been understood that the two would one day start their own independent label. Jerome, who is standing, propped against the wall with no shirt divulging his slim 6'4" cut physique, plays in his afrolength dusty brown twists, giving him an even greater height daunting appearance. Justin currently seated at the mixing console—head bobbing as he adjusts the various controls tweaking each individual sound. They reflect on the early days as teens just discovering their love for the music.

"*Maaan*—remember when we ain't have shit but dem two mixmatched Technics' wit dat lil' ass two channel Gemini."

Jerome jumps in. "Yo—hold up! ...Remember how we used to hide dat shit from mom. We'd close the room door—pull da stuff out from under the bed—I'd mix and scratch dem ole' break beats—yo ass be try'na rap and shit."

"Hell, I remember how we wouldn't eat for weeks—try'na save dat lunch money so a nigga could hit the mall on the weekend and get dem 12 inches. ...Remember how we used ta be all in Sam Goody's switchin' stickers and shit? Gettin' whole damn albums for the price of singles. ...*Grand Master Flash, the Sugar Hill Gang...*"

"Hell yeah—I remember all that shit! We'd be into all that. ...You remember break dancin'?" Both laugh.

"Yeah, yo ass thought you were one of dem New York City Breakers or sumptin'. ...Spinnin' on your head—doin' windmills and shit."

"*Nah* hold up nigga!—But wasn't it you runnin' around callin' yo self "Jay Smooth" and shit—leavin' tags all over the city. ...Nigga thought he was some kind of graffiti artist!" More chuckles.

As the laughter subsides, Justin, now feeling sentimental, takes the conversation to a deeper level.

"Man, I miss that shit!"

"I do too." Jerome cosigns the remark.

"Nah—I'm fo real. Gonna miss all this shit. It's all gonna be so different. Nigga, you been my ace *man*—it's gonna feel strange not havin' you close. We put twenty years into this shit—me and you! ...Thru thick and thin—nigga we rose past all the bullshit. Jus look at us—who'd thought we'd be sittin' here surrounded wit all this fancy shit—makin' paper." Justin, referring to his upcoming move to Chicago, confesses his gratitude. "You've always had your shit together. ...For me it ain't been like that. All the shit you've pulled me out of... I wouldn't be here without you. And I appreciate everything you've done. …You my nigga and I love you!" The two stand and embrace.

"I love you, too. But I ain't goin' nowhere nigga. I'll be right here! It's always gonna be me and you. Don't forget we got a label to start!" Jerome comforts his now teary-eyed brother. Seconds later they're interrupted by the sound of soft tapping on the studio door.

The basement has a separate external entrance into the house. Often their visitors will use that door, knowing that much of their time is spent in sessions. It's about 11:45pm, Justin looks to Jerome puzzled—thinking, "Who in the hell is this at damn 12 midnight?" He hollers across the room, "Who is it!" A soft-spoken, yet high-pitched voice answers, "…*Shanice.*"

"Hold on girl!" The two brothers—sharing a similar smirk, return a well-understood glance towards one another. Jerome leaves the room.

Justin opens the door, where a short, conservatively dressed young woman stands before him. Still wearing her gray pin-striped blazer with matching pants, Justin—devilishly thinking to himself, invites her in as there's a lot that can be said about this impromptus young female. Shanice Norris, mother of two, represents Justin's longest running open-ended romantic relationship. For over a year, they have been intimately involved. And to Justin, she is what every playa wants—a low maintenance chick who doesn't ask many questions. He never has to spend time with her kids—he just taps that ass every chance he gets.

Shanice, who's always been enthralled with Justin's presence made evident by the Cheshire cat grin worn on her face, doesn't expect much—and yet puts up with a lot. Cute in that everyday sort of way, she wears her chestnut blonde colored hair long and pressed with highlights. She's also known for her gaudy earrings used as a distraction from the rather sizable mole under the left side of her lip. She too, is one of those women that every man dreams about—a short, nasty, closet freak who's dedicated to always pleasing her man. And Shanice has always gone all out to please Justin as she stands here tonight with a plate in her hand running over with tasty vittles. Baked chicken seasoned with lemon pepper, red beans and rice, apple cinnamon muffins, and broccoli sprinkled with cheese—she definitely knows how to take care of her man.

"Here baby. I brought you a lil' somethin'."

Though appreciative, Justin isn't exactly thinking about food— apparently it's the furthest thing from his mind as he looks at her— indistinctly clothed from head to toe, yet knowing just how fine she was by the curves she wore. While on the same page, Shanice, too, admires the view standing before her, thus unveiling the coy, seductive smile that fictitiously implies her innocence. Not all the way inside, she crowds the open doorway—her forehead glistens from the humid night air. With her prepared plate in one hand, Justin extending his reach, offers the other as they proceed upstairs.

❧   ❧   ❧

The next morning after showering together, Justin, like a gentleman, walks Shanice to her car. The two hold each other close as he gently leans her against the car door. She endorses her approval of last night's lovemaking by softly rubbing across his shirt-unbuttoned chest—whispering the words, "Bye big daddy". They exchange a passionate kiss, Shanice feeling the rapid rise of his nature, figures she better make a clean break—ASAP. She jumps in her car with that— "Damn! I wish I had more time" quickening over her still horny body, then drives off having to pick up the kids from her mother's before eight.

Noticing the flashing red light on his cell phone, Justin races back upstairs to retrieve his messages. He opens the swivel face to play back two messages. The first is from Teresha.

"Hey. I see you called. We went over to the Foot Locker at Greenbriar—Justice just had to have these shoes. …Anyway give us a call back, he wants to talk to you before you leave next week. Bye."

Erasing that message he plays the next.

"Hey lover—where are you? I thought you were supposed to call yesterday. I miss you… Call me back! Peace."

The second message is from Tonya. And now that she's made the first move, he immediately calls her back.

"Hello?"

"What up, what up?" Justin addresses her.

"Hey baby! Where have you been? I missed you boo. I wanted to kick it with you last night." Tonya responds, excited to hear his voice.

"I'm sorry baby—a nigga was busy in the studio last night. I'll tell you what—how 'bout I make it up to you tonight?"

"Talk—I'm listening!"

"Let's do dinner—then we can go check out Club Esso—go back to your place—and kick it."

"Uh hmmm." Realizing it's a set-up—but one which she'll enjoy, she accepts his offer.

"I'll pick you up 'bout eight—cool?"

"I'll be waiting—*bbbyyyeee.*"

"Holla." Justin hits End on his cell. But before he closes the face—he places another call. Again he dials 404-419-2727, Teresha's home phone number. And this time she answers.

"Hello…"

"Hey yo—it's me."

"Hey," she says in an apologetic tone. "I'm sorry about yesterday. I shouldn't have hung up on you—I was wrong."

"Nah we cool.—Has lil' man left for school yet?"

"*Yeeeah.* You just missed him. …Please make sure you call him back tonight—*he's waiting* ta hear from you."

"I am. But hear me out. What y'all doin' in the morning?"

"Nothing I can think of. *Why?* What's up?" She said, obviously curious about his question.

"Let's go to Six Flags. …Me, you, and baby boy."

Surprised she quickly agrees. "Okay—what time?"

"I'll be ova there 'bout nine—straight?"

"Yep!"

"Al-ight we'll see ya then."

"Okay—bye bye!" While in shock Teresha disconnects—now even more baffled by Justin's motive.

Justin recognizes that he has just screwed with Teresha's head, as he sits at the foot of his bed, smiling—knowing that she's going to be pondering, analyzing, and guessing—all day long! And that in itself for Justin will be well worth the $50 admission price per person of tomorrow's outing.

For a change, he's early—by at least 45 minutes. Dressed and ready in a Dolce and Gabbana multicolored striped silk shirt, tie, and black trousers with black leather Chelsea boots trimmed in gold, he parlays the kitchen, seizing the rare opportunity for breakfast. From his seat he peeps in on the Channel 2 morning news for the weather while tackling toast and coffee. The breezy, overcast day will make it easy on his attire as he heads for the office. Today's agenda includes setting a production schedule for Sho' Nuff's top-selling artist—R&B sensation Kyra and her upcoming album, projected to be released exactly a year from now—next May. Kyra, who borders the eccentric, is just in town for today—which means Justin and his team needs to be flexible enough to accommodate her demanding schedule. He and Rico also have a planned meeting to discuss the final details of his Chicago trip on Monday. Foremost on the agenda is a last second walk through of

Justin's strategy to sign hopefully what turns out to be Sho' Nuff's next big thing—ENVY. The two talented young female singer/songwriters make their home in Southside Chicago—Rico's old stomping grounds. And finally, last but not least, Justin must meet with the Marketing and Promotion Department to coordinate plans for BeeGee's promotional campaign.

With all cylinders clicking, Justin and his team breeze through the day's workload. He delegates the Marketing and Promotion assignment to Shantel because of her business savvy. She's usually able to weed through the bureaucracy of bullshit to get what they need done. He puts Dee on getting together Kyra's production essentials—song selection, producers, studio, etc., while Justin meets with Kyra personally over lunch. She has requested for him to meet her at Balazaar's—a pricy, trendy, Mediterranean restaurant located in Buckhead. Here he sits with one of today's biggest musical icons—mingled amongst the general public, she's continuously signing autographs and promenading amidst her many adoring fans, leaving Justin highly annoyed and unable to tend to the business at hand. His attention is diverted elsewhere as he explains.

"I'm looking at this bitch—who da hell does she think she is? ...*Whitney?* Had me ta come out here and ain't talkin' 'bout shit! Hell—we coulda did this at the office. Got me out here wastin' my time. ...I got otha shit I need ta be doin'! Hell—she ain't the only muthafucka selling records!" Justin impatiently taps his heel against the laminate flooring while observing the melting pot of personalities who frequent the establishment.

He sees from across the crowded restaurant, standing by the swinging double doors leading to the kitchen—a tall, dark Amazonian queen fixed on his position—and staring dead in his face. He plays it off, returning his focus to the neglectful Kyra. Waiting for the right opportunity, he glances back toward her general direction—she's still looking! This time, Justin takes a more informative glimpse, noticing her long white half-buttoned satin blouse and tight fitting short black skirt. He concludes that she's a part of the working staff—maybe a hostess or something. By the detail of her accessorized physical package—nails, hair, makeup, and jewelry, it was easy to see that she wasn't laborious enough to be a waitress or server. He could also tell that she was without doubt high-maintenance—but damn if she wasn't beautiful! Feeling confident of her attraction to him, he boldly gestures for her to come over. And she, being very resourceful, grabs a round serving plate—writing her name and number on one of two napkins, then turning her written information face down. She places two glasses along with a bottle of White Merlot on the tray. Then she brings the "on the house" drinks over to the table, placing his glass on top of her scribbled data. She smiles, and walks away—never looking back. Flipping the napkin over, he reads, "Porsha Sparks—770-526-1888," wondering if she's also in the entertainment business as he sarcastically alludes to the *professionalism* of her name. Porsha Sparks, whose name sounded like that of a stripper's or an adult movie actress, has the potential reality of each blown off as—WHATEVER! For there are only two words to describe this chocolate, slender offering—*too sexy*. Her voluptuously proportioned frame has Justin fantasizing about the age-old myth of skinny women and the depth of their snatch. He discretely folds the napkin twice and places it in his front shirt pocket.

After an hour and a half of eating, boozing, and bullshit, Kyra's manager Dave Westin, a seasoned vet within the industry, now joins the tipsy diva at the table. His experienced presence gets the dialogue moving, as he, a man of many clients, is also pressed for time. Along with the formalities of her future project, a possible collaboration with BeeGee on the remix of his debut single is thrown into the discussion. Justin's proposal presents itself as a golden opportunity for Kyra to expand her fan base with hip-hop audiences—a win-win for all concerned. With both parties coming to a mutual agreement, the meeting is adjourned only minutes after it starts. Justin takes care of the $125 tab—courtesy of Sho' Nuff.

Now with his business finished, it's time for a little well-desired pleasure. "…Where's she at?" as Justin looks around the nearly vacant restaurant for Ms. Sparks. But—no Porsha, leaving him intrigued to find out more about this mysterious seductress. "I GOT-ta call her ass when I get back," referencing to the moment when he returns from his week long trip. On his way back to the office—his cell rings. The LED on the top of his Verizon phone flashes red, alerting Justin of a recent message. He scrolls down his menu options until he finds the envelope icon and presses send to play it back.

"Yo—it's Riq, I'm goin' to be out of da office fo da rest of the day. Hey—when y'all get ta Midway—my boy Thad Staley gonna pick y'all up and take y'all where you need to be. Everythin's arranged. Tell Tae to holla at me. Make it happen! …One."

With that, Justin's day is complete; he hits the interstate—75 south to the downtown connector, his next stop 3142 Mt. Gilead Road—

home! There he takes a minute to relax and prepare for tonight's date with Tonya. He reflects on the week's tally. Will it be three days in a row in some ass? Pondering the odds as he enters through the front foyer, Justin passes a 3x5 mahogany framed mirror, where he stops—and in arrogance, admires the larger-than-life image he sees of himself. But conviction causes question as he also feels the contriteness of his actions and begins to talk to himself in poetic-like thought.

"There's more to me than meets the eye. ...More to me than what the eye can see. And what the eye does see is just one part of me—a small part—my favorite part. But it's me—who I am; and yet it seems so shallow—right? I don't have to be like this—I just want to. ...As they love me—I love them back. They kiss me—so I kiss them back. Therefore they need me as much as I need them. I'm that someone ta hold they ass at night—and tell them that they're loved. ...There ain't nuthin' wrong wit that—right? They need me—like I need them."

A perceptually challenged Justin hustles up the stairs to change clothes, skipping every other step until he reaches the top. After a quick wash up over the sink, he rubs his neck and chest with cologne by Armani, then puts on an Olive and white silk polka dot shirt and navy wool sailor pants with leather strap detail for a more festive look.

7:24pm.

He gives himself one last look-over, brushing in the waves on his low cut fade. While standing there, he deliberates on how to put an early end to his night with Tonya, already thinking ahead to tomorrow's planned activities with Teresha and Justice. As much as he would like to luxuriate in tonight's engagement, he knows he needs to save something for the morning. It's not everyday that he gets a chance to spend quality time with his son—who idolizes him.

Justin realizes his shortcomings as a father, where he's placed family second in his quest to succeed. In his heart, he knows that it was his selfish actions which caused the collapse of his relationship with Teresha. And now he has to live with that guilt as he watches his son grow up without a father actively participating in his day to day life. In Justin's case, the pain of that liability is doubled, understanding the generational curse that he's allowed to continue in the life of his son. For Justin who spent the majority of his childhood without his father—though under different circumstances, has sealed the same fate for his son. At 34, a bit older and maybe a bit wiser, he wants to break the cycle, reversing the curse that has come between them.

four

Stiff Expectations

7:54pm

Exiting I-20 at Moreland Avenue, Justin takes a right—travels down three lights—makes a left on Wylie Street and finds the older, cottage-style home of Tonya Campbell. In a neighborhood overwhelmingly populated by aspiring artists, college students, and gays, he parks his 300C on the street to avoid scraping the front against the steep, uneven incline that leads up the driveway into the carport. Being that it's the middle of May, the trees and shrubs that occupy her less than ¼ acre lot are in full bloom and in dire need of attention. Such so, that Justin has to duck and push away the overgrown foliage to get to the front porch. He first knocks on the latched wooden screen door hoping that she's close enough to the door to hear his feeble tapping. With no response, he pushes the cracked and what looks to be broken doorbell. "Ding-dong," the corroded relic chimes. Moments later, he identifies the sound of hard bottom shoes thudding against a solid wood floor. Tonya pulls back the sheer curtain panel from across the window—sneaking a peak outside. Unlocking both doors, she steps out to greet him with a firm warming embrace.

"Hey baby—how are you? I'm happy to see you boo!"

"I'm cool—how 'bout you? …*Girl* you lookin' goood! That dress is on the bomb—fo sho!" She stands before him sporting a copper-colored half-sleeve, knee length Tonya original made from a light breathable stretch material.

She spins around in her black patent-leather riding boots, flaunting her near perfect figure. "Thanks! I'm glad you like—made it myself"

"Hell yeah—that shit's phat wit yo fine tail! …Found me a versatile woman."

Blushing, she thanks him by reaching up for a quick kiss "Yes, you did buddy boy! Are we ready?"

"Yep—if you are."

Gasping, she says, "Okay—let me get my things. I'll be right there. So don't move." She runs back inside to get her purse and makes sure everything's turned off. After locking the door, she's escorted to his car. Once inside, as Justin turns the ignition, immediately in the background blares Mariah Carey's "We Belong Together." As they drive off, Tonya leans over to Justin's side and serenades him, singing softly in his ear.

"Oh you just a triple threat—ain't cha? Poet, clothing designer—and now a singer. You must be tryin' to get a record deal or sumptin'?"

Tonya chuckles, smiles and rebuts, "Something like that." Pausing between sentences, she says, "…Do you believe in soul mates?"

"I don't know—why? Define soul mate."

"You know—having that one special someone who is destined just for you. And y'all share a love so strong that it transcends all time and space."

Justin laughs. "Girl don't believe the hype. You been watchin' too much of that WE channel."

"*Maaan*—I just know you ain't laughin' at me. …So I guess you don't believe in fairy-tales either?"

"Hell nah! Shit ain't neva like that in real life. Nothing turns out that good—that easy. Sumptin' always fucks up!"

"Not always. You mean to tell me you ain't neva been in love?" She inquisitively smiles.

"Once! And that shit didn't turn out right. So now I don't fuck wit it!"

"So I guess you just gonna be a playa for the rest of your life?"

"Yep—til the day I die!"

"*Whatever*—you just haven't run across da right one—that's all!"

"Yeah—whatever!" Mocking his date, Justin turns up the radio to avoid further conversation on the subject matter. Both get a good laugh.

"So where are you takin' me?"

"Just chill—it's a surprise."

"Really?"

"Yeah really!"

"You probably try'na take me to that new 24-hour Mickey D's— ain't cha?"

"*Gurl!* How did cha ever guess?" Justin burst out laughing.

"Boy you betta stop playin' wit me. I know fools who've tried it!"

"Word?"

"Fo real!"

"*Nah.* I don't roll like that boo. Trust me—you gonna like this place."

About 25 minutes later, they arrive in the parking lot of Houston's at the corner of Cobb County's Windy Hill and Powers Ferry. Justin knows this place from the many nights he and Jackie spent here during their frequent intervals of so-called dating. Houston's, considered a step or two up in class from other franchise restaurants such as Applebee's or Ruby Tuesday, has a quaint romantic air to it; especially the one here in Marietta—a quiet, and peaceful spot located away from all the hustle and bustle of the inner-city.

As they enter the restaurant, a surprised Tonya responds in excitement. "This is n-i-c-e! I really like this. ...Boy, you must be tryin' to work yo way up on some coochie coupons—huh?" she said, as she lightly jarred Justin in his side with her elbow. "...Well it's workin'. Finally a man who knows how ta treat a woman."

"I knew you'd like it" Justin responds as they're ushered to their table.

Tonya, who has made herself right at home, pulls her long flowing hair back in a pony-tail and looks over at Justin. "You don't mind—do ya? I like to get comfortable when I eat."

"Sure. Whatever floats yo boat," he says, as he grins and stares.

"Nah I know how some guys are—y'all expect us to look like little Barbies 24/7."

Justin continues to gawk and grin while being enamored by her raw beauty.

"What are ya starin' at?"

"You. You're beautiful."

"Well thank you—but you need ta quit cause you're makin' me nervous." She is once again blushing.

"Nervous—why?" He notices that his words are beginning to have an aphrodisiac affect.

"Cause I ain't used to all of this—most guys don't take the time ta do this—they usually want just a piece of ass and that's it. But you take your time. You like to do things. I like that. ...*It's different.*"

"Well, I guess that's because—like you said—just haven't run across the right one! ...Touché." Justin laughs at his own joke.

Amused, but ashamed, Tonya kicks Justin in the shin.

"*Ouch*—girl you betta quit! I ain't playin' wit'cha. ...Bust ya in yo titty. Keep playin'!"

"You ain't gonna do nuthin'. You jus think ya cute." she said, this time kicking him in the other shin.

"I—am! And I told ya ta quit!" Again, laughing at his own pun, he returns the favor by sticking his shoe between her legs—just below her coochie.

"Ahhh!" Shocked, she shrieks. "Boy—I don't believe you jus did that—You crazy! I don't know why I fool up wit'cha—some folks ya jus can't take no where!"

"Maybe so. But cha love it! ...Don't cha?" he states with much confidence.

They continue their frolicsome interaction until the menu arrives. "So, what do ya want?"

"I'll take whatever you're having baby!" she says, as she seems to be afraid to order without his prior approval.

"Boo, stop try'na be cute! You know what ya want—jus order. I got this! So eat."

"Well, if it's like that... I want the steak and chicken platter—big baller!"

"*Hell yeah.* Now that's what I'm talkin' about—I want what she's having and can you bring us a bottle of that Pinot Chardonnay—please?" Closing his menu, Justin relays the order to their waitress.

After finishing the dinner, both stuffed and a bit tired, Justin makes a suggestion in regards to their next destination. "Hey, it's been a long day—how 'bout we jus go back to your place—if you don't mind. Maybe we'll do Esso another time. You can give me one of those world famous massages you always talkin' 'bout. ...What do ya think—you up for it?"

She agrees without hesitation as they walk hand in hand out the closing restaurant. Tonya turns the table as she now takes on the role of the hopeless romantic.

"What's up wit'cha girl? …Why are you lookin' like that?"

"Nuthin'. I jus really enjoyed myself tonight. Thank you!"

"It's all good *baby*—get in!" He opens the door for her.

The ride back to Tonya's is much quieter. Justin becomes guarded with his words realizing the elevation in emotions. He knows that Tonya wants to be more than just lovers—and more than friends. He's confused because he, too, really enjoys the time spent together. He knows—while stealing a glimpse of her from the corner of his eye—that she's a good woman. She represents the future—someone who you could build a life with, but he also recognizes his own position—he's about to start a new chapter. He contemplates the feasibility of trying to build something with Tonya—exploring all the possibilities. "Long distance relationships never work" he thinks to himself. "Besides, look at me—who am I kiddin'? …Monogamy ain't exactly in my dictionary." He quickly blows off the thought.

While his life seems to be enviable, there's still a void. Yeah he enjoys the freedom, but at the same time he feels the loneliness—the incompleteness that his life holds. He flashes back to he and Teresha and the difficulties of that relationship—what went wrong and how things could have been different. He jumps to an image of his son who plays alone in a park while another boy plays ball with his father. He then thinks back to his own childhood and the emptiness felt for the father he longed for—the man he knew before the addictions. He remembers watching his mother being beaten repeatedly by his drunken father—how he and Jerome would close their bedroom door to muffle the screams of their abused mama.

His teeth gnash while gripping the steering wheel tighter. In his eye there's a look of rage—hatred. Tonya notices his blank trance like state. "What's wrong baby?"

"Jus thinkin'…" He lets off a sigh as she has broken his chain of thought.

"'Bout what?"

"Life—the past—the future."

"So whatcha see?"

"…Different things," he says, his response vague.

She gives up. Turning her head, she peers out her passenger side window understanding that she's reached a deep place. They arrive at her house. A bit embarrassed, Tonya warns Justin of the impending mess. He smiles.

"Don't worry 'bout it—you should see my place."

"That's the problem—I have!" She refers to the fact that Justin and Jerome's home is immaculate, partially due to the maid service that comes out twice a week to clean. She invites him in. Justin, who's never seen the inside of her home, looks around and is quite impressed by the artistic afro-centric decor with the statues, artwork, etc. He learns something new on this night—that Tonya is a gifted painter, amongst her many other talents.

"Girl, I didn't know you could git down like that. You neva mentioned anything 'bout bein' a female Picasso."

"*What you thought?* It's not good for a girl ta give away all her secrets on the first date," she chuckles.

"This is tight! ...Jerome should see this. He's into the African art thing. ...Where ya find this stuff?"

"All over. ...Friends, flea markets, different shops, and of course—online." She walks Justin through her 50+year-old home. The oak floors have been restored to their former glory—with no carpet or linoleum anywhere except for in the kitchen. She leads him to a large room in the back of the house. It appears to be a den or great room furnished with a red micro-fiber couch and love seat. She also has a matching ottoman with a rectangular glass placed on top to form a coffee table. The walls are painted in a suede texture to match the furniture and sparsely decorated with her own work—all 24" x 36" framed pieces. Approximately 15' in front of the couch sets a wall-sunken fireplace with floating mantle. Mounted directly above is a 42" plasma LCD television screen that looks like an empty frame. To the left of the couch there's an archway that leads to her exposed bedroom. Like on her windows, she uses the same beige sheer material as a scarf draped over the opening for limited visual access. The curtain is currently pulled back.

"No door ta da bedroom? ...Ain't no privacy—what 'bout when you have guests?"

"Most of the time it's jus me—myself—and I. Besides, I don't entertain guests like that—like some folks," she said while looking over at Justin as she points her finger. "I try ta stay ta myself—less confusion. ...Want sumthin' ta drink?"

"I feel ya—whatcha got?"

"Cranberry juice, water, milk—maybe a Corona or two fo y'all alcoholic folks," she said, being facetious.

"Corona please! ...And who ya callin' alcoholic? Ain't you da one wit it in *yo* fridge?" He flips up the tail of her dress as she passes by on her way to the kitchen—catching a preview of her black thong panties.

She turns, sticking her tongue back at him—further teasing him. "Don't start nuthin' you can't finish." She walks away with an exaggerated swish in her step.

"You jus hurry on back dammit!"

She emerges from the kitchen with two already open Coronas. They sit and share a drink. Justin peers into her hazel eyes.

"Come here," he commands in a low alluring tone.

"What boy?—I'm sitting right here!"

"Oh, you know what!" He removes the drink from her hand and pulls her to his lips. They share a slow sensual kiss. Looking back into her eyes, whispering, he asks, "So what's up?"

Understanding the intent of his question, she leads him to her dim moonlit bedroom where she helps him to get undressed. Shirt first— then shoes, socks, and pants. In near sculptured form, Justin's silhouette stands in the center of the room—his cup runneth over as he poses in lavender bikini briefs. Admiring the huge scarcely concealed sac-like package, she now gently bites the tip of her finger before excusing herself to the bathroom. Removing his underwear, he lies down in her queen sized poster bed—unclothed and ready. He investigates the understated surroundings. The pillow top mattress he lays upon is calm and soothing, he relaxes under thin percale sheets. Tonya returns minutes later.

"I'm back!" She stands in the bathroom doorway wearing a short fitted one-piece negligee. "You ready?" she asks, as she climbs into bed.

With both hands, she vigilantly massages his third leg as moans of gratification are indecipherably uttered from amidst Justin's craved lips. The rigid petrified nature of his cocked manhood causes the percolation of her internal juices. As she begins to seep, now smiling with anticipation, Tonya straddles Justin, inserting him inside her. Moving in slow winding circles she adjusts her motion to accommodate his large size. For it's not long after, she notices that with each stroke her movements become easier and less fulfilled. She now realizes he's gone limp! Through the darkness, Tonya catches the moony reflection of Justin's sleep ridden face. She immediately dismounts, hurling herself backwards against the pillows. Disgusted, she gazes into the night—wondering if it's her.

4:43am

While turning over, Justin sees the time on Tonya's alarm clock sitting on her dresser. He jumps up—remembering where he's supposed to be in just a few hours. For he had no intention of spending the night, but the week's episodes had finally caught up to him. Tonya, who lies asleep next to him, is resting on top of the sheets. Seeing what she has on, he is again aroused. He reaches over to kiss her on the cheek, whispering in her ear, "Good morning." With little response, he rubs his fingers over her partially exposed breast. Unaware of the reality, she groans in a dream-like state until his gentle caresses reach her bare moist vagina.

She awakens, blurting, "Stop!" as she turns opposite of Justin—facing the dresser. She murmurs in a near inaudible voice. "Oh, now you want some," covering herself while converting to a fetal position.

"*What?*" complains a confused Justin.

Tonya turns her groggy head toward Justin, "You left me hangin' last night. Am I that borin' to ya? Or is your mind somewhere else? …Ain't no man ever dun me like that!" She turns back the other way while continuing to vent. "Fall asleep on some pussy… *Pleeease!* That's some shit there—neva again." She sarcastically chuckles before making an attempt to go back to sleep.

Without a word, Justin gets up to get dressed—meditating on her vindictive comments. The more he thinks—the more ticked off he becomes. "The nerve of that bitch—FUCK her!" He clumsily puts his leg in his pants. She also gets up to use the bathroom. Justin detects the attitude in her gestures. His vainglory has been violated—exposing his insecurities. Justin, who lives for the admiration of others, has been brutally slapped in the face. Her words cut viciously through his mind, leaving a wounded pride. Embarrassed, he's prompted to silent rage.

In his anger, he approaches her as she leaves the bathroom.

"Oh, I ain't hittin' on shit—huh?"

Turning her towel covered body against the dresser, she bumps it, causing a picture to fall. He snatches the oversized cloth from her clinched arms. Roughly he gropes her, placing his hand between her legs. Scouring against her low-shaven loins, his middle finger reaches the tip of her clitoris—the sudden stimulation of his touch renders her momentarily helpless. Unprepared for what comes next, she's forcefully twisted around and thrust into a parallel space amid the bed and dresser. He removes himself from his pants, and then takes her from behind, as she grimaces upon his initial entry.

"You like that!" he says, gnashing his lower lip.

She braces herself to keep her head from colliding with the pedestal bedpost, her body folded—one leg on the floor, the other on top of the mattress resting on her knee. He pounds her again and again with savage force. Not knowing whether to receive his actions as rape or rough sex, she accepts his treatment—relaxes her marinated walls and returns his movements with harmonious rhythm prompting an early climax. He pulls himself out, releasing the rest of his sperm to drip within the cracks of the hardwood floor.

Justin, unsure of what to say, knows how his actions may have come across, and tries to cover the aspect of anger in his conduct by simply pretending as if nothing had happened. "You got time fo me tonight? Maybe we'll do a late movie. C'mon—let's wash up before I go. ...So what you think about tonight—you free? C'mon—get up!" he said, attempting to help her.

A stunned Tonya rises to her feet, "I got it—jus go!"

"What's wrong wit cha now? I thought we had a good time last night—what in da hell happened?" he comments with nervous agitation.

"*Please*—jus go!"

"Okay—whatever. ...Call me later if you feel up to it." He bends over to kiss her on the forehead. She accepts the kiss which instantly relieves Justin. For he knows his whole world could have just come crashing down. With his heart pounding a thousand beats per minute, he tucks in his shirt and heads for the door. Tonya never leaves the bedroom as he departs her home.

He dazes off into a zone—replaying every moment of what just transpired. He comes to the conclusion that maybe he should leave well enough alone by staying away from Tonya for a while. In seemingly seconds; he's already home. Justin rushes in to take a shower. He stands in the stall motionless—now numb as gelid waters run down his condemned body. He wonders what's going through Tonya's mind. At any minute, there could be a knock at the door from the Atlanta Police Department, brandishing a warrant for his arrest. The charge—Rape! "*DAMN!* What da fuck did I just do? I can't believe I did that shit. ...What ta do? Should I call ta check on her—or should I wait? ...I dun' fucked up!" He paces the floor of his bedroom. "She knows I'll be gone next week—maybe I'll jus call her when I get back? …Damn I fucked up." And because he doesn't really know her or what she's thinking—he panics.

For all intents and purposes, his day is over—shot! His preoccupation wouldn't possibly allow him to enjoy the afternoon. He contemplates whether to cancel and do Six Flags another time. If it wasn't for his Chi-town trip, he'd ask if they'd take a rain check. But knowing how important it will be towards rebuilding a relationship with Teresha and Justice, he decides to go on.

five

It Takes Two To Tango

Teresha, a usually organized and efficient individual, scrambles around her modest College Park townhome, flustered and unprepared. For on this day, a little more time has been spent in front of the mirror primping and adjusting because in just a few short minutes, Justin Vaughn will be knocking at her door. She stands there inspecting herself in the downstairs half-bath. Tilting her head from side to side, Teresha adds a touch of Vaseline to her lip gloss to give them that extra wet sheen. She then dusts a smidgen of blush to her peachy freckled cheeks. In her final step, a brush of mascara is applied to accentuate her light brown eyes. And with a self-assured wink, she gives herself the nod of approval as she departs from her bathroom vanity. While time fastly approaches, Teresha hurries to throw together a "just in case" bag equipped with the standard theme park necessities—a change of clothes, a few towels, and some between meal snacks to alleviate the expense of high-priced concessions.

"JUSTICE! Are you ready?" she hollers from the base of the stairwell.

"Yeah Mom!" he answers her as though he's being nagged.

"Well come down here so I can see you. Your dad should be here in a minute."

Down the steps comes a lanky pecan hued adolescent with shoulder length corn rolls wrapped in one long braid. The handsome young man dressed in a white Atlanta Braves jersey with matching wrist bands and a pair of baggy dark denim Polo walking shorts, carries in his hand the Gameboy Advance SP, which never leaves his sight.

"My—ain't we lookin' cute today?" says a flattered proud mom. But just as her mouth closes, there's a knock at the door.

"He's here! How do I look?" Twisting herself, she adjusts her bra to give just the right amount of perkiness to her 36 C-cup. She checks for wrinkles in her pink hip-riding tee shirt and khaki colored shorts. She skims over her white Tretorns and makes sure her ponytail is aligned properly out the rear end of the pink baseball cap summarized with silver sequenced embroidery spelling "Angel".

Again, she repeats her question. "Well—how do I look?"

"You straight!" which wasn't the non-Ebonics answer she had hoped for, yet it would suffice considering the circumstance. Justice silently giggles to himself in response to his mother's popping of the lips as she turns around to answer the door. For he knows what she feels, he sees the affect his dad still has on her.

To let Teresha tell it, who has always behaved in this manner when it comes to Justin, she claims to do it not to entice him, but as a friendly reminder of what he once had—and let get away. When in actuality, she's never stopped loving him. Yet, because they're so much alike, they repel one another like two magnets set on the same polarity.

"Hello—c'mon in." She checks the time. "*Whaaat*—you're on time for a change. I betta write this down—you ain't neva on time. …What's wrong wit cha?" She makes jokes sarcastically taunting Justin without knowing what he's actually gone through.

"What up girl? Hey, there's my man—what's up baby boy?" Justin steps by Teresha to get to Justice where they extend hands to give dap—pulling together in a warm embrace.

"Hey Dad!"

"So, what's been goin' on—every time I see ya you get taller. Nigga betta slow down, ya might catch up ta me. …Oh, here ya go. I got sumptin' for ya before I forget." He hands Justice a yellow manila envelope.

"What's this Dad?"

"Go head—open it!"

Justice quickly opens the package. "Oooh snap—that's the shit!"

"Justice! ...Boy you better watch yo mouth!" Teresha reprimands Justice for his foul language.

"Sorry Mom." He pauses briefly, and then resumes examining the contents of his gift. "Thanks Dad. It's cool—I like it!" he says, as he gives his dad another tight squeeze.

In the package, Justin has given his son some promotional items from the office—CD's, photos, and flats—all personally autographed by the various artists. For Justice—who like father, like son—loves the attention, and this kind of ammunition will earn him top bragging rights at school, as he grabs at any and every opportunity to boast of his big shot father.

"Guess who I had lunch wit yesterday?"

"Who Dad?"

"Kyra."

"*Daaag* Pops. ...Fo real? Why you ain't git me?"

"Hush nigga—you was in school."

"So! You coulda came and got me."

"Yeah right. I can see yo mama's face now—all frowned up and shit—talkin' shit! You know good and damn well—I ain't tryin' to hear that. You know your mama be trippin'."

"Mama—you heard that? Dad had lunch wit Kyra! And he didn't take us. ...What's up wit that?" Justice says to his mom, trying to intentionally provoke a little harmless jealousy.

Teresha rolls her eyes. "*And?* ...So what—who cares!" While under her breath she mumbles, "Ain't like I wanted to eat wit the bitch. ...Wonder what else his sorry ass did besides eat? Dirty dick fucka!" Now agitated, Teresha summons the fellows. "Y'all ready? Let's go!" She scuffles out the door, still muttering obscenities under her breath. Justin and Justice leave the apartment together right behind her, giggling like two juvenile chums.

They spend a beautiful afternoon together enjoying one another. And at least for the moment, Justin is able to forget about his other troubles. Concluding the day, he decides to take everyone back to his house.

All three return from the park, soaked after participating on several water rides. Justice, who hasn't seen his Uncle Jerome in a few months, spots his SUV in the driveway.

"Good—Unc's home. Can I go find him?"

"Yeah—go head. He's probably in his room…knock first!" Justin cautions his son, as he is unaware of whom his brother might be privately entertaining, having had the house all to himself.

Justice worships both men, and wants to follow in their footsteps with his own aspirations of becoming a rap star. Finding his uncle, he persuades Jerome to take him downstairs in the basement to the studio. Teresha, who wants to change her dripping wet clothes, helps herself to the upstairs bathroom. Justin tries to follow, but Teresha intercepts.

"Where you goin'?"

"I'm tryin' to be polite—direct a nigga to the lil' girls room."

"*Excuse me*, but I think I know my way around *thank you*. So you can stop right there!" she said, as she points to the bottom step, teasing Justin before proceeding upstairs.

Having regained his playful nature, Justin waits a second and then follows her. Once he gets to his room and sees that the bathroom door is slightly open—like a sneaky child, he peeks in. Wearing nothing but a support bra, he stares tenaciously at her light freckled skin. He then remembers the brownish birthmark on her lower back. She is still as beautiful as the day they met. His hearts races as he watches her half-naked body. Unaware of his presence, she turns, facing the door, while her head continues to gaze into the mirror above the sink. Her well-maintained shape mesmerizes Justin. Although she has thickened up over the years, her love for physical fitness has proven worthy as she now displays a muscularly toned hour glass physique. He is drawn to her bikini-trimmed pubic bush, which is as reddish-brown as the hair on her head. Having seen enough, he steps back—retreating to the living room. When she returns downstairs, she's wearing a short navy blue tennis skirt with a half sleeve top made to fit.

Justice, having had his fill of the studio, races upstairs to the guest bedroom tailored especially for him. Already equipped with XBox and PlayStation 2 consoles, he helps himself, leaving his mother and father alone to talk.

"So what's new wit you?" Teresha starts in with her third degree questioning.

"Nuthin'—same ole' shit."

"How's what's her name? *Shanice*—right?"

Justin grinning, "She's al-ight—I guess."

"You know. Speak!"

"It ain't all like that."

"Yeah right! Jus remember who ya talkin' to."

"So what's that suppose ta mean?"

"Boy, you were chasin' every piece of tail long before you got all this. Remember I was there!"

"Boo, you know I'm too busy fo all that. I'm out here try'na make shit happen!"

"Whatever—bet ya still find time for a piece of ass?"

"Yo—you trippin'."

"But cha know I'm tellin' the truth!"

"Whatever man. Let's play some Spades," he said, while attempting to divert any further discussion on the subject

"You still playin' that?" Teresha asks, amazed by his longevity.

"Ain't shit changed!"

"Then I know ya still have Yahtzee?"

"Yeah, you right. Let's do it! …*C'mon!*" They go upstairs to his bedroom, pulling out a dusty Yahtzee game from his closet.

"So who do ya play wit—ya can't play by yo-self?"

"Girl, you still on that? You see the dust! …Ain't played since we were together."

"Rrright—now whose trippin'?"

"What? …I'm fo real!" He sets the game on the bed.

"*Pleeease*—jus roll the dice." Relieved to hear such words, she playfully shoves him.

"Why ya got ta be pushin' a nigga?"

"Boy, that ain't hurt you!"

"Oh really? Well, then take some of *THIS*." He scoops her just below the knees and tosses her on the bed while he inadvertently falls, landing on top of her. Laughing, they make eye contact. The mood suddenly changes as he leans in to kiss her—she doesn't make a move to stop him. With parted mouths, they engage in a tongue to tongue union. He then nibbles her robust saliva saturated lips. Both apprehensive, Justin nervously lifts Teresha's skirt to remove her panties. He too undresses as she makes a powerless plea for him to stop.

"Don't—please Justin."

Ignoring her petition, he continues. Once inside her, he remembers why they had once fallen in love. From her overflowing juices to her panting whine of fulfilled pleasure, nothing had changed. It was even better than he could recall. When they finished, both lay stunned—too afraid to move or speak. A tear rolls down her face as she gets up to clean herself. Snatching her underwear, she takes them into the bathroom. Justin, sprawled across the bed, tries to analyze what just happened. He's been down this road before—and within the last 24 hours. Different situations, yet the same psychological outcome. Again he's left speechless as he listens to the sound of running water spewing from the sink. Quietly collecting her things, Teresha reenters the bedroom. She gathers Justice from the room across the hall and without another word goes downstairs to take a seat on the living-room sofa.

Reluctantly, Justin, who has no other choice, gets himself up. Unlike with Tonya, he has to face the uncomfortable feat of overcoming his emotional paralysis. He must decipher his feelings by internalizing his motive. Was what happened a matter of the heart or selfish desire? ...Was it love? Or was it lust? As he embarks on a new life, he wonders—why now? Juggling his thoughts, he makes the descent downstairs where he finds Justice sitting on the love seat, seemingly into his Gameboy. Teresha sits poised at the corner of the couch with her head propped in her hand now resting upon the arm of the sofa. The room is silent.

"Why y'all so quiet?" Justin plays ignorant to conceal the obvious. But there's no response. Justice, from the corner of his eye, peeks over at his mother. He can see the sickened look on her face as her eyes begin to well up again. He knows that something his father has done has caused hurt to his mother as he has bore witness to such agonizing torment—time after time. For as much as he loves his father, he knows that it's probably best if they don't be around each other. It pains him to see his mother go through the roller coaster of emotions concerning his dad. Her love is real while his remains questionable. Justice returns to his game without a single utterance.

"Okay—well I guess y'all are ready to go?" Justin snaps up his keys and waits by the door. In his mind, it's not like what happened was his entire fault. The sex was consensual. He knows Teresha, her plea was casual. She wanted to as much as he did. Now he was left with the burden of liability, and that infuriated him. Needless to say, the ride back to Teresha's was one of cautioned conversation.

While driving, Justin sorts through his repertoire of clichés and clever babblings in search of the most politically correct way of addressing the situation. And yet the best that he could do was to poke her in the thigh and say, "*Hey you*" in a sweet, smooth, charismatic voice. And just as he expected—she ignores him. Taking plan B into action, he grabs her left hand in a friendly but assertive embrace. He looks over to her to engage eye contact as she turns to him with hurtful eyes, and then quickly rotates in the opposite direction. Their hand-held embrace becomes a floodgate of emotions as she begins to weep profusely. "…What part of the game is this?" Justin now inner-speculates, having not anticipated this reaction from a generally hardhearted Teresha.

"What's up?—What's going on? I don't get it?"

"Do you ever?"

"What are you talkin' 'bout? What do ya mean?"

"I mean really—do you ever think about anybody but yo self?"

"*What?* Stop talkin' in riddles and say whatcha mean?"

"It's you Justin!—and yo selfish bullshit! She cries aloud, snatching her hand away.

"Hold da-fuck up! *It's me?* Hell, let you tell it—it's always me! So you mean to tell me—what happened back there was all my fault? …Don't put that on me!"

Justice, who had been pretending to be intently involved with his game, puts it down after hearing the elevation in his father's voice. He has never risen against his father but can no longer take watching his mother go through the habitual frustrations attached to their relationship. Scared that his father might be angry enough to possibly put his hands on her, he clinches his fist together—ready to do what he has to, in order to protect his mother.

"You really don't git it—do ya? You have absolutely no-fuckin'-clue do ya? It's always been 'bout you Justin. Nobody else matters—except you! Fuck what I needed or even Justice. It's always 'bout you—Mr. Justin—*FUCKIN'*—Vaughn. And I have put up wit your shit—over-and-over again!" Teresha, now pointing her finger in Justin's face, has positioned herself about six inches from his ear as she persists in making her feelings known. "When have you ever put us first in your world? …When? Did you ever stop to think even once how your decisions and actions would affect us? When you was out there doin' want you wanted to do, where was I? At home takin' care of yo baby! Feedin' yo seed! I gave my life up fo you—my dreams—my aspirations and for what? Bullshit! …Nuthin' but bullshit! You know what? …You right—what happened tonight ain't all yo fault. I blame my tired ass 100%—for lovin' a dumb selfish ass nigga like you!"

Keeping his composure for the sake of his son, Justin just listens. For much of what she says is truth—he doesn't deny that. It's no secret of his self-sighted nature. Though he doesn't feel that she's justified in her bias one-sided remarks, he has read between the lines—her love for him is evident. While he feels bad for hurting her, there's a part of him that smiles in knowing he's maintained a place in her heart.

"Look—let's not go there. It was more than just me that went wrong wit us. I wanted it ta work—I wanted to be there for y'all. But *you* left me—remember? I ain't like you—I ain't have my shit together—like you. I had dreams that didn't fit into yo plans. In yo little perfect world—you painted this perfect little picture. But shit changes—and you couldn't accept that."

"No Justin! You couldn't accept it! You expected everything to go yo way—you thought you had everything worked out! You had yo little degree—women at yo beck and call. And you thought ya had it goin' on! Then when shit didn't go yo way, that life that you thought you shoulda had, neva materialized and you panicked! Be honest. We were neva in your plans were we? We were just an accident on top of everything else that didn't go right for you. An extra responsibility—and you couldn't handle that! It ain't that *SHIT* changed—you changed!"

"*What?* You thought I ain't want y'all around? So I guess you thought I was jus playin' house—right? I guess ya figured I'm jus some triflin' ass nigga who ain't about his—right? Now that's that bullshit! I loved you—and you left me! When shit got hot—you hauled ass jus like my father!"

"*Your father?*—This ain't got shit to do wit yo father. That's yo problem right there. You use him as an excuse fo everything that is wrong in yo life. Let it go! …He ain't made you do half the shit you dun did!"

Her words have touched a sensitive area, and like a thorn in the side—here's one wound that refuses to heal. They say that scars are our reminders of where we've been—and what we've come through. Yet the thing about "scars" is that usually over time, we become disassociated from the pain once felt from the initial injury. But what of those wounds that never close? Those hurts that not only linger—but also metastasize—spreading to other areas of our mind, and later becoming the malignant impartations that feed the soul. In Justin's distorted reality, he uses his past to fuel his behavior in the present, refusing to release those demons of days gone by.

Balling a hand over his mouth as maybe a way of containing his emotions, Justin momentarily eats his vulgar words; but in an unprompted outcry, he lets Teresha know just where he stands in this disillusioned relationship.

"Know what—I fucked up! This was definitely a mistake—a BIG mistake! I can't fuck wit you—neva could. I shoulda just came over ta get baby boy and dipped out! But nah—tryin' ta be Mr. Nice Guy... Maybe have all of us share a quality moment—create a positive lasting memory or some shit. But like usual—sumptin' always fucks up! And here we go again—back in the same fucked up place—goin' through the same fucked up shit! Wanna know sumptin'? ...I'll tell ya. Fo a minute there—I actually thought I could be wit cha. ...Get shit straight. ...Try and fix what's broke—then make it work. But that can't and won't happen wit us. I see that. And I jus keep wastin' my time. ...Like puttin' a square peg in a round hole—Our shit jus don't fit!"

Teresha, who's been unaware of his feelings, is overcome with extreme exuberance. Her knees begin to knock while her stomach churns—sweat begins to drip from her armpits. She's unprepared to reply. This was all her subconscious had hoped for. Those feelings she kept tangled within her pride—had just broken free. In her mind she would have thrown all caution in the wind, and said, "Let's work it out. ...Pick up the pieces and try again." But her mouth, on-top of being a black woman who's sick and tired—of being sick and tired, and very used to having the last word, responds from a much different perspective.

"I think we all get the picture. ...Our shit don't fit!" She mocks Justin by throwing her hand up forming quotation marks with her fingers to emphasize his exact words. Teresha, once again, turns in the opposite direction to hide her remorseful expression. She closes her eyes and with a sigh of regret, deliberates to herself. "Girl why ya do that? Ya know ya love that man. ...Who ya foolin'? Pride don't keep yo bed warm at night—nor pay the bills—or even take out the trash. Why ya doin' this to yo self? ...You *need* a man. Hell—you want that man! Boo, ya fuckin' up!" And on that note, Teresha finds it better to just call it a night as she sleeps through the rest of the ride. Justice, having already heard an earful, decides to do the same.

six

Roses

Later that night after everything settles, Justin, alone in his own bed, relaxes with hands behind his head—reflecting on recent events. As he lays there a song comes to mind. One that loosely parallels his own life. In almost nightmarish fashion, he places himself as the lead character in the song "Poor Georgie" by MC Lyte. In that song, Ole' George—a renowned playa, believes he has life by the balls until one day he finds out he doesn't have long to live because of his own carelessness. With his disease-infested body, George decides, in a drunken stupor, to end it all by smashing his car into an oncoming truck.

Justin's greatest fear is to die young—or worse, die slow. He often imagines himself with AIDS, desolate and removed, having reaped the consequences of years of careless indulgence. In the end, Justin sees himself lying in an open white casket, dressed in a white Armani suit— white shirt, tie and handkerchief. The only thing of color is the brown paper bag pigmentation that depicts his face. Two people mourn his passing—Jerome and Justice. They watch his still remains being rolled into a white room with one other door besides the entrance. It's small opening is just large enough and high enough to slide his casket through. Once reaching the back of this ill-boding chamber, an impassive attendant opens the miniature orifice, revealing a black hole of darkness that dances with the incandescence of roaring flames. In the literal—it's a crematorium incinerator, but in Justin's mind—it represents Hell. Certainly not the way he wants his final draft to be written. Yet he doesn't know how to change it.

After careful introspection, he immediately detaches himself from that thought, concluding, "What a tangled—ass backward life we weave." It's been more than a day and he still hasn't heard from Tonya. She's already proven that she knows how to pick up a phone and call a nigga—yet she hasn't done so. He concedes the short lived relationship to be all but finished. On the other hand, with Teresha, there's a thin line between love and hate—and she walks it well, but he feels there's something still there. He's just unsure of what it is. At a time when he should be concentrating on other pressing matters, such as his job and impending business trip, like usual, he's somehow managed to bring a bunch of unnecessary drama-oriented distractions in the mix—the unadulterated story of his life.

Hours have gone by, and he has literally watched the sun come up from Saturday night to Sunday morning. Unable to rest, he contemplates his next move. For he knows he needs to have his ass in somebody's church for some oil tossin', tongues talkin' Holy Ghost prayer. Instead he opts for a sermon of a different kind.

Normally, if for no other reason than of convenience, Justin would discuss such intimate matters with his baby brother Jerome, who's always loaned a willing ear for Justin's inconceivable and unimaginable dilemmas. But on this occasion, needing more than a listening participant, he—in search of sound advice and consoling, elects to make the journey to Marietta, giving his ace boon coon, Jackie, a surprise visit.

As he brushes his teeth, it dawns on him how he forgot to go over there the other day. He knows she'll probably be trippin'. So, thinking fast like any playa should, he figures he'll rectify the situation with a dozen of white long stemmed roses—a gesture of peace. Any other color might symbolize love or "can you please break me off some of that booty," which wasn't necessarily his intent—at least not today. Besides, knowing Jackie like the left-sided curve of his own dick, he knows he can't bullshit a bullshitter!

He quickly learns that his suggestion creates a problem. It's Sunday morning and locating a dozen of *white* long stemmed roses in the ATL is like trying to find a needle in a haystack—it doesn't easily happen. Luckily, his second stop proves to be pay dirt, as he shoots by the Kroger on Cascade Road, seconds before the 285 on-ramp. There, helped by a gold tooth, blonde wig wearing, dark chocolate sixteen— possibly seventeen-year-old female floor associate, they pull together a fairly decent arrangement of leftover unwithered white roses. With some flirtatious coercion, he persuades the naïve employee to redress the grouping in a more attractive and decorative presentation. It's not exactly a dozen but along with the other floral garnish mingled in—the arrangement looks agreeably full. Satisfied, he slides the associate an extra twenty, then proceeds to the register.

Now here's a smart man, Justin has learned from experience that the quickest way to a woman's heart or into her bed is through the gift of flowers—especially roses. Roses say to a woman—I'm thinking of you, but in that extra special way, because a rose is something that comes from the heart—and not necessarily the pocket. Unlike other such permanent material endowments such as jewelry, clothing, or even money—a rose's splendor may only last for a mere matter of days before withering hideously away. And yet the impression felt by its recipient may be savored as long as any diamond or pearl. A rose, while representing the beauty of a woman, also tells that woman that this man has gone out of his way to acknowledge his feelings for her— whatever they may be. Therefore, Justin, by knowing the heart of the receiver—Jackie, who also happens to be a sucker for the sentimental, becomes quite confident that he can manipulate his way back into her good graces—if need be.

For his venture north, Justin pops in a Lil' Jon and the Eastside Boyz CD to get it krunked early on this Sunday morning. No offense to all the spiritual folks out there—but gospel music ain't exactly his gig. And the fact that it's about 9:30 in the am when all the major black radio stations are still bumping Dottie Peoples doesn't fair favorably well with his sinner's spirit. Even the contemporary stuff like Mary Mary and Dietrick Haddon played on 97.5 aren't watered-down enough to penetrate his carnal skin. As of right now, he just wants it rough, rugged, and raw—straight with no chasers. If nothing else, the music will keep his mind off his other stresses long enough until he can get help from his personal therapist—Jackie. With her, he knows he can say anything without worry—for they're one in the same. She, like him, loves a good time and a good lay. The only difference here is that she's willing to give it all up—whomever and whatever, if it means having a life with him. There's a unique connection shared by the two.

Jackie, since her divorce, has adopted a perverted and cynical outlook on love and relationships. Like Justin, she herself, a victim of an abusive past, in her case, by a possessive husband, is the mother of a ten-year-old daughter—Shayla Marie, whom she shares custody with her estranged spouse. Unbeknownst to Justin, before the divorce, she wore many an ass kicking behind their friendship. Like many, she thought she had married the man of her dreams—her knight in shining armor, only to have the dream shattered upon that first lick. The weakness that she lives lies in her inability to be alone. She justifies herself by the company she keeps. She represents the woman who falls in love with the idea of being in love. And with each passing relationship, she wears those very hopes and dreams on her sleeve—leaving the door of hurt wide open. Her insecurities about weight and what men define as beauty, keeps her bound in bad relationships. A lack of self-esteem causes her to cling to the crap at the bottom of the barrel. As different men pass through her life, disappointment progresses to pain as each failed relationship bestows an increasing bitterness.

♡ ♡ ♡

It'd been eight and a half long years and counting since that fateful day. Justin, needing immediate assistance, flipped through the yellow pages. He called a childcare placement agency trying to find a sitter for Justice while Teresha was out of town on a work-related seminar. At the time, he was between jobs when MSC—a warehouse facility, phoned him for an interview the following morning. The agency recommended Jackie as an in-home daycare provider for the Austell-Lower Marietta area. Without a choice, he contacted her to find out whether there were any walk-in openings available for the next day. She accepted his plea, but to his surprise, the brief conversation, which started as business, somehow took a personal turn. Jackie, who's silly by nature—and a straight fool, but funny, openly discussed everything from men to marriage. Her candor was shocking as she divulged intimate aspects of her life. In minutes, Justin knew all about her husband, Michael, who at the time was whooping her tail on a regular basis—to how she liked to walk around the house with no underwear. And for the life of him, he couldn't understand why this woman was telling him—a complete stranger, all her dirty laundry. But her confidence and utter forwardness intrigued him. Just by the conversation he knew she had to be bold as hell. By her own account, she professed to be tall, attractive and beige, also indicating her unusual fetish for feet. Just a big ole' freak—so Justin thought, though right up his whorish alley. If nothing else—from by what he heard, she was at least worth a walk-through—maybe ask a question or two about her operation to peep the image behind the voice.

Justin, with a then four and a half year old Justice propped in his arms arrived at Apt. 631B, formerly Flags West. Before he could even raise a hand to tap against the faded deep emerald green door, the sound of crying infants and whining toddlers could be heard from through the weather beaten entrance. He looked around with skepticism, realizing that he was not in the most desirable of locations. The crumpling stucco multi-unit complex resembled a Mexican hacienda of the early 1900's. Not at all smitten by its charm, he made a concession considering his options—in time and urgency, figured he'd make do for one day. Jackie, having anticipated his arrival, cracked the door open slowly—revealing the full semblance. "Damn, she is cute!" a stunned Justin remarked—astonished by the truth of her description, which was right on the mark. That insidiously smiling, beige bombshell stood before him in a shape-flattering, yet simple lime green spaghetti-strap sundress.

"Hey—how ya doin'? I'm Jackie—and this must be Justice? Y'all c'mon in!" She turned around to lead them into her humble abode. Justin's eyes went straight to the ass—the round mounds of jiggle. Her small waist was no match for her double portioned bouncing buttocks and thick thighs. In all his days, he had never seen such a booty-wondrous marvel as he could practically feel the gyration permeating off of each of her steps. "Can't believe this shit—No draws either!" He imagined the juicy lips of her vagina flapping loosely beneath her thin cottony attire. The mere thought placed his nature on high alert. His lips puckered in sexual captivation as they took a seat on her plastic covered light cream colored couch.

The sofa made that annoying sound of crackling vinyl as Justin maneuvered himself into a comfortable position. A sleepy Justice made swift perch on his father's knee. He observantly took notice to the other five small occupants that littered the room, each ranging in age from about three months to three years old. First, over against the far wall, sat a small Graco playpen with attached musical mobile—its nearly newborn male resident rested soundly while sipping a bottle. In front of the cherry veneer entertainment center, two male toddlers, probably a year or so younger than Justice, played loudly amongst a few scattered toys. A Barney tape ran unwatched on a 25" color console. Looking out the vertical blinds of the sliding patio door stood a cinnamon colored nappy headed little child wearing nothing but a red tee shirt and diaper. She sucked a thumb as she appeared to be waiting on a missing parent—her nose ran, dried tears were painted upon her sober face. Another girl sat quietly underneath the breakfast bar of the look-through kitchen. She pretended to read an upside down book— she looked very familiar. Her portrait decorated the wall. Wearing in neatly applied ponytails, it was two-year old Shayla, Jackie's daughter.

Also on the wall, Justice paid especially close attention to the family photo. Along with Shayla and Jackie, there was a buff, pretty nigga in the picture—lighted skinned, guessing the obvious—it was Michael. He could then place a face to the deplorable images she described. As she talked, offering the two of them an ice cold glass and cup of grape Kool-Aid, her words became oblivious, for Justin heard nothing more than the smacking of her succulent lips. Before he knew it—suckered by a big booty and a smile, he was signing medical release forms and emergency contact information. Yet ringing in the back of his mind, a bitchful Teresha all in his ear.

That was almost nine years ago. While some things change, others remain the same. Justin makes that same walk up to that same apartment—now under new management and renamed Summit Ridge. The brown door is also new. The tired tan stucco repainted with a fresh white. He knocks and a now single, heavier and still attractive, just older Jackie answers the door. All smiles, she comments on the beautiful bouquet of roses.

"Ool—pretty. Those for me?" She snatches the bouquet from his grasp and gives him a grinning, tooth clashing wet smack on the lips. "Thanks boo—come in, come in!" And like usual, an underdressed Jackie leads the way. Wearing a see-through black teddy—she gladly exposes all her glory. Justin's focus point becomes her huge baseball sized areolas and protruding nipples. He contemplates on whether or not he needs to make an advance. But in hindsight, he's been in the pussy enough to know that it doesn't quite live up to the hype or complications affixed to the act. She willingly entices with legs amply open to divulge a glimpse of her slightly parted vulva while sitting on a slate coffee table directly in front of him. Justin recognizes game and regains his composure.

"Girl—I'm goin' through it."

"Poor baby—what's goin' on?" Again all smiles, anticipating dirt, she rubs her hands together as if she's standing outside on a cold winter day. Discarding her prior quest, she readies herself to give Justin her full-undivided attention. And despite her own emotional investment, she, a woman who lives vicariously through his life, listens.

"I'm fuckin' up again!"

"Why—watcha do?"

"Shit—where do I start?" he responds with a condemned smirk.

"From the beginning fool! And boy you betta not leave anything out!"

"Ya know Tonya—right? We went out Friday—and we kicked it. I thought we had a good time. So we go back to her place—right? Shit pops off—gits a lil' hot…takes a nigga back ta the bedroom—she's feelin' on my shit—the coochie gits wet ya-da, ya-da, ya-da…"

"Boy didn't I tell you? Don't be skippin' nuthin'!"

"Shut-up—let a nigga finish! Anyway—she goes to the bathroom— I'm laying there—ain't got shit on. And she's up in the bathroom like she try'na build shit—takin' forever. Ya know a nigga was tired—her shit was all comfortable—time jus goin' by…"

"*Uh-uh*. I know you didn't!"

"What?"

"Oh *hell* no!"

"*What?*"

"Boy—I know ya didn't take your ass ta sleep."

"Shit I was tired. She shoulda brought her ass out the bathroom!"

"*Uh-uh*. I woulda canceled yo ass right there. You woulda neva got another piece of this." Jackie, now laughing, is fully entertained by Justin's mishap.

"Nah, but that's not even the worse part. All I remember she was ridin' a nigga and that's it!"

"You fell asleep while she was on top? Ool—poor girl. I know she was pissed. …I woulda beat yo ass."

"Yeah, she was, and that's where she fucked up!"

"Sweetie, whatcha do?"

"I fucked the shit outta her fo talkin' smack."

"I wouldna of gave ya nuthin'."

"She didn't—I took that shit!"

Jackie shrieks back, unsure of how to take that last statement. "Whatcha mean?"

"Like I said—I took that shit. Hell, she pissed me off!"

There's a brief pause. Jackie is quite stunned. Even for Justin, that's going overboard. The thought takes her back to her own past and the spousal abuse she had finally separated herself from. *"How? ...Why?* I mean, it ain't never that serious."

"Nah—I'm fo real. She pissed me off and I threw her ass across the bed and fucked her from behind."

"And she let you do that?"

"Hell yeah! She ground da shit outta my ass. ...Made a nigga cum."

"That's 'bout a stupid bitch! ...Uh uh! I woulda fucked you up! Boy, you lucky you ain't sittin' up in Fulton County right now!"

"I know. That's why I'm here. What should I do?"

"Oool if I was you—I'd be tryin' to kiss that girl's tail. Justin, you better start using yo head—and I ain't talking 'bout that lil' one," she said, pointing to below his belt. "I thought cha was tryin' to move up in the world.—*Huh,* I don't know. ...Bad move boo. Have ya talked to her?"

"Nah. *Should I call?* "

"Yep. I would."

"Alrighty then—next scenario."

Recapturing her sense of humor, *"There's more?* "

"Hell yeah! Yesterday I took Justice and Teresha ta Six Flags..."

"How's he doing?"

"He's good. Nigga tall though. Got ta be 'bout 5'9" and ain't even in high school."

"Why you surprised—he's jus like you and Rome."

"You right. So how's Shay? ...Where is she?"

"She's okay—she's with Michael. He took her with him to Charlotte. Supposedly he's got people up there. Now ask me how come I don't already know those folks? He never mentioned having family in *Charlotte.* ...And how long were we married? But ain't no tellin'—lying bastard! Now what were ya sayin' about Six Flags?"

"Nah—but I took them up there. It was actually pretty nice. Wasn't too crowded. ...Weather was straight. It was nice! Ya know and we all enjoyed ourselves. So then I took everybody back to the crib. Ya know, chill out fo a lil' while—let Justice see Rome and shit. We chillin'—me and Tersha go upstairs—we start playin' Yahtzee..."

"Ha ha ha—Ha ha ha..." Jackie falls to floor laughing hysterically. "Boy, you don't have to say no more. You fucked her didn't you?"

"Maaan—that shit ain't funny"

"I told you—you gotta stop thinking wit that lil' head. *DAMN*, when you gonna learn? You knew better than that one."

"Yeah-yeah but now she's trippin' like that shit's all my fault. Hell, it takes two ta tango!"

"*Eeeh*—you know me. I ain't never liked her psycho ass. If I were you—I'd leave her silly tail alone." She eyes Justin. "…Ain't that easy though—is it? You still want that little silly girl—it's on your face. …Boo, you can't fool nobody—especially me!" Jackie laughs.

"What ch'ou talkin' 'bout?"

"Don't play dumb wit me boy—you still want her."

"Whatever. …Anyway, but what should I do? She trippin'!"

Still amused, "Sweetie, it's been about fifteen years—she ain't goin' nowhere. That's one you ain't got to worry 'bout—she'll be there. Like some otha folks," she said, mumbling the last sentence—referring to herself.

"*What?*"

"Oh nothing. So, what do you want to do?"

"I don't know, that's why I askin' you!"

"But I can't answer that boo. You know what you feel. Life's too short not to follow your heart." And as hard as it was for her to say— especially in this case, she remains true to the unconditional nature of their relationship.

Justin reflects on that thought.

seven

A Done Deal

Chicago Midway Airport, Concourse B—12:27pm

Arriving on Airtran flight 824, the trio of Justin, Shantel, and Dee gather outside of gate B7. The flight having left on time from Atlanta approximately 11:40am has reached its destination in just under 60 minutes. A time zone change over Tennessee has set the actual time back by an hour. All three a bit exhausted from the whole ordeal, hurry through baggage claim, knowing that first-class hotel accommodations awaits them. Midway—a far cry from the scene at Hartsfield-Jackson, and the nearly two-hour security screening process, is a virtually hassle free facility serving only 25% of the air travelers as its cross-town counterpart—O'Hare International. The group finds it to be considerably less aggravating to deal with. Justin describes the mood.

"Ya know—we're walkin' thru the terminal—and Dee wit his silly ass, like always, gots ta be the center of attention. So jus fo the hell of it—he starts fuckin' wit Tae. Guess cause he knows how easy it is ta push her buttons. But ta be honest wit'cha—I think he wants the bitch. Actually I wouldn't be surprised from the way they be actin'—if he wasn't already bangin' the shit out of her lil' skinny ass. Anyway, this fool wit his headphones loud as shit—bumpin' some ole' crazy Jamaican shit—tryin' ta sing and dance—ya know jus being Dee. Got everybody lookin' at his silly ass. I'm like nigga—wrong geographical location. We ain't in the Islands nigga! …Cut that shit off! But he's right behind Tae—she jus rollin' her eyes and shit—lookin' pissed. Dee, he's practically in her ear wit that shit. Nigga all up on her booty, which I might add—looks rather nice today. She got on this phat denim outfit wit those tight ass hip hugger jeans—the boot cut wit the splits up the leg. Her shoes are those two-toned denim joints made like a stiletto boot. Under her jacket, she's got on her lil' wifebeater top so a nigga can finally see a lil' cleavage from those pointy titties. I gotta give her props. She looks good! Even her hair is tight, she dun took down that bun. Got her shit pressed out. I say it hangs ta 'bout her shoulder. Real cute though! Hell—I'd tap it.

But Dee, he's doin' his thing. And I guess homegirl had jus had enough of his silly ass. Damn if she didn't slap the shit out of him. …Knocked the headphones clean off that niggas' beany head. I couldn't do shit but laugh. Even Dee had to grin on that one. Tae, her ass was laughin' too. But that nigga had it comin'.

We made our way over ta the baggage claim and that's when we met our hookup—Thadius McPhail. Dude was sittin' off ta the side sippin' a Coke and half-assed readin'—I assume a Chicago Sun-Times. He spots us first of course, since we ain't know who we were lookin' for. But when I first seen the nigga—he reminded of that dude on Mad TV… *What's his name?* Yeah—Aries Spears. I could tell he was different from most niggas in the industry jus by the way he carried himself. He wasn't all 'bout image. And judgin' by first impressions, I believe the nigga was saved or sumptin'. You should of seen him—wit his platinum cross, wearin' a long sleeve Jesus tee shirt that said sumptin' like; 'To know what love really means you have to—read between the lines'. Had a picture of Jesus hangin' from the cross—beat ta hell. …Had whip marks and shit. I didn't get it—but I knew it was sumptin' deep. While he introduced himself, I'm still tryin' to figure out where he fit in. I knew he was one of Riq's boys—but I ain't see the connection. Riq, he this lil' wannabe hard ass nigga, and Thad was somewhere on the otha end of the scale. I'm pretty sure they ain't run in the same circles. Maybe they jus repped the same hood. I don't know. Now don't get me wrong—the nigga was cool as shit—jus different. We corralled our shit—nigga Thad took us to the hotel."

❦   ❦   ❦

The three are taken downtown to N. Columbus Drive in Thad's Silver 2003 Cadillac Escalade ESV. Reservations have been made for The Fairmont Chicago—a luxury hotel overlooking Millennium Park. All are impressed and in awe of the magnificent lakefront view. Shantel rides shotgun.

"I never realized Chicago was such a beautiful city." Tae remarks as she peers through the tinted glass, attempting to absorb the vast spectrum of sights.

"*Wwwhaaat*—this is your first time? I can't believe that. But yeah the Chi is a beautiful place. I love it!"

Shantel fumbles through five or six empty CD cases in search of the mysterious artist that blares from the Bose sound system. "Who is this?" She grooves in place to the infectious track.

"Tye Tribbett."

"Isn't he Gospel?"

"Yep—you got it!"

"That's what I thought. In fact, everything we've listened to has been Gospel—right?" She glances again at the empty cases.

"You're absolutely right!"

Dee interjects in the conversation. "Yo—I was wonderin' 'bout dat dude. What's up wit all da religion man? You a Jesus freak or sumthin'?" Dee having asked the very question that burned in Justin's mind.

"Yes sir! Born again and krunked for Christ.—Ain't no otha way broa!"

Justin and Dee both give each other that contentious look as Thad continues in his testimony. "I'm blessed—truly blessed. Ain't nuthin' but Jesus broa! Saved a no-good wretch like me—and still placed favor on my life! …ME!" He strikes a chord of curiosity amongst his visiting peers.

"So you're saved. You don't see that too often in our business. It's nice to know there's young brothas out there—like yourself, who stand for something besides money and booty." Shantel venerates.

"Thanks—but all the glory be to my heavenly Father. If it wasn't for His grace—and His mercy…we wouldn't be having this conversation here today. *Mmman*, y'all don't know—but I hail from the Southside. Ya might be from the dirty south—but I'm sorry cause— the ATL ain't got doo-doo on Southside Chicago—that be that real dirty-dirty. I'm sayin'…GD's baby. …Grand Boulevard representin'!

But yeah—I used to be out there doin' my thing—I got my hustle on sellin' pharmaceuticals and what nots—just killing my people softly. Ya know—try'na live that life of a thug prince. But every star gots ta fall. ...Sooner or later we reap what we sow. And let's just say—God had otha plans fo this one here!"

"How do you know Rico?" Tae asked, having clung to his every word.

"Riq—that's my dawg. ...Heaven sent! Truth be told—same story, but my man had a God given talent to sing. ...Sung his way right off the streets. Even when he got that contract—he never forgot us. So when he made it—we made it! In my darkest days—my man Riq was the light that brought me through—I'll never forget that. Riq—now he's the real deal. But yo, I thank God for second chances—gave my life to Him. For I ain't *neva* seen the righteous forsaken. And it's been all-good ever since."

They pull up at the front entrance of The Fairmont Chicago. A sophisticated setting summarizes the thirty-seven floor high rise's charm and elegance. The concierge, headed by an older caucasian gentleman, is very helpful as each receives a lakefront suite on the sixteenth floor. The view is stunning, a mere three blocks from Lake Michigan. The large rooms a bit dated, but very clean—the furnishings comfortable, as this will be home for the next five days.

Justin and Demetrius travel between rooms, congregating indiscriminately while Shantel retires to a moment's peace, taking a nap as tonight's agenda will be full. The two men go downstairs for a bite to eat at the Aria Restaurant & Bar. In approximately three and half-hours, the evening will be kicked off with an Arista and Associated labels "meet and greet" at the Foundation Lounge located inside the House of Blues. The night will be concluded with a concert from J Records recording artists Gavin DeGraw and Cassidy. Justin and his team will use tonight as a first step in wooing potential hitmakers—the mega-talented Envy. A limo service has been scheduled to pick up the girls about two hours from now—at around 4pm, and expected to reach the hotel no later than five, giving the separate parties a minute to get reacquainted. Justin and Demetrius discuss the game plan over Hong Kong bbq duck and lobster.

"Six more weeks and we're here. ...Nigga you ready?" Justin says, as he pulls for support.

"Fo sho—we 'bout ta do dis damn thang. *This city...* Man they ain't gonna know what hit they ass—believe that!"

"Al-ight cause I'm gonna be leanin' on you and Tae. Gots ta show strong. We do this right—we'll da fuck blow up."

"Like popcorn baby!" Dee takes a sip of his Sauvignon Blanc.

"Yo while we up here—we need to be lookin' fo a crib. …No complaints, the hotels are straight, especially when it's Riq footin' the bill, but I ain't try'na be cooped up like that fo too long. Nigga got an image to uphold," Justin gaffs. "That's why I need my own shit. I gotta girl over at Remax—Denise, supposedly she's got the hookup. Got me lookin' at these condos off Lake Shore Drive. They look like the shit—but we'll see. I'll check 'em out before we leave—keep from makin' another trip up here."

"Yeah I got ta do that—ain't even got all my shit out of storage yet. And here my ass goes again. …From Connecticut ta Atlanta and now da Chi—all in six months. Ain't that some shit there! 'Yo, but it's all good now—cuz we out da hood now'," he said, reciting a line made famous by Nas and later infamous through a R. Kelly remix. "We comin' up like an early morning sunrise—jus me and my nigga." Justin shakes his head to Dee's foolishness as Demetrius continues to talk. "Yo, hook me up wit your girl—see what she can do. My shit ain't got ta be no loft on da lake—some of us ain't ballin like you nigga. Jus give a nigga like me somewhere ta lay his head—and pop some of this Chi-town pussy—then a nigga straight. Fo sho'!"

"Nigga, are you ever serious man? Shoulda took yo ass ta Comic View or sumptin'. …Hell, ya mighta been somebody! But fo real though—I need ya ta talk that shit tonight. Get 'em loose and make them feel at home. Ya know—spit your usual game. Set 'em up and I'll come behind you wit the business shit. Jus do like we do—I wanna wrap this up early and take it to the house. We got a long day tomorrow." The two finish the high-priced meal then return to their rooms to prepare for the night.

5:06pm

The limo arrives—the girls, Alecia and Valerie have Mr. Vaughn paged. Shantel and Dee are already in Justin's room waiting. It's "meet and greet" time. Tae grabs her purse from off the bed, Justin straightens his casual blazer, and Dee combs through his perfectly sculptured afro. They leave the room looking like the glorified ghetto rendition of the "Mod Squad".

Once downstairs, they meet the young divas in the main lobby. Shantel is the first to greet the future label hitmakers.

"*Hey Ladies.* How you all been?"

"Fine—good," both answer. "How about y'all?" Alecia returns the question.

"We're good. I can see that y'all are lookin' good. *Gurl*—I love those shoes—where did you get 'em?" Tae admiring the glass-like open toe heeled slipper worn by Valerie.

"Girl, from Bakers—and on *clearance!* Fo sho!"

"O-kkkay!" Tae gives Val a girlie high-five hand tap. "Oh, you all have to excuse my rudeness—I know y'all know Justin, but have ya met Demetrius McPhail? He's the newest member of the Sho' Nuff team. He comes to us from Def Soul out of New York. Dee, here's Envy—this is Alecia—and this is Val."

"Nice ta meet cha—I'm lookin' forward ta workin' wit y'all." Dee extends a hand to both young ladies.

"Hey—likewise," they respond one after the other. "*Heeey Justin.* We see you back there playin' Mr. Shy Guy."

"Hey girls—what's up?"

"It's you boo—it's all you!" replies a saucy Alecia. "So, what's up for tonight? …I'm ready ta mingle and get my drink on."

Justin smiles, having previously been exposed to Alecia's brazen ways, he runs down the itinerary for the evening, while Dee, already impressed, especially with Alecia's bold spirited disposition, does the full physical look-over. Judging by their appearance, he clearly sees why they call themselves Envy. Valerie—23, a part-time IT student at IADT-Chicago (International Academy of Design & Technology), is an accomplished musician and songwriter. Bronze toned with straight long jet-black hair compliment her stretched slender frame. She could very well double as a supermodel in a slim sexy size six—Val represents a marketing jewel. Alecia—22, a graduate of Kendall College's business program is the featured vocalist and lead personality of the group. A shade lighter, her below the breast braids and slanted Asian eyes will cause many to drool. Alecia's shorter, thicker frame will contrast Valerie's girl next door look, bridging together the naughty with the nice. Both lifelong residents of Chicago's Southside, the former students of Percy L. Julian High have become the unsigned hype of the Midwest. For now the street smart and business savvy duo represent themselves without any third party management, giving more flexibility to potential labels for negotiations. Justin salivates over the opportunity to work without the interference of outside influences.

As the group reunites, slowly making their way to the limo, Dee figures he'll test the waters early calling for an impromptu sound bite of the girls in action—an abbreviated version of MTV's unplugged.

"Hold up. Before we go another step, I ain't cosigning shit till I at least sample da goods. Got ta give me a lil' sumthin'—Jay and them may have heard y'all, but I ain't heard shit. And I ain't tryna get caught up and assed out. We're talkin 'bout a nigga's livelihood. Where I come from—niggas got ta show and prove—don't jus believe the hype. Hell, if ya sing half as good as ya look—at the very *least* we got double platinum on our hands."

A reluctant Val tries to side step the request with a lame excuse. "*Now?* But we'll sound like crap. I haven't sung a note all day. …We got to warm up first."

While Alecia, on the other hand, without hesitation, is ready to answer the call—always the consummate performer and showoff. "Come on girl we can do this! You know which one. Ready. On one…

When I (Alecia)—*had you* (Both)
I treated you (Alecia)—*bad* (Both)
Wrong my dear (Alecia)
But since (Both)—*since you went away* (Alecia)
Don't you know I (Val)—*hang around* (Alecia)—*sit around* (Val)
With my head (Alecia)—*hanging down* (Both)
And I wonder (Alecia)—*And I wonder* (Val)
Who's (Both)—*loving* (Alecia)—*you* (Both)

A small crowd has gathered around—whistling and applauding as the young sopranos belt out their a cappella rendition of the intro to EnVogue's *Hold On*—a throwback which Justin, Dee, and Tae can all relate to being relics of the early 90's, and now in their early to mid thirties.

"Ahhh! Thank y'all—y'all so sweet" The humble divas take their bows having succeeded in winning over the diverse array of spectators. "Sooo—what did cha think? Are we in—or what?" Alecia directs her question to Dee.

Demetrius, pleased by what he's heard, grins from ear to ear as he stands between the front entrance and the limo and places his arms around the waist of both ladies. "Ladies, come step into my office. We need ta discuss our future relationship." He leads the anxious duo to the stretch Lincoln Navigator that awaits their service—Justin and Shantel trail a few feet behind.

Hours have passed—on center stage Gavin DeGraw has the boisterous House of Blues crowd bouncing to his hit *I Don't Want to Be.* The girls stay right in the thick of the action with arms swaying, screaming every word amongst the hundreds of fans, predominantly white, who have come to enjoy the featured entertainment. Through Justin, Sho' Nuff has provided the girls a quick glimpse into their future from both a business and artist prospective, having met such Arista hierarchy as Bob Parrish—VP for Marketing and Gabrelle Vasquz—Publicity Director, to a first hand peek at the life of an artist on the rise like Gavin DeGraw.

After the show, back inside the limo sitting silently, Alecia and Val ponder their impending decision. Justin makes a plea.

"Now let me ask y'all. Where do ya see yourselves a year from now—five years from now?"

It's at this time that Val voices her comments and concerns. "I don't know, but this is my dream. It's all I ever wanted to do. I mean, ever since I was a little girl, I've always imaged myself singing and performing. But I do know that I'm really ready to do this—and with a major label—boy please! Show me the dotted line. I think the only thing that makes me a lil' nervous—I mean you hear the horror stories about artist who've signed their life away on bogus deals—selling millions and ended up broke."

"Yeah—my thang is our creative freedom. I like what we do. Me and my girl here—we put it down—and it's different—unique! And I'm afraid once we sign and become a part of that corporate machine—we'll lose our voices. And we'll be made into something we're not. It happens all the time. But this is definitely what *I* want! It's in my blood! My momma did backup for many of the Chess artists when it was here in town—back in the day. My brother, he's laid tracks with both Twista and Do or Die. So music has always been a part of who we are. I'm jus ready ta do this. Arista/Sho' Nuff—here we come!"

"I know gurl! It's our time—yes!" Val then grabs Alecia's hand to touch and agree on Alecia's decree.

Meanwhile Justin, sitting next to a legs crossed, arms folded, and head back Tae, nudges her in the side in recognition of the nearly closed deal. Shantel, having heard every word, makes a slight turn towards Justin and casually gives a wink of support. Seeing the hole, Justin runs right up the middle for a touchdown.

"Well, that's one thing you don't have ta worry 'bout. At Sho' Nuff—Rico Pittman takes care of his people. I think that our reputation speaks for itself. When have ya ever heard or read where one of our artists broke camp cause of sumptin' we did? Never—right?"

The girls nod in agreement.

"And that's what I'm sayin'. Sho' Nuff is like family. We may be small, but our impact is global. Jus think about it—who's at the top of the R&B game right now as we speak?"

"Kyra." answers Alecia.

"No doubt—and what label is she on?"

"Sho' Nuff!" responses Val.

"Sho ya right! See—we are the future of black music. We have BeeGee—who's 'bout ta drop his debut. And on the real—I'm tellin' ya his shit is hot—he's gonna turn the Hip-Hop world up side down! And of course Kyra will be back out next year! Y'all hopefully—if you're down wit us, will be makin' your debut around the same time. So the sky's the limit! But it's all up ta you—and you! And what y'all want—and need," he explains, pointing to each girl individually. "If I were you—I wouldn't worry 'bout us try'na change ya. We're interested because of your originality. …We think y'all whole persona is hot! And we'd be fools ta change anything. So rest easy on that one. You'll be safe wit us."

"Jay—did ya tell 'em?" Dee purposely instigates a potential problem.

"Nah! I ain't said nuthin'."

"*What?* Tell us!" probes an already nervous Val.

"See, y'all ain't right. We haven't even signed yet and already y'all are withholding information. Do we need to keep looking?" Alecia teases light-heartedly.

"That's right—get in his ass girl! Show 'em what a Chi-town bunny is made of! I mean, come on… What's up with that? How are we supposed ta trust y'all?" Val pops Justin in the arm.

"Jay—go ahead and break them off sumthin'. Let 'em know what's really goin' on."

"Yeah Jay—listen to your boy—tell us!" Alecia eggs Justin on.

"Well, it was supposed ta be a surprise. But I see someone can't hold water." Justin pierces adamantly in Dee's direction. "Nah—but fo real though, in about six weeks or so we'll be doin' business right here in the Chi. Therefore, most of the time y'all will get ta stay right here at home."

Both Alecia and Val wear a dumbfounded look across their faces—totally oblivious to Justin's meandering.

"What he's trying to say is—Sho' Nuff is expanding and we'll be opening an office in Chicago—right on Michigan Avenue. And guess who'll be in charge? …None other than our very own Mr. Justin Vaughn, himself." Shantel reiterates to Alecia and Val from her relaxed—eyes closed, head tilted back position. She remains aware enough to keep her legs crossed for no other reason than to protect her private area from any uninvited viewing because of the loose undersized chiffon skirt she has on—especially with an ever-obnoxious Dee seated directly across the cabin floor.

Alecia and Val exchange dap as a show of approval. Justin again places the ball in their court.

"Well ladies—so what's it gonna be? Can I go ahead and call Riq—set up an appointment—discuss the legalities?"

After a long sigh from Val, the promising duo looking deep into each other's eyes, twist back toward Justin as three words "let's do it!" are boldly uttered from the mouth of their spokesperson Alecia

With that, Justin and the gang congratulates the young ladies of Envy. On a preconceived hunch, he has ordered congratulatory beverages to be stocked inside the limo. Out comes a sealed, already chilled, bottle of Moet and five crystal champagne flutes are passed around. Dee does the honors. He whistles to seize everyone's attention. "HEY! Can y'all please shut da hell up fo a minute?"

The group settles as Dee proposes a toast.

"Ladies—first of all, I would like ta say—even though it ain't official til a nigga puts a pen ta da paper… But welcome to Sho' Nuff Entertainment. Ya couldn't have picked a better company ta screw ya—I mean help ya!" He chuckles at his own funny. "But seriously on behalf of my bosses—Rico Pittman and Mr. Justin "too sexy fo his clothes" Vaughn—we say 'thank you' for choosing us ta represent ya—and may the force be wit cha so we all can make this paper. Godspeed ta da both of ya's etc., etc.—and etc. Wit raised glasses let a nigga say—Cheers!"

"Cheers!" The simultaneous response precedes the pinging of glass.

Amidst the hoopla and jubilation, laughter and frolic—Justin steals a moment to send a single simplistic text message to Rico… "SSD" meaning—**S**igned, **S**ealed, and **D**elivered!

eight

Say It Ain't So!

It's been a week of browsing and carousing the city. After adding Envy to an already stacked lineup, the rest of the week is spent in preparation for the upcoming move. Justin attends the close of the new facility as across the board renovations are due to start the following week. During his down time, he checks into a few real estate leads. He finds himself particularly fond of 1400 North Lake Shore Drive a prestigious condominium property overlooking the lake. This address will keep him close to his office over on Michigan Avenue. He takes one last long look at the impressive Chicago skyline as his flight ascends over the city.

♡   ♡   ♡

Now comfortably at home, Justin flips through brochures of his second and third rental choices while sitting on the living room sofa. Feeling festive and having mentally made a final decision on his future residence, he tosses the potential garbage on the slate coffee table and reaches for his cell. Ready to celebrate recent accomplishments, he pauses to consider his options. No Tonya—no Teresha, for neither is particularly speaking to him these days. The next likely choice—

Shanice becomes the apparent winner by default. Using voice dialing, he announces her name. "Shanice". But to his surprise a man answers her phone. He can hear children playing in the background.

"…Can I speak to Shanice?"

"May I ask who's speaking?"

"A friend." Feeling that his name is none of this man's business.

"Buddy, do you have a name?" responds the mystery man sounding a bit annoyed.

"Look dawg—if I'm interuptin' sumptin'—then my bad! I'm an old friend back in town checkin' in. Jus tell her Justin called. Peace!" As Justin hangs up the phone, he now understands why he hasn't heard much from Shanice lately. There's a new sheriff in town!

Shrugging off the slight disappointment, he remembers the pretty dark skinned female who had given him the digits that day at Balazaars. He tries to recall what he was wearing on the afternoon of Kyra's luncheon. "…Bingo! Dolce and Gabbana—striped shirt!" He runs upstairs hoping he hasn't already sent this particular piece to the cleaners.

"Cool—there is a God!" he says as he fumbles through a crowded closet clothing rack where he finds the multicolored button-down hung neatly on a wooden hanger. "It pays to procrastinate," he comments to himself. Removing the folded napkin from the pocket, the name comes back to him "Porsha Sparks. Well Porsha—let's see whatcha all about!" Justin takes a seat at the foot of his bed. And with cell in hand, he dials the number. After the first ring, she answers.

"*Hello?*"

"What's sup!"

"Who is this?"

"Guess!"

"Excuse me!"

"Guess!"

"Why I do I have ta guess? Just tell me!" she says, unwilling to play along.

"Cuz—I said so!"

"Darryl—stop playin'!"

"This ain't Darryl."

"Who is this!" She raises her voice in aggravation.

"Justin."

"Justin who?"

"Oh, you know. What, now you don't remember me?"

"Why—am I supposed to?"

"Hell yeah. …Balazaars'—Kyra!"

"Oooh—you're that guy. The cutie! …I remember. What took you so long to call?"

"Out of town on business—but I'm back!"

"Sooo Justin—what is it exactly that you do to keep you on the road?"

"I am the head of A&R at Sho' Nuff Entertainment. That's why I was there that day wit Kyra."

"Go head wit your bad self! A man with a *real* job—I was wonderin' about that. I thought maybe you were just one of her half interested boy toys."

"Oh, it's like dat? You like creepin' in the back door?"

"Why not—you didn't seem too thrilled to be there. Why let such a cute tenderoni go to waste?"

"I heard that. …Ya know what? I like yo style. Whatcha doin' tonight?"

"Workin'—but I'm free tomorrow."

"Well—it sounds like a date! Where can we meet?"

"*Huh*—I don't know. How far are you from the AU Center?"

"Not too far—I'm over in Cascade. But I woulda figured you were north of the perimeter by the 770 area code. Are you a student or sumptin'?"

"*Nooo*." She smiles at Justin's burning curiosity. "I used to go Morris Brown—but that was a few years ago. And yes—I do live north of the perimeter—over in Smyrna. And in case you're worried—I'm twenty-five and very legal." Again she smiles—then laughs as her humorous nature can be heard through the phone. "But I do still have some friends and sorors over that way. So I'll be out there all day."

"I wasn't worried—but it's always nice ta know. Let me guess—you an AKA?"

"*Nooo*—a Delta. What makes ya think I was an AKA?"

"I went ta FAM—I know how it goes. AKA's were always the pretty girls. And the Deltas were the chicks wit brains."

"No you didn't! …What I look dumb?"

"No—but ya definitely got it goin' on. I jus woulda pegged ya as an AKA."

"Thanks—I think." She's amused and at the same time flattered by Justin's explanation. "Take me to Visions tomorrow night!"

"Take ya where?"

"Visions. I ain't stutter!"

"That's what I thought. Oh, you tryin' ta hang wit the beautiful folks."

"I'm tryin' to be with you."

Justin, by her smooth lingo, recognizes he's not dealing with any ordinary amateur. She's got much game—but of course he's up to the challenge—so he takes her on. "You neva said exactly where ta pick ya up."

"Meet me in the lobby of Gaines Hall about 10 o' clock. …It's right there on MLK. Ya can't miss it. …Oh, and this time—don't have a sista waiting." She sarcastically refers to Justin's more than a week delay in calling her."

"Cool—I'll see ya then."

"Yep—goood night."

"Peace."

There's silence but neither has hung up the phone. Justin acknowledges the situation. "Whatcha waitin' on ta hang up da phone!"

"You hang up!"

Shaking his head with a smirk, he says, "Ya gots ta be a silly ass. I can see now you gonna give a nigga hell."

"Yep—that's my every intention."

"Take yo ass ta work! I'll se ya tomorrow."

"Yep."

"Bye." This time, Justin disconnects.

And for a moment, he sits there in deep concentration as he tries to understand what it is about her that has left this fidgety feeling in the pit of his stomach. The shakiness one experiences when they've had too much caffeine or taken a Stacker when it was still laced with ephedra—that nervous energy.

While Justin sits with the phone, he makes a brief call to Jackie to let her know he's made it in. As he starts to dial the next number—he stops once he realizes he's really not in the mood for Teresha's trivial yin yang. But it's been a week since he last talked to Justice. As a trade off, he leaves Sunday open for quality time with his son.

Justin spends what's left of this Friday afternoon, relaxing in green sweats with orange lettering from his alma mater—FAMU plastered down the outer side of each leg. A gray Hanes tee completes the look. In his room, he watches a marathon of old Tyson fights on ESPN 2.

Saturday night.

With his hands, Justin mocks the presence of two turntables as he, in his mind, scratches the beginning words of Schooly Dee's 'Gucci Time.'

"Look—lo-look." Pause. "Lookin' at my Gucci it's 'bout dat time." Justin flashes back to the days when he and Jerome used to mix and cut, deejaying neighborhood house parties and skating rinks. It's Saturday night and he's feelin' alright! His jovial mood transcends the quiet, dark atmosphere of an empty house. He's amped about tonight. For it's been a minute since he's felt such enthusiasm for a date. Maybe because a week has gone by from the time of his last sexual encounter—the debacle with Teresha. Yet to Justin, a week is like a lifetime.

His attire reflects the environment for which he's about to enter. Helmut Lang—Jean Paul Gaultier headline his topnotch apparel. Vision—formerly Club Kaya, once known for its Northern Exposure Fridays' hosted by V103's Frank Ski, attracts a plethora of sports and entertainment personalities amidst its 27,000 square feet of interior space. After two million dollars of renovations, the new look Vision is hands down one of metro Atlanta's hottest nightspots. Without a doubt, Justin will use his industry influence to impress the outgoing Porsha.

The drive over to the AU Center is casual as Justin encounters minimal traffic, which is highly unusual for a Saturday night. One good reason could be because the Braves are away playing in Cincinnati to face the Reds. Even so, traffic is still very light compared to the normal weekend buzz. Yet, the scenario plays in Justin's favor who—like tradition declares, is running behind. As he approaches the Morris Brown campus, he rides slowly down through MLK to ensure he doesn't miss his mark.

The surroundings, similar to that of his alma mater, takes him back to his collegiate days. He remembers also having a MLK Boulevard. And what everyone called "the set." A single block stretch from Barbourville Drive to Palmer Avenue—also described from the Paige Building down to Lee Hall. Party central in those days was none other than McGuinn Hall—an all female dormitory. One of three that populated the area as there were many skipped classes spent sniffing around this godsend. Across the street was the student union building and campus bookstore where on any given afternoon you may see the Que's—stomping and stepping to "Atomic Dog" while howling their signature dog call. Or the Caribbean Club spinning Dancehall vibes to promote one of their frequent island affairs. With a proud grin, he reflects upon those college years as many of the lessons learned took place outside of the classroom.

His moment of reminiscing comes to an abrupt end when he spots what he thinks to be an accompanied Porsha walking across the campus yard. Instinctively he peeks down at the platinum Movado that decorates his wrist. He realizes it's 9:47. He's actually early rather than late—convinced that the smooth traffic has saved at least fifteen minutes on his arrival time. And like a Private Dick, he peers across the university commons in scrutiny of her anonymous beau. A short distance away the two seemingly smitten souls reach the intended destination of Gaines Hall. Justin sees the couple with outstretched arms colliding to partake in what appears to be a very compromising embrace. The outdoor lighting of the presumably vacant building illuminates the two subjects—he instantly notices the overnight bag thrown over her shoulder. The moderate glow cast from sparse lighting clarifies the images. Justin takes a good intense look at the tall mulatto brother with an afro of untwisted braids supported by a white headband. His goatee is tightly manicured while his frame exudes athleticism. He wears a dark colored pullover with some type of unfamiliar wording. Justin assumes it represents his school—Morris Brown. After finishing their departing words, the anonymous figure disappears into the darkness. Porsha's eyes are affixed to the fleeting image until he finally vanishes. Justin toots his horn to grab her preoccupied attention.

Porsha, having no idea of Justin's means of transportation, cautiously approaches the vehicle. Seeing her hesitation, he flicks on his interior lights to identify himself. Once confirming his identity, she waves as she picks up the pace in her step. Before jumping into the car, she walks around to the driver side window. Justin pushes the button to roll it down.

"I see you made it!" she said, as she leans over the door.

"What's up? Were ya worried?"

"Not exactly, but I don't think it's too copesetic ta leave such precious cargo unattended." she said, referring to herself. "Someone may actually try and snatch my cookies! It seems safe enough—but ya neva know… The world is full of crazy people. Damn, you smell good! Armani—Acqua di Gio?" She leans through the window to take a deeper whiff. Her nose rest less than an inch away from his cheek as she intentionally teases him.

"I'm impressed—I see ya know your shit."

"Yep! Nice ride—2005 SRT8?" She delights herself on the interior specifications such as the leather seats, simulated wood-grain, analog controls and the satin chrome accents.

"Yeah man! What da fuck? You try'na size up my pockets or sumptin'?" he said, realizing that he might very well be out with a gold digger.

"Yep. …I like a man wit style and finesse."

"*Really.* At least a nigga's honest. So what's up? Must we continue ta have this conversation between a closed door? C'mon around and git in!"

"You a trip!" she says grinning as she trots around to the other side. She places her small duffel on the floor between her legs.

"And you a journey! So now what?"

"Good-lookin'—intelligent—paid and jus so happens to be a pompous asshole. …It figures," Porsha elaborates on her first impressions.

"And as you would so eloquently put it—Yep! I aim ta please darlin'."

"Oooh I'm gonna hate you!" Both laugh.

Until now, Justin hasn't made a single comment about Porsha's dress—or the lack of it. She wears a black lace halter ensemble and open toed high heels where the straps wrap halfway up her calf. It's actually quite amazing that she wasn't harassed—with or without a man at her side considering the area.

"Yeah and by da way—You-Look-Marvelous!" he says as he tries to pull off his best Billy Crystal impersonation.

"Why thank you—and of course so do you."

Just by the conversation, Justin knows Porsha isn't about shit. Another high maintenance hoe looking for a handout. He's seen it all before—he knows what he's dealing with. Yet he's still game to amuse his curiosity. They prance around half naked flaunting that tight pretty ass. Sexy as hell, but still just a high-class trick trying to survive with your paycheck. Ass for cash as Justin often referred to it. And knowing this—he continues in his pursuit. The way he sees it—if anything, she is a definite dime-piece. Heads would forever turn with her at his side. And by his own rationale—impression is everything!

Her flawless cocoa butter skin monopolizes his mind. He can't help but to stare at her obvious external features. The humid night air has caused her moistened body to stick against the leather interior, bringing a revealing rise to her exhibitionist worthy attire. Her lace dress though backed with a nude lining doesn't leave much to be desired, but only adds to her titillating mystique. Porsha's thin long, yet defined legs sparkle as the heat has caused the Cucumber Melon lotion to restrict her pores, leaving the sweat to rest atop of her moisturized skin. Justin imagines having Porsha in the buck—legs flicked over his shoulders as he rides knee deep in pussy.

"What's in the bag?" His thoughts have brought him to inquiry about the contents of the duffel lying between her legs.

"Sooo—what is this? Tit for tat are we? Now why you all up in my business? Naw—let me guess?" he says while laughing. "You're probably thinking I'm some insane psycho bitch like that woman down in Florida… The one they made the movie about. You're afraid I might slice your ass up and leave you on the side of the road—gank you for your goods. …I know that's what you're thinkin'." She chuckles.

"Hadn't thought about it—but now that you mention it… Ain't no tellin'—I don't know ya fo shit but got yo ass sittin' up in my car—late at night. What da fuck was I thinkin'?" Justin gives a quirky smirk. "Nah, but fo real though—Inquiring minds wanna know."

"Well, in that case Mr. Inquiring minds—being that we hit it off so well on da phone last night, I thought maybe we could—that is if you don't terribly mind, possibly make it a night. Either we can go back to my place or yours and hang out. …Play it by ear and see what happens. If necessary—I don't mind sleepin' on the couch. That is, of course, if you don't have other plans." Porsha picks up the small bag from off the floor—opens it and rattles through her inventory. "So, I brought a toothbrush, makeup, perfume—my thongs, a tank top… Oh—and another dress!"

Surprised by the blatant forwardness—he's all in as he thanks the Heavenly Father above. For this type of shit only happens on TV. Even for a playa like himself, a chick of this caliber—this easy, may randomly transpire once every blue moon. "You serious?" He makes sure he's heard right.

"Yeah—why? You must be surprised?"

"A lil'. Hell, it ain't everyday a nigga gets seduced by a gorgeous woman."

"Well, let's just say it's your lucky night."

"How 'bout we jus skip the club—and head to the house?"

"Hold up lover man.—Now you try'na play a sista cheap. Didn't your mama tell you—ain't nuthin' in this world for free. ...Not even pussy!" Laughing, she says, "And if you thought that—better think again. Child support, alimony, jewelry, clothes, shoes, light bills, gas bills, cell phones, drinks—baby daddies, AIDS, herpes, the clap... Don't get it bent—everything comes with a price tag." She counts every example with each finger. "And my price just happens ta be an all expenses paid, night out on the town. Such a small investment to reap such bountiful returns."

Once Justin lifts his jaw from his lap, he's thinking, "This damn girl is off da chain! ...And crazy as she wants ta be." He knows he shouldn't even be fuckin' with this girl. But then he ponders a really tough question. "Pussy vs. Principle, Principle vs. Pussy. "Hell, I'll take the pussy!" And there it is, once again, Justin throws his dick to the wind.

As they get to Vision, just judging by the parking in and around 10th and Peachtree, there's little doubt that the venue will reach its 2,400-person capacity. Finding parking would become a bitch having driven up and down 11th and 12th Streets. It's just after 11—long lines have formed already from the entrance. The cheapest lot Justin finds is $40—he takes it.

Taking Porsha by the hand, they move to the shorter of two lines because of his VIP status. He drops a couple hundred dollars—they enter. The reinvented megaclub now has six mood varying spaces with state of the art lighting and over sixty 42" plasma televisions. The scene is breathtaking. Justin heads directly for the orange room a.k.a. the overlook. An exclusive VIP area overlooking the dance floor. Decked in orange textures, suede banquettes, and hardwoods, Justin drops another undisclosed amount for a table. He and Porsha take their seat.

They start the night off with a couple of Martinis. Porsha points out the celebrities who dot the VIP section. A notable Atlanta sports personality stops by the table to say a few words to Justin. Then a popular Hot 107.9 deejay follows suit. Justin orders a bottle of Cristal. It's quite obvious that Porsha is enjoying herself. They talk over the loud music—until they hear a remix of Amerie's "One Thing". Both jump up to hit the huge dance floor. Porsha moves circles around Justin, as her fluid motions work him from top to bottom. Realizing that he's outdone, he then takes the easy route—moving to a simpler more repetitive step. At one point, during a break in the song—Porsha reverses direction, her back faces Justin. In a motion reminiscent of something from a booty club, Porsha shakes her butt in rhythmic fashion, bouncing backwards, closing the gap between her and Justin. As her juicy booty grinds against his pelvis, his second head lifts to full attention. Feeling his python brushing across her protruding ass, she turns around to experience him from the front. She takes quick liking to his above average size as she throws her arms around his neck, pressing her enhanced breasts to his muscular torso. He reciprocates by placing his hands around her slender waist. They now operate in a frequency all of their own as they move to a different beat. Their chemistry is undeniable. After thirty minutes of aerobic activity, they leave the floor, to retreat to the intimate setting of their private table. Sweat has caused Porsha's bone strait doo to cling to her face, partially covering her eyes. Her wet body gives her the appearance of a Sports Illustrated model who steps from ocean waters onto a fresh sandy shore. She looks stunning!

It's 3am—the club is closing. Through the vast emptying crowd, they make their way to the car. They walk and talk.

"Did ya enjoy yourself?" Justin asks.

"Sure did!" Pausing, she says, "Thank you baby."

"No problem. The pleasure was all mine. Are you hungry?"

"Hmmm—you know what? I am feelin' a lil' famished. Whatcha got in mind?"

"I'm not quite sure. What are our options? Say—you in the mood for chicken and waffles?"

"I'm game—Gladys's?"

"The one—the only. It's right down the street, so let's get on over there. If I'm right, they don't close until four—we got 'bout an hour."

"You know they're gonna be crowded."

"I know. Everybody and they mama gonna be up in there. But as long we git in the door—get us a plate, we straight. Shit, we ain't got ta sit down and eat… Take that shit back ta the crib. A nigga can eat in peace—know what I mean?"

"Whatever you wanna do bae." She clinches on to Justin's arm while resting her head on his shoulder. As her tiredness sets in, she releases an uncharacteristic yawn.

"Hell, I've been lookin' up in niggas faces all night. What I wanna see tonight is yo Hershey ass—butt ass naked, laid up in *my* bed!"

The comment causes Porsha to immediately rise up. She wasn't expecting such vulgarity from Justin—but she likes it. "You nasty." They walk huddled together with her head again at rest—pressed against his collar.

As anticipated, the cozy homey-inspired restaurant is fairly crowded—mostly bar hoppers and club-goers. Just the same, they would have to endure an extended wait. While they stand, Porsha repositions herself, now wrapping her arms around his waist, she uses his broad physical dimensions for support. She's secure within his strong presence. Justin is soothed by her affection. He delicately fixes her mildly ruffled hair—setting each misplaced strand back in its proper location. He then lightly kisses her on the forehead. Looking up, she moves her lips to his and they interchange a quick peck.

"You Al-ight?"

"Um-hmmm."

But the romantic mood is broken by their animated feminine order-taker.

"May I help you?" asks this frail, over processed hair wearing mere shadow of a man.

Justin's first thought is "Hell, fuck naw!" But what actually comes from his mouth is more like "Yeah—I want the chicken and waffle combo—yo make that two!" also thinking about Jerome. "Yeah and hook me up wit a piece of that sweet potato cheesecake. What ch'ou want?" now looking toward Porsha.

"Hmmm—give me an order of waffles—*annnd* some grits and eggs. Bae, you gonna share a couple of your wings wit me right?"

"Man, jus give me another order of them wings." He looks to Porsha, "I don't know 'bout ch'ou but I'm hungry."

"Justin, look at me—I can't eat all of that."

"Don't worry 'bout it—I got cha!"

"Is that all sir?" the worker says as he begins losing his patience.

"Yeah—that's it!" Justin takes care of the damage with his Visa. Ten minutes later they head to the house.

Justin rolls in the yard about four-thirty. In the driveway, Jerome's modified Expedition sits glistening from the moonlight. It catches Porsha's attention.

"That's you too?"

"Nah, that's my brother Jerome's."

"You live here with your brother?"

"Yeah. Well, at least fo another couples of months."

"Why is that?"

"A nigga gotta promotion a few weeks back. So my ass is headed to Chicago."

"Oh, so you a shot caller huh?"

"I guess you can say that."

Justin shuts the car off. They enter through the studio door. As he turns on the recessed lighting by way of the dimmer switch, Porsha goes from side to side—corner to corner, digesting the many extravagant features of the space.

"Damn! Do y'all even use this?" she says, impressed by its cleanliness.

"All the time. Actually it's probably the most used room in the house. Do ya remember the remix ta 'It's All You'?" referring to the Kyra classic.

"*Yeeeah*. We used ta jam off that!"

"Conceived right here in this room."

"No shit!"

"C'mon girl let's go eat."

The studio leads directly through to the kitchen. Once there, Justin places Jerome's order in the fridge. The two sit down next to one another at the bar-like counter. Justin is quick to stuff his face while Porsha takes a more methodical approach to devouring her meal. She even takes time out to feed Justin from her plate. Pulling two glasses from the cupboard, he returns to the fridge and fills them with sweet tea. A few minutes later, he licks the saucy remains from his fingers and dumps the empty tray in the trash. Porsha closes her lid to signify her being finished. He puts her food away, and then kindly snatches her hand as they tip quietly up the stairs.

As soon as he walks into his bedroom, he picks up a few floor thrown articles of clothing—especially his draws, and tosses them in his bathroom closet hamper. He sprays a squirt or two of Renuzit smell good to freshen up the stale air—strolls over to his Sony DVD/CD player—pops in a Ready for the World greatest hits CD and turns on the surround sound. Meanwhile Porsha, who has laid her overnight bag against the closed bedroom door, has made her way over to Justin's king sized bed—plopping down on it as if she's taken her last possible step. She sits leaned back on her elbows. Her legs lay spread open while her head tilts forward as she watches a silly Justin try his very best to lip sync. His efforts bring a warranted smile.

"Oh—Oh—Oh—Oh—girrrl tonight. Oh—Oh—Oh—Oh…" Justin, a legend in his own mind, attempts to croon the 80's love song. Maneuvering himself closer to the bed, he moves seductively between her inner thighs. He stops, holds out his hand and says, "Get up."

Porsha agrees, placing her hand in his, as Justin helps her up, pulling her very close. "May I have this dance?" Porsha accepts.

They twirl the floor till the wee hours of the morning. The sensual atmosphere has given Porsha a second wind. Simple sporadic pecks become a continuous French kiss as their maple syrup and barbecue saturated tongues dance melodiously together. The intense passion has each clinging desperately to one another. Undoing the neck, Justin lifts her tight stretch fitted dress above her head—her lacy panties match the removed garment—nothing else is left. Without warning she unloosens Justin's Nautica belt, unzipping his pants. With one strong tug he now wears his polyester blend down around his ankles. Not wasting another second, she drops to her knees, grabbing his man sized penis with both hands and opens wide. Like a woman who aims to please, she sucks him with excruciating fervor. Up and down, in and out, and around and round—she slobs the bob, placing most of her emphasis on his overly sensitive tip—the urethra. Justin, having a hard time staying still, can't handle the pleasurable agony, as he stumbles backward, falling to the lush carpeted floor. Porsha doesn't miss a beat, resuming her work between his now quivering knees. In under a minute, she takes him to the next level. His eyes have rolled back, which is then followed by a relieving gasp, his milky cum oozes from the corners of her still full mouth. She swallows, and then lies across his rapidly beating chest.

"Did cha like?" She slowly runs her airbrushed fingernail over his moist lips.

"Shit, what ch'ou thought? …That shit was the bomb!" The mere thought has caused his saliva-ridden penis to recuperate.

"Ah—I feel someone's tryin' ta tell me something."

"Hell yeah—c'mon let's get in the bed."

As they crawl under the covers, she flings her already dampened panties to the side of the mattress. Justin positions himself over top of her—but doesn't touch her. Without hesitation, he starts in on her two Hershey kisses. While sucking the right nipple, his fingers caress the left. She groans and squirms as she strokes her hand over his nearly bald head. His mouth and tongue continue south, taking a short layover at her once pierced navel. Returning to his travels, he discovers that the grass has been cleared—his path is now smooth. He glides into his destination. Justin tickles her pearl with his sharp tongue. She responds by attempting to push his determined head away. In the process, she scoots her body forward, bumping her head against the cast iron frame. He resorts to softly sucking her clitoris—her moans soon turn to tears of pleasure as she cums profusely. The combination of their separate juices cast a stringy trail of excreted fluids that journeys from his lips to her cunt. Moving up, he then rotates her limber body sideways. As Justin adjusts himself, he's now up on his knees straddling her left leg. Her flexibility is apparent as she lifts the other leg straight up. It's held in place by her arm of that same side. Justin guides his unprotected manhood into her creamy split. Her small frame takes his large offering with no resistance. She runs deep. ...It's the perfect match.

For the next hour, her screams and hollers can be heard throughout the quiet quarters. Their salty, sweaty, exasperated bodies have completely drenched the bed. She may be deep but he's managed to work every nook and cranny of her juice flooded hole. With one final frenzied push, they, like two-wounded animals, howl together in the barren night, signaling that both have reached climax at the same time. They lay one inside the other—collapsing into a hard unconscious sleep.

nine

Played

A brand new day—in fact it's Sunday around brunch. It's funny
what a difference a week makes. Just seven short days ago, Justin felt
his life was in a shambles. Sour women, the struggles of parenthood,
and the pressures of his high profile job all came to a head. That was
one week ago. But as seasons change, so do our circumstances. And
we see—just one short week later, he's back on top—the man of the
hour at work, and one who is at this very moment enjoying the spoils
of new pussy. As for now—life is good!

Awakened by the sound of a nearby riding mower, Justin stretches
and looks towards the time projection which reads 11:24am. A now
moving Porsha turns to Justin with content smiles and greets her newly
acquainted lover.

"*Heeey.*"

"Hey."

"*Heeeeeey.*" Still half sleep, they both laugh at Porsha's repeated
remark.

"How ya feel this morning—hell I might as well say this afternoon.
It's already after eleven."

"I'm good. …Shit—real good!" She reaches toward the ceiling with outstretched hands. "Oow I need ta pee!" Porsha abruptly bounces from the bed and scants to the toilet. "I love this bathroom. You all have a nice house." The resonance of gushing urine nearly drowns the compliment.

"Thank you. …You almost finished? I need ta get in there too. I gotta pee."

"Shit—has anyone ever told you that you need a license for that thang?"

"Whatcha talkin' 'bout?"

"Your dick! That fucker is a concealed weapon. You tried ta wear me out last night. …Got my stuff throbbing."

With boosted ego, Justin grins, "Word. Yo ass shouldn't have come up in here with some shit that damn good. Had a nigga's toes curlin'. And that's sayin' sumptin'."

"Well, I'm glad you enjoyed! So what are we doin' today?"

"Shit—I have no clue, but I know what we're 'bout ta do right now!"

"What?"

"Fuck. …Then eat!"

"Ain't cha had enough?"

"Hell nah. So hurry up and bring your ass back up in here!"

"*Hello*—Don't we need ta wash up first? If ya haven't noticed but I'm covered with dried cum—that's nasty! …Thought you said you had to pee."

Justin laughs, and then throws a pillow from off the bed and into the bathroom. "I know yo lil' freak ass ain't talkin'. Besides, it's all-natural? …Shit—I bet that pussy is real good right 'bout now. Juices all marinated and shit. I know ya still wet!"

"Boy shut-up!" She reaches down and hurls the stray pillow minus its case back into the now day-lit bedroom.

"…Yo, do me a favor?"

"*What?* …Whatcha want?"

"…Don't wipe!" He makes a rather unusual request.

"Bae—you got ta be crazy! Ole' nasty butt."

She finishes having honored his wishes—a sticky Porsha climbs back in bed, Justin gets up to relieve himself. He returns to more of the same—more screams, more exchanging of bodily fluids, and more sheets in need of a good washing. They grind it out for the better part of the afternoon, only coming up for air to refuel their empty stomachs. Justin goes downstairs to the kitchen where a currently seated Jerome curiously interrogates.

"Damn man. Where you been? …Who ya wit?"

"This chick named Porsha."

"She fine?"

"Hell yeah—her shit's on point. Ain't had no ass like that fo a minute. Fo sho'!"

"Word. That's all I heard last night—homegirl screamin' and shit. Loud as hell too. Ya had ta be rippin' that shit up!"

"Yes sir-rie buddy—I put it on her! …Hell, you heard! I fucked that bitch till she 'bout couldn't walk! Fo real!"

"I hear ya." Jerome cuts his comment short as in bops a nosy Porsha. She graces the room wearing nothing but Justin's Helmut Lang shirt worn the night before.

"Hey Jerome. What are y'all cookin'?" Porsha says, boldly injecting herself between the two brothers.

Jerome trips by the way she just jumps right in the mix—almost as if she's known a nigga all her barely grown life.

Being sarcastic Jerome asked, "Do I know you?"

Justin intercedes with an introduction. "Rome meet Porsha. …And Porsha, of course this is my baby brother Jerome—Producer extraordinaire."

The two strangers give a mutual nod and smile. Jerome breaks the ice. "I guess that makes it official. How ya doin'? It's nice ta met ya girl!"

"Likewise."

"Let me get out of y'alls way—I'll holla at cha later."

"Peace." Justin endorses his brother's 'three is a crowd' departure.

"You don't have ta run off. You all can talk. I'll go back upstairs," pleads a guilty Porsha.

"Nah it's cool—I got shit ta do. I'm sure I'll be seein' ya around. …Peace out y'all." Jerome waves goodbye as he goes through the studio and out the door.

"Damn! I see cute runs in the family," she says, as she helps herself to an ice-cold glass of orange juice.

"That's right! And I'm sure he has a big dick too. But I'll be sure ta ask him fo ya. …Trick!" A jealous Justin slings the unwarranted comment.

"*Whatever.*" She puts her half-empty glass back down on the counter and waltzes up the steps.

Justin, attempting to be incognito, peeks around the corner to the staircase making sure Porsha is out of sight. He grabs their seldom-used home phone mounted on the kitchen wall and dials Teresha to talk to Justice.

"Hey. Whatcha doin'?"

"Aaah—jus washing clothes. I think Justice is upstairs on that game again." Her demeanor is surprisingly cordial.

"Will he be free later?"

"*Yeeeah.* I can go ahead and have him prepare for school now, that way we won't have to rush in the morning—why?"

"Nah—I wanna see if it's alright wit you if I take him over to Magic Johnson's. ...Catch a flick or sumptin'."

"Okay. I'm sure he'll love that. Around what time?"

"I'll be over there 'bout 6:30—let me talk to 'em."

She covers the receiver. "JUSTICE! ...Pick up the phone!"

"Hello." Teresha clicks off on her end.

"Hey lil' man."

"Hey Dad."

"Feel like hangin' out tonight?"

"Yeah, that's cool! Where we goin'?"

"I'm thinkin' the movies. ...That straight?"

"Yeah! Can we see *Four Brothers*?"

"Doesn't matter—whatever ya wanna see. I'll scoop ya round 6:30. So be ready."

"Okay pops—bye!"

"Al-ight—bye." Justin places the phone on the wall, checks the time and returns upstairs.

He enters the room to see Porsha lying on her stomach across the unmade bed—still wearing his designer shirt which has risen above naked ass. She's watching television. Justin, wanting to ease the tension created by his earlier remark, jumps in bed next to Porsha, nudging her with his much larger body. He cheeses, attempting to be silly.

"Will I see ya tomorrow?"

Porsha, who never takes her face out the television, blandly replies, "Maybe. We'll see. Jus call me tonight."

"Al-ight—let's take a shower so I can run ya home. I got some work ta catch up on for tomorrow. I'll call ya later."

"Yep." She then convincingly converts her standoffish disposition—turns to give Justin a kiss and promptly exits the bedroom to take her shower.

Some forty-five minutes later, Justin takes Porsha home. He's somewhat surprised to learn that her Smyrna residence is actually in the Vinings—a high market area similar to Buckhead mainly composed of yuppies. Not necessarily what comes to mind when he thinks of Porsha. He knows the area well having lived in Cobb County for a number of years. From Paces Ferry Road, they enter the 360-unit AMLI residence through the access gate. He counts two swimming pools, a tennis court, and detached garages—definitely a nice place. In his mind he's thinking that either the restaurant is paying that damn good or she shares the apartment with a roommate. They pull in front of her building located at the back of the complex. She thanks him for a wonderful time. They get in one last smack, Porsha jumps out the car with her duffel strapped to the shoulder and trots upstairs to a third floor corner unit. She waves, leaning across the wrought iron banister before opening her door.

Justin vacates the complex making the sizable hike in the opposite direction to pick up his son. Having discussed the ground rules with Teresha before leaving, he alters the game plan, deciding that it would be best if they instead see *"The Underclassman"* because of its PG-13 rating. Justice obviously a little disappointed, understands that a night out with dad—is just that! Therefore, he'll relish the time spent regardless of what movie they see. The two fellas catch the 7:10 showing. Justin does it up, allowing Justice to have his run of the snack bar. Popcorn with extra butter, nachos with cheese, Mike and Ike's, and a large pop are carried into the stadium-seated theater. Two hours and a few laughs later, they head down the 166 to College Park. After saying their good-byes, Teresha then follows Justin out the door. She takes a seat on the brick step in front of her door while Justin leans against the hood of her Ford Explorer. They share a few minutes of friendly conversation under starlit skies.

"Ya know—one of these days we have to work through our differences for the sake of that little boy in there."

"I know. You right. I've been thinkin 'bout that too. It hurts him ta see us actin' the way we do. It's like we're forcin' him ta take sides when he loves us both."

"Yeah—I see it on his face everyday. It's already hard enough not having us together as a family. And now, I think it's beginning ta effect on his grades. ...I don't know—I hate ta see him hurtin' like this. What do we do?"

"Maybe I'll take up some more time wit him over these next few weeks. Do some things we haven't done… Maybe go fishin' or some shit. …Sumptin'. I don't know, but we'll work it out. I know the boy needs his father though."

"*Yeeeah*—he does." She stands up, dusting off her rear end. "Okay—well I better let you go. I need to get back up in here and finish washing. I know you got places ta go—and probably people to see. So I guess I'll talk ta ya later."

"Girl come here—you so silly." He gives her a big warm hug, fitting of a deep friendship.

As soon as Justin hits the 285 expressway, having just left Teresha's, he calls Porsha now, anxious to hear her voice but gets no answer. It's 10:03pm. When he arrives at home—he stops to talk to Jerome for a minute, goes over the logistics of the coming work week—then prepares for bed. The last thing he intends to do before falling asleep is talk to Porsha. Again he dials the number—and again he gets no answer. It's now 12:35am. Apparently Justin has come down with a sudden case of insomnia—he calls a sound slumbering Jackie and annoys her for the next hour or so. Her eventual snoring between their once two-way conversation finally convinces him to let her go back to sleep. This time it's after 2am. And now it's becomes a matter of wondering. If she's not at home, then where the hell is she? He thinks back to the guy he saw her with the night before. "…Who was that nigga?" Justin reminds himself—there are no ties here. He calls one last time and still no answer, only this time after the beep, a usually reluctant to leave messages Justin renders this little epithet.

"Girl pick up da phone. …Where da fuck is you? Ya told a nigga ta call—I'm tryin' ta coordinate my schedule for the week. Wanted you ta have first dibs. …Hit me back!" Justin sends the message feeling like he's just played himself. For him it's out of character to do such a thing. It's almost as if he had to beg—a definite no-no! But her shit was good—damn good! And to his recollection, he was stranded with the thought of perfect sin—two consenting adults having mastered the act of fornication. With his loins now tainted with the cured remnants of her rich creamy walls, Justin crowns himself whipped. And just like that—with one simple taste, he's caught out!

The next day would come and go, as day would turn to night. Again Justin sits up like a crack fiend, anticipating his next high. He impatiently waits for a call that is to never come. Feeling abandoned and betrayed, he attempts to again try his luck, breaking a long-standing tradition of male chauvinist pride. Her number is now saved for automated dialing. He calls but gets the same response—no answer. He leaves no message. Disgusted, Justin deletes the number from his address log and takes his tired ass to bed.

❧ ❧ ❧

He wakes to another day—and of course another dollar, Tuesday offers Justin some new interesting challenges. For starters he spends the greater part of the day—at least half of it, on the phone in a conference call with Steve Stapanovich, a second-rate entertainment lawyer from Evanston, IL., who just so happens to represent Envy. There seems to be some type of misunderstanding with the structure of the contract. Something with the points and term of the agreement—publishing has also come into question. They foolishly want to retain all rights, but that's not going to happen being that they're new, untested and unestablished artists. Maybe in a few years that'll be something to discuss, but as for now, Justin ain't try'na hear it. If Mr. Stapanovich had been seasoned in the game, he would have known better, but he's being fed by a meddling, uninformed Alecia. Having majored in Business, she thinks she knows more than she does—while in reality, only helps to further complicate matters. Tae, at some point during the morning, brings Justin a cup of straight black coffee with a raspberry filled Krispy Kreme doughnut. Knowing her newly appointed boss well, she discerns when he's either having a generally bad day or if his buttons are being pushed. Today, she perceives a little of both and tries to, if nothing else, relieve some of his distress.

Once that fire has been extinguished, Justin sits at his desk. With both elbows resting on the tabletop, he uses his index fingers to rub the corresponding sides of each temple. Shantel happens to pass by his partially open door as she glances in to check on him.

"You alright boss?"

"I will be—it's been a rough couple of days. Ain't been sleepin' like I should. Thanks girl—I really appreciate cha though. Oh, and will ya please do me one otha favor—*stop* callin' me boss!"

"Whatever you say—boss!" Tae quickly closes Justin's office door and dashes down the hall to her smaller administrative suite. She's brought a long awaited smile to Justin's otherwise gloomy face.

Next on the books, Justin returns a call to Arius Kitchens—a Rough House Records defector, looking for a new deal. He's released two previous projects; neither well received. But Justin realizes his potential—also knowing the debatable business practices of his competitor, understands there may be good reason why neither project took off. His sensual lyrics and good looks should have already taken this St. Louis R&B crooner to the top of the charts. Justin's plan is to reinvent the image and sound—to appeal a younger more hip audience. He's thinking maybe implementing Jerome's fresh sound into Arius's classic style—pull another Carl Thomas out the ole' hat. After a promising dialogue, Justin sets the stage for Arius's arrival to Atlanta to further discuss particulars in this more than likely merger.

As the rest of the afternoon goes by without a hitch, Justin, having evidently regained some of his original testosterone level, puts the flirt on Tae. With most of the office personnel having left for the day, he notices a still hard at work Shantel standing over her computer with her back facing the door. She appears to be reading some type of short fax or memo—but oblivious to Justin's presence. Knowing this, he sneaks up behind her—puts his arms around her petite waist, wrapping her firmly in his grasp and leans down as though he was about to whisper sweet nothings in her ear. "Let's go eat," he persuasively commands with soft words. He next caresses her barren neck with un-moistened lips, exposing her unfulfilled desire for attention.

Tae responds with a subtle coo. She relaxes her tense body, placing her hands over his firm grasp, then tilts her head to the side to receive Justin's advance. She melts like butter in his arms.

"Where?"

"You still like ta shoot pool?"

It's not exactly what she has in her dreamy mind, but decides to count it a blessing anyhow. "Yeah."

"Or do ya wanna chill?" Based on the tone of her voice, he could sense that sitting in front of some pool tables wasn't exactly tops on her list.

"Let's do that!" She turns to face him with puppy eyes—still under his seductive spell.

"Al-ight—then Jocks and Jills it is!"

They share an engaging and entertaining meal under the upscale atmosphere of the CNN Center. The two laugh and exchange light conversation over hot wings and fajitas. Far removed from their normally complicated worlds, they share an intimate moment of endearing friendship. It turns out to be the release that each needed—therapeutic in all regards. They leave with a renewed respect and appreciation for one another.

With a clear mind, Justin returns to his residence on Mt. Gilead Road. That evening, he finds himself down in the studio, sipping on a Corona while flipping through the yellow pages for a moving company. He figures he'd better start making arrangements now before time creeps up on him. Through the monitor speakers he bumps a *Best of the 70's Slow Jams* CD. His mood is nostalgic. He relives simpler times—he and Jerome playing in the back yard, tossing the ball around and pretending to be their favorite sports heroes—Lynn Swann, Tony Dorsett, Harold Carmicheal…from sunup till usually sundown. He recalls how their mama, like clockwork, would call them inside to take a bath as soon as the first street light came on. While he sits and reminisces, pages are turned without being read. "Mama used to do it all" he mumbles. He misses her dearly.

From upstairs he can hear the distant ring tone of his cell. He remembers throwing it on the couch when he first walked in. Initially he's not particularly enthused about charging to answer it as he enjoys this rare lazy moment. But the fact that it could be Porsha, whom he hasn't heard from in a few days, provokes him to get up. He listens to the message. It's not Porsha, but the call does amuse him—it's Shanice!

"*Heeey*—it's Shanice! Sorry I missed you the other day. Hope everything went well on your trip. I'll try and call you back later. Bye!"

After he clears the message, he laughs—it's hilarious to him. He knows she ain't calling back. He suspects by now—her new nigga has about got her on lockdown. And that's cool—as fine and as sweet as she is—he really can't blame the nigga, as Justin recognizes that she's a good little ole' girl who deserves someone to take of her and those kids. He accepts his maintenance man role and is completely willing to stay in the backdrop on this one.

1:10am

Justin's phone rings again. Startled and disoriented from a deep sleep, he fumbles to find the phone. It has slid under one of the pillows on the other side of the bed. Once he locates it, he answers.

"Hello?" he says in a near inaudible voice.

"Hey sleepyhead—wake up!"

"What's up—where you been? …What time is it?" Justin instantly recognizes the voice. He finally gets his wish. This time it is Porsha!

"After one—I've been workin' hard and missing you."

Her words have a way of easing his discord. "How come ya didn't call?"

"I told you Bae—I've been busy; besides this gave you a chance ta miss me—right? You did miss me—didn't you?" she asked, in a sexy seductive voice.

"*Yyyeah,*" he answers like a love struck, pussy whipped adolescence.

"Are you comin' over?"

"When?" Justin props his sleepy ass up.

"Now—I'm horny!"

"Whatcha wearin'?" he asks as he rubs his stiffening cock.

"Nuthin'—oool and I'm wet." she said, having reached down between her own legs to sample the vaginal overflow.

"Hold that thought. I'll be right over!" And he wasn't bullshitting. 'Right over' for Justin meant in reality about forty minutes. That's after a quick shower and a nearly thirty-minute jot under favorable driving conditions. Remembering the building and her third floor door—he knocks. He hears her remove the chain. The door cracks open. He waits, thinking that maybe the door will be fully opened as she comes to greet him. But that never happens. He pushes the door forward slowly following behind it. He enters what he believes to be a living room—dark, while illuminated by only two scented candles—a baby fresh aroma overpowers the space. Appearing from around a blind corridor, Porsha emerges wearing nothing.

"Hey Bae. What took you so long?" Her fake tits and inflated ass bounce in near flawless accord.

"Traffic." Of course he's lying, but it sounds good. He then walks up to her, reintroducing his tongue to her mouth. He can taste the alcohol on her breath. "I want some."

His statement confuses her. She wonders if he's talking about sex or something else. "You want some of what?"

"Whatever you're drinkin'."

"Oh, that's all? I'll fix you one."

She parts his company long enough to fix a Malibu and pineapple drink. "Now, where were we?"

Justin takes a single swallow, and then places the fruity beverage on a nearby table. He picks up where he left off. The room fills with sounds of foreplay—lips smacking, fervent passion expressed through the moans and groans of two people in desperate need. Unable to withstand the heat, she strips him of his clothes—a Patriots jersey and a pair of 501 button-fly jeans. As their naked bodies mingle together, her wet juices bathe him—the smell of her turns him on. Nibbling her nipples, he lifts her agile body in the air. She secures herself by wrapping her long lean legs around his 34" waist while he aggressively sucks her neck. She holds on—clinging to him as he pins her to an adjacent wall, inserting himself raw inside her mocha slit. Her hands tightly grip the chair rail molding—she scratches and claws like a trapped animal. Her screams seem inhumane as they move from the wall to the floor and from the floor to a chair. She's now on top as he hangs on for dear life. And like a volcanic eruption, he spews inside of her. She continues to work, blending their juices until his wilted love slides out of her soakened twat. Their sticky bodies remain together, extended across a burgundy chaise. The sun soon rises.

With the onset of a new day, the morning light brightens the sparsely furnished room. He notices what he couldn't see before—the exterior far exceeds interior. He then assumes that all of her money must go towards paying the rent. No TV or stereo—no pictures nor vases to speak of—just a stark white room with a couple chairs—expensive ones of course, but other than that, basically an empty canvas.

As they lay on the floor, side by side—covered only by an Afghan throw, Justin contemplates whether or not to make it a day. Porsha doesn't make his deliberation any easier as she gently kisses and caresses his naked chest.

"Are you busy today?" Knowing her answer will undoubtedly influence his decision.

"Nope."

"Wanna kick it?"

"Yep." She never once relents from her teasing touch.

Taking a pause for the cause, Justin reaches for his pants—his cell is still strapped to the belt. He calls Tae to inform her that he won't be in today—important personal business. He assures her that everything is okay and if she needs him to just call his cell. He then asks if it isn't any problem to relay the message to Rico. She agrees—they hang up. After which he tosses the phone over by his balled clothes, he and Porsha begin to make love—again.

ten

Consequences & Repercussions

Three weeks and a day have since passed—but here's the thing; it's been three very non-eventful weeks. And that's what worries Justin. That sense of calm before the storm, when you get that feeling deep down, waiting for all hell to break loose. That day when "Murphy's Law" comes to bite a nigga in the ass.

As for Justin and Porsha, nothing's changed—same ole', same ole'. She calls when she gets ready or whenever a need arises that somehow benefits Porsha. It's been the same story from day one. The only thing that differs is the script. Justin may have had his nose wide open once upon a time, but has long since put the relationship in its proper perspective. He now files it under "booty calls". Just another glorified piece of ass.

He anxiously counts down the days until his departure. At last toll it was ten, all arrangements have been made. His new residence is secured. From here on out it's a waiting game, the only loose ends left to mend are those of personal relationships—the people he'll miss the most—his son, his brother, and his best friend—the irreplaceable Jackie.

And what of the women he leaves behind, his attitude is like "Whatever! ...Fuck them hoes!" A new city with new avenues to explore, new trails to blaze and new pussy to be gotten, he looks surprisingly forward to this new day in his life.

Of course there's still that matter of fulfillment—the voids that incapacitate his life. One can only run for so long—or hide but so many skeletons. But what does one do when those walls start to close and the claustrophobic nature of our being becomes compromised? What do we do when there's no one else to blame—when we reap what we sow? Justin has yet to come to terms with himself. He has yet to come to terms with his life. The past continues to haunt him—he's allowed it to bend his future. Amidst even the successes he finds no joy. And so he keeps looking and chasing, and invariably there will always be a price to pay—a debt to be collected for the choices he makes.

Justin, before he heads for the door, gives Tae some last minute instructions. The team operates understaffed because Demetrius, who's on a short hiatus, has taken a few weeks off to go home to New Haven, Connecticut to visit the folks and handle a burdensome legal matter before the move.

"Yo, tomorrow—first thing in the morning, I need cha to get with Maurice down at 112—make sure everything's in place for Saturday. Then call BeeGee's Manager—I forgot that nigga's name."

"...Alonzo Whitten," Shantel interjects.

"Yeah—that nigga. Anyway, make damn certain he has his man in da club by ten—10am! We don't need em' showin' up late for his first video shoot—time is money on this one! Oh—and the last thing I need ya ta do—get in contact with Delmar Productions—make sure we have an understanding—we need at least 250 extras on this one— pretty muthafuckas please! Da last time they sent some busted fugly folks up in there—ended up editing half of them niggas out. And we're paying too much for this shit ta be goin' through all that! ...Anyway ya know what ta do—I'll be in meetings most of da day—so if ya need me, ya know how ta reach me!" He pauses for a split second because he feels the vibration of his cell at his side, which he then momentarily ignores in order to finish the conversation. "Thank ya boo—I owe ya one!"

"Yeah, ya do! So let's just say dinner tomorrow night—my choice—your treat!"

As he walks out the door he bellows from around the corner; "Yeah yeah—I got cha!" Phone already to his ear, he plays back the message.

"Hello Justin—it's me Tonya—long time no talk to. Jus wanted to see how you are doing. So if you happen to get this message—call me back whenever. Be good—talk to ya later."

Justin, ticked by the call, reacting out loud responds, "The bitch got her nerve. Ain't said shit ta a nigga in over a month—fuck her! I ain't wit that 'sometimes ya is—sometimes ya ain't shit'!" Her long exile has made it easy to justify his position—avoiding any future drama. Fooling up with her now—nine times out of ten, could possibly mean leaving himself open to the potential fallout of his previous actions. Bitch might get mad or even one day holla rape! Women have a way of remembering—storing shit for a rainy day. And best believe Justin has calculated all the possibilities, and as much as he hates to—knows he better let it go! A little less pussy now could save a whole lot of unnecessary stress later. He rushes off to pick up Porsha for tonight's date.

Seventy minutes later, Justin sits in front of Porsha's apartment. She's not home. Having fought the I-75N traffic hasn't done much for his patience. He tries to rationalize the situation being that he's not exactly the one who should be talking, considering his own seldom punctual track record. But what he's having a hard time comprehending—the trick doesn't even have a car and yet she's never around. And not only that—but her total irresponsible nature. She never calls when she's supposed to. Rarely does she do anything that she says she's going to. And that's what has begun to wear thin—her sorry ass trifling ways. Another fifteen minutes goes by, he entertains himself as he raps along to Porsha's unauthorized anthem.

"Now I ain't sayin' she a gold digga'—but she ain't messin' wit no broke nigga!" He repeats the chorus. "Get down girl—go head get down. Get down girl—go head get down…" Justin blares the Kanye West track which tops Hot 107.9's "Hot 8 at Eight," meaning that it's pretty damn close to nine o' clock. But then speak of the devil! Just as Justin has made up his mind to haul ass—an older model brown Jeep Wrangler with the no top comes pulling up behind his 300. From his rearview mirror Justin can see Porsha, who's somewhat dressed down—hair wrapped in a bun and wearing a long sleeve white button-down with black polyester slacks, giving the young caucasian female driver wearing similar attire—a hurried thanks. No doubt she's just returning from work. As the Jeep speeds off, Porsha meets Justin at the car window.

"Hey Bae—sorry I'm late. Come wit me upstairs right quick so I can change."

Justin nods in agreement, then follows Porsha up the stairs. He notices her signature duffel which looks to be full and wonders why she hasn't already changed—assuming that the bag is stuffed with her street clothes. He meditates on that thought as he walks through the doorway. His nose twinges to the smell of spoiled garbage or the souring of dishes left in a sink for more than a day—cosigning his suspicions of a home away from home. Normally he could care less, but due to the expensive nature of this union, he's become a bit leery as to overnight whereabouts of his investment. He finds a familiar seat on the chaise situated in the front room. Today Justin has taken special notice to the incredibly minuscule footage of this one bedroom—one bath efficiency. No dining room—the kitchen is too small to eat in... There's a short corridor that leads to the bedroom with attached bath—and that's about it! He assumes by the stripped floorplan—the small front area is supposed to sufficiently double as the living and dining quarters. But of course that's a joke! There's also the balcony, which has made for more than a few exhilarating intimate encounters between the two, the only other space of noteworthy interest. The perfect low maintenance address for the always-on-the-go, high maintenance ho. If it wasn't for the extraordinary sex—he would have been eight-sixed the trick!

Porsha promptly pops from behind the sealed bedroom door. As she graces the hallway with her uncompromising beauty and enhanced curve appeal, Justin is again reminded why he puts up with her shit. She cleans up well as she stands before him in a strapless tube dress—coffee colored with yellow floral print. The short flowy handkerchief asymmetrical hem emphasizes the sexiness of her slim shapely legs. And in a mere minute, all that talk has somehow eluded Justin's memory.

"Whatcha think Bae?"

"*Cute!*"

The sexual tension erupts as their loose lips come together to grant each other the proper and more accustomed greeting. Justin receives a much needed stress reliever as she sucks him off before leaving to get a bite to eat. She knows the way to his heart—and to his pocket is through the abundant pampering of his curved black dick. At least in that regard—she does her best to keep him happy.

How sad but true, his pleasure seeking principles have for so long defined who he is. How he has allowed his ego to script his true identity. For what he has failed to realize—his ego represents only the self-image of himself—his social mask. The man he sees in the mirror every morning before brushing his teeth—that façade he wears for the world to see. Yet in the process, he's confused himself and through the manipulation of his own public persona—he's lost himself. Justin's self image and his true identity are not one in the same—but only the consciousness of his identity. While his *true* identity relates to purpose of his being—and what he was fashioned for, therefore, because he doesn't know who he is, then he doesn't know where he belongs or where he fits in. Thus he's committed himself to chaos—and will always question himself and his significance always taking the extreme route to validate or prove himself—a drama seeker.

In satisfying Porsha's seafood whimsy, they travel back to the city to Buckhead and over to the Atlanta Fish Market. The spot no one can miss with that sixty foot copper statue out front boasting the best seafood restaurant in the ATL. Definitely not the cheapest place, but their extensive ever-changing menu speaks well for itself.

With no reservation, they enter the restaurant expecting to wait on a table. After being informed that the delay will only take a few minutes, Justin and Porsha head for the bar. As they walk in that direction, he does a double take and says in a hushed tone, "Oh shit!" To his utter surprise, seated at the bar along with a nondescript female companion is Tonya. Recreating the hostile climate after her phone message, Justin, wanting to send a clear and poignant message, makes it a point to be seen. Stepping over to the bar just 10 to 15 feet away, he orders two Long Island Ice Teas. Almost immediately he catches the exuberant attention of an unsuspecting Tonya, whom at first doesn't notice Justin's clingy single member entourage as she displays her familiar bubbly smile. But before a word is spoken, she catches a nauseating glimpse at his scandalously dressed acquaintance. He glares into her sullen face with an arrogant cock-mouthed smirk, then turns back to his date—never saying a word. The couple step away from the counter after receiving their drinks. Tonya, belittled and bothered by Justin's insensitive behavior, vacates the busy restaurant within a span of minutes. Now seated across the floor, a smug Justin grins behind a raised menu thinking, "mission accomplished."

Porsha's taste buds crave for the broiled coldwater lobster tails while Justin is down for the Blue Point Oysters Rockefeller. They eat in near silence as each drift into separate immersed worlds, both surely unaware of the other's thoughts. Justin wanders back to a month ago—and his times with Tonya. He compares her to Porsha—the differences are like night and day. With Tonya—time was meaningful; her compassion made for intimate conversation—her sincerity genuine. Sex was slow and expressive. What she gave came from the heart, even if it was one-sided. They shared a compatibility to compliment the chemistry. He regrets the outcome—a wasted opportunity to maybe grab something real. How he misses the creativeness of her spirit.

Justin then looks across the table at the beautiful two-dimensional work of art that sits before him—something lovely to look at, but that was it. Here is a relationship full of fire, but shallow in depth. They share nothing except a tenacity for sex. It is said—things that burn effortlessly also extinguish in the same manner—all chemistry and no compatibility. His life with her was lived underneath the sheets and no where else. And that wasn't enough.

Justin picks up the nearly $100 check. He shakes his head in disgust either because he was paying too much for the food—or the woman. Porsha catches his facial expression and questions its origin.

"What's the matter Bae?" She grabs his hand holding the check, turning it so that she can see the amount. "*Uh-umm*—no way! …Was it that much?" She plays pitiful as though she's so sorry that she's inconvenienced him. "I can't believe you treat me this good—you spoil me Bae. I'm such a lucky girl ta have a man around like you—thank you baby!" She reaches across the table to give Justin a wet and juicy smooch—then whispers, "I'll make it up ta ya tonight" delicately in his ear. Yet little does she know his generosity is about to run dry. For behind his fake smile, the wheels are turning and looking for loopholes and excuses to be up and out—adios, sayonara, and arrivederci! The free ride is almost over. Though of course, tonight will be business as usual—dick for dessert, booty for breakfast, and maybe a lick for lunch. He figures she still has a debt to work off!

They wind up back at her apartment—in her clutter-infested bedroom. Clothes, purses, and shoes make up the interior décor. Articles of designer wear, or at least its knockoff, occupies every wall, door, and roughly every inch of floor space. It's obvious this is where her money goes. To her credit the space is that of organized confusion—neat, but just overwhelming. Nevertheless, it offers a functional place to lay.

Approaching midnight with shoes off, eyes closed, and hands resting beneath a pillow, Justin relaxes his weary bones across her jacquard bedspread. Porsha, now positioned over his upper body, delivers kisses in pecks to the forehead, nose, and lips. Removing his hand from under the pillow, he reaches for the top of her strapless dress, tugging downward just enough to expose an aroused nipple. He caresses around her areola with his thumb and forefinger. Feeling the heat, she decides to dispose of any further suspense as she weaves herself across his clothed body. She then vacates her barely existent under-apparel and pulls down the other side of her tube top to match an already visible twin. As they get into the moment, there's faint knocking of a door. And because the bedroom's entrance is shut, the sound's location becomes almost undetectable—whether it's a neighbor's door or Porsha's. Justin, engrossed by other thoughts, pays no attention, while Porsha, in contrast, develops a paranoid flush over her unveiled torso. She tries to ignore it, but the knocking continues.

Justin stops, as he becomes aware of the sound. "...Is that your door?"

Porsha, not knowing how to answer his question, tries to play it off. "*What?*" She proceeds with her advances.

"You don't hear that?" The knocks intensify.

"It's probably somebody on the wrong door Bae. Forget about it and pay attention ta me!" she said continuing to kiss.

As the knocks resume, Justin gets agitated. "Are you expectin' someone?" This time Porsha doesn't answer. For whoever's outside that door knows she's inside.

Curious, Justin tells her "Get yo door!"

Pulling herself together, Porsha obeys with extreme hesitation. Once she opens the door—Justin, now standing in the hallway, can hear a deep male voice blurt; "We need to talk!"

"Not now—I'll call you later!" Justin senses the nervousness in her voice.

"No, I need ta talk ta you right now!" he demands with assertion.

"I can't!"

"What da fuck you mean—you can't? What da fuck is goin' on? ...Who's in there?"

"Shay, don't do this right now. I'll call you!" She tries to close the door, but he forces his way in.

Justin steps from around the corner and makes his presence known. "Is everything al-ight?"

Before Porsha can answer, their third wheel interruption intercedes with, "Who da fuck is he?"

"Nigga, it ain't none of yo concern—Girl, is everything cool?" Then it dawns on him—he's seen this nigga before—that night when he first picked up Porsha outside of Morris Brown—the light-skinned muthafucka. For Justin the fog begins to lift.

Again the mulatto brother interjects, "Porsha—who da fuck is this?"

"A friend Rashay—a friend!" The stress of the ordeal has brought tears to Porsha's eyes—she's visibly distraught. "Why do ya keep doin' this Rashay? …It's over. Please jus let it go!"

"Let it go! What da fuck… Oh, I'm supposed ta jus let it go like that, huh? So I guess last night didn't happen? What about last week? I guess ya forgot 'bout that too? …Fuckin' bitch! How could cha? …I loved you—and you played me like this!" Her estranged lover places a rolled fist in front of his mouth and starts to weep.

"Leave Shay—go!" Porsha's tear stuttered words manifest into festered anger as she points to the door.

"Fuck you bitch!" replies her jilted ex-lover.

"Fuck you too Shay! Now get out!" She stands holding her front door wide open.

Apparently those last words would be the straw that broke the camel's back. Rashay lunges forward, grabbing a screaming Porsha by the hair, easily slinging her to the floor. Justin, who's been standing there absorbing the all the hidden truths, jumps across the small room and into action. Like they say, "punks jump up to get beat down"— well this punk jumped and Justin commences to whoop his ass unmercifully. In a state of rage, he pummels her defenseless ex against the floor. Blood gushes from Rashay's busted mouth and possibly broken nose, but Justin refuses to yield. Porsha panics and is screaming and begging for him to stop. But in his zone, her voice remains a faint yet distance after-thought.

From nowhere Justin is confronted by a hard, painful thud to the right side of his face. The blow is hard enough to shift his momentum to the opposite direction. He staggers to the side, catching himself with the open door. He feels the blood trickling from the outer corner of his eye. His first thought "I know this bitch ain't jus hit me when I'm tryin' ta save *her* ass. Oh hell no!" Without thinking, he reclaims his balance and pounces toward Porsha. Fortunately, he trips over the ailing Rashay who lay half conscious across the living room floor. The stumble gives Porsha enough time to scramble around the corner to her bedroom where she slams the door shut. Realizing what's at stake—his career and his freedom, he ends his pointless pursuit—quickly gathering himself to leave the premises. A shoeless Justin bounces down the exterior stairwell. Luckily his keys were still in his front pocket—and wallet still in the back. He and his 300C haul ass off the property.

As he drives on bare footing, he's floored by the obvious reality—muttering, "Ain't this 'bout a fuckin' bitch!" The whole episode has left a familiar bad taste in his mouth as his thoughts teeter-totter from his shell-top Adidas that now reside in her barricaded bedroom to the realization that this bitch has been lying the whole time.

He enters his home through the basement door, with no shoes and a swollen and bloodied eye. Jerome, who happens to be headed for the studio, meets his wounded brother in the kitchen.

"Damn man, what da hell happened ta you?"

"Long fuckin' story!"

"I'm listenin'." Jerome takes a seat at the breakfast bar.

Justin takes a spot on the other barstool and begins to tell the abbreviated version of his pathetic story.

"Yo, that trick bitch man…"

"*Who?*"

"Porsha! Ya know all this time she was fuckin' some otha nigga?"

"*Word?*" He said, looking surprised.

"Yeah man—I'm over to her crib 'bout ta get my dick wet. This nigga knockin' on the door talkin' 'bout 'we need ta talk'. And Porsha, her ass all scared and shit basically tells the nigga ta go the fuck on. But this crazy nigga wasn't try'na hear that. Nigga cryin'—talkin' 'bout he love her and shit—lookin' like a bitch! I'm over to the side listenin' while this muthafucka tellin' all their business. Punk nigga sayin' sumptin' 'bout bein' wit her last night and the week before. Ain't no tellin' if a nigga tellin' the truth or not—but she ain't deny shit either. That's why a bitch ain't neva around. …It makes sense! But she tries ta put him out and this nigga jumps crazy—starts draggin' her ass on the floor and shit. Regardless of the situation—I wasn't 'bout ta let a nigga do that. And so I kindly proceeded ta fuck-dat-nigga up!

"You whooped his ass man?"

"Hell yeah! That nigga had it comin'. But wait—you ain't heard the best part! I'm over there stompin' this nigga silly—and da bitch hits me! Clocks me upside my fuckin' head. …That's how I got this shit." Justin points to his swollen eye.

Jerome shakes his head while walking over to his brother for a closer look. "Damn man—that's fucked up! Yo, ya might wanna have this checked out—looks pretty bad."

"Naw—fuck that! I ain't tryin' ta sit up in no emergency room half the damn night ta get some fuckin' nonprescription pain reliever. I can get that shit right out of my own damn medicine cabinet. Know what I mean?"

"Yeah." Jerome takes out some ice and places it in a quart size Ziploc bag, then passes the fresh pack to his brother.

"Thanks. Yeah, but I'll jus ice this shit down tonight—see how it looks in the morning. …Damn!" Justin remembers having a meeting scheduled for first thing in the morning. "I forgot 'bout that planning meeting tomorrow!"

"Jus get Tae ta sit in for ya."

"I can't—I got her doin' some otha shit."

"When's Dee supposed ta get back?"

"Monday. Oh well—whatever. Guess I'll be sittin' up in that muthafucka wit some shades and shit!"

"Word!" Jerome again shakes his head—but this time with a smile on his face. "Yo man—you stay in some shit—but you always liked that ole' drama. I don't know how ya do it—it couldn't be me. Yo, ya need ta start takin' it easy before all that unnecessary shit catches up wit'cha."

"I know right. Drama jus always seems ta find me though." Justin elaborates before walking out the door. Both take route to their previous intended destinations.

eleven

Revolving Doors

Monday morning.

Shantel and Demetrius are gathered in Justin's office. They trade cracks at the expense of his still blackened eye.

"Let me see nigga!" Dee steps closer as Tae removes Justin's Ferragamo sunglasses.

"Look—see I told you!" Shantel remarks to Dee as if she's confirming an earlier comment.

"Damn nigga! She told me a bitch had kicked yo ass. …I'm gone fo a minute—and look. Nigga can't stay out of trouble. What's up Jay?— Talk to your boy." Demetrius had received a full second hand account from Tae—blow by blow, as soon as he walked through the office doors having just returned from his trip to Connecticut. Shantel had collected her version of the morning's water cooler gossip straight from the horse's mouth, on that previous Friday night over dinner at Copelands.

Justin causally changes the subject. "How was the trip nigga? Ya got your shit straight?"

"Fuck no! I mean the trip was straight except fuckin' wit the State. Muthafuckas try'na make those charges stick. Nigga gotta go back to court at the end of next month. Ya know—got ta hang out with my peoples—eat some of my mama's home cookin'… I'ma always miss that shit! But all and all—it's all good."

"Cool. Oh your girl, she's been showin' out handlin' shit. Told me yo ass ain't shit but dead weight. Said she got this! You coulda kept yo ass up in Connecticut." Justin winks over at Shantel sitting behind his desk.

Laughing, "Who Tae? She knows she can't touch this! This nigga gets grimey. Tae don't know nuthin' 'bout that! Ain't cha learn yet nigga? …Tae don't do ghetto! That's why I'm here—as an advocate for all da BeeGees of the world. Feel me?"

"Fo sho'!" They touch fists as a show of agreement. Tae—in contrast, flashes both men the finger as a sign of her discord.

"That reminds me—when I was home, I talked ta some folks. I got this demo from a kid over in Hartford. Son! The shit's tight—I got a feelin' on this. We still tryin' ta tap into a wider urban market— broaden our horizons right? Cuz this kid's gully. Nigga straight raw!"

"Where is it at?"

"In my bag—I'll bring it over." Dee leaves to retrieve the CD.

Meanwhile, Shantel, plundering, runs across a sealed white Tyvek envelop approximately 6"x9" on Justin's desk.

"Jay, you seen this?"

"Yeah, but I ain't really looked at it. One of the girls up front signed for it and brought it back here. …Why?"

"I was just wondering. There's no name—just a label from the messenger service. That's kinda odd but there's a small box in it. Take a look!" She hands the package to Justin, where he examines it by feel.

"It's probably jus another unsolicited demo. You know how muthafuckas do… Send the shit wit no name thinkin' that it'll up their chances of getting heard. You know the game—I'll open it later!"

"Boy, you know that ain't no tape—feel the size of that box. A cassette tape wouldn't fit in that. It's too small, besides who sends tapes anymore?"

By this time, Demetrius has returned with CD in hand. "Here nigga." He passes the CD over to Justin. "…What cha'll doin'?" Dee senses a different vibe to the room.

"Justin got a bomb!" Tae teases.

"I wouldn't doubt it—probably from one of them silly bitches he dun fucked over." With little restraint, both Dee and Tae snicker in synchronous reply.

"Get out—both of ya! Find ya some business. Try actin' like ya got a job!" Justin insincerely dismisses the duo.

Once alone, he opens the package—and there's a small box laminated in silver foil. It appears to be a jewelry box—maybe something a necklace might come out of. There's an attached card. Justin immediately recognizes the familiar Sand and Sable scent. He reads its short but sweet contents;

> To Justin with luv
> XOXOXO
> Tonya C.

The card blows his mind considering their last few encounters. It's the last thing he would've expected—was a gift from Tonya. He opens the box. Instantly his heart drops to his stomach. For in the box is an EPT—early pregnancy test with a "+" symbol and a message;

Congratulations

A stunned silence.

The thought takes some time to digest. It's been longer than a month—so it's quite possible that she could already be experiencing some early symptoms. Then again, this could all be just a ploy to get even with him for the other night, but that wouldn't jive with Tonya's character. "Damn!" Justin pounds his fist against the top of his desk. He paces the floor a few rounds and walks over to the window. He tries to find peace amidst his chaos while considering the possibilities. He looks for some symbol of tranquility amongst the city's infinite skyline. But it's not working. He picks up the phone to contact Tonya, as the truth will always set you free. Of course his efforts are in vain— because she's either not there—or not answering. Both results lead Justin to where he started—searching for answers.

Having taken the rest of the afternoon off, he drives the city— headed for nowhere. From I-20, he takes the 285 perimeter loop passing all stops along the way—Glenwood Road to Covington Highway to Memorial Drive on around to Lavista Road, Buford Highway and Peachtree Industrial Boulevard. There's just something about the open road—it's hard to explain, but it seems to soothe the spirit. Justin uses the time to clear his crowded head—and reflect on where he went wrong. Was it after his mother passed or when his father turned his back on a wife and two little boys? It wasn't always like this—he once had dreams of raising a family—having that loving spouse, a few kids with a big house and white picket fence, as he vowed never to make the same mistakes as his father—he couldn't do that to them. But seldom do things work the way we want them. Now he regrets bringing a child into this world to feel what he's felt. And in spite of his better judgment—his irresponsible actions continue to play like a broken record. He wonders if his son will ever forgive him—as he has yet to forgive his own father. The thought of another child—with another woman—living, again, in separate homes sickens his soul.

Exits come and go as he continues to cruise the loop. Reaching the top of the perimeter he now passes Ashford-Dunwoody Road, the Georgia 400, and Roswell Road. Traffic slows to a snail's pace. Before long, as far as the eye can see, cars line the expressway—bumper to bumper. The smell of urban swell fills the air. Enough so, that he rolls up all windows and turns on the AC. It's almost quiet—and once again, he can hear himself think. He scrolls the memory bank through his most current listing of sexually implicated females—Shanice, Porsha, Tonya, and Teresha, all of whom could make the same claim. For with each he leaves a trail of unbridled cum—from one bed to the next, as the cycle of careless consequence soon becomes a repercussive habit.

For a time, under selfish cause, Justin has forgone the use of any prophylactic protection. He knows the obvious dangers—the potential room for error, yet he continues to roll the dice with his life and future. The desire goes far beyond the tasting of raw juices as he longs for the happiness of completion—when two are joined together as one. Not necessarily in matrimony—but of one flesh—that "us against the world" mentality. Subconsciously implanted, is the thought that every women romantically encountered could represent Ms. Right. Because with each he gives a piece of himself—as does she, the combining of two to make one. And he confuses that with love.

To the world, he lives a lie—every man's envy—God's gift to the black woman. For himself—from whom he can't hide, he lives alone—always alone, as his circumstance has only helped to heighten the sentiment. Of course it wasn't beneficial that he would spend much of his rearing years without a father. Neither did it help losing his mother to cancer as a young adult. And matters would only worsen as the woman he loved and the child she bore of his name's sake had, too, walked out of his life as did all the others who held a place in his heart. Circumstance had created a condition of loneliness that life couldn't compensate. His insatiable quest for redemption causes the calamity he now faces. Justin looks for love in all the wrong places.

Finally traffic again moves with brisk rhythm. Riverside Drive, I-75, and Cobb Parkway become passing thoughts. Continuing south, he crosses Atlanta Road, then Fulton Industrial Boulevard—at last exiting the perimeter at the I-20 junction. Justin then dials a familiar number.

"Hel-looo?" answers the upbeat recipient.

"Whatcha doin'?"

"Not a thing—why? …What are you doing?"

"I'm in your neck of the woods. Feel like company?"

"Sure—c'mon!"

"Al-ight. I'll see ya in a minute."

"*Byyye.*"

As both parties disconnect, Justin departs the expressway on the nearest off ramp which places him back at Fulton Industrial. Taking a left, he travels to MLK where he makes another left. Justin, at that point, journeys north up MLK as it changes to Mableton Parkway and then to Floyd Road. He intersects the Austell-Marietta border—reaching the income-rated community of Summit Ridge. There he finds refugee within the arms of a cherished friend. Jackie stands at the door to greet him.

"*Awww* boo. Come let mama take care of her baby." She expresses herself in a tone that would comfort even her youngest patrons. With outstretched arms, she pacifies her wounded buddy. While they hold one another Justin breaks the news.

"Tonya's pregnant!"

Jackie releases her grasp to scold him. "Naw boo. Please say it ain't so!" Disappointed, she stands with her hand on her hip, her body language oozing of shared disgust.

"I messed up!"

"Boy, you forever messin' up. …So don't make it sound like it's your first time." Recognizing the despair written over Justin's pitiful face, she eases from her chastisement. "What's our next move?" she asks, as she grabs Justin by the hand.

"I don't know. I tried callin' her but I got no answer."

"So how ya find out?"

"Oh…" Justin goes on to tell the story. Jackie hangs on to his every word. When he finishes, her look says it all.

"DAMN!" A short pause. "But boo—let's be honest—you had that comin'! I mean, come on… Why you keep doin' the girl like that?"

Justin has no comment. And because of his surprise bombshell, Jackie, who hasn't given much thought to his blackened eye, now brushes across his brow.

"Anotha rough week—huh boo?" Her smile mollifies the tension.

"Yep!"

"But jus think—in anotha week or two, you can put all of this behind ya."

"And ya know what? …I damn sure can't wait!"

Jackie turns Justin toward the door as she walks behind him with her hands on his shoulders, leading Justin inside the apartment. Shayla Marie, who watches the television and keeps an eye on the five other children, meets him by the door.

"Hey Uncle!" She rushes to his side for a big hug.

"How's my favorite girl?"

"*Finnne.* You have some money Uncle?"

"Fo what?" he responds laughing.

"So I can go to the store."

"Damn, if ya ain't jus like your mama. …Here!" He's reached in his pocket to pull out a crinkled ten-dollar bill. "Ain't ya supposed to be in school?" He looks at his watch, realizing it's only two-thirty.

"Yeah, Michael dropped her off this morning talkin' 'bout, 'She don't feel good. I think ya need to let her stay home'. She jus played his ass—daddy's little girl. …Yeah right!" Loud laughter. "Ain't nuthin' wrong wit that child. Look at her—she's been bouncin' around here all day." Justin grins at Jackie's no nonsense motherly approach.

"Shayla Marie—watch da babies while I go talk to your uncle." The two adults move to the back bedroom. Jackie shuts the door behind them. "You gonna be alright?"

"*Yyyeeep.*" Justin yawns.

"Okay. You jus lay down and take a nap for awhile. Let me tend to these babies and I'll fix us some dinner—then we can talk. Will that work?"

"Yes Ma'am." He takes off his shoes and relaxes in familiar quarters.

Once the other children leave, Jackie prepares a full course meal. Shayla helps.

"Mama, is Uncle Jay gonna spend the night?"

"I'm not sure—I think so. Why ya ask?"

"I miss him—he's not around as much as he use ta be."

"I know girl—I miss 'em too." she says, as her attitude switches to one of hopeless avail.

With the table spread, Shayla knocks on the bedroom door to awaken her sleeping uncle. Justin freshens up before entering the small dining area. Like most apartments, the walk-through kitchen adjoins the half open space considered as the dining room. He praises the feast in front of him.

"Girl, that looks great!" Justin relishes the idea of some good ole' fashion home cookin'—for home cooked meals come few and far between. He gives rare thanks to God—then takes his seat at the head of the table opposite Jackie—Shayla is positioned between them. He glances across the table, inhaling whiffs of the various aromas—collard greens with bits of ham, sweet potato casserole topped with melted marshmallows. She's apparently remembered because it's one of his favorites. For breads, there's a combination of dropped garlic biscuits and corn muffins. The main course is stuffed fried pork chops smothered in country gravy. He can hardly wait to dig in as he openly appreciates her effort. "Ummm that smells wonderful."

"I helped too Unc!" Shayla throws in her two cents—guaranteeing her place amongst the praise.

"Whaaat! …So you can burn like yo mama then." A grinning Shayla agrees. "Cool—I say let's eat!"

"Wait a minute Uncle—we have ta say our grace!" And with bowed heads, they link hands over and under the table as Shayla blesses the food.

"Dear God—thank you for letting me call you God. Thank you for my mommy and my daddy. Thank you for my new shoes. Thank you for the hot food that me and mommy cooked…" Jackie taps Shayla in the thigh with her knee to move things along. "Thank you for my Uncle. And God, help me to tell my uncle that he can call you too. Amen."

Justin is touched by Shayla's heavenly request. He can't remember the last time a prayer had been sent up on his behalf—at least not since his mother. They eat. It feels comfortable—too much like right, a quiet dinner at home with family. Justin absorbs the moment. He devours his first portion and compliments the chefs.

"Damn that was good! Y'all put cha foot in this here." Justin reaches over the spread to collect seconds. The ladies enjoy his presence as much as he cherishes theirs, as it's always nice to have a man around the house. Shayla, excited about having her play uncle around, bombards Justin with the latest 411 at school—as he thought his life was drama filled. And he soon comes to appreciate the fact that he doesn't have any daughters to worry about. Jackie shares her adventures in daycare, she reiterates what he already knew—kids can be hell too! But what Justin relishes and maybe even envies is the sense of normalcy—the mundane details of their everyday lives. What he wouldn't give for their seemingly peaceful existence. Jackie brings out the dessert—a Mrs. Smith's Peach Cobbler straight from your grocer's freezer, but looks tasty just the same. She perks it up with a little Cool Whip—and there you have it—a delicious gourmet treat.

Before they leave the table, Justin raises his half-consumed glass to propose an iced tea toast. "Here's to great food—great conversation—and most importantly—great friends! Thank y'all!" With the verdict in—the decision is unanimous. Tonight was one of those rare wonderful nights—one he'll not soon forget.

Once Shayla is excused to prepare for bed, Justin volunteers his services to Jackie to share in the clean-up duties. Jackie busts the suds while Justin dries and puts away the dishes.

"I miss this." Jackie bumps Justin's hip with hers while standing over the kitchen sink.

"What?"

"You and I like this."

"Oh really." Justin chuckles through his response.

"Yeah *really*. It's what I love about you boo!"

"And what's that?"

"You're attentiveness—and patience, your sense of humor…"

"Keep goin'!" He soaks up the excessive flattery.

"With you it was never about rushing. You always took your time. We did things together—none of that wham bam thank ya ma'am stuff that most guys try and run. But best of all—we could talk to each other. …I miss that. And now you're 'bout ta leave me." She pokes out her bottom lip and looks despondently downward just to fight back her tears.

Justin pauses a second, then looking at her side profile, he turns her delicately by the chin to make direct eye contact. "Hey—I'ma miss you too. Girl, ya jus' don't know how much you mean to me. I couldn't have done any of this without you. Come on—look at me. Who do I run to boo? …To you. It's always been you. You're the real hero. Without you there would be no me. Girl, you've been down from day one—like four flat tires. I ain't forgot that! I'll be right down the road—no more than a phone call away. And as long as I have free nights and weekends they'll always be yours boo!" With his tongue between his teeth, he cracks a big smile, and then wipes her tears away.

Jackie wails out loud enough to wake the neighbors with her annoying high-pitched laugh. Twisting a wet dishrag, she pops Justin in the butt. "Boy—that's that bullshit that use ta get me in trouble. …Have me laid up all the time foolin' wit ch'ou. I ain't forgot how you use ta feed me that ole' crock of shit—had me walkin' around here wit my coochie wet all day." She taps him once more and chases him out the kitchen. They stop long enough to acknowledge their exhaustion.

Huffing, "I don't know 'bout you but I'm tired. …You ready for bed? You are spendin' the night right?"

"Yeah girl—I'm all yours tonight."

"Goody—goody!" She claps her hands while jumping for joy like the silly overgrown child that she is.

The two would lie innocently together. After some words of encouragement and revelation, Justin spoons Jackie to sleep. He leaves early that next morning, before any of the children arrive. Even though he can't seem to find the right way of expressing it—he already knows that he's going to truly miss her.

twelve

Foolish Pride

5:46am

Just down the street from Jackie's apartment, Justin pulls into the Quiktrip at the corner of Floyd Road. With a little more than a ¼ tank of gas remaining, he darts to the nearest pump. As he reaches for his bankcard, he notices the inflated prices—$2.89, $2.99, and $3.09. Outraged by the spike in unleaded rates, Justin decides to hold out until he makes it back to the city. There he'll save at least 10¢ on the gallon. While a dime may not sound like much, especially to someone like Justin—it comes down to principle. Frustrated with the current administration, he holds the belief that the rising fuel costs are all just a political ploy to help the rich get richer. He can't even fathom how OPEC continues to raise the price of oil when there's no shortage. Well in actuality he does know why—because they can, and that's what ticks him off—"price gouging fuckas!" Justin expresses his malcontent before choosing to bypass the pumps. Yet while he's here, he might as well pick one of those Sunrise sausage and egg biscuits along with a hot cup of coffee.

From the parking lot, Justin enjoys his biscuit on this mild pre-dawn morning as he watches a sea of bustling headlights converge the congested intersection. His attention then shifts to the convenience store constituents who scurry in and out before journeying to work. Dusting the crumbs from his shirt, he takes a hasty sip of his generic java, which instantly burns the tongue. "Shit!" he says as the piping hot beverage drools from his throbbing mouth. Once he gathers himself, he looks up to see an attractive young light skinned woman wearing a blue medical uniform. Their eyes meet and she smiles as she walks by en route to her vehicle. Yet what stands out in Justin's embroiled mind is her state of maternity, as she appears to be in her last trimester. The encounter reminds him of his current situation. Grabbing his phone, he exhales and proceeds to call Tonya—the earlier the better.

She answers but does not speak. Surely her caller ID has told her who's on the other end. Justin also holds the phone a second before talking.

"Hello… Tonya?" He hears the echoes of what sounds like a television playing in the distance.

"Yeah." She speaks without the usual vivaciousness in her voice.

"What's up?"

"I don't know—you tell me!"

"I got the package. …Is it true?" His question is followed by an awkward silence. "Hello. Are ya still there?"

"Yep."

"Did ya hear my question?"

"Yes Justin—I heard you. And as if you really care—but yeah, I'm carrying *your* baby."

"So how do ya feel?" Though he wants to ask the question that burns in back of every man's mind—"Is it mine?" But he chooses not to do so at this time, fearing it may add further insult to injury.

"*What?* …Just out of ignorant curiosity—how do you think I feel?" The sarcasm is her way of suppressing her anger.

"I don't know—that's why I asked!" Justin rejoinders her question.

"Well, I'll tell you what… Let's jus say the shoe was on the other foot. How would you feel if you woke up every morning sick—vomiting, nauseated and having to pee every five minutes? And if that wasn't enough—let's jus pretend that the father of your child is someone of whom you—yourself wouldn't exactly want to have anything to do with? Let alone have a child by. Catch my drift Justin?" She finishes with even more sarcasm.

"I hear ya. So what do we do?"

"Pardon me! But *we* ain't gonna do shit! What *I'm* goin' ta do is to make an appointment to go see the doctor this morning—then I'll go from there."

Knowing that what he's about to ask given the situation may sound stupid—he sucks in his pride to ask anyway. "Do you want me to go wit cha?"

She responds in rejecting laughter. "No—that's quite alright! Jus keep your distance."

"What 'bout the baby?"

"What about it?"

"Tonya, quit wit the fuckin' games! Ya know what I mean. Are you try'na keep it?"

"*Why*—what-cha worried? Ya scared I might fuck up your life!—Take your money? I don't need shit ya got! …Arrogant selfish bastard! Tell me Justin—why are we even having this conversation? I don't need you—and you don't want us. So why are we even wastin' our air?" Tonya loses her ascetic calm.

"Why ya trippin? It ain't like that. I ain't like that! You see I take care of the child I have now. This won't be no different."

"Yeah it will—cause you ain't neva got to see this one!" She hangs up.

He tries to call back but she doesn't answer. A minute later, he tries again—but it's more than obvious she doesn't want to be bothered. Incensed, he's ready to head straight for her house—discuss the matter face to face. The last thing he wants is to have that scenario hanging over his head before changing zip codes. But the inner man tells him to sit his ass down—stay cool, for he's already messed up enough as it is. Thoughts race through his head a mile a minute. He's got to remain focused—keep his eye on the prize. Yet his concentration weans—his vision blurs, though not in an ocular sense—but in his mind's eye, he keeps climbing up to be pulled back down by his own self-destructive vices. "What would mama think?" As he can only imagine the repeated disappointment she would have encountered if she were alive today.

Justin suddenly loses his train of thought as he's startled by the sound of screeching tires. Two vehicles veer opposite one another just missing a potential head on collision about fifty yards away. The near crash causes Justin to topple his cup of coffee onto the interior floor panel just under his feet. Literally sickened by the mishap, he knows it's time to go home and get dressed for work.

♥♡ ♥♡ ♥♡

Justin, having just walked through the Sho' Nuff headquarter doors, takes a deep breath as it's already been one of those days. He steps into his office to find things thrown about his desk. Already being tested by Tonya, and having to ride to work with the irritating stench of fresh ground coffee percolating amidst the unprotected fibers of his now stained floor board, he's brought to his very wit's end—irked by the disarray of his usually well-organized desk. The culmination of occurrences simply causes him to close and lock his office door for a second of undisturbed privacy.

It would be some twenty minutes or so before anyone would cross the quarantined boundaries of his personal space. His first interruption comes from Marcus Miller over in finance wanting to later discuss the reimbursement procedures pertaining to the trio's relocation expenditures. The next breach comes directly from the Queen Bee herself—none other than the infamous Renee Sedwick—Rico's boss! Ms. Sedwick is the Chief Executive Officer over all of Arista's associated labels such as Sho' Nuff Entertainment. She's a short, wiry, very cultured white woman of her late forties entrenched with a New York state of mind, and notorious for her clean-house reputation. Whenever she comes around it's usually the first sign of trouble. But it's the end of the fiscal year, she and a few of her cohorts have come to floss off of Rico's fourth quarter earnings. A billboard number one album, two number one singles along with four other ten top appearances and numerous Rap and R&B chart toppers have made for a very profitable year. Therefore, she and Rico will be involved in some special photo ops—as today Ms. Sedwick has a chance to get ghetto—make the company look good for the hood by dirtying up her pristine image for the cameras. Justin realizes its all propaganda and politics—a game he knows all too well. But he also understands that it's a very necessary part of this industry, as image is everything.

Ms. Sedwick and her aide enter Justin's office. "Justin! How are you?" She reaches out to shake Justin's hand.

"I'm fine Ms. Sedwick—thank you. And how about yourself?" Justin perks up, perpetrating and adjusting his demeanor to appease his high ranking guest.

"Oh, I can't complain—how's the family?" She exposes her fake compassion for the little man, because for as long as she's professionally known Justin, he would have thought that somewhere in her memory bank it would have been implanted that he's single with a deceased mother and non-existent father. And because he's a non-custodial parent himself he's never really mentioned anything to her about Justice.

"Fine!" To keep matters simple he plays along.

"I don't mean to bother a busy man—but I wanted to personally congratulate you on the promotion to our new satellite office in Chicago and wish you the best of luck on that venture. We're all pulling for you, and I'm sure you'll do a great job! Okay?"

"Thank you Ms. Sedwick. I appreciate that."

"We're going to get out of your way now—take care!" She and her associate begin to walk out.

"You too!" He throws up a half sincere wave.

He shakes his head with cynicism to the political dog and pony show reverting to his prior distractions. A moment later Tae enters the room.

"Good morning—having a better day?"

"No!" Justin glances up to do a double take at the exceptionally radiant Shantel "You're lookin' good—what's up!"

"Thank you. ...You know how it is—gotta keep up with the competition. Can't have y'all all the time drooling over these half-naked prostitutes around here. ...Show theses little wenches how a real woman does it—ya feel me?"

"I hear ya—and damn sure see ya!" His eyes span the extended split of her ankle length tailored skirt. Her French-manicured toes between a thong strap sandal finish the coordinated look—Black low cut top, burgundy bottom, and black shoe.

"I came by to give you this." She passes Justin a single page memo.

Justin scans the memorandum, which outlines the changes for the upcoming BeeGee debut release. The single "One Life 2 Live" is already due to hit the airwaves next week while the album release date has been pushed up to capitalize on the unusually soft summer market. Set for early August, "Commercialized Superstar" will be in stores nationwide. Justin also notes that the album release party will be at Club 112—a month from now where the first video was shot.

"Make sure we mark that date on our calendar. We'll need ta make arrangements ta get back here for that one."

"Yeah, I figured as much. That's why I wanted to bring it to your attention boss."

"Appreciate. Say—ya got everything together right? The movers are scheduled for Friday morning. Oh and don't let me forget, Marcus wants to talk to us today 'bout gettin' our money back."

"I know that's real! But yeah I'm ready for the most part. So when will our stuff get there?"

"Supposedly next Wednesday—but we'll see." Concluding the brief meeting, he lays the letter on his desk. As Shantel exits the room—he grabs one last peek at her petite apple bottom and smiles. "…Who's the lucky guy?"

"You!" Without missing a beat, she responds as she closes the door behind her.

6:57pm

Justin pulls into his garage after a long day. He sits for a second to talk to his son on the cell. "So ya mean ta tell me—yo mama is cookin' tomorrow and me and Jerome are invited."

"Yeah Dad."

"Shit! What's the occasion?" Justin inquires with astonishment.

"You're leavin' Pops—and we're gonna miss ya."

"We! Your mama ain't gonna miss me. She 'bout glad ta see me go!" Justin chuckles.

"She gonna miss you—trust me. I know."

"Boy—whatcha talkin 'bout?"

"Dad—please stop actin' like boo-boo the fool! Cause it ain't workin' for ya. Mama still digs you Pop—but she knows ya—she knows ya got your otha scootchies. So she keeps her feeling on the down low—that's why y'all neva seem ta get along. She be pissed at cha!"

"Boy ya know you got some imagination!"

"Dad—fo real! You ain't neva wonder why mama be always lookin' good and smellin' good when you come around? She always be askin' me 'how do I look?'."

"You ain't learned by now—that's jus what women do!" He pretends to be in denial.

"No Dad. Look, what she be wearin'—coochie cutters and mini skirts. That ain't mama! She be doin' it for you. Dad—come on… Have ever known mom to be seein' anyone?" Justice makes a true and convincing point.

"Naw—but she wouldn't let me know that anyway. Jus like you said, 'that ain't her!' She's always kept her business to herself—that ain't nuthin' new."

"But Dad, you're forgettin' I'm here everyday. And there's no one. Ever!

There's brief silence. "You really believe that—don't cha?" Justin stores the unsuspected information to the back of his mind.

"Yeah Dad—I'm tellin' ya—she still loves you." His words are sincere.

"So Son—why ya tellin' me this—especially now?" he's confused by his son's motive.

"I've been wantin' ta say sumptin'—but you know Mom, she'd deny it anyway. Besides, you're leavin' at the end of the week. ...It can't hurt nuthin' now—so I figured you should know."

"But that's what I'm sayin'—it's a lil' late in the game I think."

"Pop, you know as well as I do—it ain't too late. It's two outs in the ninth inning with the winning run at plate—so there's always a chance. Ain't that whatcha used ta tell me?"

Smiling, Justin holds the phone with pride. "Ya wise beyond your years boy. Jus a chip off the ole' block. A lil' smart ass nigga—but that's alright. Well, on that note baby—Daddy's gotta go. But I'll keep everything in mind. ...Me and your uncle, we'll be there tomorrow night, okay? I love you."

"I love you too, Dad—see ya."

"Peace."

As Justin gathers his belongings from the car—a Targus satchel and his cell, he experiences a broad range of emotions. Thoughts of Porsha are still swimming in his head, while the impending drama of Tonya reigns ever so eminent. And now this... "Could it work?" He speculates. Yet, as fast as he entertains the thought, another revelation enters into the picture. Tonya's pregnancy and what's up the road ahead with that?" He envisions telling Teresha—which won't go over well. With his most primal of thoughts, as an escape, he wishes for the sexual fix of Porsha.

Justin, now starving, enters to make a beeline straight for the kitchen. He surveys the empty cupboards. He and Jerome's busy lifestyles leave much to be desired concerning everyday essentials such as food. Disappointed, he decides that tonight is going to be a pizza and wings night as he looks to the Domino's magnet posted prominently on the refrigerator. By this time, Jerome strolls through the door.

"You hungry?"

"What's up—you cookin'?" Jerome remarks ridiculously, knowing that his brother doesn't cook—nor attempt to.

"Naw nigga—you know better than that. I was gonna order a pizza and some hot wings—want some?"

"Yeah, I'm in."

"Whatcha got?" Justin points to the Circuit City bag in Jerome's hand.

"Man, check this out! I found those Bill Cosby and Sidney Portier joints on sale." Jerome removes the DVD's from the bag.

"All three?"

"Yep! *Uptown Saturday Night, Let's Do It Again*—and *A Piece Of The Action*—all $6.88!"

"Well hell! Let's do that. We'll chill and watch a flick. …Whatcha got goin' on?"

"Nuthin' that can't wait. We can do that! I'm 'bout ta run up here and take a shower. Go ahead and call in the order—I'll be down in a minute."

"Cool!"

The brothers convene in the living room, propped against the couch. They sit on the floor in front of a high-definition television. Open pizza boxes on top of spread newspaper separate the two men.

Justin, between bites of his chicken and pineapple pizza, remembers their dinner engagement.

"Yeah dude—peep this. Teresha invited both of us over for dinner tomorrow night."

"Word, that's a trip. Y'all must be cool again. You ain't hittin' that are ya?" Jerome speaks with distracted words. His attention is on the first flick of tonight's triple feature.

"Ain't like that nigga. According to Justice, supposedly it's a goin' away present."

"Yeah, I bet she's glad ta see yo ass go!" Jerome laughs as he licks the spicy buffalo sauce from his fingers.

"That's what I said—but my son seems ta think she's still feelin' a nigga."

"Shit—it ain't hard ta tell. Ya shoulda been figured that. I jus thought ya weren't try'na fool up wit her schizo ass."

"Why ya say that *man*?"

"Man c'mon—she's always been like that. Even when y'all weren't together. …Wasn't she like stalkin' ya?"

"Yep! She used ta try and keep tabs on me—but that shit wasn't happenin'. She was always accusin' me of *fuckin'* some ho."

"Yeah and most of the time ya were." Jerome jokingly confirms the accusations.

"Hell, but she neva knew that."

"I remember that time—I think ya had jus moved over ta my place right after y'all broke up. She brought Justice around ta see ya and you had went upstairs fo a minute. I caught the heifer sneakin' round in your closet, sniffin' through your clothes—doin' that crazy shit."

"What did she do when you seen her man?" Justin's laughing incites his brother to finish the tale.

"Man, you know what she did… Bitch jumped like hell then tried ta play it off. Bitch knew she was busted. She's one of them silly hoes! Didn't she use ta start shit if ya even jus spoke to anotha female? …Like maybe Jackie mighta bumped into ya at a store or some shit?"

"Hell yeah—that's her!

"Well nigga, you a bigga man than me. I couldn't deal wit that shit. …*Hell nah!*"

"I know ya remember that night when she pulled the plug out the socket cause we were watchin' *The Best Man*."

"Of course—how could I forget, the lil' bachelor party scene when homegirl was givin' ole' dude wit the dreads a lap dance. Teresha nutted up over that shit."

"*Maaan*—now that I think 'bout it—you were right, she's always been a trip—jus as jealous as she wants ta be. Like Martin said 'Crazzzy—derrranged'…" Both complete the memorable phrase together from Martin Lawrence's *You So Crazy* video. "I'll neva forget the time when that condom broke. Man—she had me runnin' my ass ta that 24-hour Eckerds on Godby Road. Had ta be 'bout 3am. I'm up there try'na get her birth control prescription filled and shit. She took them shits as soon as I got back too—like it was gonna do some good. Dumb ass! She made a nigga wanna cheat—always naggin'." Justin continues venting. "Use ta nag 'bout washing dishes and cleanin' the bathroom all the damn time. …Like I ain't have a job—fuck that! And that's when she wasn't workin' either—hell nah! Then she be tryin' ta run that guilt trip—make it seem like I ain't care 'bout her cause I wouldn't fold clothes and shit. She thought she was Dr. Phil or sumptin'—tryin' ta use reverse psychology on a nigga! …Didn't work! Then a nigga complained 'bout me bein' away from the house all the time. But shit—what else was I supposed ta do—her ass was always trippin' and shit. What the fuck I wanna be around fo? …Damn that! I hauled ass every chance I got." Justin rambles on—so much so that by the time he finishes, the credits are rolling on the first feature.

Jerome changes the movie—then changes the light-hearted nature of their conversation by discussing a forbidden topic.

"I talked ta Dad da otha day."

"Did cha." Justin answers very nonchalant.

"He's doin' much better. Maybe you should call him sometime. …He's changed."

"*What!* That's only cause he doesn't have Mama ta push around any more. I don't wanna hear that shit! Fuck that nigga! He ain't shit! Neva has been—neva will be."

"Yo Jay man—he's still our father."

"Nigga please! …*Father!* That muthafucka ain't my father. Rome—what has he ever done for us? Not a damn thing!"

"But Jay that shit ain't right, he's sick—he needs us. We're all he's got. …You know what I'm sayin'."

"So-da-fuck-what! Where was he when we needed him? Nowhere ta be fuckin' found! So fuck him! I ain't studyin' that shit."

"Maaan—has he even seen Justice? That's his only grandchild. Don't take that from him man!"

"Ain't my problem! He shoulda thought 'bout that before he started abusin' folks and walkin' out on his family. I ain't got no sympathy fo him. Fuck 'em!"

Jerome abandons his plea. And no doubt the subject has dampened the mood. For all is quiet during the second movie, as Justin's emotions float somewhere between pride and self-pity. Jerome's words have struck home—his heart beckons for reconciliation. Yet how do you forgive what you can't forget? How do you separate what was—from what is? For that's Justin's struggle. Here lives three generations of Vaughns, yet one can not celebrate the other because of circumstances of the past. "We reap what we sow," echoes through Justin's mind—understanding that the tables could one day be turned as he could be the one sick and in need—and left all alone. If he could only bring himself to ask Jerome for the number. He sits with nervous contemplation as pride refuses to allow his lips to speak. He realizes that it's much easier to just hide behind his anger—remaining a prisoner to his past, rather than confront his pain and move forward.

thirteen

Second Chances

Entertained by his nephew's PlayStation 2, Jerome battles Justice on the latest Madden. Justice easily manhandles his uncle, having mastered the Atlanta Falcon running attack of D-V-D—Dunn, Vick, and Duckett. Jerome does his best to maintain with Philly's lethal one-two combination of McNabb and Owens.

"Unc, you suck!"

"Maybe on PlayStation—but that's al-ight wait... After this, we'll take it to the court and see whatcha really got. Your father told me ya think you can ball now. Time ta show and prove kid!" Jerome figures to even the score—one on one, being the avid "Run N' Shoot" baller that he is.

Justice scoffs at the challenge, "Unc—you know ya can't hang—you old school."

"Oh really—I see I'm gonna have ta school ya right quick rookie!"

"We can do this!" Justice turns off his PlayStation. "Let's go Unc!" The two race downstairs while grabbing a basketball from a storage closet, and head out the door and around the corner to the community playground.

"Dinner will be ready in a few minutes y'all!" Teresha reminds the guys as they run out the door. Justin, who is by her side, remains in the kitchen posing as the designated taster. She mixes the simmering contents of her secret pasta sauce recipe then raises the spoon to Justin's awaiting mouth. "See if this is too sweet."

He blows the spoon before tasting, "Yeah that's on point there!"

"You sure it's not too sweet?"

"Girl it's fine! …So when can we eat?"

Smiling, "Slow your road greedy gut. Feel like choppin' the lettuce for the salad?"

"Your wish is always my command baby." He retrieves the unopened lettuce from the fridge.

"So what's gotten into you? Why you such a willing vessel these days?" she says, weary of Justin's attentive behavior.

"Whatcha mean?"

"Since when has it been a part of your nature ta offer a sister a helpin' hand. All them times I use ta slave over a hot stove and neva once did cha *ever* lift a finger. So what gives now?"

"And how long ago was that? …Can't a nigga change?"

"*Yeeeah* right! So what woman has gotcha domesticated?"

"Girl ya need serious help—why everything gotta be 'bout *some woman?* I mean damn—give me a lil' credit!" His voice excretes the frustrations of constant belittling.

"My bad! Don't get your feathers all ruffled. I guess I jus gotta get use ta the *change.*" She puts emphasis on the last word as she's still suspect of its legitimacy.

After Teresha finishes preparing the meal, she and Justin walk around the townhome community over to the playground. Justice and Jerome are competitively immersed in a game of two on two with some neighborhood boys. Not wanting to interrupt, Justin leads Teresha to the swings. "…Get on! I'll push ya."

"I haven't done this since I was a little girl."

"So then I take it's a first." He pushes lightly.

"First what?"

"First time a man's taken ya ta play on the swings."

"You can say that. The last time a man took me to the park it sure wasn't to play on no swings."

"Umph!" He pushes her with force rejecting her insinuation, causing her to swing out of control.

"Stop boy!" She sways about afraid she might fall.

"So who was he?"

"Quit! I know *you* ain't jealousy."

"Who was it?" he says as he continues to push.

"Nobody. Now quit!" she said, realizing she's at his mercy.

"That's what I thought!" Grinning, he brings the swing to a halt.

The game concludes; Justice and Jerome leave the court congratulating one another on their victory. The four walk back to the house.

Reminiscent to the other night at Jackie's, Justin is once again treated to a plethora of mouth-watering vittles. Teresha, considered somewhat inept in the kitchen, holds her own with tonight's menu. Spaghetti drenched with a rich meat sauce that includes diced pepperoni, Italian sausage, and ground chuck with Parmesan cheese gingerly sprinkled over top. As sides, a chicken Caesar salad with Romano cheese, Roma tomatoes, and garlic herb croutons accompanied by fettuccini noodles topped with a creamy Alfredo sauce. A sliced roll of slightly baked French bread and a saucer of garlic butter finish the all-Italian meal.

The fellows joke as all gather around the table. "Damn—it's like Olive Garden all up in here." Jerome makes the first crack.

"Now I get it... I forgot yo daddy was a Guido. That's why ya so light, ain't that right boo? She done got all-Italian on us and shit. ...Looks good as hell though."

"So y'all shut up and eat—talkin' all that noise 'bout bein' so hungry. Stop runnin' your mouth! Y'all go ahead and work it out," speaks the hostess.

There's a quick bowing of heads, grace is silently rendered by each and every man, woman, and child digs in for his or her self. They eat until they stuff themselves silly—seconds, thirds, and even fourths. Young Justice, the smallest of the group, complains about not being able to get up. Jerome makes way to the sectional where he soon nods off to sleep. Teresha empties the finished plates as Justin remains seated gazing at her face.

"Whatcha lookin' at?" Teresha inquires while cleaning up.

"I like ta see ya work."

"Yeah—whatever. Now that's the Justin I know—sittin' on your ass while I do everything."

"My bad!" He immediately springs up to offer his assistance. "Fo real—ya look good. ...Cute as shit in them Capri's." he says as he grabs a couple of plates from the table.

Flattered while refusing to make it apparent, she says, "It figures. That's all ya ever notice—any female wit something on showin' her ass. …That's all you think about—be honest!"

"C'mon now—give a nigga a break. I ain't that bad—am I?" He narrows the space between the two of them.

"Yes! And why ya all up on me? …Back up off me!"

"Girl, ya know you like that shit. Besides, I ain't got on you yet!" Justin remarks with a devilish grin across his face. Justice, still seated at the table playing his Gameboy, promptly removes himself, comprehending the direction of their conversation.

"And you ain't either!" She shoves Justin back. "I ain't one of your hoes ya jus screw whenever you get ready."

"Whatever—ya know ya still love me," he boldly comments, based on privileged information as he ties the garbage bag up in the kitchen.

"Say that again!" she says, not believing what she's hearing.

"You heard me. You still love a nigga!"

"Boy, please—I can't be foolin' up wit ch'ou. Ain't no future in your wishy-washy ass. …That's jus like wastin' my time."

"Yeah—that's whatcha mouth say—but you heard what I said."

Teresha gets quiet. She continues to put away the leftovers then pauses and turns to Justin. "Why would I put myself through that again. We've been down that road—what would be the point?"

"Cause sometimes we can't help what we feel. Sometimes things change. Hell, people can change!"

"Maybe. But sometimes they don't."

"True. But now answer this… Why after all these years ya still holdin' a grudge towards me? If it wasn't all that then you woulda jus let it go."

"That's easy. Cause the way ya treated me—the way ya treated us. I was always there for you—I gave you my heart. There's been no one else who can make that claim. I let my world revolve around you. And I put you on this pedestal…" Her words become broken as her wounds remain deep. She peers straight into Justin's eyes. "See, when I love something—it may sound silly, but it's for keeps. I don't get jus involved wit someone for the sake of messin' around—wastin' time. I have ta see some type of future. I had a child by you out of wedlock…"

"But you be makin' it sound like I jus straight dawged ya out! The reason we ain't together is because *we*—not jus me—had some major issues and it got to the point where the shit didn't feel good anymore, right? I mean, tell the truth, were you honestly happy? And be real!" Justin inserts his own take of the situation.

"Yes Justin we had issues. But they were what they were because of what we let them become. You wouldn't talk to me—you shut me out—and that hurt. I mean *baby*..." The word inadvertently slips. "...I woulda died for you—that's how strong my feelings were. Nuthin' shoulda stood in our way—nuthin' shoulda ever come between us."

Justin stands there frozen and remorseful, realizing the things that he valued and desired the most were always in front of him. So much wasted time—time he could never reclaim. He repentantly gazes into her flushed beige face. They say the eyes are the windows to our soul—then hers are wide open. He takes the plunge. "You're right—I did that. I let some stupid things come between us that should of neva happened. And I turned my back on y'all. I made life difficult for all of us—and you did what you had to. You took more than ya had to—I know that. And I don't blame you for doing what ya did. ...I woulda dun' the same thing. I'm sorry—for everything I've done ta y'all. I've blown a life wit my son..." A tear begins to roll down his cheek—he pauses to try and compose his emotions. Seeing his hurt causes a tear to form in the corner of her eye. A revealing moment as he repeats himself "I-am-so-very-sorry—so sorry." His words fade to a whisper. They lean over toward each another resting forehead to forehead—arms wrapped around one another. Time seems to stand still. The outpouring continues over the next few minutes.

By this time, Jerome has awakened out of a snoring stupor. He looks around confused with no earthly clue where he is until he catches a double-taking glimpse of Justin and Teresha hugged up against a wall. He's thinking to himself, "What da hell's goin' on here!" And he takes it as his cue to get on. "Excuse me—I hate ta disturb y'all, but I'm 'bout ta go. Teresha, I enjoyed myself—dinner was on the bomb! Thanks. Bro, I'll see you later. Tell baby boy I said goodnight."

The absorbed couple disengage to acknowledge Jerome's parting.

"Al-ight I'll holla at cha later tonight" replies his older brother.

"See-ya Rome—thanks for coming!" answers Teresha.

"By the way man—it's not what cha think." As Justin tries to give an explanation for their unforeseen open display of affection, he feels awkward being caught in such a comprising position by his brother—especially after yesterday's discussion of Teresha.

"Whatever man—that's y'all! Peace." He chuckles as he walks out the door.

Teresha waits until Jerome leaves, then rudely taps Justin on his shoulder. "Now excuse me! But um'—what's up wit that, '*by the way man it's not what you think*'." She alters her voice to sound like his. "So then tell me Justin—what was it?" She poses with her hands on her hip—demanding an answer.

Justin rewraps her in his arms, smiles and says, "I don't know—you tell me?" With eyes closed they lean in to exchange a sensual open-mouthed but tongueless kiss. Teresha quickly pushes away from him, afraid of getting too close—too fast.

"...You still ain't gettin' none." Teresha, though wanting to rekindle some old flames, reaffirms her earlier stance.

"I wasn't tryin' to!"

"Okay, as long as we got an understanding. Go tell your son it's time ta go to bed. Can you handle that for me please?"

Justin agrees and takes off upstairs, he returns about thirty minutes later. Teresha is comfortably situated on the sectional—her legs propped across the arm of the sofa watching television.

"Whatcha watchin'?" he asks as he grabs the cushion next to her.

"The Chicago News," she replies as she watches WGN Chicago.

"*Why?*" He's completely dumbfounded.

"Me and Justice watch it every night ever since ya told us that's where you were goin'."

Again his heart relents, he settles himself on the sofa as she places her head in his lap. Stroking through her hair, Justin admires her innocent beauty. He reaches down delivering a peck on the cheek and whispers. "Can I let ya in on a lil' secret?"

"What?"

"That's why—in my heart, I neva stop lovin' you." He kisses her softly on expectant lips.

fourteen

Transitions

Chicago, Illinois

From his twelfth floor two-bedroom condo, Justin scans the cityscape through the caddy cornered living room window. He then glares to the traffic below on Lake Shore Drive. There's a sense of slight disappointment—it's not what he's used to. Here everything's on top of each other, buildings and people—no space, no room to breathe. The city is cold and uninviting. Things were different a month or so ago. Maybe because he knew he was just visiting. But now it feels distant—removed, it's not home. Everything's changed.

He leaves behind two lives—one he runs from and one he runs to. He leaves behind much unfinished business—many loose ends. He's tried time after time to reach Tonya, as all efforts have been unsuccessful. She makes no attempt to return any of his calls. To Teresha and his son, he gives the rest of his energy, they share a new dialect—one of renewed hope. He seizes the unique opportunity of a second chance, attempting to rectify some previous wrongs.

With the slightest of smirks, Justin ponders backwards to Porsha who'd tried her damnedest to work her trifling ass back into the picture—calling Thursday, Friday, and Saturday to no avail. Only on Sunday, he decides the answer the call minutes prior to he and Demetrius's departure from the ATL. She actually has the audacity to offer Justin back his shoes he left the night of Rashay's beatdown. In fact, she does her best to persuade Justin to spend the evening in bed making up for lost time. At one point, she places the phone to her moistened cunt then stirs a finger down deep inside her hole so Justin can hear the sound of sopping wet juices. He admits that was hard to pass up. She goes on and on and on—promising to kiss and lick his ills away. She apologizes for the blow to the eye and explains that she thought that he might kill Rashay, and that she was only trying to protect his best interest. He reflects as he's listening to her—he's thinking, "Her ass is missin' the money and shit. That nigga ain't doin' shit for her! That's why a bitch 'bout ta bust her ass tryin' ta call a nigga. She needs shit—that's all!" And by the end of the conversation, after allowing her to plead her case, he causally declines all offers and even tells her to keep the shoes as a beloved keepsake to commemorate the day he walked out of her life. He finds power in self-restraint.

His cell phone rings, he's since changed the ring tone to Mario's "*Let Me Love You*".

"Hello."

"What up nigga!" The voice is unmistakable—it's Dee. "Nigga, it's 5:30 and I'm bored as shit! Come scoop a nigga—let's do sumthin'— let's bounce!"

"Word! Al-ight give me a few minutes. Call Tae—see what she's doin', then hit me back."

"Nigga, don't be takin' all day—bring yo ass on."

"Nigga jus call Tae!"

"Hurry up nigga—one."

Dee calls back a few minutes later; Shantel is on the other line of a three-way call.

"Yo—I got Tae. Here she go." Dee clicks over to bring Shantel into the conversation. "Girl, you there?" Dee looks for confirmation.

"Yeah it's me. ...Hey Jay—what's up for tonight?"

"You tell me—what y'all wanna do?"

"I was thinkin' when you go get Demetrius, swing back ova here and we'll go chill at the Shark Bar. I wanna see if it's anything like the one in New York. You'll be already ova this way anyway. I'll drive— that way if y'all wanna get your drink on, I'll have y'alls back!"

"Whatcha think Dee?"

"It's straight—we ain't got shit ta do tomorrow right?"

"Hell naw. Jus gotta check in. The contractors are supposed to be through by Thursday. So we got another day ta waste. …Sounds like a plan to me. Dee, I'll be over there in a few—Tae, I'll see ya after while—al-ight?" With last parting words the trio disconnects.

5:56pm CST.

Still holding his cell—he checks the time. It's about seven o' clock back in the ATL, Teresha and Justice should be home. He's had them on his mind all day. Without another thought he dials the number. The phone is picked up on the third ring.

"Hey!" answers a winded Teresha.

"What's the matter wit ya?"

"I knew it was you—so I didn't wanna miss the call, but we just walked in the door. I had to run to the phone."

"Where were y'all?"

"At the store—we went ta Winn Dixie ta grab a few things. What are you doing?"

"'Bout ta catch up wit Dee and Tae. Get sumptin' ta eat. Where's baby boy?"

"He's standing right here. 'What's up pop?'" Justice, partially listening in on the conversation, gives a shout out to his dad.

"Tell that nigga I said what's up! …You think ya gonna be up later tonight?"

"*Why?* What's on your mind?" She softens her voice expecting to hear something that illustrates his longings for her.

"You." He lowers his voice to a baritone mumbling.

"What about me?" She turns the corner—stepping out of the audible reach of Justice's young ears.

"Everything—I'm missing you baby."

"You jus saw me a few days ago."

"So what! I still wanna see ya. Shit, I wanna kiss those sweet thick lips—touch that pretty kitty again."

She blushes, knowing that the other night she gave in a little more than she wanted to. As that old couch provided a place of viewing pleasure for something other than television. "I bet! I don't know why ya workin' yo self up—I'm down here—you up there. Can't nuthin' happen."

"Still—it doesn't hurt ta dream. …Take a vacation! Y'all come up here. I'll pay for the flight!"

"Justin, don't be playin' wit me. You know I can't. So stop talkin' like that." Her soul melts at the thought but prior obligations at work prevent her from jumping at the opportunity.

"Why not? The Taste is just around the corner in a few weeks, too. Y'all would love that! Ain't cha always talkin' 'bout getting away? …So jus do it! Ya can't tell me that office can't survive without ya fo a couple of days!" Justin emphatically pleads his argument.

Teresha, after listening to Justin's plea, is silent. Then with reluctant words, she murmurs, "I can't."

Justin pauses with disappointment. "Al-ight, ya said ya gonna be up later right?"

"Yeah." Her tone somber.

"We'll talk then—cool?"

"Yeah."

"Bye baby."

"Bye." She hangs up knowing that she's deeply disappointed him—which saddens her. Dejected, Justin grabs his keys and heads for the door.

fifteen

Amongst Friends

As Justin rolls through the unfamiliar city streets confused by the grid of countless one way routes, his mind wanders to the day he must confront Teresha with the truth before the truth confronts him. As the possibility of yet another bastard child looms over his head, for now, he concludes that there's no need of rocking the boat—just let things be for the time being. Justin figures that maybe after he and Teresha can solidify a foundation—rekindle what they once had, then perhaps the power of love could possibly withstand the agony of deceit. Maybe!

Justin approaches the corner of Clinton and Adams. Seeing the signage directing him to the Dan Ryan—Interstate 90/94, and the Eisenhower—I-290, he tries to remember which one will take him to Independence Square over near Garfield Park. It comes to him—290 is the west loop, which he memorizes from being at North Riverside Mall over on Cermak the last time they were in town. Dee resides in this undesirable Westside neighborhood. Naturally he doesn't have to, but as some would argue, "You can take the nigga out the hood—but you can't take the hood out the nigga." Dee loves the hood.

He chooses to remain inner-city bound, living ghetto fabulous for two primary reasons. The first of which is due to his current

Connecticut Department of Motor Vehicles dilemma of a revoked license. Therefore, he needs to be somewhere he can depend on CTA—Chicago Transit Authority, to get to and from. The other is because his cheaper living arrangement will help to support his renowned weed habit, which brings us to the reason for his unfortunate predicament. He was previously stopped while driving with a suspended license and no proof of insurance—and having just finished one of his signature Philly blunts laced with honey to produce that slower burn. Thus, the lingering aromatic impression led the ticketing officers to do a probable cause search, where of course they would recover small traces of marijuana concealed in a tin Altoids container. It was enough to warrant a misdemeanor charge of possession, which he now fights in the state court system.

Dee stands on the stoop in front of his leased renovated two-flat as he pulls on a Black & Mild. He shoots the shit with three other brothers while he waits. He soon spots Justin coming down the street, and after giving the young men some parting dap, Dee flicks the burnt butt on the sidewalk and strolls over to the curve. It's no secret that his comedic wit and swagger has made him an icon in whatever community he resides.

Justin slows down, then using his hazards, he stops in the middle of the street. Dee darts between the parked cars which line the busy boulevard and jumps in. An impatient motorist toots his horn from behind. "Suck this—bitch!" With harsh vernacular, Dee voices his disapproval as he eyes the perpetrator who also returns some vulgar words of his own. "Yo mama!" Dee retorts as the assailant passes around the improperly parked vehicle. "What up nigga?" He now turns his attention to Justin.

"What up."

"Asshole right?" he says, referring to the motorist.

"*Yeah.* Ain't no surprise. Heard the city's full of them."

Justin can see by the discolored red eyes of Dee that he's already started the party without him. "Save me some nigga?"

"Baby, I gotcha!" Out the pouch of his Mecca pullover pocket comes a pre-rolled blunt with Justin's name written all over it.

"Not now nigga… Put that shit up. I'll catch it later."

Dee sniggers at Justin. "You a paranoid lil' bitch—ain't cha?"

"Nigga, I ain't try'na be like you—catchin' cases ova dumb shit. Ya think ya stupid ass woulda learnt a lesson or two by now."

"Nigga… *Fuck* da po-po! They ain't stop shit. …Didn't even slow a nigga down."

"Yeah al-ight. That's why yo ass runnin' round hitchin' rides and shit." he says, referring to the revoked license.

"Only temporary my nigga—only temporary."

Justin, who usually partakes in only the occasional puff-puff-pass, has come the Chi understanding that with Dee, weed is like water—he can't survive without it. So you either tolerate it or step the hell on. And it's because of their friendship that Justin therefore chooses to put up with it.

They travel back through downtown. And like Justin, Shantel's preference is to reside right in the thick of things just north of him in the River North district. Her one bedroom apartment inside a vintage art deco nine story building on N. Dearborn boasts an area filled with a cornucopia of nighttime entertainment. Finding a rare street park, the fellows gain entry through the time-access wrought iron gate surrounding the property. They buzz her second floor apartment, and through the hand-crafted decorative door front, the block glass distorted image of Tae is seen hopping down the staircase. She opens the cumbersome door.

"*Hhheeeyyy!* What up, what up!" She greets each with a hug. "Y'all c'mon in." Then she leads the way to her apartment. The guys are perplexed upon entering the space. It's been just two days and her shit is already hooked up. Pictures on the walls, curtains hung—everything coordinated.

"Damn girl. Whatcha have shipped?" Justin comments on the sheer amount of stuff already in the apartment.

"All the big things. …Bedroom suite, sofa, and the rest of my clothes and shoes."

"You were right behind us coming down. You ain't have that much in the Montero."

"I know right! But I've been on it. I went up to Schaumburg today ta Ikea and picked up a few things on clearance. You know how we do."

"I heard that. …It's nice though fo sho'." As Justin looks around, Dee has made his way over to the refrigerator.

"In all that shoppin' and shit—you ain't buy shit ta eat? Know a nigga hungry!" Dee rubs his belly while standing in the open doorway of an empty icebox.

"What you thought! What's wrong wit yo…"

Justin cuts the two of them off "Damn y'all be killin' me! Nigga sit yo high ass down somewhere. Girl ain't cha 'bout ready?"

"Hold on." Tae prances to her bedroom.

The two sit patiently waiting—ten minutes, then twenty. After about thirty minutes, Justin looks at his watch but Dee expresses himself first. "*Maaan*—What da fuck! What the hell she doin'?"

"I thought I heard her on the fuckin' phone man. I bet she's in there runnin' her mouth. Dun forgot all 'bout us and shit."

"Nigga go knock on the door and tell her ass ta hurry up!"

"Word." As Justin gets up, Tae vacates the room. The first thing he notices is how cute she looks in her Diesel jeans and fitted Chicago White Sox tee. But quickly his attention is drawn to the desolate look draped over her face. "Girl, what da fuck wrong wit ch'ou?"

She doesn't answer. Both Demetrius and Justin look at one another with that shrugged shoulder "I don't know what to do" look as Justin restates his concern. "You al-ight?"

Tae pulls herself together before responding "*Nooo*. But I'm gonna be alright. Let's go!" They say no more as they exit the apartment.

It's Tuesday evening—so as expected, the Shark Bar's normally ghetto fabulous crowd is considerably light. For this warm summer evening, the group elects to enjoy the city view as they sit outside on the patio roof. Justin and Demetrius waste no time devouring through the southern menu—smokey black-eyed peas, pork chops, etc. while Shantel opts for the seafood gumbo. Dee, still high, tells exaggerated tales of growing up in Connecticut. Between laughs, the fellows do a little sight-seeing of their own, evaluating the female prospects who also engage the muggy climate.

Dee signals Justin with a head nod. "Six o' clock."

Justin, seated to Dee's left, attempts an unassuming backward twist and confirms the warranted interruption. "That's what I'm talkin' 'bout!" he says as he acknowledges the four sexy Chi-town honeys that have just enhanced the view. "Maybe I can get use ta this after all."

"Fo sho'!" Dee cosigns the remark with spying eyes.

"Work it out nigga. Go introduce yo self! Give em' a lil' taste of that Dee magic."

"Ya right! …I think I might do that." He stands up to adjust his gear before walking over to their table. "Ya got my back nigga?"

"Always nigga. Now go make me proud."

Dee bombards their conversation as Justin waits a second to make sure his partner's featherweight mack isn't instantly rejected, and then turns his attention to a distant Tae. "Girl, what's up? Ya ain't hardly said two words since we been here. I thought comin' here was your idea. What's up wit that?"

"Nuthin'. I'm straight."

"No, ya ain't. I know ya better than that. So what's up?" He rubs the top of her hand to reassure his concern.

Wanting to talk, she hesitates then offers some divulgence. "Y'all"

"*Y'all?* I know ya ain't talkin' 'bout me and Dee!" Justin jumps in defense mode—curious about what she's referring to.

"No silly—not y'all per say, but all men in general. ...Y'all ain't shit! Jus look at you... Ain't been here a week and already chasin' skirts. Justin, I thought you were tryin' to work things out wit your baby's mamma. Now look at cha—ready ta fuck the first thing ya see!"

"Whoa, hold up! Maybe we need ta backup. For starters ya don't see me try'na fuck shit. Ain't I sittin' here wit you? If it was the otha way around I'd be ova there spittin' my own game. What you see is Dee—not me, so let's get that straight—al-ight?"

"But you're lookin'—I heard y'all. Now am I lyin'? Ta me it's all the same thing. I bet if one of those hoochies brought their triflin', no clothes wearin' ass ova here and offered her pussy on a platter—you're sayin' you'd refuse, right?"

Laughing, Justin skirts around the question. "Girl, ya trippin'. Fo real—what's all this about?"

"Don't change the subject. Answer my question. You'd fuck her! Tell the truth!"

"I mean, I don't know. Depends on the situation. *Why?*"

"You're just like the rest—full of shit! ...Depends on the situation!" She mocks his words. "I told you the situation—and what does that have ta do with anything? If you're with somebody—then you're supposed ta be with *just* that person. But y'all don't think like that. It's always about the next conquest—the next piece of ass!" She shakes her head in disgust as she finishes her closing statement. Dee returns to the table all smiles having succeeded in obtaining the seven digits—ten if you include the area code.

"How ya like me now!" He tosses on the table a business card with a home number written on the back—flaunting to his partner in crime.

With their discussion having met a premature end, Justin silently mouths across the table. "We'll talk later." She interprets his lips and agrees. He then addresses Dee. "Let me see nigga!" Like two high school buddies scheming on the same girl, Justin picks up the card.

"Alexus Andrews—Shear Magic Custom Hair Boutiques. I know that place. Ya hear 'bout them in the ATL. Supposedly they da shit though. From what I've heard—anybody who's anybody gets they shit done there. ...I hear ya nigga—gotcha a beautician. Maybe she'll keep yo shit hooked up *fo free!*" He grins at Dee. "So which one is she?"

"Right there. The dark skinned chick on the right."

"Damn cuz—she fine as shit! I heard that. ...Homegirl got ass fo days." He gives Dee a quick congratulatory soul tap underneath the table. In his over zealousness for his boy, he's forgotten the self-righteous talk he spoke just minutes earlier to Tae. He glances her way to catch the sour expression. He can't help but to smile—her thoughts are written all over her face. He knows she's thinking, "Triflin' ass niggas." But Justin takes it in stride because he also knows—deep down she's right.

Later, Alexus gets up from her table with one of her pretty friends. They head inside—probably to use the ladies room. Dee clears his throat to get Justin's attention. Justin turns, for here's his chance to catch poetry in motion—as her walk should be illegal. He spots nothing but ass cheeks bouncing from side to side as they creep from under the tattered hem of her daisy dukes. Her long smooth legs, chocolate complexion, and down the back Yaky weave puts her in the category of Porsha—not as pretty, but every bit as sexy.

"That shit there is nasty cuz. I sure hope ya hit it cause if you don't I sure as hell will. Shit."

"Nigga don't hate. There's three otha fine ass bitches sittin' ova on the same table. Show and prove nigga!" Dee throws a challenge at Justin.

"Can y'all jus get the check—I'm ready ta go." Tae having heard enough is sickened by the blatant sexism portrayed by her male counterparts. Justin, wanting no part of Dee's proposition, is saved by the bell.

Leaving the Canal Street rooftop, the trio runs into Alexus and friend headed back to the patio. The two parties stop just inside the doorway as Dee and Alexus trade good-byes and "I'll call you." promises. Justin takes a deeper look at Demetrius's prize catch. He glances over her tattooed street scarred body and skimpy hooker clothing then concludes that the chick is a damn hood rat. And yet she's right up Dee's alley. He's tickled by the verbal exchange of urban ebonics from the gangsta Bonnie and Clyde wannabes. "A fuckin' match made in heaven." Justin utters under his breathe, as he and Tae stand close—looking very much together.

Amidst all the intermingling, he can't help but to notice Alexus's silent partner who stands lurking in the shadows—purposely positioned away from the action. A tall tan sista—conservative, at least judging from the standard set forth by her tablemate—Alexus. She seems a little tense as her attention indiscriminately drifts about the swelling crowd. Justin browses the tangible outline, evaluating her bumps and curves, as she's fine as hell too—especially from the waist down. Yet what she lacks up top is compensated by a pretty face—undoubtedly very doable. In fact, tempting enough that Justin now wishes to some extent he hadn't asked Dee to call Tae.

Those desiring to get in or out of the lounge-like establishment break up the gathering as the two parties block the only entrance. Tae begins to walk off linking arms with Justin. It's her contemptuous way of saying, "let's go!" Taking the hint, Dee puts in a final word then catches up with his ride.

After first taking Demetrius back to his apartment, Shantel and Justin sit parked in front of her residence absorbed with their earlier discussion.

"Yo, ya neva did say exactly what that was all about earlier. We established you were referring to us so called triflin' ass negroes. …Now elaborate. What's on your mind?"

Half smirking with a hint of sarcasm, she says, "And why would I waste my time tellin' you. You're one of them. And from what I can see… shit, you're probably worst!" She laughs.

"Girl, you don't mean that."

"*Psss*—yeah I do. You a dawg with a capital D boy! Remember we talk—and I register everything ya say. …Even take notes. So ya can cut the bull and get real. You got quite a list goin' buddy—and that's jus ova the last few months. So let's not play games cuz I know ya Jay."

"Yeah-yeah whatever. But ya forgettin' one thing."

"And what might that be?"

"I'm jus a friend. I ain't tryin' ta stick my dick in ya. *Therefore*—I have nuthin' ta gain. And besides, we work together. Ya may be cute and all that, but I ain't tryin' ta go there. Business and pleasure don't mix. …Been there and done that! And the shit ain't neva worth it. So ya ain't got nuthin' ta worry 'bout here! Jus a friend lendin' an ear. That's 'bout it. So talk."

"On the real—I'm jus tired of all the games and the bullshit attached to y'all. I'm serious—all the bogus promises and lies…. A sista gets fed up! And it ain't worth it. …Have us puttin' our lives on hold for some shit y'all ain't tryin' ta do no way! My thing is—so why lie? Jus let me go 'bout my business. Ya wouldn't think that would be too much ta ask."

"Whatcha mean booby?" With a big smile Justin listens to Tae bash the male population.

"I mean, why go through all the games? …Have us believing ya really want a relationship—and wanna build a life together. …The bullshit! You know what I mean—I'm sure you've said it many times. You know how y'all do when ya want the draws. Ya tell us anything! That 'I'll give ya da world' crap! I'm sick of it! Y'all all the same—bunch a wannabes."

"Calm down boo. It's gonna be al-ight. Jus chill! Damn, what nigga done got ya all worked up and shit? …Don't hurt 'em hammer. Hell, I'm scared of you! Now let's take it from the top. Who are we talkin' 'bout and what he done did?"

After a much needed exhale, she relents. "I've mentioned him to you before—Quentin."

"You still hangin' wit him? Thought that shit was ova a long time ago. I thought you said ya couldn't deal wit long distance relationships right? Ain't he in Baltimore or some shit?"

"Not anymore—and that's the problem. He's here—well close to here, in Milwaukee. …It was his idea ta keep things going. I was doin' fine all by myself. But he called a couple of months ago and I told him I was relocating to Chicago. And that's when he said he was already up here. …Then comes the bullcrap. Starts filling my head with the possibilities—makin' it seem like distance would no longer be a factor. '…*More time for us.*' he'd say. So then he comes up for a visit maybe a month later. …One thing led to another. Next thing I know we're back together again."

"Ya ain't neva tell me 'bout that."

"Was I supposed to. I'm not like you. I don't go kiss and tell after every booty call like some folks."

"Oh, it's like that?" he says, grinning.

"Well, if the shoe fits. What can I say?—Sometimes the truth hurts."

"I hear ya." Sullen in expression, Justin remarks after the put down.

"I hope ya do. Anyway ole' Mr. Reid decides he's now all of a sudden busy—too busy for me, who he doesn't see but maybe once every few months. ...But I'm supposed ta be his lady. He canceled our plans today for this weekend. Just like something came up when we were here last month. I mean, jus tell me, I'm not stupid. ...Jus say ya don't want to be bothered! What's the point in stringin' someone along like this? Jus say the word and I'm out!"

"Yeeeah right! You wish it was that easy. He got ya caught right where he wants ya. That's why ya sittin' here spillin' your guts now. ...*Quentin Reid?* Ain't he that muthafucka that be in Black Enterprise?"

"*And?*—So, what's that got to do with anything?"

"Girl, don't be stupid. That's yo problem right there. Stop and think 'bout that shit. Here you have Mr. Entrepreneur of the Year—seen by millions in a popular magazine... So ya know he knows he's got it goin' on. ...Money, power and position boo! Keep it real. You ain't his only piece of ass. ...Jus face it! That muthafucka can have his pick of the litter. You're probably jus a sideshow. What I call geographical pussy—ass by area code."

Tae says, "I betcha jus loved ta say that! Quentin may not walk the walk, but he isn't that trite. That's your department."

"Ain't we condescending. Don't think I'm try'na rain on your parade sweetie—cause that's where you're wrong. I'm doin' what he ain't. And that's tellin' the truth—and bein' honest wit a nigga. ...He's tellin' ya one thing—but doin' sumptin' else. Actions speak louder than words baby. Don't' jus talk 'bout it—be 'bout it! Shit—you know!" Shantel looks at Justin with malcontent, but remains silent. "Don't get quiet on me now boo—talk! Ya say this nigga ain't stereotypical—then show me how he's any better than the rest of us?"

"Jus drop it—I'm tired." Tae stretches her arms and yawns. "I'm going upstairs." She recognizes where the conversation is going and has had enough.

"Al-ight. ...Still my booby right?" He squeezes her thigh as a friendly gesture.

"Yes sir boss. Now get out of my car!" she confirms that she's over the somewhat combative nature of the conversation.

"Whatever. But I'll see ya tomorrow. What time y'all want ta meet up at the office?" she asks as both exit her SUV.

"I'm not sure. Jus call me in the morning."

"...Wanna flip ta see who picks up Dee?"

"I'll go get him if you'll take him home," Tae volunteers.

"Shit—that'll work. I'll holla in the morning. Sleep tight!" He walks her to the access gate.

"You too." She goes inside.

Walking to his car—inspired by the eye-opening discussion, he takes out his phone to return a promised call. "Hey baby—what's up?" "Yeah fo real…"

sixteen

Touch Me, Tease Me

Like a blink of an eye, the first month soon becomes history as Justin begins to settle into his new routine. Running a satellite office in the Midwest, he learns has its advantages. Even though Chicago represents a mega metropolis—the third largest city in the United States behind only New York City and Los Angeles, it's still not considered the music mecca as other smaller cities like Atlanta or Nashville. Sho' Nuff Midwest reaps a much lower profile—much to the liking of its Commander and Chief Justin Vaughn. Here the staff performs its day to day functions without the office politics or pressure of central headquarters—Sho' Nuff South.

After settling some contractual differences, production finally begins on Envy's debut release. Alecia and Val have become regular fixtures around the office, as their project is this division's top priority. Rescheduled and rerouted, Arius Kitchens finally joins the Sho' Nuff family and is number two on the depth chart.

Justin, while enjoying the spoils of his executive suite, sits behind an oblique honey maple desk with rustic granite tabletop. He glances

through an advance copy of Vibe magazine. The cover features Sho'
Nuff front man Rico Pittman and next generation heavyweight
BeeGee, as the issue discusses the recent resurgence of southern Hip-
Hop. Flipping forward to the article, Justin reflects a proud moment as
a picture of Jerome graces page 51, depicting him as one of the key
elements in the south's urban market reconstruction. "Yeeeah—that's
baby boo! …Go'on nigga!" Justin pages his personal secretary.

"Yes Mr. Vaughn."

"Rhonda—can you please get in contact with my brother. I'm not
sure if he's at home. Ya might have to reach him by his cell. If you
would have him contact me ASAP please."

"Yes Mr. Vaughn. Anything else?"

"Naw that's all fo now Rhonda. Thank you."

Within the hour Justin's secretary informs him that Jerome is on
hold on line two. He zealously takes the call.

"*Yooo!*"

"What's up man!" Jerome is thrilled to hear his big brother's voice.

"Chillin' nigga. I jus peeped our spread in Vibe and congrats on the
write up. Now what the industry already knew the heads will know too.
…You runnin' shit!"

"Word. Thanks man. But enough about that. So what's been up?
Don't get ta hear much from you these days."

"Shit—so far, so good. Everything's flowin'. Ain't got no
complaints. Jus handlin' business nigga.

"Yo—they playin' the remix up there?" Jerome inquires about the
BeeGee/Kyra remix that he recently produced.

"*Heeell* yeah! WGCI is blowin' da shit up! So I know it's got ta be in
heavy rotation down there. Word—I even caught the video on 106 &
Park the otha day."

"Yeah—me too. I think we did it again—anotha number one!"

"Oh, no doubt—we puttin' niggas on the map. …That reminds me
man—I need ta holla at cha wit a game plan for Arius. Nigga itchin' ta
get in the studio. Yeah—me and Dee are supposed ta be down this
weekend for the release party. So don't forget ta squeeze a nigga in on
your ta do list man."

Jerome, inflicting his usual classic sarcasm says, "I'll make sure ta
pencil ya in nigga. We gotcha! …Man, whatcha think 'bout that
cover?"

"What Rico—Mr. Smooth Criminal? Can't front—the shit is tight.
Had a nigga on that Capone shit—Zoot suits and all. Whose concept?"

"I think that was all Vibe. Naw—but I'm talkin' 'bout BeeGee. Ya see that shit?"

"Oh, that nigga." Justin takes another look at the cover photo. "Yeah, I see his clown ass. Lookin' like a Snoop reject wit his press and curl wearin ass! Thought that shit went out in the 90's."

Laughing, he says, "Yo, why they let my man go out like that?"

"I don't know." Justin flips back to Jerome's picture on page 51. "But look at you—all fly and shit. I know that's gotta up the ante on pussy—fo sho!"

"Maybe. But you know me—that ain't my steelo. Ain't wit all dat shit. So fuck em'—ain't nuthin changed!"

"Yeah-yeah—I know. Got ta give it to ya though—always the one-woman man. That's some rare shit in itself."

"Yep. But what 'bout you? How's everything wit Teresha? …Or are you up there already breakin' new ground?" It's at this point in the discussion when Dee walks through the door. He makes himself at home in the private sitting room, reclining in a black leather chair with his feet propped on Justin's honey maple coffee table. Dee picks up a magazine. Justin's face contorts as he continues with his conversation.

"Naw—we straight. I'm tryin' ta chill. But I'll tell ya what… I'll be glad ta get back home. I already dun told Teresha she better have her ass rested up cause I'm a put sumptin' on her lil' beige tail come Saturday night!"

Grinning, Jerome acknowledges his brother's changing ways. "That's good man. I'm happy fo y'all. I imagine it's a lil' different for ya—but jus think how that shits gonna feel on Saturday. Like gettin' some pussy fo the first time. It'll all be worth it—you'll see. I know Justice will be glad ta see ya."

"Yeah, I hope so. That's my nigga. You right though… No ass! That-shit-ain't-me! I'm getting ta know myself a lil' too well—know what I mean?" he says, as he chuckles at his own short-comings.

"I heard dat! But yo, let me bounce. I need ta finish playin' wit this beat. Got a session tonight. Some new kid—Riq wants ta check him out."

"Word. Al-ight then." He pauses. "Oh, I meant ta ask ya. If it's cool—I'm wanna stay at the house this weekend."

"*Maaan*—ya ain't got ta ask me that. It's still your place too! Ain't nuthin' changed!" Like an echo, Justin joins in to finish the familiar phrase with his brother.

"Peace nigga." He then redirects his concentration to Dee. "Nigga—I know you ain't got yo feet up on my furniture!"

Demetrius drops his Averex boots to the floor. "My bad nigga. How's my ho?"

"Oh nigga I got your ho!" Justin gestures by grabbing his crotch. "Y'all early today. So where's Tae?"

"I don't know. Ain't seen her!"

"Whatcha mean nigga? Didn't she bring ya?"

Dee pulls from his pocket a set of keys and dangles them in front of Justin.

"Whose are those? ...Oh hell—I know those ain't Alexus's?" answering his own question. "I know da bitch ain't lettin' ya drive her car." Dee just snickers. "Nigga, you ain't got no license! Dude—she's got ta be a stupid bitch!"

"Whoooa—don't hate cause some bitch got ch'ou whipped almost a thousand miles away. I heard your ass on the phone... You chillin'," mocking Justin. "Nigga you in the Chi—that bitch don't know what ya doin'. All this ass up under your nose and a nigga ain't sniffin' shit! Jus for that nigga—you need your playa card straight revoked. Jus throw that shit away cause you out da game nigga! A *has* been!" Dee stresses the last three words, solidifying his sentiment.

"Oh, don't trip. Nigga, I wrote da book on bitches. Even taught ch'ou a thing or two... How soon we forget that shit! Ain't that right Dee?"

"When? ...Ten years ago!" Amped, Dee's voice elevates to a falsetto tone.

"Muthafucka don't go there. I ain't even know you ten years ago. You trippin'!"

"Old news Jay! That's all I'm sayin'. What's a nigga done lately—know what I'm sayin?"

Taking Demetrius's comments personal, Justin is beside himself. He shakes his head in disbelief as he walks away still talking, as if another person was in the room. "I don't believe this muthafucka... Finally got em' a lil' shot of ass—and a nigga think he all that! ...Call himself a playa. Please! Nigga don't know nuthin' 'bout no pussy!" Justin smirks while still moving his head, but calms the conversation. "So, where's ole' girl at now? You left her at the crib?" he says, creating small talk.

"Yeah, she ain't have shit ta do. She's off today."

"Where the kids?"

Grinning, "I don't know. Guess ova her mom's. What's up?"

"They started callin' you daddy yet?" Justin being sarcastic throws in a cheap shot.

"Naw nigga it ain't like that! A true nigga don't get caught up ova a piece of ass." Dee peers directly at Justin as he counters with a low blow of his own—then changes the subject. "Ya know Tae ain't goin' this weekend."

"Naw, the last thing she told me—she'd let me know. So what happened?"

"She's supposed ta be drivin' up to Wisconsin ta see ole' what's his face."

"Talkin' 'bout Quent—fo real? She need ta let his ass go. Stop foolin' up cause he ain't tryin' ta be wit her. Jus some convenient pussy—that's all. But she'll learn."

"But ya can't tell that girl nuthin'. Watch—she'll be cryin' on a nigga's shoulder in a minute. Mock my words."

"Yep. Oh well, that's on her. And yeah, while I'm thinkin' 'bout it, have your bags ready ta bring ta work on Friday. Since our flight leaves at around two, I'll have the limo service take us straight to the airport from here. Save a lil' time—straight?"

"Yeah." Dee tosses the magazine back down on the table and readily vacates the plush office suite.

It would turn out to be just that kind of day. The kind where Justin wishes he had never gotten out of bed. His conversation with Dee has set the tone for the rest of the afternoon. Today, Justin finds out exactly what it means to be on top, as it becomes one thing after another—from haggling over production budgets to negotiating details of a twenty city promotional tour for one of the company's lesser known acts. Not to mention the growing pile of garbage once considered the undiscovered magic stacked neatly in a cabinet behind his desk as the next big thing continues to elude his ear. By the end of the day, he would find himself begging for a rock to crawl under. He discovers temporary solace by way of his administrative assistant.

"Rhonda—can you please hold my all calls for the next hour. I need a lil' cat nap if you don't mind."

"Having a rough day sir?"

"Rough ain't the word. …Check on me in an hour."

"Will do."

That night, submerged in effervescent jet soothing waters, Justin relaxes in his oversized porcelain tub—it's one of those Calgon moments. For it's been a long day—almost stressful. Two tropical melon scented candles line the rim of the tub as Boney James sets the mood. He soon drifts in and out of consciousness. Between his stints of la-la, he sips on a glass of Cognac, chilled by cubes of swimming ice. He feels like those white women on television whose husbands are never home—alone and horny. And without realizing, he catches himself gently encircling his protruding nipple with the fingernail of his unoccupied hand. His body tingles, as both nipples become fully aroused. While fantasizing with self-gratifying intentions, he preferably anticipates the day he and Teresha will reunite. Justin's bemused hand then moves from his chest, sliding beneath the warm massaging sea of bubbles, to the increasing erectness of his manhood. Just as his fingers begin to wrap around the swollen cylindrical mass—the phone rings. "Damn!" Full of sexual frustration, he reaches for his cell stationed nearby answering the untimely call.

"Talk!"

"What's the matter with you?" as she detects the displeasure in his voice.

"Heeey baby. What's goin' on?" Her voice instantly changes his mood.

"Nothing. I should be askin' you."

"I'm glad cha called girl!"

"Well good. I'm glad I called too. I wanted ta make sure you were still comin' this weekend."

"Why. You ready ta see me?"

"Ummm—you can say that."

"Well then that makes two of us. Cause I'm fo sho ready ta see you."

"Why? So you can screw me?" she says, being facetious.

"That too!"

"That's all you think about. It's probably all you want!"

"Yep. I wouldn't doubt it." He teasingly plays with her emotions. The remark causes a pause in words until she hears the distinct sound of swishing water in the background.

"Are you in the tub?"

"Maybe," he says, sounding mellow.

"Don't play with me. Why you sound like that? ...*Whatcha doin'?*"

"Playin' with my nipples. Wanna join me?"

"How? Want me to touch 'em through the phone?"

"Hell—that'll be nice. Go for it!"

"You're serious!"

"Very! Now give me your hand—and close your eyes."

"*What!*" she says, not understanding his point.

"You heard me. Give me your hand and close your eyes." He hears her blowing as her patience is tested. "C'mon—jus do it! He waits. "Are they closed yet?"

"Yeah."

"Good. …Now can you feel that?"

She takes a deep breathe. "Where are you?"

"Right there between your legs." He gropes his now fully erect penis with his eyes closed and in deep concentration. "Touch it!" Her breaths become winded stutters as her obeying fingers follow his lead. "Can you feel it?"

With a deep flustered sigh. "Yes."

"Now how does it feel?"

"G-o-o-d" She exhales. "…Real good," she says while touching herself.

Justin strokes his subterranean reef while she speaks—imagining her every move. "So what does it feel like?"

Moving fingers around her moist kitty she describes the obvious. "It's *reeeal* wet—*tight*." She pauses to enjoy the moment. "I want you," she soon confesses at a low octave.

"*Shhh*—I know. Now touch your nipple."

"Hold on," she considerately mentions before stretching across the bed to reposition the phone between her cheek and shoulder—freeing her other hand. She removes her bra and now wears only a long Mickey Mouse tee shirt.

"*Ummm*." She moans.

"Feels good?"

"Uh—hmmm," she says as the positioning of the phone has distanced her preoccupied voice.

They continue to pleasure one another with verbal manipulation, as each oral stroke brings the deprived couple closer to a heightened intense climax. Thus after a few magnificent minutes of masturbating—the session peaks. "Are you ready ta cum baby?" Justin speaks with anxious words as his hand speed and friction increases.

"*O-o-o-o-o-l baby.*" Teresha squeezes her nipple—rolling it between her thumb and forefinger. While on the opposite end—two fingers perform a quick furious gyration of her clitoris.

"*U-m-m-m.*" His body tenses as he releases. The excreted evidence floats amidst the fading bubbles. She immediately follows. The dialogue ceases as the recovery process begins.

Moments later, "Did cha enjoy?"

"Yes—I sure did." She sits up surveying the aftermath. "Oool damn—that's nasty! …Boy you made me get my sheets all messed up!" she says as she lingers back to reality.

Justin cheesing, remarks, "So go change them."

Popping her lips "I swear—I don't know why I be foolin' up wit you." She dries her sticky fingers on her floral bedspread.

"Cause you love me," comments an almost cocky Justin.

"That's why?"

"Fo sho!"

"So that's what's wrong wit me—huh?"

"*Yeeep!* You can live wit that—can't cha?"

"I guess. Let me go wash up," she says as her feet hit the floor. "Call me back in twenty minutes."

"How 'bout fifteen?"

"I love you." With the truth now out, she allows those revealing words to flow freely from her tongue.

"I love you too baby." And with some profound measure, he hesitates before saying; "Bye." For it has been quite some time since he last uttered those three little words—and meant them.

seventeen

Home

Hartsfield-Jackson International Airport, Atlanta, GA.

It's an overcast day when the incoming Delta flight touches down. Enthused, Justin breathes deeply. "Home sweet home" gushes over his hushed lips. He turns to Dee, aisle seated next to him, sleeping—apparently lullabyed by something solacing in his Walkman. Justin smiles, his head soon reverses direction as he gazes out the window across the tarmac. And like a soldier returning home from a tour of duty, he craves to be received by an adoring family. He visualizes his son zealously rushing to his side to welcome him. The force of the embrace is enough to topple his larger than life presence. Teresha follows just behind, she greets him with tears of joy—hugs and kisses. But that's the stuff fairytale wishes are made of. Justin realizes as he and Dee exit at the boarding gate to no fanfare.

Judging by the midday patronage, it's convincing to see why Hartsfield is regarded as the busiest airport in the world. Dee insists that the two stop at Sbarro for some fast food Italian cuisine before heading downstairs to catch the train back to Terminal. Justin, pressed for time, loses patience.

"Damn cuz… Let's go pick up the car first—then get sumptin' ta eat."

"Relax nigga we got time."

"You mean you got time. I got runs ta make. Maybe if ya stop smokin' that shit so much ya wouldn't be so hungry all the damn time." Justin delivers the causeless flippant remark. For hot on his mind is his intention to pay someone a little surprise visit—tend to some deferred personal affairs.

"Oh, it got ta be all like that? Let me get out your way then nigga. So forget it—we can go. Jus drop me off." He pulls the headphones over his ears, mumbling near indecipherable obscenities under his breath. Justin gives little thought to Dee's meanderings as they hurry through the crowded concourse.

Once claiming their bags, they take the Hertz rent-a-car shuttle to the reservation pick-up facility where a GMC Denali awaits their arrival. They part company not far from the airport over in East Point. There Demetrius plans to rendezvous with an old friend—Scoob, a reformed street hustler from around the way up in Connecticut now residing in the *SWATS*—Southwest Atlanta. Justin then heads straight for the ATL city limits—specifically Moreland Avenue. For its time that he and Ms. Campbell sit down face to face.

But as he makes the southbound turn onto Wylie, the surprise ends up being Justin's, as the now vacant home displays a "For Rent" sign on the curb in front of the driveway. "I'll be damned! …Where da *fuck* this trick done went to?" He scopes the neighborhood as if she lurks somewhere close—watching and waiting for him to take a hint and leave. It all feels like a bad joke, as there's nothing funny about the punch line. He circles around the block twice miraculously hoping for something to change. Of course nothing does.

"Oh, this bitch wanna play games. …Al-ight—fuck her then! Hope ta neva see da bitch again." But another side of the scenario also plays in back of his head. What if seven months or so down the line she ends up on his Chicago doorstep—or worse, Jerome's doorstep looking for him with a baby in her arms. He knows the advent of that dilemma will destroy everything, which makes it incredibly difficult to enjoy the relationship he now has with Teresha. Already he's keeping secrets and hiding skeletons. He wonders—when will it ever end? There's been many nights that he contemplates telling her. But why create unnecessary waves? As there's always the chance that Tonya could be lying. It's been done before—and on more that one occasion.

But the odds don't weigh in his favor. And that's what gnaws at him—the possibility.

With both hands firmly gripped on the steering wheel, he taps erratically in complete wonderment as though his mind vigorously paces the floor. He snatches his cell phone and punches in her number—something he hadn't done in nearly a month. "The Verizon customer you are trying to reach is not in service," answers the automated disconnection administrator. "Fuck!" He becomes beside himself because of the lack of forwarding information. His disgust causes him to carelessly sling his phone to the back of the vehicle, where it bounces off the seat and hits the floor as it snaps in two. "Shhhit!" He moans, and then smacks his lips—muttering to himself while glancing down at the separated pieces. He forgot to close the swiveling receiver before lashing out his founded frustrations. So basically he's just thrown away three hundred dollars—give or take a few pennies. And on top of that—he's lost his prided primary source of communication—as not having a phone for Justin is like being constipated. ...The shit hurts!

It's at this point where Justin concedes to the obvious. With nothing left to say—and nothing left to do, he goes home. In his moment of calamity, he hopes this isn't any type of premonition of things to come. It's funny, but Justin's initial plan was to stop by the office and check on things—maybe run into a few people. Yet hindsight is always 20/20, as he now regrets having not gone there first. Because now he's definitely not in the mood. "...*Fuck* Sho' Nuff! ...*Fuck* Rico! ... *Fuck* all of it!" With fullest of intentions, he journeys towards the house.

Overcast skies transform from light drizzle to a heavy downpour as the sound of working windshield wipers become almost hypnotic. The traffic slows—as does time. The blinding pellets of rain play seemingly orchestrated rhythms against the tempered glass. Like déjà vu, time once again presumably repeats itself. He thinks back to that day at the office—and to the package. He remembers his reaction to Tonya's big announcement and he recalls his remedy—to run as fast and as far away as he could. He vividly remembers the drive. He reminds himself that no matter where he went or how fast he could get there the facts remained. And neither time nor space could separate that reality. He finds himself again traveling the same throughways and possessing the same downtrodden spirit—feeling overwhelmed and helpless. "What ta do?" Justin deliberates amongst self, realizing he's done all he can.

And with nowhere else to turn, he relents to a higher power. "Lord if you get me out of this…" Yet he shrewdly doesn't finish the petition. While he may not fully understand or follow the faith, as the bible in his words represents little more than 'a glorified book of morals used to scare folks into living right', he recognizes that there must be something more to the story—something immensely deeper to have so many ensue His mercy.

Having endured the inclement journey, he congers a partial smile as he enters his old residence. "Hell yeah! Ain't no place like home." Dropping his bag just inside the doorway, he treks to the living room, plopping down on familiar furniture. He grabs the remote from off the coffee table and immediately starts to channel surf. He curiously looks around noticing subtle changes in the décor—some new vases, more African-influenced art, and even some faux foliage in the form of potted plants and trees have been added. Overall the changes are to be commended but a bit suspect. Though the images spell Jerome, the efforts don't say it. Justin senses something in the mix and gets up to further investigate. His first stop of course is the refrigerator. Once he opens the door—all speculations are confirmed. "The damn fridge is full. So who's the ho?" Justin jokes, speaking solely to himself. For during his tenure, he and Jerome couldn't keep any food in the house. And for good reason, their lifestyles had forbidden it. And now all of the sudden, miraculously shit changes. He knows the deal as baby brother appears to be playing house these days. Justin wonders, "But with whom?"

He pauses on that note realizing he might best go ahead and handle his own business by checking in with his better half before she puts an APB—all points bulletin out on his ass. He corrals the wall phone. Seconds later, he's conversing with his boo.

"Girl, ya know I'll be over there tonight."

"*When?* …Cause baby I'm tired of talking on the phone. We want ta see you." The distance has gotten the best of Teresha. She's ready to see her man. And knowing that he's just around the corner doesn't help matters.

"Look girl. We could have spent the whole night together. But yo ass actin' like ya can't indulge every now and then. I asked ya ta go wit me to the party. Shit it was only gonna be fo a minute. …Them folks don't bite. Hell, ya mighta even enjoyed it! But naw—not Ms Uppity… The funny thing is that a lot of them industry folks are just as prissy and conservative as you. Yo ass would fit right in!"

"But baby you know I don't get in ta all that. And for your information—I'm not prissy. Maybe a lil' traditional—but I'm definitely not stuck up! Ya would think you'd want a woman who carries herself wit a lil' dignity. I thought by now you'd been tired of them fake sluts you deal with everyday."

"Now why must ya always take it there? I mean shit… I keep tryin' ta tell ya—let that shit go! That was yesterday boo. Both of us have matured since then. All I was tryin' ta say is—jus live a lil'. Shit—jus look at it as an opportunity fo us ta do sumptin' different. When was the last time we had a night out on the town? …Jus me and you? So chill. Stop actin' like everything I do has sumptin' ta do wit some bitch! Ya know as well as I do, I gotta job ta do—and we all reap the benefits of that shit. So enough is enough man—I mean damn!" Justin, about at his wit's end, drops his complaint just to sidestep the possibility of any conflict. He hears the faint thump of music playing outside and moving closer to his position. It's got to be Jerome—whom he can't wait to talk to. Justin rushes to get off the phone. "Al-ight baby, I got ta go get dressed. So I'll see ya tonight."

Teresha, not satisfied with that conclusion, changes her approach. "Baby." Spoken seductively.

While Justin, being a bit standoffish responds, "*What?*"

"Do ya still love me?" Her soft irresistible voice beckons for his forgiveness.

"Yeah, ya know I do. Always and forever boo."

"Good. Because I'm sorry. I know I'm buggin'—so pay me no attention. I'm jus lookin' forward ta seein' ya—that's all."

"It's all good. Of course the feelin's mutual. But let me go and I'll talk to ya later—okay?"

"Can I ask one last thing?"

"What's that?"

"Around what time shall I expect you?"

"Ummm. I'm pretty sure no later than eleven or eleven-thirty—cool?"

"*Yeeeah.* I can't wait. …Thank you baby. *Byyye.*"

They hang up. Justin waits for Jerome to walk through the studio and into the kitchen. His ears follow the footsteps. Just as Jerome breaks the plain to the upstairs door Justin, seated at the breakfast bar, blurts out, "So who is she man?" In almost rude fashion, he does this before any words of cordial address can be uttered. And yet it's because of his zeal to be nosy which causes the subsequent embarrassing moment. From around his baby brother's slim physique peeks a Salli Richardson look-a-like except maybe ten years younger and with glasses. As usual baby boy has done real well for himself. Justin's thinking, "Fool done straight hit da jackpot wit this one."

"Well, I take it you're Justin? And it sounds like apparently you're wondering who I might be. So without further ado, I'm Monique— Monique Shelby and it's nice to finally meet your acquaintance." She reaches to shake his hand.

"Oh the pleasure is all mine—believe me!" All share in on a casual laugh. The two brothers exchange a manly hug. "Seems like somebody's got real good taste. ...*Man* she's done wonders for this place cuz." Justin compliments the fledgling couple on the numerous enhancements throughout the house. He wonders why Jerome had failed to mention his latest and probably greatest inspiration—Ms. Monique Shelby. Justin can see why—and it's no wonder Jerome said what he said about the Vibe article and his rising stock in the bachelor world. At least from external appearances—who could do any better? But then again, in Justin's skin deep world, don't much else matter— only the beautiful ones. Everything else falls into a category of "nondescript"—and not worth being mentioned.

Justin sizes up Monique, and from the looks of it, she stands about 5'7" or 8. It appears she has some caucasian mixed in her bloodline judging by her thin naturally silky hair which is wrapped and pinned up—more than likely because of the wet weather. She wears brown spandex tights and brown nearly knee high riding boots worn like paint against her thick calves. Her shiny pearl sleeved blouse with big collars, big cuffs, and big buttons, being long enough to cover her spandex bottom, deters any unwelcomed previews. Her northern prim and proper vocab, confirmed that she wasn't of your normal ghetto variety. If anything, it was probably the other way around. To look at her, she obviously wasn't hurting for anything.

Justin kicks it with Jerome and his new lady for a little more than an hour. He watches the interaction between the two as he tries to determine Monque's motive. She could be just looking for an easy paycheck. Justin knows his brother represents the cream of the crop when it comes to eligible suitors. Besides being young, good looking, and damn near rich, his brother is one of the rare good guys—honest and sincere. While yet he's in the position to do so, he's never played the game for his gain. He elects to go against the norm—and against the temptation. And silently, Justin has always respected that about his baby brother. Therefore, it's his brotherly duty to be Jerome's other eyes—the unbiased ones unaffected by emotion.

They talk, and having heard an earful, Justin seems to be satisfied that Monique could very well be the one—Mrs. Jerome Vaughn. Her subservient personality is reassuring, as she's not afraid to get her hands dirty. He wouldn't have thought that by just looking at her. He observes—taking careful note to the minor trivialities, the way she compliments Jerome. Not in the regard of verbal admiration, but rather where his brother may be weak—she will bring strength. At one point, Justin notices how her eyes wander—secretly diagnosing the negligible untidiness of the kitchen. "Excuse me guys," she says as she gets up from her stool—rolls up her sleeves and starts washing the few dishes left from breakfast. After which she offers to *fix*—not buy, the two brothers something to eat. "Actions speak louder than words." Justin recalls his conversation with Shantel a few nights prior as he agrees with his own summation. Monique reaffirms the fact that not *all* women are the same. He's reminded of what qualities he has in Teresha. Yet to Justin, it's still funny to see Jerome in this position—playing house; but it's cool to see his younger brother happy—and completed.

Checking the time, Justin breaks the union, removing himself from the kitchen. He heads to his old bedroom—now the guestroom, to get dressed. "*Whoooa*—shit!" Surprised, he enters the totally redesigned room. Undetected, Jerome follows Justin inside the room.

"Whatcha think?" Concerned by his big brother's reaction.

"The shit's fly! I'm impressed. What made cha do all *this*?—Or should I be askin' who?"

"Naw. Mo—she's finishin' her bachelors' at the Art Institute. ...I think for the Fine Arts program. Anyway, I know she's majoring in Interior Design. ...But she needed a space fo a project in one of her classes. And since she lives in an apartment—she came ova here. You know how it is. Ya can't trust them property management companies. Take your deposit and charge out the ass in penalties. ...Remember we went through that shit ova in Austell?"

"Hell yeah. I remember. Fo real though—it's cool. She's got a lot of talent that should take her far. Looks like ya got a winner Rome. Surprised ya neva mentioned her. ...What's up wit that?"

"Appreciate. But naw—it's like that shit just happened. We were kinda kickin' it when you were still here. Nuthin' serious. But the more we talked—the more we were alike. The shit jus started clickin'. So we went wit the flo'. Gotta roll wit it and see what's up. She's straight though."

"I know whatcha sayin'! …Shit—look at me." Justin said, being empathetic.

"Cool. Yo, da remote is ova in that top drawer. The towels are on the shelf in the armoire. I think you'll pretty much find everything else. But if not, jus holla." Jerome feels better after receiving his brother's blessing.

"Al-ight then—appreciate. I'll be down in a few."

Jerome walks out closing the door behind him. Justin, now alone, stops to take in the incredible overhaul. The room views like an episode of *Trading Spaces*. No doubt she's stuck to Jerome's afrocentric taste as the room carries a "Back to Africa" theme. From top to bottom and corner to corner, the entire space is covered in zebra print. The furniture all appears to be handcrafted—very simplistic with a bleached weather-beaten finish. The mattress only bed sits on a low platform. An oversized table, wider and taller than the bed itself, rests down by the foot. It brings new meaning to having breakfast in bed. Two spiny palm-like trees occupy each corner from the headboard. The dangling limbs crisscross to form an arch that overhangs the bed. Accent lighting over various framed art pieces dimly illuminate the space, while meticulously plotted tea candles offer the only other source of light. She uses an occasional dash of red by way of pillows and window treatments to ease the monotone pallet of black and white. A single contemporary element—a Panasonic 32" widescreen LCD television perched on top the armoire, is sole slice of American tradition. Fun—yet the arrangement isn't quite Justin's idea of *fun*ctional living. He spreads his Oleg Cassini garment bag across the satin comforter.

"Hmmm—now let's pick our poison." Unzipping the bag, he skims through his arsenal of flossy afterhour essentials. "*Yeeeah*. Here we go!" he says as he pulls out a James Perse cotton twill tailored fit button down—black with reverse stitching. He loves how the classic cut accents his broad shoulders. And from his duffel, he grabs a pair of True Religion distressed jeans, which are easy to match any shoe— particularly his black square toe slip-ins. With this ensemble, he feels he can't go wrong—rain or shine. He hops in the shower.

Justin rejoins Jerome and Monique downstairs in the living room, where arranged on the loveseat, he encounters the affectionate duet engaged in mischievous foreplay. She sits in Jerome's lap—arms around his neck, as they swap enticing kisses of restrained passion.

"Hey-hey—y'all cut that shit out! Are y'all still goin' or do ya need a moment? ...Cuz I can leave." Justin teases his brother as this time, roles are reversed—and he's the odd man out. He gestures with his hands pointing to the door.

"Nigga, shut the hell up! We goin'." With Monique still embracing his neck and laughing, Jerome playfully dismisses his brother's silly ramblings. "Let's roll! ...Yo, we still takin' separate cars?"

"Yeah, I guess. I don't know how long I'll be out there...Teresha— she already trippin'. I promised ta be ova there at a decent hour. Maybe I'll catch baby boy still up."

"Word. That's cool then. We'll see ya there. ...Comin' back through tomorrow, right?"

"Yeah, I'll be here."

"Alright."

"Al-ight then."

As Jerome and Monique leave, Justin goes upstairs to get his bag together for his stay at Teresha's. Once packed, he then heads out to the club. From cloudy evening skies brings continued rains. The summer air remains humid—almost muggy; typical for an August night in Georgia. Challenged by the weather, he takes his time traveling back to the city. Traffic flows despite the wet pavement. In his thoughts, Jackie crosses his mind. He hasn't spoken to her since his afternoon arrival. A reminder of how handicapped he feels without his cell. He exits I-75/85 at 10th street, takes a right—goes down a few blocks to Peachtree, and there it is—Club 112.

It's been almost a year since the club was relocated from its celebrated Cheshire Bridge Road location. The popular nightspot, now pseudonymous and forever immortalized by another hometown hero—Jermaine Dupri of So-So Def fame, is already jumpin' as the early crowd gathers to see such local acts as TI and Young Jeezy performing. Yet this night will inevitably belong to Sho' Nuff and its family of artists representing in full force to celebrate BeeGee's highly anticipated debut release *Commercialized Superstar*, due to hit the shelves this coming Tuesday.

Justin cruises through the crowd making his way to the VIP, where Rico has the whole section on lock. Women and men, fans and haters alike, stop to acknowledge his illustrious presence. This is what Justin loves and misses about the ATL—here he still reigns large amongst the players and ballers. Looking around, he stops first at the table with the finest women—undoubtedly Rico's spot, who shares the spotlight with his guest of honor, none other than the "trillest nigga in showbiz"— BeeGee.

"What up nigga!" An intoxicated Rico, holding an unlit cigar, stands to greet Justin.

"What's up Riq? …Still know how ta throw a party—huh nigga?"

"Fuck yeah. Sit down nigga! Whatcha want? Bottle of Moe—Cris? *What?* …Some pussy!" he says as he points to the three half-naked beauties who also occupy the small booth.

Chuckling, Justin refrains. "Naw—I'm good!" He turns toward BeeGee. "Here's da man of the hour. What's up?"

"Me niggah! How you livin'?" answers the frail, charcoal complexioned bad boy—grinning with teeth dressed in platinum.

"It's all good. Jus try'na come up like you nigga!" Justin unintentionally stares at BeeGee's long braided hair. With a smirk, he reflects to the Vibe cover and his preposterous doo. He's glad to see that someone has set him straight. "Yo, let me motivate fo a minute— al-ight?" Justin prepares to walk away.

"Alright folk." BeeGee refocuses his concentration on one of the three women. Rico nods while continuing to sip on a glass of Courvoisier.

Before he can get ten feet from the table, he's tapped from behind on the shoulder. He turns around to an unfamiliar face. The muscular figure, without saying a word, gestures over to another booth. It's his favorite diva—Kyra, surrounded by security, waves him over to her table.

"Hey gorgeous—what's goin' on?" He kisses her on the cheek. "As always I see you're lookin' lovely." He stands back to fully observe the neosoul package—attire and appearance, while holding her hand.

"Why thank you Mr.Vaughn. Ya know flattery can get you everywhere." She smiles and winks as she flirts. "And as always—you yourself look quite delicious. Can I taste?" she propositions on the low.

"Maybe later." Gnashing his bottom lip, he lustfully looks her up and down—agreeing with himself that under any other circumstance prior to he and Teresha, he'd probably take her up on her offer. Her earthy, short blonde curly hair against golden skin, and above average body can be, at times, quite appealing—and worth at least one night. But as of now he's just blowin' smoke in an attempt to shrug her loose as he tries to stick and move—mix and mingle. He pretends to spot his brother off in the distance, which ultimately becomes his excuse. "Baby girl I gotta talk to ya later—I see Rome ova there. I need ta holla at him"

"Okay. Well contact me later. You got my private number. So don't be a stranger."

"Sounds good. I'll do that!" He kisses her a second time on the cheek, then vanishes amidst the growing crowd.

It takes Justin just under two hours to make his rounds. He reappears in the raised VIP section after having crashed the DJ's booth as Hurricane and Skillz do their mix thing on the ones and twos. Justin seeks asylum from his playboy, man-about-town reputation—doing his best to duck and dodge all female pursuers. He finds Jerome—with his lady, seated in a corner relaxing.

"Damn! Where y'all been?" He takes a seat next Jerome.

"We've been here man—fo at least an hour. …Where *you* been?" Jerome's vocal pitch lifts. Just as he can get his last word out—a strange woman emerges at their table.

"Hey Justin. How you are? I see you ain't tried ta call anybody." The attractive young woman grooves in place moving to the latest Chris Brown joint *"Run It."*

"Hey you. …Long time—no see. It's been a minute." He tries to recall who he might be talking to. "My bad boo—I couldn't find your number. So what's up?" Justin avoids using any names, as her face is familiar, but every other detail seems to have escaped his memory. Like most men, he doesn't enjoy surprises. Thus this encounter causes some apprehension.

"Nuthin' new." Still gyrating, she waits for Justin to get a clue. When he doesn't—she comes clean. "Wanna dance?"

He momentarily contemplates deciding, "Hell—why not?" The taut blue dress wearing mystery woman takes initiative to lead the way.

Sweaty, Justin returns to the table minutes later where Jerome has one very curious yet justified question. "…Who was that?"

"*Shhhit.* I don't know," shrugging his shoulders. "…I left her talkin' wit somebody."

Jerome flips to Monique—peering with raised brows, as if she can answer his question. But her replying look exudes the attitude of "So why ya lookin' at me?" He then turns back to his brother. "All this time—and you don't know who you were wit?"

"Naw!"

"*Damn man.*"

After a brief lull in conversation, Justin concludes. "Man—I ain't try'na do this tonight. I got somewhere ta be—know what I mean?" He leans over to Jerome.

"I hear ya man. So whatcha gonna do?"

"Yeah man—I'm up!" He rises to his feet. "Mo—y'all try and stay out of trouble." Then he winks, "Don't do anything I wouldn't—al-ight?"

All laugh. "That's where niggas fuck up right there—followin' yo ho ass." Jerome makes light of his brother's risqué reputation.

Justin just smiles while reaching to shake Jerome's hand. "Y'all be cool. I'll see ya tomorrow." A quick thought then enters his mind. "Yo, I'll probably bring the whole crew through—cool?" he says, referring to Teresha and Justice.

"Yeah, that's cool. Can't wait ta see lil' man. ...But yeah—we'll be there."

"Al-ight, y'all be safe."

"You too—and tell Teresha I said, 'What up!'"

Justin shakes his head to agree as he squeezes through the now packed house. He vacates the building before any of the featured acts perform, including his reason for being in town—BeeGee.

eighteen

A Rainy Night in Georgia

Standing in a steady mist just outside of Teresha's door, Justin knocks. "Bap! Bap! Bap!" It's half past twelve, he taps harder than usual, making sure he's heard, with Teresha having more than likely fallen asleep. The rain has caused his twill top to uncomfortably cling to his damp body. All lights are out—so he knocks again. And this time, he receives a response.

"*Justin?*" responds Teresha, sounding cautious.

"It's me boo!" He firmly confirms her intuitions.

Locks unhinge. The front door swings open. A thrilled Teresha stands in the doorway with outstretched arms to receive her prince. Justin, taking the less than subtle hint, tosses his bag in the foyer—bending to meet her extended reach.

His weight collapses the overjoyed couple backwards. Their awkward posture causes laughter and giggles as they are very content with finally sharing the same space. The sound of loose lips and tongues soon follow as their arms wrap even tighter.

"Ya jus don't know girl—I've missed ya so much," he says after he catches his first available breath.

"Baby—I love you," she speaks while holding his soft malleable cheeks. "I miss you baby." Her heart-spoken words cause a resuming of passionate mouth-infiltrating exchanges. Justin somehow manages to break away.

"Let me see ya." She takes a step back revealing her lingerie—a silk wrap-tie nightie. "So this is what I've been missin', huh?" He slowly twirls her. "Damn, you're fine."

Her grins and blushes prevent the uttering of any words. Teresha grabs his hands—again pulling him very close. She's now where she has always wanted to be. At last she can exhale. Realizing the hour, she moves to the next phase. "Come on." finally allowing herself to let go. As an extra incentive, she unties her silk robe. The loose garment soon slides down her naked body. Teresha picks up a burning candle positioned on the floor further down the narrow pathway. She uses the faint lighting to guide her steps.

It's with eager anticipation that Justin follows, yet he can't help but to wonder. "So where's Justice?" as his words are delivered by mere whispers.

"In the bed silly. Ova two hours ago." She then places her finger over her lips and says, "*Shhh*," signaling for Justin to be quiet. Having led him in darkness through the entire first floor, she eventually stops at the last possible door. Already closed, she secures the passage by tightly grasping the knob. She turns herself so that her back faces the door exposing her fully unclothed frontal. "Close your eyes," she says as her hands still cling to the handle from behind her back.

Before obeying, Justin casually attempts to fondle her proportionally endowed breast. Giggling—tickled by his touch, she orders Justin to stop, swaying frantically from right to left, never releasing the knob. "Behave yourself please! You're gonna spoil the surprise. …Now do as I say and close your eyes." Justin does as he is told—closing his eyes and placing his hands over top. "No peeking. Stop cheating! …Gotta always be a knucklehead—gosh!" She catches his roving eye peering through a partial opening between cracked fingers.

"*What?* I ain't did nuthin'!" he says while laughing through his own lie. "Al-ight—I'ma stop fo real." He regains his composure and complies with her wishes.

"You ready?"

"Yeeeah—now c'mon!"

He next hears the squeaky separation of an opening door. He's instantly chilled by the cool breeze flowing from obviously raised windows. A hint of jasmine fills the air.

"Open your eyes baby."

He uncovers his eyes to a haven of romance—an oasis of erotic pleasure. "*Oooh* shit!" he says as he gazes with astonishment. "Damn, you went all out."

"For you." They again start to kiss. Her nude frame presses against his grown but concealed nature. He impatiently pulls away to undress himself.

"No wait—let me do that," she insists in a hushed yet desirous tone. As she strips him—she teases, caressing and kissing all his sensitive zones. Now naked, Justin stands before her—his dangling manhood floats horizontally in mid air. She touches it, gently stroking it with deep longing. And yet despite her own desires, she follows the agenda.

Taking his hand, they enter her staged candlelit bathroom where she prepares to bathe him. He glances back into the bedroom for one more look—still in awe of the fragrant wax-lit decor. He's thinking how much this isn't like her—not Teresha. Romance has never been her cup of tea. And yet here they were. Stepping next to the shower, she pulls open the glass door unveiling the now cold tub waters littered with multi-colored rose petals. She refreshes the bath bringing the room to a steamy fog. "Get in." He obliges without hesitation.

His body flinches as the warmer than room-temp waters touches first his toes, then his feet—followed by the rest of his lower extremities. Teresha is nothing but smiles watching the grimacing looks of Justin's anguished face. "You alright baby?"

"I guess I will be huh? But cha can cut the water off," he says as he submerges himself to near scorching depths. She props an inflatable bath pillow under his head.

"Lean back." On bended knee, she reaches across the tub grabbing a fuchsia spongy along with a tube of Amber Rose shower gel. "Relax baby. Think happy thoughts."

With a boyish smirk, he responds. "What type of happy thoughts?" he asks, referring to those of a sexual nature.

"Whatever you wanna imagine." She erotically rubs around his neck and chest.

"Well, in that case—help a brotha out. Come give me a kiss."

"Only if you close your eyes first."

"Look now girl—this is the last time I'm closin'..."

She cuts him off in mid sentence, covering his mouth and face with her wet hands. Leaning forward she licks his anxious lips with gentle caresses of the tongue. In pursuit of more, he moves aggressively towards her, attempting to pull her on top. To stop him, she pushes back, accidentally causing him to slip and fall against the tub's rear rim. He catches hold of the edge to protect himself, but the splash douses Teresha along with the entire ceramic tile floor. Laughing, with water dripping from her hair and face, she slaps Justin's chest. "...You weren't supposed ta get *me* wet." She examines her drenched surroundings. "Look at the floor! Boy, standup—I gotta getcha outta here. Messin' up my bathroom wit yo silly self."

"Like it's my fault! You the one pushin' folks." He rubs his burning chest while standing to his feet. Several rose petals cling to his legs and thighs.

"Yeah, but I ain't tell ya ta do all that either. So slow your role tiger—*I got this,*" she says, quoting one of Justin's favorite replies. She scrubs his back with a good lathering, and goes down between his legs and on around to his ankles. Once finishing, she dries his dripping body wrapping the damp towel around his waist—then points to the bedroom. "Go on now—run along. I'll be there in a sec." She pinches his booty to get him moving.

"*Ouch!* Dammit girl! Why it gotta be all that?" The simple pinch causes Justin to vent. "See, that's what I'm talkin' 'bout. Always startin' shit—then wanna go blamin' yo shit on someone else. There's a perfect example—right there!"

"Oh boy quit cha whinin'—ya big baby! Take yo tired ass on in the room and wait on your woman. I said I'll be right there." This time she rears back and straight blasts his butt-naked bottom with the palm of her hand, catching every nook and cranny of his raw tender ass. And she does it for no better reason than to cause further pain and aggravation.

"*Shhhit!* ...Damn you!" He limps away, holding his ass and mumbling words of revenge. "But that's all al-ight though. It's quite alright... Jus remember that shit when I'm tappin' yo ass. So don't be screamin' mercy cuz I ain't try'na hear it!"

Teresha replies, "Whatever. Don't flatter yourself!" She then slams shut the bathroom door. Yet it's all in fun—every last word. For no matter how it sounds—the taunts, the teases, and the bravado all comes down to this long-awaited moment as the past fades a million miles away.

The toilet flushes, Teresha opens the door. She walks into the room concealing something behind her back. Justin, now in the bed, lies on his stomach—unwinding against satin bedding. The night-air cools his uncovered body. Seizing the opportunity, Teresha climbs on top, mounting his legs. More than twenty slow burning candles light the room as she dispenses a foreign liquid substance over his barren back. The warm solution touching his chilled flesh causes Justin to cringe with a tingling sensation. She commences to massage the oil-like lubricant onto his dry ashy skin—instantly turning it smooth and silky. Aroused by her own actions, she leans in, trailing kisses from the neck down. Having been teased for long enough, Justin turns himself over as she next nibbles his chest. He grabs her straddling hips, lifting to place himself inside her. Their initial contact causes Teresha an immediate orgasm. She can't ever remember feeling so free—so secure. For the first time she allows herself to release all those bottled emotions—the hindrances that kept her from once again trusting—or forgiving. Her body responds, causing a cascading flow of juices as their assembled bodies continue to quiver in the heat of passion. It's at this very moment when Justin finally realizes the difference between making love and having sex. He recognizes that the contrary is in the transfer of energy—from one heart to the other. The power that brings two people together and the bond that never separates them. It's in this time—and place, which gives that fervid feel of home. Here he's not preoccupied with breaking any records or tryin' to knock the ball out the park. But rather he takes his time to enjoy the ride. For there really is... *no place like home.*

nineteen

Sunday Mourning

The inviting aroma of hot bacon and buttermilk biscuits brush the nose of a still slumberous Justin. He flips from his belly to his side, grasping hold of the vacant pillow beside him. Drawing it close, he apprehends the reality that he's not dreaming and that he's all alone. He sees the half turned back sheet and the now empty spot next to him. The morning light and chirping birds introduce the new day. Dwindled candles exuding the sweet scent of jasmine and the slick touch of satin against stripped flesh bring comforted validation. Justin soaks in the authenticity of last night. Deciding to enjoy the solitude for a spell longer, he tosses once more in search of the perfect position. Yet before he can reach that distinct place, Justice, without knocking, crashes through the cracked bedroom door excited to see his father.

"Hey Dad!"

"What's up baby boy?" Justin reaches for the thin linen, making sure his body is fully covered.

Justice takes a seat next to his dad at the edge of the bed.

"When you gettin' up Pops?"

"In a few—what's up?"

"Nuthin'. So what are we doin' today?" he says, as he makes a sly play for quality time with his father.

"*Shoot*—whatever. We'll have ta play it by ear—al-ight?"

"Yep!" He pauses before the next statement. "I see mama's happy."

"*Huh?*" Justin says, baffled by the remark.

"Shit. It's Saturday Pops! Mama don't cook on the weekends. Especially no breakfast! Saturdays I'm usually on my own. ...Me and a bowl of Fruity Pebbles."

Justin, boastfully smirking says, "So what's she cookin'?"

"Everything. ...Eggs, grits, biscuits, sausage and bacon. She's in there hookin' you up Pop!"

"Word." he says, feeling smug.

"Yeah. Whatever ya did ya need ta do it more often. Maybe we'll eat a lil' better 'round here—ya know?"

"I hear ya." Still grinning, he shakes his head to his son's suggestive remarks. "Lil' man—let me get up and put some clothes on."

"Okay." Justin gets up to leave the room.

"*Nooo.* I want you to stay right there." Teresha enters the room holding a portable-folding tray filled with a smorgasbord of morning vittles.

"*Yes Ma'am.* That's what I'm *saaayin'.*" She places the tray over his lap. "Good morning baby. Where's my sugar?" Justin pokes his lips out ready to receive his kiss.

But Teresha, being silly, drops packet of Sweet N Low meant for his coffee down on his plate and says, "There you go." After a good laugh, she relinquishes, giving Justin what he wants. "*Hey baby.*" She offers up a quick smooch. "Let me know if you need anything else. I'll be in the kitchen."

"Thanks baby."

Once breakfast is over, Teresha rejoins Justin in bed, leaving kitchen clean-up duties with Justice. They lay together holding one another while talking.

"So, what got into ya last night?" Justin asked, referring to Teresha's aggressive foreplay and surprising preparation.

"*What?*"

"Girl, you know what I mean—the whole seductress act. That ain't like you."

"And it ain't like you ta cum after five minutes either—is it?" She teases his initial short-lived performance.

"Oh, we got jokes huh?" Then, with a cocked smile, he counters, "Oh, but I more than made up fo that shit. Ya know what I'm talkin' 'bout. Had yo ass climbin' walls and shit that second time—now didn't I? Don't lie!"

"Ummm huh. So ya say." she says, toying with his ego.

Justin turns to Teresha, facing her with undeviating attention. "On the real though—last night was deep." With elbows resting squarely on the mattress and forearms upright, their fingers dance, intermingling together with the slightest of touch.

"Whatcha mean?" she asks, confused.

"Neva felt like that before. It was different—much deeper."

"How so?" Teresha smiles while enjoying Justin's emotional confessions.

"I don't know. ...I felt you."

"I betcha ya did!" she says, being sarcastic in a sexual sense.

"Naw, I mean as if you were a part of me—a piece of my body. Sounds crazy but I think ya know what I'm tryin' ta say."

"*Yeeep*—I sure do. It's always been like that for me—with us. But I'm glad ta see you finally feelin' what I've always felt." A tear trickles down onto her ear before saturating upon the sheets as she stares at the ceiling to confess her feelings. "I used ta pray fo this everyday—us together as a family. I remember how I used ta blame God for not answering my prayers. How I would cry myself ta sleep at night—wonderin' what had I done ta deserve so much disappointment and hurt. And I literally allowed myself ta hate you for everything you put me through. And I actually promised myself ta neva forgive you for as long as I had breath in this body. ...I solemnly meant that! And for a long time I wasn't tryin' ta hear nuthin' ya had ta say." She pauses. "But then—which seems so funny now, but something clicked. Ever since that night in the car—that weight I carried around my heart—was lifted. It disappeared—vanished! I mean, of course there were those occasions afterwards where ya still may have pissed me off..." Justin laughs. "Shut up—I'm serious. But I got over it—unlike before. And then I was able ta talk ta ya—and listen ta ya. But in a different sense! Like my mind had this huge gapping hole—jus really open and receptive... Are you listenin' to me?" She checks to make sure he hasn't drifted off to sleep.

"Yeah—I'm still witcha!"

"I guess what I'm tryin' ta say—God's gotta purpose in everything—and maybe sometime we have ta go through something to help us understand later. I mean I'm sayin'—we live and we learn. And I believe everything we went through—together and separately, helped ta bring us ta this present place. And my biggest question now—where do we go from here? ...*What is this?* I mean—what are we doin? How can either of us be ready for any type of commitment?"

"I hear ya—I feel whatcha sayin'. If you're askin' if *I* really want this too, then the answer is yes. I wouldn't be here if I didn't." He stops to ponder, taking extra time with his words before speaking again. "To play games with this relationship—what would I gain? If anything, we're taking a risk of creating a deeper wedge—causin' mo' problems. I mean seriously—jus look at the history and how volatile it's been. *Shit!* Look what we've done to our son. The po' boy stays confused. No doubt I want my family back. But ta reopen old wounds... Then who benefits? What goes through my mind is whether our past will ever really be a dead issue. I mean, that night in da car—and even otha times, I've seen—and heard cha express yo pain ova things that happened a long time ago. And I'm sayin' now—are ya sure you can move past the way it was before? Or is it goin' ta be this thing where I have ta constantly be provin' myself ova and ova til' you decide ta trust me again? And if it's gonna be like that—then maybe we are makin' a mistake."

"Baby, you say that as if I've questioned your reason for being here. And if that's whatcha think... I can tell ya now that's not my intention. Ova this last month—since we started talkin' again, have I shown you anything that even resembles that?"

"Naw—not so far. But I'm sayin'—ya know it's like all of a sudden everything's different. It's got me trippin'! Almost too good ta be true. I keep thinkin'—why couldn't we be like this before? I don't know—but it seems like we wasted a lot of time."

"Maybe so. But I'm jus happy we are where we are now. At least now I can see the effort. I mean—you're doin' all I could ever ask." She smiles, "If it could jus stay like this always. ...Jus continue ta be honest wit me cuz I got your back baby. I love you! And no matter where you are—or how many miles between us—I'm there for you—and there with you. So jus neva forget that!" Teresha pauses. "If this is what we both want—then we can do this!"

"Fo sho'! Ya know I love ya too." But just as he finishes his endorsing remark, it comes to him—her comment about *being honest*. His imminent predicament with Tonya comes to mind. Its unpredictability metastasizes through to the rest of his body, taking root in the pit of his stomach. The sickening thought causes Justin to become silent—and preoccupied.

♡   ♡   ♡

3:34pm

Teresha and Justin are in the shower. Their hearts race as they find themselves again making passionate love. Within the warm stall, a vaporous cloud conceals the essence of the experience. Bellowing moans sustained by clinching embraces as neither can let go. Fifteen minutes later, remnants of the moment drain down their erect bodies. Justin continues where Teresha left off the night before. Sudsing a washcloth, he carefully cleanses her.

"Y'all goin' ova ta Jerome's wit me?"

"Sure, if you're invitin' us. We ain't lettin' ya off the hook that easy. Ya know I ain't try'na let ya outta my sight." She moves in to wrap herself around his waist—arching to kiss his neck.

"Why, whatcha worried 'bout?" Sensing her jealousy, he grins—then reciprocates her show of affection.

"*Please!* You must think I'ma fool. I ain't forgotten where we at. …Gotta protect my interest. Dun waited too long for this!" They both giggle.

5:12pm

With all three standing at the front entrance, Justin does something he has never had to do at 3142 Mt. Gilead Road—he rings the doorbell. Jerome answers the door with Monique at his side.

"What up! What up!" "Hey y'all!" Jerome and Monique greet the recently reunited family. After all the formal introductions, everyone then moves to the living room. Teresha and Monique, having already found a common interest, take a seat together on the sofa while the fellas disperse amongst the floor and loveseat. Jerome and Justin talk shop while Justice squats and listens. But hearing nothing that fascinates his curiosity, Justice stretches across the floor grabbing the Sunday early edition of the Atlanta Journal-Constitution. Now lying in the middle of the room, he scans the paper, previewing next week's sale ads—specifically for electronics. Jerome speaks.

"Yo—I ain't see Dee last night. I can't believe dat nigga missed a party. Especially when a muthafucka could drink all night fo free! That nigga know he can drink like a fish."

Justin laughs as he concurs with the nodding of his head. "Word— but you're right. I ain't see that nigga either. Which reminds me… Don't let me forget to call his ass tonight—so we can be on the same

168

page for our flight in the morning. Ain't tryin' ta have ta hunt his ass down when we got a plane ta catch. I wanna get there early so we ain't got ta be foolin' up wit security at the last minute?"

"Yeah—so what time y'all flight leave out?"

"10:30!"

"Whatcha doin' 'bout tonight? You stayin' ova here or are y'all chillin'?"

"I'ma chill. But before we leave I got ta go up here and get my stuff."

"I take it everythang must be pretty straight then?" Jerome comments with a sly smirk.

"We good—know what I'm sayin'. It's all love!"

Geeked, Justice, who hasn't heard a word, interrupts the conversation.

"Dad! This is what I want right here!" Taking a Best Buy sales ad over to his father, he points to one of those Sony PSP handheld gaming consoles similar to his Gameboy, but about a $150 more.

"Boy, ain't that da same thing ya got!"

"Nah! SP's can't play MP3's and download off the Internet." He tries to bring his out-of-touch dad up to date with the latest technology.

Justin turns to Jerome. "Da shit ain't like it use ta be when we were growin' up. Remember that Atari 2600 we had?"

"Yeah—we had Pong and shit!" Both erupt in laughter. Justice just shakes his head with pity as he watches his two idols reflect on glory days. Their laughter is loud enough to also break up the ladies' seemingly involved discussion.

"While y'all ova there having such a good time and all—what are we goin' to do tonight?" Monique's inquiring mind wants to know.

"*Shhhit*—I don't know. That's up ta y'all!" Justin answers with some indifference.

"I wanna go eat!" Justice quickly throws in his two cents.

"Oh, that figures comin' from ole' mini mouth ova there. I know his growin' ass *always* ready ta eat! ...So whatcha got in mind lil' man?"

"Ryan's!" He rubs his hand in circles across his belly, signifying his obvious appreciation for that particular restaurant.

"Look! lil' greedy bastard. Dun picked himself out one of dem all-you-can spots." Jerome slaps Justin in the thigh as he teases his nephew. "I don't blame ya lil' man—mo' fo yo money. I'll tell ya what—dat fried chicken be right on point though. ...Count me in—I'm wit it! What cha'll say?"

The masses agree—and Ryan's it is. Within the hour, all load into Justin's rented GMC, venturing to the location on Tara Boulevard in Jonesboro. They eat, drink, and be merry while fully enjoying themselves—and each other for just under fifty bucks. Jerome gladly picks up the tab.

Once back at the house, the group talk and chill until about nine-thirty when Teresha and Justin, looking wantonly distracted, decide to call it a night, craving a minute of quality time before the morning. Justin runs upstairs to grab the rest of his things. He meets his crew waiting by the door where he tightly embraces his brother.

"Appreciate it man."

"No problem bro."

"When ya comin' up? We still got ta holla 'bout Arius."

"Well, that's my excuse right there. Have Rico's ass pay fo that one. We'll do that real soon then."

"Al-ight—we'll be waitin'. Girl, take care of my baby brother." Justin bends over to hug Monique.

"Oh, I will." She reaches to put her arm around Jerome.

"Alright lil' man—behave yo'self. Keep them grades up and we'll talk 'bout dat game you saw—cool?"

"Thanks Unc." Justice enwraps his uncle.

"It was nice meeting you."

"You too," as the ladies exchange their good-byes. Monique runs her hand through Justice's locs. "Take care handsome." Justice, already smitten by her beauty, cracks a huge smile.

"Alright sis—you be cool." Being silly, Jerome extends his balled fist forward to give his future sister-in-law dap.

"Whatever Rome—you know better. I ain't no nigga so don't treat me like one!" Having shown her saucy nature, Teresha opens her arms to receive a more fitting farewell. She and Jerome hug. "Be good Jerome."

"Girl, you know it!" he says while still embraced.

Justin, Teresha, and Justice make the quiet journey back to College Park. Yet, the lack of conversation speaks volumes for what is actually being felt and thought by each. For Justin, he's thinking ahead to tomorrow and on to the following week. As he knows—it's back to the grind again. The weekend having served as a battle won, settles one impasse directly affecting his future. Justin can now rest easy having explored the reconcilable plausibility of the relationship. Though the road may be rough, the prognosis looks bright. The reconstructing of a bridge once burned. While Teresha, on the other hand, has already begun to dread the separation—fearing tomorrow. Her mind moves ahead to a time when all parties can be together, sharing their day to day lives under one roof. She dreams of the day of becoming Mrs. Justin Vaughn. The thought brings a smile to her face as she envisions herself in the kitchen of their *new* home, cooking and living the celebrated life of a domesticated diva. She now regrets the time wasted in grieving—blaming herself. Thinking if she had just been able to get beyond the bitterness, things could have been a lot better—a lot sooner. As solace, she tries using her own advice with the adage, "everything has a time and place." And yet these once wise words have somehow lost their effectiveness and power when pertaining to herself. From her passenger side seat, she stares intimately into Justin's drive-focused face while affectionately massaging his tapered nape. She realizes just how much she loves her man. Even young Justice drifts in thought—edifying the moment, as he's happy to see his estranged parents finally back together. Maybe soon he'll have his life back too. He speaks in reference to his thoughts.

"So Dad, when do we get to go witcha? I wanna see Chicago too," he said, bluntly.

"I'm not sure baby. We'll have ta wait and see. But we're workin' on it." He looks to Teresha with a warm smile. Her heart flutters as possibly dreams do come true. Unbuckling her seat belt, she slides close, resting her head on his shoulder. She savors the moment, though Justin worries. "Girl, you know better. That's not safe," he says, referring to her nonexistent seat belt.

She sits up grinning. "Oh, ya worry 'bout me now. …That's right baby, protect your woman." She refastens the belt, then, out of the blue, Jerome crosses her mind. "Your brother looks happy. Monique, she's really cute. They seem to get along real good."

"Mama—she ain't cute, she's *finnne*! Unc's lucky." From out the mouth of babes, speaks raging adolescent hormones.

"Damn!" Justin cleverly intervenes.

"*What!*" Teresha jumps.

"I forgot to call Dee. Baby, don't let me forget when get back to the house."

She recollects her nerves. "Okay!"

Yet by design, Justin successfully eases the recourse of his son's statement—avoiding any mood changing, conversation ending, recoiling remarks from Teresha. For he knows his woman—and it doesn't take much, as young Justice still has that lesson to learn concerning his mother's jealousy and how to discern the moment— particularly when she's having a good day. Justin figures why mess up a good thing as he breathes a sigh of relief.

Teresha makes good on her word. Upon unlocking the door, she reminds Justin of his request. "Baby—call Demetrius."

Using the house phone, Justin calls his cell. When Dee answers, it's evident by the commotion in the background—he's caught him at a bad time. "What up nigga! Where ya at?" Beyond the loud music, he hears numerous voices—male and female.

"What up? I'm still at Scoob's." A woman then interrupts. Justin can tell by the muffled voices that Dee tries to cover the phone. "Ay yo—nigga let me call ya back."

"That's al-ight—do ya thing. I'll be through 'round 8:30—a quarter til nine. Jus be ready!"

"Yeah nigga."

"Al-ight." After hanging up, Justin focuses on his family, as the rest of the night is spent in front of the television watching BET. Justice soon falls asleep on the couch. Teresha and Justin, leaving the TV on, but muting the sound, walk back to the bedroom. Teresha, stripping down to her bra and panties, grabs a V-neck tee from out the drawer and jumps in bed. Justin does the same, as he lays down, wearing only a pair of gray Calvin Klein boxer briefs. The two cuddle beneath the covers.

"So, are ya gonna miss me?" He directs his question to a near sleep Teresha.

"More than you'll ever know," she says, as she snuggles closer, positioning herself underneath his chin. While resting on his back, hands tucked comfortably behind his head, she lays partially on top— her arm across his torso, her leg over his. The night ends here as sleep conquers both.

7:00am

"Uuur-uuur-uuur…" The alarm sounds. Justin rolls over, disoriented. He realizes that once again, he's awakened to find himself all alone. The sound of running water affirms that Teresha is close— and already in the shower. Being the stickler she is—always on it, and always together, Justin figures that at some point in the middle of the night, she had enough sense to set the alarm. He also notices his two bags already by the door, packed and zipped. His outfit for the day hangs on the doorknob just beside them. He smiles, remembering some of the finer advantages attached to this woman. Teresha appears from the bathroom.

"Good morning sunshine. How are we this morning?" She sashays in the room with her pink terry robe—tied tight, accentuating her every curve—her brushed back hair, lays loosely atop her shoulders.

Justin, readjusting his focus, wipes the sleep from his eyes. "I'm fine—but obviously not as fine as you. Now come here!" he says, as her shower fresh radiant appearance causes Justin to feel a little frisky.

"Whatcha want?" she says, knowing exactly what he wants just by the predatory tone of his voice.

"Shit—I wanna see!"

"What? ...These?" She opens the top of her robe, exposing her aroused nipples—then quickly closes the garment, leaving Justin to fiend for more.

Smacking his mouth, "Girl, ya know ya wrong for that."

"Give ya something ta think about while up there with all those other women. Maybe you'll remember whatcha have at home." She approaches Justin, putting her arms around his neck. "So, whatcha want for breakfast baby?"

"You!" he says, as he replies without a second thought.

"*Nooo!* Besides—I just took a shower."

"So! Take another one!"

"No, because you need ta get up and get ready. You have a plane to catch—remember?"

"Yeah-yeah, you right. Let me get up. Feel like fixin' some pancakes?"

She pulls away, heading towards the kitchen, "Want some sausage too?"

"Yes please. ...By the way, thank you for getting my stuff together."

"Anything for my baby. Now hurry up and go take your shower!"

Justin, after getting dressed, goes upstairs to spend a few last quality minutes with his son. They talk until Teresha summons everyone for breakfast. The three share a quick meal. Justin, watching the wall clock, announces his departure. "Al-ight y'all—it's 'bout that time. Baby boy—go get my bags out of yo mama's room please. ...Thank ya!" Now on his feet, drawing Teresha close, he places his finger under her chin, lifting her head—sweetly pecking her full lips. He inhales deep the fragrance of her Curve Crush. "Thanks fo everything boo. I'll call ya when I get there. Ya know I love ya."

"I love you too. Call me 'round two-thirty. I'm supposed ta go to church wit a couple of girls from the office—but I'll be back by then."

"Al-ight. Make sure you take care of yourself and that boy of mine." He tilts down for another kiss. But this time, the connection is longer and much deeper. Justice walks in with the bags.

"Y'all need a room."

"Hush boy. Gimme those." He takes the luggage from his son. Teresha, still attached to his side, blushes vividly. "Watch over yo mama fo me." He then kisses his son's forehead. "Be good! I'll call y'all this afternoon." As he leaves, Justice and Teresha stand in the doorway waving.

♡ ♡ ♡

8:39am

Justin, parked outside of Scoob's East Point residence, beeps his horn, alerting Dee of his arrival. Demetrius drags from out the first floor apartment—backpack thrown over his shoulder. With a garment bag in one hand, he wheels a smaller piece in the other. Sporting an Enyce fleece cocoa colored sweatsuit—a Black & Mild tucked neatly behind his ear, Dee gets in the Denali.

"Long night nigga?"

"Sumthin' like that." he says, being unusually short with his words.

Sensing his attitude, Justin responds with another question. "What da hell wrong wit ch'ou?"

"Same ole' shit. ...Bitches!"

"What's up?"

"Nah—Alexus, she buggin'. Try'na fuck wit my head."

"*Shhhit*. From the looks of it—it must be workin'." Justin smirks as he leaves the parking lot. "So, what she do this time?"

"Bitch called last night...ya know how it is. Talkin' shit cause I ain't called her this weekend. But shit—caught up wit my man Scoob—and a nigga was out! She do da same shit! ...Let it be one of her girls—she'll get ghost on a nigga quick!"

"*Maaan*—but that's how they do. If we out—then we got ta be fuckin'. But let they ass go somewhere—they jus kickin' it. Niggas—we get a bad rap every rip. Shit, ya might as well live up to their expectations...they think we fuck everything that moves anyway—ya know?"

"Yep—and that's exactly what I did!" Dee laughs as he lights his Black & Mild. "That's why a nigga neva made it inside da club Friday night.

"Yeah, I was wonderin' where yo ass was at."

"*Shhhit*. Me and Scoob ran up on these two silly ass hoes standing around outside. Shit, next thing ya know—we back at Scoob's." Dee reclines his seat grinning and reminiscing. "Kept them bitches high and naked da whole weekend!" He takes a pull from his cigar.

"So where's the problem nigga? …Why ya even sweatin' that shit wit Alexus? *Shit*—ya did cha thing! Some out of town ass at that!" Justin shrugs his shoulders with insensitivity. "Fuck her! I'm not understandin'—where's the dilemma? She ain't all that no way!"

"Nah—after she hung up on my ass da first time, I waited awhile and tried ta call her back. Bitch ain't answer. I called this morning—still ain't answering. I bet she fuckin' wit Jarrod's daddy. The muthafucka been hangin' around lately."

"What?—that's her little boy's daddy?"

"Yeah. That nigga ain't slick. He's schemin' on that ass. Hatin' and shit—now the muthafucka wanna try and play daddy."

"Aaah nigga—don't act like it's a surprise. Look who ya fuckin' wit. Her ghetto ass ain't nuthin' but drama. Ya knew that shit from day one." He pauses. "If it's all like that—kick her ass to the curb and keep steppin'. Ain't like ya can't do no better nigga." But the silence alerts Justin of possible security breaches in Dee's "playa" mystique, realizing that much of the persona is all mouth—and just talk. The truth of the matter is that Dee needs Alexus or someone like her. Justin, who cuts his eye at his colleague, concludes that beyond the flossy exterior there's not much else. Lacking anything of real substance to offer any female, Dee represents a man whose dependence on a woman exceeds far more than just her mobility. Justin tries to empathize—but can't. "Yo nigga let me use yo phone?"

"Where's yours?" he says as he passes his Nokia cell to his boy—and boss. And without going into much detail, Justin gives his explanation—then calls Jackie.

"Hey girl—whazzz-zup!" Justin mimics the once popular Budweiser commercial. He uses humor to break the ice.

"Boy—where are you?"

"Headed to da airport." He cringes as he waits for a rebuttal.

"Justin, I don't wanna talk ta you!"

"Why ya trippin'?"

"You been in town—for how long? …And you just now callin' me."

"Boo—now ya know I've been busy the whole time." He looks to his partner who coincidentally just went through a similar situation. But Demetrius, uninterested in Justin's conversation, stares in another direction—still puffing on his cigar.

"I can only imagine."

"Whatever. But anyway, I wanna say thank you."

"For what booby?"

"*Everything!* …Past, present—and the future."

"Well, you're welcome." She guffaws. "Boy, you so silly!"

"Guess what?"

"What?" she says, still laughing.

"I took your advice yesterday. Remember what you said awhile back 'bout following your heart?" He lowers his voice in a false sense of privacy.

"Yeah-yeah-I-do," she says, as she curiously awaits his next word.

"Well, I did that!"

"Wit who—carrot top?" referring to Teresha's reddish brown—fiery Auburn hair.

"Yep!"

"Ummm huh." she says, as though she's not convinced.

"I'm fo real!"

"So now let me ask you—honestly… Are you really being sincere—or are ya jus lonely? 'Cause you all up there in Chicago—probably don't really know anyone yet, and sittin' on the phone half the night jabbering with that girl. Both of y'all horny—all hot and bothered." Again, with an eruption of laughter, she gives an already formed assumption. "She's jus sumthin' ta occupy your time boy! I know ya boo!"

"Naw—it's legit! I love her—and I can honestly say I'm actually 'in love'. I know that shit sounds funny but if you know me like ya say—then ya know I ain't lyin'! That ain't sumptin' I'd jus say—especially ta yo ass. You'd see right through the shit. You know it!"

Silence.

♡♡   ♡♡   ♡♡

10:16am

Teresha, having dropped Justice off at a friend's house in the same townhome community, heads to Douglasville to meet Cynthia—one of her co-workers. The plan is to pick up Cindy then rendezvous with another co-worker—Stephanie in Lithia Springs; eventually ending up at Faith Fellowship Church of God in Christ located in Powder

Springs. Justice narrowly escapes the outing—by default only, because the ladies had already decided that after church they would treat themselves to an "all girls" luncheon at Red Lobster.

Though somewhat familiar with Douglasville, Teresha—unsure of the best route, debates whether to take Camp Creek Pkwy or the interstate to Cynthia's apartment. Using her V3 Razor, she contacts Cindy to collaborate.

"Gurrrl—where you at?" Teresha confuses Cindy with her question, then clarifies herself by saying, "No girl—I'm talkin' 'bout is it faster for me to take the streets—or the interstate?" Laughing, Teresha repeats back the directions. "Oh we got jokes! But cha say—take 20 to Fairburn Road. Make a right at the light—a left on Highway 278, then a right on Broad—where I cross the tracks. And go about a mile—and look to the right. I should see the entrance. I got it girl!"

The conversation then switches to earlier events of the weekend. Cindy inquires about Justin's visit. Teresha elaborates. From Old National Highway, she enters the 285 perimeter loop. "Yeah girl—we had a *g-o-o-o-o-d* time—ya hear me. Lord have mercy! *Gurrrl*—best believe I'll have my butt on that altar today—beggin' fo forgiveness!" Swapping their scandalous tales, Teresha loses her Bluetooth wireless ear-piece. And without thinking she looks to the floorboard—reaching, unaware that the swift-moving traffic has slowed due to the weekend road construction schedule. A mere second later, she returns to her original position. Startled by the unavoidable stalled traffic before her—she screams "JEEESUS!" As an image of her son flashes through her mind as she veers left, changing lanes. The vehicle behind her already in that lane catches the tail end of her Explorer, careening the out of control SUV toward the concrete median. Without time to react—she closes her eyes.

twenty

Beyond Our Understanding

A week later, Yazoo City, Mississippi—Teresha's birthplace.

More than two hundred family and friends gather inside the small community church of New Bethel AME to say farewell to Teresha Latriece Rozier. Amidst sweltering temperatures, the ushers distribute hand fans to compensate for the airless facility, as one by one, mourners fill the pews paying their final respects. Behind the pulpit—a choir of four women harmonize a beautiful rendition of "Take My Hand, Precious Lord".

Standing a few rows back behind the immediate family, a solemn Justin watches his tearful son being consoled by Teresha's mother. The surreal surroundings paralyze Justin as he stands, shaking visibly at the knees. Jackie, by his side, takes his hand for support. Jerome from the other side, places a hand on his wounded brother's shoulder. Monique and Shayla also stand in solidarity.

Justin stares towards the closed pristine cherry casket placed front and center. As reality sets in—he again turns to his son. The heat, along with his tightly wound tie, makes it increasingly difficult to breathe. Beads of sweat form over his brow. The last time Justin had set foot inside a church was under these very same conditions at his mother's funeral. He remembers that day—he remembers the hurt of knowing he would never see her again. The thought overwhelms him. Now looking toward the ceiling, he wonders why. As tears begin to stream down his face, Justin avoids looking to the front—for he's not ready to let go. And for the time being he averts closure.

As the service continues, words are just garbled noise as each speaker speaks—and each song is sung. It isn't until Teresha's sister, Tracey, reads the eulogy does Justin restore focus on the program. She recites a poem.

"To My Beloved Sister

We can shed tears now that you are gone
Or we can smile because you have lived

We can close our eyes and pray that maybe you will come back
Or we can open our eyes and see all that you have left

Our hearts can be empty because we can't see you anymore
Or we can be full of the love that you shared

We can turn our backs on tomorrow and live yesterday
Or we can be happy for tomorrow because of yesterday

We can remember you and only that you are gone
Or we can cherish your memory and let it live on

We can cry and close our minds, be empty and turn our back
Or we can do what you would want: smile, open our eyes, love and go
on

Sis, keep smilin' down on us as we continue to smile for you
We love and miss you
Rest in Peace"

The words touch home as Justin must now learn to pick up the pieces. Unlike coping with the loss of his mother—losing Teresha meant gaining the full time responsibility of raising a teenage son. He recalls a particular conversation with Teresha. The discussion dealt with the possibility of Justice coming to live with him in Chicago. Then—what appeared to be improbable, now becomes a reality only months later. The resonating theme in Justin's life is "transitions"—one after another.

The presiding pastor gives his sermon and final remarks. Justin mentally jumps forward to the immediate needs of his son—and how to make this latest transition work. He recognizes and embraces the fact that his entire life is about to change. He understands, that now, he has to be strong for the sake of his son. Plagued by his own selfish grief, he must come to terms with the realization; though his personal loss may have been great, Justice's is even greater. He loses a mother.

After the acknowledgments are read, the scene shifts outside for the burial. Her body is laid to rest in the church cemetery—directly behind the sanctuary beside her grandparents, aunt, and a cousin. In a sobering farewell, Justice places a dozen red roses over his mother's casket before being lowered into the vault. The crowd thins. Justin's distraught son remains seated under the funeral home tent, clutching a rolled home-going program. His face reflects the anguish and bewilderment of the event. Justin, feeling helpless, is at a loss for words and watches from afar as Jackie steps in, placing her loving arms around his grief-stricken child. The sight causes Justin to again weep. He cries for two.

Jerome, who feels his brother's pain, walks over to Justin with words of encouragement and advice.

"You gonna be alright?"

Justin answers with only a nod—signaling yes. Jerome proceeds.

"Neva makes sense—does it? It's crazy how things seem to work in life. …I remember when mama passed. It was like a piece of me died along with her. And for a long time I was mad at the world. Ya know—I ain't understand all that. Like a rug had been snatched from under my feet. Why me? …Why us? Seemed like we had been through so much already." With arms crossed he pauses for reflection. "Humph. And it took awhile—a long while, ya know, to grasp that life goes on. I had ta start livin' again, and cherish what we had. Not only the memories, but what she taught us."

Justin takes a deep breath, while removing the handkerchief from his blazer pocket and wipes the tears from his eyes. For through the madness, there is a message. As bad as it hurts now, he knows that time will ease the wound. Therefore, who better to be there and help his son understand than he himself. Jerome's point is well taken.

"Go be wit your son! We're witcha."

"Yep." The tone of Jerome's words could, by many, be misperceived as harsh, yet Justin heeds to their significance. He thanks his brother and goes to be with his son.

Jackie gets up seeing Justin approach. She whispers something in Justice's ear then gives him a big hug. As she and Justin pass one another, she touches the arm of his sport coat—again in support. Under his breath Justin mouths, "Thanks. I need ta talk to ya later." She agrees and rejoins Shayla, Jerome, and Monique. Justin sits next to his son, draping his arm around the backside of the chair. Justice, with his elbows resting firmly on his knees, head positioned between his hands, stares off into space. Together they sit in silence. Finally, Justin, having carefully put his thoughts in order, speaks. "Walk wit me." He taps his son on the leg and uses his head to motion the direction.

Justice rises up to follow his father's lead. They walk away from the burial site facing a field of cotton in front of the church. Justin, speaking candidly, talks to his son about the setbacks of life.

"I loved your mama—and I'm goin' ta miss her more than most will ever know. And it hurts like hell knowin' that I didn't do what I should of. I didn't take care of y'all like I was supposed to. ...I didn't seize what was important. And now it's too late." Justice, unmoved by his father's words, continues to hold his head low. They tread through the lush adjoining tract of land until it's end where they stop, and Justin faces his son.

"I wanna be honest son. I've been avoiding this moment. Because I ain't know what ta say to ya. Ya know—I was scared. I mean—what do ya say? *'I'm sorry'*. ...Is that what ch'ou wanna hear? I mean—I know you hurtin' and nuthin' I say today—or tomorrow is gonna change that." he hesitates. "I'm hurtin' too son—bad. And I keep askin' myself—*why?* I'm tired of losin' the people who mean the world to me. And then when I thought it was safe to let go—and trust life again... Now this!" Justin's voice quivers as he expresses his feelings—which garners Justice's attention. He looks to his father yearning for help. "Baby, I don't know what to tell ya. But we're in this together. ...You and I. And we gonna be al-ight—*together*. Ya know?" Tenderly, he places a hand to the side of his son's tearful face.

"Yes sir." And for the first time since the start of the funeral, Justice speaks. Stepping closer, Justin grabs his son. They embrace.

"I love you baby," as the two chat, eventually walking back to the church.

Following the service, gathered at the home of Teresha's mother in nearby Rigdeland, Justin and Jackie sit under an oil-stained carport on rusted folding chairs escaping the pounding mid-afternoon sun and continuous parade of people who stop by. From many summer visits, Justice, being very familiar of the area, walks down the street to the corner store with Shayla. The time alone gives the adults a minute to talk.

"Boo, I need a big favor." Justin's reluctance is evident by the humbled volume of his voice.

"Anything Sweetie, I'm here. All ya have ta do is ask." She knowing the situation anticipates his question.

"I need ya ta take care of Justice for me over the next few months. I need a minute to rearrange some things before he gets up there wit me—ya know?" He hates to ask such much of a burden of her—but feels left without any other choice. Teresha's people would love to take Justice in, but he can't trust their sincerity, as he's afraid that any sign of weakness on his behalf may prompt an unnecessary custody battle. The rocky history of him and Teresha's past relationship has always fueled ill feelings from her family. Nevertheless, his need makes it a hard pill for his pride to swallow.

"You know that's no problem. We'll love to have him." She smiles. "I can see Shayla now—she loves herself some Justice. He's like the big brother she never had. Patient, like someone else I know." Leaning forward, still smiling, she looks directly at Justin.

"Thanks baby. I don't know how I'll ever repay y'all. I mean for everything. I couldn't ask anything more of someone—than what you've already given me. I'll neva forget this." Fighting a roller coaster of emotions, Justin manages to return a smile, then reaches over to take Jackie in his arms. Rocking slowly they share a special appreciation and love.

twenty-one

Joy Cometh (Psalms 30:5)

Two months have passed. Justin stares out his bedroom window into an empty twilight. In the backdrop, the constant ringing of an unanswered phone provides the pity-party theme of the early evening. Turning toward his bed, he picks up a glass from the nightstand—hastily tipping it to his lips. He sips on his second serving of a Hennessy and Coke mix. Again reaching to the same piece of furniture—from the top drawer, he removes a folded previously opened envelope addressed across the front in bold cursive, simply written—"To Justin". He takes the single wide rule sheet of paper from its bent packaging—unfolding it, as the author of this handwritten letter lives in immortality through the expressiveness of her emotionally charged words. Its daily reading is a permanent reminder of what was—and could have been. For in Justin's every mind, body, and soul—Teresha lives on. And like every other day since her tragic death—he again reads the letter.

Dearest Justin,

My feelings are getting stronger & stronger again for you every day. I am totally beholden unto you …my soul, spirit, mind, and body. When I look into your eyes all I see is us holding each other close. Time just stands still as our souls are brought together to experience true and eternal love. You are my very breath, I am obsessed with you, I see you when you are not around as my body aches for you. Only you can put that look into my eyes, and I want to please you in every way …emotionally, mentally, and sexually.

Justin, you are head and shoulders above all. My body screams for yours. When you touch me …all my juices start to flow. And that time and moment can't be interrupted. You give me a sensation that truly can't be expressed with words. So I wait with bated breath until that time when we can be together again. I love you always.

Forever your lady,
Teresha L. Rozier

He finishes the letter wiping watery eyes. A lump fills his throat as a straying teardrop manages to make its way onto the wrinkled paper. Ironically, the moisture dissolves the ink which produces the words "I love you always," blemishing the instigant of his sorrow.

184

Ridden with guilt, pity, and letdown—life has become far from what he expected. Justin meditates on every adverse experience attached to his life—past and present. And he convinces himself that his life has been lived in excruciating vain. As the liquor begins to talk, he wishes he could sleep through it all. Pacing the floor in deep reflection, Justin turns the glass up, emptying his temporary peace. At least, if only for a few hours, he knows through the drinking he can escape the devastation of his disappointment.

The phone rings again. He answers out of sheer frustration. The constant interruptions have disturbed his embattled thoughts—and broken the flow of self-degradation.

"What up!" he says with a raspy slur.

"*Heeey*. How are you?" A feminine voice speaks with concern.

"I'm cool. What 'bout cha'll? How's my son doin'?" He's immediately bombarded with guilt knowing that he's been very non-existence in his son's emotional recovery. He's gone against his word as he hasn't been there like he promised. Justin reflects on the motivational pep talk he spoke after the funeral to Justice—about working through the hurt together. Yet the past seven or eight weeks have been anything but. His evasive attitude causes Jackie to worry.

"Aaah, he's doin' okay. As well as ya would expect—given the circumstances. ...He's been really quiet lately. *Well*—he took it pretty hard. So of course it's an adjustment. ...It's gonna take time. So how are you doin'?"

Justin sighs. "*Hmmm*. I'm makin' it." But the struggle is evident. "Did I send enough last week?" referring to the $800 of care money for Justice.

"Oh yeah—more than enough. There's no problem there!" Jackie snickers in retort of Justin's question.

"Lil' man not doin' so good then—huh?"

"I've seen him better. Got an idea though... Why don't you ask him yourself? He's in the room helping Shayla with her homework. So hold on—let me get him."

Jackie puts the phone down. A sense of anxiety sweeps over Justin's body as goose bumps rise on his forearms. He chaotically rehearses his approach—what excuses to use. It's been almost two weeks since they last talked. And even that conversation was prompted by a call from Jackie. But before he can get his lies together, Justice's meek voice resonates in his ear.

"Hello."

"Hey buddy—what's goin' on?" Justin tries to sound chipper as though nothing's wrong.

"Nuthin'."

"*Okay*. So how's school?"

"Alright." Justice answers but says nothing else. There's silence. The conversation then becomes strained—and unnatural.

"Well alrighty then. Heard from your uncle?" Not knowing what else to say.

"Last week. He bought me a PSP—like he said."

"Oh shit—that's cool! What games ya got wit it?" Justin talks beyond the subliminal implications of Justice's remark, realizing that his son is well aware of his futile promises. The comment hurts his feelings, but he refuses to let it be known.

"Grand Theft Auto—Liberty Stories and Midnight Club Dub Edition." And again he answers, but offers nothing more to the discussion. Both sit holding the phone.

Justin finally gives up. "Well—I'll let ya get back to helping Shayla. I'll call ya later in the week. …Be good. Maybe I'll send ya a game or sumptin'—al-ight?"

Slow to respond, Justice ignores his father's generosity. "Bye Dad."

The phone clicks—followed by the dial tone. Justin has the receiver still to his ear. He feels small—and a little embarrassed, because he realizes he's just tried to buy his son's forgiveness to no avail. Justin marches into the kitchen to refill his drink. Jackie's phone call has diminished his buzz.

The next morning with a French vanilla cappuccino and plain bagel in hand, Justin arrives at the office an hour earlier. Expecting to be alone, he unlocks the suite to find one lone light illuminating the otherwise dark and vacant facility. The source leads Justin around the corner to a space designated as the employee break room. Through the all glass door, he spots his secretary—Rhonda Craig seated at one of three small round gray tables. She sits leaning motionless over a leather-bonded bible. He peeks in to speak.

"Hey there. …Mighty early this morning."

"*Ooo!* " Startled, she sits straight up placing her hand across her chest. "You scared me Mr. Vaughn."

Smiling, "I'm sorry. I ain't mean ta surprise ya. Next time I'll knock on the glass first."

She catches her breath before speaking again. *"Jesus."* Still holding her heart, "Well, good morning... I try comin' in a lil' early most days—catch up on my readin'. We have bible study tonight. Pastor teachin' out of Matthew 24—signs of the end times."

"Oh okay—sounds interesting. I'll be up in my office if you need me—al-ight?" He attempts to politely duck out of the room, wanting to be nice, but at the same time avoiding any in depth discussion—especially on religion.

"Mr. Vaughn?"

"Ma'am?" He reenters the room.

"Jesus loves you." She removes her reading glasses and smiles warmly.

Perplexed, he looks at first confused before returning an amicable smirk. "Thanks for the info Rhonda. I 'bout needed that."

"Oh we all do from time ta time sir." She puts back on her glasses and continues to read.

Still facing his employee, Justin stands at the door pausing to marinate on her words of assurance. He smiles then turns to head out. "Talk to ya later Rhonda." he says as he walks away feeling a little better about his day.

"Yes sir."

By 9am—with everyone in place, Justin calls an impromptu communication's meeting to discuss the current state of affairs pertaining only to his office—Sho' Nuff Midwest. During the time since Teresha's death, work has been Justin's primary focus—pouring all of his energy and time into the company. He uses his position as a crutch to cope with his loss. They gather inside the conference room.

"Good morning everyone."

"Good morning." said by all as the fifteen person staff shuffle around the elongated oval cherry table equipped with leather reclining chairs. The swirling scents of mixed colognes and perfumes fill the space. Coffee and donuts occupy the hands of many as Justin gets straight to the point of today's meeting.

"I know most of y'all are probably wonderin' the reason for this happy gathering." he says, smirking with sarcasm. "Though we have done well with what we had—by signing Envy and bringin' aboard Arius—it ain't enough. Let's just remind ourselves of the Sho' Nuff legacy—and Rico's vision. No doubt a hard act to follow—*but* I believe, with talent of our personnel—*right here.*" Justin motions to everyone gathered around the table. "We have the ability to carve and create our own place in history. Now it's been more than 50 years since the establishment of such label giants as Mercury and Chess, who ruled the industry from theses very streets. ...And I know fo a fact—at one time Chess had practically a monopoly on the Rhythm & Blues market. So we know it can be done. Rico believes this—and so do I. But what I'm seeing is folks restin' on their laurels because of the success of our sister company. Therefore, let me remind you... This is not a free ride folks. We have ta earn our keep. So in otha words—we can not, nor will not tolerate complacency people. ...We jus won't!" With calm sternness, he over emphasizes his point. "Sure Sho' Nuff South is definitely doin' its thang—always has. I know personally— along wit few othas sittin' here because we were there! And most of us from the very beginnin'. So I know first hand what it takes ta be the best. ...And all bullshit aside—we ain't there yet! Excuse my French," as he looks specifically towards Rhonda. "I'm jus not seeing any emphasis being put on fresh new material. Hell, let alone any real talent! What I am seein'—everybody's tryin' to land the big manufactured copy cat acts. ...Shit that's played out! But that's not it. That's not how we do. Our survival depends on staying ahead of the industry. Not blendin' wit 'em! We're the trendsetters—remember that! They want ta be like us!" His is voice passionately elevated.

Justin glances over the silent room observing the head nods and facial expressions of his staff. Some seemingly inspired—while others hide yawns under carefully placed hands. He continues his motivational sermon, detailing what he believes is the way to drive this division forward. He outlines the necessary reassignments and realignments needed to relive the stalling subsidiary—though to the stunned dismay of many. He ends the meeting by opening the floor to any questions. A young brotha at the far end of the table—Jeff Spivey, a recent graduate of DePaul University now working in marketing, delivers the meetings only question.

"Mr. Vaughn—why now? What I'm trying to say is that—this office has only been up and running for a few months. So why the urgency? Or at least what I sense to be some form of pressure. ...Is this an internal—or external issue? I would think the expectations of duplicating the success of Rico Pittman and Sho' Nuff South would be unrealistic in the Midwest. The market forecast here isn't as robust as the southern markets. How do we expect to *compete*—for a lack of a better word?"

"Good question Jeff—but here's the thing. From what are we drawin' our expectations of success? By some demographic that says that folks in Midwest aren't as talented as the folks in the south? Bullshit! Maybe not as exposed—but definitely not lacking the potential. Maybe that means gettin' off our asses ta dig a lil' deeper… Then so be it! That why we're here—ta cultivate sumptin' unseen and hopefully untapped. …Oh, it's out there. Now it's our job ta go find it! And Jeff, to answer your first and second questions… No. We haven't necessarily received any outside pressure—as of yet! But let me also add—if you been around this business long enough, then you'd know when it's time ta revise the script. And that's where I come in. Someone has to have the foresight to see the upcomin' storms and figure the best ways to weather them—stay afloat—and ride da waves. And that's what I'm doin' as we speak—simply by determining what is best for the longevity of this company—and our livelihoods. And with that being said—are there any otha questions?" Justin scans the room. And to his surprise there are no other question or comments. "Good! Then on that note—this meeting is hereby adjourned. Y'all have a good day!" They all scatter.

Just as soon as Justin can gather his papers and get back over to his office, he's intruded by a zealous visitor. Shantel, having practically followed him into his suite, plops down taking the seat behind his desk. And by knowing her and her presumptuous nature, he elects to close the door for privacy.

"What's up?" He flips through the contents of a miscellaneous file folder while awaiting her answer.

"Can you please explain to me why exactly I'm bein' reassigned?"

"Because it makes sense."

"But haven't I dun the job out in the field?"

"Yes you have."

"So why am I bein' moved from A&R to Marketing?"

"I thought I jus answered that—because it makes sense!"

"I'm not followin' ya—so explain."

"Well—it's pretty simple. We need someone in that area who can not only act as an intradepartmental liaison between us, Rico, and Arista—but also someone who has some working knowledge of the artists we're representing. Therefore, who better than you? Nuthin' against ole' Bill Beck—cause I got ta give it to him—he knows Sales, but doesn't know shit 'bout the artists we put out. His approach is mechanical—predictable… Hell, almost like clockwork. I wanna try and get away from that—broaden the spectrum. See—wit you, you know exactly what we're fightin' fo—and I need someone scrappy ta get things done—*from our perspective.* Know what I mean? So hopefully ya can see where I'm comin' from."

"I guess. ...Hope ya know whatcha doin'," she says, showing her reluctance.

Smiling, he says, "I think so." He's amused by Tae's lack of confidence." Relax girl—it's a promotion. Now it's your department—and your headache. So work it out!"

Shantel lifts herself from the seat, "Well, let me go ova here and start crackin' my whip. I would say thank you—but I have a feelin' I'm the one about ta be screwed."

"Yep! And I'll be sure ta bring the Vaseline," he says, turning her statement into sexual innuendo.

"Ah, ya make me sick!" as she storms out his office. Justin enjoys a good laugh for the first time in months.

twenty-two

Natalie

Like the rest of the nation and much of the world, Justin, in the wee morning hours, unable to sleep and flipping channels, tunes in to Fox News' around the clock coverage of the horrific devastation of Hurricane Katrina. He watches the on-going debates and finger pointing between the federal and local governments over what went wrong. His heart goes out to the millions affected in New Orleans and Biloxi—and thousands still homeless in its aftermath. It's just so hard to imagine having to go through something like that, he empathizes with the trauma of sudden loss and displacement. His son, Justice, comes unexpectedly to mind—and the correlation of events; how life can appear in order one minute and turned up side down the next, as every aspect of his existence has been disrupted. Even now—almost four weeks later, Justin still vividly remembers the tearful reporting of Shepard Smith as he stands on a desolate overpass while the body of a dead man lingers some fifty yards behind. How Smith passionately pleads for help—from FEMA, and anyone willing to aid in the relief efforts. Justin recalls his own plea to God—with him wanting refuge of his situation with Tonya. He somehow connects his words of petition to Teresha's untimely death. Blaming himself, his conscience brings about an agitated energy from which he springs from the couch.

♡   ♡   ♡

Just before sunrise, amidst the brisk October morning air, Justin jogs along a North Beach trail wearing only cotton sweats and a skully. The gale blowing off the Lake Michigan coast gives confirmation to the city's "Windy City" alias. Running—the latest addition on Justin's daily regiment, helps pass the idle time providing much needed solace. The routine becomes a welcomed distraction. In recent weeks as sleep comes sparsely—if at all, he clings to this one positive. His drinking—which he isn't considering a problem yet, consumes most nights and weekends. With his social life all but non-existent—he indulges alone. Bright spots come in the form of a heightening friendship with Shantel. He also distinguishes that his relationship with Demetrius is held together by spit rather than nails, as the slow dissolve of their fair-weathered friendship couldn't come at a more opportune time. Outside the office, he keeps the social congregating to a limit. He chalks it up to the changing seasons. Justin pounds the pavement prior to work for maybe an hour—iPod attached to his elastic drawstring waistband.

♡   ♡   ♡

The morning starts with a conference call from Rico, after which Justin prepares to spend most of the day out the office overseeing a photo shoot for Envy's cover art. But first, he tags along with Dee to take the girls over to Shear Magic for some last minute touch-ups. Alecia called the day before ranting and raving—disappointed with the job done by another boutique, needing a re-braid of her micros. Dee pulls some strings with his girl, Alexus, to get a nearly impossible early appointment.

They arrive at the Westside shop and are met at the door by Tracie—owner of the popular salon. The drop-dead gorgeous entrepreneur personally greets her prestigious guests—welcoming each to her establishment. Neither man, Justin or Demetrius can seem to pull their attention from her lacy see-though get-up. The sheerness of her dress causes Justin to perspire through his rayon shirt. Months of inactivity and recluse have made him forget what it is to be man. He eyes the gap between her legs until he can almost see the lips of her vagina. "*Damn*, that's one pretty ass bitch," he comments to himself. Long and bouncy—her crimped hair, flawless caramel skin, and sculptured shape make her a tough act to follow. Not wanting to expose his zeal, Justin checks his manhood to make sure nothing's showing. Once he sees everything still in place, it's now time for business.

From the corner of his eye, he catches Dee practically drooling, which is funny considering Alexus stands only a few feet away as she watches his every move. He foresees trouble brewing in paradise. As Dee introduces the girls, Justin strays noticing that this chick—Tracie, really has her shit together. He wanders the shop in daunting reverence. Parquet floors, chrome fixtures, marble counters all through—a stretch from its ghetto Madison Avenue exterior.

Continuing to be nosy, Justin works his way to the back of the salon. He can see up front where Tracie has already set Alecia up with a stylist—some dude. As he observes the room, he counts, "One, two, three…" men working in booths—all of the feminine variety. Over where he stands, there's a tall, slim red girl working the corner station. Headphones in her ears, she's apparently oblivious to everything else around her. Seeing her makes him stop to pay closer attention to the music being broadcast over the salon's sound system. It's Syleena Johnson's latest, one of Justin's favorite artists and fellow Chicagoans. So it really strikes a chord with his curiosity—he wonders what she might be listening to. And for a minute, he watches closely as she works magic, putting in blonde extensions on her nearly bald client. Just by what he's seen—he can tell that she's very good at what she does. The girl, perhaps feeling Justin's glaring eyes, looks up smirking in what appears to be his direction. She cocks her head slightly to one side as if to wonder why he was staring. Once caught, Justin does his best to hide the trespass by affixing his eyes on any trivial object he can find. He spots the Paul Mitchell display bordering her booth where he attaches focus until the heat blows over.

With the coast clear, she continues on her customer's head. Justin again observes, this time taking particular notice to her clothing. The orange and white nylon wind suit—one leg pushed above her calf revealing its muscular tone, reflects a sort of thuggish around the way look. He's brought back to his earlier thoughts, assuming that she's probably listening to Ying Yang or Mike Jones—something light with a hard edge. While her loose gear conceals the true definition of her body, from what little he can tell, there's not too much happening up top. Even the length of her deep brown hair is questionable, as much of it is covered by the hoody of a thin sweater worn underneath her nylon jacket. She's cute though! And now, once he thinks about it— her face is also very familiar.

"Jay!" Justin's nickname is blurted from behind.

"What's up?" He quickly spins around to see Alexus's grinning face in front of him—quite close.

"What's been goin' on Jay? …Long time—no see. Where ya been hidin'?"

He first takes a step back to make some space between them. "Nowhere. I've been around. Jus keepin' low these days." He looks off without giving direct eye contact—thinking that maybe she'll take the hint.

"I'm sorry ta hear 'bout cha girl. Dee told me what happened." She offers a pitying stare.

"Thanks." Her genuine condolence justifies his courtesy. He delivers a direct look.

"So, where's your son?"

"Still in Atlanta."

"You bringin' him up here?"

"That's the plan." He begins to wonder why all the small talk until he sees Dee. Then the picture becomes clear. Dee's still up in Tracie's face. Justin covertly smirks thinking, "Bold move. …Nigga got balls." He realizes Alexus wants to play "tit for tat". He settles for no part of the game and flips the script.

"What's up wit your girl Tracie? Is she single or what?"

Alexus turns to see her man sweating her boss, "Her bull-dikin' ass?" with her face frowning. Then she turns back to Justin. "She keeps company wit some bitch. Supposedly they live to together. *Why? You lookin'?*"

"Maybe. What 'bout cha girl back here? What's her story?"

She starts smiling, "*Her?* She's straight! Trust me—she ain't your type!" she says, still grinning.

"Why what's up? She a dike too or sumptin'?"

"*Ssshit*—try the opposite."

"I don't git it?" Not understanding the analogy.

"She says she's saved. So she fo sho' ain't your speed! Neva seen her wit anybody—but then I ain't neva asked. She good peoples—a lil' flaky at times. But we cool."

Justin nods with interest, "I know her from somewhere though… Can't figure it out."

"That night I met Dee—remember at the Shark Bar? She was standin' there when we talked at the door."

It comes back to him. "That's it—she looks different now though," he says, as he takes another look.

"Oh, we were out that night. Usually dresses down any otha time." Both eye the hard at work girl.

"Okay. So what's homegirl's name?"

"Natalie."

"Huh." He appears to be scheming on something.

By day's end—satisfied with the shoot, Justin runs back to the office to touch base with Rhonda, check mail, etc. Wanting to just run in and out—he in a hurry, swings open the main entrance door and carelessly enters, nearly knocking over an exiting pedestrian.

"I'm sorry man—my bad! I ain't see ya." He apologizes for bumping into the man, then immediately realizes that he knows this guy. "What's up man? What's goin' on?"

"Hey—how you doin' broa?" They shake hands and address one another with exuberant admiration and surprise. "It's been a minute cuz. …Jus the man I wanna see!" he says, still joined by a firm grasp of hands.

"Al-ight. So how's everything man?"

"Broa, I'm jus blessed wit livin'." It's Thadius McPhail, Justin's original Chicago contact and longtime friend of Rico. "I came down here cause I need your help man. Got a lil' proposition for ya." Grinning, he squeezes Justin's shoulder.

"Okay. Well, let's go up to my office." Justin leads Thad inside. They run across Rhonda in the hallway as she prepares to leave the building. Justin attempts to introduce the two but he's late as they've already met acquaintances a few minutes earlier. After a short briefing of the day's events, Justin excuses Rhonda and the two men enter his office.

"Man, grab a seat—make yourself at home!"

"Thanks broa. I'll try not ta take up too much of your time."

"Naw, no rush man. Now tell me what's goin' on?"

"Well a few of us have gotten together with Alderman Samantha Lewis of the 3rd ward—and we formed a community outreach program called 'Reach to Teach'." The program—ya know, it focuses on reachin' underprivileged inner-city youth, predominately Black and Hispanic kids from the Southside—Bronzeville and so on. There's teen mentoring and tutoring—preventive health fairs. It's a good program."

"Okay—cool!" Justin reclines his chair back, making himself comfortable to give Thadius his utmost attention.

"Yeah—and what we wanted to do was to have a community block party to drum up some outside support. Plus—ya know, it'll be great for da kids…"

"Aaah man—we'd be happy to help. Got ta give back to the community! So how much we lookin' at? I can get wit Riq tomorrow…" While Justin jumps the gun, Thad politely interjects.

"Financial donations are great broa—we can always use those. And we appreciate that! But what we're really lookin' fo—is entertainment!" …Named entertainment! Homegrown Chicago entertainment! See what I'm sayin'? We need hometown heroes to inspire those kids man. Sho 'em that they ain't relegated to a life in the hood—they got options, especially if ya willing ta work hard!" His words come from the heart and are filled with much passion.

"Okay. So now how can we help ya?" Justin strokes his freshly grown goatee with curiosity.

"We need your girls man!"

"Y'all want Envy huh?"

"Yes sir! Southside homebred!"

"So, when are we talkin' 'bout?"

"In three weeks!"

"Al-righty—let me see what we can do. Who else y'all got comin'?"

"We're talkin' to Jennifer Hudson's people. I know ya remember her from American Idol. Yeah, well she grew up in da Southside—singin' in church. Michelle Williams—she's been invited. Got WGCI's Crazy Howard McGee hostin'. So ya know we tryin' ta do it big in da hood!"

"I'll tell ya what—count us in. Jus let me make sure there's no scheduling conflicts. Call me sometime tomorrow ta confirm—and we'll go from there. Cool?"

"Broa—we really appreciate that." He stands to shake Justin's hand. "You don't know what it'll mean to them kids man. They our future! And yet it's up ta us—ta give them the tools they need ta carry this country. We feed 'em garbage—we get garbage! See what I'm sayin'? For the word says, 'Train up a child in the way he should go: and when he is old, he shall not depart from it—Proverbs 22:6'. Jay—I don't know if ya read the bible man, but if ya get a chance check it sometimes. But yeah man—that's all we're tryin' ta do. Give em' sumptin' ta work wit."

"It's all good—anything we can do ta help. And it ain't got ta end here. Jus call whenever ya need sumptin' dude. We here—and ya know where that's at. Al-ight?"

"Thanks again Jay! I'll give ya call tomorrow—now let me get out cha way broa!" Thadius makes his way to the door.

"Hold up Thad—give me a minute ta grab my things. I'll walk ya down."

♡   ♡   ♡

That evening after dropping his bag at the door, Justin walks over to the couch—plops down, then kicks his feet up on the ottoman. Now that he's finally stationary, he realizes the extent of his exhaustion. It's been a full day—time to relax. He sits there—arms folded, legs stretched, head tilted back—hungry but too tired to move. He eventually closes his eyes for a minute's nap.

As blurred images begin to clear, he hears the distance screams of what seems to be a crying baby. He watches as nurses and doctors rush by—yet no one sees him. He follows the frantic workers down the long white corridor. At first he's walking, then sprinting to catch the distancing crowd. He finds that what he thought to be the sound of a weeping child is actually the hysterical screams of an undistinguishable woman crouched against white cinder walls. They reach a set of double doors with no windows. The sign thereupon prohibits all non-medical staff. As nurses and doctors barge through the swinging doors, Justin continues to follow. All converge chaotically to a profusely bleeding black male, his body still resting on the EMT gurney from which it arrived. There's a severe chest wound—the man's body convulses as it enters shock. Valiant efforts are made to save the injured man, but it's too late—he flat-lines. A doctor announces the time of death. One by one, medical personnel leave the area. Again Justin's presence goes unnoticed. An eerie chill suddenly comes over the room. There's an unexplainable yearning to approach the dead man's side. With cautious steps Justin nears the still warm corpse. His body quivers with a nervous uneasiness. As he steps within feet of the lifeless body, his worst fears are confirmed. He stumbles backwards gasping for air. Once composing himself, he takes one more look. His heart skips. For the man that lies before him—is himself, cut down in his prime apparently by a gunshot wound to the chest—his dilated eyes left partially open. Who would do such a thing? And why? Sickened, he wonders if it could have been just some unfortunate random act of violence—or was the perpetrated crime premeditated? He then ponders the identity of the weeping woman. Who might she be? Justin squirms in his seat, sweating—tormented by his dream.

"Bzzzzzz—Bzzzzzz" Justin pops straight up—eyes wide open, disoriented—his dream seeming so real. He relaxes as he leans back, stretching his arms up high.

"Bzzzzzz—Bzzzzzz" He realizes he's been disrupted by the doorbell. "Dunk, dunk, dunk…" The visitor then resorts to knocking.

"*Yeaaah!* …Hold on!" Jumping to his feet, he looks through the peephole to find Shantel standing on the other side. He lets her in. "Girl you right on time—and a nigga's hungry too." Styling her Gucci shades and faux fur leather coat, Tae stands there holding two bags of take out.

"So are you gonna invite me in or what?"

"C'mon in—ya ain't got ta ask." He takes the food from her hand. "Gimme your coat."

"Hope you up for Chinese. …It was on the way." She makes her way to the couch. "So what we watchin'?"

"Turn ta whatever. …Hope ya grabbed some egg rolls?" as he peeks through the white cartons. "Wanna beer or sumptin'?"

"A Heiny please—if ya don't mind!"

"Yes ma'am. Comin' right up!" He brings the beers and a couple of trays—fixing their plates in front of the television.

"Missed ya. So how did everything go today?" She finds a Bulls' preseason game on, instantly stealing her attention.

"Straight! Alecia's lil' bratty ass pissed me off, but otha than that it went. A good shoot I think. I'm sure Rico will be happy. And you?"

"The same—it went! Jus tryin' ta grasp everything. And ya know Bill ain't no help. I don't think he likes answerin' to a sista—ya feel me?"

"I can believe that—but he'll get over it." Sneering, he says, "Especially if he wants to keep his job."

"*O-kkkay.*" She raises her bottle for a toast—cosigning Justin's threat.

twenty-three

Opposites Attract

"Hey girl—let me speak to Justice right quick."

"*Heeey!* I'm surprised to hear from you so soon—but I'm glad. …Everything okay?"

"Yeah—everything's straight. Jus checkin' in."

"Well good. Hold on—he's in his room watching TV." There's a short lapse of dead air as Jackie goes to get Justice.

"Hello." he says, sounding bored.

"Hey bud! Whatcha doin'?"

"Watchin' TV."

"Uhhh. Guess where I'm at?"

"I don't know."

"That wasn't much of a guess. But anyway I'm standin' here in the middle of GameStop.

"Why you in there?" The answer finally sparks some enthusiasm in his voice.

"Stop perpetratin'—boy I can feel ya smilin' through the phone." Justice releases a muddled snicker. "Now, what games ya want?"

"Ummm—I ain't sure. That's hard I can't think—hmmm."

"Betta think of sumptin'!"

"Alright-alright! How 'bout Socom?"

"*Socom?* What the hell is that?"

"A military game Dad."

"Oh okay—I'll ask the guy behind the counter. What else?" Like a dyslexic, Justin searches the racks backwards out of ignorance.

"Get Madden 2006!"

"Thought ya already had that!"

"Dad—that's on PS2."

"PSP—PS2, what's the damn difference?"

"There's a difference Dad," making his father seem stupid.

"Okay—anyway. What 'bout this Xmen Nemesis? Looks pretty straight."

"Yeah—that's cool. I forgot 'bout that one."

"Ummm huh—I bet. Al-ight—need me ta send ya anything else?"

"Some money!" he says, being completely forward.

"Nigga please—I know betta than that one. You straight! Jackie gives you an allowance every week. Now say she don't!" The sound of laughter fills the other end of the conversation. "That's what I thought. Al-ight then—I'll send those games out tomorrow from work. I'll call ya sometime tomorrow night—cool?"

"Yeah Pops."

"I love you son."

"Ditto."

"*Ditto?* What's that?" he says, frowning sarcastically. "Oh, so now we too grown ta say I love you to your old man—is that what it is?"

Laughing, "Naw Dad—I love you too," he succumbs.

"That's much better. I'll talk to ya tomorrow. Good night—sleep tight. And oh—don't let them bed bugs bite. Al-ight?"

"Bye Dad!" he says, smiling at his father's silliness.

"Bye!" Justin disconnects.

He pays for the games and exits the store. Finding a bench near JC Penney, he waits for Shantel. The funny thing is Justin hates mall shopping. But somehow Tae has managed to hoodwink him into the experience, with Carson Pirie Scott's yellow dot specials being the latest motive.

Tae, a gifted manipulator and thrifty shopper, convinces Justin that the fresh air will do him some good. He agrees, knowing it would probably be his best chance to do what he promised for Justice. Having already shopped at Water Tower Place Mall over on N.

Michigan Avenue—close to his home, they frequent a second mall—Ford City, some thirty minutes away on S. Cicero. And like most men after a few hours of aimless plundering, the patience tends to wear thin. Justin uses the wait to call Jerome.

He gets only his brother's voicemail and leaves a brief message. "Yo, what up nigga? …*Man* clear your schedule fo the next few weeks. We're gonna fly you and Arius in. Found the perfect studio." He grins. "It'll be like old times. I've already worked it out wit Rico. So pack your shit and let's do this! Hit me back!"

As he starts to put away his phone, suddenly warm moist hands cover his eyes. His nose tingles taking in the potpourri of fragrances absorbed around her fragile wrist. The culprit is obvious.

"Guess who?"

"*Ahhh*—let me think. …Halle Berry!"

"Nope. Guess again."

"Well if it ain't Beyonce—then I give up." Shantel releases her hold. Justin turns around to act surprised. "Oh, it's your skinny ass."

"Shut up. Now look." Tae, who's also an impetuous shopper, opens one of three Carson's bags, revealing a sexy shimmering satin number—a backless sleeveless evening gown, one of those special occasion dresses. "Whatcha think? Will that be showin' too much?" She shows Justin the low bust line and lengthy split.

"Who's that fo? …*You?* " he says, laughing.

"And what's so funny?"

"Quentin must be dun turnt yo lil' ass out!"

Having folded the dress over one arm, she reacts by punching Justin in the stomach. "Why ya say that?"

Holding his belly but still laughing, he says, "Cause. Since when you started wearin' some shit like that? Thought you supposedly miss goody-goody conservative or sumptin'." He points to the folded garment. "That there is a 'fuck me!' dress.

"*A whaaat?* "

"You heard me—a fuck me dress! …Da shit that says take this shit off—and *fuck* da hell outta me! Play if ya wanna… I know if ya fool up and wear that shit around me—I'm gonna fuck ya! *Word*, now try a nigga!" He gives Tae a "take it how you want" confident head-nodding dare.

With the notion practically making her loins tremble, she smiles internally—keeping her willing thoughts to herself. "Jay, you always runnin' your mouth. Besides, you wouldn't know what ta do with me if you had me." She passes Justin a bag. "C'mon—I gotta run in Bakers. I need some shoes," to which he abides like a child obeying a parent.

twenty-four

The Next Big Thing

"Uf-haaa, uf-haaa, uf-haaa, uf-haaa…" Justin breaths with heavy trots through dried autumn leaves scattered along a narrow Lincoln Park trail. He strays from his usual Lake Shore route, avoiding the monotony of habit. Justin, who prides himself on his unpredictability and spontaneity, explores the new path, hoping to spark some subconscious tucked away thought—or idea. He's in search of the next big thing. Of course realizing the odds of finding something entirely new and original as far as talent goes falls somewhere around slim to none. But maybe crossbreeding styles—like with Arius, may actually work with other genres. The success of BeeGee's now platinum debut has laid the foundation and formula for Sho' Nuff's own unique blend of southern Hiphop. Yet he ponders how to play off that emerging concept. This time his iPod deliberately remains at home—hung next to the microwave on a hook reserved for keys. He runs in complete accord with nature.

What were once furious strides of determined intent have stalled to a slow stroll. Hands now at his hips, his mind percolates with thoughts of revelation. Reversing his course, he sprints back to the condo. His inspired theory provides a second wind. Over treeless stretches of rolling landscape, Justin with Edwin Moses-like fervor, hurdles all obstacles standing between him and 1400 North Lake Shore Drive.

Bypassing the lobby entrance, Justin jogs about another block down the street to where his car is parked. It's the one thing he can't quite get used to about living in the city—street parking. It's definitely a bitch—especially for a born and raised Georgia boy who's never had to parallel park. His sudden zeal voids any thought of running in to take a quick shower or even just changing clothes. He jumps into his Chrysler wearing navy blue hooded sweats—two white strips down each arm and leg, long johns hidden neatly underneath.

And without thinking, Justin heads to the Westside, forgetting that it's only 8am on a cold Saturday morning. Passing Garfield Park, he finds a spot to pull in along the crammed roadway. Excited, he exits his vehicle making haste up to Dee's door. The structure's sandstone veneer opens to a foyer like area with one door to the right and a stairwell leading to the second floor apartment on the left. Justin opts right and starts ringing the ancient twist style bell. He doesn't give Dee a decent chance to answer before he begins banging on the door. Through hollow walls Justin can hear the obscene mumbling of Dee's irate mouth.

"*Who da fuck*… Fuckin' eight in da morning—*fuck!* …Who is it?"

"Yo, it's me—open up!"

"*Jay?*"

"Yeah nigga—open up. It's nippy out this muthafucka!"

The door opens, Justin is struck immediately by the intoxicating aroma of Endo. Dee's pink tinted eyes confirm the obvious. With no shirt, he bears beaded speckles of hair across his chest while scratching his ass wearing only a pair of white cotton boxers. Dee removes a Newport from behind the ear with his free hand. "What's up nigga—ya comin' in?"

"Yeah." Justin steps in to see two kids—a girl and a boy, spread over the floor fast asleep in front of the television. That could mean only one thing—Alexus is somewhere close. "My bad dawg—I shoulda called first. Didn't mean ta interrupt a family moment," he says while snickering. "Yo—can you still get in contact wit that kid up in Hartford?"

Looking dumbfounded at first as he tries to remember who Justin is talking about, it clicks. "*Yeeeah*—Dat nigga *Nigel the Great*. Thought ya weren't feelin' his shit? Said sumthin' 'bout da nigga bein' too raw. Gotta change of heart nigga?"

"Maybe. I need ya ta see whatcha can find out. If it pans out—how ya feel 'bout makin' a trip?"

Lighting his Newport, Dee takes a long pull—exhaling its cloudy extracts. "Shit—we can do that."

"Do what Dee?" Staggering from the back enters Alexus—all in the Kool-Aid without knowing the flavor, interrupting, "Hey Jay!"

"What up girl!" Justin answers.

"Why ya all up in here!" Dee—becomes heated by her rude entry. "Nosy Bitch!" He looks over at Justin as though he's waiting for a cosigner of his derogatory comment. Justin smirks but avoids eye contact.

"Why da fuck ya gotta be sayin' all that Dee!" She too raises her voice, as she walks up to him, divulging her two to three inches of height advantage.

"Take yo nosy ass back in the room and stay da fuck out my business!" Dee points to the bedroom—then degrades her even more by blowing smoke in her face.

"Fuck you Demetrius!" Alexus screams at Dee, clutching her leopard satin robe tightly closed—her hair all over her head and no makeup. She's an ugly sight as her baggy eyes—even redder than Dee's, and dark lips reveal her obvious smoking habits. She throws her hand up as if to put a finger in Dee's face, but gnashes her bottom-lip to restrain from any comment. "Ain't got time ta put up wit this shit." she says, muttering to herself as she walks off.

"Good—then haul ass! Ain't shit stoppin' ya!"

"Fuck you Dee," she says, now speaking with a surreal calmness as she makes her way down the hall. Their elevated words have awoken the children who sit up—still under the influence of sleep, staring into Demetrius' pasty mouth.

"What da fuck y'all lookin' at? Y'all can haul ass too! Pick up yo shit and go back in the room wit yo mama." The children scramble to leave the room, afraid of what Dee might do. Justin observes the spastic chaos.

"Al-ight Ozzy and Harriet—do I need ta holla at cha later?"

"Nigga, sit yo ass down!" Dee walks over to his see-through kitchen where a half-empty bottle of Vodka resides. He pours himself up a glass—chasing the potent drink with cranberry juice. "Want some?"

Justin hesitates, knowing his growing obsession, yet he gives in to his craving. "Yeah, hook me up!"

Over drinks they discuss the demo. Justin tosses around his thoughts while the two converge on a strategy. An hour into the discussion, standing to shake hands, they agree on a game plan. Before leaving Justin reminds Dee of the benefit "street party" concert to be held that night. He urges indirectly for his participation. Though Dee agrees, Justin won't hold his breath. On his way home, he grabs the demo from the office. He rides down Michigan Avenue bumping the low budget CD. He now listens with different ears. The last time, Justin blew the recording off because of the poor sound quality, giving less than thirty seconds for each track to develop. Since the CD was never professionally mastered—a sign of inexperience, Justin figured "too much nurturing" would be involved. But it was also the day Tonya sent her little surprise package to his office, which undoubtedly had his focus anchored elsewhere.

As the first song plays—Justin, without identifying track titles, absorbs the slow hypnotic groove laid under raspy prophetic vocals. The kid foretells his rise to power in the music game, paying homage along the way to his many fallen comrades—a halfway decent track with potential. In his head, Justin substitutes the generic beat with one of Jerome's creations. "Hell yeah that shits gonna work!" Before the song ends he skips to the next track. After the first few bars of the lead-in chorus, Justin's enthusiasm nearly halts traffic as the light changes green and he remains stopped. His attention is caught by the catchy uptempo groove, definite commercial material. The third offering seals the deal, another uptempo, but dark track, with political overtones capturing the essence of much of today's domestic headlines from poverty to the war in Iraq. Just by the lyrical content alone, Justin recognizes the author has to be somewhat socially conscious. He realizes that most young kids couldn't touch such depths with credibility without having a solid academic background. He removes the CD from his Infinity deck having found a much closer parking spot. He walks less than a half block to his condo where he retreats to ponder the possibilities.

twenty-five

...Excuse Me?

Saturday afternoon.

Justin finishes some much needed cleaning around the house. Since his self-induced exile, he admittedly has allowed many routine responsibilities to go undone—trash, dishes, laundry, etc. He even tries eliminating the lingering stale odors associated with such neglects by burning incense and potpourri throughout the space. He's been very fortunate to have Shantel around doing much of the dirty work and realizes he's been at her very mercy.

For tomorrow Justin has to pick Jerome up from the airport, justifying his rush to get the house in order. In preparation of his brother's arrival, he listens to Arius's first two CDs—on shuffle, hopefully to get a better feel of the artist's strength—maybe jump start the creative process. It's been a long time since he's had the opportunity to mingle in the studio with the artist while in production. He credits his absence to his brother's success. Yet he misses the late nights—and late mornings sleeping in. He recalls the thrill of creating the next masterpiece—that next #1 smash, as the only feeling that can possibly compare is perhaps having great sex. He can't wait as he embraces the change of pace.

Once placing the vacuum in the closet, he checks his time—a quarter past two. Mumbling, he recites his "to do list". He's got to call Envy's attorney/manager Steve Stapanovich to go over the details of tonight's performance. Yet he holds that thought remembering his common sense need to contact Thadius first before giving Steve any final plans.

He talks to both men—then takes a second to relax on the bed. But as soon as he lies down, his sixth sense tells him to check on Alecia— the group's diva in the making. He calls to make sure his investment is ready and also happy.

For a change Justin manages to get through to Alecia on the first try. Usually the two end up playing phone tag—sometimes for days before any one on one connection is made. Frustrating to say the least, but this time she answers his call.

"Hello!" she says, sounding rushed—or winded.

"*Daaamn*—I don't believe this shit! I actually got through. That's a first." Justin beams with sarcasm.

"Hey stranger—how ya doin'?" responds Alecia.

"I'm fine! The real question is—how are you? …Y'all ready? Need anything?"

"*Yeeeah*—we're ready. A lil' nervous—but nuthin' we can't handle."

"Well, that's expected. It's been a minute since y'all last were on the stage—huh? What's Val up to?"

"I think she's studying for an exam… Something about Advanced Algorithms. But that was about two hours ago."

"Ya got ta be kiddin'! Hello, but um—did someone forget to tell her she's doin' a show tonight? I mean damn! I know it's a beautiful thing to pursue an education and all, but shit, first things first…" His pitch heightens with quick words as he expresses his apprehension.

"Relax Justin—it's goin' to be okay. In case you've forgotten, we've been doin' this for a while. We aren't exactly new to this. …It's goin' to be a piece of cake." She coaxes Justin's needless worry.

"Al-ight, if ya say so. Jus don't want y'all all tense and shit. We need a good showing. Y'all remembered what we discussed. Two songs— "Sobeit" and "Slow Motion". …That'll give us a chance to measure the public's feedback on those singles. Maybe give us a taste of what to expect in the near future—especially as far as marketing goes.

"No problem boo!" she says, now laughing. "Damn—I thought I was nervous."

"Whatever—I'll let ya go though. And I'll see y'all after while…call me if sumptin' changes."

"Yes Mr.Vaughn." she says, still grinning.

Justin hangs up knowing how ridiculous and overbearing he must have sounded. He shakes his head then starts to take out his clothes.

♡ ♡ ♡

5:24pm

Arriving at the street festival converted Bronzeville neighborhood, Justin socializes with Thad who introduces him to some of the key organizers of the event. He shakes hands with such notable community activists as Ray Croft, CEO of the WeCare Foundation, a respected nonprofit organization responsible for such charitable programs as "Meals on Wheels" and "Empower to Employ"—a training program geared towards technical skills education for the underprivileged. There's also Alderman Samantha Lewis, co-founder of "Reach to Teach," the program sponsoring the all day event. She takes Justin aside, officially welcoming him and the Sho' Nuff family to the greater Chicago community. Ms. Lewis—a savvy veteran politician having served on City Council and the Cook County School Board, shares her vision.

"Justin—if I may?" she asked as she seeks his approval before continuing to address him on a first name basis.

"By all means ma 'am." he says, extending his respect and courtesy.

"I've been serving this community for more than twenty years now. And what I've seen over the last few years is the widening gap between meeting the needs of our community—and having the resources readily available to meet those various needs. For instance Justin—if we look at today's inner city African American or Hispanic family, the average medium income is well under $20,000 a year—which also falls far below the state standard of poverty. That means the type of employment sustained by many of these families is unskilled, menial labor—jobs that barely pay minimum wage. One factor—just looking at this area alone, well over half of our young people drop out of high school. Thus, joblessness becomes the norm. And without jobs people are forced to rely on welfare and other insufficient governmental aid programs. That's why so many people are trapped and condemned to places like this." She points to what's left of the largest high rise public housing community in the nation—Robert Taylor Homes located about a block away.

Justin views the poverty stricken area in solemn wonder. "So, how do ya ever get beyond all this?"

"One life at a time Justin… One life at a time." Samantha stops to absorb the sheer magnitude of the job ahead. "Yep—starting with these babies. We've centered our focus around helping these children to break the patterns of their circumstance—and resist negative behaviors associated with peer pressure. And how do we do that? By increasing the skills needed to achieve their dreams. Give them something to look forward to. If we teach them that education is the foundation of success and help them to realize that every person has the ability and talents to succeed, then maybe they will want to stay in school—graduate, and lead productive, prosperous lives," she says while pausing. "Every child deserves a chance—and this world is full of opportunities."

"Ms. Lewis, you're absolutely right. If we can reverse the curse—and feed these youth with positive images and role models, ya know—using our experiences to sharpen their leadership abilities enough so that they will be able to go out and create positive contributions to society—then maybe we'll have sumptin'. It's all up here." Justin points to his temple signifying the mind. "On one hand it can be our greatest weapon—and yet on the other, it can also be our biggest nightmare. It all comes down to the way we see ourselves. And how we value what we see. …Self-esteem is key! And yet everyday, we watch and encourage the devaluing of ourselves through the media, television …and *MUSIC!* And these are the influences that dictate who we are—and that's wrong!"

"*Yeees!* We have to take back what's rightfully ours… our families and value systems that make us the God-fearing people that we are."

"Huh." Justin reflects over the eye-opening discussion. He now understands the plight and passion of Ms. Lewis' vision. They stroll through Taylor Park towards the two-stage setup. A live Deejay spins a variety of music—from classic soul to hiphop. As hundreds congregate amidst the maybe five or six-acres of park, Justin observes the unity and mix of young and old converging to support the cause. He can't help but to feel good about what he sees—from the dense crowds gathered to spectate the three on three co-ed basketball tournament to watching the little kids running around just enjoying themselves. He sees in one corner a mobile book fair passing out free literature to all ages, while on the other end a tent has been set up by the community medical clinic to do free health screens. Various booths providing a variety of services are dispensed amongst the festival site.

"Justin, I can still remember as a little girl growing up in this very community and seeing such a different picture. Jobs were plentiful, black businesses were thriving, the church strong—there's such a rich cultural heritage here. So many at one time have called Bronzeville home—Ida B. Wells, Thomas Dorsey, Gwendolyn Brooks—and that's just a few!" She finishes her retrospective; an event contributor has summonsed her presence for a private word. "Justin, you'll have to excuse me—but duty calls. But it was nice meeting you."

"Oh the pleasure was all mine ma'am. …Take care." He watches Ms. Lewis walk away. And with time to kill before the concert, Justin ventures through the festivities where he wanders upon a particularly interesting sight. In a trailer behind the stage, a makeshift barbershop is erected offering free cuts and shaves to the men and boys of this impoverished area. There Justin encounters a familiar face. Standing outside the mobile facility, talking to a fellow stylist is Natalie—the girl from Shear Magic. Apparently, she's volunteering her time in support of the program. And once again—from afar, his attention is drawn to her engaging presence. Even today, she displays a vastly different look. With temperatures now in the low sixties—having jumped some twenty to thirty degrees from Justin's early morning run, Natalie has on a red ribbed turtleneck shirt tucked inside a pair of low rise jeans accented with red high heel pointed toe boots. She plays in her dark mahogany beyond shoulder length hair, swooping the ends toward her chin and neck—a bang cut just above her brow add a tinge of sexy to her already cunning face. Justin debates whether to approach to her.

"Whatcha doin' back here!" A female voice to his left catches him off guard. And walking hand in hand with her beau, Shantel appears with Quentin. "I just ran into the girls. I think they're lookin' for you. And you can see what the cat jus drug in," she says, referring to her elusive boyfriend.

"Hey Quent—it's been a while man. How's everything?"

"Good. And yourself?" The smug pompous Adonis of a man extends his hand, placing a tight firm squeeze against Justin's palm.

"So what brings ya ta this neck of the woods?"

"Well, I just finished inking a production deal with Viacom. My company will be responsible for developing a pilot on Black finances to be aired on BET next summer—and of course starring 'yours truly'.

So to celebrate, I decided to make a special trip to see my baby." Grabbing both her hands, he turns to peer into the gullible eyes of Tae. All smiles, she returns an endearing gaze. "My schedule hasn't afforded me the luxury of spending the quality time due to this beautiful woman right here. So maybe in some small way I can begin to make it up to her this weekend." And with a big fake smile, he bends down to kiss his naïve sweetheart on the side of the mouth.

"*Bullshit!* Betcha this nigga got some more pussy nearby. Put my last dollar on da muthafucka havin' an excuse not to stay at her crib. ...Watch!" With no love loss between the two men, it's the first thought that comes to Justin's mind. From day one, he's never trusted Quentin's intentions as he's also made those feelings abundantly clear to Tae. Yet when it's all said and done—all he can do is be there to pick up the broken pieces. "Well congratulations! I hope everything works out for ya." Lying—but just the same, he reaches again to shake Quentin's hand. After which, Justin tells Tae he'll see her later following the concert. He then takes a glance toward to where Natalie was standing—which she's no longer there. "Damn!" Disappointed, he now sets out to find Alecia and Val.

Nearby Justin hears the amplified voice of WGCI's on-air personality "Crazy Howard McGee" who takes the mic on stage two. The spread crowd now begins to gather together around the portable platform. As the mini concert is set to start, Justin uses his cell to make quick contact with the girls.

"Yo! I'm standing here in front of the first stage. ...Where y'all at!" With no answer, he posts that message on Alecia's voicemail and stands around for a few minutes, waiting for a response. But it isn't long before—beaming from around the corner comes the women of Envy—Alecia and Val.

"*Yooo—What's up!*"

"*Hey now!*" Alecia speaks. "*Heeey!*" Then Val speaks.

"How's my favorite girls?" Holding his arms wide open, he collects the femme fatales for a group hug. He also compliments their all-leather pants and jacket wardrobe. "I like that! Sophisticated sexy—yeeeah I'm feelin' that fo sho'!" giving both a good look over.

"You know we're performing next to last—right?" Alecia gives Justin the 411.

"Naw—I didn't. So who they got last?"

"Jennifer," mumbles Val.

"Well—no biggy! Y'all cool wit it—ain't cha?"

"I guess we'll have ta be. Kinda wanted to go on earlier—before it gets too dark—and gets cold!" And of course, it's Alecia with the complaint.

Teasing, "C'mon now—y'all can handle it. You should be used to this. …Born and raised in it—right?"

"Whatever. *Shhhit*, cold is cold! I don't care if you're born in it—or not! I ain't up fo all that." Alecia looks to Val to cosign.

"Ummm huh. Gurl ain't that the truth!" she says, giving a delayed reaction.

"Poor babies." Justin drapes his arms around each, comforting their delicate dispositions.

7:12pm

After watching comedian Tony Sculfield do his thing—along with two other local unsigned acts perform, the time has finally come—the moment Justin's been waiting for as Envy gets ready to take the stage. Pretending to be an innocent bystander, he stands nearby off to the side with arms crossed to gauge the crowd's response. He fills with eager anticipation. Once host Howard McGee finishes the introduction, Alecia and Val take their place under the spotlight. Greeted by a warm reception, the Southside products—still very much remembered, thank the adorning audience.

Under the crisp night air, the sizable crowd—huddled close to beat the falling temperature, bounces to the uptempo groove "Sobeit"—the first single off their upcoming debut release. Receiving a generous ovation, the girls—Alecia and Val, having already pre-positioned two stools behind the platform, bring both forward to center stage. Going against what had been decided as the second number, Val, whose been given a Gibson acoustic guitar from backstage, starts to strum a beautiful melody that momentarily hushes the crowd. As the song plays, Justin—displeased by their undiscussed decision to change song selection, soon recognizes the track. It's "Cupid" of 112 fame. "*Damn. A good move.*" He bobs his head, receiving the mesmeric sing-a-long, clap-a-long response of the reminisced crowd. Alecia nails the Marvin "Slim" Scandric lead as she serenades the surprised audience. Her voice—a cross between Toni Braxton and Mariah, echoes powerfully over the multi-block area.

Justin watches the performance as an awed spectator—for it's the best he's seen of them. The crowd loves every minute of it—so he's more than satisfied. Already thinking ahead, knowing that the original recording is a part of the Arista catalog, he starts pondering "remake".

And why not, he figures it's an easy way to tap into an already established core market. Again—with waves and smiles, the girls thank the enthusiastic crowd. "We love you Chicago!" is the praise given to the audience as they exit the stage. Justin moves in that general direction to congratulate their efforts. He works his way through the buzzing mass and around backstage where he finds that Tae has already beaten him to the punch. There she is talking to the girls amidst a small growing entourage of friends and fans. Unwilling to be outdone, Justin makes his presence felt as he walks toward the gathered group applauding loudly and shouting "Bravo! Bravo!" He adds a few whistles for extra measure.

"Thanks Justin. Hope you're not too mad at us." An apologetic Val steps forward.

"Yeah, I have ta admit, I was a lil' pissed at first. But y'all tore that shit up! I'm curious though—what made y'all choose *that* song? Cause fo real—I'm seriously thinkin' 'bout usin' it on the album."

"I thought that too!" Tae rushes to add.

As both of their young faces light up in approved pleasure, Alecia explains the reason for their timely noncompliance. "We always wanted to do that song. ...*Wow!* We were like eleven or twelve when we first heard 'Cupid'."

"Yeeep. We were jus gettin' into boys then." Val nods as she dwells on those early memories.

"Yeah girl. But we used to be up in my room—in front of the mirror—jus singin' our lil' hearts out. And we played that song ova and ova fo hours—day after day!" She chuckles. "Shaun, my older brother, would get so mad. Girl, remember when he took and hid the CD from us—cause he was tired of hearin' us sing?" Both laugh. "Talk 'bout hurt! I think I cried fo a week. But that was the first song we ever sung together. ...almost ten years ago. Now look where we are. I still can't believe it. So we had ta do it—*sorry*." She too apologizes.

Justin, with a subtle smirk, accepts their repentance. "I hear ya. Oh well, what can I say? It all worked out.

For a few more minutes the conversation continues before the two groups separate, Justin and Shantel walk back around front to catch the last performance.

"So, where's ya boy?" Justin soon realizes that Tae is alone.

"I don't know. Said something 'bout he had ta go back to the hotel. He's supposed ta meet me at the apartment a lil' later. ...But *whatever*." The disappointment is obvious by her attitude.

"…I knew it!" Justin keeps his negative comments to himself not wanting to add insult to injury. He abruptly changes topics. "Yo, what's goin' on wit Dee?"

"I don't know. Why ya ask?"

"Naw—I was jus wonderin'. I knew things between me and him had changed, but I've noticed the distance between y'all too. What's up wit that?"

"*Demetrius*—that's always been your boy! We cool and all—but we were neva like that." Shrugging her shoulders, she says, "He's an asshole. If it wasn't for my association wit you I would of neva been around him like that anyway. But I feel what you're sayin' cause it's definitely different. But I'm not complainin' either. I think it's jus one of those things. …When we were in Atlanta we were all he knew—he didn't associate wit too many people outside of work. And here, I think it's jus more of what he's used to—so he's kinda off in his own world."

Justin agrees. "You probably right. I don't know though—I jus hate ta see it be like that. I look at us as the three musketeers—all fo one, one fo all type shit. We went into this together—ya know? Y'all my squad—da 'A' team! Know what I'm sayin'? We're suppose ta make this thing happen together…"

"Justin, you know betta than anyone… Things don't always turn out the way we want them." Shantel takes a serious sullen glance into Justin's eyes, and he instantly knows exactly where she's coming from.

"Yeah—and I blamed myself fo awhile. I mean after Teresha died—I pulled away. …I literally took myself from everything I was close to. I jus wanted ta be alone! And unlike you, I don't think Dee knew how ta handle that—I think my hurtin' overwhelmed him and fo once, he didn't have the remedy to my situation. So he didn't know what ta say. And so it was jus easier ta stay away. I know exactly what he was feelin'. I was there too!"

"Still, that's no excuse not ta be there for someone. That's jus lame!" Tae expresses herself with conviction. "That's anotha reason why I can't put up wit him—I hate a triflin' pathetic ass man. *Aaah.*" she says, mumbling and shaking. "Jus does something ta me."

"But ya know what? I don't blame him—or the situation. What happened wit us was already in the makin'. I jus didn't see it at the time. We see shit different—ya know?" His look sincere, "But I'll tell ya what… You've been right there," he laughs. "I don't know why—

cause I know it's been a bitch. But I must say—you been a troopa. And I couldn't have made it without cha. …Thank ya baby."

Blushing through her cinnamon cheeks, she adds a bit of humor, "So, I guess this would probably be the best time ta ask for a raise—huh?"

"*Nope!*" he quickly declines her request. The conversation pauses as Jennifer Hudson takes the stage. Gazing over a sea of folks, Justin, wanting a better view, finds a seat on top of a folding table used earlier to display employment opportunities posted with the city. Tae follows his lead, her butt barely touching the tip as she leans against the front edge. From the back of the crowd they exchange critiquing comments—poking jokes as people pass by. Justin relaxes—his arms propped behind his back while his feet dangle. His job is done. He now enjoys what's left of the show. He and Tae—facing one another, engage in mischievous conversation until—out the blue, Justin catches wind of an all too familiar sound. "Cluck, cluck, cluck, cluck…" The approaching swift paced cadence immediately hooks his radar. He inadvertently cuts his eye towards the sound of hard-bottom shoes tapping the tattered concrete. The speed of each step foretells the hastened stride of a rushed woman. "Oh shit, it's her!" blares across his mind. With a fluttered heart and focused eyes, Justin loses his train of thought—unintentionally cutting Tae off.

Natalie flies by the table—nearly running and looking straight ahead. Wrapped in a brown leather trench with her Dooney & Bourke bag clutched at her side, she hurries to the bus stop. Justin pursues with a stare as he's forgotten about Tae.

"Ah hello—earth to Justin." She waves her hand in front of his face. But he pays no attention. "Do you know her?" she says, feeling disrespected by his blatant gawking of another woman.

"Maybe. …Hey, I'll be right back." He hops down off the table to follow Natalie.

"Where you goin'!" Flustered, Shantel interrogates him.

"Hold on. I said I'll be right back!"

"Oh, it's like that!"

"Jus hush girl," he says as he trots after his target.

Reaching the corner of 47th & State, Natalie takes her place between the other ten or so CTA riders. Two adolescent boys—maybe late teens, stand under the hooded bench dressed in classic street garb. Bubble jackets, baggy jeans, doo rags and fake ice around the neck, they whisper amongst themselves—staring, as Natalie waits just behind the Plexiglas structure. She spots the thug wannabes through the smoke-tinted shelter—turning her head just enough to avoid any eye contact, but not far enough to lose their peripheral position. After some hushed words, the two make their way toward her. She girds herself expecting a verbal confrontation. Justin appears from her blind flank.

"*Natalie?*"

Startled, she turns quickly to the masculine stranger. "...Excuse me?" And with frowning brows she says, "Do I know you?"

"Yeah, sort of." Justin smiles having heard practically the same question just five minutes earlier from Tae.

"No, I don't!" She answers with blazing earnest.

"Yes, ya do—but ya jus don't know it yet. Hi I'm Justin Vaughn." He reaches for her hand. The teens reverse their course seeing her much larger suitor.

Not returning his friendly gesture, "Okay—whatever. I don't have time for games." She attempts to move away.

"Hold on. Can ya please let me finish?"

She sighs with displeasure, but stops to let Justin say his peace. His cause is helped by her reluctance to face the two young gangsta look-a-likes—if Justin should happen to walk away. She contorts her lips and gazes in another direction as Justin explains their couple of previous coincidental meetings. She remembers the night Alexus and Dee met—but doesn't recall seeing him. She vaguely recalls the morning Envy came to the salon—but again she doesn't remember Justin—or his peeping antics. But the fact that these chance occurrences happened does seem to spark her interest. "Well—I guess it's a small world after all," she says, breaking a slight smirk.

"Oh fo sho! And very glad of it!" Ecstatically, Justin responds. Her smirk widens to a smile, as her perfectly white teeth gleam from the city lights. "My, we have some pretty teeth. I betcha ya make your dentist proud—huh?"

A slight giggle somehow seeps through as bus #29—State Northbound approaches the corner. She finally extends her hand "It was nice to meet you Justin." They shake—then she moves to the back of the line.

As she's about to board the nearly vacant bus, Justin poses one final thought. "*Hey.* Is there any way by chance that maybe we can continue this discussion at a later date?"

Standing in the doorway as the bus begins to move—smiling while firmly holding on to a chrome pole, she responds, "I suppose. I guess I don't see any problem with that. ...I'm sure you know where to find me." The doors close, she waves and takes a seat behind the driver. The bus departs down State Street. Justin holds the corner, watching until the transit vehicle vanishes. He returns to the park to find Tae.

twenty-six

My Brother's Keeper

Justin and Jerome, on their way back from Midway Airport, enjoy the downtown drive along empty streets—taking full advantage of all the Sunday morning late sleepers. Justin travels the more scenic route up on North Michigan, giving Jerome a full tour of Chicago's famous Magnificent Mile.

"Man jus look at this shit… Stores every damn where!"

"Yeah man—the shit is phat," Jerome remarks, having never visited Chicago. "The skyline is like endless dude."

"I know—right. That's the same thing I said when I first got here. The shit is pretty though—especially at night. …Romantic as hell!"

"*Word.* I need ta bring Monique through. She'll eat this shit up. All that girl does—is shop and shit!

Justin, cracking a big grin, "Yeah man, I hear ya. Reminds me of Tae—that trick loves ta shop. And is good at it! Shit—her lil' thrifty ass—I know fo a fact she can squeeze a dolla out of fifteen cents. Seen her do it—*shhhit!*"

"Oh so y'all be kickin' it?" Jerome tries to pry on the sly.

"Not like that but she's been a big help though. Baby girl kept me sane through everything."

"Well, that's cool." Jerome readjusts himself in his passenger seat knowing he's about to delve into uncomfortable territory. "Yeah dude I've been meaning ta talk to ya. Jackie called me about a week ago. She's worried 'bout ya. Said you were avoiding Justice." He stops there for a response.

"I don't know man—I was fucked up. I ain't know what ta say. That shit still hurts man. Feel like I'm lettin' him down by makin' him stay there. But I know I got ta get myself together first before I bring him up here in all this shit. I ain't want him sittin' up here havin' ta be by himself while I'm runnin' around handlin' shit fo Sho' Nuff. ...Know what I mean? At least not right now! ...Shit is kinda crucial. I wanna try and get everything on track—crack the whip on some of these lazy asses who ain't doin' shit!"

"Jus remember though man—what's really important. Fuck all this Sho' Nuff shit—it don't mean shit. "We're all we got. ...Me, you, and baby boy—that's it! So we gotta look out for each other. That's what's important. Hell—Riq understands what's goin' on. He ain't gonna hold it against ya if you need some time off." Jerome tries to convince Justin that it's okay to stop and grieve.

"It's jus so crazy man—I still can't believe she's gone. I mean everything was straight—I finally had my family back... Fo a second I was actually happy dude. Been so long since I could say that. I mean damn man—*why?* She ain't neva do nuthin' ta nobody—so why He have ta take her? That shit's fucked up!" Shaking his head, Justin fights his emotions.

"You alright man—want me ta drive?" Jerome says, fearing a lapse in his brother's concentration.

"Nah—I'm straight." He wipes a stray tear from his cheek. "I jus don't get it man—that's some cruel shit! It's like He's tryin' ta punish me for all the dirt I did. And it's like no matter what I do right—it makes no difference cause I still owe for some shit I did five years ago. And like it's useless cuz I can neva get out of debt. So why try. *Fuck* it!" He throws his shoulders up.

"So whatcha sayin' man? ...What, you wanna give up? ...Throw in the towel—stop livin'—*what?* I mean do ya hear yourself?" he asks, showing his brother little empathy. "So what 'bout Justice? Wanna quit on him too? Hasn't he been through enough?"

"I'm sayin' man—I been through a lot..."

"And ya still here—so now what? Ya keep pushin' and survivin'. How that sayin' go? 'Whatever don't kill ya—only makes ya stronger'," he Laughs. "Well, in that case—we should be some strong ass muthafuckas—I'm sayin'."

Justin sneers, realizing his baby brother is right. Though they've been through a lot, they've always managed to make it through. With their destination being Jewtown, he turns onto Roosevelt crossing over the bridge, for an authentic Chicago style polish. The latest expansions to UIC—University of Illinois-Chicago, has shifted the old landmark from its original place of glory, but with the city being synonymous for Gangsters, Jordan, and such renown delicacies as Polishes and Italian beefs, Justin stops here still for a taste of history. Jerome gets a Polish with fries while Justin grabs a pork chop sandwich with grilled onions.

After experiencing his tour of city sights, Jerome is most impressed with Chicago's lakefront. They eat and ride as Justin cruises up and down Lake Shore Drive—from Navy Pier to Fullerton beach. He's amazed at the vast mix of culture and personality concealed in one package. Jerome now understands the draw and sees why so many would leave the south to come here. They finally make it to Justin's high-rise, high-cost abode—entering the enormous French paneled lobby where the serving of coffee and muffins pleasantly surprises the two of them.

"*Shooot!* That's pretty cool right there. Like being in a hotel." Jerome secures his luggage strap over his shoulder then aggressively attacks the limited menu—seizing and sampling all on the table.

"Do ya need some help man?" Justin inquires, being sarcastic.

"*Naaaw*—I think I got it." And with a silly smirk, Justin's hungry younger sibling situates his second meal and motions for his brother to lead the way. Both speak to the attractive young blonde behind the front desk before jumping on the elevator. "Some nice shit man—a lil' older than I thought. ...fancy as hell though. A nigga can get used to this shit!" Jerome compliments before sipping on his coffee.

"Oh fo sho! But yeah—24 hour fitness center, a big ass all night laundry room and shit. ...A hot tub on the sun deck. The shit's tight!"

"I see."

They exit the vintage elevator—making a right at the end of the corridor as Justin pulls out his key to unlock the door.

"C'mon in dude." He taps a touch lamp to give light to the dark curtain drawn room.

Jerome, dropping his bag, looks around the surprisingly plain décor. "Definitely a bachelor pad big bro."

"Yeah—ain't had a whole lotta time ta do too much. Maybe we can get Mo up here and spruce it up a bit."

"Word. I'll call her ass tonight." Smiling, he squeezes his big brother's shoulder with amused understanding. They spend the rest of the day inside relaxing, ordering in, and catching up.

♡ ♡ ♡

Monday morning at the office, Jerome, hanging with his brother, listens to the demo of Dee's homeboy. "So this the kid from Connecticut—huh?"

"Yeah. So whatcha think? …Hype or what?" Justin sits behind his desk checking email.

"He's got potential. Needs some more music! …Whatcha tryin' do?"

"Splice that shit! Take that nigga's Eastern flow and fuse it wit yo shit. The question is… Can we make it work?"

Jerome spins around in a leather recliner, concentrating. "I don't know man—ya might be reachin' on this one. At least his delivery is original—maybe a lil' gimmicky…" He takes an even deeper listen before saying another word. "I don't know—I have ta get the nigga in the studio." he says, not convinced one way or the other.

"So whatcha sayin'? You'll take him on in a developmental deal maybe?" Justin throws the suggestion out there as he tries not to push the issue. But his brother doesn't want to commit to anything.

"I ain't say all that—we'll have ta see."

"*Maaan*—let me know sumptin'. Shit, before I go sendin' Dee up there tryin' ta chase a nigga down!"

"Didcha talk ta Rico first?" Jerome gets amped from feeling the pressure.

Rhonda buzzes Justin because Thad is on line two. While at the same time, Tae and Demetrius enter Justin's office to say hello to Jerome.

"Hey boy!" Shantel heads straight to Jerome for a hug.

"What's up girl—how ya doin'?"

"I'm good."

"What up nigga" Dee follows with some dap.

"Yo, what up dude?"

Justin hangs up the phone complaining. "I guess y'all niggas forget we runnin' a business up here!"

"Why? …Who was that?" Shantel asks, showing concern.

"Thad. He jus wanted ta thank us again fo getting involved with the program. But that's beside the point—y'all know better. All loud and shit!" He scolds the trio like little children.

"Oh yeah Jay! I talked ta Arius's people jus a few minutes ago—a change of plans. They'll be here 'round one instead of five. He rescheduled for an earlier flight. Sumptin' 'bout an endorsement deal wit Captain Morgan." Dee gives Justin the latest information.

"*O-kaaay.* Al-ight—let me think." He ponders his agenda. "Al-ight call the limo service. Make sure they can do that. If not, I may have to send one of y'all down there ta meet them at the airport—al-ight?"

The room answers with silent nods. Tae and Dee both volunteer to show Jerome around to meet the rest of the staff. Justin uses the time alone to call Natalie. Yet he's reluctant as he continues to struggle with the guilt of moving on—past Teresha, and wonders if maybe it's too soon. Natalie is the first woman he's pursued since losing the woman he loved. Even with the passing months, he can't seem to find closure. Justin picks up the phone only to put it back down. Finally, after seemingly minutes of rocking back and forth in his chair, he gains enough nerve to dial information for the number.

She's been on his mind constantly. Her smile and confident soft-spoken demeanor reign foremost. She's cute—but with a different vibe. He thinks back to what Alexus said—about being saved; yet nothing she did or spoke about gave him that impression. He then blows Alexus' comments off as mere jealousy. He dials the number, which rings—at the very least four times before anyone answers.

"Hello Shear Magic, this is Davin. How can I help you?" greets the male but feminine sounding voice.

"Yes. Can I speak to Natalie please?" Justin drops the ghetto from his usual tone. Her coworker—placing his hand over the receiver, proceeds to ask another nearby colleague if she's made it in yet.

"Aaah sir?" he says, smacking his lips. "If you could jus hold one second. She's coming."

Justin, rubbing a pencil across some meaningless document, doodles as he waits.

"Hello?" Her tone distressed.

"How ya doin' Smiley?"

"Who is this?" She relaxes.

"Justin from the otha night—remember?"

"*Oooh.* I'm sorry. Thought ya mighta been the school callin' again. So how are you? I see you found a way to contact me."

"Oh, no doubt. But yeah—we good! So ya in school?"

She chuckles. "*Nooo*—not me. ...My daughter."

"Wow. Ya look too young ta have a kid!" Justin says as he runs game.

She scoffs at his lame compliment. "*Right!*"

"No, I'm fo real! How old is she?"

"Twelve."

"*Naw.* So how old are you?" he asks as he pries for details.

"Ain't we nosy—I'm twenty-eight? And you?"

"Thirty-four."

"Almost ova the hill." Natalie smirks with facetiousness.

"Maybe so. ...See you started early." He refers to her age as compared to her daughter's.

"Yep. Let's jus say—I was young... ready... and willing." Her blatancy throws Justin for a loop as he's left speechless. "What's wrong—cat gotcha tongue?"

Chuckling while stroking his head he says, "Maybe. But dang girl—you a trip! So what's your daughter's name?"

"Asia. So what's up? A playa like yourself can't hang?" She's relentless in her taunting.

Justin sits up. "So what's this—bash on a nigga day or what? A nigga only called ta invite a sista out ta lunch—I mean damn..." He's just about ready to throw in the towel.

"Oh, so what you're sayin' is—you wanna go out on a date?"

"Hell, I did!" he says, sounding discouraged.

"Well, in that case—why didn't ya jus say so?" She laughs to herself. "When we goin'?"

"I don't know. ...Tomorrow. ...Wednesday. You tell me."

"Oh, you suppose ta have that together playa!"

"Damn, if I ain't have you pegged wrong. Thought you were quiet and shit."

"Looks can be deceivin' babes!"

"Tell me 'bout it. *Shit.*"

"Oool baby... We have ta work on your mouth. I'm off on Wednesday so let's do it then? Where and what time do ya wanna meet? ...I tell ya what. I'll come to you. It's the least I can do. How's that?"

"Yeah, that works for me." he says, surprised by her generosity.

"So, where are we gainfully employed?"

"Sho' Nuff Entertainment. It's downtown on North Michigan—817 suite #2.

"So let me guess? You're a stripper." Again she teases.

"Yeah right—I wish. I'm actually the head of A&R over the Midwest.

"Sounds important—so what's A&R?"

He laughs. "*Whaaat*—you don't know everything? But seriously—A&R simply means Artist & Repertoire. In otha words, I help cultivate careers of artists signed to our label. You've heard of Kyra—right?"

"I've seen her on TV."

"Well, she's one of our artists. And I help oversee her career on the creative end."

"*Oooh*. So you are important." She strokes his ego.

Smug and smiling, he says, "I wouldn't go that far—but it has its perks."

"I don't even wanna know—so Wednesday around twelve sounds okay?"

"Yeah ma'am!"

"I'll see ya then. Be blessed!"

"You too." Justin barely gets the last word in before Natalie disconnects. She abruptly rushes the latter part of their conversation.

Walking back into the office, fifteen to twenty minutes later, Jerome who is still cackling from cutting up with Tae, catches his brother daydreaming. "Whatcha thinkin' 'bout man?"

Justin just shakes his head "Nuthin'."

"C'mon man—I know you better than that. What's up?"

Jerome's persistence pays off as Justin comes clean. "How soon do ya think is too soon—ta start seein' someone? …Ya know after Teresha and all." He stutters through the last part of his question.

"Really, the only one who can answer that—is you man. Are you ready?" Jerome takes a seat.

"I'm not sure. I know I wanna be."

"You met someone?"

"Yeah—kinda."

"Well… How ya feel 'bout the situation?"

"It's like I really want things to go back to the way they were—but I know that can neva happen. And sometimes I can't handle that. I mean—I can't sleep—don't wanna eat. Shit! I don't know—it's like I can't function. Like maybe I'm goin' crazy." Justin gets emotionally flustered.

"I know you're not blamin' yo'self! *Maaan* look... What happened wit Teresha, as sad as it is, was not yo fault. The girl was happy. And that was because of you. ...Y'all were doin' your thing—workin' it out! So ya got nuthin' ta be ashamed of. Stop beatin' yo'self up. ...Nobody blames you!"

"Shit, I wish it was that easy. But it goes deeper than that."

"*How?* " Jerome, not understanding his brother's survivor's guilt.

"I ain't neva tell ya this—but..." He is reluctant to say another word.

"Go ahead man—say it!" Jerome becomes impatient with Justin's stalling.

"You remember Tonya—right?"

"Yep. What's up?"

"Well, according to her, she's pregnant and supposedly I'm the father."

Jerome leans back—taking a deep sigh. "Damn—that's fucked up. Whatcha gonna do?"

"Shit I can't do nuthin'. She took off and I don't know where she's at. So I don't know shit!" he says, sounding like the victim.

"*Damn.*" Jerome, who's in shock, can't do anything but repeat himself. "Did Teresha know?"

"Hell naw! Shit, it was enough jus try'na keep our everyday shit straight. Besides—I didn't know if Tonya was actually tellin' the truth. We weren't on the best of terms—remember?"

"That's the shit fuckin' wit cha right there! Hell, no wonder ya can't sleep and eat and shit. I don't know man. Don't know what ta tell ya. That's some shit!" Both sit quietly for a second.

"But yeah dude—all this shit keeps swirling through my head. And I jus want the shit ta stop—hell!" With his elbows resting on the desk, he rubs his temple. Justin sits, frowned in the face.

"Man—I hate ta say this, but ya might wanna seek some professional help—know what I'm sayin? Either way, if I was you—I wouldn't rush into anything wit this new chick."

"I hear ya."

"But are ya listenin'?" Jerome asks, knowing his brother—and his unwillingness to take heed to sound advice. He knows Justin won't slow down for much of anything.

"*Yeeeah man.*" Already frustrated, Justin feels patronized by his younger brother. The two continue to talk on until lunch. Justin treats his visiting brother to Joe's Seafood on E. Grand Avenue. They over indulge themselves with stone crab and prime rib.

After an extended meal, where already waiting in Justin's office is Arius Kitchens and his manager—Kim Carson. He opens the door to find Arius behind his desk on the phone. He's peeved at the fact that Rhonda didn't page him upon Arius's arrival, but then realizes that he's actually left his cell on the charger—in his office. A careless move on his part as he addresses his latest visitors.

"There he is—Arius "Superbad" Kitchens! Sho' Nuff's next multi-platinum superstar. …How ya been man?" Justin walks over to his desk to greet the still sitting—still very comfortable prima donna.

"All gravy baby!" Arius stuck in permanent pimp mode, responds in a retro Isaac Hayes like fashion, as Versace covers his eyes. Justin smiles and nods over at the pacing—cell phone consumed Kim, who from the sounds of it—is up to her usual intimidation persuasion tactics. She hangs up once she's aware of Justin's entrance.

Grinning—exposing the noticeable gap between her two top front teeth, she marches straight to Justin—hand already extended. "Hello Justin—good to see you again." Her small softened tone a direct contrast to her ferocious tenacity.

"Hey Kim—good ta see you too. How was the flight?" He gently embraces her smooth delicate hand.

"Tolerable."

"And the hotel accommodations?"

"Grand."

"Good. …Nuthin' less than the best for you." He pours on his usual flattering charm.

With a smile now frozen to her face, the slanted eyed, copper toned, over middle aged diva swooshes her plaited straight-back Micros over her left ear. Her public propensity for younger men, especially her own clients, nearly precedes her long-standing reputation as a top-notch professional manager.

"Kim, I want to meet my brother, Jerome Vaughn. He'll be in charge of overseeing production on the project."

"It's nice to finally meet you Jerome. It seems you're the latest industry wonder boy these days. So, it will definitely be a pleasure working with you."

"Likewise Ms. Carson." Jerome adds a plagiaristic smirk to the mix.

"Jerome, this is Arius. If I'm not mistaken y'all have neva met—right?" Justin introduces the two key players.

"Naw—so what's up Arius?" Jerome speaks first.

"It's you baby! You the man wit the plan."

The two shake and exchange a touchless embrace. Jerome's already thinking, "…dis corny ass muthafucka!" and begins to second-guess the whole endeavor. After which, Justin gets right into the details of the studio arrangements and schedule.

twenty-seven

Vital Impressions

Sho' Nuff Entertainment Midwest—48hrs later.

Rhonda informs Justin that he has a visitor up in the front lobby. He immediately stops what he's doing—first adjusting his clothing, then opens his top desk drawer grabbing a Listerine breath strip from the newly acquired pack. With today being special, and second impressions just as important as the first, he's taken extra precautions and gone great lengths to be at the top of his game. With a charcoal Calvin Klein single breasted three-button jacket, matching pleated trousers—taupe colored tie and gray shirt, he pretends to pop his collar before heading to the lobby.

A dapper Justin makes his grand appearance where he finds Natalie and Rhonda already engrossed in conversation—looking well acquainted.

"Ms. Rhonda—I know you're not tryin' ta steal my date!" He interrupts their deep discussion.

"I didn't know you knew Natalie—Justin." Rhonda says, surprised by the young couple's association.

"And I didn't know you knew her either," he says, being a bit facetious. "So how do y'all know each other?"

"Church! We both attend Faith Fellowship." A prided Rhonda tells of their shared affiliation.

"Oh, so where's that?"

"Oak Park." Natalie speaks with subtlety—her arms crossed as she checks out Justin's designer suit. "My, aren't we sharp. I feel a lil' underdressed." She stands before her luncheon date with her hair pulled back wearing jeans and a simple gold off-the-shoulder blouse. But again, she coordinates with gold heels.

"Thank you! But no—you look nice." He notices her Tommy book bag sitting on the floor beside her. "Thought ya said you weren't in school?"

"I'm not silly. I jus came from the library. …Had ta grab a few books." She stoops down to open the bag showing Justin and Rhonda her sign language texts.

"You know how ta talk wit your hands?" Being silly, Justin acts astonished.

"*Yes.*" Amused, she answers as if he shouldn't be so surprised.

"Justin, she's a part of the sign language ministry at church." Rhonda eagerly explains.

"Oh, so you translate the sermons for the hearing impaired?"

"Ah-huh—amongst otha things. I also work with the kids in the youth ministry—teaching them!"

"Whoa—a regular Ms. Do-it-all, huh?"

"I's try!" She uses some southern ebonics flava.

Shantel enters the lobby carrying an undisclosed document. "There you are… I've been lookin' all ova for you!" She hands Justin the paper.

"What's up?" Pausing, "Oh—Tae, this is Natalie…"

"*Broussard,*" as she divulges her last name to everyone, including Justin.

"Thank ya. And Natalie this is Shantel Norris. She's the head of our Marketing Department, and a long-time friend—my partner in crime."

"Hi—nice to meet you." Natalie cordially greets Shantel.

Tae nods with a fake smile remembering her face from the park, but doesn't say anything and then picks up where she left off with Justin. "I need your signature—right there please. If ya don't mind."

she says, pointing to the space. Her malcontent is obvious, especially in the eyes of the other females.

"What is this?" Justin asks as he tries to quickly look over the document.

"Jus our latest budget report. Finance wanted me to verify Marketing's figures for the quarter. And of course—as our fearless leader, your John Hancock is most appreciably needed on the last page—as always."

"Al-ight. Looks like everything vibes. Make sure ta leave a copy on my desk please."

"Eye-Eye captain!" Mocking her boss, Tae about faces before disappearing around the corner and up the hallway to her office.

Rhonda, shaking her head, mumbles. "She's a funny one."

"Oh, I can believe it." Natalie agrees, while wearing a cynical smirk on her face.

"C'mon, you ready ta eat?" Justin rubs Natalie's upper arm strategically cutting short the female bantering before it gets brutal. "If you would excuse us Rhonda. I'll be back in a lil' while. …You know what ta do if you need me."

"Okay. You two enjoy yourselves. And *gurrrl*—I'll talk ta *you* Sunday!"

"Alright girl—be blessed!" Natalie hugs her sister in Christ.

Justin opens the lobby door, allowing his date to pass through. "You first!"

"Thank you very much sir. I see chivalry isn't dead after all."

"Not-at-all!" He follows close behind, covetously checking the "junk in her trunk". He admires the rather large unproportioned bubble that describes the seat of her pants. And for what she lacks byway of breast is more than compensated for in booty.

"Why ya walkin' behind me? I hate for a man ta be laggin' behind! …Please get up here beside me. I wanna see your face." she says, sensing Justin's wanton eyes on her backside. He promptly obeys, realizing she's not one you'd easily pull the wool over.

"So, where ya parked?" Justin leads Natalie down a short alley to a small reserved parking area to the side of the building where he unlocks his car by remote.

"Nowhere—I caught the bus."

"You don't own a car or sumptin'?" he says, surprised.

"Nope! My transit card takes me wherever I need ta go." She settles in her seat as Justin, once again being the prefect gentleman, holds open the door. He walks around to his side of the car, stopping first to remove the jacket from his suit. Next he undoes his tie, tossing both on the back seat. Finally unbuttoning the top two buttons of his dress shirt, he gets in. "What are you doin'?" Natalie curiously wonders—though she enjoys the innocent striptease.

"Jus tonin' it down a lil'." he says in his considerate attempt to help her feel comfortable. She smiles, now fully comprehending his gesture. As Justin drives to an undisclosed location, Natalie relaxes—taking the quiet approach, never once inquiring as to their destination. Justin, puzzled by the sudden change in demeanor, forces a conversation. "So, judging by the otha night—do ya volunteer your time often?"

Natalie expresses a frown of bewilderment, "What are you talkin' about?"

"At the benefit block party—weren't ya one of the barbers giving free cuts? I saw ya standing outside that trailer—talking to some guy."

"Oh—you saw all that? ...So what, are you stalkin' me?" She speaks with playful candor.

"Naw—nuthin' like that. Jus anotha one of those coincidences. The last thing I would have expected ta have seen that afternoon was your pretty face."

"Humph. That's right try and sugar coat it. ...Stalker!" she says with a big sarcastic grin.

"Damn girl—ya dun caught me! Dun blown my cover! ...Guess the truth is out."

"*Heeey*. ...And ye shall know the truth and the truth shall set you free!"

"Oh, so now ya gotta be quotin' scripture on me—huh?"

"But He answered and said, it is written, that Man shall not live by bread alone, but by every word that proceedeth out of the mouth of God."

"C'mon now. Give a brotha a break. I ain't quite so spiritually abounding as you. Ya losin' me."

But despite Justin's plea for mercy she continues. "Ask, and it shall be given to you; seek, and ye shall find; knock, and it shall be opened unto you. For everyone that asketh receiveth; and he that seeketh findeth; and to him that knocketh it shall be..."

"Okay, okay, okay—I give! So what's your motivation?"

"My motivation?" She chuckles. "That's easy. ...I woke up this morning to see anotha day. I have a beautiful daughter to share my life with. And both of us are of good health. Our bills get paid. We have roof ova our heads—clothes on our backs. And we ain't hurtin' for food—*Praise God!* Humph. Need I say more?"

"I hear ya."

"So, what's your story? 'Cause everybody has one. …What brings ya to the Chi?" Natalie flips the question.

"Who says I'm not from here?" he says, playing dumb.

"For starters—your Georgia license plate silly. Not to mention your southern drawl. You know that lil' twang you have—*'naw'* and *'y'all'.*" she laughs as she mocks on his southern heritage.

"Hold on!" Justin pauses the conversation as he pulls up to The Capital Grille where a valet attendant awaits. "Have ya ever been here before?"

"Can't say that I have. Seems nice though." She surveys the marbleized polished granite and glass entry.

"Well, if ya like red meat—then this is your place. …Best steaks in town. And they also have a wine list that's out of this world. C'mon!" Justin unbuckles his seat belt while the attendant opens Natalie's door. She accompanies him inside the dignified corporate-clientele frequented restaurant.

As Natalie looks around at the predominantly Caucasian well-dressed quiet crowd, she begins to understandably feel out of place—instinctively glancing down at her own attire. Tugging Justin's arm, she whispers in his ear. "Ya coulda warned me."

"But then that woulda took the fun out of surprising you—right?" And grinning from ear to ear, he softly recites "Surprise!"

Rolling her eyes, Natalie pops her lips—securing Justin's arm like a bride being escorted down the aisle during her processional march. "Jus remember what they say about payback!" She cautions her date before revealing the biggest Sanaa Lathan smile as the couple is cordially greeted by their host.

"Reservation for two please—under Vaughn." And with a quick confirmation of the list, they are immediately seated.

Natalie, who peeks through the menu, and the prices, tilts her carte du jour down to leer at Justin. "Why you doin' this?

"Maybe cause really I'm a nice guy in disguise—who jus so happens to want to treat a very deserving—and beautiful might I add, young lady out to nice a lunch," he responds as though he anticipated her question. He talks from behind his menu—completely concealing his face.

Speaking slowly she says, "So then, we have a mutual understanding in which it is safe to say... that in no way, shape, or form will you be expectin' anything kinky, immoral, twisted, perverted, masochistic, narcissistic or anything deemed as disgusting, demeaning, or degrading. In otha words—I hope you don't think you can simply waltz in here and buy my chocha with an expensive meal... 'Cause it's not for sale! Am I makin' myself clear?" She finishes her statement with a serious straight face.

Justin calmly tilts his menu forward—revealing an equally unmoved piercing stare. "To be honest with cha—the thought neva crossed my mind." And again he covers his face. "So, what are ya gonna order? I've neva tried it—but I hear the Calamari is really good."

"What's that?"

"Squid." The expression on her face says it all. Both laugh, breaking the seriousness of the moment.

"*Well*, help me out here... What do you usually get?" Natalie, maybe a little naïve when it comes to fine dining, seeks Justin's advice.

"Meat and potatoes—all cow! I'm gettin' ten ounces of that dry-aged Black Angus beef—well done wit some mashed potatoes. If I was you—and guessing by your slim—but on-point bodily dimensions... I'd say try the grilled salmon. It's real good! Whatcha drinkin'?"

"Water."

Justin laughs, then imitates in his best female voice, "*Water*." Shaking his head, "C'mon now—ya got like 5,000 different wines ta choose from—and you talkin' 'bout some water. Gurl, ya betta live a lil'."

Carla—their waitress takes the order. Natalie follows Justin's suggestion—ordering the salmon, but sticks to her original drinking choice of water. While they wait, Natalie gets curious; "You started to tell your story before we came inside. So, are you dating—divorced, married? ...Children? What's up?"

"Single—one son, Justice, who's thirteen goin' on thirty. He's back in Atlanta right now stayin' wit a friend..."

"So, where's his mother?" Natalie interrupts.

"Aaah—she passed away a few months ago in car accident." Justin drags his words.

"I'm sorry. I didn't mean..."

"Nah, it's cool. We had been separated for a long time. But jus before her death we were tryin' ta work through some things. I mean..." Justin pauses as he starts stuttering, his lip sputters.

Natalie instinctively moves to a lighter topic. "So, how long have you been up here?"

"Three months or so. Whenever I got this promotion. But I actually really like it here! There's a lot ta see. I mean—of course there's no place like home, but I've really enjoyed myself since I've been here."

"So, what have you seen?"

"*Aaah*—the beaches, Navy Pier, Buckingham fountain... Ya know—pretty much most of all the famous stuff." he says as he runs out of things to name.

Natalie grins, then chuckles. "It's one thing to pass by them on your way to work everyday. But what have you actually gotten to experience up close and personal? Have you ever walked along the shoreline with your pants rolled up—sand between your toes and have the afternoon waves cover your feet every few minutes—washing away the sand? ...Or maybe sat on a bench late in the evening up over on North Pier—soaking in the infinite view of Lake Michigan as city lights reflect off its surface?" Like a true romanticist her thoughts are spoken with passion while poetic in delivery. "Even Buckingham Fountain at night—with all the colorful lights... It's beautiful—so peaceful."

"Wow. I sure like the way ya make it sound. But naw, I ain't quite experienced it like that! Maybe I need a tour guide or sumptin'. You offerin'?"

"Maybe. We'll have to see." Her long lashes bat as she teases with alluring eyes. Justin, now hooked, gets a lump in his throat; he's rattled—all hot and bothered by her unrefined erotic nature.

"Well, I hope so." Justin wishes. They spend a second gazing at one another—it's funny the difference a minute makes. The moment is interrupted by the partial delivery of their food.

Over a hot meal—and good company, the two swap stories of parents lost—and of parenthood, sharing historical accounts of personal tragedy and hysterical misadventure. Having similar backgrounds in common, Natalie, whose estranged mother will have nothing more to do with her or her daughter, was raised by her oldest brother—Brunell. Molested as a child, she wears the guilt of her father being incarcerated for much of her rearing years. She tells of the traumatic effect it's had on her life—the mistakes made, her early promiscuity and rebellion. They discuss their dreams along with their disappointments. Justin, wanting to one day start an independent label with his brother, while also talking of the pain and voids left after losing loved ones. Natalie dreams of going back to school and earning a degree in law. Yet, she details the reality of dreams deferred because of the pitfalls of raising a child as a teenager. They talk and eat for more than an hour, mixing moments of intense adversity along with the lighter side of lessons learned. The conversation becomes therapeutic for both. Justin admires the fact that she's a good listener.

Justin, realizing he needs to get back to the office, looks to his watch with displeasure. "*Damn*—1:40. …Funny how time flies when you're havin' fun."

"*I knooow*. But I need ta let you get back to work. Maybe we can do this again real soon. Maybe my treat. …Get a lil' ghetto on ya. Take ya to a few spots I know!"

"Definitely!" Justin signals to Carla for the check. After taking care of the bill, he drops a twenty on the table for a tip. As always, the food was excellent and the service—impeccable.

The valet attendant brings Justin's car around to the front. Once inside he offers to take Natalie home. She refuses, insisting for him to drop her off at the nearest El stop. He doesn't want to hear of it, "Girl, let me take you home."

"No. What did I say? …You're already late." She takes a firm stand.

"So what, I'm the boss!" He laughs.

"I'll let you take me home the next time—okay?"

Blowing, he concedes. "Al-ight. Where do ya want me ta drop ya at?"

"Right-over-here…" She directs Justin to the corner of Michigan and Ontario where he pulls to the curb. "Thank you—I really enjoyed myself." She reaches into her Tommy bag, grabbing a piece of paper—tearing off a corner. "Here's my number—so call me!" She jumps out the car. "Bye."

"See ya girl. Be safe." He's a little disappointed having to end the date on this note.

"I will. Go so you can get back to work. Jus call me tonight." She waves—then turns, hitting the pavement in full stride.

2:34pm

Feeling pretty good overall by the way things turned out, Justin whistles a tune as he returns to his office. Tae prances in right behind him. "'Bout time! So where did cha'll go?"

"The Capital Grille."

"Huh. Ya don't say. A bit extravagant for a first date—you don't think?" She drops on his desk the copies he had asked for earlier.

He instantly detects the funkiness in her attitude. "What's your problem?"

"Ain't got one!" she says nothing more as she prances back out of his office.

Justin jeers, mumbling, "Whatever man." A few minutes later, Tae buzzes his line. "Justin speakin'!" he answers rudely.

"Hey—I'm sorry. I was buggin'—wasn't I?" Tae says, sounding remorseful.

"Don't worry 'bout it. Must be that time of the month or sumptin'?"

Sighing deeply, she says, "Nope, jus one of those days. So, what are you doin' later?"

"Remember me and Rome are suppose ta be in the studio wit Arius tonight."

"Oh, I forgot. Alright then—once again I jus wanna apologize…"

"*We cool.* Go home and getcha some rest tonight. And we'll do it again in the morning. …And cheer up! It ain't neva that bad."

"Alright—bye." Her voice exudes a sense of despair.

"Peace." Justin hangs up. After disconnecting he feels bad about ignoring the fact that maybe something was really wrong. He decides to call her from the studio later to at least check on her—and say "goodnight".

twenty-eight

Threesome

That night at the Sound Station—a leased recording facility in downtown Chicago, Justin, Jerome, Engineer—Mike Kozlowski, Arius and entourage, and musicians Damian Foster and Bernard Wright fill the session. The building, a brownstone located on West Huron, once halfway house now state-of-the-art studio, Justin chooses for its multistory home like setting. Three and a half hours into the session with things progressing slowly as Arius, being seemingly more preoccupied with entertaining his tag along female groupies—two half dressed twins—Tamequa and Shemequa, isn't responding or being as productive as Jerome feels an artist of his caliber should. Frustrated, Jerome halts the recording.

"Shit—stop! Dude, ya sound flat as hell. C'mon man we been here damn near four hour and ain't accomplished shit! Now, what's up? Mike, rewind that shit back—let's run it again! Arius, look now... Gotta show me sumptin'! Two albums—you ain't no rookie nigga!" Jerome barks his instructions. Justin paces the floor, monitoring his baby brother's demanding leadership. It's funny watching Jerome work—a total contrast to his everyday disposition. Usually reserved any other time, yet in the studio—it's like a beast unleashed, a totalitarian bent on perfection. "Stop! Jus stop man... *Fuck it*—everybody take ten." Unsatisfied, Jerome calls for a break. With a few suggestions, Justin converses with his brother while Mike steps outside for a smoke. Damian and Bernard go hang in the lounge where a 60" plasma television resides. They tune in to the World Series to watch the White Sox try and finish off the Astros for the pennant. Arius and company make their way to the kitchen—their pre-session high has left them with the munchies. They pilfer a well stocked fridge.

After finishing his discussion with Jerome, Justin, fulfilling his promise, takes a minute to call Natalie. He walks and talks, finding a vacant, much smaller session room on the second floor. "Hey there whatcha doin'? ...I hope I'm not callin' too late."

"No, you're fine." There's a short pause. "I wasn't thinkin' when I told you to call—I forgot we had bible study tonight." Another pause. "Me and Asia jus got in not too long ago."

"*What are you doin'?*" Justin wonders the reason for the choppy conversation until he hears in the background a blaring television and what sounds like the ball game. "Never mind. I can answer my own question. Ya got the game on too—huh?"

"Yeah—I think we're about to do it. So, you're watchin' too?"

"Naw—but it's on in the lounge. ...I got too much goin' on to pay any attention to baseball. Hell—it wasn't until the otha day that I found out that Chicago was even in it."

"Uh-ah! *Whaaat?* I wouldna even claimed that. Eighty-five years in the makin'—and you didn't know?" She laughs. "Oo-oo—yes!" she says as she reacts to a play in Chicago's favor. "So, where are you?"

"In the studio. My brother is up from Atlanta workin' wit one of our new artist—Arius Kitchens. You familiar wit him?"

"*Yeeeah.* Didn't he have that one song *Tasty Love* a few years ago." Remembering, "Oool child—yeah I definitely remember that one. ...Of course that was before I was saved and all," she adds with a bit of humor.

"That is he."

"He's fine!"

"Can ya even say that?" Justin, now feeling a tad inadequate, refers to her Christian beliefs.

"Why not? I'm saved—not blind!" she says, chuckling at her response. "AAAAAAAAAH!" She starts screaming. "WE DID IT! I CAN'T BELIEVE IT! GIRL WE DID IT!" Then the phone drops.

Justin can hear the sound of jubilation in the backdrop. She picks the phone up. "Hey, let me call you right back—I have your number on my call ID—okay?" Her excitement is evident.

"Yeah, that's cool. Bye." As soon as he closes his cell, the resonance of beeping horns and popping firecrackers fill the air. From upstairs, Damian and Bernard rejoice in victory as the city celebrates their Southside heroes. Chicago wins the pennant!

Uninterested, Justin ignores the commotion and figures it's as good of a time as any to check on Tae. He reopens his phone—punches in her speed dial code and seconds later her line is ringing. She answers—her voice practically inaudible as she was sound asleep. She perks up, realizing it's Justin on the other end.

"*Auuugh*," Tae stretches. "Hello dear. What time is it?" she says, still groggy.

"Late."

"So, what's goin' on?" She yawns during the question.

"You. I jus wanted to say goodnight and make sure everything is alight. By the way, did I mention how sexy you sound when you're sleepy?"

"Aaah, that's sweet Jay. Although not very original—but I thank ya for the compliment anyway." Tae sarcastically adds—being one to never leave well enough alone. "Y'all still in the studio?"

"Hell yeah," he says, chuckling after his reply.

"*What?* What's funny?"

"Jerome. He 'bout dun went off on Arius's sorry ass. Triflin' bastard ain't hittin' on shit. …Bunch of damn hype. All this damn time—and we ain't recorded shit! Best believe I'ma make sure we recoup all recording costs right out his damn royalty check—straight off the top! …Now play wit me!"

Tae laughing, says, "So, what's he in there doin'?"

"Jus fuckin' up! Wastin' my damn time—cause he can't get his shit together!" Justin's wired antics have Shantel in tears—laughing hysterically she tries to talk.

"I can see Jerome's face now. …Lookin' all fruity-faced. I know he's pissed." She sniffles from all her crying.

"Hell yeah—you ain't said shit. That muthafucka is mad! That's why I'm talkin' to ya now. Nigga was so frustrated he told everybody ta take ten!"

"*Nooo*—stop lying! For real?"

"Yep! Besides man—the damn city is in pandemonium. Them White Sox dun won the damn championship. ...You don't hear all that racket? All them damn horns and shit?"

"Jay, you know me—I sleep like a rock. I don't be hearin' a damn thing—you know that." And as she completes her thought, Justin's other line starts beeping.

"Hold on girl, let me get this." He clicks over. "Hello?"

"Hey there! I'm calling you back. Are you busy?" It's Natalie returning their earlier interrupted call. "If you are I'll jus talk to ya later." she says, not pressing the issue.

"Naw—naw. Jus let me get off this otha line. Won't be but a second—hold on." He clicks back over. "Tae baby—I gotta get this one. Let me call you back. Better yet—I'll jus talk to ya in the morning—al-ight?"

"No. Call me back! I'll be up waitin'. So make sure you call me back."

"Al-ight! I'll call ya afterwhile. Bye!" He once again clicks over to Natalie. "You still there?"

"Yyyeeesss," as she drags her words.

"I'm glad ya called back. I was jus thinkin' 'bout cha."

"Really. And thinkin' what?"

"How much I really enjoyed our time together today. It was definitely liberating. It's been a minute since I had that much fun—ya know? Your conversation—sense of humor... The fact that you actually *listen*. The whole package was jus really nice. Thank you."

"Well, it was the same for me. You're a nice guy. And I had a wonderful time. I thank you—for being so kind and considerate. You were such a gentleman. And you jus don't know how much I appreciate that. Some of the men ya run across these days—I'm telling ya—they're a mess."

"And so wit that being said—when can we do it again?"

"Let me check my schedule. I know my daughter will be with her father this weekend—if he does what he said. I won't hold my breath on that one though. But let's jus see how it all plays out and maybe we can get together Saturday night—if that's good for you?"

"Hell yeah! Whatever. I know how ta make concessions. ...Maybe rearrange a thing or two."

"Oh really?" She observes how Justin spits game. "Ya don't say. You're quite the smooth talker—aren't ch'ou?"

"*Huh?* What are ya talkin' 'bout?"

"Nuthin'. Jus runnin' my mouth." she says, opting not to reveal her hand.

"Yeah right—but anyway… So what time do ya have ta go in tomorrow?"

"Aaah—I'm goin' to try and make it in around seven-thirty or eight… The closer to the weekend the busier the shop is. And I have a few customers that like ta pop in early."

"I would assume so—y'all got it goin' on down there. When it comes ta hair that's all ya hear 'bout—Shear Magic. Ya girl Tracie dun tapped into sumptin'."

"Yeah she's smart—*very resourceful*, good ta work for…"

He cuts in. "Hey, I meant ta ask you this the otha day. How cool are you and Alexus?"

"We're okay. We hung out a few times—that's about it. With Alexus you jus have ta know her. *Why?* "

"I was jus wonderin' how close y'all were. I guess tryin' ta make the connection. Y'all two don't seem… What's the word I'm lookin' fo? …Compatible maybe? Ya know what I'm sayin'?"

"I know exactly what you sayin'. And you're right I have to keep my distance. 'Be ye in the world—but not of it'." Her biblical reference goes straight over Justin's head. Again his phone beeps.

"Nat, hold on a second I need ta click over."

"Okay."

From his cell's call waiting caller ID—he sees that it's Tae. "What's up girl?"

"Thought you were suppose ta call me back. Ya still on the otha line?"

"*Yep!* Whatcha need?"

"I can't sleep… Who ya talkin' to?"

"*Why?* " she asks, being insistently nosy.

"Jackie!" He lies to keep her from saying anything more.

"Tell her to call you back!"

"Naw. She's tellin' me sumptin' 'bout Justice."

"Oh, in that case—go ahead. How's he doin'?" she says, satisfied with his reason.

"He's straight. But I'll talk to ya tomorrow." he says as he tries to hurry her off the line.

"*Well bye!* "

He clicks back over. "Yeaaah—now what were we talkin' 'bout?" Justin speaks but there's no one there to respond—just dead air as he

242

himself is now on hold. Meanwhile, he sits waiting—having totally forgotten where he is, the faint sound of music seeps through the ceiling. "*Damn.* They dun started without me." He ends the call, and then dials Natalie right back. She answers, apologizing.

"I'm sorry. I didn't mean to have you on hold for so long. Say, can we talk tomorrow? I'm still on the otha line."

And with no other choice, he agrees, "Sure. I'll call ya tomorrow. You and your daughter have a good night."

"You too—bye." She quickly clicks over.

Justin runs upstairs. He stops by the kitchen to grab a beer before heading back into the studio. With his mind now off business—he can hardly wait until Saturday!

twenty-nine

Forgotten Kisses

With the street lights illuminating the dust flurry of falling snow, Justin and Natalie, on this cold brisk November night, walk hand in hand along the city's famous North Pier. As the flakes begin to cover the ground, Justin talks about having never played in snow while Natalie vividly replays her days as a child—making snowmen, and having snowball fights with her brothers. Both bundled from head to toe, stop to enjoy the view of Lake Michigan. They celebrate their kindling relationship by expressing their innermost feeling towards each other.

"You know what?" Justin, now facing Natalie, speaks determined, yet very gentle.

"What?" she softly speaks as she peers into his serious eyes.

"I really like you." He removes a leather glove to touch flesh to flesh by carefully caressing her cheek with the back of his fingers. "And I wanna get this right. I've enjoyed us—and everything 'bout us ova these last three weeks. And it's like I've been reborn. Jus when I wanted to give up on life you breathed fresh air into this tired old soul. ...I'm alive again! And I so sincerely thank you fo allowin' me to be a part of your life. You don't know how much that means to me. You actually saved me. …I truly believe that." He pours his heart out.

With a tearful smile, she responds with poignant words. "Baby—as much as I would love to take credit for that—I can't! I know you probably won't understand all that I'm sayin' but—baby it's no accident you and I. …It's not luck or some chance coincidence. It's God baby—he's predestined everything! This time, this place—our hearts… For the first time in a long time, I am finally able to again open myself to someone. …Trusting again to give my heart—that shattered piece of me to a man—*you*." Pointing an index finger at herself, she reaches across to then touch Justin on the left side of his chest directly against his pounding heart. "And He's brought two needy hearts together for a time such as this. I really like you too Justin…" Justin doesn't give her the chance to say another word before planting a soft sensual kiss upon her thin moist lips. Caught by surprise, Natalie, while fully into the moment—eagerly accepts his expression of affection. The rest of her body hesitates—slow to respond, not knowing how to handle the temptation. This display of passion goes against her every belief—breaking her every rule. And as a child of God—a new creature in Christ, she's ill-equipped and ill-prepared to face the reality of own her feelings. She gives in, invoking God for help. As they slowly pull apart—her eyes still closed and saliva generously mounted around her mouth, she, with her knitted glove wipes away the dampness upon her lips.

Justin, lavishing himself in the taste of her succulent tongue mutters, "I've almost forgotten how good that can feel." Natalie smiles, resting her slim 5'10" frame against his solid 6'1" body. They embrace as she's overwhelmed and without words. "Are you al-ight?" He speaks out of concern. And with a simple nod, she expresses her secured sanity. "C'mon let me take you home." She agrees, and they leave the isolated pier, again walking hand in hand—arms swinging.

He takes her back to her Austin Avenue Westside address. Fortunately, Natalie lives in the more decent—and preferable section of the street where a Currency Exchange and Baptist church reside in eye's view.

A thin blanket of snow has covered the streets, and it's obvious by Justin's creeping travels that he's not used to driving in these hazardous conditions. While Natalie offers to take the wheel, his pride will not relinquish the honor. He even goes as far as to teasingly question her driving capabilities having not seen her ever once behind a steering wheel. She puts his insecurities to rest by explaining the sob story of her 96' Taurus GL—purchased by her baby's daddy and taken back upon their split which was more than two years ago.

"What an asshole! Didn't he think 'bout his daughter?" he says, voicing his opinion.

"Humph. That's what I said. But ya know how y'all men are… Afraid I was goin' to have anotha brotha ridin' in something he brought. Anyway, God gave me two feet and of course the CTA. And we've managed this far—so we won't complain." Justin pulls along side another parked car in front of her apartment and turns on his hazards. Natalie redirects him a spot about four cars down, "Grab that park there!" as she points to the vacant space. Justin obeys and once in the space, Natalie turns to Justin—squinting one eye, she rattles off an opposing question, "If I ask you to stay tonight—you won't be expectin' anything more—will ya? And you know exactly what I mean!" Peering out her passenger side window, she observes the falling flakes. "But I'd hate for you to have to drive home in all this."

Justin, who's only ever gone as far as the front door, is quick to accept her offer and terms. "I'll be a good boy—I promise!"

"Let me see your fingers." She looks to see if they're crossed.

"See!" He exposes spread fingers. "What? You wanna see my toes now?" he remarks with an asinine grin.

"Shut-up." She leads him inside the aged vestibule and upstairs to her apartment. They enter the quaint two bedroom second floor flat. With the lights in the living room having been left on, Justin examines the many pictures on the walls. He's—until this day, seen only dated wallet shots of Asia as now he witnesses the abundant homage is paid to her only child. Justin walks up to one picture in particular sitting prominently on a shelf on the entertainment center just above the television.

"Is this him?"

"That's him—my baby's daddy, Christopher Mariq Richardson. The one—the only."

"Nice lookin' guy. Is he a model or sumptin'?" Justin holds the picture in his hand, comparing the genetic similarities of Chris and his daughter posed side by side.

"*Please.* He'd love that. Conceited bastard! …Lord forgive me." She chuckles. "When I think about all he's put us through, it jus makes my blood boil." She grimaces then makes her way to the kitchen. "How about some Cocoa ta warm ya up?"

"Please. Thank you." He continues to investigate her dwelling. Soon he runs across another framed point of interest. A diploma from the Cornelia School of Cosmetology—Class of 98' awarded to one Natalie Nicole Broussard. "So, your middle name is Nicole?"

"Don't tell no one?" she says, ashamed of the name.

"Naw, it's funny, I always said if I was ta have a daughter I would name her Nicole—Nicole Brittany."

"*Really?* I woulda figured you for a Shaquita—or Darneisha or something." She brings to him the promised mug of Hot Cocoa.

"Oh, so whatcha try'na say—I'm ghetto?"

"Not necessarily by appearance—but definitely by the way you speak. I've always assumed it was because of the people you surround yourself with—especially dealin' with all those music folks. All that filth has corrupted your mind."

"So now we got ta be baggin' on my job—huh?" Though laughing, he gets defensive.

"I wanted to ask you something for awhile now. But I'm kinda afraid of how you might take it the wrong way."

"*What?* Don't beat 'round the bush. By all means, speak your mind." he says, as he claims to be approachable.

"Come to church with me Sunday."

Grinning and giggling, Justin squirms at the thought of setting foot in a church—especially for something other than a funeral. "Does it have ta be this Sunday?" he says, procrastinating, in hopes that maybe she'll forget.

"Pleeease?" She uses her female persuasion to get what she wants by delivering a quick peck to the cheek.

Sighing he says, "Well, I guess if that'll make ya happy."

"Thank you baby!" His extorted consent has made her night. And now she's ready to end the day on a good note as she prepares the couch for Justin. Not being able to touch is one thing, but sleeping in another bed—in a separate room wasn't exactly what he had in mind. Yet having gained leaps and bounds in other areas of the relationship, he takes it all in stride, clutching his pillow and wrapping himself tight in a Korean quilt. He soon falls asleep.

♡   ♡   ♡

Bright and early that next morning, awoken from his dream-filled slumber by a kiss to the forehead, Justin opens his crust-stuck eyes to see a vibrant Natalie looming over him. With no makeup and her hair combed down and feathered, she stands in a one piece silk lavender gown—her spaghetti straps covered by the matching robe. "Baby get up—I wanna show you something."

Justin sits straight up, having slept in his tee shirt and plaid boxers. He twists his back from side to side, doing the same with his stiff neck. "What's up?" He stretches.

"Come look." She stands by a window peeking through the mini-blinds of her sunroom.

Justin, crowding over her shoulder, peers outside at the beautiful view of snow covered sidewalks, yards, trees and homes. The urban backdrop now takes on the serenity and peace of the Catskills in the winter. "That's pretty."

"Get your clothes on baby. Let's go outside."

"You're serious?"

"As a heart attack—c'mon! …The last one ready buys breakfast." She sprints to her bedroom, locking the door.

"*Heeey*—no fair. Can I at least get a rag ta wash my ass please?" he asks as he's left with no towel or wash cloth or hygiene products to freshen up with. A minute later, her door partially opens, offering a new white towel set, bar of Irish Spring soap, an unopened soft bristle toothbrush, and a tube of Crest toothpaste. He takes the goodies from his bare armed host who immediately retracts her disrobed limbs to close and lock the door. "Thank you!" But before he retreats to the guest bathroom in the hallway, he poses a spontaneous question. "Say—ya wouldn't happen to be standing behind that door naked—would'cha?"

"Hush. Go get ready!" she echoes through the sealed door.

"Al-ight. Jus wishful thinkin'." Dragging to his destination, he mumbles to himself "*Shit*—it neva hurts ta ask though."

Not even fifteen minutes has gone by, and already at the bathroom door pounds an impatient Natalie. "Hurry up slow poke! The snow will be dun melted by the time *you* get finished. Lord… You worse than a woman." She pounds the door some more.

Unlike other women, Natalie doesn't waste much time in preparation. But then again she doesn't have to, as what you see is what you get—a testament to her natural beauty. Justin opens the door to find Natalie standing there—hands on her hips and rolling her eyes. "Are you ready?"

He chuckles, "Yeah, I guess." And he's thinking, "She a trip." as he's yet to catch her uncoordinated. Baby blue suede snow boots, faded blue jeans, baby blue Perry Ellis bubble jacket, baby blue scarf, mittens, and hood with the attached knit ball. "Damn!" He imagines her closet. Better yet, her bedroom as there's no way in hell she could have room for anything other than clothes and shoes. From the bathroom counter he grabs his keys—she grabs hers from the kitchen as they go outside. But before Justin can get out the door good—Natalie attempts to clobber him with a snowball. "Oh shit! …Two can play that game homegirl." Justin grabs a wad of snow and takes off after her.

"*AAAAAAH!* Justin quit!" Natalie runs away screaming. Jumping steps, she makes her way down the slippery sidewalk where it isn't long after that she loses her balance, falling face first to the ground. Justin drops his snow and charges to help her. From where he stood—the force of impact could have caused serious injury.

"Natalie baby—you al-ight?" And he's not laughing as he crouches beside her panicked. "Say sumptin' baby!" he says, turning her on her back.

"Gotcha!" She startles Justin who slips back, landing on his butt. She sits up—her front covered in snow, just laughing and clapping as she flicks snow in Justin's face, adding insult to injury. Soon both are laughing as Justin returns the favor with an unpacked snowball to Natalie's nose.

After dusting each other off—Justin asks, "So, where are we goin' ta eat?"

"To Division and Karlov. There's a lil' ma and pa diner I wanna take you to."

"Cool!" Justin reaches in his pocket and tosses Natalie the keys.

"*Whhhat.* You trust me wit your baby?"

"*Huh.* Somebody might need ta take my temperature—cause I must be sick. Fo real!" Justin makes an exception to his "look but don't touch" rule concerning women and his car. She proves his preconceived notions by gunning the car out of the park and into the street, causing the vehicle to hydroplane slightly but beating the coming traffic behind her. "*Shhhit.*" He can't do nothing but shake his head and pray.

The conversation on the way over to the restaurant thickens as Justin brings up a crucial topic—their children. "I was wonderin'? How come you ain't introduced me to Asia yet? I mean, I thought we were tryin' ta do something."

"So, tell me Justin—what are *we* trying to do?" she asks, wanting his words to be spelled out.

"C'mon nah—ya know what I'm sayin'?"

"No, I don't—so tell me."

"Hell, I thought we were workin' on bein' together in a relationship. I mean, that's the impression I got. But I don't know…"

"Well—first of all, I'm glad at least we're on the same page. Othawise I wouldn't be sittin' here wasting my time. …I've done enough of that. Secondly—until now, we never really defined our relationship. And I can't read your mind, so how was I to know what you were wanting—or thinking? I couldn't!" She hesitates for a second to get her thoughts straight. "But as of right now—I can't afford to put my daughter through anything else that's not real. And see, her father has been in and out of her life several times like a revolving door. …And ta be honest, in the past I allowed men to come and go sometimes between and during the times when he was there. I knew it was wrong, but I also knew where we'd end up. But he kept telling me that it was going to be different—and I kept listenin'. But nuthin' ever changed—and so my precious pooh became the one true victim in all of that. Justin baby—I dig ya… But until I know—that I know—that I know, without any doubt that this is for real… you won't be exposed to her—and that's jus me being honest."

Justin, who doesn't quite know how to respond, remains quiet. She has a valid point and he knows it. Of course it doesn't make him feel any better, but in all actuality, he understands. "So now what? …Where do we go from here? I mean, are we jus spinnin' our wheels?" What were once clear and sunny skies have become cloudy and gloomy in his mind. His natural high has been reduced to a sobering low.

"Well—it's really up to you. I just explained to you how I felt. Now what do you wanna do? And since we're on the subject… What about you and your son? I know you thought about it. He's just lost his mother. And now here I am. So, what do *you* say? I don't think it's fair to jus throw me in his face 'Son, here's your mother's replacement'. So how do you handle that?"

"I mean, I don't know. I'll cross that bridge when I get to it." He shrugs his shoulders.

"You'll cross that bridge when you get to it," she sneers. "Isn't your son moving up here after the Christmas break? I guess I wasn't that far into your plans…?"

"Look—let's back up. Ya know this Tuesday I'm driving down to Atlanta to bring him here for Thanksgiving. I think we should use that time to test the waters so ta speak. Let's get together wit the kids and jus do sumptin'—anything. …I wanna do this. So, whatever it takes—I'll do it. Al-ight?"

"Okay. Well, maybe I have an idea. My brother, Stevie, is having a big dinner at his house. …Always plenty of people, so how about if I invite you and your son…"

"…And my brother and his girl." Justin makes sure to add Jerome and Monique to the invitation list.

"Okay—all of you to share dinner with my family. Like you said… Test the waters—especially not knowing how the babies will take to each other."

"Yeah, that jus-might-work." Pondering, he strokes through his five o' clock shadow.

❤ ❤ ❤

12:43pm

Justin returns home. Jerome, still in town finishing his part on Arius's album, sits on the couch with a pair of headphones over his ears as he taps beats on his Akai MPC 4000. The TV is on—but the sound is on mute.

"What's up dude?" Justin puts his keys and coat down on the ottoman.

Jerome removes the headphones, "Yo."

"Ya see all that snow? …Funny ain't it?" He and Jerome, being Georgia natives, are unaccustomed to seeing snow.

"I know. Last night I figured your ass was out somewhere stuck in it." Jerome remarks about his brother's overnight disappearance.

"Almost—shit! I ended up stayin' ova at Natalie's. …She was worried 'bout a nigga."

"Word."

"Monique gets in tomorrow—right?"

"Yep—one o' clock. I need ta confirm our hotel reservations right quick while I'm thinkin' 'bout it."

"*Maaan*—now ya know ya ain't got ta do all that. Y'all can stay right here. There's plenty of room."

"We appreciate that man—but ya know how it is. Ain't seen my boo in almost a month. You know… Gotta make up fo some lost time bro."

"I hear ya man—but the offer still stands. So, what did ch'all have planned fo Thanksgiving?"

"I'm not sure. We ain't decided yet. Probably jus kick it at one of them restaurants. The Westin or sumptin'."

"Well, if y'all are up fo some home cookin', we're all invited ova ta Natalie's brother's house ta eat."

"They don't know us man. ...You met em'?" Jerome, being very skeptical.

"Naw—but Nat said it's cool."

"I don't know 'bout that man. We should jus all go out and eat. ...Baby boy will be up here too. Ya know what I'm sayin'?"

"Yeah but she said it was cool though man." Justin tries to convince his brother otherwise.

"That's y'all's thang dude. I said what we gonna do." He is adamant about his decision. "Yo, I wasn't goin' ta say nuthin', but I jus gotta ask man. Do you have a problem wit being alone or sumptin'?"

Justin looking confused, "Why ya ask that?"

"Cause man—what maybe three weeks ago ya were still grieving ova Teresha. And now—miraculously this new chick is all that! C'mon man! ...What is ya doin'? It ain't right man—you rushin' shit! And I don't know why." He pauses, "And what 'bout Justice? It ain't fair ta him. How ya gonna bring him up here without jus you and him havin' spent any time together? Then throw this bitch in his face..."

"Rome—her name is Natalie man." Justin feeling disrespected by his brother.

"So what! All I know is ya fuckin' up! I can't even talk to ya right now." Pissed, Jerome goes to puts his headphones back on but stops to add to his already inflamed opinion. "Man, ya need ta check yo'self! Stop and think sometime... You ain't in this by yo'self anymore—remember that!"

Heated, Justin retorts, "Oh, so I don't have the right ta be happy anymore—is that whatcha sayin'?" Yet in the back of his mind he takes heed to the fact that he's basically heard the same comment twice concerning Justice.

"You know that's not what I mean."

"Look man—I loved Teresha with all-my-heart. And I planned ta spend the rest of my life wit her—no doubt! But that's not goin' ta happen. ...I know that now. And yet wit Natalie, I've neva grown so close—so fast wit anyone like I have wit her. I mean and it's jus been wit conversation..."

"Jay, listen ta yo'self man. You ain't even slept wit the girl and already tryin' ta spend yo life wit her. Be honest wit yo'self man...

How are *you* gonna maintain a relationship where there's no sex involved?" Jerome laughs. "Whatcha ya smokin' bro? C'mon, when have *you* ever stayed in a relationship where sex ain't the primary factor?" Justin remains quiet. "That's all I'm sayin'. Think 'bout what you're doin'." Jerome picks up his MPC and goes into the guest bedroom.

Justin plops down on the couch. Drained, frustrated, and confused, he starts second-guessing himself about everything. He recalls the many conversations he and his momma would have. Even in her dying days, she was always his rock—and his comforter. In that hospital—on her death bed, the talks they would have about life and making the right choices. How he now yearns for her presence. "Mama, what am I doin'?" He throws his head back and closes his eyes.

♡　　♡　　♡

Sunday morning.

After a wake up call from Natalie reminding him about church, he thumbs through his closet in search of what he feels is the appropriate suit. A nervous anxiety creeps into his system; he's always avoided church like a bad habit—especially as an adult. To be honest, he's afraid of the truth. And being well aware of how he's lived—and still lives, he runs from the condemnation of his lifestyle. The excuses come easy, "Church folks are hypocrites. They sin as much as anyone else. Always judgin' folks for the same shit they do in the dark." The reasons can be numerous, but the bottom line always equates to one common factor—the fear of being exposed.

The ride to Natalie's apartment is slow as Justin prolongs the inevitable. Hoping for a miracle, he takes the longest route possible. His wish goes unfulfilled as he arrives at her front door—where evidently she'd been watching from her sunroom window. She meets Justin at the car.

"Baby, what took you so long? We're almost late." Rushing, Natalie settles in and buckles her seat belt.

"Hell, I was tryin' ta find sumptin' ta wear." he says, sounding serious.

In disbelief, Natalie just looks at him. "Not Mr. GQ. I'm pretty sure you have a different suit for everyday of the year."

"Okay—*whatever*. So how do we get to where we're goin'?"

"Easy. It's a straight shot. Stay on Austin until we get to Oak Park. You'll see the church on your left." She takes out a brown Cover Girl pencil—and pulling down Justin's sun visor for the mirror, she applies

253

the Liner to her lips—outlining the outer edge. She then follows with a wet look sand colored gloss to fill in the rest. She turns to Justin, "How does this look?"

And with one glance, his dick swells. "Damn—you look good! But ain't it a bit much fo church?" he asks, referring also to her hazel contacts and large gold hoops.

"Well, we know you haven't been to church in a while. Times have changed baby. This ain't grandma's church! I'm pretty sure you'll like Faith Fellowship. It's anything but traditional."

"*I forgot.* …Won't cha be doin' the sign language stuff?" he says while thinking that he's probably going to be left sitting alone during the service while she does her thing.

"Normally I would—but I called my girl Neicy last night and told her that I was bringing a guest—so I asked her to take my spot today. I wouldn't do you like that baby. I'll be right there with you." And with a sweet smirk, she reassures an apprehensive Justin.

In no time, the church appears in plain view. Justin turns into the huge parking facility. The church itself—with the grounds and two or three adjoining buildings, nearly takes up an entire city block. To Justin, it looks like one of those mega-churches he's only seen on TV. "This a big ass church!" he says as he looks around in awe.

"Justin—baby, today is Sunday—the Lord's day. Can you please watch your mouth maybe—for me?"

"I'm sorry—my bad!" He walks around to open her door. Taking her hand he helps her out the car. "Yeah girl—I'm likin' what I see."

"Thank ya!" She struts her stuff in a brown pinstriped blazer and duplicate fitted medium length skirt—brown boots with the thick four-inch heel exposing only her stocking covered knees.

"So, where's my kiss?" Justin asks as he shops for a cheap thrill.

"You shoulda got it before I put on my gloss. Now c'mon before we miss the sermon."

From outside the beautiful antique brick structure, the joyous harmony of the Faith Fellowship choir permeates the atmosphere. The hand claps and stomps of the congregation vibrate the ground they stand on. Just by the exterior noise—Justin, experienced in venue crowds, can tell that there's at least a thousand people inside causing him to get even more nervous—more sick on the stomach.

They climb the steep steps, entering the antechamber just outside the sanctuary. Two church mothers first greet Natalie—then Justin, "Praise the Lord Sista Broussard—God bless you young man." The second lady asks Justin, "Is this your first time visiting with us sir?" Her voice is small and cracked.

"Yes ma'am."

The elderly woman hands Justin a visitor sticker to place on his jacket and a program. "Welcome to Faith Fellowship Missionary Baptist Church—hope you come back to see us young man. Enjoy the service." She then shakes his hand. "Thank you." he says, humbled by her hospitality.

Natalie steps in with a late introduction. "Sista Jackson—Sista White, this is my friend Mr. Justin Vaughn, he recently moved here from Atlanta.

"Oooh that's nice sweetie." The first lady speaks.

"How y'all doin'?" Justin addresses the women.

"Just fine young man. I'm blessed and covered in the blood. Ain't that the truth." The two seniors speak respectively. Natalie leads Justin inside. And just as he thought, the massive cathedral boasts a huge inclined orchestra section and balcony easily exceeding a thousand in capacity. Natalie grabs Justin by the hand as a male usher takes them to their seats. As the choir finishes the "Praise and Worship" portion of the service—with many already slain in the spirit, the anointed atmosphere overwhelms Justin. Natalie wastes no time getting involved.

"GGGLLLOOORRRYYY! Glory Jesus!" Standing, she hollers at the top of her lungs—her arms flail back and forth. The choirs sings *Praise Is What I Do* as their animated director breaks down the chorus to a harmonious, "What I do—What I do—What I do…" repeating the phrase over and over. A speaker comes to the mic shouting above the choir's continuing chant.

"Look at your neighbor and say, 'Neighbor—I don't know 'bout *you*—but *I* came to rejoice, I came fo my blessing, I came fo my healing'…" The now frenzied crowd caught amidst sporadic euphoric shouts of "Hallelujah" and "Thank ya Jesus," reacts to the speaker. "I came here today with the spirit of expectancy. God's gonna move in this place! And if you believe God's got something for you. Say *YEEEAH!*

"*YYYEEEAAAHHH!*" The congregation explodes.

"Say *YEEEAH!*" As he repeats.

"*YYYEEEAAAHHH!*"

Natalie now in the spirit, "*Oooh* thank ya Jesus! *Oooh* thank ya Lord!" Her body convulses as tears stream down her face. "Thank ya. HALLELUJAH!" Justin sits stuck to his seat—knees shaking, he's never seen anything like it. He feels something that he can't describe. As Natalie shouts and sobs almost as though she's in pain, Justin—now horrified, remains motionless and feeling helpless.

thirty

Far From Perfect

Marietta, GA.

Some twelve hours and five interstates later, tired but back in familiar surrounding, Justin exits his late model Chrysler in front of Jackie's apartment. He takes a deep breath before knocking. "Tap-tap-tap-tap…" Lightly striking the door he steps back—then looks toward the ground. He can hear Jackie giggling through the door—obviously happy to see him.

"*Heeey* booby!" She anxiously answers. And with a small child still tucked neatly in her arm, she pokes her lips out preparing to receive a long overdue smooch. Justin delivers an arousing sustained kiss—backing Jackie into the apartment.

"What up, what up!" he says as he breaks the exchange.

"Oh nuthin'. Jus glad you're here." Her eyes tell the tale as she stares with lecherous reverence.

"So where is he?" Justin scans the apartment. He's disappointed that his son isn't nearby to welcome him.

"In his room perpetratin'."

"'Bout what?"

"About not bein' excited that you were comin'. …Going to Chicago. The whole bit."

"Fo real? I shoulda figured as much."

"*Yeeeah*. But he's back there."

"Al-ight." Justin makes his way to the once empty space. The door is pushed up but not closed. He knocks while simultaneously entering. He finds his son lying stretched across the bed—Pumas on his feet, headphones attached to his ears as he plays his PSP. Justice pretends to be so involved with his game that he doesn't realize his father is standing there. Justin walks over to the bed—playfully popping his son in the gut.

"Get up and give your father a hug." Justice takes out the budded earpieces—placing them by his side. He sits up to receive his dad. The embrace is nonchalant and unmoved—not the expected show of endearment by a father and son who have been separated for months. Justin does notice however two neatly stacked bags against the wall—a black leather bomber lays next to them. "I miss ya baby boy—what's been goin' on?"

And with an unenthusiastic response, Justice answers, "Not much." It's at this point Justin realizes it's going to be like pulling teeth—he knows he has his work cut out for him. "So, are you ready to hit the road?"

Through a nod, Justice expresses a *yes*.

"Al-ight—well hold up. Let me talk to Jackie to see what she has planned. He heads up front to the living room where Jackie sits feeding an infant—the one she was holding when she answered the door. "Say boo—when are y'all leaving fo Texas."

"Tonight. Whenever Michael brings Shayla back. *Why?*"

"Nah—I'm sayin'… Me and baby boy are 'bout ta get out of here."

"*What?* Uh uh! Now boo, you jus drove how far?" The stupidity in his thinking pisses Jackie off. "Nope. I ain't even try'na hear it! Boy, sit yo ass down somewhere and rest for a while. …Have me runnin' round here all worried. I ain't the one!" She rants like an over protective mother. "In a minute, when his mother gets here, I'll go pick up something ta eat for y'all. So ya might as well go in the room with Justice and lay down!"

Justin doesn't argue, but he does voice his concern for Jackie and Shayla. "What 'bout y'all? Ya ain't tryin' ta leave out here tonight by y'all selves—right? …How far is Houston from here anyway?"

"Needen fret booby. Linda and Vince are going too. But it's about eleven or twelve hours—pretty close to the same drive you have."

"Hell naw! I know ya ain't talkin' 'bout Linda Jarrod."

"The one and the only boo." as she confirms Justin's worst nightmare.

"I know I gotta get da hell outta here now. ...Can't believe ya still fuckin' wit that girl. That chick is crazy!"

She laughs, "You didn't think so when you had your lil' dick stuck all up in her."

"Shit, that was before I knew exactly how crazy that bitch was. So who the fuck is Vince?"

"*Child*... Her latest and greatest."

"He's gotta be a damn fool if you ask me!"

"It slipped my mind but she asked about you the otha day." Jackie then explodes with laughter.

"That shit ain't funny. I don't know if I ever told ya this—but I remember this one particular night she paged my ass 911 real late. Had ta be 'bout one in the morning. Well you know me, I was jus turnin' ova good so I wasn't try'na answer no page—especially from her ass! But she jus kept on paging me every few minutes. So I cut my shit off but then the heifer calls the apartment. Rome, he's sleep and shit, so I answer the phone ta keep from waking him up—right? This muthafucka gets on the phone and starts sayin' some ole crazy shit 'bout she all depressed and shit—and if I don't come ova there she's gonna kill her kids! She's cryin' and gaggin' and shit, talkin' 'bout she gonna leave the gas on, 'cause she can't take it no more—she wanna die and all this psycho shit. And I'm thinkin', 'Oh shit—she crazy— right? So I'm takin' her stupid ass seriously. I go runnin' ova there... Dun left my child in the bed by himself. I get there—and you know what this stupid bitch is doin'?"

Jackie practically in tears humors Justin, "*What?*"

"Sitting on the *damn* couch eatin' muthafuckin' ice cream! Talk about a mad muthafucka—*whoa!* Man, I coulda whooped her muthafuckin' ass right there! But after all that... Needless-ta-say, I wasn't fuckin' wit her ass too tough anymore."

The end of Justin's story sends Jackie over the edge. She's laughing and crying—which takes a minute before she even regains her composure. Wiping her eyes, "I remember that girl use ta love herself some Justin. Callin' me lookin' for you. ...Had me tired—*shit!* Boo, I don't know what ya did to that girl—but she had it bad."

"Yeah, I remember how jealous she was of our relationship. ...I know ya remember that?"

"Uh-uh!" she says, surprised.

"Yep! She ain't want me around you. You were trespassin' on her territory boo!"

"But I knew you before she did. Hell, I was the one who introduced y'all! You were still bringin' Justice around—and I was keepin' her son, Marcus. Y'all met at the door that day bringin' the babies ova. I haven't forgotten that. So how she gonna trip? I coulda had ya whenever I wanted to!" Then being sarcastic she says, "Oh that's right—I did!" There's another hysterical outburst.

Justin, who joins in on the fun, reminds Jackie of his earlier thought, "Still ain't said how y'all got ta talkin' again."

"Long story. But the poor girl called me needing some *dire* expert advice..."

"Expert advice on what?" he asks, sounding skeptical.

"What else? ...Y'all triflin' behind men!"

"Oh, so she came ta you—out the clear blue fo advice?" He finds it a little hard to believe.

"Boy, don't hate!" As Jackie toots her own horn.

"Whatever. But 'um... don't worry 'bout gettin' me and baby boy anything ta eat. I ain't try'na be here when she gets here. So I'ma stretch out fo a minute then we'll be on our way. Know what I'm sayin'? I ain't got time fo her mess."

Jackie, who finds the whole situation amusing, reluctantly agrees. Justin goes to retire to the bedroom with his son. He reenters the room where Justice now lays sideways—propped on his elbow and still on his game. He takes more than his fair share of space.

"Move ova man! Give your old man some room." Justin makes a light-hearted request to share the full sized mattress. Justice obliges, but with contempt as minutes go by before another word is said. Sprawled on his back with his eyes closed, Justin blurts. "So, how ya feel 'bout movin' to Chicago?" Cynicism fills his voice. He releases the culmination of compiled frustrations as he struggles to understand his son's continued hostility. In Justin's mind, while he knows he hasn't lived up to the role of responsible parent—conceding his erratic and inconsistent behavior was a mistake, yet not one worthy of such hardened animosity. He now faces the bridge he dreaded to cross—especially in light of recent developments in his personal life. He realizes there's nowhere to run. "I didn't hear ya. ...So how ya feel 'bout it?" He repeats the question.

"How do you want me to feel 'bout it?" Justice sardonically answers while continuing to play his game. Justin pops up furiously, yanking the Sony console away from his son's unsuspecting hands. "I'm serious— now what's the problem?"

"WHY YA DO THAT?" Justice shouts. "*DAMN!* ...You always messin' everything up!" With bowed chest, he pants in deep breaths. His light complexioned face reddens with malice.

"What do ya mean son?" Justin becomes a voice of soothing reason as he tones down his previous temperament.

Welled with tears, Justice unleashes his vented version of his father's competency as a man. "YOU ALWAYS THINK 'BOUT YO'SELF! Mama was right..." His tears become apparent. "You neva cared 'bout us..." He's overtaken with emotion.

Justin, who can't believe what he's hearing, looks to his hurting child, stunned but with compassion. His son's words echo Teresha's very beliefs. There's a subtle knock at the door. "Yeah!" as he bellows in reply.

"Y'all alright in there?" A worried Jackie, having heard Justice's heated comments, awaits some confirmation of peace.

"Yeah—we straight." Justin calmly answers with a hint of anguish.

"Are you sure?" Jackie chuckles slightly sensing Justin's distress.

"Yep."

"Alrighty then—if ya say so." she says as she goes about her business. The discussion picks up.

"Baby, why are you sayin' that? I'm not understandin'. Where's all this comin' from? I know what I did in the past—and I explained how so-very-sorry I was. I thought we were past that. I mean, I thought I reconciled everything wit you—and your mother. And now I'm hearin' all this! I don't get it son."

"Then why am I here Dad—and not wit you?"

He responds with a deep sigh, "Cause I thought I was doin' the right thing. ...It's stable here son! I knew Jackie would do a wonderful job providing all those things I felt you deserved." Justin places a hand on his son's shoulder. 'I mean—I know how hard it's been and I didn't want to take anything else away from you. I thought that being here would at least allow ya ta keep some sense of home—know what I mean? Even though I know ya had ta change schools but I also knew ya would still have your friends. Plus wit Jackie and Shayla both being here *everyday*... I knew ya wouldn't be alone. Baby, you know how I work. You know how hectic my job can be. I don't know where I might be from one minute to the next. I don't want that for you—at least not right now. ...I thought we talked about this—I thought it was understood. ...It's not a permanent arrangement son—you're comin' up there ta be wit me. I'm not jus try'na stick you somewhere 'cause it seems more convenient! That wasn't my intention baby."

"But I don't wanna be here. Can't you see I'm still alone even *here!* It's like I'm an orphan wit both my parents dead." He continues to sob. "Why can't I be wit you? If you really loved me—then I would be wit you!" Justice turns his head to avoid facing his father. Justin hesitates before uttering another word as he begins to realize where exactly he went wrong. It's through all his material acts of giving where he actually thought he was being a "good dad—a cool dad". Never once has he ever disciplined Justice—or ever said anything that might create conflict between he and his son. Gifts and trips became his way of expressing love—relieving the personal guilt of not being there for his family. And somewhere along the way, he missed what really mattered most—his cherished presence.

"So, that's whatcha want?" Justin looks to his son with an explicit sternness. Justice cuts an eye towards his father, wanting deeply to say *"yes,"* but his inherited stubbornness prohibits such an easy surrendering. "It's a simple question—with an obvious answer son."

"So, why ya askin'?" the cocky teen retorts.

Justin grins—then smirks, "Okay I guess I walked into that. But alight... That's it—it's done! Get the rest of your shit together—you're goin' to Chicago fo' good!" In his spontaneous solution, Justin, who has yet to work out the specific details such as school records and extended care if he needs to travel, vows—on this day, to never again neglect the needs of his son.

thirty-one

To Whom It May Concern

Thanksgiving morning.

An exhausted Justin collapses across his bed—still dressed, as his snoring wakes his son in the next room. The journey up and right back has taken its toll. Justice, having slept through the bulk of the trip, wanders around his new surroundings. And now, for better or worst, ready or not—he's here! It all sinks in as he peeks out the twelfth floor living room window. While all is still not well between the two of them, deep down he knows he's been unfair to his father. He acknowledges that the hurt and disappointment he feels is much in the same as what swirls inside his dad. As Justice walks the dull uninspired space—lacking the usual vibrant flair of his father, he realizes the emptiness his dad feels. "I'm sorry Dad." An empathic Justice apologizes to an audience of one.

11:28am

Justin staggers from the bedroom holding his back and walking stiff legged like Fred G. Sanford. He catches Justice on the couch eating a bowl of Fruity Pebbles. "Ya coulda woke me up ya know." Scratching, he takes a seat next to his son.

"I didn't want ta bother ya. ...As loud as you were snoring, I figured ya needed the rest." He pokes an innocent jab in on his old man.

"Was I that loud?" Justice just looks at his father—and without a word both burst into laughter, "I guess so—huh?" Justin rubs affectionately through baby boy's unbraided afro. "Start gettin' ready, your Uncle Rome and Monique should be here 'round one."

"Where we eatin'?" he asks, being curiously concerned as he shovels a serving spoon full of cereal in his mouth.

"Oh don't worry—we gotcha covered."

"Baked macaroni and cheese—and broccoli casserole?"

"I guess so. Shit—I hope so." He gets up to call Jackie's cell—make sure she's made it in alright. He wishes her and Shayla a happy thanksgiving and thanks her once again for everything. Justice's premature departure has thrown Jackie for an unexpected loop. Baby boy had been her lil' man of the house—a big help, especially concerning Shayla. His presence will be missed. After their brief conversation, Justin immediately follows with a quick call to Natalie. He dips to his bedroom to be discreet. "Hey baby—Happy Thanksgiving!"

"Thank you—and you too. So how was the trip? I know you're about ta pass out."

"Been there—dun that one, but I'm cool though. Are we still on for later today?"

"Yeah—of course, if you're up to it."

"Yep!" He pauses. "Yo—we really need ta talk later too." His tone is resolute.

"Why? What's goin' on? I hate for someone ta do me like that. Don't sound all serious and not tell the whole story. I hate that!"

He chuckles, "Naw, it's nuthin' like that. There's jus been a slight change of plans... Justice is here ta stay. He ain't goin' back!"

"What happened?"

"We talked. And he doesn't want ta be there anymore. Said he rather be here."

"Are you ready for that?"

"No. But I might as well be. 'Cause he's here—right? I may need your help though. ...You know more 'bout Chicago than I do. I'ma take a few days off after the holiday ta get everything situated—but I need ta get him registered for school next week. That's my first priority…"

"I'll call Tracie tomorrow and tell her I won't be in on Monday—so she can fill that chair."

"Naw—don't do that. I appreciate it—but I got it! That's your livelihood and I ain't tryin' ta interfere wit that. That's really sweet though. If anything—help me wit maybe findin' out 'bout the school system. I haven't had ta deal wit that stuff. Gotta find out what I need—and which school is in our district. And I know ya know how all that works—so…"

"That's why I'm goin' to take the day off silly. And I don't wanna hear anything else about it!"

"Al-ight—ya know whatcha doin'. I thank ya though. So what time we gettin' together?"

"Four. *'Mama. I don't wanna wear this. …It's ugly!'* Augh—this child, she gets on my last nerve! Ya still got the directions?"

"Yes ma'am. Now go handle your business."

"I guess we'll see ya then."

"Yep—*byyye!*" He smirks.

"Bye!" Natalie places the handset of her cordless phone down—redirecting her attention to a disgruntled Asia. "You know betta than ta interrupt me while I'm on the phone! I'm not playin' witcha gurl!" She boisterously warns her ill-mannered daughter.

"But Mama—I'm not wearin' that!"

"Why? What's wrong wit it?" She walks over to Asia, picking up each piece—one after the other. "It's a skirt—and a blouse! …*What?* Ya think you're goin' ta wear that ole' tight tacky mess all up in yo butt? *NO MA'AM!* Not here—not under this roof!" Asia mumbles something under her breath. Natalie immediately responds. "*What?* I didn't hear ya. …Repeat that!"

"Why I couldn't go wit my daddy today?" A defiant Asia speaks her mind.

Visibly upset, Natalie settles herself, "I don't know Asia." She picks up the phone. "Call him—see what excuse he gives ya this time." She stands in the middle of the floor—her arm extended toward Asia, holding the handset.

Asia reluctantly takes the phone and dials the number. The pale expressionless look on her face tells the entire story. She holds the receiver for a second before embarrassingly having to lay it back down on the table. As usual she gets only an automated message.

❤❤ ❤❤ ❤❤

1:20pm

Jerome and Monique arrive at the condo rushing. Based on Monique's suggestion, Jerome has booked a two o' clock reservation at the luxurious "Signature Room" atop the John Hancock Center—95 stories above the city.

Unlike the lukewarm reception given to his father at Jackie's, Justice races to greet his uncle at the door. "*Yooo*—what up, what up!" As Jerome says hello to his nephew, the two meet in a causal embrace.

"Hey Unc. Hey Monique."

"Hey baby." Monique kisses Justice on the forehead, leaving just a hint of her cherry lipstick.

"Guess what Unc?"

"What's that?"

"I'm stayin'. I'm not goin' back!" Justice's zeal is finally revealed.

"*Whuuut.*" Jerome acts surprised though his brother has already told him. Hours earlier the two talked while Justin journeyed back from Atlanta with baby boy lying right beside him sound asleep. "Lil' man— you ain't gonna be able ta handle all this cold weather."

"Ah-hmmm. Watch!" he says, accepting his uncle's challenge.

"Naw, you can't hang. Jay, betta tell this boy! Whatcha gonna do when it's five below and the wind chill makes it feel like it's fifty below—*say?* And y'all right on the lake too. ...Ssshit!" Jerome laughs. "Snot freezin' on your lips... Whatcha gonna do? They don't close schools 'round here fo shit! Tell 'em Jay! Rain, sleet, or snow—best believe you'll be right there!" Jerome taunts his nephew.

"Lil' man, don't listen ta that crap. You a Vaughn! That means ain't no punks up in here! It's all in the mind baby boy. Don't let nobody tell ya any different. ...Jus all in the mind," Justin says, as he protects his son from Jerome's silly mind games.

"Yeah—believe that if ya want to. Jus wait until ya lil' nuts freeze standing outside waitin' fo the bus. You'll see!"

"Rome!" Monique calls out—reminding Jerome that Justice is still just a child. Both father and uncle laugh while baby boy grins uncomfortably.

"Let's bounce y'all!" Jerome makes the round up call to head out. "I know we ain't the only noncookin' mo-fo's in the Chi—so we might wanna hurry up." And as Monique and Justice walk ahead, Jerome hangs back while Justin locks the door. He lightly tugs on his brother's

266

cashmere sweater—lowering his voice, "Jay—y'all still gonna do that?" he asks, referring to dinner at Natalie's brother's.

"Yeah we supposed to. What's sup?"

"Nuthin'—jus hoped maybe ya thought 'bout what we discussed. I think ya should reconsider man—especially considerin' how things have gone so far wit you and baby boy."

"I thought 'bout it—but he'll be al-ight. Right now she's jus a friend—know what I'm sayin'?"

Jerome, smirking with skepticism says, "If ya say so." Which of course he doesn't agree—but what else can he really say. It's Justin's call.

"Man, don't do that!" He senses his brother's changing attitude.

"Do what?"

"Oh you know nigga… Make that face! Everytime we don't vibe on sumptin' that's what you do! Throw up that cocky ass smirk! You do it all the time!" Justin shakes his head. *"Maaan*—it may not seem like it, but we know what we're doin'. She's practically in the same boat wit her lil' girl. …We know ta take it slow." He does his best to reassure Jerome's doubts.

"Whatever man. Like I said—that's yo thang! I dun said what I had ta say. So it's squashed!" The two clashing siblings walk the hall soon catching Monique and Justice at the elevator.

thirty-two

Trouble In Paradise

One of the more pleasing aspects of living in the downtown area is convenience. Justin revels in his decision to call this section of the city "home" while Justice—quietly impressed by the "bigness" of Chicago's skyline, nearly breaks his neck looking from one sight to the next. Amused by his son's overcoming amazement, Justin watches with pride, "Ya like that don't cha? A far cry from Atlanta though. …Definitely more hectic." He too joins in on the sight gazing. Within minutes, they arrive at The Hancock Center.

The panoramic view of the city and Lake Michigan from the restaurant's human-sized windows earns Monique sweeping compliments from Jerome and Justin. "Gurrrl you knew what you were talkin' 'bout. This the shit here! …Where ya hear 'bout this place?" Admiring the simple art-deco decor, Justin praises the comfortable atmosphere.

"Actually the last time I was in Chicago my parents brought me here for Sunday brunch. And when we finished—I remember we all went up to the observatory to take pictures. …But I thought it was real nice…"

"Family vacation?" Justin interrupts.

"Well sort of. I guess you could call it that. My father often mixed business with pleasure. And so my mom and I were usually the benefactors. He's a Kazan consultant. So a lot of times when a company calls for his services—depending on how long he's needed, we'd get to go if it was only for a few days."

"Musta been nice. Pops had it goin' on." Justin enviously points out.

Monique smiles, "I thought so." She agrees, being one who has never taken her very fortunate upbringing for granite.

After receiving the menu, it becomes quite clear that this wasn't exactly what Justice had in mind as far as Thanksgiving dinner. With appetizers like seared Ahi Tuna served with a Sishan peppercorn crust and seaweed cucumber salad, he soon longs for the traditional turkey potluck extravaganzas once prepared by his mother. Coming to the rescue—his dad aided by his uncle and future auntie, converge to save the day by summonsing the waitress. Once explaining their dilemma, she in turn talks to the head chef, requesting a personal favor. The outcome is the preparation of a special holiday dish combining main course elements such as a stripped chicken breast minus the artichokes, a generous portion of grilled pork without the raab, steamed broccoli sautéed in a creamy cheese sauce, and whipped garlic potatoes. With much appreciated regards to the staff, and Justice now more than squared away—all enjoy the delicious high-priced meal.

Yet it's in the smiles seen on all four faces—the conversation and laughter, which justifies every penny. As for these kindred souls, it's about being there—sharing in the victories as well as the pains. It's on this day that they take time out of otherwise busy lives to celebrate one another—giving thanks for the chance to fellowship one more time.

For the Vaughns, this is all there is and possibly all there will ever be. The last of a fading clan—two men and a boy left to carry on the family name and tradition. And so in the spirit of commemorating today—and those things which are not promised, each will raise a glass in honor of themselves—and in honor of each other.

❧   ❧   ❧

4:03pm

Running behind after being dropped off by Jerome and Monique, Justin—standing out front of his Lake Shore address clinching his overcoat closed, unclips his phone and says to his son, "Baby, hope ya have room fo more." He then turns for privacy while dialing Natalie's number. "Heeey—what's up? We're a runnin' lil' late." And after listening to her bark, he pleads his case as she's not at all thrilled by his tardiness. "...But we're on our way right now! ...*Yeeeah*—y'all ate yet?" But she continues complaining on until he ends the conversation. "...Al-ight. We're be there in a lil' bit. *Bye*." He closes the face of his cell—blowing in frustration. "C'mon lil' man—let's get out of here."

Justice, looking baffled and shivering, has no idea what's goin' on. "Where we goin' now?" His question sounds more like a complaint rather than an inquiry.

"I promised a friend we would stop by later. I bet ya up fo some banana puddin' or some sweet potato pie—right?" Justin, moving at a jogger's pace, makes quick haste. He uses his son's weakness for sweets to persuade him to come along quietly—much like a bribe.

Justice struggles to keep up. "I wanna see who won the game." He refers to the Atlanta-Detroit NFL early game on Fox.

"*Maaan*, I'm pretty sure the game will be on ova there too. Since when have ya ever known a Thanksgivin' dinner ta be at somebody's house without football on? C'mon nah—get real!" Justin makes his point as they reach the car. The just below twenty-degree partly cloudy weather becomes Justice's new reality, as he's quick to get in. "Thought ya was cute runnin' 'round here wit nuthin' on yo head—huh?" Justin snickers at his son's ignorance. "Oh, you'll learn." From his coat pocket he pulls out a folded piece of paper—a computer printout from Expedia.com with the directions to their next destination.

"Thought ya knew where ya was goin' Pops." Justice makes the flippant comment while frantically rubbing his hands together and blowing on them.

Realizing his son's unspoken request, Justin starts the car—immediately turning on the heat. "Boy jus hush. I got this! ...Jus put a CD in or sumptin'." he says, with his eyes glued to the paper.

Taking full advantage of the situation, Justice inserts the Ciara disc—jumping straight to track 5—"Oh". Bouncing and bobbing as the music blares, "...How come ya neva got a DVD player put in?"

Struggling to concentrate, Justin unintentionally ignores the question. "*Huh?*" His face frowned.

"Neva mind." He sees his father's preoccupied state and decides to drop any further conversation. Justice resumes to his one-man party over in the passenger's seat. With arms up, he raps along with Ludacris. "...Southern-style, get wild—old skool comin' down in a different color whip ...whip ...whip. Picture perfect, ya might wanna take anotha flick, flick, flick, flick, flick…" He flows until finally Justin feels he can't take any more and lowers the volume.

"Dude, ya gotta chill fo a minute. I gotta figure out where I'm goin'." Utter frustration becomes his temperament.

"Damn Dad how hard can it be? …*Shit.*" he says, showing little empathy toward his father's plight.

"I knew we shoulda met up at her place." Confused by the directions, Justin talks to himself out loud.

But the *her* is all Justice hears. And right away he gets defensive. *"Her* who?"

"I told ch'ou… A friend of mine!"

Knowing his father's flare for women, he gets quiet as his blood curls—pissed that his dad would even think about betraying his mother's memory so soon.

"It's not whatcha think son." Seeing Justice's reaction, he lies to keep the peace. Yet the fib fails to change anything. And the code of silence continues.

Not being too concerned with Justice's present disposition—figuring he'll get over it, he studies the sheet for the Downers Grove residence.

♡♡   ♡♡   ♡♡

4:46pm

Stopping at a gas station on Butterfield Road, Justin tries for more detailed directions. He's confused by the road name change, but the clerk behind the counter isn't exactly familiar with the street or the subdivision on the paper. With no other option, he calls Natalie. She answers after the first ring, anticipating his call. "Where are you!" she says, sounding stressed but at the same time relieved.

"Well hello to you too. But yo—we're here."

"If you were here—then I'd see you."

"And that's why I'm callin'—we're on Butterfield Road. Now how do we get ta where you're at?"

"Alright. First ya need to get back to Ogden Avenue…" She explains the route to Justin and ten minutes later, he and Justice arrive in front of the two story—two car garage, mixed vinyl siding and brick dwelling. Natalie, standing behind a storm glass door, waits with anticipation. Four newer model vehicles take up the spaces in the driveway—a Dodge Magnum, Nissan Armada, Cadillac XLR convertible, and a Ford F150 extended cab. On the street two more cars occupy the property's anterior—a late 90's Jeep Grand Cherokee and an 80's model Caprice classic tricked out with twenties and a ragtop. Justin is forced to park on the other side of the neighbor's driveway. With her arms crossed to keep warm—wearing only an Angora two-piece sweater dress, a beautiful Natalie rushes across the yard to greet her man.

Smirking wide, Justin bubbles with exuberance. "Let's go lil' man— I want ya ta meet someone."

Justice, who isn't thrilled by any means, exits the car under watchful suspicion as Justin and Natalie collide for a restrained but endearing embrace. They pull apart wanting more—yet continue to behave for the sake of the kids. She strays over to baby boy—holding her hand out, "Hi… You must be Justice. Your father has told me a lot about you. I'm Natalie." Her smile is very likable, but Justice doesn't buy into it for a second. He shakes her hand with cautioned generosity. "You all c'mon in out of the cold. I'll introduce ya to the rest of my crazy family." Taking Natalie's place in the doorway is a curious Asia, who without shame, stares at the two strangers. "That nosy child standing right there is my daughter Asia." She points to the door as they approach the house.

And after finally seeing Asia in the flesh, Justin acknowledges the unmistakable resemblance. "*Damn*. Couldn't deny her if ya wanted to. She looks jus like you."

"Yep. That's my baby."

Switching his attention elsewhere, he scans his surroundings. Impressed by the house—and the middle-class neighborhood, Justin speculates the market value of real estate in this area. Even at conservative estimates—a home like this one couldn't be anything less than $200,000. Thinking in terms of the future, he keeps an open mind about possibly owning property in the upwardly mobile Downers Grove community. He walks in behind Natalie where he and Justice are formally introduced to Asia. "Baby, this is the friend I've been tellin' you about—Mr. Vaughn. And this is his son Justice. I think I may have told ya this already… But they just moved here from Atlanta."

Asia, looking unconcerned, smacks on a piece of gum—hand on one hip, "You datin' my mama?" She directs the very blunt question to Justin, who's caught off guard, not knowing how to respond. He looks to Natalie.

"Asia! That's not nice. And you know betta! *Gurrrl*—don't get me started up in here!" Gnashing her lip, Natalie gives her crass daughter the evil eye. "I'm sorry. You have ta excuse my baby's manners. ...She acts like she doesn't have any home training sometimes."

"Oh, I bet she gets it honest." Grinning, Justin makes the sly comment. Natalie doesn't entertain the remark with a response but rolls her eyes—offering up the same evil look given to her daughter. Justin simpers—keeping his head down, knowing he's just gotten away with one.

Again amazed at the likeness, Justin sizes up the bright skinned, tall and slender adolescent. Brash—just like her mama, Asia is underdeveloped up top and plenty healthy downstairs—especially for a twelve year old. He also notices that she's very pretty like her mama too. The only significant difference between them—is in hair length. Asia wears a much shorter flipped bob cut falling just below her ears. She looks much older than she is—and in some sense more street savvy than her mother—who is almost ghetto fabulous. But what Justin does fail to notice is the way she undresses his son with desirous eyes—unbefitting of her age, while Justice by the same token is more than compliant to her cause. He too engages in lustful looks, admiring the baby fat of her thick thighs and calves peeking through the split of her denim skirt.

"Follow me guys. Everyone else is in here." Natalie directs her guest to the living room where the sound of whooping and hollering men fill the room. The familiar noise confirms Justin's earlier statement—like white on rice, thanksgiving dinner and football go hand in hand. "Ay everyone excuse me for the interruption, but I would like you ta met my friends Justin and Justice!" She boldly burst upon the scene interfering with the testosterone fest.

"That's nice! Now if ya don't mind—can you step from in front of the TV please?" A well-spoken, well-dressed younger brown skin male speaks. Everyone in the room laughs.

Walking over to the spokesperson Natalie makes her first introduction. "Justin, this ignant soul here is my brotha Avery—the baby."

Placing his half-digested plate on the floor and wiping his hands on a nearby napkin, he says, "What's up dawg? ...Ay shorty?" he says, as he gives dap to both before returning attention to the Dallas-Denver game. Sharing the sofa, is another of her siblings—a tall very fair skinned, built, professional looking fellow to whom Natalie moves next. "And next we have Arthur—the brains of the bunch. Some would think we were twins—but we're not! …We jus favor," she says, as she's quick to point that out.

"How are ya?" He reaches to give Justin a firm shake. His tone leaks an air of Caucasian capitalism. A forced smirk permeates from his face upon greeting Justice as maybe he's a bit appalled by baby boy's trendy hip-hop accessorized attire, which consist of a diamond stud in his left ear and gold 24" necklace worn over an Ecko purple and black rugby top. Not to mention his six inch curly afro.

"We cool," as Justin duplicates his grasp.

Over in the corner, sitting in his Lay Z Boy recliner is the host and family lush—Stevie. Older, darker and decked in a Dallas jersey, his forehead shines from the many shots of Patron tequila. A ravished plate sits on the carpet next to the clear bottle. "*Stevie,*" Natalie snaps her finger. "This is Justin and his son Justice."

Unconcerned, he looks past his sister trying to watch the game. He jumps from his seat. "*Wwwoo!* Damn—now that's a hit! …Laid his ass OUT!" he yells, responding to the action on the screen.

"Excuse you!" She reacts to his rudeness.

"Oh. A pleasure ta met ya young buck." He throws his hand out loosely for Justin to grab. "Nat, go fix that man something ta eat! Make yo self at home." He sits back down, helping himself to another drink. His belly jiggles on impact, representing years of inactivity.

Finally, seated on a loveseat perpendicular to the couch, is Natalie's oldest and closest sibling—Brunell. The one dearest to her heart, for he's the one responsible for taking care of her during her turbulent teenage years. At a time when Natalie and her mother could no longer live under the same roof, he stepped in to relieve a volatile situation. He is quiet yet commanding figure—mocha complexioned like Stevie, with long dreads tied back in a ponytail. His slim brawny physique gives the impression of a much younger man. "This my boo here. Justin this is my brother Brunell."

Standing to his feet while nursing a Bud Light, Brunell welcomes the two guests, "Good ta finally meet cha. Dun heard so much 'bout ya."

"Likewise," Justin amicably replies while they shake hands—by far the sincerest of all the greetings.

"Hey there," speaking to Justice, who in turn says hello. "Boy, he's almost as tall as you."

"Yeeeah. He thinks he's grown," he says, nudging his son on the arm.

"If you guys are hungry there's still plenty in there—so help yourselves." Brunell places a hand on Justin's shoulder.

"Thanks man—we appreciate that." Justin opens up as he's made to feel like something other than an intruder.

"C'mon let fix y'all some plates." Natalie leads them to the kitchen—her most dreaded stop of the tour. For propped against the archway, blocking the narrow entrance, is the matriarch of the Broussard clan—Camille Broussard. Arms folded, she sips on a champagne flute of sparkling bubbly.

"Hey mama—this is…"

"I know who they are, I heard ya before." Impolitely interrupting mid-sentence, the tall mannish woman of her late fifties imposes her domineering will from the very start. With eyes glazed over—and skin matching that of her two eldest, she stares at Justin while taking another swallow. "So, where ya meet this one? …On the bus again?" Her baritone chuckle is as distinctive as the quarter-sized mole prominently positioned on her jugular. She intensifies the moment.

"Excuse me Mama!" Natalie forces her way by.

"Child, don't put yo goddamn hands on me." As tensions escalate, Cassie, Stevie's wife, intervenes by pulling Natalie on into the kitchen. Justin and Justice follow. Camille finishes her glass and enters too.

"Fellas, look ova there on the counter and y'all grab a plate! Gurl, jus sit down and rest yourself. I'll fix their food." The mild mannered hostess tries her best to separate opposing sides, but a tipsy Camille continues to provoke.

"What da hell she needs ta sit fo? …What *she* cook? But ya don't cook—now do ya girl? …Cassie let her do that. She needs ta do something besides eat!" Taking every functional muscle contained inside her petite frame—with clinched fists, Natalie heeds and takes a seat at a table on the other side of the room. Feeling sorry for her, Justin makes sympathetic eye contact—raising his brow and flattening his lips as show of support.

"Mother Broussard, it's alright" As Cassie uncovers the leftovers. "Whatcha want baby?" She directs the question to a quiet Justice who's being surprisingly entertained by all the shenanigans—far from the ho-hum outing he expected.

Having already eyed the spread, Justice rattles off his request. "*Aaah*—some macaroni and cheese… That sweet potato casserole, some deviled eggs, and a piece of ham Ma'am."

"No greens baby?" She packs his vegetable-less plate.

"No Ma'am."

"What else baby?" Justice turns to his father for approval before showing any sign of greed. Justin nods—giving his okay. "Ma'am" He points to the Key lime cake on the counter and the dish of banana pudding right beside it.

Cassie laughs showing the protruding and separated nature of her top row of teeth. And like her husband, her more than healthy tummy gyrates in perfect rhythm with her mouth. "Both baby?" Her dumpy configuration compliments her jolly character.

His head quivers, "Yes Ma'am." Baby boy accepts his plate, and walks over to share the table with Natalie. Meanwhile armed with china in hand, Justin surveys the buffet of delicious looking dishes that decorate the counter and disguised five-foot table situated in the middle of the floor.

"See whatcha want hon? Y'all jus help yourselves." Cassie extends an open invitation.

"Thank ya. It all looks so good," he says, as he goes straight for the dirty rice and baked chicken wings. He adds some collard greens marinated in neck bones—then recovers the trays.

"I'll get that baby. Jus eat!" The hostess chuckles.

Camille, standing off to the side, momentarily quiet, helps herself to another glass of Ernest & Julio Gallo. "*Pah.*" She sighs with contempt before leaving the kitchen. A relieved Natalie exhales as Justin joins the table.

"You al-ight?"

"Una-umph." She lays her head on the table—embarrassed and feeling disheartened.

Cassie comes over gently rubbing her back—consoling her. "Baby—ya know we have ta overlook your mama sometimes."

"*Huh.*" Lifting her head, she looks to Justin. "I'm so sorry. I didn't mean for y'all ta see all that." She starts mumbling. "I thought maybe things woulda been different… At least for one day."

"Don't worry 'bout us. We straight! Jus wanna make sure everything is cool wit you." Justin expresses his concern. Even though in the back of his mind, he's thinking what she feels. "*Big mistake …I shoulda listened ta Rome.*" He glances over at Justice stuffing his face while pretending not to be paying any attention. "Where's Asia?" he then asks Natalie—thinking that maybe his son is taking in a little more than he should.

The thought strikes a curious chord with Natalie also—who looks around baffled. "Probably in the living room wit her Uncles I imagine. That gurl, she jus loves the attention." Still exasperated, Natalie places her head back down on the table. A moment later the doorbell rings—breaking the minute of respectful hush. The sound of pit-pattering feet race to the door.

"*DAD-dy*!" As all about-face to the mention of those dreaded and unexpected words. None more surprised is Natalie, who raises up—almost primping herself, forgetting the fact that Justin sits only a few feet away. He catches her slip—causing an instant red flag.

From the front, the jovial expression of grown men embracing one of their own can be heard back in the kitchen. Justin frowns—but with restraint, feeling a sense of resentment. A bit jealous by the less than enthused welcome he and baby-boy received minutes earlier. Natalie attempts to downplay the moment—and her indirect involvement into the incident. "Why is he here? Nobody invited him!" She blows as though she's being unwillingly imposed upon. Cassie—speechless, shrugs her shoulders having no answers. But the naïve act doesn't hold much weight against an always distrusting, guilty until proven innocent Justin. He attentively listens to the conversation in the other room.

Following the exchange of holiday tidings and other small talk, a willful Camille escorts Natalie's ex to the kitchen. Asia's, of course, glued to their every step.

The setting unnerves Justin. It's just the thought of encountering a ghost from Natalie's past that invokes an internal cringe. In steps the opposing trio. A shocked Christopher, surprised by Natalie's male guest, plays off the obvious. "Happy Thanksgiving Ladies." Possessing a smooth and charismatic demeanor, he walks over first bending down to give Cassie a kiss on the cheek then proclaims his dominion by taking a seat next to Natalie and immediately starts in on a personal discussion—never once acknowledging Justin's presence. He makes it very clear to all comers—that he's the past, the present, and the future. The transpiring of the events unravels the normally composed Natalie—who wilts under pressure, stammering her words.

"Chris *s-s-stop it!* …Jus quit it! You see I have company. Don't do this here!"

"What? What da hell did I do?" He then turns to Justin—instantly recognizing the error—and the threat. "My bad my man! I'm Chris Robinson—Asia's daddy."

"Justin. Justin Vaughn." Dissed—and quite pissed, he extends the courtesy despite the flagrant foul.

"Look man. I ain't mean anything by that—I ain't know. Nat never mentioned anything 'bout having a friend. Hopefully no harm dun folk! Jus came by ta see my peoples." After the insincere performance, Chris stands to his feet to excuse himself.

"*Daddy*, where you goin'?" A confused Asia whines.

"Angel, I gotta go. Come walk Daddy to the door."

With bowed eyes, Asia complains. "But Mama..."

"Don't start Asia! You don't understand," she responds, warning her daughter.

"*MAMA!*" She repeats herself in near tears.

"BE QUIET GURL!" Infuriated, Natalie yells back.

"Look, I betta go. Angel, jus call me later," he says, as he places a hand under his daughter's chin. And as quick as he entered—he leaves, though the damage has already been done. Camille, who revels in the wake, finishes another glass of White Zinfandel. While Justice—enjoying his banana pudding wonders, "What jus happened?" And with the exception of Asia's whimpering—all is quiet.

thirty-three

A Simple Misunderstanding

Three days after Thanksgiving about nine-thirty on a frigid Sunday night, Justin answers his front door. In the hallway—still dressed from church service, paces a distraught Natalie. "*Girl*, whatcha doin'?—it's late! ...How ya get here?" Automatically his eyes scan the hall. "I know ya gotta be freezin'." Justin talks while still standing in the doorway—not instantly inviting her in.

"Justin, why haven't you called? If you're mad at me—I thought I explained to you I had nothing ta do with him jus showin' up ova there. ...Why can't you believe that? Baby, there's nothing goin' on!" With her eyes showing the wear of a few sleepless nights, she jumps right in with a clarification of Chris's unannounced visit on Thanksgiving Day. And without saying a word—keeping his hands clasped behind his back, Justin leans in delivering a quick peck upon Natalie's chilled lips. Under normal circumstances—he more than likely would have made her suffer for a little while longer. But seeing that she's come so far out of her way—with no transportation of her own, he cuts her a break. Also working in her favor is the fact that even in her Sunday's best, she exudes a sexiness that he can't resist.

"Girl, bring yo silly tail on in here." He embraces his pitiful mate. "How come ya didn't bring Asia?"

"Cause she's wit you-know-who." she says, not wanting to mention his name.

"Hmmm—I shoulda known. So, what brings ya ta this neck of the woods?" he asks, as they face one another still tightly cuddled.

"I missed you. And I thought you were mad at me."

"And you were right… Cause I was!"

"But why baby? I already told you… This is where I wanna be, nowhere else!" She tries selling Justin on her sincerity

"If ya say so 'cuz I ain't puttin' myself through all that! I'm fo real—that's some ole' bullshit! And I ain't try'na have no part of that. …If y'all still tryin' ta figure sumptin' out—maybe see what's still there. Then by all means go right ahead. …Don't let me stop ya! *Hell*, mo power to ya! Jus don't be expectin' me ta be somewhere standin' 'round waitin' and shit." Justin vents.

"Shhh." Smiling, she puts her finger across his mouth, removing it only to replace it with a kiss. "I love you," words which catch Justin completely off guard. "Don't say anything—jus kiss me," as he more than happily complies.

Once inside it doesn't take Justin much to convince her to stay. With Justice sound asleep, like two teenagers sneaking past dozing parents, he leads her to his bedroom and locks the door. In the absence of candles, Justin illuminates the room by drawing back the vertical shading exposing the festal glow of Chicago's lakefront. "Baby, what are you doin'? …Won't someone see us?" She whispers.

"*See what?* Girl, who's gonna see us? We're twelve stories up and facing the lake." With a twisted smile, he turns his attention to the spectacular view. "It's pretty though—ain't it?" Natalie removes her coat—tossing it on the bed, and then disperses of her shoes, allowing her toes to breathe. She joins him by the window.

"Yes, it is." Caught in the moment, she corrals him from behind, comfortably resting her chin at the base of his neck. "Know what I wish?" She poses the question.

"What?"

"I wish we would have met sooner."

"*Why?*" Justin burns with curiosity.

"Cause things might have been different—my life. I don't know… Maybe coulda skipped a few things." She sighs.

"Humph. Not necessarily—as much as we wanna think that." He turns to face her. "...but I know whatcha mean." Eye to eye—only inches apart, they stare in deep debate—deciding whether to give in—or not. Both mindfully weigh in on the consequences of taking that much-anticipated next step—Natalie in her Christian walk and Justin's embattled guilt of moving past Teresha. Enticed by their overwhelming passion, they yield to temptation. Justin pulls off his tee shirt. He reveals a leaner, more defined look. Top heavy and sculptured, Natalie outlines his tightly stretched torso—gently touching every erotic zone of his naked chest. Doing what comes natural, she moves to his nipple—kissing it and teasing it with her tongue. Her hands now rest on his waist. Justin rejoices in its result as his nipple hardens, "Ummm I like that. ...Are you nervous?" he asks, detecting her taut touch.

"A lil'." She continues drifting higher toward his neck—up around his throat. Her lips are now in contact with the stubble of his unshaven face.

"So, how long has it been?" Again, he interrupts her flow.

"Why ya ask?" Her face contorts in disbelief.

"Cause I wanna know."

She turns to an alarm clock on the bureau. "Twenty-four months, six days, and three hours. Now you satisfied?"

"Guess so." He proceeds to undo a single button to the beige jacket of her Donna Vinci sleeveless dress. He endorses her firm petite figure. With one snap now separating the joining of stripped flesh, he removes her last line of defense—the beaded neckband. Backing her towards the bed, the garment falls to her hips. Justin immediately attacks in true aggressive fashion—necking the region above her breast. She unzips the back—releasing the gown to the floor. The sultry sequence exposes her bra and panties. "...Was it Chris?" he asks as he comes up for air.

"*What?*" she says, completely confused by the line of questioning and exhilarated foreplay. "Why are you doin' this?" She rubs her delicate hands over his warm body.

"Was it Chris?" Speaking softly, he repeats his question.

"*Yeah*—now please let's drop the subject." she says, conceding, in hopes he would have nothing more to say.

"So, what was it like?" But he continues—seemingly obsessed with her past while further frustrating her with his tantalizing touch.

"C'mon baby—please I don't wanna talk about that." Between gasps, she pleads for mercy.

Turned on by her begging, he commences to passionately kiss her—nibbling through the lace of her satin bra. They fall upon his bed. "Go ahead—I'm fo real. What was it like?" He is poised atop of her nearly nude body.

Blowing—but again conceding, she blurts, "Rushed—always rushed. ...Hip hop instead of Jazz. To him romance is usin' a bed."

The description invigorates Justin. "But'cha liked it—didn't ya?" He speaks with perverted undertones.

"*Sometimes*. ...So why are you playin'?" Her words reduced to a breathy whisper.

"And what 'bout this?" He hunches her nakedness—grinding his concealed love against her moistened loins. She drips with anticipation. So much that her cum produces a spot on the mattress. Justin—no longer interested with playing games, abruptly pops up rushing to undo his army green khakis.

"Let me," she says, as she does the honors placing his penis in her waiting hands. She carefully massages it—licking her lips as her thighs open. Reaching down, Justin gingerly parts her thong-like panties over to one side revealing the hairy prize. He leans in—face first, ready to explore. Yet with a sudden unexpected change of heart, Natalie squirms sideways—pulling back. "*No*. ...I can't. Not like this." She pushes against his chest—preventing any further progress. For it's better late than never, as it seems her spiritual values and common sense have prevailed.

Stunned, Justin resorts to begging—thinking that she might be retaliating from earlier distractions. "Nat—c'mon baby—*please*." With caressing kisses to her wrist and forearms, he hopes she'll reconsider.

"I'm sorry—but I can't baby. ...Please try and understand. But I have ta know without any doubt..."

"*What?* Whether I love you or not?" Disgusted, he rolls from on top of her—throwing himself beside her. "Well I do—if that's what you're worried 'bout." Staring into the ceiling, though very disappointed—he tries to understand.

"Please don't say that unless you mean it. ...Don't play wit those words! ...Why ya toyin' wit my emotions?" She sits up to speak seriously. "Let me say this once. ...First of all, define love. What's *your* definition?" She looks directly into his eyes. Justin offers no answer—wishing to avoid the looming speech that follows. With attitude, she begins to explain her interpretation; "Well baby, let me help you. Love is patient Justin—and kind. …Not jealous or conceited or proud. And when we do make mistakes—love forgives. It doesn't hold our past against us. Most importantly—love never fails. No matter who or what it comes across." Her account unintentionally targets the pettiness of Justin's recent behavior. "Secondly… Don't jus say something because *I* said it—or cause ya think that's what I want ta hear…" She pokes a finger to his temple. "So consider this a warning—don't just say something like that unless you really mean it!"

"Girl, lay yo lil' wannabe gangsta ass down and get some sleep. Got a lot ta do in the morning." With this being the first time they've shared a bed together, he relinquishes his usual spot. Rotating opposite of her, he reaches for his tee shirt on the floor and passes it to Natalie before snuggling underneath warm covers. "I love you."

Overjoyed—but trying not to show it, she repeats the same. "I love you too." *It's funny how things seem to come so much easier—the second time around,* as that cliché becomes the sentiment of both their slumber time thoughts.

thirty-four

Familiar Territory

In what seems to be a rarity these days, Justin and Shantel spend a quality moment in Schaumburg's Woodfield Mall. Doing some last minute Christmas shopping, Justin checks over his list a second time—being careful not to leave anyone out. In his world, holiday shopping usually means waiting a day or two before the actual date and running to the nearest mall grabbing gift cards—the exceptions being, of course, Justice and Jerome. But hanging with Tae changes his usual routine, instead of having only a day, he now has the comfort of a few weeks. He contemplates whether or not to get more personal with his gift giving this year—especially for Natalie. He seeks indirect advice from the Mall Queen herself—Tae.

"So, whatcha try'na get ya boy Quent this year?" He walks holding Tae's usual assortment of bags.

"His sorry ass will be lucky ta get anything from me—*ever again*!"

"Girl please! ...Always be talkin' that ole' ying yang. You know ya 'bout dun already bought that man sumptin'. So fess up—what is it?"

Admitting the truth, "Anyway, you know me... I like ta try and get my Christmas shopping out the way early—have it ova and dun wit—

that way I jus sit back and relax without foolin' up at the last minute. ...*Who* wants ta deal wit all that chaos—feel me? So what I did was... Before we left Atlanta I picked out these two really nice Italian suits from the Men's Warehouse—with the shirts and matching ties. ...I jus went on and got the whole ensemble...And then I went online and found this really cute leather Nautica travel bag—which I went ahead and had Quentin's initials engraved on it. And since he's always on the go—at least let him tell it, I figured he'd like that. But that's about it." In nonchalant fashion, she finishes her impressive list.

"But shit, that's enough—don't cha think? Ya dun went all out for—*let you tell it*, somebody who ain't doin' ya right no way. That don't make any sense boo. Stop always sellin' yourself short. There's niggas out there who'll do right by ya—respect ya and all that shit. Ya jus gotta be patient," he says, adding his two cents.

"Yeah whatever. So show 'em to me...Where they all at—tell me that? I've been patient and look where it's gotten me. ...No where!" She pauses. "Anyway, my mama always taught me ta treat people the same way I wanted ta be treated. And that's why I do what I do. So don't be surprised if on Christmas day you jus so happen to get two brand new designer Italian suits!"

Justin just smiles. "Girl, you crazy! I know one thing—I sure miss these days." They reminisce on the way they used to always kick it— the relaxed candor of conversation. No facades—just a straight up "whatcha see is whatcha get" type of vibe.

"Well, whose fault is that? The last time I checked, I was still employed by the same company. ...Still livin' at the same address. ...And still reachable by the same seven digits. I'm not the one who acts like they've dun run off and gotten married—like someone else I know—feel me?" Eyeing Justin, she makes a valid point.

"Ha-ha, very funny!" he says, being sarcastic. "But riddle me this! The last time *I* checked—a certain someone whom shall remain nameless—was all in love wit some jet settin' Negro whose pretty face jus so happens ta be plastered on every major financial magazine in the damn country! ...So now what?"

"You're jus jealousy!" Grinning, she throws the quick rebuttal in Justin's face.

"Whatever." Then changing the subject, he says, "So what should I get Nat? She ain't one of those women easy ta shop for—know what I mean? ...You're a trendy gal. What would you suggest?"

"Huh. That's a loaded question. What's the price range?"

"Hell, I don't know. Jus name sumptin'—shit!" He throws up his shoulders.

"*Okaaay*—hmmm… What ta get lil' Ms. Tacky?" She mumbles under her breath.

"*What?*" Justin inquires, suspecting some type of crude comment—having not heard a word.

"Oooh nothing." Tae keeps her personal opinion to herself. "How about some *mildly* expensive perfume?" Pointing to a particular fragrance, "…Especially since you haven't known her long enough for any *diamonds* and what not." She drags Justin through Nordstrom's—stopping at the cosmetic counter.

♡   ♡   ♡

Having polished the final touches on six tracks of Arius's upcoming album, Jerome, later that evening, is taxied back to O'Hare International by his brother and nephew. After two months, he's going home to the ATL. Justin congratulates him on a job well done.

"Yeah dude—ya did it again. Ya neva cease ta amaze me Rome! …A genius and shit! Ya keep pullin' that fly shit out yo ass. If the rest of the CD is anything like those ya finished—we talkin' platinum baby! Sho' Nuff Midwest—we'll be on our way ta framing a second plaque—know what I'm sayin'? Thanks man." Justin hugs his brother.

"No problem. Ya know how we do." Over the intercom the last boarding call for Jerome's flight is announced. "Yo, y'all stay tight—I'll hit cha when I'm at the house. Jay, thanks man. We'll have ta do it again real soon. Baby boy be good and listen ta yo father. …Don't think I forgot 'bout Christmas!" Jerome trots to his gate with a knapsack over his shoulder. He jumps to the back of the line.

Using his hands like a megaphone, Justin shouts across the terminal. "Yo tell Mo—'thanks fo the hookup'. I owe her one!" he says, referring to the quick room makeover she pulled off on Justice's room before leaving after the Thanksgiving weekend. As they turn to head for the exit, Justin questions his son about homework. "Did ya finish your report yet?"

"Nope. I gotta do the bibliography and redo my outline."

"What 'bout everything else? Are you straight fo tonight? That paper ain't due until next week—right?"

"Yes sir. I finished my Social Studies in the car."

"Al-ight. Feel like grabbin' a bite ta eat ova at Nat's house? She said for us ta drop by cuz she's cookin' tonight."

Justice, having grown tired of Italian beefs and pizza puffs, longs for the taste of a real meal. "Sure Pops." The 8th grade Schiller Elementary scholar has learned to tolerate Natalie's big sister persona and no longer feels threatened by her—as he puts it, "*temporary presence*". In fact, he sees her as a pushover—someone wrapped around his dad's finger, to which Justice uses to his full advantage. Besides, he's always up for the latest 411—and that's where Asia comes in. Like two life-long friends, who haven't seen each other in years, the two easily pass the time catching up with the latest gossip on the streets.

On the ride over—quiet, as has become customary, Justin peeks across at his nodding son. Though they talk, he can feel a distinct difference in the relationship. He knows there's something missing— he feels his son slipping away. He attributes a part of the reason to Justice becoming a young adult—his mind rapidly maturing as his parental needs and dependency are steadily diminishing or at least changing. But even beyond that, there's a void where Justin feels that he's failed as a father and followed in the footsteps of his own father. He realizes there are those times, when as a parent, he will be called upon by his child to meet a very specific need. He also recognizes he may have missed one of those significant, critical moments—a moment that may very well change permanently the strength of their bond. In his selfishness Justin recognizes his mistakes.

From the street—now parked, Justin glances to Natalie's second floor window where he follows the shadows of moving occupants pass the shaded blinds. He makes a quick call upstairs for Nat to unlock the vestibule door. "Hey!"

"Hey—are you on your way?" As always, she sounds as though she's in a hurry.

"Gurl, you late! …Actually we're here. So unlock the door." Natalie dashes to the window. Justin sees the slit in the blinds open as she peeks out.

"Okay bye! …*AAASIA*!" She disconnects, but not before a beckoning blurt of her daughter's name. They exit the car to be met at the door by a grinning Asia. Her smile registers the reprieve of her mother's constant wrath.

"What's up Just-Ice?" Popping on her usual wad of gum, she picks at Justice's name while holding open the door.

"What up!" Baby boy responds with a head nod and an extra dip to his step. He likes it when she says his name like that—anything using the word "ice" has got to be cool.

"Hey Jus… I mean—hey Mr. Vaughn." Now very comfortable with Justin, she slips in properly addressing him. Like Justice, she looks up to the fact that he works with all the hottest music celebs. In her mind having Justin around is like having a live version of "Right On" magazine at her dinner table. And despite the interfering infraction against her dad on Thanksgiving Day, she otherwise enjoys their company.

It's half way up the stairwell when hit with the combined aromas of onions and baked apples—Justin and Justice engage one another with thrilled euphoric smiles. Natalie leans out the doorway to greet her two favorite men. "Hey guys. Hope y'all brought an appetite?"

"Oh, ya ain't gotta worry 'bout that!" Justin passes dap with his son who cosigns the comment with a big grin.

"Hey baby." Natalie meets her man at the top of the stairwell. She greets him with a tight hug and kiss to the cheek—whispering, "I miss you" in his ear. She turns to reciprocate the act to Justice, minus the endearing utterance.

"*Boo*, whatcha got goin' on? …Whatcha in there burnin'?"

"Come and see. Asia, go get the plates and glasses out—and fill them with ice please!"

"Yes Ma'am." Pouting, she pokes her lip out but promptly abides.

"Justice go help her." Justin offers his son's service.

"Okay Dad." He jumps right to the task.

"See—I wish Asia would do like that. I don't know what ta say about that girl. …Jus lazy. But I guess she'll learn—huh? Life ain't as easy as she thinks." She stares in the direction of the kids.

Half listening, Justin entertains other thoughts. "Come here girl. Now let's do that again." And with the children occupied, he pulls her gently by the belt for a more intimate greeting. The proceeded smacking of lips echoes down the hallway. "I've been thinkin' 'bout you all day." He holds her in his arms.

"Justin, stop lying." She blushes.

"Who's lying?" Pinning her to the hall wall, he plants sucking kisses to her neck.

She squirms, "Stop baby—please don't leave a mark." she says as she finally wiggles from his grasp. "C'mon on—let's eat." She grabs him by the hand and leads him inside—politely subduing his advance. Yet, his silent chagrin loudly portrays his growing frustrations.

From the door they enter directly into the living room to find the kids darting in and out—chasing one another through the kitchen and into the nook-like space posing as the dining room. Behind the laughter and frolic neither notices their parents standing idly by. "Asia—I thought I told you to set the table!"

"And Justin—what are you doin'? I said come in here and help— not play!" Startled by the stern voices of their guardians, both stop dead in their tracks.

"*Aaaugh.* If you want something done, ya gotta do it yourself!" Natalie mutters amidst gnashed teeth. Agitated, she impatiently storms in the kitchen to complete the task—pausing along the way to remind Asia of her immature behavior. "Gurl—you know damn betta!" She scolds with a menacing sneer as both young perpetrators step out of her way. Justin, shocked by her use of the "*d*" word—stands back also to let her have her moment. The silence gives recognition of her rash actions, which she immediately reverses. "Y'all go sit down! I'll bring the food to the table." She restores the bliss in her voice. All congregate around the small glass table as she introduces each dish. First is a simmering pot roast seasoned in onions, diced potatoes, and carrots. She follows the main course with a green bean casserole garnished in French fried onions—each dish contributing to the mouthwatering aromas. She finishes with a bowl of Au gratin potatoes and a tray of Jiffy cornbread. Her final treat remains in the oven. Nat takes her place amongst the gathered. Bowing her head, she volunteers grace. "Oh heavenly Father, we thank you for this food and all the blessings you've bestowed upon us. Oh heavenly Father, come be our guest, and take your place at this humbled table. Oh heavenly Father, as this food feeds our bodies, so we pray that you would feed our souls. Aaamen! ...Now y'all eat!" She breaks away from the table to check on dessert. The men waste no time preparing their plates. For it's always nice to enjoy a full course meal as Justice has quickly become all too acquainted with the bachelor lifestyle. "Sweetie, don't forget about tomorrow." Natalie reminds Justin about taking her car shopping. She's ready to make her life—specifically her blossoming love life, more convenient—stressing independence over dependency.

"I haven't. Ya figured out whatcha lookin' fo yet?"

"I'm not sure. Maybe a Nissan Altima or a Toyota Camry. I don't know, but something along those lines." She takes the pan of piping hot apple pastries out the oven—then pours a homemade butter cream icing on top.

"I hear ya. We'll do that tomorrow afternoon." Justin notices her little surprise concoction. "*What's that?*"

"If you close your eyes I'll let you taste." She spoons off a piece of the turnover like dessert—blowing it with her hand under the spoon as she walks the sample over to Justin's chair. "Open your mouth. Be careful cause it's hot," she says as she eases the apple stuffed croissant into his expectant mouth. "Chew," she says as she takes a step back.

"Ummm—that's good." He devours the treat in one swallow. "So, what do ya call it?"

"Don't worry 'bout all that. As long as you like—that's all that matters." She stands over Justin grinning and gawking, as her body language sends blatant flirtatious signals. Meanwhile Asia and Justice look on with sheer intrigue–fully aware of what's going on. The fact that Justin and Natalie are still attempting to conceal the depth of their relationship is beyond comprehension as the kids have suspected the obvious from day one.

"*What cha'll lookin' at?*" Justin says as he catches their snooping glances. Natalie straightens up—poising herself to maintain the proper example. Asia and Justice pretend as though they have no idea what Justin is referring to. "While I'm thinkin 'bout it—I got a lil' surprise for y'all." Pointing to the children, he says, "Y'all know the *Holiday Jam* kicks off here in the Chi next week. Bow Wow, Ciara, Chris Brown, Omarion, Marques Houston… All them hot teen acts. Well, it jus so happens that Sho' Nuff Entertainment and yours truly has the inside track on a couple of front row floor seats—plus some backstage passes. So, what cha'll think?" Asia almost loses her eyes from falling from their sockets as she covers her mouth in disbelief. Justin gives a smug nod as a sign of his enthusiasm. "Y'all ain't sayin' nuthin'. Wanna go or not?"

A giddy Asia turns to her mother. "Can I go Mama—*pleeease.*"

"I don't know Asia. …Justin, where is this going be at? And on what day exactly?" she says, instantly having her doubts.

"The Allstate Arena. And it's on the 22nd—a Thursday I believe. But school will be out for winter break on Friday—so *that* shouldn't be an issue."

"And you're gonna be there with them—right?" she says, again voicing her reservations.

"*Yeeeah* baby—they'll be in good hands. …You worry too much."

"I need ta talk to ya in private please." she says, delivering her request with a frown.

"Sure." He wipes the smirk off his face, heeding the stark contrast in expressions. Justin follows Natalie to her bedroom. Asia sulks, fearing the worst. "What's up?" he wonders after seeing Nat push the door up.

"Baby, I don't think it's a good idea—at least not for Asia. I know you meant well, but that's not something I really want to expose her to..."

"Boo, it's jus a lil' teeny bopper concert. I sure you went to your share at her age. Nuthin' ta be overly concerned 'bout. I promise!"

"But see, that's jus it. I don't want her ta be like me! By the time I was twelve I was already sexually active. I don't want that for her! ...No, she can't go!" as she's resolute in her answer.

"*Look*... I feel whatcha sayin'. But let's do this... Since I've already mentioned it—and now the poor baby got her lil' hopes all up, let her go this once. I'll be right there monitoring everything. So nuthin' is gonna get out of hand. And after this, I'll neva again mention anything even remotely resembling the subject ever again—deal?" Natalie stands with her arms crossed—not saying a word. "Pretty please?" he says, pleading his cause, "Wit sugar on top?" He pokes his lip way out being silly.

"*Ehhh!* Put your lip back in—don't nobody wanna see that," she says, finally cracking a smile.

"You gonna let her go?"

"I'm thinkin' so. But I'm holding you completely responsible! Don't bring my child back here with her lil' head all up in the clouds, then I got ta deal wit her. Have me sittin' here try'na bring her hot mess behind back down to earth. And please have her home at a decent hour. I don't want her thinkin' she can do whatever she wants whenever she's around you. We're not gonna start that!"

"I got the point boo!" he says as he cuts her off. "Thank ya. Now c'mon, let's go back in there before they think we're back here doin' sumptin'. Ya know we ain't foolin' nobody—right? ...Trust me, they know what's up. They may be young, but they ain't stupid." He smirks. "They know what's goin' on wit us." Nat offers no comment as Justin escorts her out the room with his hand on her shoulder. He winks at Asia once reentering the dining area, giving her reason to celebrate. And she does so by hi-fiving Justice and squeezing his neck with a big over exuberant hug almost choking him.

"That's enough Asia—finish eating!" Natalie immediately bounces her daughter back to reality. "You got the dishes tonight."

"Yes Ma'am." But not even the menial chore can steal her joy. As Justin and Natalie rejoin the table, the conversation soon splits into separate discussions. While the kids chat over the life and times of public middle school, the adults converse on the trials and tribulations of the passing day. The phone rings. Asia races to answer—grabbing the loose cordless handset from the seat of the couch. "I got it!"

"Gurl, it ain't that serious—that's why we have an answering machine. …Jesus!" Natalie remarks on the abrupt sequence.

"*Heeey* Daddy!" She plops on the couch commencing to converse. "Are you still comin'?" Guarding her words, she steals peeks over at the now intruding guests. "Yeah. …Yeah. okay. …MAMA!" She holds the phone out for her mother.

Natalie, who avoids eye contact with Justin, rises up to take the receiver and starts talking. "Hello," knowing all too well who's on the other line.

"When yo folks leavin'? It's time fo ole' boy ta be runnin' along. …Ain't it past his bedtime?" Chris makes his presence felt with the crude comments.

"Shut up!" Natalie starts to walk towards her bedroom. Justin follows her path with observant eyes. He sits full as he rubs his stomach—having pushed away from the table. A toothpick hangs from his lower lip.

"Strike two!" Is what goes through his mind. "What the hell she gotta leave the room fo?" Justin flips the script as his whole mode changes. Ten minutes seem more like an hour while he impatiently waits for Natalie to resurface. With no love lost between Chris and himself, he suspects there's more going on than a father wanting to spend quality time with his daughter. "Why all of a sudden? …Fool jus throwin' salt on a nigga's game," he rambles within his head. Showing a look of distress upon her face, Natalie appears from the bedroom. "Who was that?" Justin barely lets her enter the room before he starts his interrogation.

"You know who it was. Nobody important."

"Still doesn't answer my question!" Justin lifts his voice.

"Asia's father." To cut the confusion she plays along.

"So what's up?"

"Nuthin'!" She is already aggravated.

"Must be sumptin'—look at ya!"

"What did I say? …Don't start—I'm not up for it Justin!" She raises her voice.

Pissed, Justin then makes a quick assumption. "He must be comin' ova or sumptin'?"

She walks away. Her silence confirms his answer. Justin looks to his watch. "Fuckin' late ain't it? What the fuck he want?" Justin tries to hush his words so the kids—who are now in the living room, will miss the wrath of his anger. Though a verbal confrontation is eminent, Natalie refuses to respond. "Oh, cat got your tongue all of a sudden?" Waving his head up and down, "Okay—I hear ya. Justice, c'mon baby—let's get ready ta go! School day tomorrow man."

"Justin don't!" Natalie tries to grab his hand but he snatches it away. "Why you actin' like this!"

"Jus don't fuck wit me right now. …Don't say shit to me! …It's always sumptin'. Ain't ya told that muthafucka you wit someone?" Natalie, copping an attitude of her own, stands with folded arms, looking away as she ignores him. "Didn't I ask you a question?"

She snaps forward, "You said don't say *shit* to ya!" speaking from behind closed teeth.

"Fuck it!" He grabs his coat. "C'mon Justice!" Justice doesn't hesitate. Acknowledging his father's angered tone, he moves to the door. "Oh and thanks for dinner!" Full of sarcasm, he and Justice walk out the door. Arms still crossed, Natalie follows them out—stopping atop the stairwell. While Justin never looks back—Justice does, he flashes a look of pity for Natalie. She waves from her folded arms.

Walking back inside, she closes the door. Moping her way to the dining room, she takes a seat at the table. All is quiet. Asia plays it smart by straying to the kitchen to start on her chores. Natalie sits nearly comatose as she picks at the bamboo place mat in front of her. Her mind cluttered—her head spinning. She wonders why after almost two years, is Chris trying to re-enter their lives—attempting now to be the man and father that he wasn't. "Is it because of Justin?" She ponders, but then in the same thought, "Why should he care?" She recalls how easily and frequently he moved on to other relationships after the split. Yet it still deeply bothers her, having vested so much time and energy into that relationship. Thus a part of her actually likes what she's now seeing. She's especially glad for Asia, having for years missed such an important component in her life. She knows her daughter longs for his attention.

thirty-five

Eve

Like any other morning, Justin drops Justice off a couple blocks up the street at Schiller Elementary. The all-black public middle school caters to an atmosphere much to Justice's liking. It's like being at home in College Park—only more of everything, especially girls. He loves to step from his dad's Dub edition Chrysler to the envious smiles and whispers of doting females and jealous, playa-hatin' fellas. In a few short weeks he's quickly become a popular figure around campus being that he's the new cute guy with an almost famous father. "You got your key—right?" Justin checks with Justice, as he always does, to make sure he's able to get inside the apartment after school.

"Its right here Dad." He pats the front pocket of his Girbaud jeans.

"Ya know ta call as soon as you make it in—al-ight?"

"Yep." Justice opens the door having spotted his boy Natron approaching the car.

"Make sure ya get straight to your homework as soon as ya get settled. Should be a pizza in the freezer. ...Al-ight then. Be careful and y'all have a good day. Pay attention to your teachers! ...NO BAD

REPORTS—AL-IGHT?" He barks his last request as Justice gets out. "I love you Son."

"Love you too Dad." He quickly closes the door to catch up with Natron.

Justin takes one last look at his son before pulling off. If it's one thing he's learned since Teresha's death, it's not to take anything for granted, particularly time. The thought instantly brings him to last night's unfortunate episode with Natalie. He feels pretty bad by the way he acted, but yet can't quite bring himself to call and apologize. The incident has caused him to toss and turn most of the night—being guilt-ridden over the triviality of his reason for walking out.

Loss has caused Justin to socially shutdown, decreasing his already limited circle of close trusting friends. He refuses to expose his weaknesses to others. So he remains content with concealing his hurt. And now that he's taken a chance by opening up to Natalie, his expectations of her have gone beyond reasonable. Therefore, he can't handle her concessions towards Chris and thus struggles to control the relationship. Jealousy has become his primary release of repressed anger. He feels Natalie isn't making a real commitment to the relationship by continuing such an open dialogue with her ex. And so he feels second. He sees a lot of himself in Chris, having used Justice in some ways to remain close to Teresha. It's the agony of knowing that his vested feelings for her may be in vain because of emotional ties to the past. As a result, he's forever haunted by Chris's ghost, whether it's just a figment of his own imagination—or not.

It's just before eight o' clock. Having noticed Shantel's car in the parking lot, Justin storms into her Feng Shui influenced office suite.

"Well, good morning Mr. Vaughn. And to what do I owe this pleasure?" A poised Shantel sits behind her mahogany desk—reading glasses positioned low on her nose as she skims through a small pile of papers.

"Man check it out…" Justin says, as he goes straight into what's on his mind. "Last night me and baby boy were ova at Nat's—right…" Tae puts the documents down, removing her glasses. She leans forward, clasping her neatly manicured hands upon her desk, with Justin's boggled tone warranting her full attention. "Everything's goin' fine until her baby's daddy calls. She leaves the room ta go talk to the nigga. And homegirl stays gone fo awhile! You know how I get… That shit pissed me off. Then she brings her ass back after she dun took her sweet ole' time on the phone—and ain't sayin' shit! I'm sittin' there askin' her shit—but she ain't try'na answer me either. Come ta find out, the muthafucka comin' ova after we leave. And it's already late as hell! I 'bout dun got tired of his ass. Tired of the whole situation! …Try'na play like nuthin's goin' on. Like I'm over exaggeratin' shit! …I ain't got time fo all that—so we bounced!" He pauses to analyze his own words. "I mean, what ch'ou think? Am I trippin'?"

Shaking her head, she says, "I honestly neva thought I'd say this but—boy you pitiful. Pit-ti-ful! …You hear me? Jay—that girl got your nose wide *open!*" She laughs. "Damn, I gotta give her credit—the girl is good if she got yo ass out like that! C'mon Jay—think about it! Look at the big picture baby. 'Ms. Holier than thou' has got all the bases covered boo. …The best of both worlds! Wit your gullible ass—she mentions something about being saved and she's got you thinkin' she's some sweet sanctified prize. …*Syke!* Meanwhile, ova here she's got Mr. Luvaman—triflin' as hell I'm sure, but probably the sorry behind joker she really wants, who has only walked back into the picture because she's dun went and got wit someone else. It's all game boo. Even I can see that!" She sneers at Justin as he stands there looking completely miserable. Tae has successfully made him out to be a fool. And yet, at this moment, that's exactly how he feels. She takes the opportunity to dig the dagger even deeper. "Jay, she's always going ta use their daughter as an excuse—and you jus have to understand she's neva really going ta ever let that man go. He's always gonna be that "in case of an emergency—break glass" crutch—if things jus so happen not to work out with you! Boo, I bet she sees you as her ticket out of a bad situation. …A way out of poverty, possibly a way to achieve a better life for her and her daughter." She smirks. "And let's be honest—who wouldn't?"

"C'mon now, I don't think she's that bad!" Justin tries to give Natalie *some* credit.

"Whatever! She's usin' you—plain and simple. But of course, that's only my opinion." She restores her glasses to their original position and goes back to what she was doing prior to Justin's little interruption. He towers over her desk as if he's waiting for Shantel to say something else, which doesn't happen.

"Thanks for your time," he remarks before leaving.

"Sure anytime." She delivers a wicked smirk from behind her work.

It's two hours later when Tae drags Dee into Justin's office while he's on the phone. And after a brief discussion—looking puzzled he ends the call. *"What's up?"*

"Tell him what you told me!" Tae nudges Dee to speak.

"Why ya got ta be puttin' me in this. That's that man's business! Shit, I'm Paul and that's on y'all—know what I'm sayin'? I ain't tryin' ta get into all this!" Dee snickers, as he's reluctant to say anything.

"Shut up and tell him what's goin' on!" Tae insists.

"Hell yeah—what's up?" Justin, now curious, urges Dee to say whatever it is.

"Naw nigga, my girl says she's seen your boy up in the shop lately. And according to her it ain't look all innocent either—ya know? Said they be lookin' cozy and shit. Ya know—and she brought that shit ta me—askin' me what's goin' on. Shit, I told her I ain't know—ain't none of my business. And it ain't!" He starts giggling—showing little concern for Justin's feelings. Justin looks first to Tae wondering why in the fuck she went to Dee discussing any of his personal business. She's supposed to know better, being well aware of the situation between he and Demetrius.

Sucking his lips, he nods, "Okay. So I guess it's like that, huh?" as anger doesn't begin to describe the emotions flowing through his veins. Just seeing Dee grin at his expense causes a fist to ball. Embarrassed by the chink in his manhood, he tries to play it off. "Fuck it—it's all good! Two can play that game—right?"

"Now that's my nigga talkin'!" Dee gets excited with the reemergence of his partner's old attitude. "Sounds like we goin' out tonight!" he says, still giggling.

"Damn right! Tae, you in?" Justin gives his consent. "It'll be jus like old times girl."

"Fuck yeah—bring your bony ass on and have a drink wit some real niggas!" Dee adds to the invite.

Tae returns a menacing glance towards Dee but overlooks the wisecrack to answer Justin's question. "I'll go. Where we goin'?"

Justin turns to Demetrius for the answer. "Where are we goin'?"

"Shit it's Wednesday night nigga! We headed ta Palatine. ...Durty Harry's nigga!

"Palatine! What the hell we goin' way out there fo? That's all the way out west nigga! I ain't goin' way out there!"

"$1 drinks on everything muthafucka. That's why!"

"Man, then somebody's got ta be the designated driver. That's too far ta be playin'." Justin makes it a point to get that part of the plan straight before going any further. Turning to Tae, he says, "Girl, you don't drink that much—know what I'm sayin'? ...Help a brotha out!"

"I'll do it. You're the one wit all the issues anyway. I'll let ya drown your lil' sorrows away this time." Being sarcastic, she complies.

"Al-ight. That's it then. After work it's on! So we good until then—right?" All agree. "*Sooo*, now get the fuck out my office!" Though teasing, Justin displays a serious face. They leave. He takes a minute to soak in the news. A part of him doesn't want to believe what all's been said. Yet, what really bothers him is the fact that he didn't see it coming—not from Natalie. He regrets having even brought up the situation with Tae—yet he had to talk to somebody. And instantly he's reminded of just how much he misses Jackie.

In looking at his so-called friends, Justin analyzes his sources and it's funny how misery always loves company, as neither is happy in their own relationships. But as much as he hates to admit it—Tae has a point. For someone who professes to be so saved, Natalie does seem to have more than a few bones poking from her closet. Yet, despite everything, he feels funny about reneging on his promise—adding to his initial guilt. But by no means is he about let himself be made a fool of. Come five o' clock, he knows she'll be waiting—ready to look for a car.

4:11pm

Justin gets the call he's been waiting for—it's his son calling to check in. "Yo, everything's al-ight?"

"Yeeeah—I finished my homework. Can I cut the TV on?"

"Yeah, that's straight. Yo—ya think you'll be al-ight by yourself fo awhile?"

"Ummm—I think so. *Why?* I thought we were takin' Ms. Natalie somewhere."

"Nope—change of plans. What's up? You ain't scared is ya?" Sensing the apprehension, Justin grins through the line. "Boy, you'll be al-ight. I'll be home before too long. Hey, while I gotcha on the phone—go in the kitchen, look in the fridge and tell me what you see." Justice follows his instructions. With the phone attached to his cheek, he leans in the open chrome door.

"I see some of them ribs we had the other night …a lil' potato salad left. Ummm some pastrami…"

"We got any bread?"

"Yes sir."

"Anything ta drink?"

"Some Minute Made fruit punch …and some Hennessy.

298

"Well, you jus stick to the fruit punch and fix ya a sandwich. I'll bring some hot wings home or sumptin'. So sit tight. Hit me if anything comes up. I'll call ya 'round seven ta make sure everything's okay—cool?"

"Yep."

"Don't answer the door ta any strangers—and stay in the house. No wild parties and all that other good shit—understood?"

"*Yyyep.*"

"And I'll talk to ya later."

"Bye Dad."

"Peace out." He hangs up feeling confidant with leaving Justice home alone.

4:46pm

Demetrius and Shantel met at Justin's office. The two try and be patient while Justin finishes up. Both relax in the suite's separate sitting area. Tae plays with her nails as she pulls an emery board from her purse while Dee—antsy as hell, flips through a Billboard Magazine, pretending to be interested. "How much longer man?" Speaking his mind, Dee pops the question.

"Chill nigga. Gimme a couple minutes. Tae we're takin' your ride—right?"

"If that's what you all decided," she says, continuing to touch up her nails.

"Yeah, I think that'll work out a lil' betta. I'll leave my car here. Dee, she'll drop you off on the way back. We'll run back by here—I'll scoop my ride. Then Boo you can head to the house—sounds straight?" The group agrees. Grinning, he says, "Dee, ya dun talked ta 'Lex already? Don't wanna hear 'bout ya gettin' that ass whooped now." Justin tries to be funny.

"Nigga, I ain't ch'ou! I ain't got ta call no bitch ta tell her where the hell I'm goin'. That's yo bitch ass nigga!" Dee just laughs.

"Whatever nigga. Al-ight I'm ready." He turns off the computer and puts a few files in his satchel. "Let's go!"

But before Justin can get out the building his cell phone is ringing. He checks the face for the caller ID—and like he suspected, it's Natalie.

"And this nigga got the nerve ta be talkin' 'bout somebody. Why ya ain't answerin' nigga?" Dee's having a ball throwing Justin's taunting remarks back in his face. "Nigga ya know ya wanna answer it." He snickers. "Go ahead Jay, I ain't gonna say nuthin'."

"Shut up boy!" Tae, laughing too, shoves Dee so he can back off.

"Fuck y'all!" Justin smirks pretending to be a good sport, yet deep down Dee's right. He wants desperately to take the call—but he also wants to save face. So he plays along with the program—perpetrating to be hard. He changes his ring tone to vibrate, ignoring the message.

6:05pm

After fighting an hour of traffic, Tae, who's been behind the wheel, vents her frustrations. "Hell nah, I know you ain't! Wake yo ass up! …Dee where ya got us goin'?" Exasperated, she drops her head against the steering column, tapping her nails on the grips. She's stuck behind a non-moving vehicle. "Aaarrruuugh—damn!" Growling, Tae pounds the wheel. She once again sits up to watch for the congested traffic in front of her. "Do you even know where we're goin'? …*Ssshit*—I'll need a drink after this," she says, not giving Demetrius a chance to respond. Caught underneath a pair of DKNY sunglasses, Dee lifts his head and wipes his mouth for possible drool. He's a bit disoriented after the short catnap, but checks for the nearest road sign.

"Yo, get off at the next exit." Dee cocks his head back—reclining the seat as if he's about to finish an interrupted dream. Stretched out in the back, Justin—detached from his immediate surroundings, quietly reflects. And unlike with his fellow companions, time has slipped by quickly. His cell hasn't helped matters as it continually vibrates at his side every few minutes. He can't help but to wish he could switch places and be riding to the dealership with Natalie instead of stuck in traffic headed to a bar out in the middle of nowhere. He knows now he should have kept his mouth shut and worked through his own problems as his every thought contains her.

"Right or left Dee?" Approaching the Palatine road exit, Tae gets her directions together.

"Make a right!" he says, sounding disturbed by the question.

"Look ass—don't make it sound like I'm gettin' on *yo nerves! Pleeease*—you the one who drug us out here!"

"Jus drive STUPID! If your yo ass was lookin' you'd see the shit! It's right there!" Dee points to the displaced, run down, barn-like structure facing Shantel's side of the street.

"Like I'm suppose ta know that's a bar!" She makes a left into the gravel parking lot enclosed by a wooden picket fence. "…Dammit Dee!" she yells, attempting to slow down over the bumpy terrain. "I know you ain't got us at no damn honky tonk! Should of known not ta listen to yo simple behind! …Jay, you see this?" The ride over has gotten the best of Tae as her mouth reflects her obvious agitation.

Dee turns to Justin, "Why we always gotta be bringin' her raggedy ass? Shoulda left her ass at the office."

"Raggedy! …Who the hell you callin' raggedy!" Tae just about comes across the console at Dee. From the back Justin emerges between the two.

"Damn! We got ta go through this every time? I knew this shit was a mistake! …Knew I shoulda took my ass to the house." Eyeing both, he gives an ultimatum. "Look, either we're goin' in right now—or turn this shit around and take my ass home—shit!" He only momentarily waits for an answer. "So, what's it gonna be Dee? …*Tae?* 'Cause fuck all this—I got betta shit I could be doin'.'"

The two short-lived adversaries engage in offsetting confrontational stares before conceding to Justin's terms as Dee is the first to give in. "I don't know 'bout cha'll but I'm try'na get my buzz on—and we wastin' time out here—know what I'm sayin?" He starts giggling.

Finally they pull themselves together, entering the three-space establishment after paying the $10 cover. A large full service bar welcomes all comers, as it's the first thing anyone encounters upon walking through the swinging saloon doors. The rustic exterior is consistent with the inside décor with bullhorns and lassoes, whips and wagon wheels attached along the walls. The authentic western memorabilia theme is carried throughout the bar area. Straight back—a lesser area used as the game room houses six regulation pool tables, several dartboards and a small-scale bar. Four televisions are strategically hung amidst the intimate, more contemporary space. To the left, another room separated by glass doors conceals the Dancehall conveniently called Club Harry's—illustrated by the neon sign above the tinted doors.

The very loud, very packed mixed yuppie crowd makes for the lively atmosphere and instantly all prior events are forgotten by the trio. Dee soon wanders off to explore. Tae tugs at Justin's arm to get his attention. "Buy me a drink!" He tilts down so she can speak into his ear. He looks around to grab one of the many servers hustling through the masses carrying drinks and food orders, as he's only able to identify them by the Santa hats worn by all the staff.

"Whatcha want boo?" He tries talking over the boisterous crowd and loud music.

"*WHAT?*" But Shantel doesn't hear him.

"WHATCHA WANT!"

"Oh—a Rum and Coke!"

"Hold on—I'll be right back!" And in a few minutes he returns with drinks in hand—Rum and Coke for her and a Corona for himself.

"Thank you!" And in one gulp she finishes her drink—handing Justin her glass.

"Al-ight. Betta slow yo role designated driver."

"Don't worry 'bout me, I can handle mine! Get me anotha drink please!"

"Al-ight now—I'm watchin' you."

Tae pulls his ear to her mouth. "Good, I'm glad somebody is." She grooves sensually to the mid-tempo Caribbean beat, exposing her flirtatious nature. Justin smiles, taking her pass as an innocent tease amongst friends.

"You want the same thing?"

"Yes please. …Hurry back!"

And again he returns with another Rum and Coke. She takes a longer time to consume the second drink but still finishes before Justin can down his first Corona. Her moves are now more pronounced—the drinks seem to have taken away any inhibitions as she shakes her round petite ass against Justin. "Whatcha doin' girl?" He stops drinking to enjoy the show.

"C'mon, I wanna dance."

"Naaaw. You go ahead, I'm straight!" he says, as he resumes to sipping on his beer.

"Ole' fuddy duddy! C'mon—I'm not takin' *no* for an answer." She hauls him kicking and screaming all the way from the door to the dance floor. They jig to Bobby Valentino's *Tell Me*. Justin loosens up once he sees the competition. He watches his mostly Caucasian counterparts twirl and fling across the fog filled floor with absolutely no rhythm. He gets a kick out of their intoxication. His focus then turns to Tae. He's impressed because she's actually workin' it!

"Girl, I ain't know ya had all that in ya!" He smoothly converses in her ear.

"So, whatcha thought?" she asks, throwing her arms around his neck.

"I'm not sure—but it wasn't this." Justin moves in close, wrapping tight around her waist. The close quarters causes each to sweat. Their bouncing bodies create a tantalizing friction, which both willingly act upon. It's the closest he's been to Tae and he likes it. He brings his hands around to her ass and gently squeezes.

"Found what you were lookin' for?" She enjoys his full-undivided attention.

"Yep—most definitely."

By the third song, she's removed the jacket to her skirt suit revealing everything her mama gave her as she quakes in a black brassiere top. Justin bites his lip with approval. The session continues for the next few songs until both mutually agree to step out for some air. Holding hands Justin and Tae walk back into the bar where they spot Dee over in a corner huddled with some Hispanic chick—sharing drinks. Smirking, Justin turns to Tae, "Should we go over there?"

"*Nooo*—I don't wanna be 'round him and his lil' skank!"

"Al-ight. Are ya enjoyin' yourself?"

"Sure am!" she looks heavily into his brown eyes. "I'm ready for anotha drink."

Justin takes the cue, finding two seats at the bar. And before they know it an hour has gone by. They trade four or five shots of Alabama slammers before both realize the depth of their inebriation. Shantel's smaller frame rejects her abnormal consumption. She tries standing to her feet but slips back on her stool. "Girl, are you al-ight?" Justin laughs.

"It's not funny Justin—I have ta pee," which she shouldn't have said as Justin practically falls out his own seat laughing even harder. He takes full advantage of the situation.

"Hold up girl let me help ya. ...Thought ya said ya could hold yo liquor." He grabs under her arm lifting her up while she throws a hand around his shoulder. With the help of a waitress they get her to the ladies restroom. But she barfs in the sink before reaching the commode. The girl comes out informing Justin that he's gonna have to go in and get her because she's laid out on the floor. "Damn!" he says, as he waits for the other women to clear the room. By this time a small crowd has gathered outside the lavatory, wanting to see a very drunken black woman, including Dee who happens to pass by en route to relieving himself. He catches Justin walking out the john with Tae in his arms—she looking completely out of it.

Dee, like all the other spectators, can't help himself from laughing as he approaches his boy. "What's up witcha girl man?"

"Man, I fucked up! ...I don't mean to rain on your parade, but we need ta get her out of here—like right now! So unless you straight—

looks like I'm the taxi then, huh?" And without any argument Dee doesn't hesitate to come on. He briefly stops to talk with the cute young senorita he was kicking it with earlier. She scribbles what looks to be her number on a napkin before saying goodbye. Dee then grabs Tae's coat and jacket, tossing them over her underdressed top as Justin carries her to the truck. They try sitting her up in the back seat—but she doesn't stay there long before slumping lifelessly across the bench. They leave her there, turning the seat into a temporary bed. "Ain't this some shit!" Justin shakes his head while closing the door.

"Nigga, what she drink?"

"Shots mixed wit Southern Comfort and Amaretto …I knew betta." Dee pulls out his camera phone savoring the hilarious moment. "Don't do that man." Justin says, not wanting to take advantage of the situation.

"Damn that—future ammunition nigga!" Both chuckle.

As planned, Justin drops Dee off first, who actually offers to ride over to Tae's apartment to help get her inside. But he tells Dee, "Thanks—but he's got it", not wanting to push the issue because of having to drive back to the Westside to take him home. He's still buzzing himself—and a DUI wouldn't exactly be at the top of his list of favorable accomplishments, though Tae has already blown most of his high since having to suddenly sober up to deal with her predicament.

9:14pm

Justin calls his son from outside Tae's apartment—two hours later than he was supposed to. Justice, like he figured, was sitting in front of the television playing his XBox. He then explains to his son that he'll be home shortly. Once off the phone, Justin glances to the back seat where Shantel is sound asleep and snoring. He turns to check around the front gate—quickly skimming the block to see if there's anyone milling about. He realizes he has to unlock the gate, the building entrance, and her apartment door before he can carry her inside. Locking the Montero, he runs upstairs and turns on the lights, as he prepares his path. And as usual, her apartment looks like something from *Better Homes and Gardens*—with not a dust particle anywhere. He darts back downstairs to grab Tae. Positioning her dead weight in his arms, he thanks God for her 120-130 lb. body. The commotion momentarily disturbs her sleep. Justin gazes down into her half-opened eyes "Girl, you silly."

"No I'm not—I'm where I wanna be," she says as she snuggles under his chin returning to her nap.

‚ Like a husband carrying his new bride across the threshold of their honeymoon suite, Justin totes his intoxicated frail friend through the corridor and into her living room. Her incoherent babble amuses him. "*Shhh*—go back ta sleep boo." He places her down on the couch— then walks to her room to prepare the bed. Pulling the covers back and adjusting the ceiling fan to low, he takes her to her room and proceeds to tuck her in. As he turns to the kitchen for a cup of coffee, she snatches his hand. The sudden grasp startles him. "Girl, I thought ya was sleep!"

"Uh-um. Where you goin'?" she asks, still tanked.

"Make some coffee. …Want some?"

"Uh-um." As she musters enough sobriety to yank Justin down to her level, she says, "Don't go."

"I'll be in kitchen girl!"

"Nooo—I'm talkin' 'bout don't leave me tonight." She tries planting her tongue across his lips. But Justin leans back, figuring it was the alcohol talking.

"Boo—you know I can't do that. Lil' man's home by himself. But I'll be back in the morning to pick you up." He smiles, whispering; "I left my car at work—remember?"

"You don't want me Justin?" Stroking her finger across his thigh, she speaks with soft sincerity.

"C'mon Tae… What are ya talkin' 'bout? You're drunk baby," he says, confused by what she's asking.

"I'm not that drunk to not know what I want—so whatcha waitin' on? …Come and get it." She slides off her skirt and panties while underneath the covers—then tosses back the comforter exposing her cleaved cunt. The moment seems almost surreal, as Justin practically pinches himself to prove what's going on.

"Baby don't…"

"*Shhh*. Jus respect me in the morning." Catching his wrist, she pulls him on top. …He doesn't resist.

thirty-six

You, Me ...and She?

11:45pm

Justice, who sits with his legs crossed on the edge of his bed in yoga-like position, is still on the game. With the lights out and the sound turned down on the TV, Justin walks into his son's room. "Sorry I'm late baby," as he kisses Justice on the forehead. "In case you're hungry—I gotcha sumptin' ta snack on." He doesn't have the heart to tell his son to turn everything off and go to bed after leaving him alone for so long. And so he compromises by saying, "Don't stay up too late baby—it's a school night." Justin vacates the room, tired and ready to go to bed himself.

Reeling in the aftermath, he still can't believe what just happened as he never intended to cross that line with Tae. He jumps in the shower and it's there where he feels the reality of his actions. The normally soothing spray of warm water burns his back as he rubs the bar of Zest over his drained body. For in the heat of passion she's left scratches around both shoulder blades. Though it was good—in hindsight he realizes it can't happen again and therefore hopes nothing will change between them. His thoughts fast forward to Natalie and the confusion he now adds to that situation. He wonders how he can love one woman—and yet screw another, but then remembers it's always been a way of life having done it for years with Teresha. Justin steps out the stall, moving to the mirror and turns his shoulder to view the damage—whelp marks decorate his back.

♥ ♥ ♥

The alarm sounds, Justin searches for the snooze button—forgetting his intent to get an early start. He shoves his face under his pillow, refusing to acknowledge the time. Ten minutes later he's once again reminded to get up. Turning over on his back, he stares at the ceiling—takes a deep breathe then glances at the clock—5:45am. Justin, now sitting straight up, doesn't move for another five minutes or so before rubbing his tired eyes. As his head pounds and his ears ring, he climbs out of bed, dragging his way to the kitchen. He stops to tap on Justice's door. "Wake up lil' man—we need ta be out of here by seven!" His toes twinge once touching the cold tile floor as he reaches for the Maxwell House from the cabinet and starts the coffee maker. He pauses for a second, leaning over the counter, then picks up the cordless. Dialing ten digits, the line rings with no answer. He disconnects prior to the machine starting, hits redial and after three more unanswered rings, Tae picks up.

"H-e-l-l-o." Her voice low and nearly inaudible.

"How ya feel?"

"H-e-e-e-y," she says, sounding as though she's stretching. "What time is it?"

"Six."

"What time did cha leave last night?"

"Had ta be 'bout eleven-thirty. ...I'll be ova there after I drop lil' man off. So get up."

Yawning, she asks, "Bout how long?"

"Hopefully no later than seven-thirty."

"Okay."

"I'll se ya in a few minutes."

"Bye."

As he puts down the phone, he's surprised there's no mention of last night's exploits—and probably for the first time ever, he feels almost uncomfortable talking to her.

He rushes Justice to get ready. And as planned, they leave the house about five minutes to seven. His inquisitive son questions him about the reason he has Tae's Mitsubishi instead of his Chrysler. "Cuz Tae got sick while we were out yesterday. So I drove her home and kept her truck. That' why I'm takin' ya ta school so early—so I have time ta go pick her up and still make it ta work on time."

"That's why you got home so late?"

"Yep. Had ta make sure she was straight before I left."

"Ms. Natalie called 'bout four times last night. Said she called your cell but ya neva called back." Justice wonders what his father is *really* up to.

"*Huh*—that's funny I don't remember gettin' any calls. ...Maybe my phone was off. I might need ta check my messages—huh?" he says, nonchalantly telling the intentional lie. The conversation ends when they reach Scott Road as Justice gets out. "Have a good day baby!"

"Bye Dad!"

Within the half-hour, Justin stands, freezing outside Shantel's River North residence waiting to be let in. Tae finally bounces downstairs in a long thick Terry robe with a toothbrush still stuck in her mouth and opens the door. "Well, good morning sexy." he says as he teases her for the uncouth entrance. She rolls her eyes. And without saying anything she leads him upstairs.

"I fixed a pot of coffee—so help yourself," she says while walking back to her bedroom.

"Girl, I thought ya said you were gonna be ready." He rinses out a mug sitting in the dish drain, helping himself to his second serving of the morning.

Tae pokes her head from around the bedroom door. "As I recall—that was you runnin' your mouth. I didn't promise anything!"

"Whatever—jus hurry up!" She slams the door shut. A second later Justin hears the shower running. He's astonished that still a word has yet to be said about last night. It's to the point now that it begins to affect his pride. And he's starting to think that maybe it was just he that enjoyed the experience. He then recalls that it was her doing all the screaming. "...So what was all that?" as he speculates with himself.

When Shantel reemerges from her room, she's half dressed wearing just a bra and skirt which she needs Justin to help zip. Turning her backside in his direction, she blurts, "Get this for me." While he attends to that, she puts in a pair of large hoop earrings. "Are you having trouble?" she asks, wondering why he hasn't gotten the zipper all the way up yet.

"Jus a lil'."

"Is it stuck?"

"Not now." Reversing the zipper back down, he turns Tae around facing him. "Why ya fuckin' wit me?" Justin then drops the skirt to her ankles. Lustfully, he stares at all that she has to offer. Her red bra and panties set against cocoa butter skin speaks louder than words. From the middle of the kitchen they stand hand in hand—both thinking the same thing. With a smile intent on seduction, she plays coy—asking, "So, what am I doin'?"

"Oh, you know. So how much time do we have?"

"You tell me. You the one barkin'." She rebuttals softly as their lips meet and every heed of warning goes out the window—and every room except the bedroom becomes their playground.

Forty minutes later—his head cocked over the couch, and eyes rolled back, Justin breathing heavily, attempts to catch his breath. Sweat covers his stark naked body.

"Get up! Get up! ...Jay, I don't that on my couch!"

"*What?*" he says, not wanting to move.

"Your cum silly! ...I don't want it all over my couch!"

"Hell, I should have left it in ya."

"No, ya shouldn't have! We were wrong for that anyway. I was suppose ta do like I did last night—and make ya put a cap on it! I can't trust you like that. ...I don't know where ya been." Justin knows that Tae gets a contraceptive shot every three months, so he shows no concern over their unprotected sex. She jumps up from on top of him, dashing to the bathroom before any of his dripping sperm can touch the sofa. She wipes off her inner thigh along with the rest of her lower body—returning with the same damp washcloth for Justin. "Here." she says, tossing the rag on his belly. "Why ya still layin' there? Get up so we can get in the shower." Rather wishing he could get in his bed and go back to sleep, Justin finally pulls himself up—slowly motivating himself to follow.

Though they share the tub—neither touches the other. Even after the great sex; they wash up—and get out. Justin, wrapped in only a towel, scours the apartment for his clothes—shirt and shoes on the kitchen floor, pants over by the TV, and his underwear sits on the arm of the sofa. He steps into the bathroom where Tae stands—still naked in front of a fogged mirror applying makeup. From behind, he pops her bare bottom, causing her to smear her eye shadow. He aggravates her before pressing his now clothed body against hers. "Stop boy!" But he proceeds to kiss the base of her neck. "Uh-uh—stop! You've done enough damage. ...Look at me!" She reveals three sizable passion marks located just below her ear. She tries to cover them with foundation to no avail.

"My bad! Hell, it was gettin' good!" Already late, Tae hurries to get dressed. As they go out the door Justin warns, "Get ready cause ya know Dee's ass gonna be trippin'—especially when he sees your neck."

"I'm not worried about him—it's Rhonda who scares me! You see the way she looks at me? ...I wanna ask her what's her problem."

"Oh that's jus Rhonda—she's like that wit everybody. I know one thing though—she's got my back! I wouldn't trade that woman for *nuthin'*." Justin pledges his loyalty.

"Any who, jus lock my door. You got the keys." She shows her lack of accord. It then occurs to Justin that he stood outside in the freezing cold for nothing—her keys were in his pocket the whole time.

"So, I guess I'm driving," he says, being sarcastic as Tae makes her way to the passenger side.

"Guess so." She waits for him to use the remote to unlock the door.

"Can I be honest 'bout sumptin'?" Both get in.

"By all means, go ahead." Tae says, insisting on the truth.

"I wasn't sure of what to say after last night."

"*Why?* That's silly."

"I don't know. I mean, it makes for a potentially uncomfortable situation. Shit, we work together, side by side. ...Hell, we play together! You know, who wants ta jeopardize *that*? ...I mean, and both of us are involved in other relationships!" he says, voicing his concern.

"*And*—so what?" She shows no remorse or regret for her actions as she takes down her sun visor for the lighted mirror—adding gloss to her lips.

"So, then what 'bout Quentin?"

"What about him? Like he has ta know what I'm doin'. I have no clue what he does up in Milwaukee—or anywhere else for that matter. ...And I can only imagine. Besides, it's different..." She stops there.

"Whatcha mean?"

She looks the other way before saying anything. "The relationships are different." She pauses. "Why do ya think I let this happen?"

"I don't know—horny maybe?" he says, giving her a silly smirk.

"Because doofus—I like what we have and I know that above all else... you'll be *here*. And I don't mean here in Chicago, but I know you'll be here for me. And you always have, whether you know it or not. …I can count on you. I can't say the same for Quentin. And that means a lot."

"Friends and lovers—huh?" Justin says, as he tries to make the correlation.

"A lil' deeper, but something like that."

"Were you ever jealous of Natalie?" He throws the question out there.

"You damn right. And I'm bein' honest! I don't like her. …It's jus something about her. She's not you! And it does something to me ta see you wit her. …I don't know why—I can't put my finger on it. But it jus does. It's sickenin'. But it's no different than what you feel for Quent. …You can't stand ta see us together—admit it? I could see it in your eyes when I used ta talk about him." She grins.

Again Justin returns a smirk—because she's right, "I know ya can do betta. I see how he treats ya. Yet ya keep puttin' up wit his bullshit. And I don't get it… You're intelligent, motivated… *Shit*—you're a beautiful girl! You ain't got ta go through half the shit you do—and I don't understand it!" He vehemently makes his point.

"It's no different with you. I've watched you go from relationship to relationship jus fuckin' up!" She laughs. "Why? Because they don't understand you! You're like a piece of fool gold—you glitter on the outside but once you flake off the top, what's left ain't worth shit!" she says, as she laughs even harder.

"*Damn*, am I that bad?" he asks, looking dejected.

"Yes Jay—you are! I hate ta be the bearer of bad news, but you have issues boo. …A whole lot of them!" she says, still laughing. "Jus keepin' it real."

Justin takes her comments personal. "*What?* You think I'm incapable of maintainin' a healthy relationship? You don't think I would know how ta love somebody or sumptin'?"

"Jay, neither one of us knows anything about love. Not from the standpoint of a relationship. But at least you have a son ta fill the void. All I have is you—my ever-faithful boss. And that's it!" It's through her smile that she hides the tears—as loneliness has gotten the best of her. "But that's why I stay close—you need me…"

"Like you need me!" He reciprocates the sentiment. "So, what's goin' on wit us? …Why we in this situation?"

"Two lost souls try'na find our way boo."

"Huh." Justin ponders the thought. "Still can't believe we crossed that line though."

"Boy, don't act so surprised. Ain't like it took much—flashed a lil' of this poonanny and that's all she wrote! ...Game over! You were easy." Tae makes light of the conversation.

Grinning, he says, "I'll give it to ya—you got it goin' on!" He compliments her sexual prowess.

At the office, Rhonda greets the two with messages and schedules for the day. In departing, Tae blows Justin a kiss as they separate to their individual suites. She makes it her business to leave him with something to reminisce on. By swishing her form fitted ass down the hallway, she shows off her skirt's provocative rear center split. As expected—Justin looks.

thirty-seven

The Way To A Man's Heart

The big news on Friday afternoon is that it appears by all accounts that Demetrius has worked a verbal signing commitment from Winston Jeffries a.k.a. Nigel the Great—the kid from Connecticut. Having just heard, Justin expresses his gratitude as he passes Dee in the hallway. "Good job man. ...When ya ready ta fly out there and close this thing?" he asks, giving Dee dap.

"Should be right after the holidays. ...Looks like mama pulls the strings. So you know how that goes... Bitch wanna make sure she gets a new house—know what I'm sayin'? But it's all-good—we'll ink this thang ta start the New Year off baby!"

"Word. So then we can count on it?" Justin asks, seeking his personal reassurance.

"Like death and taxes nigga!"

"Al-ight." He pats Dee on the back before continuing to the front desk. But he's beaten to the punch as Rhonda rounds the corner headed in his direction—bearing gifts.

"Surprise, surprise!" she yells, as she grins from ear to ear. "Sir, look what jus arrived for you." She holds up a bouquet of flowers—a mixture of red tulips and blue irises, beautifully contained in a red transparent vase.

Caught off guard, Justin takes the vase as a frown of curiosity consumes his face. "Thank ya." He twirls the bright arrangement in the light—searching for the card. But Rhonda finds it first and hands it to him.

"Here ya go." She stands there smiling—being quite nosy, waiting for Justin to read the card. He thanks her again but turns around to head back to his office for the privacy. He leaves Rhonda standing in the middle of the corridor—arms crossed and looking offended. Once inside, he closes the door behind him and immediately sets the flowers on his desk. Holding the card, he wouldn't think it would be Tae sending something of this nature—not to the office; yet stranger things have happened. Justin removes the greeting from its envelope, which reads.

"Life is too short to live it without you…"

I love you,

Natalie

Simple and to the point—yet very effective, Justin takes a seat and starts his usual second-guessing. After his Wednesday evening and Thursday morning romp with Tae, things would have been a lot easier and convenient if Natalie would have just walked away after Tuesday's argument.

"Damn." Consumed with guilt, he closes his eyes attempting to relax. It's the same shit all over again. Justin, having destroyed yet another relationship, bows to the temptation of making it right. He calls Natalie at work. She answers as the sound of laughter fills the bustling background. "Hey." His somber tone expresses remorse.

"Hey." A similar drab voice speaks—followed by a long pause.

"Thank you. I got the flowers—and the message."

"Good." She speaks softly despite her coworkers' boisterous shenanigans.

"I've missed you." But Natalie doesn't respond. "I'm sorry. Can you please forgive me? …I shouldna acted like that."

"I wanna see you," she says, breaking her shroud of silence.

"When?" Justin eagerly accepts.

"Tonight," She responds with her voice hurting.

"Okay." He Pauses. "Eight sound al-ight?"

"Yep." Her voice gets more and more feeble.

"Are you al-ight?"

Again—at first, nothing's said. But she soon responds with a very non convincing, "Yep."

"You sho'?"

"I'm alright," she says, perking herself up enough to satisfy Justin's concern.

"So I'll see ya at eight then. Your place—right?"

"Yep."

After another lengthy pause, Justin dispenses with the conversation. "Bye." He disconnects, feeling funny, rather apprehensive about having to face her later and act as though everything is okay. He justifies himself by confessing his love for her. Yet, in his mind rings Tae's condemning words of delusional love. Again, he ponders the question, "How can I do this to her?" He wonders if his feelings for Natalie are really considered love—or is it just infatuation based on his need to be loved? Almost daydreaming, he reflects on that thought until Tae enters the room.

"Snap out of it Jay—we got work ta do!" She bombards his office, dropping a financial report concerning Envy's sales forecast down in front of him. "Let me show you something," she says, pointing to a particular figure on the first page. "...Look at this—now tell me what you see?" Then she makes herself quite at home by copping a seat on the corner of Justin's desk as he studies the report. She notices the beautiful bouquet of flowers also sitting there—she picks at the leaves but doesn't immediately inquire as to their sender. "Don't ya feel like dinner tonight?"

Still engrossed by the document, he says, "I can't. Got otha plans—maybe tomorrow." He never looks up.

"Oh okay." And because it's not the answer she wants to hear, she violently plucks a leaf from the bouquet—destroying it between her fingers. Justin, who's preoccupied, doesn't see her do it. "So, where did ya get the flowers? ...They're beautiful!" She sniffs the arrangement, pretending to admire them for their splendor.

"Yeah—ain't they nice? Nat sent those awhile ago. ...Yo, explain to me whatcha talkin' 'bout—I'm not seeing any problem here." Changing the subject, he refers back to the report.

"Look Jay..." Grabbing the document, "If you take the projected revenue based on this demographic right here—then why are we incurring *these* costs if our target market is ova *here!*" she says, pointing again at her initial figure along with an analysis graphic on the same page.

Justin takes another look—now understanding her argument. "*Yeeeah*—you right. Tell ya what… Call Atlanta, get in touch wit Margret LeMay since she's our Budget Manager on this project. See what she says. Otherwise, I'm like you, that's not our responsibility. …Good catch! See whatcha can find out." He returns the report to Shantel, who practically snatches it from his hand as she vacates his office. Justin immediately glances at the flowers on his desk—fully aware of her problem. It's exactly the kind of thing he was worried about as shit is already coming between their work relationship. He sighs before sitting down.

Over on the Westside, Natalie rushes through her apartment door carrying a bag of groceries. She calls out to her daughter for help. "ASIA! Come put up the food baby!" She pauses—tapping her fingers against the counter while standing in her kitchen contemplating her next move, "Now where should I start?" Answering her own questions, Natalie pulls a carton of fresh strawberries from the grocery bag—grabbing a knife out the dishwasher. She starts slicing them into a bowl. Once finished, Natalie sprinkles sugar over the top and places the Tupperware dish in the refrigerator. "ASIA! …I thought I told you to come put these groceries up!" She takes out a box of Duncan Hines cake mix and sets it on the stove. She stops—wondering why Asia hasn't answered. Her intuition tells her to check the bedroom. "Gurl, you don't hear me talkin' to you?" She pushes the door open to find Asia sound asleep across her bed. Natalie delivers a sigh of relief— happy that all is okay. It worries her having a twelve year old come home to an empty apartment most afternoons while she works. It's one of the things she wishes she could change about her life—as its hard being a single parent. She leaves Asia to sleep while heading back into the kitchen.

After the cake is in the oven, Natalie reaches for her blender stored underneath the sink. From the refrigerator she takes out a couple tomatoes, a jar of minced clams and from the freezer, and pulls down a bag of frozen cocktail shrimp. She runs cold water over the shrimp to unthaw while preparing the paste for the red clam sauce. Tonight, it's her every intention to show Justin just how special he is—above any other man.

As a pot of linguine boils on the stove, she makes a call to her brother Brunell. "Hey my favorite big brother. You still taking the kids to the movies for me?" she asks, having pre-planned the occasion. Once he gives her the confirmation, she shows her gratitude. "Thanks Nelly—I owe you dear. ...Yep—around eight. See ya then, bye!" She ends this call only to make another to Justin's cell.

"Hey girl—what's goin' on?" He answers, already knowing who's on the other end.

"Hey baby. ...Are we still on for tonight?

"Oh yeah—we'll be there! First—I'ma run and get sumptin' ta eat right quick..." He gets interrupted.

"*Ut-um!* That's why I called. Got a lil' surprise for you. Don't worry about Justice cause I already have the kids squared away. So, you all can jus come on whenever you get ready—and we'll be here—okay baby?"

"Whatcha got up those pretty lil' sleeves girl?"

"You'll see. So y'all c'mon!" She holds him to the mystery.

"Al-ight—give us a minute, we'll be there."

"I love you baby." she says, gushing with emotion.

"Love ya too girl."

"*Byyye.*" Her mood is now uplifted—a far cry from earlier as she's happy to get everything back to the way it was.

"Bye baby." And once Justin hangs up, Natalie continues devising her gourmet meal—taking the thawed shrimp and tossing them into a ready frying pan basted in butter, parsley, and scallions for the scampi. She waits to do the salad and bread until after she jumps in the shower.

"Asia—get up gurl! Your Uncle Nel will be here in a few—so fix yourself! ...Make sure ya look decent—get that hair together! He's taking you and Justice out tonight."

A discombobulated Asia arises, having only heard Justice's name. "Mama, when is Justice coming?" Her head still swirling from the deep sleep.

"They'll be here in a lil' while—so get up!"

"Okay Mama." Quickly she pops forward—bouncing out her bed in search of a comb.

"Baby, while ya doin' that—do mama a big favor and watch the food for me while I run and get in the shower."

"Yes Ma'am."

With the water on, creating a cloudy mist over the entire master bath, Natalie escapes to the tight confines of her bedroom closet as she rambles through her cramped wardrobe. "Gurl, what are we *wearin'* tonight?" she says, as she talks to herself. "...What would make my baby happy?" She takes down a few pieces—holding each up to the light before finally deciding on a comfortable, yet cute, Japanese Yukata. She lays the kimono robe across the bed and steps out of her clothes. Tipping towards the shower, she makes a pit stop at the commode for a tinkle—then hops in. From the shower caddy at the back of the stall, she snatches an apricot scrub that she applies to her face. The pulsating water rejuvenates her tired body—working wonders on those tense and worn muscles. Natalie, unraveling her pink scrubby from around the faucet, uses it to lather herself before reaching for a Bic razor to shave her thick calves and thighs. She desires for her skin to be silky smooth to Justin's touch. Removing the retractable massaging head, she rinses her every mountain and valley—but is careful not to wet her pinned hair. The slick floor causes her to almost slip as she steps out the stall. Natalie, who wraps a towel around herself—covering the top of her breast down to her bottom cheek, exits the room—still dripping wet as she drops booty first on the edge of her bed where the baby oil and lotion awaits.

Rubbing the Johnson & Johnson over her arms and legs, she applies the oil to bring a glistening sheen to her already radiant skin. The lotion relieves the dryness caused by scrub—adding the needed moisture. She slides on a crimson thong to compliment her scarlet kimono—electing to do without the bra, and then finishes her preparation with two modest squirts of Chloe'. "There. It's all for you baby," she says as she makes her way to the kitchen.

"*Oool* mama. Why ya got that on?" Frowned, Asia disagrees with her mother's choice of attire. "Ya shoulda wore yo white fleece mini wit the slit and that white halter top—the one that shows yo belly button Mama. I know Mr. Vaughn would like that!" She smiles, feeling that she's found the magic combination to her mother's drab love life.

Natalie shakes her head in disbelief. "Baby—you got a lot ta learn. It doesn't take all that ta hold a good man's attention. ...He'll look past all that otha stuff cause a good man looks deeper than the surface—past the pretty faces, fake boobs, and big butts. He looks at a woman's heart—and that's where he'll find the real you—and all that you really bring to the table baby. ...That's where yo mama will come out on top every time!" She twists and shakes her romp—flaunting her walk as she passes her daughter on the couch. "Besides baby, mama happens ta like this outfit—it's simple, comfortable ...and convenient!"

Laughing at herself and the hidden innuendo, she struts the whole way to the kitchen.

"So, if it's all like that Mama—why ya went ta Frederick's last week ta buy dat skirt den?" she asks, busting her mama out.

"Hush gurl—and stay out of grown folk's business!" Natalie tends to the meal—throwing a bit of "do as I say—and not as I do" advice toward her daughter.

She finishes the last details to her cake—adding strawberries atop the whipped icing made from cream cheese, powered sugar, and sour cream. Now some two and a half hours later—with everything ready and waiting, Natalie finds herself finally able to sit down and relax. She assumes her restful position on the sofa—next to Asia. The two sit in silence until there's a knock at the door. "Baby, get that for Mommy— I bet that's your uncle." Asia skips to the door—squinting through the peephole before opening it.

"It's him Mama." She unlocks the deadbolt.

"Hey! There's my girl. How you pretty lady?" he says, as he reaches for a hug.

"I'm fine. ...Momma's ova there." Pointing to the couch, she tries avoiding the customary chit chat that comes with talking to her much older relatives. As of right now, her Uncle is just the sideshow to her main event—Justice.

"Hey Sis—and how are you?" He steps around Asia where he sees his little sister laid back and comfy—looking exhausted.

"I'm makin' it. I can't complaint." Easing herself up, she asks, "And you?"

"The same. You know... 'Fakin' it till I make it' as always. Gotta keep sumthin' goin'," he says while walking toward the kitchen. "This is quite a spread sis. ...So, where is our guest of honor anyway?" He nibbles on a leftover strawberry.

"He should be here shortly. Thanks again Nel—I'll make sure ta save ya a plate.

"No biggie. It ain't everyday I get to see my baby sis—all in love and happy. So the pleasure's all mine. ...It's jus good ta see ya smilin' again." Stepping behind the sofa he squeezes both her shoulders— pleased by her newfound bliss.

"Dunk-dunk-dunk!" As there's yet another echoing knock at the front door. And this time, no one has to tell Asia to answer. After an exchange of greetings, she invites the fellas in. Asia then, full of her usual exuberance, rushes to tell Justice their plans for tonight—pulling him by the arm to her room. Justin can't help but to smile at the two of them, amused by their comradery. Without any hesitancy, he respectfully shoots over to Brunell—still perched behind the sofa, as they acknowledge one another with a welcoming handshake.

"Good ta see ya again man."

"You too… How's life treatin' ya? Hard gettin' used to this Chicago weather—isn't it?"

"Oh fo' sho! …And we ova by the lake too—it's a mess!" Both laugh at Justin's obvious struggle to adapt to the cold and windy conditions. "But we here—so I guess that means we al-ight then—huh?"

"Yes sir—that's one way of lookin' at it! You'll get used to it—jus takes a lil' time," as Brunell tries to encourage him.

"And what 'bout you man? …How's everything?" Justin returns the concern.

"Oh, I'm good. As long as I got my health and strength—and my family's alright..," reaching again to the shoulders of Natalie for a light press. "…then everything is wonderful."

"Yep. I know whatcha mean." Justin agrees just to be saying something. A brief pause comes over their conversation, and he uses the opportunity to say hello to his beautiful hostess. "Hey baby," he says, as he reaches down for a kiss which becomes something more.

"*Muuuah*, I love you." Natalie wastes no time in expressing her rooted feelings.

"I love you back—*muuuah*." Planting another kiss, their lips tango for a deep passionate reconciling moment.

Almost embarrassed by his baby sister's affectionate actions, Brunell humbly dismisses himself from the room to gather the kids. "You all enjoy yourselves—and have a good time. Me and the kids, we'll see ya later," he says as he tries whisking the teens past the "R" rated activity and out the front door.

"*BYE!*" shouts Natalie.

"See y'all!" Justin says, also responding. "So, where are they goin'?" unaware of her plans.

"Does it matter? They're in good hands." Natalie throws her arms around Justin, pressing her forehead against his while finishing her statement. "At least we're alone."

"I hear ya." Justin agrees, allowing Natalie to become the aggressor as she tugs her willing participant onto the sofa. They lay crammed in close quarters continuing what they started. Face to face—tongues mingled, her loose garment sags across the front, partially exposing her palm fitting pointed breast. The wetness from her still shower damp body seeps through her thin cottony robe and unto his pleated slacks and pastel shirt. Justin helps his situation by untying her gold sash—separating the two sides. He splits his time between succulent wonders—tenderly passing his mouth over each firmly aroused nipple. But he then stops abruptly, having caught a whiff of the tantalizing aromas permeating from the stove. "Hmmm—what's cookin?"

"Huh?" Swept away in the pleasure, she finds her fantasy session interrupted as she's lost track of the world around her.

'On the stove boo!" he says, bringing her quickly back to reality.

"Shit!" She pushes Justin to the floor as she jumps to her feet. "The food baby—you let me forget!" She sprints to the kitchen.

"What? I ain't know nuthin' 'bout no food!" Holding his back, Justin picks himself up from off the carpet "...Damn girl, that actually hurt."

"I'm sorry baby. I couldn't burn your surprise," she says as she turns the stove off and dashes to Justin's aid—helping him to his feet. She rubs his aching back before delivering a sympathetic peck to his cheek. "I got jus the trick for that later." Smiling, she directs him to a seat at the dining room table. In the brief chaos, she's forgotten that her kimono is wide open where she finds Justin's wandering eyes glued to her every move. "Cha," realizing his focus, she gives a bogus sneer while clutching her robe closed. "Do ya mind?" Rolling her eyes—pretending to be pretentious, she roves by the couch for her sash.

"I like your lil' oriental thingy. It's cute," he comments with his finger enfolded over his lip.

"Oh, we know. Especially what's under it." Her confidence borders the point of almost being cocky.

"Oh, so now ya think ya know me—is that it?"

"I'm pretty sure I know whatcha want." She stands at his side, holding a loaded plate. "Here! ...Now eat!"

"*Nah*. I'll wait on ya. ...Go fix ya plate."

"Ummm—oh how kind of you sir." Surprised, she compliments with sarcasm as she prepares her helping. Rejoining Justin, she sits—silently blessing her food. With a piece of garlic bread in one hand and his packed fork in the other, Justin makes little haste in satisfying his appetite. Natalie watches with blatant wonder. "Must be good?"

"Um-hmmm ...very." he says, as he's hardly able to open his mouth.

Still fixated, Natalie, having contemplated the moment, unleashes her innermost wish. "I don't wanna fight anymore—about anything. I jus want *this* to work baby." Releasing her fork, her delicate hand now caresses his ingrained jaw. "I don't want us ta ever argue over Chris— so jus tell me what I need ta do?" Her eyes fill with unwavering devotion.

Momentarily stifled by the question, Justin stops chewing— swallowing much of his mouth's contents whole. He collects himself— modifying his mood to a solemn seriousness before speaking. "I don't know what you're expectin' me ta say—I mean, he's a part of your life that I wish wasn't there—but now what? ...Cause nuthin' will ever change that—right?"

"Justin—baby! He's my daughter's father ...nothing else. He's not any threat to you and I baby. ...I don't understand why can't you see that?"

Justin takes the napkin folded next to his plate and raises it to his mouth—wiping each corner with methodical perfection. He appears completely miffed by Natalie's absolute denial of any wrongdoing. "Because for one... I've watched you. And the mere mention of his fuckin' name brings a damn glow to your fuckin' face—am I right?" His tone and words divulge a subdued anger.

Natalie's eyes bulge, realizing the topic has struck a sensitive chord with her mate. "Baby, you're wrong—and please stop cussing at me. Justin, I jus wanna talk and try and work through this baby. I'm tryin' ta be honest and open with you. But you're readin' into something that's not there..."

"So, you're sayin' that there ain't the slightest piece of your soul that doesn't still have feelings for that man? ...On the real—since ya wanna be honest and open and all. So what's up?" His gesturing hands demonstrate the rage within his scrutiny. Lowering her head, Natalie doesn't respond. "That's what I fuckin' thought! Grabbing his fork, he continues with the meal—heartbroken by the truth, yet unwilling to break. His venous forehead displays the torment. The rationale behind his erratic relationship with Tae becomes increasingly clearer. She represents his peace—an escape from within the confusion; that safe place from which to hide from all failure and frustration. And whatever guilt he once felt because of their sexual involvement, now subsides as Natalie tries to explain.

"You have ta understand that Chris came into my life at a time when no one else was there..." Her emotional words are spoken with careful adaptation. She makes contact with Justin's idle hand—playing with each of his loose fingers. "...I was alone—and I was hurting." With tears now flowing, "My mama hated me. She blamed me for my daddy being taken away from her..."

Expressing some sense of compassion, Justin interjects, "But it wasn't your fault ...You said you'd tried tellin' her, but she wouldn't listen. Your Uncle was hurting you—he stole your innocence and your father only did what any man would do for his child. ...He made it right—and ta him that was worth the price he had ta pay for protecting his family. ...I woulda did the same. ...But your momma, she can't see all that. She only sees that she lost a brother and a husband—probably the two most important men in her life—know what I mean?" And with Justin's elaboration, Natalie never gets the chance to finish her side of the story. He stops to wipe the tears from her flushed face. He begins to feel that maybe he is being too hard on her—she's been through a lot. Though it doesn't excuse what he sees as unjustified confusion on her part, he decides to seize the moment for what it's worth and deal with the harder punches later.

During the course of the dinner, Natalie stares as Justin avoids any deep eye-confessing contact. It's like she knows that something's different—it's almost as if she can smell Tae's expensive scent still attached to his pores. "I love you," unexpectedly tumbles from her mouth. She then waits for his reply. But the more those three little words are tossed about—the less they tend to hold their weight.

"Ditto girl." he responds, using the term once offered by his son. Though funny how convenient its casual reference, now relates.

thirty-eight

If Ever A Doubt...

While his son sleeps, Justin, during Monday's predawn hours, pounds vigorously away on a Nautilus treadmill located downstairs in the fitness center. It's been since Thanksgiving—the extra meals and lack of exercise, that Justin has noticed a returning bulge around his midsection. He hasn't been able to get out in the mornings for his usual jog because of the freezing temperatures and the added responsibilities of raising his son. So he finds the next best thing— taking full advantage of the amenities offered at his residence. The 5:30am opening works perfectly with his morning schedule.

Having taped a note to Justice's bedroom door, informing his normally light sleeping son of his whereabouts, he removes it at roughly six-twenty, undisturbed as baby boy silently slumbers. Winded by his workout, Justin lumbers into Justice's room—searching the wall for the light switch. But as he passes through the doorway, not paying any attention, he trips over a clutter of clothes strewn across the floor. The half stumble drops him to one knee, "Ssshit! ...All this *damn* mess!" Steamed, he blindly finds the lamp next to the bed and turns it on. "Boy, getcha ass up—time for school!" He shakes his son with disgust who sleeps through the commotion of his blundering. *"Get up!* …I ain't gonna tell you no more. Now getcha ass up!" Justin rises to his feet as Justice rolls towards his chastising father squinting—then throwing an arm across his face because of the glaring light.

"What time is it Pops?" he asks, barely coherent.

"Time ta get up—that's what! …And clean this damn room before ya leave out this house!" Justin barks, kicking his way through the junk, as he makes for the door. Justice turns back over, covering his head with a pillow as he attempts to block out his dad's nagging words.

Once up, Justice, obeying his father's wishes, gathers the mess he's neglected for weeks. He realizes he's taken a few extra liberties since coming to live in Chicago. He knows that his mama would have never put up with his sheer trifling ways. But that was always the difference between his two parents. His mother was never too busy to notice the little things while his dad, on the other hand, was always too preoccupied with everything else to notice anything until there was a problem—always a day late. Squatted on the floor in front of the TV, he separates clothes—clean from dirty as Justin pokes his head into the room, "You ready baby. It's 'bout that time." His dad's whole demeanor has changed.

"Yes sir." Justice reaches for the remote to turn off the television, grabbing his book bag as he exits the room.

At the end of another speechless journey, Justin puts his son out at the usual spot and goes through his accustomed dialogue—"Have a good day. Call me when you get home." etc., before pulling off en route to Michigan Avenue. Only this time, he doesn't leave right away. He takes a second to watch his son disappear behind the school doors. He reflects upon the days of walking Justice to his kindergarten class—how tight baby boy would hold his hand, too afraid to let go. He remembers the sense of pride in knowing his son's reliance on his protection and security—that feeling of significance and reverence. He misses that. And now Justin watches his nearly six-foot seed quickly becoming his own man—the years having passed right before his eyes. He wonders if he's missed the whole point—realizing his need to spend more time with Justice before it's too late.

♡   ♡   ♡

Like most mornings, Justin arrives at the office around 8am—about an hour early, to give himself a minute to relax and prep for the day. Usually he stops for a cappuccino and bagel before he gets to the office. But Mondays are a bitch to get in and out of the area coffeehouse because of the weekend's returning workforce in need of that extra motivation to get the new week started. Thus not wanting to be bothered with the wait or the traffic, he skips breakfast.

Justin spots Tae vacating her vehicle as he approaches his reserved park. She's holding a small white box and a carrier with two Styrofoam cups, which Justin hopes is the answer to his prayers. He drives past the parking spot, circling back around the lot to intersect Tae as she starts towards the building—her hands full. With abandon, he recklessly pulls in front her—causing a near panic attack. Justin runs down his mirror-tinted glass—proudly smirking, offers his service. "Looks like ya need a hand."

Despite the careless prank, Tae smiles—obviously smitten by Justin's unexpected presence. "Sure. ...You see I stopped by Benini's and picked us *both* up something"

"*Al-ight*. Wait a second ...Betta yet, hop in so I can park." She hands Justin both cartons through the window and jumps in on the passenger side. Moments later, the two walk inside to his office where they can sit down, eat and talk in peace.

"I started to call y'all on Saturday ta see if ya wanted to rent a few movies. Maybe grab a pizza. But I figured you and lil' Jay probably wanted ta spend some time alone... Do y'all lil' male bonding thing. I know the opportunities are few and far between. Maybe we'll get chance ova the holidays while school is out. He gets out this Wednesday—doesn't he?" Tae clears the table in the extra sitting area.

"Naw—on Friday." Justin answers with the phone stuck to his ear while standing behind his desk checking messages. "Hey, what's Mike Gradaski's extension?"

"2287. *What he want?*" she asks, being nosy.

"Hold on." Justin dials the number. "Hey Mike, it's me. ...I got your message. Buzz me as soon as you get in. I wanna go ova the schedule before the meeting. So call ASAP—al-ight? Bye." After placing the phone down, he makes his way over to Tae for an abbreviated breakfast. "Naw—Mike finally got those tentative promotional tour dates together for the girls. ... Says we're lookin' at 20 cities in thirty days. And it looks like we're still set for April."

"Good. And it's about time!" She expresses what he's already thinking.

"I know, right. I still need ta see what he's got prior to the conference call. ...Wanna make sure we're on one accord before talkin' to Riq. …Got that whole media campaign thing ta look into today, too."

"So stop runnin' your mouth and sit down. You'll need that energy—trust me. …Got a full day ahead of you. Here ya go." She slides a cup of French vanilla coffee along with a split cinnamon and raisin bagel in front of him.

"Thank ya. I appreciate this boo. Guess I'm in your debt again—huh?"

"…Who's counting?" She smiles as she spreads the cream cheese between the two slices—then feeds him the first piece. "Bite!" Tae's got that Kelly Rowland thing going this week with the long jet-black curly weave. Justin definitely likes what he sees. Yet the attraction is mutual.

"I see ya have no problem spoilin' a nigga. …Al-ight. Ya betta watch yourself—be dun started sumptin' up in here!" He sinks his teeth into half of what she has in her hand.

"*Whatever.* Shut up and chew! Ain't like you can handle this no way." She shoves the remaining piece into his mouth—partially missing her target, intentionally smearing the strawberry flavored topping across his cheek.

"Hey whatcha doin'!" Justin says as he objects to the idea of having his face made a mess of.

"Ooops—my bad baby. …Let me get that." The provocative nature of her response lends some indication of her next move as she leans over licking the creamy remains from around his mouth. But before she can finish, Dee crashes the party as he bolts through the door unannounced.

"What up—what up!" Both Justin and Tae jump. She quickly reverses her course pulling herself away from Justin—implying that nothing was going on. She inconspicuously sucks the cream cheese residue off her fingers. "So, where's mine?" As Demetrius wants to know why hadn't he been included. "Oh, I see how y'all niggas wanna be. Wanna forget all 'bout a nigga! …That's al-ight. Forgit cha'll! …Jay, I need ta holla at ya when you get a minute." Though he laughs out loud—attempting to make light of the matter, yet to know Dee, Justin is very aware of truth behind his words.

"So talk! Don't mind me." A smug Tae, now on the other side of the table, nibbles on an onion bagel while doing her best to aggravate Dee.

"Last muthafuckin' time I checked—it was supposed ta be an A & B conversation meaning... C yo ass on up outta here! And what da fuck you all ova my man fo anyway? Try'na screw yo way to the top! ...I saw ya. *What?* Y'all fuckin' now? ...I interrupt sumthin'?" Tae, having accomplished her goal, starts an avalanche of questions from Demetrius. She was fortunate the week prior after narrowly escaping his tenacious wrath, as he never mentioned the hickeys on her neck. But this time, her compromising position has caught Dee's unyielding curiosity. He then turns to Justin. "What up Jay? ...Thought ya was my man. You holdin' out now nigga?"

"Nah man whatcha talkin' 'bout?" Justin denies all accusations.

"And what if we were? ...The way I see it—wouldn't be none of your business anyway!" Tae continues her pretentious ways, causing more vexation.

"You right!" Dee says, now lifting his voice to a squeal. "That's y'all shit..."

"So mind your damn business!" Smirking, Tae interjects in a patronizing nonchalant tone—adding to the mockery.

Justin—taking his usual role, intercedes, "Let me finish eating— then I'll be ova there."

"Bet... Yo ya need ta check yo bitch!" Dee grievously eyes Tae before leaving the room.

"*Whoa!* ...C'mon nah chill nigga. This is still a place of business. Don't forget that shit!" Justin warns his disgruntled colleague. Demetrius retreats to his cubicle without any further discord.

"Let him talk. ...Like I'm scared. He must think I'm one of his whores. Cause he got the wrong one Jay!"

"Both of y'all trippin'. And if ya keep it up I'll make sure one of y'all gets a one way ticket back down ta Atlanta—fo' sho'!"

"*Anyway.* I know I'm not goin' anywhere." Tae gives Justin a light kiss on the forehead, then wipes away any evidence left by the Fashion Fair sheer clear gloss before heading towards her office. "Finish your food. I'll be back later," she says, her swagger exuding the confidence of royalty. And she's absolutely right. She wouldn't be the one to pack her bags, as she's too much of an asset—and ally. In his subconscious mind, Justin agrees.

♡ ♡ ♡

Tuesday brings more of the same as Justin and Tae have once again cornered themselves in his office—entangled amidst another precarious position, as this time it's Rhonda who happens to wander through the partly open door. She bears appalling witness to their inappropriate behavior as Tae is found receiving comfort on Justin's lap, with both seemingly amused by something on his computer.

"Mr. Vaughn!" Rhonda announces herself, not wanting to step all the way in the room.

Caught—but thinking fast, Tae turns the damning moment into one of humorous innocence. "Thanks for the seat Justin. Maybe the next time I won't be clumsy enough ta trip ova my own feet!" Laughing at herself, she hops up gathering the papers she brought in with her—handing Rhonda two envelopes. "Oh Rhonda… Can you please make sure these go out with today's mail?"

"Yes Ms. Norris," she says, reluctantly accepting the assignment.

"Thanks Rhonda." She vacates the scene with a huge condescending smirk on her face. "Talk to ya later Jay!"

"Al-ight" Turning then to his secretary, Justin inquires about the reason for the unanticipated visit. "So what's up Rhonda?"

"You have a guest waiting to see you in the lobby sir." She addresses Justin in a professional manner. Yet her tone reaps the repulsiveness of her thinking.

"Well, who is it?" Justin responds with abruptness, as he's not in the mood for playing guessing games. But Rhonda releases only a nod—gesturing towards the lobby, refusing to concede any further info. Beside himself, Justin, expressing the disfavor of her contempt, storms out of his office headed to the front. He rounds the hall corner to be met by the warm welcoming smile of Natalie—his supposed better half. "Hey girl—whatta surprise!" His expression collaborates the sentiment.

"Hey baby. I came by ta see if you had time for lunch?" She reaches for the bottom of his blazer, drawing Justin in close for a quick smack.

After the kiss, he looks to his watch, checking the time. "*Aaah*… Yeah I think I can swing it… Can you give me a minute?" It's only 11:30 in morning—and much earlier than his usual lunch-time departure.

"Take all the time you need baby. My time is your time." She exposes a subtle smirk, affirming her willingness to wait. "I'll be sittin' right here until your return—how's that?" While attempting to reclaim her sofa seat in the lobby, Justin poses a better suggestion.

"Naw baby. Ya ain't gotta sit out here… C'mon back. You can chill in my office until I finish. It's only gonna take a second." He chuckles at her eagerness and committedness to please.

"What ch'ou laughin' at?" she asks, curious to know the subject of his amusement.

"*You.*" He says, while still chuckling.

"Why?"

"Oh no reason—c'mon!" He grabs her hand and escorts her down the corridor of office suites.

"Uh—don't I feel special." She pops her lips and rolls her head being playfully animated—impressed by the ritzy surroundings. "So, I finally get ta see how y'all six-figure folks do y'all thang—huh?"

"Whatcha talkin' 'bout silly?" he asks, as he entertains the comment.

"If mama could see me now." Natalie ignites into ball of laughter. She stops in the middle of the hall—practically on her knees, while still holding Justin's hand as she tries to compose herself behind the inside joke. "*Whatever.*" Finally calm, she wipes away the tears of her hysterics before making the cynical remark.

Justin, who feels like he's just missed the punch line, is a bit confused by the outburst. "Did I jus miss sumptin'?"

"Nope. Thinkin' 'bout my crazy mama," she says, as she reflects to an earlier moment in her life when her mother used to preach to her as a young girl about what to look for in a good man. Of course finances are at the top of the list. Yet it's the hollowness of Camille's trite character, even back then, that spurs the sudden eruption of emotions.

"Alrighty then." Justin, choosing to skip past the dramatics, opens the door to his office. "Here we go. Make yourself at home."

Stepping in, Natalie looks around the spacious suite soon acknowledging its lavishness. "Baby, this is really nice."

"Yeah, that's what I thought when they first moved me in here. ...Damn sure a notch above Atlanta!" Poised over his desk, Justin picks up the phone. "Excuse me boo. I need ta handle sumptin' right quick—al-ight?"

"Go ahead baby. I'm fine." Staying out of Justin's way, she wanders the room, admiring the different paintings and personal photographs scattered around the space. She particularly gets a special kick from a vintage picture of Justin and Jerome posing in their b-boy gear—arms crossed in Adidas windbreakers and shell-tops. Justin wears a step box doo like Bobby Brown during his "My Prerogative" days. Natalie enjoys a good laugh at the expense of the ridiculously outdated piece of history. Next, she glances over a professionally produced black and white of Justin and a then three or four year old Justice—both topless, as Justin coddles his son amidst his powerful arms. She reverences Justice's handsomeness—even at that age. Just above rests another portrait—a 10"x13" oil, a recent reproduction of whom she assumes is Teresha, based solely on the undeniable likeness to that of Justice. The vibrant piece brings an eerie chill over her body—she quickly moves on.

"*Yoo-hoo!* ...Is anybody home?" Knocking and entering at the same time, Tae initiates a precipitous end to Natalie's tour. Moving straight towards Justin, she doesn't notice Natalie—coming uncomfortably close to her boss, who gives a cold shoulder to their now accustomed affectionate touches. Tae, who backs off, reacts with a baffled look—offended by the blow off. While still on the phone, Justin cuts an eye in the direction of Natalie, attempting to warn Tae. Now busted for a third time, he develops a tight wrenching burning in his chest—like that of acid indigestion, as he's sickened by this latest screw up. Comprehending the clue, Tae—not knowing whom it is she will see, reorganizes her approach, throwing on a fake smile as she turns towards the trespasser. "Hey gurl! I'm sorry. I didn't mean to be so rude! ...It's good ta see ya again." She walks over to Natalie for a hug. But the swarming hospitality is transparent after having witnessed her initial entry.

"It's Shantel—isn't it?" Natalie confronts her competition—feeling the obvious attraction Tae has for her man.

"*Yyeeaahh*. You remembered," she says, surprised by the positive ID.

"Ummm-huh. ...I don't forget names."

As the two engage in territorial chit chat, Justin nervously continues his conversation, worried that Tae may slip at the tongue. Once off the phone, he hurries their departure—avoiding further discussion between the two. "Boo, are you ready? I need ta be back in an hour so we betta get movin'!"

"Okay baby—I'm waitin' on you." Natalie proudly responds to her man's beckoning. "Girl, it was good talkin' to ya again ...Maybe we can get together sometime—have a girl's night out or something..." she says, as she perpetrates her willingness to extend open communications.

"I'd like that! ...Get Justin to give you my number and we'll set that up soon—alright?" Tae makes sure to remind Natalie of Justin's convenient access to her.

"Okay!"

"Make sure you call me now—I'll be waitin'!" she says, continuing to let it be known.

"I will." Natalie heads to the arms of Justin. "I'm ready hon," she says, openly displaying her devotion.

"Let me get my keys." But before he can get his hand inside the drawer, Natalie pulls a set from her purse dangling them in his face.

"What's those?" Looking perplexed.

"I got it!" she says, as she expresses her excitement.

"*Huh?*"

"My Nissan! …That's where I've been this morning—at the dealership signin' papers. …Wait til you see it. Jus like I wanted—emerald green, leather—a rear spoiler, sunroof—it's loaded baby! …C'mon—I'm takin' *you* ta lunch!" she says, ecstatic to show off her new Altima.

"Oh you go girl!" And while appearing elated, Justin's first thought is one of guilt for not following through with his rendered promise. As he was supposed to be the one to take her car shopping—coincidentally on the very day he eventually slept with Tae. His thoughts then move to; "how did she get there?" thinking that Chris probably had something to do with that. But his notion is quickly dispelled as Natalie explains.

"Yep. Neicy came by first thing this morning—which we were supposed ta be practicing. But we got ta talkin'—and I jus did it! …I needed a way around! So we went—I saw what I wanted—drove it… The next thing I know—I was in the office signin' for a loan. …Didn't have ta haggle on price or anything. And here I am about ta take my man out to lunch."

"That simple huh?" He smiles.

"Yep!"

"Well good then—I'm happy for ya."

"Thank ya baby," she says, bubbling with giddiness.

Tae, after watching the nauseating couple together, excuses herself, wanting no part of the congratulation ceremony. Her high is broken by her now clearly inferior position on Justin's totem pole. Neither Justin nor Natalie witnesses the exit—or at least that's the perception each wanted to give.

Following lunch—an hour or so later, Justin returns to the office realizing what has to happen. He knows what he said before about Tae—but easier said than done; especially when it comes to fighting the temptation. Having tasted Tae's fruit—and then knowing just how sweet it is, makes the task that much more difficult. Her willing attitude, coupled with the longevity of their friendship is causing Justin to quickly reconsider his decision to break it off. It's becoming comfortable. And the idea of having a "no strings attached" relationship begins to sound therapeutic. The fact of the matter is that Justin has long since been fed up with Natalie's touch and tease antics—and comes to the conclusion that he needs more from the relationship. He remembers Jerome's words about the situation—wishing now that he had listened.

As Justin sits behind his desk playing devil's advocate, he continues to mull over all the pros and cons. He brings up—of course the whole religion thing. While he sympathizes with Natalie's plight, he's also thinking, "What's that got ta do wit me? That's her life—her walk, not mine." Yet his practical mind also understands the severity of the other possible outcome. It's only a matter of time before he and Tae's little bombshell becomes public—causing a potential company-wide scandal in light of recent promotions. Justin, already paranoid of the situation, convinces himself that she'll understand, considering all that's at stake—namely their careers and reputations. Not to mention the cushy lifestyle. He deliberates just a few minutes more—recognizing the only common sense answer. For it takes more than great sex to pay the bills. Justin pages Tae to his office.

thirty-nine

When It's All Said and Done

Thursday rolls around and as promised, Justin prepares to take the kids to the Allstate Arena for the "Holiday Jam". He pulls out all the stops as a stretch Hummer has been reserved to transport the three of them backstage for VIP accommodations. Stressed, he uses the outing as a release—it hasn't been a good day, things between he and Tae begin to take its toll. It's much harder than he thought—she's got his mind. Their conversation the other day didn't go over as well as he'd hoped. While she may have understood—there's still the emotional ties. Sort of like Jackie—she's been there, and despite the wrong that he's done to Natalie, he still feels a deep sense of commitment to Tae. With now strained interaction, both struggle to conceal their natural feelings. Justin spends the afternoon reminiscing on their private moments.

It's at the last minute that Natalie arrives with Asia—about six. She chooses to rendezvous with Justin at his condo to save time—allowing the limo to go straight to the concert. As the ladies approach the door—both Justin and Justice, each in separate bathrooms, spend the awaiting moments grooming to perfection. Justice, who's first to hear the knocking, answers with anticipation—anxious to see his running partner. All gathered at the door—oohing and aahing over outfits as Justin makes his appearance from the back. Natalie takes no hesitation in meeting him halfway into the room.

"How are ya?" Justin's smooth entrance and lazy words add a sense of allure to his youthful, yet debonair look.

"Fine," she responds as she smirks while biting her bottom lip—completely turned on by what she sees.

"What's wrong wit ch'ou?" Justin infers to her expression.

"I'm about ta be a lil' jealous."

"Why?" He laughs, already knowing the answer.

"Cause my man is 'bout ta leave me—lookin' all good and all, ta be around a bunch of horny half-dressed hoochies. That's why! …You betta behave yourself!" she says, playfully shoving her beau.

Grinning, he says, "Well baby, you're more than welcomed ta join us. I'm sure I can scrounge up anotha pass."

"Nope. I'll be alright… Jus remember I got eyes in the back of my head." She ends the warning with a smile.

"I bet!" Knowing exactly that she is referring to Asia, as he figures she'd stoop that low.

"Oh! Before you all leave—let me get a few pictures of you and the babies." Natalie pulls a disposable Fuji camera from her purse. "I guess I'll go ahead and start workin' on the family album—since we have yet ta take any pictures together." She cuts a sarcastic eye up at Justin—hinting to her plans of relational permanence. "Hey, can you all come over here and sit on the couch for me please?" Asia and Justice are momentarily interrupted to accommodate her request. The two have been trading wishful thoughts and fanatic dares as they're within minutes of meeting their peer-aged pop idols. Carefully, Natalie positions the children in place with the adept eye of a professional photographer. After several shots, she motions for Justin to join in. "C'mon baby—strike a pose!"

Being silly, Justin immediately jumps to a crouched inmate stance with his fingers twisted flashing W's while barking, "*WESTSYDE!*" as everyone laughs. A call comes in from the downstairs desk informing Justin that the limo has arrived. "That's us. Y'all grab your coats!" The adolescents eagerly oblige, grinning from ear to ear. Asia throws on her Baby Phat faux mink matching the rest of her Baby Phat ensemble—from hoop earrings to her copper v-neck tee down to the Arctic wash, low rise jeans. The only item not of the same maker she dares to sport is a pair of brown wedge heel boots—presumably borrowed from her mama. The mature outfit actually surprises Justin—knowing Natalie's overprotective nature. Meanwhile Justice takes a moment to adjust his nylon skully—methodically aligning his freshly woven braids, before applying the charcoal Akademiks parka. He loosens the belt on his Triple 5 jeans—manufacturing a saggy look. "Baby, you're stayin' here—right?" as Justin confirms Natalie's plans.

"Yes baby. I'll be right here," she says, affixing a smile.

"Am I straight?" Acting like one of the kids, Justin reworks his leather blazer.

"Yes baby."

"Al-ight then—help yourself ta whatever and we'll see ya later on tonight!" He reaches for a quick taste of her lips.

"*Byyye*—and be careful. …Call me if you can!" She speaks those last words—poking her head outside the door as the trio departs down the hall. Sucking her teeth, Natalie breathes a sigh of deep concentration—ducking inside once the coast is clear. She stands in the middle of the living room, surveying her surroundings, her index finger resting comfortably against her sealed lips—reaffirming the profound thought as she theorizes on how to arrange her little surprise. Finally with somewhat of a plan, she gets her coat to go downstairs to her car.

It takes three wearying trips up and down the elevator to eventually accomplish her plight. A number of bags and one oblong box sit spread amongst the couch and floor. She pushes some of the merchandise aside—finding a small spot on the sofa to rest from her labor. "I sure hope he appreciates all this," Natalie mumbles to herself, expressing her anguish as she pulls a box of gold Christmas ornaments from one of the bags. And with only days away from the biggest holiday of the year—and no sign of the Christmas spirit lurking anywhere, Natalie takes it upon herself to bring a little holiday cheer to an otherwise depressing situation. Between stops at Target and Mernards, she's actually able to pick up a few last minute bargains— even finding a six-foot artificial tree.

Natalie, not wanting to get too comfortable, now sits straight up, as she takes another deep breath while gasping for that second wind before rising to her feet. Time is of the essence—realizing she better get started if she plans to finish before they return. She kicks off her Sketchers—then empties the bags.

Left with no other choice, she moves the furniture around by herself, repositioning the couch and coffee table away from the television, thus leaving an open area to place the tree. It's during this phase of the decorating that she manages to conger up old memories of days gone by, as she, Chris, and a much younger Asia were all united under one roof, spending holiday after holiday together as a family. Natalie tries voiding those thoughts—focusing on the future. She replaces the past with the present—remembering her fonder moments with Justin. She smiles, "My baby is so sweet." Reminding herself of his attentive and caring ways, she says, "He's so silly." Again, acknowledging his finer qualities. But even with Justin's good-natured personality, she can also clearly identify the flaws—the jealousy, and the control by manipulation. And so with history possibly repeating itself, "Lord—please not again" becomes a fleeting prayer.

Natalie, caught up in her own introspection, before she knows it, completes the first round of tree trimming as she finishes the assembly. She next opens two boxes of multi-colored lights—unraveling each and laying them down in a straight line, and then plugs both cords in the wall. It's to her delight that the kits perform to specification, giving her the green light to proceed. As she begins to hang the lights—it's Shantel, who all of a sudden crosses her mind. She's becomes a little leery of that situation. It's not that she doesn't trust Justin—but it's Shantel that she's worried about. She sees the way Shantel looks at him—the desire in her eyes. There's more to it than friendship—no matter what Justin thinks. She remembers the other day in his office, having witnessed firsthand Shantel's overly aggressive behavior, as she seemingly throws herself at Justin. "Poor child." Natalie shakes her head—while smirking to pathetic pettiness of Shantel's game. Yet, she does sometimes wonder what Justin really thinks of his dedicated colleague—since there's such a close bond.

But again, she removes that thought from the forefront of her mind—electing to concentrate on upping the ante to her game as she contemplates whether or not the time is right to take her and Justin's relationship to the next level. She appreciates the fact that he has been so patient with her—and realizing his needs along with her own, she begins to feel that the time has arrived. For months now, her flesh has been screaming to experience his large presence inside her milky walls. She convinces herself that at this point in the relationship, any procreation on their part would only be an extension of their love for one another. Yet, that explanation does little towards justifying the abomination of premarital fornication. She thanks the Almighty for His grace and mercy as her weakened spirit falls under the submission of her flesh.

It's in these days Natalie finds herself in constant need of spiritual encouragement—struggling through the day to day strongholds and falling victim to the same vices of her past as she goes above and beyond the call of duty to please man. It's because of Justin that she's willing to sacrifice her beliefs, opting for the tangible. Once the bulbs are securely in place, she wraps red and gold strands of garland around the imitation evergreen. And before long, she stands back admiring her work—dimming the living room's recessed lighting for the full effect of transforming colors. "That's nice!" After which deciding to stretch out for a minute, Natalie cleans up her mess—yawning, as it's already 9:30. She ventures to Justin's room where she collapses across the bed.

She hears the arguing of two men—their muffled voices slinging obscenities back and forth. Too afraid to move, she remains frozen in place cowering—content with just listening as the altercation escalates to a tussle. Her body quivers and tears begin to fall from the sound of furniture shifting and breaking because of the fighting in the next room. "BLAAAL!" a single echoing shot is fired. Mortified, Natalie places her hands over her ears, surrounding herself in complete silence. Yet, it's the chilling blare of sirens that soon follows, which can't be ignored. Amidst the chaos of strangers running in and out the house, she's embraced by the shielding arms of Brunell. But even the broadness of his strong shoulders against her frail frame can't prevent her from seeing the face of her bruised beloved father being led away in handcuffs. "*DADDY! …DADDY*—what's wrong? Where are they takin' you?" She screams pulling away from her older brother. But showing no regard or recognition for anything around him, Natalie's unremorsed father looks straightforward, acknowledging nothing. As she turns away in tears—with Brunell corralling her back, she spots the body of her lifeless uncle lying on the floor in the next room as his blood puddles the light colored carpet. Her monster is dead. It's then that Camille—just arriving from work, bombards the room having witnessed her husband being taken into custody and to find her only brother lying in their den in a pool of his own blood.

"*NOOOOOO! …nooo*" The eerie whimpering cry of her distraught mother reverberates across the concealed crime scene as a policeman attempts to console her. Yet, it's the sight of her frightened daughter that sets her off even further. "YOU LIAR! …YOU 'LIL LYIN' BITCH! This is your fault! …all your fault." Camille withers to the floor convulsing in obvious grief.

"No Mommy—I didn't… I didn't lie—please Momma. I promise…" Violently tossing and turning, Natalie pleads for her mother's understanding as Justin has to awaken her from the vivid nightmare.

"…Baby—wake up!" He shakes her—rescuing her from herself.

Her panicked watery eyes open, thrusting herself into the grasp of her squatted mate, reiterating her last words. "I didn't lie baby. I didn't…" she says, clinging tight to Justin' neck.

"*Ssshhh.* It's okay—you're dreamin'. …I'm here," he says, as he rocks her in his arms while whispering words of sweet solace. She takes a moment to gather her senses—remembering the time and place.

"Where's Asia?" she asks, worried that she's misplaced her daughter.

"She's fine. I let her go to sleep in Justice's room—he's in there on the couch. Oh and I like whatcha did with the Christmas tree. …Now I don't have ta feel like the Grinch anymore—thanks!"

She smiles, and then reverses the gratitude. "Nooo—thank *you.*"

"For what?" He is also smiling.

"For bein' you baby—for jus bein' you." Her soft piercing stare conveys the sincerity of her words. "Come here." Her voice trembles—faint with timid impulsiveness, knowing the inevitable outcome of her next move. And as Justin approaches—advancing even closer than his already near touching proximity, she lays back, catching his hand and slowly guiding it beyond and underneath all superfluous boundaries, grazing her moist malleable vulva lips with his fingers. "Touch me baby." Enkindled, she speaks between intermittent breaths. "…And this time don't stop," she says, allowing Justin to finally make love to her.

❧   ❧   ❧

Frustrated by recent events, Justin, tired of the growing tension between he and Tae, walks straight into her office without knocking. Determined to make amends, he delivers a peace offering. "Here!" He places the boxed gift down on her desk. Having just made it in herself, she turns around after hanging up her coat.

"What's that!" she says, appearing unfazed by the bribe.

"Hell, open it!" Justin, excited by his purchase, pushes the issue.

"I will later." She takes the box and tucks it in the bottom drawer of her desk. "How was the concert last night?"

Feeling foiled, he tries hiding his disappointment. "Oh, it was tight. You know them kids had a ball. Took a few pictures, got some autographs—hung out backstage fo awhile. They loved it! Both of 'em woke up this morning still talkin' 'bout it."

"Well, that's nice. I'm glad they had a good time." she says, still speaking as though she's hardly interested.

"So, what are the big plans for the weekend?" Justin installs the question strictly for the sake of asking.

"Oh, well you know Quentin is supposed to be comin' up for Christmas. In fact, he should be on his way by the time I get out of here this afternoon." She pauses. "…And what about you and your little family?" A sense of sarcasm protrudes from her voice with the return inquiry.

And like a dagger to the heart, just hearing the mention of Quentin's name churns his stomach. "Nah. We jus planned ta have a nice quiet weekend together. Ya know, enjoy the time off! …Nuthin' spectacular." Justin's harboring jealousy prevents him from saying much more. "Okay, I won't hold ya up any longer. I'll let you get back to whatcha were doin'. And if by some chance I don't get ta see ya this afternoon, I hope y'all have a merry Christmas and I'll see ya after the break—okay?" Now uncomfortable, Justin heads for the door.

"I just walked in Justin—so I wasn't doin' anything. And you know you'll see me. We run into each other all day."

"Well, you neva know, but just in case we didn't. I wanted ta make sure I at least had the opportunity ta say that much—know what I mean?" But she doesn't respond, instead she stares at him—arms folded looking miffed, yet feeling herself with the same bewildering strain as he. "Guess I'll talk to ya later." He closes the door behind him.

♡ ♡ ♡

Hours later, Justin sits at his desk pretending to be busy. It's Friday afternoon—prelude to the holidays, so there isn't much by way of business happening anyway. There's actually more interoffice mingling amongst the staff being achieved than work, as Justin offers no exception. Thus it's Tae who reverses the tables by entering his office unannounced. She carries a stack of sealed envelopes in her hand, dropping one upon his desk. "Merry Christmas!" Now, in a much better mood, she pokes fun towards Justin's brooding attitude. He notices the red silk corner-store rose that he bought this morning on his way in to work—pinned to the lapel of her jacket. "Thanks for my flower." She flaunts the cheap gift—recognizing its ulterior significance, as it's the premise behind its thought that matters.

Justin finally cracks a smile—now feeling a bit better about himself, and the day. "Ya welcome boo. So, what do we have here?" he asks, referring to the labeled envelope.

"Your Christmas card silly. What else would it be?" She scoffs at the lame question.

"Who knows. Coulda been anything." he says, still blissfully content.

"*Huh*. Maybe once. But nope *you* messed that up. ...Jus makin' my rounds before I get outta here." She holds the batch of cards up in plain view. "Will you be home all day Sunday?"

"Should. What's up?"

"I might drop by for a few. I have something for lil' man." She gives Justin the impression that Justice is the sole reason for the visit.

"That's cool. Actually we have something under the tree for you too." He has yet to give a second thought to the fact that Natalie will be spending the day with them. And if the truth be told—like water and oil, the two don't mix.

"Oh okay..." she says, a bit surprised by Justin's thoughtfulness, yet she doesn't get to finish the discussion as his office phone beeps.

"Hold up—let me get that!" He answers the line. "Yes Rhonda?"

"You have a personal call sir."

"Thanks Rhonda." She then immediately patches the caller through. "Hello?"

"Hel-lo Mr. Vaughn. How are you?" The soft-spoken southern falsetto accent peers through the receiver.

"Who is this?" he asks, unable to distinguish the voice.

"How soon we forget ...It's Shanice!"

Oh snap—it is you! Hey Boo—what's up!" He takes a seat, shocked to be hearing from this blast from his past.

"Nothing—it's just good to hear your voice."

"Likewise boo! So, how's the boys?" And on that note, Tae leaves the room, throwing up a hand to say goodbye. Justin covers the receiver and mouths the silent utterance, "See ya Sunday," then returns to his conversation where Shanice goes on to provide lengthy accounts of her children's lives as if Justin is remotely interested. He holds the phone until finally she brings a merciful end to the rambling.

"I know it's been a long time—but I better let you go-o-o. I wanted to call and wish you and your son a very merry Christmas—and a happy New Year. And maybe the next time you happen to be down this way—maybe we'll have a minute to get a bite to eat or *something...*," stressing the something, which of course Justin catches.

"Oh, well thank you. That sounds good. I wanna wish y'all a merry Christmas and a safe and prosperous New Year's also. And you be good. Call me soon okay?"

"I will and you do the same—*byyye.*" she says, sounding sweet as always.

"Bye." He chuckles while disconnecting, amused by the unlikelihood of having just heard from the irrepressible Shanice.

With only a few remaining stragglers left in the building—now minutes before five, Justin collects his cards and gifts, including his newly acquired Callaway golf clubs, courtesy of the entire staff. By Rhonda's lead everyone pitched in to purchase the pricy set along with a gift certificate to John Jacobs Golf Academy for lessons. Earlier, having returned the favor from his own pocket, Justin himself treats every employee from department execs to receptionists, out to a private luncheon at the Everest where all were presented a hand-blown glass wine goblet set from Crate&Barrel. It's then that Justin buzzes his ever-dutiful secretary.

"Yes Mr. Vaughn."

"Rhonda—why ya still here?" He jokingly questions her meticulous work ethic.

She chuckles, knowing exactly what comes next. "Sir, I was just finishing up..."

"Girl—go home and enjoy the weekend. We'll see ya on Tuesday. And Rhonda..." He pauses.

"Yes Sir."

"Thank you."

"You're welcome Sir."

Justin divulges his gratitude not only for the gift, but also for the dedication and professionalism she brings to the job. He realizes attitudes around the office could have been very different after the incident with Tae. But never once did she ever allow her personal feelings to interfere with her work—and he appreciates that. "Merry Christmas Rhonda."

"You too Sir."

On Saturday Justin dedicates his time to Justice as they spend the day in and out the mall mostly window-shopping. Though it's a day before Christmas, Justice manages to finagle his father into an early gift as Justin stands at the EB Games checkout counter, entering the pin number to his debit card. "Al-ight man—now that's it! ...I thought tomorrow was supposed ta be *yo* day." Griping, he takes the $147 dollar receipt from the cashier, tucking it in his pocket. "Grab the bag man!"

"Thanks Pops." Justice grins. He takes the merchandise, knowing full well that he's just capitalized on his father's guilty kindness.

"Yeah-yeah—I bet! So what's next?"

"It's your turn Pops. You decide." A deceptively sympathetic Justice offers his father the burden of choosing the next place where his money will be spent.

Justin looks at his Fossil. "Think we got time to catch a movie or sumptin' before the girls get there?"

"*Yeah*—we should if we leave now!"

With that in mind, they hustle to snag the last matinee showing of *King Kong*. After the movie—as the credits begin to roll, Justin nudges his half sleep son. "C'mon baby. ...Let's bounce!" he says, wanting to get a jump on the exiting crowd. The combination of the move's long slow drawn-out beginning and a full day of walking and looking has gotten the best of young Justice, who's slow to his feet. "C'mon now—I wanna get outta here before we end up fightin' traffic!" He further stresses his point. Justice—finally standing, stretches while staggering to gain his balance. By the time the lights are on, both Justin and Justice are already through the double doors and past the concessions—almost running to the car.

While one would believe that all Justin's rushing was for the sole purpose of meeting Natalie, yet on the contrary, he seizes the opportunity to spy on Tae, whose apartment is just minutes from their North Chicago location. For it's been on his mind all day—wondering what she was doing, and more specifically, meditating on what she and Quentin were up to. It bothers him to think that they could be intimately entangled at this very moment. Having Quentin sharing in something as special as Tae, plays noxiously with his head. He knows it's silly—yet he can't seem to shake the thought. With baby boy all but sleep, Justin passes her residence in search of Quent's car or some detectable hint of his presence. Heart pounding, he sees nothing but a darkened window and no sign of anyone—not even Tae, as her vehicle is nowhere to be found either. Despite feeling a bit foolish, he finds a comforting peace from the empty-handed endeavor. He heads home satisfied.

♡ ♡ ♡

Timed perfectly, as father and son make their way to the main lobby, they're startled by the toot of a passing horn. Justin flips towards the sound spotting the Euro-style tail lights of Natalie's late-model Nissan "There they go!" They stop just shy of the door. "Let's go see if they need us for anything baby." Both take route in the direction of the parked vehicle.

Appearing tired, the ladies exit the new Altima—Natalie carries a Marshall's bag. "*Heeey.*" She greets Justin with an unusual less-than-enthusiastic embrace.

"Long day?" he asks, detecting the difference.

"Yep! …Hon, can you get the rest of the bags out of the trunk for me please?" She rubs the base of Justin's back for extra incentive as she pops the trunk with her remote.

"Yes Ma'am!" He gladly honors the request in response to the humanitarian services performed by both women whom have just spent the day preparing and delivering food baskets to needy families; a feat that's become an annual tradition in the Broussard household. "Did everything go al-ight?"

She pauses—reflecting on the day's activities, "*Well*—all and all, we were blessed. Despite being shorthanded—and running out of food on a couple of occasions, we still managed to feed over 2,000 families for the holidays!"

"Damn, that's great Sweetie… Congratulations! Y'all should be proud."

"Yeeeah—I am," she says, her face showing the glow of her efforts. In the rear—just a few feet behind, Asia and Justice trail their parents as each—fighting for the floor, tries to get a word in. Asia flaunts her new cell phone—a gift from her father while Justice shows off his latest collection of games. Also in Asia's hands, are the eats for the evening in which she aggravates Justice by sticking the brown paper sack in his face.

"Quit girl—what's that?" As baby boy catches a whiff of the spicy smelling menu.

"Ain't tellin'! …Not until ya take my bag." She sees if Justice will take the bait—desperately wanting to relieve herself of the duffel over her shoulder.

"Nope!" He declines Asia's bribe without a second thought.

"Make me sick. Betcha neva get a girlfriend!"

"Why? Because I ain't carryin' your bag—*whatever*." he says, laughing practically in her face.

"Boy, get the bag!" Justin interjects having heard every word.

"Yes Sir." Dejected he takes the duffel from Asia with no other choice.

"*A-ha*. See, that's whatcha get!" She taunts her chastised friend—adding more lip service. "Cause that's what a man's suppose ta do. Jus like yo daddy!"

"Gurl, shut up! You get on my nerves wit that! …Always runnin' your mouth and don't know nuthin'!" A now disgusted Natalie enters into the drama.

It's once upstairs and inside the condo that Justin does realize the bags he's been carrying are actually the gifts for under the tree. "We see you've been a busy lil' bee." he says, referring to the numerous pre-wrapped presents which will be contributing to an already crowded floor.

"Like you have any room to talk—Mr. 'I don't like ta shop.' So what's all this then?" She points to the amassed array of gifts accumulated from Justin's shopping romps with Shantel.

"Well—jus considerate it a blessing. You're always doin' sumptin' for someone else… Maybe it's 'bout time for you ta be blessed ya self."

"Aaah—you so sweet baby. …I love you—*mmmuah*." she says, planting a mushy smooch upon Justin's lips—totally enamored by his endearing comment. "Everybody wash their hands so we can eat!" She parts Justin's company long enough to fix plates as she herself is ready to sit and relax. Natalie easily rips the side of the grease-saturated sack revealing four Hernandez burritos stuffed to the max with steak and peppers. "I know it's nuthin' gourmet and all—but I hope it'll do for tonight."

"Hell yeah!" Agreeing for everyone Justin is the first to grab his plate. He enjoys a Corona with his meal.

After dinner—Natalie, being the traditionalist, sets the mood by finding her Marshall's bag. Removing the contents, she distributes one to all in the room.

"Pajamas!" Justice cries out—dumbfounded by the offering.

"That's right! …Something we used ta do every Christmas Eve when Ma' dear was around. She made sure all us children had a new pair of pj's—even if she sewed them herself, and that way Santa wouldn't see us in no ratty dusty clothes. ...Yep, so that's what we gonna do. I got *ever-rybody* a nice new clean pair and once we take our baths we can all sit around the tree in our jammies—lookin' sharp while we wait on Santa. ...There!" She adamantly crosses her arms following the presentation, daring anyone to do any different. As eyes roll and mouths pop—one by one, the unwilled participants hold up—needlessly comparing, the identical two-piece sets. Justin smartly submits carrying his pajamas on into the bathroom laughing.

"Okay baby—if that's whatcha wanna do."

The kids soon do the same—Asia first, then Justice. Natalie returns last—refreshed and showing all teeth, as she plops down on the couch to join the rest of the clan. "Now this is nice!" Pausing for just a second, she then crawls to the floor up under tree to be nosy as she sorts through boxes searching for her name.

"Whatcha doin'?" Justin quickly follows.

"Jus curious baby—that's all. I wanna see what's under here for me." Acting silly, she uses a babyish whining tone.

"*Yeeeah okay*. Don't get your feelins' hurt. You'd be jacked up if ain't nuthin' down there!" He does his best to discourage her from looking.

"But baby you've already told me in so many words...," as she continues to scrounge the floor. "See, here's one right here!" She lifts it up in the air, attempting to guess the contents by the size of the box. She soon gives up and resumes where she left off. "Justice ...and Justice again. Asia ...Shantel ...and Shantel again. Justin ...one more for Shantel. Wow! We know somebody's sure about ta have a nice Christmas." A tinge of jealousy surfaces as she ambles about until she finds another gift bearing her name.

They hang out for a just a while longer—but before it gets to be too late, the kids start complaining about being tired as an early night always tends to shorten the wait. And with neither wanting to sleep in Justice's room, they settle on separate pallets on the floor around the tree. Justin and Natalie meanwhile decide unanimously on moving to the back bedroom. "You ready baby?" he asks, extending his hand to help her up off the couch.

"Thought you'd neva ask." Accepting his gesture she receives his hand as Justin turns off all lights including the tree. "Goodnight y'all!"

"Goodnight!" both babies answering at the same time.

Delivering soft nibbling kisses to the neck, Justin, from behind, leads Natalie down the hall entwining himself tightly around her waist and forcing her forward with each step until inside the bedroom. And like putty she molds to his embrace as he closes the door.

"I suppose you're ready to unwrap one of your presents now huh?" Natalie spins around reversing her position once safely inside closed quarters. She returns Justin's foreplay by pinning him hard to the wall. Her hand travels south until reaching pay dirt as she wraps firmly around his Johnson.

"Why not?" Caught by surprise, he tries maintaining his composure.

"So, have you been naughty—or nice?" Natalie toys with his stretched penis between anxious fingers then flicks her salivated tongue across Justin's dry lips.

Unsure of how to answer and unable to handle the pressure, he quivers—buckling under her spell. "Nice."

"We'll see." As a very naughty Natalie strips Justin of his nightclothes, dropping to her knees, she says, "Merry Christmas baby."

Awoken by a continuous annoying pounding at the door, Natalie rolls over shaking a sound asleep Justin. "Baby get up—it's the kids!"

"*Huh?*" peeved by the sudden interruption.

"The kids baby—it's Christmas!"

"Oh shit I forgot. What time is it?" he asks, rubbing his eyes.

"A quarter til seven." She laughs.

"Oh hell nah!" He rolls over clinging to his pillow.

"Jus a minute y'all!" Natalie hollers through the door keeping the babies at bay. "Baby don't do that—get up!" She starts smacking his exposed naked body with her pillow until he rolls back over.

"Alright, alright—I'm up!" He expels a deep sigh, and then sits up. "What cha'll want?" he asks, also yelling through the locked door.

Asia gets right to the point. "We ready ta open our stuff!"

"Al-ight hold on!" Justin collapses back down on the bed. Natalie grabs her pajama top and heads to the toilet. He lunges forward to pull her back but misses. "Where ya goin' baby? …Bring that pretty ass back ova here!"

"Later *Hon*. We might as well jus go on out there. You know they're not gonna stop til' we do." She lets down the commode seat before sitting. Justin—not wanting to get up finally does so and joins Natalie in the bathroom. He stands over the sink looking for his toothbrush.

"It's in the cabinet." She answers his thought having rearranged a few things. The sound of urine echoes within the confined space.

"Thanks." Thinking, he says, "And so it starts—she's already movin' my shit!" He quickly realizes that he's not in the best of moods. Then immediately changing his temperament, he acknowledges the day by squatting between her open toilet bound thighs and whispers, "Merry Christmas—I love you." Choked with emotion and no longer able or willing to contain herself, she kisses Justin, inserting her tongue—morning breath and all.

Asia and Justice are impatiently huddled by the tree when their parents eventually emerge.

"*Good morning y-a-ll.*" Bubbling with cheer, Natalie takes her place next to the kids. She's as excited as they are. "I don't know about you all but I say let's get this party started!" She picks up the first package with her name on it.

"We can open them now Mommy?" Asia makes sure she and her mother are on the same page.

"I don't see why not."

"Yeyah!" Justice blurts his enthusiasm as the unwrapping begins. Smirking, Justin holds post behind the sofa, observing the mess being tossed about.

"*Ool*—Mama look!" Asia proudly displays her new combination DVD/VCR player.

"That's nice baby! …Now you can watch movies back in your own room—and stay from out my front area…"

"Look y'all…" Justice interrupts, holding the box to the recently released XBox 360°.

"*Oooh*—you go boy! Santa got you the hookup." As Natalie cheers Justice on.

"*Yeeep.*" He agrees while clinging to his latest prized possession.

Natalie gets into the act—revealing her first gift. "Somebody musta read my mind." Laughing, she unveils the heated foot spa."

"I picked that out for you Ms. Natalie!" Justice lays quick claim to the idea.

"Thanks baby—I sure needed it! …And I'm on my feet all day too!" She relishes in the thought of having a foot massage accessible for those long days on the job.

"Mama look what I got for you!" Digging for the same attention, Asia presents her gift.

"So, let's see what my baby done got for her mama." Natalie tears away the silver metallic paper. "Oh my goodness! …*Girl* bye!" She opens the flat rectangular box to find an Armani gift set for Sensi. "Watch out now! Mommy gonna be smellin' good... So sexy!" she says, as she samples the soft flirty fragrance on her wrist. By the imagined cost Natalie figures that each gift has Justin's name written all over it. She looks to him with a subtle smirk. Sipping on a cup of decaf, he smiles and winks. "Hon, you have some things down here to open too," as she attempts to get Justin in the act.

"I know baby—I'll get them in a minute. I'ma go in here and start breakfast. Y'all up fo some grits and eggs?" On this rare occasion, he offers to cook.

"No, I'll do that! You can come and sit down." She gets up.

"Girl, what did I say? I said I got it!" as Justin insists. "Don't cha got some more stuff ta open?" he asks, pointing to two other boxes. "So handle that!"

"Yes sir. ...Thanks baby!" she promptly regains her spot.

"Pops, can we have some sausages?" Justices tries adding to the menu.

"*Yeeeah*, I think we can do that" He rummages through the freezer, making sure there is sausage to cook. The phone rings and Justice answers.

"Hey Auntie! ...Merry Christmas to you too!" He pauses. "Yep ...I got an XBox 360°... Sure did!" He talks for a minute before giving the phone to his father. Natalie listens in having previously heard nothing about an Aunt.

Just by the tone of the conversation, Justin has already identified the caller. "Merry Christmas boo!" His voice is charged.

"Merry Christmas boy!" followed by the distinctive laugh of Jackie.

"So, what's been goin' on? How's baby girl? ...Did Jerome bring by what I sent cha'll?" he asks, unleashing a barrage of questions.

"We're here—but otha than that everything's the same. Shayla, she misses Justice being around—and so do I. I thought maybe you all woulda made it down for the holiday, but then I figured you probably didn't have much time off. I remember how busy it gets this time of year. Oh, and Rome brought the presents ova last night—He and Mo. ...We thank ya!" Again Jackie breaks into laughter, as she's very appreciative of Justin's generous gifts.

"Yeah, cause I wasn't sure of what ta get ya—figured a gift card was as good as anything else. That way ya get whatcha want."

"And I can definitely do something with this!" she says, referring to the $500 Visa gift certificate. "So, what female you got lookin' up in yo face? Justice told me you had company. ...You know we need ta talk!" she says, realizing she wasn't up on the latest. "It's not even eight in the morning... That means she's spendin' nights. Boy, ya ought ta quit—that's ridiculous!"

Grinning, he says, "We'll talk."

"Whatever. So, what are ya doin'? Am I disturbin' something'?" she laughs. "Don't matter no way. Tell whoever that is ova there she has to wait—I knew you first... So jus tell her ta take a number—cause she'll be alright!"

"Girl you sick!" he says, shaking his head.

"*And? ...*I ain't playin'!" She defines the hierarchy of relationships.

"Anyway, but guess what? You'll neva believe what I'm doin'?"

"What boy?" she asks, having no clue.

"Cookin'!"

"*Oh hell.*" she laughs. "The world must be comin' to an end! So my question is—how is it you're the one in the kitchen boo? ...You don't cook! *What?* She don't know how?" she asks, surprised by the unbelievable feat.

"*Nah.* Ya know how we do!" he says, being smug.

"That's the whole point... We know how *you* do! ...What's gotten into you?" Jackie reminds Justin of his past persona. They continue to talk. All the while, Natalie sits back, pretending to be into the presents, but keeps an ear open on the conversation. She gathers Justin isn't talking to a real relative and begins to feel slighted. She remedies her curiosity by walking over to him while he's still on the phone.

"Thank you baby." She whispers words of gratitude for the Coach purse and Ralph Lauren stiletto suede boots she's just opened. "Who's that?" she whispers, as she cradles Justin's arm. He holds a finger up for her to wait a second, realizing the game she's attempting to play. He knows his conversation is all but over.

"Boo, let me holla at cha later! ...I'll call ya tomorrow."

"Yeah right! She's starin' in your mouth—ain't she?" she asks, recognizing the change in Justin's tone.

"Sumptin' like that." He smiles at Natalie—brushing his hand across her cheek. She kisses his fingers as they pass over her lips. "Like I said, we'll talk later."

Jackie, who despises being rushed, gets rude. "BYE!" as she immediately hangs up the phone. He knows that with Jackie, he'll have some making up to do. Meanwhile, he turns his lacking attention back to Natalie.

"So, you like—huh?" he asks, deterring her question.

She nods in agreement as she moves in close for a hug. "I love you." Her clinching embrace outlines the panic that rages through her head.

"I love you too." Justin senses her neediness. It's not like he has anything to hide with his relationship with Jackie, but he also realizes the potential for more confusion. Even though she's the woman who kept his son during those tough days—for which Natalie knows all about, it's the close intimacy of the relationship that she most likely wouldn't understand. Therefore, he prefers to keep it simple and not discuss it. And while the kids continue to open presents, Natalie elects to remain in the kitchen to help her man prepare the food.

By noon, Natalie, having spent the night and morning with Justin, gets dressed so she and Asia can do some visiting of her family early enough to return at a decent hour. While she showers, Justin uses the vacant moment to call Jerome. Dialing the house first he gets no answer—he then speed dials Jerome's cell.

"Yo, Merry Christmas man!" Jerome answers after one ring.

"You too man. What's up? Where's Mo?"

"She's right here…"

"Let me holla at her real quick!"

And before Jerome can say anything else he's passing the phone over to Monique. "…*Jay wants ta say sumthin' to ya.*"

"*Heeey* Jay. Thank you for the beautiful card …And the *watch*." With a slight giggle, she compliments Justin. "Good taste must run in the genes—very nice!"

"Cool. I'm glad you liked it. …Yeah and I wanna thank you for both me and baby boy's stuff. I know it had ta be all you cause *Rome* don't go that deep. That duvet was on point—goes perfectly with the room. I see you remembered! And the blue jean comforter set and curtains for Justice was real tight. He already got it on his bed!"

"Good I'm glad. I didn't want get him anything that has to do with those games. Between you and Jerome he gets plenty—probably more than he should. So I thought I'd do something different…"

"Well, ya came correct girl—cause we love it! Ya know we fashion illiterate up here anyway. At least when it comes to decorating," he laughs. "Rome show ya what we got 'em?"

"Yeah and he got a big kick out of it too!"

"Found it on Ebay wit the games—an original joint too!" he says, describing the vintage Atari 2600 gaming system.

"Jerome had me trying to play that thing this morning—but I don't know anything about that stuff!"

Again laughing, he says, "Word. That's cool! …Yo, let me talk back at Rome!"

"Okay. Well, you all enjoy the rest of your day and thanks again. …Tell that handsome young man of yours I said hello."

"I will girl. And you do the same. You take care of yourself—and that brother of mine—al-ight?"

"Okay." Grinning, she passes the phone back to Jerome.

"*Yooo.*" He makes Justin aware of his return.

"Yeah dude. Mo says ya diggin' that Atari joint man."

"Yeah, fo real! …It's still the shit! Jus like what we had."

"That's why I got that shit—bring back them memories."

"Man, we used ta be on that shit all day—remember Chopper Command?" Jerome recalls the exact game.

"Hell yeah. We'd battle ta see who'd turn that mofo over first."

"Shit, which was always me!" Jerome brags.

"Whatever nigga! In your dreams—hell!" Justin begs to differ as the two competitive brothers volley back and forth trading biased recollections. With neither side budging, Justin switches the subject. "Where y'all at? I called the house and y'all weren't there."

"Went ta go check on Dad. See how he's doin'."

After a brief pause, "So, how is he?" Justin's mood then changes.

"He's doin' okay. As well as ta be expected I guess. The doctors say he's strong willed. Since that last stroke they didn't think he'd be around this long."

"Does he know ya?" he asks, referring to his father's vegetable-like state.

"I'm not sure. Ya can't tell. His eyes blink every now and then, but that's 'bout it."

"Huh," Justin mulls. "How is his care?" he asks, showing rare concern.

"Man, they do a good job. Every time I stop in he's always clean and lookin' comfortable. Considering he needs around the clock lookin' after. I don't think we could'na found a better place for him ta be—ya know?"

"That's straight," he says, again switching the conversation. "Baby boy all into that 360°."

"Yeah I figured he would be," knowing his nephew. "What he say 'bout those games I sent?"

"Man, you know betta than that… Ya don't hear him do ya?"

"Nope." Jerome agrees.

"Cause he all up in the TV!"

"Word." Jerome hesitates before asking his next question. "Has Nat been through already?" he asks, being nosy.

"Yeah, actually she and Asia spent the night. She's gettin' dressed right now to go visit her peoples. They supposed ta come back later."

"So, how's that situation goin'?" he asks, as he digs deeper.

"Touch and go. You were right. I think we're movin' too fast. There're too many differences. I don't think we see eye to eye. But we'll see—know what I mean?" Justin speaks as though they're in the process of slowing the relationship down.

"I guess. Jus be careful. …Remember it ain't jus you anymore." He reminds Justin of his fatherly responsibilities.

"I know…" Interrupted by knocking—Justin pauses. "Hold up man somebody's at the door. …*Who is it?*" He probes while approaching to answer.

"*Ms. Claus.*"

"It's Shantel man," speaking then to his brother. "What's sup boo? Merry Christmas! …I got Rome on the line." He greets Tae with a kiss to the cheek and invites her in.

"Merry Christmas," she says, sounding winded as though she's just taken the stairs. "Hey Rome—Merry Christmas!" as she's loud enough to make her presence felt.

"Tell her I said hey and the same to her," he says, wanting Justin to relay the message.

"I gotcha. …But al-ight man let me go. Company awaits. Yo, but give me a buzz later in the week though. Oh and thanks again dude."

"No problem. Give lil' man a hug and stay out of trouble man. I'll holla."

"Peace bro." Justin then turns his focus to his gift-bearing guest. "Damn girl whatcha got there?" He comments as he watches her struggle through the doorway. She carries two department store garment bags and a gift-wrapped box.

"There's more downstairs." She stops to catch her breath.

Grinning, Justin relieves her of the merchandise and calls on his son to retrieve the rest. "Ya took the elevator—didn't ya?"

"Still. ...Divas don't do stairs boo—remember that!" She sashays with attitude in her turtleneck dress and leather coat despite the bitter temperatures.

"Damn, sure lookin' good though—so where's ya boy?" he asks, referring to Quentin.

"Child please... He came and went. Like I said—I'm through with that! It's been me, myself, and I since Saturday morning. I told cha— he's not gonna treat me like a piece of ass."

Relieved by the revelation, Justin responds, "I've been tellin' ya that for the longest."

"Ummm-huh." She locks eyes with Justin—expressing her cynicism over his double standing statement. They continue staring at one another until Justice and Asia enter the room.

"Hey Tae." Justice acknowledges his father's longtime friend.

"Hey baby. I brought something for you." She hands Justice the keys to her truck. "Go downstairs please and grab the rest of the presents off the back seat. ...*Thank yooou.*"

"Yes Ma'am. ...C'mon Asia." He signals for his shadow to join him.

"Hi there Asia. ...Nice to meet you. I'm Shantel and I got something for you, too." The gesture brings a big smile to Asia's adolescent face.

"Thank ya," she says as she runs behind Justice.

"Cute girl. Actually those two would make a really cute couple under different circumstances. Ever looked at that?" Tae makes the casual reference.

"Yep."

Having heard the female voice—and wrapped in only Justin's robe, Natalie emerges from the bedroom—still wet. "Hey gurl—Merry Christmas," she says, settling herself under Justin.

"You too!" Tae replies, dismissing Natalie's blatant intrusion.

The two trade idle pleasantries on the tiled entrance before Natalie offers Justin's courtesy. "Baby, where's your manners? Take her coat. Gurl c'mon and sit down!" Her hospitality obviously premeditated as she decides to keep the enemy close.

"Oh no—I couldn't intrude. ...You all enjoy each other. I only came by to drop off a little Christmas cheer. Believe me, I know how hard it is with Jay's demanding schedule to find any down time." She chuckles. "Besides I have him all week—it's about time I shared him with his family." Tae's subtle sarcasm causes even Justin to cringe. But the kids return with the gifts prior to any rebuttal being made. The comment only confirms the false pretenses of their sista-girl relationship.

"Here ya go Tae." Justin and Asia hand Tae the remaining packages—two boxes and two gift bags. She then distributes the offerings.

"Asia honey—this is for you and this one is for your mommy." She passes Natalie's beaming daughter the two gift bags from Victoria's Secret. Next she gives each Justin and Justice a box apiece.

"Gurl, thank you. That's sweet that you thought of us like that." as Natalie pulls a bottle of "My Desire" body lotion from her bag. "I feel bad now. If Justin had told me you were comin', I woulda had the chance to return the generosity…"

"Oh! Lil' man go under the tree and bring Tae her stuff!" Justin remembers. Afterwards Justice recovers the three store-wrapped parcels—all of the same paper. He then presents them to Tae.

"Gracias señor!" Tae takes the packages, hardly able to contain herself, as she recognizes the familiar Parisians' gift wrap. She realizes she's obviously receiving some nice things—or at least expensive ones. Cutting her twinkled eyes toward Justin, Tae decides that maybe it's time for her departure. "Well you all—I think I best be going. I hate to jus get up and go, but I'm sure I've taken up enough of your time. …Jay, I'll see you Tuesday," pointing to Justin. "And I'm sure I'll see the rest of y'all soon." as she rushes her exit to take a quick peek at her presents in private—concealing any unwarranted reactions in front of Natalie.

"We appreciate ya girl. …See ya bright and early Tuesday." Justin walks her to the door.

She cheeses. "It's a date then," whispering once beyond all eyes and ears.

"BYYYE!" as the kids poke their heads out after her for a final good bye.

"Bye y'all!" She turns around and smiles, amused by Justice and Asia's gleeful innocence. Once safely in the elevator Justin closes the door. He's welcomed by an arms crossed, straight-faced Natalie.

"Open your presents hon—let's see watcha got!" She seems pissed. From her noticeable silence as Shantel was leaving gives some indication of her mindset.

"I'll open them later." Justin tries avoiding the inevitable.

"Open them now!" she commands with coercion.

"What the hell is the matter with you?" Knowing what's to come, Justin immediately becomes defensive. And fearing a possible argument, the kids vanish to the bedroom—grabbing Shantel's gifts.

"She likes you, doesn't she?"

"*What?*" he asks, pretending to be surprised.

"She likes you—it's obvious!"

"What are ya talkin' 'bout? And where ya goin' wit this?" he asks, as he continues the charade.

"Do *you* like her? …Are you hiding some sort of feelings for her?" But Natalie delves deeper.

"Don't cha have somewhere ta be?" He then rudely sidesteps the question. Natalie storms into the living room—now foaming at the mouth, in search of something on the floor. "What are ya lookin' for?" Stressed, Justin tries approaching her—but to no avail, as she ignores him. Again, he restates himself. "What the fuck are you lookin' for?" He now comes across with force by profanity.

"My keys *ASSHOLE!*" She scours the floor through the ravished paper and debris, which scatters the trash making more of a mess.

"They're on the counter! I put them there maybe an hour ago… They were on the floor by the sofa." He tries to calm himself.

"Cause that's where I left them Sherlock!" After the ridiculing remark, Justin forgets that she's a much smaller woman.

"Come here!" He grabs her arm. "I don't know what the fuck your problem is but ya need ta can that shit—*like now!* What the fuck's gotten into you! …Where you gettin' all this shit?" He squeezes her arm to the point of pain without realizing.

"Get the fuck off me!" She snatches away. "Don't fuckin' touch me!" Irate, Natalie gets in Justin's face with a finger. "Muthafucker, I'll *KILL* you if you ever touch me again!" Despite her warning, Justin makes another foolish attempt to grab her arm. And whatever she'd been through before culminates into this very moment. She goes off— slapping and kicking Justin in a wild flurry. "You FUCKED her! …Don't lie muthafucker!" And like a cornered animal, she attacks Justin with everything she has—her misguided flails reaching their mark on many occasions. Justin has to do all he can to defend himself. The children rush from the room. To stop her he tries slinging her onto the couch but the force of his fling causes her to completely miss the intended target, launching her directly into the lit Christmas tree—

knocking over the whole display. Asia runs to her aid, screaming and crying. Justin panics.

"I'm sorry! …I didn't mean ta do that. Please believe me, I wasn't tryin' to hurt her. But Asia screams out.

"YES YOU DID! …You hit my Mommy!"

Justin attempts to help Natalie but Asia starts striking him repeatedly across his back with something in her hand. Natalie struggles to get up but she's tangled amidst the mess. Justin grabs Asia, embracing her just tight enough to subdue her, as Natalie finally stammers to her feet—staggering onto the couch. Justice stands by his bedroom door too stunned to respond to anything. And just like Thanksgiving—after the Chris fiasco, the room becomes silent with the exception of Asia who sobs profusely under her mother's arm. She's broken free from Justin's grasp to be by her side. And after twenty minutes of silence, Natalie raises up—collecting her daughter's hand, taking only their coats and her keys to vacate the residence, leaving everything just as it is—gifts, clothes and all. Disappointed, Justice retreats to his room, closing the door behind him, realizing that he's just lost a friend. Meanwhile—frozen to his seat, Justin looks around the room, pondering what just happened. He wishes to rewind the tape, but understands that there's no going back. No reconciliation—no do-overs, because she's gone—and yet another chapter closes. It's then when all else fails that we sometimes venture backwards to the things we know best. Reminded of Tae, he opens the garment bags beside him. As he unzips the first—he discovers it's exactly what she said it might be—an Italian single-breasted suit. He checks the size, which matches his measurements to the letter. Smiling, he thinks back on their conversation, realizing that everything she said was nothing more than a setup. And considering the substantial size difference between he and Quentin, the suits were apparently bought for him—and not the Indian giving gifts that Tae described them to be. To no surprise, he unwraps the final present to find a designer travel bag bearing the initials JV.

forty

Divine Intervention

As Sunday rolls into Monday, Justin finds himself anchored to the sofa. He lays there covered by a fleece blanket, apparently having not moved from the day before. Curled in the fetal position, he draws the cover tight to his neck so only his head is exposed as the aftermath of Christmas day lies before him. Unable to laugh or cry he stares into the darkness.

By daylight—now up a few hours, Justin manages to muster enough motivation to clear the area. Salvaging whatever he can, he packs away the tree and lights while most of the bulbs are thrown away—broken by the fight. He's disillusioned by the reversal of events—for he never saw it coming. And just as he reacted to Chris, Natalie reciprocates his actions a hundred fold. Once again, he's left with nothing to hide—freed from the stressful burden of concealing the truth.

After emptying the dustpan of the last lingering remnants of Christmas, he remains in the kitchen running hot water over yesterday's dishes—opting not to use the Kenmore. He finds that staying busy occupies the mind from further deliberation. Yet despite the effort, a few seconds of idleness provides plenty of opportunity for the mind to wander. It's in the contrast of fantasy and reality that baffles Justin. No "happily ever afters" or "Ozzie and Harriet" relationships—just one apocalyptic crisis after another. In his pursuit of happiness, the act of chasing love has left him empty handed and embittered—though he blames no one but himself. He slides his hands in the near scolding water without even realizing.

In the moments following, the cracking of Justice's bedroom door breaks the morning calm. No words have been spoken between father and son in the last 24 hours. Justin clinches his stomach bothered by what feels like hunger pangs, and instantly a nervousness comes over his entire body. He reaches for the Maalox in the cabinet above the sink. "You al-ight this morning?" He forgoes the use of a spoon, and drinks straight from the bottle.

"I'm alright. ....What 'bout ch'ou?" Baby boy returns the concern.

"I'm straight." Neither engages in any eye contact. Justice grabs a bowl from the drain and the milk from the refrigerator before pulling up a stool to the edge of the counter.

"Pass me a spoon Pops."

Justin, in the middle of his washing, searches underneath the suds for a clean utensil. "Here," having fulfilled the request. "...So how ya like that XBox?" It's with not knowing what else to say that he goes for the easiest subject of conversation. For as much as he's been blessed with the gift of gab, he often finds himself at a loss of words when it comes to his son. Embarrassed by his own example, it's his overwhelming sense of failure as a father that continues to stymie his ability to be parent. Constantly replaying and reliving his every mistake and oversight—now he realizes just how much he's taken for granted over the years. It's in a father that every child expects to find refuge and stability, but as he ventures backwards to the past, he regretfully concedes to not having supplied either. Under his own admission, he acknowledges his use of material *things* to compensate for his unwillingness to involve himself emotionally. That was always Teresha's job. And up until today he's always patted himself on the back—often priding himself for having fulfilled his monetary obligations. It's looking at their relationship now that brings Justin in full recognition of what he's actually accomplished—a distant dysfunctional relationship with his only child. He realizes as he rinses dishes that he's not the hero that he thought himself to be.

"It's tight... Especially 'Gun'!"

"And what's that?" Justin extends the discussion.

"A first person shooter. It's phat though! ...That's the one Unc sent," he says, expressing his implicit gratification.

"Word." As usual—not at all sure of the techy terminology, he quickly switches topics. "...So, what else did ya get?" He dries his hands with a paper towel, propping himself against the kitchen wall in front of his son. Justice fills his bowl with Fruit Loops.

"Unc got 'Call of Duty 2'..."

"What did Tae bring ya?" Justin jumps in, more curious about Tae's offering.

"*Aaah*... Hold up—let me get it!" He drops his spoon in the bowl to run to his room. Baby boy returns holding a still in the box, Toshiba laptop—DVD burner and all.

"Goddamn boy—she hooked you up! Ya need ta go call her right now and thank her again. You realize 'bout how much she paid for that? ...Man, that's a nice ass gift!" as Justin shows more enthusiasm than its recipient. In all the excitement of receiving his new XBox—very little attention was given to anything else.

"No, but look Dad... Ms. Natalie gave me these!" Justice unwraps the ear plug style headphones from around his neck which came with the 1GB MP3 player tucked safely in his front shirt pocket. The contagious nature of his father's excitement now too oozes from his voice.

"*Damn*. Make me wish I was a kid again. ...Shit was different then—cause we definitely ain't get shit like this!" Justin opens the carton containing the laptop.

And from nowhere Justice poses the question, "Do ya think we'll ever see them again?"

Shook, Justin isn't exactly sure of how to answer, nor does he want to, much rather wanting to skip the conversation all together. "I don't know baby. I wouldn't count on it." The candid response instantly resets the mood. "I'm sorry baby, I know that's not what ya wanted to hear, but I don't know what else ta tell ya. I'ma miss 'em too man." His expressed regret adds little consolation.

"But they left their stuff!" Justice whines as he's become quite attached to girls being around. "Asia's presents are still in my room!"

"Jus put 'em up! ...We'll make sure they get 'em later. Ain't like we don't know where they live!" His tone becomes increasingly harsh. The conversation then deadens after the exchange. Justice finishes his cereal and returns to his room. Justin does the same but not before grabbing an unopened bottle of Merlot from the fridge as the rift between the two couldn't be more apparent.

CD   CD   CD

Once tucked away behind the four walls of his bedroom—with the door closed, Justin sits at the far corner of the bed. He slouches forward with his elbows entrenched upon his knees. Massaging his temples, he agonizes over the outcome. Another failed relationship— another failed attempt at happiness. The residue from its aftermath already forming the stale taste that later becomes advent of unconscionable actions. His path of loneliness and disappointment continues to haunt him as his desire to fulfill a void of love has led to questionable life choices. Adding to his misery, he loads a Babyface CD—appropriately repeating a track called "The Loneliness." And as the song plays over and over, the words manage to penetrate his thinking—saturating his every thought.

In his evaluation of everything, Justin confronts the rebounding of Natalie—admitting his inability to be alone. Unable to release the past, he's allowed it to become his excuse—and his curse. It's the scarred little boy still raging on the inside of Justin's mind that has him now selfishly trying to overcompensate for a lacking childhood—attempting to reclaim a discharged debt forgiven by God. Removing the cork from the Tobin James, he takes his first swallow.

Within the half-hour he finishes the bottle, chugging the last swig before passing out across his made bed—the empty remnant still in his hand. It's there after developing an impetuous urge to pee—unable to move as the room spins slowly, that he slips into a hallucinate state of eternal sleep.

Dressed in all white, Justin envisions he and Teresha standing before a crowded church, full of family and friends, as they exchange their self-written vows of matrimony. Justice, who stands as his father's best man, passes the multi-karat ring to be placed upon his mother's eager finger. And by the power vested in the officiating minister, the two are then pronounced as husband and wife—the culmination of a dream come true. It's as if her beautiful freckled face and dimpled smile are actually before him—so real, so alive. He then drops the empty wine bottle, reaching to touch his new bride. Accepting his hand, she lays her cheek delicately in his grasp.

"I love you Justin." The fervidness of her tone coincides with her words.

"I love you too baby." His sleep-ridden inebriated mumbling enacts the stolen moment. But as vivid as this joyous vision is rendered—it quickly disintegrates, leaving behind a black void that represents the emptiness in his life. Unaware that he's actually dreaming, Justin's face contorts in confusion seemingly lost by the darkness. He hears voices—at first indecipherable, but is soon recognized as a single sound from a familiar source. Unmistakably he identifies the voice to be that of Teresha—laughing, apparently deeply involved in some sort of discussion. And like the brilliant flash of a snapping camera the image brightly appears as Teresha is seen driving while talking on her cell. Her radiant glow illuminates the setting. She looks happy and at peace. Just by the tidbits of conversation, Justin soon conceives that's he's the topic. It's seeing the smile over her face—the delight in her voice, which brings a warming comfort to his soul. He too smiles remembering the blue shoulder-tie church dress that she's wearing— and how he used to tease her about how snug it fitted, as it clung to her every curve. He joked about how she would mess up a sermon once the preacher had seen her in such temptress attire as so often she tipped into the sanctuary late. And how every time without fail she would act all offended by his remarks, yet he always knew how much she enjoyed the attention.

In the fleeting seconds following, Justin sees Teresha drop her earpiece and without thinking reach down to pick it up. When she looks forward again her expression reveals the panic of her imminent peril. Behind the steering wheel, her subsequent frantic maneuvering tells the tale of those last desperate moments. It's in her eyes that Justin sees the horror and sheer fear of confronting the unknown. He's left with no doubt that in that final moment she knew her time had come.

The image then switches to Justin arriving home after his hour long flight from Atlanta, but before he can lay his keys on the counter, his cell phone rings. It's Jerome bearing the tragic news. And like it was yesterday, he relives his disbelief—the violent denial, as his head erupts back and forth, disputing Jerome's every word. With tears streaming, he gibbers for his son—afraid that he might have been with her. Despite learning of Justice's safe whereabouts, everything fades to black. His knees begin to buckle as he nears the point of passing out. "Jay! ...JAY!" Worried, Jerome calls out, feeling his brother's pain, yet receives no answer. Justin, who's suffering from a shortness of breath, stammers behind the kitchen counter for a glass of water. He's precariously laid the phone down, having totally forgotten that Jerome was still on the line. He can't believe she's gone.

The realism of his dream awakens Justin in a hyperventilating fret. Struggling to catch his breath, he looks around the room sensing the urgency to figure out his location. Once realizing he's in his own bed, he immediately finds himself at the bathroom sink splashing cold water upon his distressed face. He stares deep into vanity with drips of mixed perspiration and doused H2O profusely descending onto his pajamas. Standing disoriented, Justin now remembers the Tobin James consumed no more than forty-five minutes ago—and resorts to a cold shower to counteract the effects. Yet, what the shower doesn't remedy is the nauseating swirl within the pit of his stomach. He then forces himself to puke, relieving the queasiness. After rinsing off, it's with a pronounced sigh that he exits the stall shivering—a towel wrapped around himself as he takes an uncomfortable seat on the bathroom floor. Eyes closed, he leans his head back against the tiled wall while in the backdrop Babyface remains on repeat. "*Fuck.*" His low obscene utterance singing the sentiment of a distraught soul—wondering what good has his life been to anyone. A hand hides his face as he sits alone, with his knees tightly bundled and pointed toward the ceiling.

It's with the lyrics of the song that he begins to torture himself—drowning needlessly in the desolation of lost love. His spirit tires from the constant failures of life. And like images etched in stone, the unrelenting memories—and retrospections, all playing their part in Justin's continuing downward spiral. And within that one split impulsive second he entertains the thought of committing suicide. Mentally, he inventories the medicine cabinet for any past-prescribed sedatives, wanting emphatically to be able to just sleep—only permanently. With Justice and all assets already willed to Jerome, his plight begins to make sense as he can't rationalize any fathomable reason for wanting to disillusion himself any longer. Enough is enough, as his shitty short changed existence has never made sense. Plagued since birth, he follows a legacy of letdowns. Compiling his flaws, he recognizes the internal anger—desiring so desperately to erase everything. Its then that Justin jumps to his feet and without hesitation, he opens the cabinet and reaches for a barely used box of Rozerem—a doctor prescribed sleep aid. He anxiously begins removing the little white pills from their foil packaging—quickly he pops seven or eight into his hand. Realizing the Rozerem wouldn't be enough by itself, Justin grabs a bottle of Paxil from the shelf—easily pouring out another twenty or so tablets. Between the sleep aid, anti-depressants, and alcohol—the combined dosage he figures should prove to be lethal. A tear rolls from the corner of his eye—his loaded hand shakes as the other retrieves a plastic cup residing on the sink which he now uses to collect water.

As the handful of pills begin to dissolve amidst his sweaty palm—Justin takes one last *good* look at himself in the mirror before doing the drastic deed. He finally concedes to the unending battle that wavers within his mind. So many issues, so many past hurts—the lacerating wounds eventually becoming fatal. *"I'm sooo sorry baby."* He ushers a muffled early apology to his son for the inevitable finale of all his selfish acts—the burden of discovering his lifeless body. Unable to cope, he brings the sleep-inducing mixture to his lips.

"POPS! …Come check this out!" Startled by the unsuspecting interruption, Justin loses his train of thought—immediately disposing the fist full of evidence in the toilet as an excited Justice enters the room ready to show him something.

"What's up?" Not believing the timing of the intrusion, he blows in frustration.

"Jus c'mon Pops!" Justice urges for his father's willing participation.

Talking between the partially pushed up door, Justin having no other choice, gives in. "Al-ight jus hold up. I'll be out in a minute!"

"Whatcha doin' anyway—takin' a dump?" he asks, being sarcastic.

"Got jokes huh?"

"Jus hurry up!" Now badgering, he rushes his father.

"Go ahead boy! …Didn't I say I'd be in there!" Justin loses his patience. Once hearing the patter of his son's parting feet vacate the room, he releases his tight-wound composure, again sobbing. With balled fists he pounds the ceramic basin—bellowing in anguish before falling upon the floor. Whimpering and laughing hysterically—completely exasperated by the chain of events, Justin—unable to believe his own luck, finds himself now hilariously pathetic, as even in death he fails.

forty-one

For Better, For Worse

7:25am Tuesday morning—Sho' Nuff Entertainment.

It's back to the grind again as Justin sits in the empty parking lot, reluctant to go inside. With Justice out of school for another week and the alarm going off at its normal time, arriving to work early becomes an understatement. For he's been sitting there ever since a few minutes past seven. He shakes his head in disgust thinking, "What a fuckin' weekend!" having experienced the extreme highs and lows of the past 72 hours. So in need of a good laugh and a welcomed ear, he decides to kill time by aggravating Jackie. "What's up boo? Sorry I ain't call ya back yesterday."

"No biggie. I knew as much anyway. …So how are you?" The early morning rise has her sounding congested.

"Cool."

"And my baby?"

"Good! …Still enjoin' his stuff. Had me on that game all day yesterday." They both laugh.

"So, what's wrong?" She senses that something's not right.

"...Why ya ask?" he asks, seeming somewhat surprised when of course he shouldn't be.

"Boy, I know you're not callin' me at 7:30 in the morning for no reason boo! ...So let's have it—*spill it.*"

Justin releases a smile knowing he's made the right call. "That's why I love ya girl. ...Nobody knows me like you!"

Laughing, she says, "Whatever. So start talkin'!"

"*W-w-well* let's jus say... *Oops* I dun did it again!"

And now cackling even harder, she says, "She's gone ain't she?"

"Yep!"

"Boy, what's your problem? I mean, my goodness! You can't keep a woman. ...Wasn't it jus the otha day when she was in your face grinnin'—and wouldn't let ch'ou talk?"

"Yep."

"You know I ain't appreciate that. Hell, it was Christmas..."

"I know boo. My bad! ...I'm sorry," as Justin tries to pacify the situation.

"See, that's why ya shoulda stayed your black ass right here—married me and made beautiful babies!" She expresses her own wish.

"That's what I'm sayin'." He cosigns her every word.

"You'll know the next time though—won't cha? ...Go runnin' off ta Chicago when ya could have had everything ya needed right here!" she says, unconsciously complaining.

"Oh fo sho!"

"So, what happened this time?"

"Same ole shit! She started talkin' crazy—a nigga tried ta calm her down. But then she went ta swingin' and shit! ...Next thing ya know da bitch is try'na pick her ass up from off the floor. Well, actually the Christmas tree. ...Knocked the whole shit over!"

"Uh-ummm. Did cha hit her?" she asks, concerned.

"Naw. I was try'na get her to quit! She jus flipped out and shit!" he says, telling only half the story.

"*Over what?*" She's now angry herself.

"*Tae!* ...She got all jealous and shit cause she brought ova some Christmas gifts for me and baby boy."

Jackie gets quiet for a second, realizing that there's got to be more to it. "Um-huh." she says, conveying a tinge of sarcasm.

"So, what's all that for?" he asks, feeling offended.

"Cause Justin, I jus know you." She shows her rare serious side as she uses his actual full first name.

"Meaning what?"

"Meaning, I know there's more than whatcha tellin' me. That girl didn't jus get like that over a Christmas gift. I don't even know the girl and I still think there's more to the story boo! ...You been dippin' again?" she asks, using her intuition. "Have you tripped and fallen into anything new lately—like maybe Shantel—hmmm?"

"Please. I got enough goin' on than to be try'na fool up wit her. That's my girl and all but I ain't try'na go out like that!" he says, lying.

"Neva stopped you before."

"Okay, whatever man. ...But hey, let me holla at ya later—al-ight?" Justin cuts short his conversation after seeing Tae pull into the parking lot.

"Bye Boy. Call me back!"

"Al-ight—peace out!" He immediately closes his cell as Tae parks right beside him. He jumps out to meet her. While standing in sub freezing temps—each obviously enamored by the other's presence, her smile says it all as she leans back against her Montero door, hardly able to maintain just a smirk.

"I tried calling you on Sunday—but didn't get an answer. I woulda called back but I wasn't try'na get anybody in trouble. But thank you Jay." Grinning, she steps in front of him. Her voice cracks while attempting to hold back an outpouring of emotions. "Gimme a hug. That was so sweet." The two share a lengthy embrace.

"Oh, you're more than welcome. I told Baby boy to call ova there yesterday ta thank ya again. That computer was a really nice gift. He needed it fo sho."

"That's what I was thinking—since he'll be in high school next year..."

"And yeah... You ain't got ta be worried 'bout when and what time ya call anymore. Homegirl—she up outta here ...ancient history— know what I'm sayin'? So from now on—jus call or come whenever ya get ready!" he says, boldly introducing his new unrestricted freedom.

"Oh really? And for how long this time?" she asks, knowing the nature of the relationship.

"For good. I'm for real! Ain't no goin' back after this weekend. ...All hell broke loose, *shit!"*

"Yeah right! Heard it all before—*we'll see!* But I am curious to know what happened?"

"I'll tell ya later. But jus know this—it's over! And I can sure show ya better than I can tell ya." He puts his hand under her jaw gently guiding her lips to his. The soft sensual kiss momentarily silences Tae—along with her doubts. "And jus for the record—ya know you a trip!"

"And why is that?" she asks, still taken by the kiss.

"Cause that ole' bullshit you ran 'bout my gifts!"

Now perky, she looks up at Justin grinning, "Oh, you like that? Was kinda smooth wasn't it? …Even if I say so myself."

"Yeah. Pretty tight. Definitely had me buggin'. Thank ya!" He kisses her forehead.

"Always obliged. So, I take it everything fit to your satisfaction?"

"Yes Ma'am …And yourself?"

She removes one of her leather gloves and pushes back her jacket sleeve to reveal her shiny new diamond encrusted Baume & Mercier watch.

"Lovely. I knew it would look good on ya."

"And yes it does. But so does this!" She looks first for any passerby's before opening her shirt just enough to give Justin a quick glimpse at her other bestowed offering—a sexy cleavage bearing black push up bra, just one half of a lacy see-through ensemble from Victoria's Secret.

"Damn, you wearin' the shit out of that!" he says, admiring the view.

"I was going ta tease ya wit it later, but I guess now is a good as time as any. …So how ya know my size?"

Smiling, "Oh, I've gotten pretty good wit numbers…"

"I bet ch'ou have chump!" she says, playfully rejecting the comment.

"Figured if nuthin' else, ya boy Quent would get a good kick out of it."

"Anyway, next subject!" She adamantly dismisses the thought, linking herself to Justin's arm to hurry him along.

♡ ♡ ♡

10:37am

On the phone with Rico, Justin discusses the focus for the upcoming new year. As Rico gives the final green light for the forward pursuit of Nigel the Great, he makes sure Justin "gets the picture" of the company investment about to be put forth. The dicey gamble attached to the creative direction harbors some doubts over Sho' Nuff's long term ability to recoup its vested interest. But purely on Justin's gut instinct, Rico commits—with only a few stipulations. The conversation ends after a brief undebated discussion. Like a scripted plot, Demetrius enters the room on perfect cue. "Speak of the devil... What's up man?" Justin gives his fellow colleague a warm reception.

"You nigga. How was Christmas?"

"Huh, we ain't even gonna talk 'bout that. But yeah man ya came thru at the right time. I jus talked ta Riq. On that first Wednesday after the new year—I think it's on the fourth. But ya get your wish—you're goin' to the crib! ...See whatcha can do wit this kid—*straight?* "

"Yeah we straight! ...You know who's got da skillz nigga. I'll have his ass on lock within the week!" he says, boasting with the utmost confidence.

"*Al-ight.* ...Say, while you're in here... When me and Riq were talkin', the subject came up of you maybe workin' back out of the Atlanta office—*whatcha think?* "

Dee frowns—wondering where all this is suddenly coming from. "So, what's up man? Talk ta me nigga. I ain't understandin'!" he says, as he voices his concern.

"They need cha down there. I mean, we do too, but ch'ou know what I'm sayin'... Especially if we sign this kid. I think he'll be betta served there. Of course you'll be the one ta head up the project. ...Could mean big things for you! I know we talked 'bout expandin' into more diverse markets, but I'm beginning ta agree wit Riq. ...Now jus ain't the time. But either way there'll always be a place for you here. So we put the ball in your court—and it's completely up ta you. When you're ready jus tell us what ch'ou want."

Stunned but pleased. "Shit nigga—ya need an answer now?"

"Nah. Mull that shit ova! I know ya jus started layin' some roots here, so weigh your options. I'll get up witcha when ya get back—al-ight?"

Dee nods his head. "Thanks Jay," he says, extending his hand.

"Shit, you earned it! ...Hell, I'm jus glad that here there's always enough love ta give a nigga a chance—know what I'm sayin'?"

"*Hell yeah.*" Dee snickers in full agreement.

Some thirty minutes later Tae pops on the scene. "I heard!"

"Heard what?" As Justin's eyes are glued to his laptop.

"I jus talked to Demetrius. Said he might be leavin'."

"That's possible but nuthin' concrete. ...Sumptin' we're tossin' around. I thought a nigga woulda kept it to himself at least for a minute."

"From the way it sounds he's already made up his mind."

"Well, that's his choice. I'd probably do the same thing if I was in his shoes. ...I mean it's a great opportunity. *Heeey* that's how a nigga like myself came up. ...Started wit Kyra—remember? Finally turning his attention to Tae, he says, "So more power to a nigga."

"Yeah I guess you have a point." She pauses. "...Oh and he also seems ta think that I already knew about all of this—I guess insinuating that he knows we have something goin' on."

"Whatever. That nigga knows how I get down! He knows betta than that shit! ...Business is business when we up in here. ...No *ands*, *ifs*, or *buts*—I don't play that shit!"

Tae just looks at Justin as he goes through his whole Mr. Man spiel. She knows he's just saying all that to hear himself talk. Once finishing his sermon, he jumps to an entirely different subject. "You feelin' like pizza tonight?"

She seems surprised. "That's fine."

"After work I'll scoop up Baby boy and we'll do Home Run Inn— that's straight?"

"Sounds copesetic ta me! ...Which one?" she asks, thinking of several locations.

"Probably the one ova there on 31st. But what we can do—this time we'll jus leave your ride here and you roll wit me to the house for a minute..."

Remembering something, Tae interrupts. "On second thought—I do need ta run home first. But I can swing by your place afterwards and then from there we'll decide which vehicle ta take."

"*Al-ight?*"

"Then it's a date. I'll let you get back to work. ...*Chow!*" she says as she bounces out of his office, high on life.

"Yep." Justin turns back towards his laptop. Yet its focus eludes him. Pausing from everything, he takes a minute to himself before lunch as he puts his life in perspective. Just venturing back to a day ago, it's crazy to even image—if he actually did what he had set out to do. If he had just swallowed those pills, the lives that would have been affected by this one selfish decision. He knows all too well he's battling a conflict within himself—in which the list of potential casualties keeps climbing.

❧   ❧   ❧

2:11pm

In his office, Justin sits in an interview with Tomar Rutledge from *Upscale* magazine. The Atlanta based publication is featuring a two-part story on the mega success of ATL's own Sho' Nuff Entertainment. Laughing and giggling the entire time, the two old acquaintances trade flirty rhetoric and industry gossip amidst the private casual setting. "...So Justin—to what do you attribute your own personal success story since joining Sho' Nuff?"

"Well, that's easy. I can sum it up in two words—*Rico Pittman* ...No doubt! It was his vision that inspired many of us to even wanna take hold of our own destinies. You know—this brotha took a bad situation and did sumptin' about it! And he neva ...and I do mean *neva*, let this industry deter him from his dreams. He's a maverick—a role model for all of us! And when I look back on my own life—you know I graduated from FAM—had my lil' degree and went out here and thought I could conquer the world! ...*HAAAD NO CLUE!* Fo' real. I started out in Retail Management." Quite surprised, Tomar flares her eyes. "...Yep—as an Assistant at Upton's department store. After that, I tried my hand in sales—sold everything from insurance ta used cars—all that shit failed! ...Found out right quick how hard it was ta feed a family off a 3% commission—especially when ya ain't sold shit!" He laughs. "...Kept goin' from job to job. I even ventured into a few of my own businesses—but nuthin' panned out. And at the time he and my brother, Jerome, were workin' on some things in the studio. I would hang out wit them from time to time ...*Shit*, I ain't had nuthin' else ta do!" He smiles. "So, we would kick it up there... And Riq—he noticed how opinionated I was and how I loved to talk. He'd bounce ideas off me—I told what I thought and it went from there. Next thing you know we're up in the clubs and showcases tradin' thoughts on a few of the local artists at that time," he says, releasing a big smirk. "I ain't know what he was doin'. But after several months—lo and behold, next thing ya know he's tellin' me about this venture he has wit Arista. And the rest is history!"

"That's good—real good. So, what was it like during those first few years? What signified the turning point—when you officially knew that Sho' Nuff Entertainment was going to be a force in the music industry?" The attractive Tomar knocks back the hair from in her face—attentively leaning forward with a mini recorder in hand.

"If I could answer the second question first; ...We knew from day one!"

She smiles. "Seriously Justin—what marked that defining moment of success?"

"Nah I'm for real! Since the moment we started this journey—from the very second the name was ever attached to this endeavor… We honestly knew! There was jus so much untapped talent right there in Atlanta that simply needed an open outlet to the rest of the world! I mean—look at all our early stuff… Hell, 100% of it was homegrown. And once the word got out there—we ain't have ta look for nuthin'. The talent came to us! …Made my job easy! There was always a different vibe to the way Riq went 'bout his business—always straight up! …Was neva 'bout the bullshit. You could take his word as bond. And you ain't see that wit many companies. Soon artists' jus gravitated to us!" In the backdrop, Justin's office phone has been continually buzzing for the last few minutes. Unable to ignore it any longer, he gets up to answer it. "Excuse me girl—I need ta get that!"

"Okay." Tomar kicks back in her recliner, making herself comfortably at home.

Judging by the nervous expression on his face and tense turning of his back—it's obvious the call is of major importance. He returns to the session uptight. So much so that at Tomar's request the rest of the interview is postponed to a later date. Once the room is clear, Justin immediately calls Tae into his office. When she walks through the door—pacing and without any greeting, Justin gets to the point. "We need ta talk."

"Do I need to sit down? …What's wrong? You're almost scarin' me." as she too starts to fidget.

"There's sumptin' I neva told ch'ou. …Remember that day in my office when I got that package in the mail wit no return address—and I ended up sendin' y'all out the room?"

"*Yeeeah*—vaguely."

"*Well*. Do you remember Tonya Campbell?"

"That Bohemian girl you were dating—I think! …The one that was into poetry."

"Yeah well, that package she sent was actually a positive pregnancy test—claiming me to be the father. But what's fucked up though… After that I kept try'na contact her to talk, but she neva returned any of my calls. And when I went to her house—she had moved. So all this time I've been runnin' round here not knowin' what da fuck's up!"

"That's why you ran out of here so fast that day. …But *why* are ya tellin' me this now?" she says, disgusted and shaking her head.

"What, I shouldn't?" he asks, as he tries to make her feel guilty.

"*Go* 'head!" she yells, immediately hanging her head low.

"Well, anyway she jus called!"

"And what did she want?" Then thinking about it, she says, "How did she even find you? ...When all that happened weren't we still in Atlanta? And you haven't talked to her since—right?"

"*Right!* But she said she called the main office there asking for me. And they gave her the number here! ...Said it was easy."

"So what did she say?"

"The same shit I jus said ta you, '*we need ta talk* '. What it is—she's supposed ta be in town for New Year's Eve. ...Some poetry slam or sumptin'. So she wants ta meet before the show..."

"Did she say anything about the baby?" she asked, concerned more for that fact.

"Nope. Said we'd talk on Saturday."

"So why she gotta be playin' games? When you tried talkin' to her—she was nowhere to be found!" Frustrated beyond belief, she expresses her personal feelings on the subject. "*Man*, I hate triflin' ass people!" Justin sits back quietly—yet confident in knowing that, for better or for worse, he's gained Tae's full support. He neglects to inform her of the intimate details surrounding Tonya's ambiguous departure.

forty-two

A Dream Come True

From his inside coat pocket Justin unfolds a small sheet of memo paper containing the address and directions, along with a phone number to The Zodiac Café—the place of he and Tonya's long-awaited meeting. Having anxiously anticipated this day all week, he double-checks his instructions as he makes the tedious drive up N. Broadway. Being that it's Saturday night—New Year's Eve, the streets soon begin to stir.

Encircling a three-block area, he finally stumbles across the inconspicuous converted lot—the one that Tonya spoke of supposedly near the club. Justin creeps slowly into the crammed part-time parking tract, leaving the engine running and fog lights on. With a slight sigh, he squints—peering through the windshield to see if he can catch any sign of the café from there. "…There that muthafucka go!" he says, once spotting the venue about 100 yards to the right. After which he tries settling himself in his seat while impatiently finger tapping the steering wheel to the beat of Power 92. It's 7:45—now fifteen minutes late, he wonders if he's already missed her. Somewhat tense, he then slows things down a bit—opting for an Anthony Hamilton CD over the radio. Another ten minutes passes before Justin lifts his cell to make the call.

Emerging from the darkness, leaving behind a dense trail of white cloudy breaths—a lone silhouette appears under the lit street lamp. Justin pauses before dialing as he identifies the brisk paced strides as that of a female. Finally able to make out the face—he realizes it's her! She approaches Justin wearing a full-length fringed buckskin coat—cloaked tight by a wide sash-like belt, hiding any hint of her pregnancy. Immediately he starts calculating the months—figuring she should be at least seven months or more. His evaluation leaves one thing for certain—she looks better than he remembered. He unlocks the door as she heads straight for the passenger side of the car—her clinched folded arms signifying the bitter cold conditions. Their eyes briefly connect once she jumps in. Seeing no bulge, bump, or any visible sign, anything but a well-built—perfectly fit woman, he instantly asks, "So, where's the baby?"

Not being nearly as serious, Tonya replies, "Why hey Justin," as she chooses to ignore his question. "…So how are ya?"

Reversing the understandable zealousness of his approach, "I'm sorry—I'm good. …And yourself?"

"I'm okay." She pauses. "And as you see …I'm not pregnant!" she says, looking down at herself. "That's why I wanted to talk to you in person. …I was never pregnant Justin and I wanna apologize for ever telling you that I was." She attempts to show her sincerity by making direct eye contact but with no success. Relieved in some respects—yet disappointed in others, he turns opposite of her as he stares out his driver side window, knowing full well he dodges yet another bullet. Justin's obvious contempt is conveyed through his silence. "I know you're mad—and I'm sorry, but so much happened then. …At that time—honestly, I was hurt and so angry at *you*, I woulda done anything to get back at ch'ou!" Reliving the moment, she says, "The way you did me! …Even after that night at my house—I forgave you! Then that day at the restaurant…"

"I understand…" His voice trails off after the interjection.

"But do ya?" she asks, wanting nothing less than his full empathy.

"*Oh*, I get it! My ass could be sittin' in county lockup if ya had gone anotha route. …I realize that!" Now biting his top lip, "I know my life could be very different right now. …So I do thank ya—and *I'm* sorry fo' all that confusion I brought into your life." Turning his head in

disgrace, "...'Cause no woman should ever have ta go through that."
And with a deep prolonged breath, he continues the confessional, as
Tonya becomes inundated with more than she bargained for. Justin
begins to reveal the tattered portion of his tormented soul. "I have a
lot goin' on wit me—you know inside my head. And it's like I know I
need help ...*real* help. And I keep tellin' myself that shit. But I still ain't
done nuthin' 'bout it." He chuckles. "Probably cause I really don't
know what-the-fuck ta do! I be wantin' ta jus wish all the bad shit
away. ...My father ...Mama. A lot of shit!" He frowns. "It's like my
mind stays cluttered wit everything that ever went wrong. And it sits
there buildin' until I can't take it anymore. ...Then I pop. And then it's
too late—shit gets all fucked up! That's why I try and keep ta myself.
And don't fuck wit too many folk. I can't trust like that no more. Ya
know—cause lurking somewhere 'round every corner is the next
fuckin' disappointment! ...But do ya see what I'm sayin'?"

"Sort of. But my thing is... why put yourself through all that when
you can't change what's already happened? So why not just let it go?
...We can continue ta be mad at the world—but for what? Cause when
ya really look at it—who ends up losin'? ...*We do!* And you never allow
yourself to experience the good in anything. Never take time to enjoy
what you actually have in front of you. ...I find myself now really
understandin' what it *really* means to smell the roses. ...Our
tomorrow's are not promised Justin. Remember that." She lays a hand
of encouragement on his thigh.

"Wanna know sumptin' funny?" he asks, still aimlessly gazing
through the window.

"*What?*"

"I can't count how many times I dun messed up—or fucked ova
the good in my life. I mean everything that was ever sound—ya know?
And it's like that very thing I need can jus be staring me in the face—
like this close!" he says, placing his spread palm just inches from his
nose. "And I still miss it everytime!" He manages to laugh at himself.
"I know ya think I'm crazy!"

"*Nooo*—jus wild!" She herself giggles.

"So whatcha sayin'?" He smiles.

"I'm sayin'. This night sure ain't what I expected it ta be..."

"Meaning?"

"I don't know. I guess I thought the conversation would have been
more of you being angry—and more of me tryin' ta defend my
actions."

"Nah. We cool. I think we both may have learned a lil' sumptin' and that's why, again, I wanna say thank ya." He finally faces her. "And I'm really sorry—for all *my* dirt. Cause you're absolutely right. I ain't have ta do ya like that!" He smirks. "Jus wish ya woulda returned jus one of them calls though. ...Coulda saved a brotha a few sleepless nights. But its all-good!" now engaging a full smile. "I am curious of one thing though?"

"*Whaaat?*" she says whining.

"When you left and got the heck out of dodge. ...Where the hell you went? ...Nigga got ghost quick! I came to the crib one day and the shit was empty. ...Where the *FUCK* you go?" he asks, humorously repeating himself.

She laughs. "*Maaan*—I had to G-O boo—no joke! I got the heck on! I couldn't take Atlanta no more—I'm serious!"

"*Why?*"

"Cause everything was headed in the wrong direction. My writing stalled—then *YOU!* ...A combination of a lot of things. One day I decided that I had jus about had enough. Called my aunt then went ta South Philly. Thought I'd lay low for awhile. Get some much needed R&R. ...Regroup and recharge."

"Oh I feel ya. Been there, dun that! We all need a break from time ta time," as he can definitely identify with her decision.

"That's what I'm sayin' though... It worked! After a few weeks— picked up my pen and flowed. ...Nothing beats that groove when it all comes together. It's what I do—that's why I'm here!"

"In Chicago?"

"*Y-Y-YEAH!* ...Had to get back out there again—and feel my peoples." She says, expressing her joy for the stage.

"How long are ya here?"

"Tonight. I leave in the morning."

"And where to after that?"

"Believe it or not—Pittsburgh!" They both laugh.

"Word. Think ya ever end up back in Atlanta?"

"Who knows. Never can say." She lifts her wrist for the time. "Stayin' for the slam? You haven't seen me do a show in awhile. Hang and watch a sista do her thang."

Justin smirks. "Maybe the next time boo."

"*Pleeease?*"

"I can't this time," he says, surprised by the pleaded offer.

"*Pretty please?* ...Always nice to have a familiar face in the crowd." She says, bargaining for sympathy.

"Yeeeah—I know. But fo' real—I have ta *definitely* take a rain check though. But since ya know ta reach me now—jus call a nigga whenever and we'll hook it up—al-ight?"

"Ummm-huh—betta be a promise," she says, expressing her slight disappointment.

"Got my word. ...Let me take ya back ova here." And he does just that—ending the brief meeting by releasing Tonya in front of the "weekends only" club. Amiable smiles and parting waves closes that chapter of his life. With a now cleared conscious, he heads next to enjoy an evening out with his son. Forgiveness becomes the reigning thought.

♡   ♡   ♡

Over on N. Dearborn, only the light of an unwatched television illuminates the single bedroom flat. A bowl of raspberry Haagen-Dazs sorbet sits melting on an end table while Tae lies across her Broyhill sofa—feet in the air, her face in front of a Vaio notebook. There's been some ongoing debate over the CD title and cover art—amongst the department, of Sho' Nuff's latest signing. She compares the design samples received from a contracted freelance artist and tries matching his artwork against the teenage trio's personality and sound—yet doesn't find any applicable connection. She determines her best bet is to just simply hire a new artist.

Assuming that her problem is solved, Tae lays her reading glasses on the floor and rolls off the couch to her feet. She lifts her nearly forgotten bowl—and walks to bedroom, taking a swallow of the soupy dessert. Sipping, she stops at her already opened closet—then steps in to pull the cord to the light. From the middle of the small well-organized space she stands in vigilant contemplation of tonight's attire. "Ummmh—so what's the move?" She talks to herself out loud while her bowl soon finds itself a new home on a top shelf—next to several boxes of shoes. She figures if she goes out—and hopefully has a good time tonight, then maybe it would be a way of negating the stress of Justin's latest paternity drama. Tae then thumbs through racks on both sides of the room. "Here we go!" as she stumbles upon a sexy sophisticated black mini dress—equipped with collars and long sleeves. Buttons run up the front to adjust for cleavage. She places the hung piece against her wifebeater tee and cut-off shorts. "Eat your heart out Justin!" Her once conservative taste giving way to her long hidden feelings for Justin, "Okay—I can wear that silver tiara choker wit this! ...Put on some leggings..." She pulls an oblong shoe box down— dropping it to the floor. An outburst of laughter follows, "Oool—I'd be such a slut!" Having removed the lid from a pair of glossy stretch thigh high boots with chrome heels bought over a year ago as part of her seductive wicked witch of the west Halloween costume. She reminisces on the heads that were turned that night. "Uh-ummm— NOPE! ...I wouldn't dare," she grins. Tae shakes her head as she returns the outfit to its proper slot. She leaves her closet with second thoughts on even wanting to be bothered with all hoopla of watching the ball drop over at the Navy Pier. "Seen one—ya seen them all." She picks up the remote—finds a comfortable spot on the carpet and turns on the TV back in her bedroom. "Dick—it's me and you tonight boo," she says as she flips to the annual New Year's Rockin' Eve broadcast.

Twenty minutes or so into her latest relocation—now posed fully stretched over the floor, Tae, with her head propped under a pillow, nods in and out until she hears the phone ring. It's the house phone up front so she doesn't bother moving to answer it. Instead she waits for the beep—listening for a message.

"Hey Love—it's Quentin. ...Aaah—since you're not at home and I don't like talking on machines," producing a smug chuckle. "I'll make this quick. ...I miss you baby—I miss us. We really need to talk. You know how to reach me." He pauses. "I love you. ...Happy New Year's baby." Click.

The smooth delivery of his reconciling message comes a little too late, as it does absolutely nothing for his cause. Quentin, who calls more now than when they were together, has just made the top of Shantel's shit list. "Tired A-S-S! All y'all jus alike. Always go ta missin' sumthin' when it's gone—huh! ...Didn't do shit wit it when ya had it—so arrivederci asshole!" she says, immediately pressing the erase button on the answering machine after having gotten up, ticked off at the audacity of Quentin's out of the question request.

She turns off the TV in the front room on her way back to the bedroom—but the door buzzes, sending Tae in a frenzied tirade. She wasn't expecting any company. "Shit!" She runs to the window looking for any familiar vehicles. "Damn you Justin!" Popping her mouth as she spots his 300 parked across the street in front of the building. She tries pinning back her loose bushy fro with no success for having recently removed the weave to allow her natural hair to breathe. "Shit!" Remembering her lounge-a-bout wears, she runs around in circles trying to get herself together. He buzzes again. She darts to the bathroom—checks for any trace of mote in the corners of her eyes, then squirts a dab of Colgate on her finger and proceeds to swish toothpaste around the inside of her mouth. She spits and quickly rinses, realizing she needs to go ahead and answer the door.

Feeling busted—and caught at less than her best, she trudges downstairs to open the door. Justin, himself stunned at the raw, nearly unrecognizable—but still cute Tae, laughs. "Bad hair day—huh?" Smirking, he runs his fingers through her nap.

"Shut up! Where's Justice?"

"Ova at Natron's! ...I jus came from there. Ya know we were suppose ta be hangin' out tonight. But when I got there ta pick him up, he said he wasn't ready and wanted to stay. ...Ended up talkin' ta Natron's dad—said he was more than welcome ta spend the night. Told lil' man, 'al-ight—call me if ya need me and I'll see ya in the morning'. So here I am—surprised?"

"Obviously," as she looks down at herself. "But *a-n-y*-way... Oh, so I gotcha all to myself then?" she asks, wrapping her tiny arms around him.

"All night long."

Changing subjects, she pulls back—yet still clasped to his waist. "You're smilin' so things must have gone well with Tonya?"

"Well, if you're askin' if she's pregnant—*well*, she's not."

"Thank ya Jesus!" she says, breathing a sigh of relief. "...Still in the business of answerin' prayers." She tearfully looks toward the ceiling—her hand covering her heart.

"I know whatcha mean. *Oh*, I know." He gives her a comforting embrace before heading upstairs.

Once inside the apartment, Justin makes his way to the kitchen. "After all this drama—a brotha could use a bite ta eat. ...I'm hungry!" he says, while bogarding the fridge. "Boo—ya ain't got nuthin'?" he asks, surveying the empty appliance.

"Like you've ever seen me cook! You know I'm a wine me-dine me kinda girl. Betta recognize!" And from the pantry she tosses Justin a rubber banded rolled bag of Jay's Hot & Spicy Kettle Krunchers. "Maybe that'll work for ya!"

"Well damn—I guess!" he says as he makes the no choice sacrifice. He eyes his homely dressed companion from behind as she enters the living room, taking her lazy place on the couch. "My, ain't we a sight for sore eyes today. ...I see someone ain't been out the house. I was kinda figurin' you'd be dressed and ready ta hit the streets tonight—out there try'na get your party on or sumptin'. What's up?" he asked, while continuing to tease.

"My friend's here—that's what's up!" She plays solitaire on her laptop.

"*What?*—who?" At first he's confused, then immediately assumes that Quentin is in town. "…Where is he?"

"My period silly! My monthly cycle—comes once every 28 days in case you've forgotten," she says, being sarcastic. "…I took some Midol earlier—but still don't feel worth a damn."

"So, in otha words—whatcha try'na say is… You won't be very good company tonight—right?"

"And if I'm not—you're still not goin' anywhere!" she says, as she's dead serious.

"Oh really?" he asks, unsure of how to take her.

"*Really.*"

It's after maybe an hour of dallying on the couch—and what not, as neither could care less about what's on television, that Justin temptingly watches Tae with her feet propped up on the coffee table—her loose shorts exposing gapping opportunities of the imaginable. He mischievously licks his lips as he pops her braless tit as she tries filing her nails in the dark.

"Ouch. Stop foolish!" She rubs her burning breast.

"Why?" he asks, as he does it again.

"Cause I said stop!" Tae pops his naughty hand with the emery board.

"Quit man!" he yells, now fanning his hand in pain.

"Well try keepin' your hands to yourself," she says, continuing her filing where she left off. But no more than a minute later, he's at it again—this time Justin tries running his hand under her flared bottoms.

"Ya jus don't quit—do ya?" As she puts the emery board down, Tae—who's not one to waste time with the formalities of foreplay, takes Justin's preoccupied hand—guiding it through the loose siding of her shorts and on up to the opening of her moist cookie. Justin gladly takes over from there. One finger—then two, enter her warm confines, penetrating deep then returning for a silky gliding massage over her erect clit. He soon makes a startling discovery.

"Thought you said your friend was here." He remembers her earlier line—realizing she's not wearing a tampon.

Amidst her jerks and moans, she confesses. "I lied. …Wanted ta see if you would stay if ya thought you might not get any ass."

"So, did I pass?" he asks, as he proceeds on with his provided pleasure.

"I suppose—this time," she responds, pausing between words. "Uuummm—oool…"

Stopping for only a second, Justin proposes disposing of the unnecessities. "Don't think you'll be needin' these," while commencing to remove her bottoms.

"Naaah—I suppose not," she says, as she helps his efforts. "We have a bed you know," hinting to her preference of location.

A trail of discarded clothes litter the path to the bedroom as Tae jumps to the center of her sleigh bed—grabbing the headboard. "You wanna get it like this? I want some back action." And like one of those a strippers from Club Cheetahs', she works the bed like a pole, shaking all of her bona-fide ass. Justin stares at her beautifully naked body. The whole time he's holding himself—stroking the base of his penis as it grows with every second. He rolls his nipples between his own fingers—only heightening the stimulation. Ready, he climbs onto the bed repositioning Tae on her stomach. Justin licks his finger then inserts it into her creamy cunt as she squirms with exhilaration. Carefully, as he navigates his curved mass, entering her from behind—he latches himself to the top of the mattress for extra leverage. He places his legs outside of hers—making for an even tighter feel. His slow—barely moving grinds allows for his gentle acceptance. Her moanful gasps indicate that the moment is more than she can handle. "Ummmf—ummmf… AAAH!" She yells out because he's gone too deep. Yet he surrenders no relief, as her sounds of passion become almost rhythmic—and more pronounced. Tae pushes her face into a pillow—muffling her own cries. Minutes of faster, focused motions finally cause them to reach their peak. A bead of sweat descends upon his lips—the taste of salt commemorates his moment of climax.

The idle weight leaves her with nowhere to go as both collapse in exhaustion. Too tired to move, but experiencing the brunt of burden, Tae wiggles her hips to arouse Justin. "Get off me!" she makes the anything but subtle request.

"Why?" he asks, barely responsive.

"Cause you're heavy!"

"*Shoot.*" He reluctantly rolls over to accommodate her discomfort.

"Where ya goin'?" she asks as she turns over on her back.

"I'm right here," he responds, not comprehending the question.

"Come here." She begins to play in her own juices.

"*What?*" he asks, sounding perplexed.

"I want you *here*—I'm not finished." Now catching her drift, Justin,—still hard, obliges by rolling himself back on top. He enters her again—this time from the missionary position. Tae—now facing him, she gently massages his buttocks as he once again starts with slow subtle strokes. "...What if I were pregnant?" The surprise question stops Justin in his tracks. "Whatcha doin'? ...Don't stop!" she yells as she slaps his ass cheek. "Handle your business! ...I'm speakin' hypothetically."

"So, why ya askin' that?"

"I was jus wonderin'..."

"But wonderin' what?" he asks, as neither breaks stride.

She looks into his eyes—her lips now sputtering as she begins to cum. "Give it me." Her muttered beckoning begs for Justin to dispense with all the finessing and hit it harder. He answers by lifting her leg above his shoulder and commences to vigorously pump her inner walls, with their previous discharge eliminating any friction amongst genitals. Her slick slippery offering soon fills with yet another helping of communicable secretions.

Justin dismounts—twisting flat on his back. This time he loses his erection, the liquidity leftovers now drain and dry over his thigh. Tae turns to him, resting her head upon his chest—her eyes in full contact with his. Smirking, he kisses her smitten face. "What's up?" he says as he questions the look.

At first saying nothing, she then confesses, "I want one."

"*Want what?*" A hint of sarcasm peeks through while he pretends to not know what she's referring to.

"A baby." She sits up.

"*Girl*—you must be out your damn mind!" he says, laughing and scoffing at the ridiculous request. Yet he notices that she's doesn't seem to be joking. In fact, by her expression, Justin instantly realizes that she's actually serious—very! "*Why*—what for?" he asks, now panicky.

"Because we belong together!"

"Okay maybe so. But what's a baby got ta do wit all that?"

She explains, "The way I see it—you have already had the last piece of new tail you will ever dig in!" She sneaks a kiss. "So baby ya betta enjoy it because it stops right here. ...I'm not goin' anywhere—you're not goin' anywhere. Both of us are in our thirties, so whatever children we're goin' ta have—needs ta be had soon. I'm not about ta be old and runnin' after any babies—maybe grandbabies, but that's it! So…"

"So, what you are sayin' is that this is it for me—and you're that *it*—right?"

"Yep. You got it!"

"So whatcha *really* sayin' is that you wanna marry a nigga—right?" he says, blowing her off with sarcasm.

"Yep—I guess so!" Totally agreeing, she rolls over to the opposite side of the bed. Reaching into her chest-of-drawers she retrieves a small gray box. "Give this to me."

Stupefied and stunned, Justin frowns wondering, "What the fuck is goin' on?"

She opens the box flaunting the 2-karat solitaire spectacle set on white gold. "I bought this with our Christmas bonus …*Well*, I put a down payment on it." She grabs the receipt handing it to Justin. "But of course you can finish payin' for the rest." Her calm demeanor confuses Justin of her seriousness.

"You fo' real?"

"*Yeees.* I'm not playin'! …Who's waitin' around fo you ta finally come to your senses? That's like waitin' around for hell ta freeze over—it'll never happen. …I guess I have ta keep tellin' ya this—but you *need* me. Justice needs me. …And settlin' for anything else is like havin' a Volkswagen when ya coulda had a Benz! …So-here-I-am offering myself unto you. Now marry me."

Justin stares like she's completely lost it—but realizes she has a point. He does need her, as does Justice. Beyond a doubt, she's kept him straight—always having his back like only a few have. "Smart and sexy, great in bed… a friend long before ever becoming a lover…" She now owns his every thought. And most importantly, probably only the second person on the face of this earth who's ever understood him unequivocally and uniquely. She has always accepted him for who he is—never once rejecting him for what he's not. It's her actions that have consistently spoken above all other's words. Therefore—what better suitor? Just seeing her adorning face beside his convinces Justin of the unconditioned love that surrounds this room—this place. "What is love? …It's everything." Answering his own question, he finally realizes that sometimes the best things in life are never more than a few feet away. It now all starts to make good sense—actually great sense! "Okay—fuck it! …Let's do it. Will you marry me?"

Spontaneously agreeing to the union, he places the perfectly sized ring on her finger.

"Why yes I will!" Tae then explodes in giddied laughter—kicking and screaming and kissing every part of Justin's hunky stark naked body. Overwhelmed and overjoyed she surrenders all to her husband-to-be, making love until the first sunrise of this bright promising New Year.

And We Are Not Saved

And We Are Not Saved

The Elusive Quest for Racial Justice

With a New Appendix for Classroom Discussion

DERRICK BELL

Basic Books, Inc., Publishers

NEW YORK

Library of Congress Cataloging-in-Publication Data

Bell, Derrick A.
    And we are not saved.

    Bibliographical notes: p. 273
    Includes index.
    1. Afro-Americans—Civil rights.   2. Racism—United
States.   3. Afro-Americans—Legal status, laws, etc.
4. United States—Race relations.   I. Title.
E185.615.B39   1987   305.8'96073'073   87–47512
ISBN   0–465–00328–1   (cloth)
ISBN   0–465–00329–X   (paper)

To Ada Elisabeth Bell, my mother;

to Jewel Hairston Bell, my wife;

and to all our Genevas

The harvest is past, the summer is ended,

and we are not saved.

—JEREMIAH 8:20

Contents

CONTENTS

PART II
The Social Affliction of Racism

PART III
Divining a Nation's Salvation

x

Preface

THE HEROINE of my book, Geneva Crenshaw, and her Chronicles owe their being to America's most prestigious legal periodical, the *Harvard Law Review*, and its annual practice of inviting a legal scholar to write the foreword to the Supreme Court issue. The roll of past foreword authors is impressive, and, to put it mildly, I did not expect to join the list. When the editorial board of volume 99 selected me to write its foreword in 1985, I doubted whether they would take kindly to a radical departure from the doctrinal analysis of the Supreme Court's work, an analysis that previous authors have undertaken with great competence. And yet I wanted to examine from a new perspective—beyond even the most exacting exegesis of case decisions—the civil rights movement since 1954 and the *Brown* school decision: that is, to explain or justify what has happened, or not happened, and how black people (or some of us) feel about it.

The civil rights movement is, after all, much more than the totality of the judicial decisions, the antidiscrimination laws, and the changes in racial relationships reflected in those legal milestones. The movement is a spiritual manifestation of the continuing faith of a people who have never truly gained their rights in a nation committed by its basic law to the freedom of all. For my foreword, then, I sought a method of expression adequate to the phenomenon of rights gained, then lost, then gained again—a phenomenon that continues to surprise even though the cyclical experience of blacks in this country predates the Constitution by more than one hundred years.

As the deadline for the article hovered imminent, there came to my rescue Geneva Crenshaw and her tales, challenging the accepted view of how blacks gain, or might gain, from civil rights laws and policies. Thereafter the writing, while not easy, became a labor of enormous fulfillment. And to my great relief, the *Harvard Law Review* editors accepted my unorthodox approach and contributed their energy, skill, and enthusiasm to the editing process. Carol Steiker, the *Review*'s president for volume 99, Elena Kagan, supervising editor, William Forbush, executive editor, and several staff members became collaborators in the challenge to express jurisprudential matters of significant importance in a language and format more usual in literature than in law.

Encouragement and sound advice for both the article and this book came from a host of friends, family, teaching colleagues, and students. My long-time friend, Teachers College of Columbia University Professor Diane Ravitch, disagreed with some aspects of my thesis but enthusiastically recommended the work to her publisher, Martin Kessler, president and editorial director of Basic Books. Mr. Kessler graciously offered to serve as general editor and, having helped shape the book's structure, assigned copy-editing responsibility to Phoebe Hoss, whose fiction-writing skills, careful eye, and infinite patience reduced the gap between my thoughts and their expression. Linda Carbone handled the production chores efficiently and quickly. My thanks to family members, and the many friends, colleagues, and students, especially the members of my Fall 1986 seminar, "Civil Rights at the Crossroads," all of whom reviewed chapters and offered suggestions. I want to thank particularly Sharon Carter, Dr. Jane DeGidio, Paul Dimond, Lani Guinier, Elena Kagan, Elaine McGrath, Stephanie Moore, Audrey Selden, Carol Steiker, Gloria Valencia-Weber, and professors Regina Austin, Denise Carty-Bennia, Linda Greene, Joel F. Handler, Randall Kennedy, Henry W. McGee, Jr., Arthur S. Miller, Daniel J. Monti, Cass Sunstein, and Patricia Williams. Ken Diamond and Elizabeth Wilkerson at Stanford and Rodney Akers and Areva Bell at Harvard provided research assistance, and Marian Holys at Stanford and Debra Ayles at Harvard handled secretarial chores. The Harvard Law School Summer Research Project granted financial support.

And We Are Not Saved

Introduction

JEREMIAH's lament that "we are not saved" echoes down through the ages and gives appropriate voice to present concerns of those who, flushed with the enthusiasm generated by the Supreme Court's 1954 holding that segregated public schools are unconstitutional, pledged publicly that the progeny of America's slaves would at last be "Free by 1963," the centennial of the Emancipation Proclamation. That pledge became the motto for the National Association for the Advancement of Colored People's 1959 convention in New York City, where were gathered, in jubilant euphoria, veterans of racial bias and society's hostility who believed that they had finally, and permanently, achieved the reform of the laws that had been for a century vehicles for the oppression of black men, women, and children. Not even the most skeptical at that convention could have foreseen that, less than three decades later, that achievement would be so eroded as to bring us once again into fateful and frightful coincidence with Jeremiah's lament.

With the realization that the salvation of racial equality has eluded us again, questions arise from the ashes of our expectations: How have we failed—and why? What does this failure mean—for black people and for whites? Where do we go from here? Should we redirect the quest for racial justice? A response to those questions—more accurately, a series of responses—is the purpose of this book. Rather than offering definitive answers, I hope, as law teacher rather than social seer, mainly to provoke discussion that will provide new insights and prompt more effective strategies.

3

I recognize that most of what can be said about racial issues in this country has been said, and likely more than once. Over and over, we have considered all the problems, tried many of the solutions, and concluded—reluctantly or with relief—that, while full racial equality may some day be achieved, it will not be in our time. Developments in the civil rights field have been dutifully reported and analyzed by the media. And scholars have not been silent. Library shelves creak under the weight of serious studies on racial issues. Surely, one might think, the literature would not suffer, and might even benefit, from a period of repose.

For better or worse, though, race is not like other public problems. Throughout America's history, racial issues have been high among, if not central to, the country's most important concerns. Often—as when the Constitution was written, during the Civil War and Reconstruction, and throughout the decades of the civil rights movement since the Supreme Court's *Brown* decision in 1954—racial issues have riveted attention. At no time has race slipped far down the list of the most crucial matters facing both the nation's top policy makers and its most humble citizens. Consider the predictable self-congratulation as we celebrate the two hundredth anniversary of the Constitution's signing in 1787, its ratification in 1789, and the adoption of the Bill of Rights in 1790. During the conferences and commemorations, few will wish to risk discord by reminding us of what has not been accomplished. On the agenda of unfinished business, America's continuing commitment to white domination looms especially large for those citizens of color whose lives are little less circumscribed than were those of their slave forebears.

Racism is more than a pejorative hurled in powerless frustration at an omnipotent evil. As Professor Charles Lawrence more precisely puts it:

Racism in America is much more complex than either the conscious conspiracy of a power elite or the simple delusion of a few ignorant bigots. It is a part of our common historical experience and, therefore, a part of our culture. It arises from the assumptions we have learned to make about the world,

4

ourselves, and others as well as from the patterns of our fundamental social activities.[1]

Even in the face of this enormous obstacle, the commitment of those who seek racial justice remains strong. Tangible progress has been made, and the pull of unfinished business is sufficient to strengthen and spur determination. But the task of equal-justice advocates has not become easier simply because neither slavery's chains, nor the lyncher's rope, nor humiliating Jim Crow signs are any longer the main means of holding black people in a subordinate status. Today, while all manner of civil rights laws and precedents are in place, the protection they provide is diluted by lax enforcement, by the establishment of difficult-to-meet standards of proof, and, worst of all, by the increasing irrelevance of antidiscrimination laws to race-related disadvantages, now as likely to be a result as much of social class as of color.

How are we to assess the unstable status of a struggle that all but the most perversely pessimistic predicted would end in triumph many years ago? Even those most deeply involved in this struggle are at a loss for a rational explanation of how the promise of racial equality escaped a fulfillment that thirty years ago appeared assured. Indeed, logical explanation fails before the patterns of contemporary racial discrimination so close in intent to, if different in form from, those practiced in earlier times. Rationales based on political concerns and economic realities do not alone explain the increasing viability of concepts of white superiority that long ago should have been consigned to the obsolete. The discrepancy between the nation's deeply held beliefs and its daily behavior add a continuing confusion to racial inequities that undermine effective action. Thus, we take refuge in the improbable and seek relief in increasingly empty repetitions of tarnished ideals.

In order to appraise the contradictions and inconsistencies that pervade the all too real world of racial oppression, I have chosen in this book the tools not only of reason but of unreason, of fantasy. The historian Robert Darnton reminds us that fairy tales in their early versions did not always have happy endings but, rather, usually reflected, through the folktales on which many were based, the harsh life of eighteenth-century peasants. Darnton reports that many classic fairy tales "undercut the notion that virtue will be rewarded or that life can be conducted according to any principle other than basic mistrust."[2] The historic subordination of American blacks is not unlike that of eighteenth-century French peasants.[3] The role and fate of civil rights measures can be compared to those of the brides in the French fairy tale *Bluebeard's Castle*, in which Bluebeard woos and brings to his castle a series of brides in the hope that each will free him from the burden of his past crimes. But the brides are rebellious rather than redemptive, and each is condemned either to death or to a dark chamber. Thus, first after the Civil War and again in 1954, America produced symbols of redemption in the form of civil rights measures seemingly intended to rectify past racial cruelties and expunge the dark stain of slavery. But, after a brief period of hope, compliance with these measures has impeded other goals and, like Bluebeard's brides, they have been abandoned, leaving the blacks' social subordination firmly entrenched.

In resorting to the realm of fairy tale—and its modern counterpart, science fiction—I have devised ten metaphorical tales, or Chronicles, one of which opens each of the chapters in this book. These Chronicles, as my friend Professor Linda Greene reminds me, follow as well an ancient tradition in using fantasy and dialogue to uncover enduring truths.[4] As illustration, she cites the works of Plato[5] as well as law school professors who maintain that Socratic dialogue effectively illuminates essential principles.[6] A well-known example of the genre is Professor Lon Fuller's *The Case of the Speluncian Explorer*.[7] In law practice, too, as more than one teacher has observed, a "lawyer's primary task is translating human stories into legal stories and retranslating legal story endings into solutions to human problems."[8] (On the other hand, as the public knows too well, legal jargon often distorts beyond recognition legal stories claimed to be factual.)

My expectations for the Chronicles are ambitious precisely because, as Professor Kim Crenshaw has put it, "allegory offers a method of discourse that allows us to critique legal norms in an ironically contextualized way. Through the allegory, we can discuss legal doctrine in a way that does not replicate the abstractions of legal discourse. It provides therefore a more rich, engaging, and suggestive way of reaching the truth."[9] Thus, the Chronicles employ stories that are not true to explore situations that are real enough but, in their many and contradictory dimensions, defy understanding.

The book is divided into three parts. Part I deals with the intricacies of the barriers to racial equality established in law by the society at the very beginning of this nation's history. For the identifiable factors determining today's racial policy—jurisprudential, economic, political, even psychological—are neither novel nor new. They were active at the start of the colonial era; and by the time the present government was conceived in 1787, they were full-blown with consequences far beyond the bondsmen who were the objects of the policies.

Following the prologue to part I, in which the narrator introduces himself and recounts the story of the extraordinary visitation of my heroine, Geneva Crenshaw, chapter 1 opens with the Chronicle of the Constitutional Contradiction. In this Chronicle, I take the liberty of tampering with time and history to examine the original contradiction in the Constitution of the United States—a contradiction that is at the heart of the blacks' present-day difficulty of gaining legal redress. Thus, I dramatize the concerns that likely led even those Framers opposed to slavery to sanction its recognition in a Constitution whose Preamble pledges to "secure the Blessings of Liberty to ourselves and our Posterity." At the conclusion of this Chronicle, Geneva and the narrator further discuss the implications of this original contradiction for contemporary conditions. This pattern of Chronicle and discussion is followed by subsequent chapters, where the one serves as the springboard for the other in which Geneva and the narrator express their strong, and usually conflicting, views.

Thus, in chapter 2, the Chronicle of the Celestial Curia, with its otherworldly setting, raises pragmatic questions about whether law and litigation can achieve meaningful reform for the victims of racial and economic inequality. Geneva and the narrator compare the dichotomy between civil rights lawyers' unshaken belief in and reliance on the courts and the serious questions posed by legal scholars regarding the role of the Supreme Court in racial reform. Voting-rights cases illustrate these points in preparation for the voting rights measure examined in the next Chronicle. In this second Chronicle as well, Geneva begins to explain the origin of her Chronicles and their role in her quest for racial justice.

Chapter 3 examines, through the Chronicle of the Ultimate Voting Rights Act, the limitations on the voting rights of blacks and asks whether an ideal "ultimate" voting rights act would not only survive constitutional challenge but be effective as well.

Any examination of the civil rights era that began with the Supreme Court's 1954 *Brown* decision must inquire into the ensuing and widespread strife carried on in the courtrooms and in the streets. Thus, chapter 4 and the Chronicle of the Sacrificed Black Schoolchildren center on the real beneficiaries of the *Brown* school decision. Geneva and the narrator speculate about policies that might have more effectively improved the quality of education provided for black children, but were never much tried because of the civil rights community's commitment to achieving school desegregation through racial balance.

The Chronicle of the Black Reparations Foundation, in chapter 5, raises the question whether the cost of a black reparations program is the main basis for white society's opposition to improving the economic status of blacks. This question leads to a discussion about the elevation of "reverse discrimination" from an opposition slogan to a judicially recognized limit on the remediation of racial justice.

In chapter 6, affirmative action, a contemporary policy intended to compensate for the damaging effects of past racial discrimination, is examined in the Chronicle of the DeVine Gift. The frequent complaint that "we can't find qualified blacks" may be proof that the affirmative-action policy is serving its real, though unacknowledged, goal: excluding all but a token number of minorities from opportunities that previously were available only to whites. Exploring this notion in the context of whites' desire to maintain what Professor Manning Marable calls "cultural hegemony,"[10] Geneva and the narrator discuss the relative ineffectiveness of employment-discrimination law, and consider as well the civil rights community's acceptance of benign housing quotas.

Many who labor to make real Dr. Martin Luther King's idealistic vision for this country firmly believe that if all Americans faced a common crisis or extraordinary peril, the need to work together for survival would eliminate racial prejudice—a belief tested, both humanly and legally, in chapter 7's Chronicle of the Amber Cloud. Geneva and the narrator review current policies, such as civil service tests, that perform some useful social function, and conclude that such utility serves to insulate the policy from constitutional challenge even when in operation it seriously disadvantages blacks.

In part II, I move from analyzing civil rights campaigns intended to gain recognition of black rights, to the human difficulties within the black community arising from the blacks' long involuntary status as secondary members of society. The internal stresses resulting from living as "strangers in a strange land" (as Harriet Tubman put it) can, paradoxically, be worsened as a result of civil rights gains. In the prologue to this part, I explore the complex relationship between Geneva and the narrator and, by extension, the ambivalence of close male-female relationships based on respect and friendship rather than on romance and sex. Here the narrator comes up once again against the psychologically disabling fact that contemporary black men are, like their slave forebears, unable to guarantee their women and families protection against the society's racism and the violence founded in that racism. This disability, among many others, provides a cogent argument for advocates of black emigration, a subject also touched on in this interlude.

The differences in sex-role expectations between black men and black women are the subject of the narrator's own Chronicle of the Twenty-Seventh-Year Syndrome in chapter 8. This chapter focuses on how black male sexism as well as white racism has damaged the black community, and on how the tardily recognized right to interracial sex and marriage has affected black male-female relationships.

Self-help, perhaps the most frequently prescribed cure for the malaise of black poverty and disadvantage, is the concern of chapter 9 and the Chronicle of the Slave Scrolls. Here are reviewed several legal approaches that might offer constitutional protection for a black community competing successfully with whites and no longer begging for either bread or rights.

Part III brings us to Geneva's ultimate strategy, based on the Chronicle of the Black Crime Cure, and to her eloquent appeal for new ways of seeing and using old civil rights strategies in a situation where a positive outcome, while not assured, can still be hoped for.

In my plan for this book, I have been guided by the observation of Justice Oliver Wendell Holmes, Jr., that law is more than logic: it is experience. And long experience teaches that legal outcomes are not determined by advocacy alone. Nor, alas, will the justice of one's cause suffice to ensure justice. Constitutional protections, and the judicial interpretations built on them, have real importance but, all too often, work out in practice in unanticipated, and destructive, ways. Moreover, both practice and law are affected by a major, though seldom acknowledged, factor: the self-interest of segments of the dominant society. For what both elite policy-making whites and working-class whites perceive as their self-interest can be very different—a difference that can have destructive implications for all black people even as they applaud the latest recognition of their civil rights by the highest court in the land.

PART I

The Legal Hurdles to Racial Justice

Prologue to Part I

UNTIL NOW, I had thought that law faculty meetings were the most frustrating gatherings known to the Western world. But I had forgotten that special futility I always experience at civil rights conferences where seemingly every participant espouses with fervent and unflinching faith a different strategy for our racial deliverance.

And it was happening again. After two days of intense wrangling, it seemed clear that—barring a miracle—what promised to be a memorable gathering of the country's best-known black leaders, would end—as had so many others—with much said and precious little accomplished. My sense of futility was heightened as I remembered how the invitation to this "Black Bicentennial Convention," impressively engraved on high-quality paper, had lifted my spirits, wearied after a particularly unhappy session with my faculty colleagues. In accepting, I felt confident that the civil rights gathering would respond more positively to my suggestions than had my mainly white faculty colleagues whose backgrounds and outlooks on racial matters differed drastically from my own.

Foolishly perhaps, I had recommended at a recent faculty meeting that the law school commemorate the Constitution's two-hundredth anniversary by hosting a national conference devoted to the role of race in constitutional law development. After listening quietly as I explained my proposal, the faculty members— without discussion or formal rejection—simply smothered my idea under the weight of their enthusiasm for other less controversial and, as one committee member put it, more "patriotic" proposals.

At a younger age, I would have reacted dramatically, filling the room with angry accusations and then departing in a rage. Experience had taught that such displays are always good for the ego and can, on occasion, actually shock my white colleagues into taking me seriously. But, during this time when civil rights has lost its urgency, my departure not only would have been quietly applauded by members whom my suggestion had irritated, but, worse, might intensify a search—already rumored to be under way—for the appointment of another black from among those academicians who are definable less by their disparate ideologies than by their perverse willingness to denigrate their race in ways that many whites believe true but dare not publicly assert.

Hardly new are contemporary assertions that black deficiencies, and not white racism, are the root cause of our lowly status. In the post-Reconstruction era of the 1870s, the nation, weary of racial issues, prematurely proclaimed the former slaves free and able to rise or fail on their own efforts. Experts from fields as diverse as religion and social science gained prominence by proclaiming that the inherent inferiority of black people made further efforts on their behalf futile, even dangerous.[1] Today, as policy makers again seek to abandon civil rights enforcement, certain experts assert that the plight of blacks is the fault of blacks or of the social programs on which the poor rely.[2] When such claims are expounded by blacks, they obtain a deceptive authenticity.[3]

Such blacks, knowingly or not, dispense a product that fills the present national need for outrageous anti-black comment. Many whites welcome it. The black neoconservatives, as some of these black critics describe themselves, gain wide recognition for their views; while the angry denials and demands for equal time by dissenting blacks are ignored just as my law faculty had, from its position of power, ignored my proposal.

I sat. By occupying the faculty's "minority seat," I was at least not letting a black neoconservative use it as another forum in which to spout the white-racist rhetoric that obtains a spurious legitimacy because it emanates from a black mouth. It will be a measure that we have arrived in this society, I thought to myself, when whites give positive statements by blacks about other blacks the same weight whites now reserve for our disparagements of one another. In the meantime, we must deem ourselves advantaged when blacks in public positions are willing, in their unelected representation of black people, to apply the physician's cardinal rule: "Do no harm."

Now, I was sitting again, both bored with the repetitious statements, and angry with the self-righteous rigidity with which each civil rights speaker championed one cause while disparaging all others. And because participants had been transported to the conference site, I was unable simply to leave, my usual remedy for unproductive discussions. In fact, I was not even sure where we had been meeting for two long days, with one more to go. Sadly, I was sure that the sessions, while interesting, had not fulfilled the high expectations set during the exciting trip to the conference site.

At dawn on the day of the Convention, the delegates who represented every point on the civil rights spectrum, had met—as our invitations directed—on Harlem's Lenox Avenue at the Schomburg Center for Research in Black Culture, known better as the Schomburg Library and famous for its contributions to black scholarship. Rather than remaining at the library, as I had expected, chartered buses took us away to a remote area at Kennedy Airport, where we boarded a 747. We all had questions about the unusual arrangements, but the host committee members, all well-known faces, assured us that all was proceeding according to plan.

The flight was more than three hours long, but the time passed quickly as each of us greeted old friends, made new acquaintances, and discussed various racial issues. All veterans in one way or another of civil rights campaigns, we shared war stories and reported on current activities and interests. My apprehension, allayed by the welcome opportunity of fellowship with individuals with whom I had worked, returned when we began our landing in fog so thick it seemed more than a match for even the most sophisticated radar and on-board computers. After a period of circling, though, the big plane touched down smoothly.

I breathed more easily as we taxied to a landing area where, through the fog, we could see three other large planes and a long line of buses, all bearing Convention delegates from other parts of the country. If anything, the fog seemed to thicken as the buses rolled away from the landing area and headed down a tree-lined road on which as far as I could see there were no other vehicles. Perhaps the others did not notice for our hosts were distributing handsome conference folders that contained the meeting agendas, position papers, and draft resolutions.

The Convention building loomed out of the fog, which seemed to be lifting. The structure's architecture, all glass and wood, was modern but mysterious, evoking a mood that was sober, austere, serious—and far more impressive than the cold concrete monstrosities that, though called convention centers, host every activity from rock concerts to horse shows. In contrast, this was a conference center more than worthy of the name. There were elegantly equipped meeting rooms of all sizes, offices, a library, as well as impressive dining facilities. The main auditorium, the Great Hall, was designed to reflect the architecture and atmosphere of both church and courtroom. It was both the focal point and an almost sacred nucleus of the conference complex.

For the first day, the presentations were interesting and the discussions following them lively. We genuinely felt that our decisions would be important; that, in ways we could not explain, history was being made and we were a part of it. The delegates, mainly lawyers, represented every segment of the black community from elite academics to grassroots spokespeople from poverty-stricken black areas, both urban and rural. Most of the delegates were black, but some whites, long identified with black causes, were also present. At first, potentially divisive differences in political beliefs were muted as delegates worked for consensus and understanding. Spirits were high, but delegates were sobered by the continuing reminders of how much more had to be accomplished despite the gains made during the past decades. Sobering as well was the predicament of the black poor which was without precedent in our people's bleak past.

In this unique setting, the presentation of the major policy alternatives was familiar to regular attendees at civil rights meetings stretching back to the post–Civil War era. There was much urging, particularly by representatives of the mainline civil rights organizations, that we not neglect the unfinished integration agenda. Despite admitted setbacks and disappointments, advocates viewed racial integration as the only answer to discrimination. Their uniform response to critics was that "integration had not worked because it had not really been tried."

In stark contrast, delegates representing many smaller groups voiced strong separatist motifs. Then a series of "third stream" strategies were advanced as more flexible and realistic alternatives to either all-out integration or black nationalism. Advocates for the various positions generally emphasized the ability of their strategies to provide support and protection to blacks in a nation where racial hostility was again on the rise.

By the second day, the harmony the Convention hosts had worked hard to maintain began to break down in the clash of disparate views. I had heard all these arguments before. I longed for the conciliating presence of Geneva Crenshaw, the civil rights attorney who—except for a mysterious encounter some weeks before—I had not heard from for twenty years. My quick decision to rearrange my schedule so that I could accept the Convention's invitation was prompted by the likelihood of her presence; but now I was beginning to fear that the proceedings had degenerated beyond the point of saving by even her persuasive advocacy.

It did not help that I understood our basic problem all too well. Each of us, veterans of the racial struggle, have willingly risked life and career and, in so doing, have escaped the fate of most blacks whose lives are narrowly walled in by racism. By our actions, we have already gained a large measure of personal independence and overcome society's built-in racial impediments. That is, we have achieved the essence of freedom, the ideal on which our society is based. We value the hard-won ability to work through problems, to implement approaches that we find right, and to hell with anyone, white or black, who disagrees or urges a different course.

We came here because we want the same thing for other blacks, and, viewing ourselves as the leaders or at least representatives of other blacks, we willingly join civil rights organizations and attend conferences like this one. But, unconsciously, at some point our personal independence comes into conflict with the requirements of a consensus that could give a large group strong and meaningful direction. In the end, while we seek and sincerely want consensus, the need to sacrifice the hard-gained independence of personal action proves too high a price to pay. Not recognizing either inner conflict or its unconscious resolution, each of us has a personal investment in our strategy. Thus is agreement rendered impossible and conflict inevitable.

The last hours of debate before the final day's plenary sessions dragged as delegates maneuvered to get their proposals on the agenda. In self-defense, I allowed my mind to wander back in time to the early 1960s, when I first met and began working with Geneva Crenshaw as we both represented clients with civil rights cases across the South. She had come to New York right out of law school to join the NAACP Legal Defense Fund's legal staff. Despite her youth, she was soon a highly respected civil rights advocate, well known for her willingness to go South to represent blacks in rural settings where living conditions were poor and personal risk was considerable.

Strikingly tall, well over six feet, Geneva, as I soon learned, was able to display an impressive intelligence honed by hard work. She would have confounded the findings that caused the sociologist E. Franklin Frazier to characterize our middle class as "Black Bourgeoisie."[4] Apparently oblivious of her stunning looks, highlighted by a smooth, ebony complexion, she was proud of her color and her race at a time when middle-class "Negroes" (as we then insisted on being called) were ambivalent about both. Even in that pre–"black is beautiful" period, she insisted on using the term *black* because it was more direct, if less accurate, than *Afro-American*.

Geneva would have applauded Mary Hamilton, a black woman who took her case to the Supreme Court to gain, in 1964, judicial confirmation for her insistence that she be addressed in a state court as "Miss Hamilton" rather than as "Mary."[5] But Geneva did not like to spend time discussing, much less litigating about, what black people are called. What she deemed "image projects" irritated her as a sad waste of limited resources. "Titles follow status," she would say. "Those that precede it are gratuitous when they're not intended insults." These views and others like them tended to defy the accepted civil rights orthodoxy, but Geneva had, in the 1960s, espoused them with a skill and commitment not easily ignored.

I appreciate her prescience now, but must confess that in those days I was more impressed with her courage. Watching her articulate her views at staff meetings, and later working with her in Southern courtrooms, I saw her as the embodiment of the great nineteenth-century abolitionists Harriet Tubman and Sojourner Truth, even resembling photographs I'd seen of those stern black women who both fought and spoke for their cause. "I've seen those pictures," Geneva responded when I once, unchivalrously, remarked on the resemblance. "And were I given to vanity, I would hardly find the resemblance complimentary. But those women had an inner vision that enabled them to defy the limits on their lives imposed by the world around them. I try to be a good lawyer, but my devotion, too, is to an inner vision that makes me feel close to old Harriet and Sojourner—so your thinking I resemble them is not only a compliment, it is an honor."

Inner vision or not, Geneva was an excellent advocate—as more than one Southern white attorney who refused to shake her hand learned at some expense to his case and his psyche. But much as she loved litigation, Geneva decided finally that she should teach. The fateful trip to Mississippi was to have been her last before leaving the NAACP to join the Howard Law School faculty. It was fortunate that Geneva wanted to teach at Howard because in the mid-1960s, despite her academic record and litigation success that more than justified predictions of a brilliant teaching career, her opportunities were, for the most part, limited to black law schools.[6]

Of course, in those days, there were few women law teachers, black or white. Geneva's colleagues, though, confidently predicted that she would follow in the footsteps of the Howard faculty members, including William Hastie and Charles Houston, and of Howard alumni, including Thurgood Marshall and Robert L. Carter, all of whom were her mentors.[7] Geneva's intelligence and accomplishments made her a definitive example of W. E. B. DuBois's expectations for those blacks he designated the "Talented Tenth," the exceptional individuals who would save the race. It was the great black thinker's hope in 1903 that, by "developing the Best of this race . . . they may guide the Mass away from the contamination and death of the Worst, in their own and other races."[8] And yet the working-class people Geneva represented, and among whom she lived, thought of her as she did herself: an ordinary person, or "drylongso."[9]

Her concern about the common folks motivated that last trip to the South. Approximately one thousand volunteers, mainly college students, had been recruited by the Council of Federated Organizations (COFO), representing several civil rights organizations, and organized into the Mississippi Summer Project to register black voters.[10] Geneva was concerned that both the volunteers and those they hoped to help would face harassment by state officials and private vigilantes. She was right.

Neither her legal talents nor her promise as a black leader and legal scholar saved Geneva the evening she was driving to a voter-registration meeting in the Delta during what came to be known as the violent summer of 1964. She never made it. Her car, forced off the rural country road, turned over and rolled down an embankment. A student riding with her reported that the pick-up truck that hit them while traveling at high speed paused only long enough to see that no one emerged from the demolished car. Then it sped away, the sound of gleeful laughter echoing, with the engine's roar, across the hot summer night.

Given Geneva's reputation, the attempt to kill her would have provoked a national furor in some other year; but during the summer of 1964, there were one thousand arrests, thirty-five shooting incidents, thirty buildings bombed, thirty-five churches burned, eighty people beaten, and at least six murders during the period of the summer campaign. The most infamous of these were the deaths in Philadelphia, Mississippi, of civil rights workers Michael H. Schwerner and Andrew Goodman, whites, and James E. Chaney, a black, all three murdered by local whites. Lemuel A. Penn, a black Washington, D.C., school administrator, was shot and killed as he drove through Georgia, returning from Army Reserve duty at Fort Benning.[11]

Geneva's attackers were never found, and state officials denied any racial motivation to the collision—a ludicrous suggestion accepted by those who wanted to believe the pick-up truck owner's claim that the vehicle had been stolen earlier that day by "two negras." The media, confused by the conflicting stories, lost interest and turned their attention to the numerous attacks on civil rights workers where the racial hostility behind the attacks was not in doubt. Geneva's physical injuries eventually healed; but for more than twenty years, her mind wandered in realms where medical science could not follow. Those who knew her were shocked by the attack, outraged that no arrests were made, and saddened by the discouraging reports on her continuing poor health. After Geneva failed to recover, we who were her friends spoke of her in those terms of unqualified respect and affection usually reserved for the dead; and gradually in my preoccupation with my own life, I permitted myself to forget her.

"Brother! Brother! Wake up! They have adjourned for the day, and the hosts want the delegates to pick up additional reading material for tomorrow's sessions." Thanking the delegate who had roused me from my reverie, I noticed with some embarrassment that the Great Hall was almost empty. Quickly I headed for the main doors where the reading packets were being distributed. Deciding to pass up the post-meeting reception, I obtained my materials and retired to my room. It had been a long day filled with frustration and disappointment.

Then came the shock. I opened my reading packet and found it contained only a single book, handsomely bound and with a title that brought me out of my chair: "The Civil Rights Chronicles as related by Geneva Crenshaw and reviewed with a friend." I scanned the pages, my hands shaking so much that it was difficult to read. But there was no mistaking the contents, which I had experienced firsthand. I sat down, took several deep breaths, wiped the cold perspiration from my face, and tried to remember

21

how the discussions with Geneva, now recorded word for word in this book, had been arranged.

I recalled the evening a month earlier when I was both surprised and more than a little guilty to find a message from her on my computer which, through a national electronic mail service, allows me a speedy means of communication with friends and associates—a revolution in modern technology that had occurred in the decades since I had last seen Geneva. After so many years, her words, in her elegantly formal style, were appearing on my computer screen:

Dearest friend, I have folded my wings for a little while and returned to this world. I have learned all that I can from reading about our people's condition. It appears that my worst fears have been realized: We have made progress in everything yet nothing has changed. Our people's faith has altered the law of the land, yet their lives are deprived and stunted.

Like the Crusaders of old, we sought the Holy Grail of "equal opportunity" and, having gained it in court decisions and civil rights statutes, find it transformed from the long-sought guarantee of racial equality into one more device that the society can use to perpetuate the racial status quo. Our cause is righteous, but have we prevailed?

This, though, is no time to bewail our fate. I have always respected your views and now need your help. For the moment, you must not share word of my return. I have no time for reunions, for I have come back with a purpose. My mind is filled with allegorical visions that, taking me out of our topsyturvy world and into a strange and a more rational existence, have revealed to me new truths about the dilemma of blacks in this country. To be made real, to be potent, these visions—or Chronicles, as I call them—must be interpreted. I have chosen you to help me in this vital task.

The message went on to give me directions for finding her in a cottage in Virginia, not far apparently from Thomas Jefferson's Monticello, and ended: "Please come! Please come soon!"

I could not refuse. It took but a short while to clear my schedule and pack, and then, that evening, I said goodbye to my wife in the airport and flew eastward across the country. I took with me only a briefcase filled with writings that might further our discussions, an overnight case (I could spare no more than two days), and my trusty tape recorder, which I'm never without in these electronic days.

I landed at dawn and, in a rented car, headed for Geneva's cottage which, even with her precise directions, I had some difficulty finding on those winding country roads. But finally I was driving up to an old-fashioned cottage, somewhat in need of paint. The door was open, and Geneva was standing there, waiting, and then coming down the steps. It was like old times, as though the intervening years of my life as a law professor and her illness had never been, and we were about to sit down to thrash out one of the many civil rights cases we'd worked on in the 1960s.

We hugged each other, and then Geneva took me inside, into a large sitting room which, in striking contrast to the cottage's exterior, she had transformed into a library complete with books packing the shelves lining the walls, books stacked in every free space on the floor, and a legal databank terminal—but no telephone. It seemed an ideal place for serious research and writing.

Geneva sat me down in a big armchair and handed me a cup of a green herbal tea that seemed as strong (and tasted as bitter) as black coffee. As she poured her own cup, I took a long look at her. Her long ordeal had not left her unchanged. She was much thinner than I remembered; her once-black hair was gray though still in the Afro style she had always affected, even before it became popular during the black pride period of the late 1960s and 1970s. Her hair served to halo her face with its high cheekbones and eyes that seemed strangely fixed on me.

"Have I changed so much?" she asked abruptly, letting me know I was staring.

"I've likely changed more than you—and for the worse."

Geneva laughed. Her voice had not changed. It still had all the

23

warmth and richness of tone characteristic of black women's voices and reminded me of the long-running debate among classical music lovers over whether that distinctive voice quality can be discerned even in black women opera singers.[12]

For an hour, Geneva and I chatted about mundane matters, and gossiped about working associates from the old days who now occupied positions of prestige impossible to even contemplate back in the early 1960s. After reciting an impressive list of judges, law teachers, law partners in prestigious firms, and high government officials, I noted the discrepancy between the grim situation of working-class blacks and our own success, which we have achieved by representing them.

Then I reminded Geneva of my fantasy shared with her long ago in which I imagined myself going back in time to counsel the Founding Fathers about two centuries of development in American constitutional law. "How," I had asked her, "should I begin so major a teaching task?"

Geneva's response had been as quick as her keen wit. "First," she had said gently, "you would have to explain to the Framers how you, a black, had gotten free of your chains and gained the audacity to teach white men anything." Rather than join me in laughing about her quip, she immediately became serious and sad. Though surprised, I wanted to pursue my idea.

"Suppose," I suggested, "we could recruit a battalion of the best black lawyers from the era of *Brown* v. *Board of Education* (1954)[13]—Thurgood Marshall, Robert L. Carter, Constance Baker Motley, Robert Ming, William Hastie, Spottswood Robinson, and Charles Houston—and send them as a delegation back through time to reason with the Framers before they decided to incorporate slavery into the Constitution. Surely that impressive body would influence decisions made by those who knew blacks only as slaves?"

"What you suggest," said Geneva when I paused, "is precisely what I myself have done."

At my look of incredulity, she smiled. "Yes, friend, I have, in one of the Chronicles I spoke of in my message to you, been enabled by extraordinary forces to address the Framers of the Con-

24

stitution just as they were about to sign it. Of course, you don't believe me—but now that you're here, I hope you will let my Chronicles speak for themselves, and then you and I can discuss them together."

I suppose I must have been looking dazed, for she came over to me and, touching my arm, said, "Are you ready?"

"Yes, yes," I answered, and had just presence of mind to set my tape recorder going. Geneva watched me with a quizzical smile; then, leaning back in her old-fashioned rocking chair, she closed her eyes and began to speak.

Chapter 1

The Real Status of Blacks Today

The Chronicle of the Constitutional Contradiction

AT THE END of a journey back millions of light-years, I found myself standing quietly at the podium at the Constitutional Convention of 1787. It was late afternoon, and hot in that late summer way that makes it pleasant to stroll down a shaded country lane, but mighty oppressive in a large, crowded meeting room, particularly one where the doors are closed and locked to ensure secrecy.

The three dozen or so convention delegates looked tired. They had doubtless been meeting all day and now, clustered in small groups, were caucusing with their state delegations. So intense were their discussions that the few men who looked my way did not seem to see me. They knew this was a closed meeting, and thus could not readily take in the appearance, on what had just been an empty platform, of a tall stranger—a stranger who was not only a woman but also, all too clearly, black.

Though I knew I was protected by extraordinary forces, my hands were wet with nervous perspiration. Then I remembered why I was there. Taking a deep breath, I picked up the gavel and quickly struck the desktop twice, hard.

"Gentlemen," I said, "my name is Geneva Crenshaw, and I appear here to you as a representative of the late twentieth century to test whether the decisions you are making today might be altered if you were to know their future disastrous effect on the nation's people, both white and black."

For perhaps ten seconds, there was a shocked silence. Then the chamber exploded with shouts, exclamations, oaths. I fear the delegates' expressions of stunned surprise did no honor to their distinguished images. A warm welcome would have been too much to expect, but their shock at my sudden presence turned into an angry commotion unrelieved by even a modicum of curiosity.

The delegates to the Constitutional Convention were, in the main, young and vigorous.[1] When I remained standing, unmoved by their strong language and dire threats, several particularly robust delegates charged toward the platform, determined to carry out the shouted orders: "Eject the Negro woman at once!"

Suddenly the hall was filled with the sound of martial music, blasting trumpets, and a deafening roll of snare drums. At the same time—as the delegates were almost upon me—a cylinder composed of thin vertical bars of red, white, and blue light descended swiftly and silently from the high ceiling, nicely encapsulating the podium and me.

The self-appointed ejection party neither slowed nor swerved, a courageous act they soon regretted. As each man reached and tried to pass through the transparent light shield, there was a loud hiss, quite like the sound that electrified bug zappers make on a warm summer evening. While not lethal, the shock each attacker received was sufficiently strong to knock him to the floor, stunned and shaking.

The injured delegates all seemed to recover quickly, except one who had tried to pierce the light shield with his sword. The weapon instantly glowed red hot and burned his hand. At that point, several delegates tried to rush out of the room either to escape or to seek help—but neither doors nor windows would open.

"Gentlemen," I repeated, but no one heard me in the turmoil of shouted orders, cries of outrage, and efforts to sound the alarm to those outside. Scanning the room, I saw a swarthy delegate cock his long pistol, aim carefully, and fire directly at me. But the ball hit the shield, ricocheted back into the room, and shattered an inkwell, splattering my intended assassin with red ink.

At that, one of the delegates, raising his hand, roared, "Silence!" and then turned to me. "Woman! Who are you and by what authority do you interrupt this gathering?"

"Gentlemen," I began, "delegates"—then paused and, with a slight smile, added, "fellow citizens, I—like some of you—am a Virginian, my forefathers having labored on the land holdings of your fellow patriot, the Honorable Thomas Jefferson. I have come to urge that, in your great work here, you not restrict the sweep of Mr. Jefferson's self-evident truths that all men are equal and endowed by the Creator with inalienable rights, including 'Life, Liberty and the pursuit of Happiness.' " It was, I thought, a clever touch to invoke the name of Thomas Jefferson who, then serving as American minister to France, was not a member of the Virginia delegation.[2] But my remark could not overcome the offense of my presence.

"How dare you insert yourself in these deliberations?" a delegate demanded.

"I dare," I said, "because slavery is an evil that Jefferson, himself a slave owner and unconvinced that Africans are equal to whites, nevertheless found involved 'a perpetual exercise of the most boisterous passions, the most unremitting despotism on the one part, and degrading submissions on the other.' Slavery, Jefferson has written, brutalizes slave owner as well as slave and, worst of all, tends to undermine the 'only firm basis' of liberty, the conviction in the minds of the people that liberty is 'the gift of God.'[3]

"Gentlemen, it was also Thomas Jefferson who, considering the evil of slavery, wrote: 'I tremble for my country when I reflect that God is just; that his justice cannot sleep forever.' "[4]

There was a hush in the group. No one wanted to admit it, but the ambivalence on the slavery issue expressed by Jefferson obviously had meaning for at least some of those in the hall. It seemed the right moment to prove both that I was a visitor from the future and that Jefferson's troubled concern for his country had not been misplaced. In quick, broad strokes, I told them of the country's rapid growth, of how slavery had expanded rather than withered of its own accord, and finally of how its continued presence bred first suspicion and then enmity between those in the South who continued to rely on a plantation economy and those Northerners committed to industrial development using white wage workers. The entry into the Union of each new state, I explained, further dramatized the disparity between North and South. Inevitably, the differences led to armed conflict—a civil war that, for all its bloody costs, did not settle those differences, and they remain divisive even as we celebrate our two-hundredth anniversary as one nation.

"The stark truth is that the racial grief that persists today," I ended, "originated in the slavery institutionalized in the document you are drafting. Is this, gentlemen, an achievement for which you wish to be remembered?"

Oblivious to my plea, a delegate tried what he likely considered a sympathetic approach. "Geneva, be reasonable. Go and leave us to our work. We have heard the petitions of Africans and of abolitionists speaking in their behalf. Some here are sympathetic to these pleas for freedom. Others are not. But we have debated this issue at length, and after three months of difficult negotiations, compromises have been reached, decisions made, language drafted and approved. The matter is settled. Neither you nor whatever powers have sent you here can undo what is done."

I was not to be put off so easily. "Sirs," I said, "I have come to tell you that the matter of slavery will not be settled by your compromises. And even when it is ended by armed conflict and domestic turmoil far more devastating than that you hope to avoid here, the potential evil of giving priority to property over human rights will remain. Can you not address the contradiction in your words and deeds?"

"There is no contradiction," replied another delegate. "Gouverneur Morris of Pennsylvania, the Convention's most outspoken opponent of slavery, has admitted that 'life and liberty were generally said to be of more value, than property, . . . [but] an accurate view of the matter would nevertheless prove that property was the main object of Society.' "[5]

"A contradiction," another delegate added, "would occur were we to follow the course you urge. We are not unaware of the moral issues raised by slavery, but we have no response to the delegate from South Carolina, General Charles Cotesworth Pinckney, who has admonished us that 'property in slaves should not be exposed to danger under a Govt. instituted for the protection of property.' "[6]

"Of what value is a government that does not secure its citizens in their persons and their property?" inquired another delegate. "Government, as Mr. Pierce Butler from South Carolina has maintained here, 'was instituted principally for the protection of property and was itself . . . supported by property.' Property, he reminded us, was 'the great object of government; the great cause of war; the great means of carrying it on.'[7] And the whole South Carolina delegation joined him in making clear that 'the security the Southern states want is that their negroes may not be taken from them.' "[8]

"Your deliberations here have been secret," I replied. "And yet history has revealed what you here would hide. The Southern delegates have demanded the slavery compromises as their absolute precondition to forming a new government."

"And why should it not be so?" a delegate in the rear called out. "I do not represent the Southern point of view, and yet their rigidity on the slavery issue is wholly natural, stemming as it does from the commitment of their economy to labor-intensive agriculture. We are not surprised by the determined bargaining of the Georgia and South Carolina delegations, nor distressed that our Southern colleagues, in seeking the protection they have gained, seem untroubled by doubts about the policy and morality of slavery and the slave trade."

"Then," I countered, "you are not troubled by the knowledge that this document will be defended by your Southern colleagues in the South Carolina ratification debates, by admissions that 'Negroes were our wealth, our only resource'?"[9]

"Why, in God's name," the delegate responded, "should we be troubled by the truth, candidly stated? They have said no less in these chambers. General Charles Cotesworth Pinckney has flatly stated that 'South Carolina and Georgia cannot do without slaves.' And his cousin and fellow planter, Charles Pinckney, has added, 'The blacks are the laborers, the peasants of the Southern states.' "[10]

At this, an elderly delegate arose and rapped his cane on his chair for attention. "Woman, we would have you gone from this place. But if a record be made, that record should show that the economic benefits of slavery do not accrue only to the South.

Plantation states provide a market for Northern factories, and the New England shipping industry and merchants participate in the slave trade. Northern states, moreover, utilize slaves in the fields, as domestics, and even as soldiers to defend against Indian raids."[11]

I shook my head. "Here you are then! Representatives from large and small states, slave states and those that have abolished slavery, all of you are protecting your property interests at the cost of your principles."

There was no response. The transparent shield protected my person, served as a language translator smoothing the differences in English usage, and provided a tranquilizing effect as it shimmered softly in the hot and humid room. Evidently, even this powerful mechanism could not bring the delegates to reassess their views on the slavery issue.

I asked, "Are you not concerned with the basic contradiction in your position: that you, who have gathered here in Philadelphia from each state in the confederacy, in fact represent and constitute major property holders? Do you not mind that your slogans of liberty and individual rights are basically guarantees that neither a strong government nor the masses will be able to interfere with your property rights and those of your class? This contradiction between what you espouse and what you here protect will be held against you by future citizens of this nation."[12]

"Unless we continue on our present course," a delegate called out, "there will be no nation whose origins can be criticized. These sessions were called because the country is teetering between anarchy and bankruptcy. The nation cannot meet its debts. And only a year ago, thousands of poor farmers in Massachusetts and elsewhere took up arms against the government."

"Indeed," I said, "I am aware of Shay's Rebellion, led by Daniel Shay, a former officer who served with distinction in the war against England. According to historians of my time, the inability of Congress to respond to Massachusetts's appeal for help provided 'the final argument to sway many Americans in favor of a stronger federal government.'[13] I understand the nature of the crisis that brings you here, but the compromises you make on the slavery issue are——"

"Young woman!" interrupted one of the older delegates. "Young woman, you say you understand. But I tell you that it is 'nearly impossible for anybody who has not been on the spot to conceive (from any description) what the delicacy and danger of our situation . . . [has] been. I am President of this Convention, drafted to the task against my wishes. I am here and I am ready to embrace any tolerable compromise that . . . [is] competent to save us from impending ruin.' "[14]

While so far I had recognized none of the delegates, the identity of this man—seated off by himself, and one of the few who had remained quiet through the bedlam that broke out after my arrival—was unmistakable.

"Thank you, General Washington," I responded. "I know that you, though a slave owner, are opposed to slavery. And yet you have said little during these meetings—to prevent, one may assume, your great prestige from unduly influencing debate. Future historians will say of your silence that you recognize that for you to throw the weight of your opinion against slavery might so hearten the opponents of the system, while discouraging its proponents, as to destroy all hope of compromise. This would prevent the formation of the Union, and the Union, for you, is essential."[15]

"I will not respond to these presumptions," said General Washington, "but I will tell you now what I will say to others at a later time. There are in the new form some things, I will readily acknowledge, that never did, and I am persuaded never will, obtain my cordial approbation; but I did then conceive, and do now most firmly believe, that in the aggregate it is the best constitution, that can be obtained at this epoch, and that this, or a dissolution, awaits our choice, and is the only alternative."[16]

"Do you recognize," I asked, "that in order to gain unity among yourselves, your slavery compromises sacrifice freedom for the Africans who live amongst you and work for you? Such sacrifices of the rights of one group of human beings will, unless arrested here, become a difficult-to-break pattern in the nation's politics."[17]

"Did you not listen to the general?" This man, I decided, must be James Madison. As the delegates calmed down, he had returned to a prominent seat in the front of the room directly in front of the podium. It was from this vantage point that he took notes of the proceedings which, when finally released in 1840, became the best record of the Convention.[18]

"I expect," Madison went on, "that many will question why I have agreed to the Constitution. And, like General Washington, I will answer: 'because I thought it safe to the liberties of the people, and the best that could be obtained from the jarring interests of States, and the miscellaneous opinions of Politicians; and because experience has proved that the real danger to America & to liberty lies in the defect of *energy & stability* in the present establishments of the United States.' "[19]

"Do not think," added a delegate from Massachusetts, "that this Convention has come easily to its conclusions on the matter that concerns you. Gouverneur Morris from Pennsylvania has said to us in the strongest terms: 'Domestic slavery is the most prominent feature in the aristocratic countenance of the proposed Constitution.'[20] He warned again and again that 'the people of Pennsylvania will never agree to a representation of Negroes.'[21]

"Many of us shared Mr. Morris's concern about basing apportionment on slaves as insisted by the Southern delegates. I recall with great sympathy his questions:

> Upon what principle is it that the slaves shall be computed in the representation? Are they men? Then make them citizens & let them vote? Are they property? Why then is no other property included? . . .
>
> The admission of slaves into the Representation when fairly explained comes to this: that the inhabitant of Georgia and S.C. who goes to the Coast of Africa, and in defiance of the most sacred laws of humanity tears away his fellow creatures from their dearest connections & damns them to the most cruel bondages, shall have more votes in a Govt. instituted for protection of the rights of mankind, then the Citizen of Pa or N. Jersey who views with a laudable horror, so nefarious a practice.[22]

"I tell you, woman, this Convention was not unmoved at these words of Mr. Morris's only a few weeks ago."

"Even so," I said, "the Convention has acquiesced when representatives of the Southern states adamantly insisted that the proposed new government not interfere with their property in slaves. And is it not so that, beyond a few speeches, the representatives of the Northern states have been, at best, ambivalent on the issue?"

"And why not?" interjected another delegate. "Slavery has provided the wealth that made independence possible. The profits from slavery funded the Revolution. It cannot be denied. At the time of the Revolution, the goods for which the United States demanded freedom were produced in very large measure by slave labor. Desperately needing assistance from other countries, we purchased this aid from France with tobacco produced mainly by slave labor.[23] The nation's economic well-being depended on the institution, and its preservation is essential if the Constitution we are drafting is to be more than a useless document. At least, that is how we view the crisis we face."

To pierce the delegates' adamant front, I called on the oratorical talents that have, in the twentieth century, won me both praise and courtroom battles: "The real crisis you face should not be resolved by your recognition of slavery, an evil whose immorality will pollute the nation as it now stains your document. Despite your resort to euphemisms like *persons* to keep out of the Constitution such words as *slave* and *slavery*, you cannot evade the consequences of the ten different provisions you have placed in the Constitution for the purpose of protecting property in slaves.*

* The historian William Wiecek has listed the following direct and indirect accommodations to slavery contained in the Constitution:

1. Article I, Section 2: representatives in the House were apportioned among the states on the basis of population, computed by counting all free persons and three-fifths of the slaves (the "federal number," or "three-fifths," clause);
2. Article I, Section 2, and Article I, Section 9: two clauses requiring, redundantly, that direct taxes (including capitations) be apportioned among the states on the foregoing basis, the purpose being to prevent Congress from laying a head tax on slaves to encourage their emancipation;
3. Article I, Section 9: Congress was prohibited from abolishing the international slave trade to the United States before 1808;
4. Article IV, Section 2: the states were prohibited from emancipating fugitive slaves, who were to be returned on demand of the master;
5. Article I, Section 8: Congress empowered to provide for calling up the states' militias to suppress insurrections, including slave uprisings;
6. Article IV, Section 4: the federal government was obliged to protect the states against domestic violence, including slave insurrections;
7. Article V: the provisions of Article I, Section 9, clauses 1 and 4 (pertaining to the slave trade and direct taxes) were made unamendable;

"Woman!" a delegate shouted from the rear of the room. "Explain to us how you, a black, have gotten free of your chains and gained the audacity to come here and teach white men anything."

I smiled, recognizing the eternal question. "Audacity," I replied, "is an antidote to your arrogance. Be assured: my knowledge, despite my race, is far greater than yours."

"But if my race and audacity offend you, then listen to your contemporaries who have opposed slavery in most moving terms. With all due respect, there are few in this company whose insight exceeds that of Abigail Adams who wrote her husband, John, during the Revolutionary War: 'I wish most sincerely there was not a slave in the province; it always appeared a most iniquitous scheme to me to fight ourselves for what we are daily robbing and plundering from those who have as good a right to freedom as we have.'[25] Mrs. Adams's wish is, as you know, shared by many influential Americans who denounce slavery as a corrupting and morally unjustifiable practice.[26]

"Gentlemen," I continued, "how can you disagree with the view of the Maryland delegate Luther Martin that the slave trade and 'three-fifths' compromises 'ought to be considered as a solemn mockery of, and insult to that God whose protection we had then implored, and . . . who views with equal eye the poor African slave and his American master'? I can tell you that Mr. Martin will not only abandon these deliberations and refuse to sign the Constitution but also oppose its ratification in Maryland. And further, he will, in his opposition, expose the deal of the committee on which he served, under which New England states agreed to give the slave trade a twenty-year immunity from federal restrictions in exchange for Southern votes to eliminate restrictions on navigation acts. What is more, he will write that, to the rest of the world, it must appear 'absurd and disgraceful to the last degree, that we should *except* from the exercise of that power [to regulate commerce], the *only branch of commerce* which is *unjustifiable in its nature*, and *contrary* to the rights of *mankind*.' "[27]

"Again, woman," a Northern delegate assured me, "we have

---

8. Article I, Section 9, and Article I, Section 10: these two clauses prohibited the federal government and the states from taxing exports, one purpose being to prevent them from taxing slavery indirectly by taxing the exported product of slave labor.[24]

heard and considered all those who oppose slavery. Despite the remonstrations of the abolitionists—of whom few, I must add, believe Negroes to be the equal of white men, and even fewer would want the blacks to remain in this land were slavery abandoned—we have acted as we believe the situation demands."

"I cannot believe," I said, "that even a sincere belief in the superiority of the white race should suffice to condone so blatant a contradiction of your hallowed ideals."

"It should be apparent by now," said the delegate who had shot at me, but had now recovered his composure and shed his ink-stained coat, "that we do not care what you think. Furthermore, if your people actually had the sensitivities of real human beings, you would realize that you are not wanted here and would have the decency to leave."

"I will not leave!" I said steadily, and waited while the delegates conferred.

Finally, a delegate responded to my challenge. "You have, by now, heard enough to realize that we have not lightly reached the compromises on slavery you so deplore. Perhaps we, with the responsibility of forming a radically new government in perilous times, see more clearly than is possible for you in hindsight that the unavoidable cost of our labors will be the need to accept and live with what you call a contradiction."

The delegate had gotten to his feet, and was walking slowly toward me as he spoke. "This contradiction is not lost on us. Surely we know, even though we are at pains not to mention it, that we have sacrificed the rights of some in the belief that this involuntary forfeiture is necessary to secure the rights for others in a society espousing, as its basic principle, the liberty of all."

He was standing directly in front of the shield now, ignoring its gentle hum, disregarding its known danger. "It grieves me," he continued, "that your presence here confirms my worst fears about the harm done to your people because the Constitution, while claiming to speak in an unequivocal voice, in fact promises freedom to whites and condemns blacks to slavery. But what alternative do we have? Unless we here frame a constitution that can first gain our signatures and then win ratification by the states, we shall soon have no nation. For better or worse, slavery has been the backbone of our economy, the source of much of our wealth. It was condoned in the colonies and recognized in the Articles of Confederation. The majority of the delegates to this convention own slaves and must have that right protected if they and their states are to be included in the new government."

He paused and then asked, more out of frustration than defiance, "What better compromise on this issue can you offer than that which has been fashioned over so many hours of heated debate?"

The room was silent. The delegate, his statement made, his question presented, turned and walked slowly back to his seat. A few from his state touched his hand as he passed. Then all eyes turned to me.

I thanked the delegate for his question and then said, "The processes by which Northern states are even now abolishing slavery are known to you all.[28] What is lacking here is not legislative skill but the courage to recognize the evil of holding blacks in slavery—an evil that would be quickly and universally condemned were the subjects of bondage members of the Caucasian race. You fear that unless the slavery of blacks is recognized and given protection, the nation will not survive. And my message is that the compromises you are making here mean that the nation's survival will always be in doubt. For now in my own day, after two hundred years and despite bloody wars and the earnest efforts of committed people, the racial contradiction you sanction in this document remains and threatens to tear this country apart."

"Mr. Chairman," said a delegate near the podium whose accent indicated that he was from the deep South, "this discussion grows tiresome and I resent to my very soul the presence in our midst of this offspring of slaves. If she accurately predicts the future fate of her race in this country, then our protection of slave property, which we deem essential for our survival, is easier to justify than in some later time when, as she implies, negroes remain subjugated even without the threats we face."

"Hear! Hear!" shouted a few delegates. "Bravo, Colonel!"

"It's all hypocrisy!" the Colonel shouted, his arms flailing the air, "sheer hypocrisy! Our Northern colleagues bemoan slavery while profiting from it as much as we in the South, meanwhile avoiding its costs and dangers. And our friends from Virginia, where slavery began, urge the end of importation—not out of humanitarian motivations, as their speeches suggest, but because they have sufficient slaves, and expect the value of their property will increase if further imports are barred.

"Mr. George Mason, of the Virginia delegation, in his speech opposing the continued importation of slaves expressed fear that, if not barred, the people of Western lands, already crying for slaves, could get them through South Carolina and Georgia. He moans that: 'Slavery discourages arts & manufactures. The poor despise labor when performed by slaves. They prevent the immigration of Whites, who really enrich & strengthen a Country. They produce the most pernicious effect on manners.' Furthermore, according to Mr. Mason, 'every master of slaves is born a petty tyrant. They bring the judgment of heaven on a Country ... [and] by an inevitable chain of causes & effects providence punishes national sins, by national calamities.'[29]

"This, Mr. Chairman, is nothing but hypocrisy or, worse, ignorance of history. We speak easily today of liberty, but the rise of liberty and equality in this country has been accompanied by the rise of slavery.[30] The negress who has seized our podium by diabolical force charges that we hold blacks slaves because we view them as inferior. Inferior in every way they surely are, but they were not slaves when Virginia was a new colony 150 years ago. Or, at least, their status was hardly worse than the luckless white indentured servants brought here from debtors' prisons and the poverty-ridden streets of England. Neither slave nor servant lived very long in that harsh, fever-ridden clime."

The Colonel, so close to the podium, steadfastly refused to speak to me or even to acknowledge my presence.

"In the beginning," he went on, "life was harsh, but the coming of tobacco to Virginia in 1617 turned a struggling colony into a place where great wealth could be made relatively quickly. To cultivate the labor-intense crop, large numbers of mainly white, male servants, indentured to their masters for a period of years, were imported. Blacks, too, were brought to the colony, both as slaves and as servants. They generally worked, ate, and slept with the white servants.

"As the years passed, more and more servants lived to gain their freedom, despite the practice of extending terms for any offense, large or small. They soon became a growing, poverty-stricken class, some of whom resigned themselves to working for wages; others preferred a meager living on dangerous frontier land or a hand-to-mouth existence, roaming from one county to another, renting a bit of land here, squatting on some there, dodging the tax collector, drinking, quarreling, stealing hogs, and enticing servants to run away with them."

"It is not extraordinary to suggest that the planters and those who governed Virginia were caught in a dilemma—a dilemma more like the contradiction we are accused of building into the Constitution than may at first meet the eye. They needed workers to maintain production in their fields, but young men were soon rebellious, without either land of their own or women, who were not seen as fit to work the fields. Moreover, the young workers were armed and had to be armed to repel attacks from Indians by land and from privateers and petty-thieving pirates by sea.

"The worst fears of Virginia's leaders were realized when, in 1676, a group of these former servants returned from a fruitless expedition against the Indians to attack their rulers in what was called Bacon's Rebellion. Governor William Berkeley bemoaned his lot in terms that defined the problem: 'How miserable that man is that Governes a People wher six parts of seaven at least are Poore Endebted Discontented and Armed.'[31]

"The solution came naturally and without decision. The planters purchased more slaves and imported fewer English servants. Slaves were more expensive initially, but their terms did not end, and their owners gained the benefits of the slaves' offspring. Africans, easily identified by color, could not hope to run away without being caught. The fear of pain and death could be and was substituted for the extension of terms as an incentive to force the slaves to work. They were not armed and could be held in chains.

"The fear of slave revolts increased as reliance on slavery grew and racial antipathy became more apparent. But this danger, while real, was less than that from restive and armed freedmen. Slaves did not have rising expectations, and no one told them they had rights. They had lost their freedom. Moreover, a woman

39

could be made to work and have children every two years, thereby adding to the income of her master. Thus, many more women than indentured servants were imported.

"A free society divided between large landholders and small was much less riven by antagonisms than one divided between landholders and landless, masterless men. With the freedmen's expectations, sobriety, and status restored, he was no longer a man to be feared. That fact, together with the presence of a growing mass of alien slaves, tended to draw the white settlers closer together and to reduce the importance of the class difference between yeoman farmer and large plantation owner.

"Racial fears tended to lessen the economic and political differences between rich and poor whites. And as royal officials and tax collectors became more oppressive, both groups joined forces in protesting the import taxes on tobacco which provided income for the high and the low. The rich began to look to their less wealthy neighbors for political support against the English government and in local elections.

"Wealthy whites, of course, retained all their former prerogatives, but the creation of a black subclass enabled poor whites to identify with and support the policies of the upper class. With the safe economic advantage provided by their slaves, large landowners were willing to grant poor whites a larger role in the political process."

"So, Colonel," I interrupted, "you are saying that slavery for blacks not only provided wealth for rich whites but, paradoxically, led also to greater freedom for poor whites. One of our twentieth-century historians, Edmund Morgan, has explained this paradox of slave owners espousing freedom and liberty:

Aristocrats could more safely preach equality in a slave society than in a free one. Slaves did not become leveling mobs, because their owners would see to it that they had no chance to. The apostrophes to equality were not addressed to them. And because Virginia's labor force was composed mainly of slaves, who had been isolated by race and removed from the political equation, the remaining free laborers and tenant farmers were too few in number to constitute a serious threat

to the superiority of the men who assured them of their
equality.[32]

"In effect," I concluded, "what I call a contradiction here was
deemed a solution then. Slavery enabled the rich to keep their
lands, arrested discontent and repression of other Englishmen,
strengthened their rights and nourished their attachment to liberty. But the solution, as Professor Morgan said, 'put an end to
the process of turning Africans into Englishmen. The rights of Englishmen were preserved by destroying the rights of Africans.' "[33]

"Do you charge that our belief in individual liberty is feigned?"
demanded a Virginian, outraged.

"It was Professor Morgan's point," I replied, "not that 'a belief
in republican equality had to rest on slavery, but only that in Virginia (and probably in other southern colonies) it did. The most
ardent American republicans were Virginians, and their ardor was
not unrelated to their power over the men and women they held
in bondage.' "[34]

And now, for the first time, the Colonel looked at me, amazed.
"My thoughts on this slavery matter have confounded my mind
for many years, and yet you summarize them in a few paragraphs.
I must, after all, thank you." He walked back to his seat in a daze,
neither commended nor condemned by his colleagues. Most, indeed, were deep in thought—but for a few delegates I noticed
trying desperately to signal to passersby in the street. But I could
not attend to them: my time, I knew, must be growing short.

"The Colonel," I began again, "has performed a valuable service. He has delineated the advantages of slavery as an institution
in this country. And your lengthy debates here are but prelude to
the struggles that will follow your incorporation of this moral evil
into the nation's basic law."

"Woman! We implore you to allow us to continue our work.
While we may be inconsistent about the Negro problem, we are
convinced that this is the only way open to us. You asked that we
let your people go. We cannot do that and still preserve the potential of this nation for good—a potential that requires us to recognize here and now what later generations may condemn as evil.

And as we talk I wonder—are the problems of race in your time equally paradoxical?''

I longed to continue the debate, but never got the chance. Apparently someone outside had finally understood the delegates' signals for help, and had summoned the local militia. Hearing some commotion beyond the window, I turned to see a small cannon being rolled up, pointing straight at me. Then, in quick succession, the cannoneer lighted the fuse; the delegates dived under their desks; the cannon fired; and, with an ear-splitting roar, the cannonball broke against the light shield and splintered, leaving me and the shield intact.

I knew then my mission was over, and I returned to the twentieth century.

G ENEVA had related the Chronicle of the Constitutional Contradiction as though she were living it again—and, indeed, I felt, as she talked, as though I, too, were in that hot and humid hall arguing along with her. Now she sat back in her chair and looked toward me in anticipation. She was waiting for me to say something, but what? Clearly she didn't consider her Chronicles mere flights of high fantasy. She would never have asked me to cross the country simply to listen to her recount a series of dreams. She had always been pragmatic—a realist in an idealist world, she had said back in the early 1960s while trying to explain why she could not accept the idea that the evil of racial discrimination would be swept away in a sea of legal precedents generated by the Supreme Court's decision in the 1954 school-desegregation case of *Brown v. Board of Education*.[35]

And, just as during the 1960s when we traveled across the South as co-counsel in dozens of civil rights cases, I resisted the unblinking pragmatism that was a part of Geneva's strength and the source of our constant arguments. But she was obviously still waiting for me to express an opinion about the Chronicle.

"The story was very real for me," I told her honestly enough. "Knowing the difficulty I have trying to get bicentennial committees on which I serve even to acknowledge how the Constitution handled the slavery issue, I can understand your frustration with the Framers themselves, but——"

"But, had you been there, you might have succeeded where I failed?"

"I'm not sure I could have done better, Geneva. Your presence shocked them, and any black person seeking acceptance as a peer in that group would have been a shock, but a black woman——" I struggled without success for some suitable analogy. "I kept waiting for you to dazzle them with a devastating analysis of the increasing tension between slave and nonslave states, its threat to the Union, the Civil War, and the amendments that, in granting blacks full citizenship rights, altered the dimensions but not the essence of the racial contradiction."

"I wanted to, but I sensed that they did not want to know a future that lay outside their imagination. Their rhetoric spoke to the ages, but their attention was focused on events close at hand. I guess contemporary policy making is not much different."

"Perhaps," I agreed, and then ventured unwisely, "but if you had provided more information about the future, you might have better demonstrated your superior knowledge and your entitlement to be heard."

"*When* did you last win an argument with a white man by proving you were smarter than he was?" And certain she knew the answer to that question, she continued, "I hope you have not missed the real point of the Chronicle. It was not a debate. The Chronicle's message is that no one could have prevented the Framers from drafting a constitution including provisions protecting property in slaves. If they believed, as they had every reason to do, that the country's survival required the economic advantage provided by the slave system, than it was essential that slavery be recognized, rationalized, and protected in the country's basic law. It is as simple as that."

"And not so simple, to judge by the Colonel's revelations," I suggested. "As a result of your aggressive advocacy, you forced him and the rest of the Convention to think through motivations for the slavery compromises that went beyond the Southern delegates' refusal to compromise on this issue."

"The Colonel's reaction surprised me," Geneva admitted, "but his insight into the political as well as the economic importance of slavery simply added more compelling reasons for recognizing and providing protection for slavery in the Constitution."

"The implications for current civil rights work are a bit too close for comfort."

"Exactly right." Geneva leaned forward in her chair to give emphasis to her words. "Even in that extraordinary setting, what struck me as I fought for their attention was how familiar it all was. You know, friend, we civil rights lawyers spend our lives confronting whites in power with the obvious racial bias in their laws or policies, and while, as you know, the litany of their possible exculpatory responses is as long as life, they all boil down to: 'That's the way the world is. We did not make the rules, we simply play by them, and you really have no alternative but to do the same. Please don't take it personally.' The Colonel's speech revealed components of those rules far more complex than ignorant prejudice."

I smiled at her vehemence. "No one will be surprised to learn that you've not become a racial romantic during your long absence."

"Maybe not, but I am surprised that after all these years you continue to believe in this nation's Fourth of July fantasy which most people pack away on July fifth with the unused fireworks."

"We've all got to have faith."

"Faith is not foolishness, my friend," Geneva countered, serious now. "And, as we are reminded in Scripture, 'Faith, if it hath not works, is dead, being alone.' "[36]

"We in civil rights have worked hard," I said. "Why are you so ready to criticize those who try to end the evil of racism rather than those who perpetrate it?"

"Because," she said flatly, ignoring my irritation, "you seem so complacent even though you have lived to see your faith betrayed, your hard work undone. Through it all, you pretend that all is well or that 'real freedom' is almost here. The reports and statistics I have been reading about the current state of most black Americans make that character of belief seem closer to cowardice than to courage."

Before I could respond to the charge, Geneva continued on a less challenging tack. "Of course, I understand that, with the removal of formal segregation barriers, it is a rare area of endeavor where at least a few blacks have not made notable achievements—a progress in which civil rights workers can take pride. But all but the most optimistic among you must concede that the once swiftly moving march toward racial equality through law reform has slowed to a walk, leaving millions of black Americans no better off that they were before the civil rights movement."

Geneva handed me a sheaf of news clippings and reports along with a summary of each which she had copied out in long hand. "Though you know this material, I am sure," she said, frowning, "you can imagine how, after the many years I had been unaware of what was happening, it hit me to learn—as these data indicate—how little had in fact happened."

The reports were all too familiar. One study showed that "blacks in every income strata, from the poorest to the most affluent, lost ground and had less disposable income in 1984 than in 1980, after adjusting for inflation." In sharp contrast, the top 60 percent of the white population experienced income gains; and, worst of all, the study found "a consistent pattern of widening income inequality between blacks and whites since 1980."[37]

The National Urban League in its annual report, *The State of Black America*, charted the decline in the economic fortunes of many black people. In his overview written for the 1985 report, the Urban League president John E. Jacob found that, in virtually every area of life that counts, black people made strong progress in the 1960s, peaked in the 1970s, and have been sliding back ever since. In 1975, he reported, black unemployment was 14.1 percent, about double that of white unemployment (7.6 percent). At the end of 1984, black unemployment was 16 percent; white, 6.5 percent. Constituting some 10 percent of the labor force, blacks account for 20 percent of the jobless. Then in his 1986 overview, Jacob noted that "the median black family had about

56 cents to spend for every one dollar white families had to spend, which was two cents less than they had in 1980, and almost six cents less than they had in 1970."[38]

The long-term impact of joblessness and underemployment on the economic well-being of black households was traced with depressing figures in a Bureau of the Census report. Based on a sampling of 20,000 families, the study revealed that white families, whose median income is almost twice that of black families, have accumulated assets almost twelve times as high. Figures varied by age, income, and marital status; but while the median net worth of all families was $32,667, the overall black median was $3,397, compared with assets for the median white family of $39,135.[39]

"I would think," Geneva remarked, "that few civil rights proponents can feel much satisfaction about the progress of some blacks when the statistics on the woeful state of so many loom large even as they, month by month, grow worse."[40]

"You're right. We all acknowledge the devastating impact of these statistics on the black family. Focusing on female-headed households, a recent summary by a group of black academics pointed to statistics showing that 48 percent of black families with related children under eighteen are headed by women, and that half of all black children under eighteen live in female-headed households. The 1979 median income for black female-headed households was only $6,610 compared with close to $20,000 for all families.[41]

"We must, of course, keep in mind," I cautioned, "that, despite the disparate statistics on virtually every measure of black/white comparison, not all blacks are adrift on the sea of poverty. In the deluge of statistics concerning the plight of the black family, we must not lose sight of the fact that over half of them (53 percent) are intact, married-couple families. Such families represent the most economically viable family unit, boasting a median income in 1983 of $26,686 when both husband and wife were in the labor force. Unfortunately, the married-couple family as a percentage of all black families has declined over the last two decades from 68 percent in 1960 to 53 percent in 1983."[42]

"Isn't the major issue here," Geneva asked, "the disappearance of black men, whose absence has led to the tremendous growth in black-female-headed families and the accompanying rise in poverty among black families?"

"It would seem obvious," I replied, continuing to skim through the reports. "One paper here suggests the 'economic status of black, adult men is the other, largely unnoticed, side of the troubling increase in single-parent black families.'[43] The report focuses on your word *disappearance*, Geneva. Unemployment is only one cause of black male absence. As of 1982, there were 8.8 million black men from the ages of sixteen to sixty-four. Only 54 percent of them were working, compared with 78 percent of white males. The balance of these black men were unemployed (13.1 percent), not in the labor force (20 percent), in prison (2.1 percent), and unaccounted for (10.5 percent). These percentages are not only much higher than those for white males but are higher for black males than in 1960 when, according to the report, 'nearly three-quarters of all black men included in Census data were working; today, only 55 percent are working.'[44]

"But, beyond overt racial discrimination, these grim figures are influenced by a great many factors, including the automation of many jobs at low-skill levels and the loss of so-called smokestack industries where great numbers of blacks used to be employed. The severe cutback in social service programs has also worsened unemployment statistics for black workers, though whites have been hurt by all these factors as well."

"There is, I gather," Geneva broke in, "a widening income gap between the top and bottom of U.S. society. In fact, some of the most distressing data relate to income distribution of American families. In 1983, the wealthiest two-fifths of all U.S. families earned 67.1 percent of the total national income, while the poorest two-fifths earned only 15.8 percent, and the poorest fifth—where nearly one-half of all black families fell—earned only 4.7 percent of the national income."[45]

"What percentage of blacks are in the top fifth?" I asked, looking for some positive note.

"Only 7 percent of all black families are in this group. Worse yet, the top fifth of American families earned 42.7 percent of the income, or nine times as much as the bottom fifth—hardly a basis for your perverse optimism since 9.9 million blacks, nearly 36 percent of our population, are living in poverty. This is the highest black poverty rate since the Census Bureau began collecting data on black poverty in 1968."[46]

"Let me anticipate you, Geneva," I suggested. "Yes, these statistics reflect many ruined lives for whom the oft-heralded legal gains have been fatally tardy. Professor William J. Wilson, one of the most perceptive of contemporary observers, reports: 'The pattern of racial oppression in the past created the huge black underclass, as the accumulation of disadvantages were passed on from generation to generation, and the technological and economic revolution of advanced industrial society combined to insure it a permanent status.' "[47]

"My conclusion may be premature," Geneva interjected, "but my reading indicates that because the Supreme Court is unable or unwilling to recognize and remedy the real losses resulting from long-held, race-based subordinated status, the relief the Court has been willing to grant, while welcome, proves of less value than expected and exacts the exorbitant price of dividing the black community along economic lines."

"Precisely one of the points Professor Wilson makes as he compares the ever-worsening situation for unskilled black workers with the increased opportunities for educated blacks with skills. In fact, Wilson has upset some civil rights advocates by noting that 'affirmative action programs are not designed to deal with the problem of the disproportionate concentration of blacks in the low-wage labor market. Their major impact has been in the higher-paying jobs of the expanding service-producing industries in both the corporate and government sectors.' Furthermore, Wilson shares your concern, Geneva, about the 'deepening economic schism . . . developing in the black community, with the black poor falling further and further behind middle- and upper-income blacks.' "[48]

"So," said Geneva, "to sum up this discussion before moving on to my second Chronicle, there seems little doubt that the abandonment of overtly discriminatory policies has lowered racial barriers for some talented and skilled blacks seeking access to opportunity and advancement. Even their upward movement is, however, pointed to by much of the society as the final proof that racism is dead—a too hasty pronouncement which dilutes the achievement of those who have moved ahead and denies even society's sympathy to those less fortunate blacks whose opportunities and life fortunes are less promising today than they were twenty-five years ago.

"Despite your optimism, you seem ready to agree that the future for a great many black people is bleak. The necessary question that I hope we can decide during our discussions is whether this result—this economic-political disadvantage set in motion by the Framers—is beyond any known power to halt or even alter. Or, whether different strategies might make the annual observances of the *Brown* decision celebrations of great expectations realized rather than increasingly sorrowful commemorations of what might have been. And finally, whether, as I tried to suggest to the Framers, the real problem of race in America is the unresolved contradiction embedded in the Constitution and never openly examined, owing to the self-interested attachment of some citizens of this nation to certain myths—myths that I hope my Chronicles will allow us to examine in detail."

"Your summary, Geneva, is a good place to start, but my optimism about the future doesn't mean that I'm not as disturbed as you are about the current condition of black people in this country. It is all too true that much of our effort in the courts and in getting civil rights laws through Congress fell far short of eliminating our subordinate status in this society."

Geneva looked suspicious. "I sense a thinly veiled *but* in your statement."

"Not really. I am troubled, though, by the challenge you faced in your first Chronicle, and continue to wonder whether there wasn't some way to get the Framers to acknowledge that their compromises on slavery could only have dire human consequences."

For far from the last time that day, Geneva was exasperated. "And what makes you think that the Constitution's Framers who saw us as slaves, and used that lowly status to convince themselves that we were an inferior race, would have been more likely to recognize our humanity than are the country's contemporary leaders who, having every reason to know that we are not inferior, seem determined to maintain racial dominance even if that aim destroys us and the country?"

"Yes, white policy makers' racial motivations seem hardly to have changed at all over these two centuries—but, Geneva, before you go on to your next Chronicle, tell me, what was the main lesson you derived from your debate with the Framers?"

She answered at once. "That they would not, or could not, take seriously themselves or their ideals." Noticing my puzzled look, she tried to explain. "The men who drafted the Constitution, however gifted or remembered as great, were politicians, not so different from the politicians of our own time and, like them, had to resolve by compromise conflicting interests in order to preserve both their fortunes and their new nation. What they saw as the requirements of that nation prevented them from substantiating their rhetoric about freedom and rights with constitutional provisions—and thus they infringed on the rights and freedom not only of the slaves, who then were one-fifth of the population, but, ultimately, of all American citizens."

"If this situation is part of the nation's basic law, how are we to reach the whites in power today and gain redress?"

"That's a hard question," said Geneva, standing, "and one even the Celestial Curia has had trouble answering. Indeed, that's why they sent me here."

"The Celestial what?"

"Curia," she said calmly, heading for the kitchen, "a sort of supreme court with more than the usual judicial power. You'll understand in the next Chronicle—the one with which my visions began. But before I start on it, let me put on some more tea."

Chapter 2

The Benefits to Whites of Civil Rights Litigation

The Chronicle of the Celestial Curia

I ARRIVED after what seemed a long but very swift journey and was ushered into a great hall, like that of an ancient temple. The walls of highly polished rosewood were pierced from floor to ceiling at regular intervals by narrow windows. A double row of intricately carved columns supported the high ceiling, on which were painted frescoes of scenes depicting humans engaged in heroic struggles. The only light came through the windows, whose stained glass cast shadows of rose, indigo, gold, and green over the expectant faces of the throngs of men and women assembled there. Those faces, I later learned, belonged to social-reform activists from all over the world. Until I recalled that people of color populate most of the earth, I wondered why there were so few Caucasians present.

Everyone was dressed in plain black robes and spoke a formal language that I was able to understand but not identify. Suddenly, just as I was about to ask why we were there, there was a fanfare from an unseen organ, and a burst of spontaneous applause from the gathering.

"All rise for the Celestial Curia," the audience said in unison as they stood. Their applause now became rhythmic, as they provided accompaniment to a hymnlike chorale they were singing. The music was as infectious as its rhythms were intricate. To my great satisfaction, I was able to join in their singing though I had never before heard either the melody or the lyrics.

I glanced toward the massive doors behind us, seemingly the only entrance to the hall, but they remained closed. Somehow, in that instant, two of three ornately carved, thronelike chairs arrayed on a dias at the front of the hall were occupied by black women dressed in robes of some rich and gleaming fabric like lamé.

When the audience—with some reluctance—brought our song to a close, the Curia Sisters welcomed us, speaking in harmonic unison, and immediately launched into a concerned discussion about the delay in a much-needed transformation of an industrial nation's social structure that, as presently organized, espouses liberty for the individual but prospers through the systematic exploitation of the lower classes, particularly those who are not white. The women of the Curia seemed to agree in their criticism of suffering and injustices being visited by the system on the exploited groups, and were appalled by the uncaring stance of the upper classes who justify their superior status by reason of their ability, merit, and skill, and ignore the role of economic class, contacts, and luck.

"How can it be," the Curia asked, "that the exploited working-class whites—lulled by a surfeit of sports, sex, and patriotic fervor—readily acquiesce in so oppressive a system? And who would expect that this white majority could find solace in the knowledge that they are of the same race as the upper-class elite who hold most of the money and power and control the police and the military forces?

"Reform is also impeded," the Curia added, "because leaders of the benighted colored peoples shun economic and political transformation, and strive instead for pseudo-liberal social-welfare programs wholly incapable of really improving the lot of the lower classes. Accepting the majority's prattle about a society of equality under the law, minority activists limit themselves to the predictably inadequate remedies available within the existing socio-economic status quo. They know, or should know, that in a society where money is fundamental, equality that does not include economic equality is not equality at all."

America was obviously the country in question. It became just as obvious that, while united in describing the country's failings, the Curia Sisters were far from agreeing on what, if any, events would bring about the long-overdue social reform that would conform the nation's policies with its often-proclaimed ideals of equality and justice for all. The Curia member seated on the left urged disruptive protest and strident resistance to the multiple injustices suffered by the people of color. The tone of her declamations was fierce and fearsome. Her sister to the right, while deploring these racial wrongs, clearly despaired of their correction. She advocated a massive exodus by the nation's colored peoples and a new beginning in some more receptive land.

Suddenly, calling me by name, the Curia summoned me to stand before them. Addressing me, they again spoke in unison: "Great power does not always bring great wisdom. You hail from this country. Your commitment to ending its injustices is known by all. We want your counsel regarding a bold plan we call the 'Conservative Crusader' which will displace the rhetoric of complaint with firm action. Even now, the plan is being transmitted to your mind and heart. Share the plan's details with those assembled here, and tell us your honest views."

As I started to protest that I did not know of any such plan, it suddenly unfurled in my mind, and I understood it clearly. The Curia's means of communication was no more shocking than the diabolical scheme they had devised.

Surely, the audience of advocates would join in my objections to this devious design. Whatever their response, I seemed to have no choice. With unmistakable firmness, the Curia urged me to begin:

> Come now. Detail for all our plan today
> To place the poor where now the rich hold sway.

I took a deep breath, and the words came almost without my volition. "The Conservative Crusader will gain appointment to the land's Highest Court, and there will wage a ceaseless campaign against the liberal orientation of its decisions. In particular, the Crusader will oppose protections that shield the poor from the worst abuses of the system. This vigorous and militantly conservative crusade will be designed to convince the upper classes and their representatives that their selfish interests can best be protected by an even greater than usual lack of concern for the plight of the working classes and the poor. Most important of all, the Crusader will further policies designed to make clear to even the most ignorant of lower-class whites that their enemy is not the blacks but those responsible for economic and social policies that maintain both poor whites and poor blacks near the bottom of our society.

"While the political stance will be conservative, the intent will be to incite radical reform by the only means possible: hardening the hearts of the upper classes against those whom they exploit, and eliminating the present social programs, which even now manage only to stave off starvation while keeping the masses too weak to recognize their true status."

The audience, far from appalled, greeted my recitation of the Conservative Crusade plan with applause—enthusiasm that the Curia shared: "The disinherited will surely be stirred by this stimulus toward revolt or reasoned Emigration." Then the Curia member on the left rose and sang a solo in a voice like that of the great gospel singer Mahalia Jackson:

> The exploited poor will not be made whole
> By liberal souls of good intent
> Ringing changes on the golden rule.
>
> Separate but equal is not the way.
> Integration is not the way.
> And begging for rights will not suffice—
> For those who would be free
> Must free themselves.

In response, the audience sang, "Oh, Curia, when will they come to know?"—a line that became a new background beat to a series of statements and responses in harmony, just as the congregations responded to the preacher in black churches when I was a child. First, the Curia Sisters would chant the beginning of a question, which the audience would then complete:

"When will they come to know ——"

"That equality cannot be obtained merely by enacting civil rights laws or winning cases in the courts?"

"When will they come to know——"

"That equality will not come through an array of social programs which serve to provide minimum relief for the needy while providing the upper classes with stability, regularity, and the poor's acceptance of the status quo?"

"When will they come to know——"

"That while protecting upper-class privilege, liberal social programs too often offer the poor food without nutrition, welfare without well-being, job training without employment opportunities, and minimal legal services without real expectations of justice?"

"When will they come to know——"

"That true reform movements are motivated by adversity not by the beneficence of do-gooders who themselves are profiting from the misfortunes of those they claim they wish to help up— but not up too far?"

The music had now reached a crescendo of emotion, and I could not help but join in. Then, after several choruses in which both Curia and audience spoke together, the Curia Sister on the left stood and, in a deep contralto, sang:

> A revolution, with neither sword nor shield,
> And wrested through law alone,
> Is no Revolution. It is mirage:
> A changing of guards under
> Orders from unchanged rulers.

In response, the soaring soprano of the Curia Sister on the right floated out over our voices in a song that was new though it seemed to arise out of the one we were singing:

> Our Revolution must be an Emigration
> From causes lost and dreams long dead.
> Unchained from the old, we can sing a new song
> In a strange land any place but here.

When the singing ended, the Celestial Curia seemed ready to move on to the many other problems before them. They beckoned me to come forward and whispered an invitation to remain for some time to consider their plan. I accepted and for a happy period enjoyed that feeling of belonging that American blacks often sense while visiting a Third World country, but seldom feel at home.

T HAT'S ALL?" I asked when, after a few minutes of silence, it was clear that Geneva was waiting for me to say something.

"For the moment," she replied, and I thought to myself how clearly she recalled the details of her so-called Chronicles, not like most people recounting a dream. "For the moment," she went on, "I would like your thoughts on what you have just heard."

"Well, it sounded very much as though the Celestial Curia was trying to recruit you to join and exceed even the most conservative members of our Supreme Court. In fact, certain legal commentators would, on hearing your Chronicle, launch an even more careful review of Chief Justice William Rehnquist's ideological motivations than those already undertaken.[1] I rather doubt, though, that he will concede, or his biographers find, more than a lifetime of conservative experience to explain his judicial outlook. Indeed, there is reason to believe he would find your Chronicle rather humorous."[2]

"I hope," Geneva responded, without smiling, "that you found more than humor in the story."

"I did! I did! Much in the Chronicle is thought-provoking, though perhaps unrealistic."

"Well, think about it," she suggested, rising, "while I brew more tea."

When she returned, Geneva spoke with an air of anxiety foreign to her usually cool and commanding demeanor. "Before I recounted my Chronicle of the Celestial Curia," she reminded me, "we were discussing the ineffectiveness of civil rights litigation. Clearly, the Celestial Curia are convinced that social justice will gain a perverse impetus through the adverse decisions handed down by a conservative and uncaring Supreme Court. Do you agree?"

"Well, Geneva," I said, trying to relieve her nervousness, "it's your Chronicle, what do you think?"

"I asked you," Geneva said sternly, "to come here to help me interpret the Chronicles and not practice your Socratic classroom techniques on me." While Geneva's appearance may have changed during her long illness, the quick temper I well remembered had survived the years intact. The difference now was that I had adopted Geneva's less praiseworthy characteristics as well as her more estimable ones, and I was unwilling to submit to her browbeating. I said as much, adding, "I know you didn't ask me to cross the country simply to reminisce about the old days or engage in bickering. Why not tell me what's all the urgency?"

Geneva raised her hand slightly in a gesture of concession. "I apologize, friend, but I earnestly need your help. Your interpretations of the Chronicles are very important, though for now I can't explain more. Please trust me."

It was hard to imagine Geneva pleading for anything. Back at the Legal Defense Fund offices, the joke was that, even when she went to court, she made "demands" rather than "pleaded" for relief. But she was clearly pleading with me now, and after so many years of illness, it seemed both humane and politic to comply with her request.

"While they did not identify the country," I began, "it appears the Curia's concern is America, and that they, like many blacks, have lost hope in racial reform through the existing democratic mechanisms, particularly the courts. The Curia have concluded that only a major disruption in the society, precipitated by some form of revolt by a coalition of minorities and working-class whites, will bring substance to the nation's long-held myth of equality.

"I agree that a conservative Supreme Court hostile to existing rights and protection would certainly bring hardship to people whose lives are now desperate, but whether this would lead to some form of revolt or simply more passive despair is another question. And, Geneva, it's not an either/or question.

"For example, Frances Fox Piven and Richard Cloward would agree with the Celestial Curia 'that the poor gain more through mass defiance and disruptive protests than by organizing for electoral politics and other more acceptable reform policies.' But Piven and Cloward, two of the most thoughtful commentators on social-reform issues, caution that it is hard to get the poor involved in protests, particularly those involving serious risk of arrest or retaliatory violence. The poor usually remain acquiescent in the hardships of their lives, conforming 'to the institutional arrangements which enmesh them, which regulate the rewards and penalties of daily life, and which appear the only possible remedy.'[3]

"In any event," I concluded, "while the Celestial Curia have impressive powers at their command, they seem to lack real understanding of America's race problem and the limited role courts can play in its solution. Let me discuss a few areas in which your Curia miss the point.

"First, the duty of the Supreme Court as well as of others who exercise power in a democratic government is, as Justice Felix Frankfurter has said, 'not to reflect inflamed public feeling but to help form its understanding.'[4] In that role, however, the Court can seldom stray far from prevailing public moods, particularly on racial issues. Race has always been a politically sensitive subject in this country. And as the Court learned from its attempt in the *Dred Scott* case (1857)[5] to 'solve' the slavery issue by both invalidating a Congressional compromise between slave-holding and free states, and finding that blacks could not be citizens under the Constitution, the Court's reputation can be harmed more easily than enhanced. So, while members of the Court may hold wildly varying views on how to decide particular racial issues, they seem unified in the task of harmonizing those decisions with their determination to preserve and protect the Court as an institution."[6]

"If that is so," Geneva inquired, "why do civil rights people place such great faith in the courts?"

"I think that the judicial role as reformer rather than regulator may be overemphasized by representatives of relatively powerless groups who, lacking either economic or political power, feel they must rely on the courts for both the correction of injustices and their elevation to equal status in the society."

"And they maintain this stance," Geneva asked in exasperation, "even when the history of civil rights law teaches that reliance on courts for so heavy a responsibility will lead to disappointment?"

"Well," I hedged, "a growing number of civil rights advocates have been forced by the trend of judicial decisions to abandon their 'we can do anything' approach to the courts so prevalent in the heady years after *Brown*. Even so, it's difficult for any civil rights lawyer, past or present, to be objective about the worth of litigation in bringing about racial reform. Because legislatures and executives were so unresponsive, we and the organizations we represented came to rely on the courts as a matter of necessity; and for a very long time, criticism of our strategies was neither welcome nor well received."

"Yes," and Geneva sighed, "I guess I can remember how I felt when I was racing around the South like some light-black knight trying to save the poor defenseless cullid folk from segregationist dragons. Nobody could tell me I was not performing a wonderful work."

"Exactly. I can almost guarantee that the Curia's suggestion that Justice Rehnquist is secretly pursuing egalitarian ends with conservative means would be accepted by him with better grace than some civil rights proponents would accept the Curia's implication that their litigation efforts do more harm than good.

"You know, Geneva, there was a time when criticism of the Supreme Court which went beyond disagreement with individual decisions was deemed serious heresy by civil rights groups. It happened after your accident, but I must tell you that differences of precisely this character led to the resignation of the NAACP's legal staff back in the late 1960s."[7]

"What happened?" asked Geneva.

"A young NAACP staff attorney, Lewis M. Steel, published without prior approval a criticism of the Supreme Court's decisions during the fifteen years when Chief Justice Earl Warren presided over the Court. In his article, Steel argued that the Court's decisions were primarily intended to meet the needs of the white community rather than those of blacks. For example, in criticizing the Court's vague mandate requiring the elimination of segregated schools with 'all deliberate speed,'[8] Steel wrote—and I have his article here so I can quote it exactly:

> Never in the history of the Supreme Court had the implementation of a constitutional right been so delayed or the creation of it put in such vague terms. The Court thereby made clear that it was a white court which would protect the interests of white America in the maintenance of stable institutions.
>
> In essence, the Court considered the potential damage to white Americans resulting from the diminution of privilege as more critical than continued damage to the underprivileged. . . . Worse still, it gave the primary responsibility for achieving educational equality to those who had established the segregated institutions.[9]

"Coming as it did during the height of the civil rights movement, this was too much for the NAACP. As it happened, the organization's national board had a meeting scheduled on the day after the article appeared. The matter was discussed and Steel was summarily fired.[10] General Counsel Robert Carter and the rest of the legal staff resigned when the board adamantly refused to offer Steel a hearing.[11] Some months later, the NAACP published a brochure, 'The Issues in the Lewis M. Steel Case,' explaining that Steel was fired not because he criticized the Court for not moving fast enough or not doing enough, but because he charged that the organization's court victories 'have been merely symbolic and not substantive.' 'It was thus,' the essay concluded, 'a reflection upon the NAACP and a rejection of its many victories in civil rights cases in the courts, including the United States Supreme Court.' '"[12]

"That was regrettable," Geneva acknowledged, "but it was also a long time ago. Surely the civil rights community must now understand and accept the limits on the Court's role in bringing about racial reform."

"They do to a certain extent, but I think there is a continued faith in the courts that is jarred by criticism. Several liberal scholars, on the other hand, might agree with the Curia's assessment. For example, Professor Arthur S. Miller's articles have reached conclusions quite like those that cost Lewis Steel his job. In Professor Miller's view, 'the Supreme Court before Warren was mainly concerned with the protection of the established property interests; under Warren, the High Bench, by moving to protect many of the poor and disadvantaged, also helped those highest in the social pecking order.'[13]

"Professor Miller might agree with the diagnosis offered by the Celestial Curia, though he would probably disagree with their prescription for a cure. He, like Lewis Steel, maintains that the civil rights decisions of the Warren Court were profoundly conservative and protected the economic and political status quo by responding to the pleas for justice by blacks and other severely disadvantaged groups just enough to siphon off discontent, thereby limiting the chances that the existing social order would pay more than minimal costs for the reforms achieved."

"A strange dichotomy," Geneva mused. "Civil rights people argue strenuously that the relief they seek will help the nation prevail in war or other crisis, but later forget and almost resent the implication that their hard-earned victory was likely brought about by outside events or strongly influenced by the perception that relief for blacks would serve interests of identifiable classes of whites."

I agreed. "I often cite the NAACP and government briefs in the *Brown* case, both of which maintain that abandonment of state-supported segregation would be a crucial asset as we compete with Communist countries for the hearts and minds of Third World people just emerging from long years of colonialism.[14] As far as I'm concerned, the Court's decision in the *Brown* case cannot be understood without considering the decision's value to whites in policy-making positions who are able to recognize the economic and political benefits at home and abroad that would follow abandonment of state-mandated racial segregation.

"Other civil rights advocates have seen the tie between our rights and the nation's foreign policy posture. As far back as 1945, NAACP lawyers William Hastie, Thurgood Marshall, and Leon Ransom argued that it would be unconscionable to allow segregation in interstate travel facilities after the end of a world war in which all of the people of the United States were joined 'in a death struggle against the apostles of racism.'[15]

"Our lawyers, though, tend to view such arguments as enhancements of rights based on the Constitution. They are reluctant to believe that vindication of even the most basic rights for blacks actually requires a perceived benefit to whites. And that's why Dr. DuBois didn't endear himself to civil rights advocates when, years after the *Brown* decision, he observed that 'no such decision would have been possible without the world pressure of communism,' which he felt rendered it 'simply impossible for the United States to continue to lead a "Free World" with race segregation kept legal over a third of its territory.'"[16]

Geneva had heard enough to interrupt and make sure she understood my point. "Would civil rights lawyers today not agree in any respect with the Curia's plan?" she asked.

"They would certainly concede that the disruption that might follow a loss of faith in the law is one way (though a dangerous one) to bring about change. It is, after all, how this country gained its independence. And when blacks rise up in some form of direct action, civil rights lawyers support those efforts—as was shown during the sit-in protests of the 1960s.[17] But lawyers representing a long-subordinated group of relatively powerless black people, in a country supposedly committed to justice under law, would not seem to be following an unreasonable course in continuing their reliance on the courts that have given them many important victories over the years.[18]

"Now I know you want to move on with the discussion, but a last story should explain just how disillusioned some of us have become. A few years ago, our best-known legal advocate, Justice Thurgood Marshall, returned to his alma mater, Howard University, to speak at some special occasion. Eschewing the usual homilies of hope, he spoke frankly and bitterly of what he and his fellow civil rights lawyers had failed to achieve:

> Today we have reached the point where people say, "We've come a long way." But so have other people come a long way.... Has the gap gotten smaller? It's getting bigger.... People say we are better off today. Better than what?
>
> I am amazed at people who say that, "the poorest Negro kid in the South is better off than the kid in South Africa." So what! We are not in South Africa. We are here. [People tell me] "You ought to go around the country and show yourself to Negroes; and give them inspiration." For what? Negro kids are not fools. They know when you tell them there is a possibility that someday you'll have a chance to be the o-n-l-y Negro on the Supreme Court, those odds aren't too good."[19]

"It seems to me," Geneva remarked, "that all you have said adds to rather than detracts from the Curia's view that further progress will come through tactics other than litigation."

"No, I do not go that far, but as a law teacher I've had the luxury denied most civil rights activists to examine the legal precedents, and there is no doubt in my mind that reforms resulting from civil rights litigation invariably promote the interests of the white majority."

"The classic example of that truth," suggested Geneva, "is the Fourteenth Amendment. Although it was enacted to give blacks the rights of citizens, for most of its early history it was utilized, as Professor Boris Bittker put it so well, to nurture 'railroads, utility companies, banks, employers of child labor, chain stores, money lenders, aliens, and a host of other groups and institutions . . . , leaving so little room for the Negro that he seemed to be the fourteenth amendment's forgotten man.' "[20]

"It is a truth," I conceded, "that most people would rather not remember, but the Fourteenth Amendment's due-process protection of 'liberty of contract' rights has proven of far greater value to corporations—to cite only one example—than to black people.

"While not going as far as those of us who claim the society benefits more from our victories than black people do, Paul Freund observed years ago that 'the frontiers of the law have been pushed back by the civil rights movement in many sectors that are far broader than the interests of the movement itself.'[21] Professor Freund cited the impact of several decisions: *New York Times* v. *Sullivan* (1964), which held that the defamation of a public official is not actionable unless the statement is published maliciously, with knowledge of its falsity, or with reckless disregard of its truth or untruth;[22] *NAACP* v. *Button* (1963), proclaiming that group representation of potential litigants in desegregation cases is constitutionally protected speech and association, not subject to attack by state bar rules;[23] and *Shelley* v. *Kraemer* (1948), finding unlawful 'state action' in the judicial enforcement of privately made, racially restrictive land covenants."[24]

"Well," Geneva said, "though not a law teacher, even I know that Professor Freund might have extended his list to include other civil rights precedents, including *Dixon* v. *Alabama State Board of Education* (1961), establishing a constitutional right of due process for students facing summary disciplinary action at state colleges.[25] In that case, the Court reversed the summary expulsion of black college students who had protested segregated public facilities. Then in the voting area, we cannot forget *Smith* v. *Allwright* (1944), one of the long series of civil rights challenges to the white primary.[26] This litigation made clear the need for oversight by the federal judiciary in the election process to ensure constitutional rights for blacks and whites alike."[27]

"Speaking of federal oversight," I observed, "all criminal defendants have gained from the century-long effort blacks have made to eliminate racial discrimination from the jury box."[28]

"That is true," Geneva admitted, "but the effort to make the right to a nonbiased jury more than silly symbolism will not be won as long as prosecutors can use their peremptory challenges to rid juries of prospective black jurors—a practice at least acquiesced in by the Court until quite recently."[29]

"Wait!" I said. "We shouldn't omit *NAACP* v. *Alabama* (1958), in which the Court responded to Alabama's effort to intimidate NAACP members and found that the state cannot use its power to control domestic corporations to interfere with First Amendment rights to 'engage in association for the advancement of beliefs and ideas . . .';[30] and, of course, *Gomillion* v. *Lightfoot* (1960), where for the first time the Court found it appropriate to apply constitutional standards to the apportionment of districts for elections.[31]

"Actually, that subject is worthy of a lengthier discussion, but let me mention first Professor Robert Cover's conclusion that 'although the Court had never treated them as race cases, there can be little doubt that decisions . . . made in *Moore* v. *Dempsey* [1923],[32] overturning the mob-dominated conviction of a black man on due process grounds; *Powell* v. *Alabama* [1932],[33] where the Court for the first time found a limited right to counsel essential to due process in capital cases; and *Brown* v. *Mississippi* [1936],[34] reversing as violative of the due process clause a state conviction based on a confession resulting from "physical brutality," all made new criminal procedure law in part because the notorious facts of each case exemplified the national scandal of racist southern justice.' "[35]

"Getting back to *Gomillion* v. *Lightfoot*, the *Tuskegee* voting case," said Geneva, "I seem to recall that it was one of NAACP general counsel Robert L. Carter's greatest Court victories. Since it is close to the definitive illustration of what we are talking about, I would hope that a review of what we civil rights lawyers did there, and how the precedent has been used subsequently, should bring you around to the Curia's view on the value of trying to obtain favorable race decisions in the courts."

"Geneva," I said, more testily than I had intended, "I see no reason to support the Curia's crazy plan just because I agree that *Gomillion* has become, as you predicted years ago, an excellent example of a civil rights case that helped increase substantially judicial involvement in electoral politics. Keep in mind, though, that the state's effort to frustrate black voters, by changing the town's boundaries from a square to what the Court found to be a 'strangely irregular twenty-eight-sided figure,'[36] was sufficiently shocking to gain relief from even the most conservative court.

"And don't forget that Justice Frankfurter tried his best to limit the *Gomillion* case to its extraordinary facts, carefully basing relief on a finding that the Alabama gerrymander had violated the Fifteenth Amendment rights of blacks to vote. His continuing opposition to judicial intervention in reapportionment cases did not change.[37] And he later dissented from the Court's change of view on the issue in *Baker* v. *Carr* (1962),[38] the case that set the stage for the 'one person, one vote' cases that made suffrage a fundamental right and recognized that the right could be denied both by unequally apportioned districts or by a 'debasement or dilution of the weight of a citizen's vote.'[39]

"Of course, in *Baker*," I admitted, "the Court majority did not actually rely on *Gomillion*, but Justice Tom Clark in concurring found 'the apportionment picture in Tennessee is a topsy-turvical of gigantic proportions'—and, moreover, that the majority of the people of Tennessee had no 'practical opportunities for exerting their political weight at the polls' to correct the existing 'invidious discrimination.'[40]

"In subsequent cases, the Court found similarly indefensible gerrymandering in other states.[41] Reapportionment suits from virtually every state led to the major precedent in *Reynolds* v. *Sims* (1964), where Chief Justice Earl Warren wrote that, despite 'political thickets' and 'mathematical quagmires,' the Court was required by 'our oath and our office' to hear cases in which constitutionally protected rights were denied."[42]

"I have not been able to catch up on all the reapportionment decisions," Geneva said, "but while the value of judicial oversight has been great, I gather that it has been as thorny an experience as the Court feared. With the computer becoming an increasingly useful tool, the courts are now being asked to determine the validity of district lines that are no less gerrymandered because they hardly deviate from pure equality."[43]

"Yes, Justice Frankfurter's warning that apportionment cases are a 'political thicket' the judiciary should avoid has returned to harass if not to haunt the current Court. And you won't be surprised to learn that, to complete the circle of protection provided blacks against racial gerrymanders in the *Gomillion* case, the Court has now agreed that purely political gerrymandering can be challenged in courts as violative of equal protection."[44]

"That is all well and good," Geneva observed, "but, while the Court is fine-tuning standards in the political gerrymandering cases, blacks whose litigation efforts in the voting field sparked the reapportionment revolution are still trying to beat back both simpleminded and sophisticated schemes designed either to keep them from voting or to dilute the impact of their vote below the minimum needed to elect anyone who will advocate their interests and be responsive to their needs."

"The two sets of cases have followed divergent paths as to proof," I explained. "In the reapportionment cases, the Court decided that the Constitution prohibited any substantial variation from equality among districts in drawing district lines—without regard to legislative intent or motivation."[45]

"Big deal!" Geneva scoffed. "The Court militantly insists on almost mathematical equality in weighing the validity of apportionment plans, while ignoring the fact that much of this legislative districting, supposedly undertaken to meet the 'one person, one vote' standard, is actually used to dilute black voting power by carving up the neighborhoods of racial minorities and placing them in majority white election districts."[46]

"A few cases," I responded in the Court's defense, "did suggest that the right of suffrage would prohibit at-large or multimember voting schemes; that is, those plans where all voters in a legislative district are able to vote for each candidate seeking office in that district, where—'designedly or otherwise'—such districts operate 'to minimize or cancel out the voting strength of racial or political elements of the voting population.' "[47] Unfortunately, as the voting rights case law developed, the Court concluded that, in attacking at-large district schemes that diluted black votes—the technique that had supplanted the white primary as the favorite means of discriminating against black voters[48]—civil rights litigants must prove that the legislature adopted or maintained at-large or multimember districts with the intention of diluting the value of minority votes."[49]

"One would think," Geneva suggested, "that if a state could deny the right of suffrage either by reapportioning a district or by establishing at-large districts, both dilution schemes should be subject to the same effect-oriented standard of proof."

"Think about it, Geneva! There is a distinction. The Court found that unequally apportioned electoral districts were in complete conflict with a meaningful right to vote. Requiring legislatures to draw district boundaries that aim for mathematical equality of voters was deemed a benefit to all and a harm to none. But at-large and multimember districts, while sometimes serving as vehicles of discrimination, can also serve legitimate functions. And single-member districts, the alternative to the at-large approach, are not a perfect remedy. Such districts are susceptible to gerrymandering. Lines drawn to favor some blacks, for example, can lead to charges of discrimination by other blacks[50] or by other ethnic groups."[51]

Geneva was unimpressed. "I see the distinction, but I also know that all too often the legitimate potential of at-large plans serves as a convenient shield for discriminatory intent. If plaintiffs have the burden of proving that intent, the task can be almost impossible."

"Not quite impossible. The Court has ruled for plaintiffs in a few cases.[52] But, yes, the task is very difficult."

"Does the Voting Rights Act help at all?" Geneva asked.

"One would have hoped so, but a plurality of the Court held, in *City of Mobile* v. *Bolden* (1980),[53] that proof of discriminatory intent was required to invalidate at-large election plans, whether the suit was brought under the Fourteenth and Fifteenth amendments or under the Voting Rights Act. Congress finally interceded and enacted amendments to the Voting Rights Act in 1982[54] to restore the pre-*Bolden* effects tests for proving discriminatory intent.[55] Even though the Justice Department argued that the amendments require proof of purposeful intent,[56] the Supreme Court upheld the new provisions."[57]

"And while the interpretation battles go on and on," said Geneva impatiently, "black voters face discrimination hurdles while trying to exercise the most basic right in the Constitution. The hard-to-meet intent requirements serve to insulate black vote–dilution schemes that would be struck down under the 'one person, one vote' rubric were they challenged in reapportionment suits."

"True," I conceded, "but the 1982 amendments have encouraged civil rights lawyers to continue their voting rights litigation, and the Court has remained responsive to voting complaints."[58]

"Well, friend, I am impressed with your review of the cases in the voting rights area, but the overall results of all this activity seem mainly to have sparked more opposition to the meaningful participation of black people in the election process. To my mind," she added, with more than a touch of acid in her voice, "the voting rights cases prove to a shocking degree that litigation—while perhaps a guaranteed employment program for lawyers—is a never-ending detour for blacks, at least for those seeking protection of their own rights as opposed to their lawyers seeking new and more exciting cases."

"That's a low blow!" I protested. "Why do black women transfer to their men hostility that should be hurled at the real culprit—society's racism? Moreover, I didn't come here to have my evaluation of the cases measured by some otherworldly standard of yours!"

"Now wait a minute," Geneva admonished, her own voice rising. "In the first place, you are not my man, and I resent your generalizations about black women. And, in the second place, I am upset not with your review of the precedents but with your sense that you have to defend them or at least defend civil rights lawyers' continued reliance on a freedom train that has run out of steam."

"I'm discussing, not defending."

"Wrong! You are defending, and I hear you also admitting that civil rights litigation, although no longer a primary weapon, is necessary 'busy work,' occupying those who feel that 'something should be done' even if it is not particularly helpful and may be a harmful delusion. Why cannot you simply concede that my conclusion is the correct one?"

"Sure, Geneva, litigation may be a leaky boat whose engine has run out of gas—to change metaphorical vehicles—but one can still paddle through treacherous waters. It's prudent to be aware of all of the boat's defects, making adjustments for them, even trying to fix a few of them as time permits. But it is not prudent to abandon the boat, particularly if you can't swim to shore."

"And what do you do, Mr. Prudent Man, when you look ahead and see that your leaky boat is heading toward the falls?"

"I stay with that boat, Geneva, unless and until a better option presents itself. Swimming is not an option for the nonswimmer. And talk of revolution makes for bravura rhetoric but is no more realistic or, I think, necessary for black Americans today than it was back in the 1930s when the NAACP's executive secretary James Weldon Johnson rejected it in favor of a strategy of 'creative disorder.'[59] A pragmatist, Johnson viewed violence in self-defense as an obligation, but urged blacks to eschew violence not on any moral or pacific grounds but because it would be futile. Now, Geneva, tell me what has changed since the 1930s that leads you to a different conclusion from Johnson's when he said: 'We would be justified in taking up arms or anything we could lay hands on and fighting for the common rights we are entitled to and denied, if we had a chance to win. But I know and we all know there is not a chance.' "[60]

"That," Geneva said, "is exactly my point. There has been less change than either of us would like because there has been too little creative protest, and too much focus on changing laws that are the products of racism, not its cause. I do not like the idea of blood being shed any more than Mr. Johnson did, or than you do, or do most black people for that matter. But does the alternative to litigation have to be violent revolution?"

"Several movements in this country have achieved major change by direct, nonviolent activity. And, Geneva, as I said before, lawyers have played important roles in direct-action campaigns. It was strong legal defense efforts that limited the risk of protestors being sentenced to long prison terms under laws that violated constitutional rights."

"Fine, but the question remains. How long do you expect our people will be dependent on the leaky boat of litigation? Surely, it keeps us afloat, but its deficiencies are obvious even to you. How long should we be kept, by continued reliance on litigation, from attacking the real causes of our subordinate status?"

"A typically militant statement, Geneva, but until you come up with a more effective technique, I guess I'll stay with litigation—along with, I might add, most other civil rights lawyers I know."

"Well," she said after a long moment's silence, "now that we have gotten that out of our systems, let me make sure I understand your position on the voting rights cases. As a starting point, I assume you agree with the statement that 'as a constitutional rule, the principle of one person, one vote actually is derived from cases decided under the fifteenth amendment, the explicit purpose of which is to protect against the abridgement of racial minorities' voting rights.'"[61]

I nodded.

"Then would you also agree with the statement that 'any evidentiary standard in racial vote dilution cases demanding a greater quantum of proof than that required to challenge population malapportionment works an intolerable inversion of constitutional and historical priorities'?"[62]

"I do also agree with that statement, Geneva, but I've never said the courts are always fair, or legal principles are always construed in our favor. But there's a world of difference between admitting that litigation is hard, uncertain, and frustrating, and concluding, as you do, that it's an impossible approach. The Court today has difficulty handling civil rights cases in which allegations of discrimination are not accompanied by proof of actual intent.

71

The Court has a real fear that, if blacks could successfully challenge the validity of government policies by simply proving that they burdened or were less fair to blacks than to whites, then—through the use of such a disparate-impact test—'they would raise serious questions about, and perhaps invalidate, a whole range of tax, welfare, public service, regulatory, and licensing statutes.'[63]

"Our challenge, Geneva, as lawyers and legal scholars is to move the Court beyond its current reluctance to redress racial harm in the absence of discriminatory intent—a difficult task, I admit, particularly because intuitively I feel that proof standards like intent and motivation are used by courts to conceal other concerns."

Geneva was on her feet, her arms raised high in mock supplication for heavenly strength. "It's not just a matter of feeling, friend. It's history! From the very beginning of this nation, blacks have been the exploited, the excluded, and often the exterminated in this society. For most of that time, racial policies were blatant, vicious, and horribly damaging, leaving most of us in a subordinate status when compared with all but the lowest whites. And now that the Court has, as a result of our ceaseless petitions, been forced to find that overt discrimination is unconstitutional, we are for all intents and purposes still maintained in a subordinate state by the so-called neutral policies of a still-racist society because—for God's sake—we are not white! Though I have been out of things during much of two decades, I can see the hypocrisy here. Why can't you?"

"It's not a matter of seeing," I said, trying to remain calm, "but of doing something about it. Civil rights lawyers do not have the power of your Celestial Curia. We're simply trying to do what we can in the courts and in the country to make white people understand that blacks continue to face discrimination based on their race, despite the legal advances of the last few decades. You and I know that this country's people of color—blacks, Hispanics, Asians, Native Americans—have given more and received less than whites and yet, for the most part, have, as Harlem's Congressman-preacher Adam Clayton Powell used to admonish us, 'kept the faith.' We want nothing more than our rightful share of opportunities long available to whites."

"An old sermon," Geneva interrupted, "and it seems always to fall on deaf ears. It is simply too comforting for many white people to ignore the facts, to hearken to their fears, and say with real belief that blacks are demanding privileges they have not earned to remedy injustices they have not suffered. And under the steady reiteration of the marvels of 'freedom' and 'equality,' whites not only become anesthetized to the injustices blacks suffer, but also are rendered incapable of comprehending the fact that, as the historian David Brion Davis put it, 'Americans bought their independence with slave labor' and then have systematically denied blacks both freedom and equality."[64]

"Well, while you'll find more understanding in today's society than you got from the Framers, the real history of slavery is certainly not on the nation's educational agenda."

"In other words, less has changed in racial attitudes than meets the eye?"

"No, Geneva. Much has changed. But a great many whites view black claims for justice in the voting area as elsewhere as unjustified bellyaching, and secretly harbor a deep-seated belief that the real cause of the blacks' plight is the inferiority of the black race."

"You spoke a moment ago of the Celestial Curia's power. Tell me, friend, if you had such superhuman power, what would you do to gain for blacks a fair shake in the electoral process?"

"To be honest, the devices used to prevent blacks from voting are effective because many black people are so low on the socio-economic scale that they see no value in voting. Whites are still the majority in most electoral districts and have the economic power in virtually every area. This is a majoritarian system, and, as you well described, whites tend to oppose those policies that blacks support."

"*You* describe the problem well," Geneva remarked, "but I ask for your solution."

"I'm not sure I see a solution other than to keep on chipping away at the dilution and other anti-black-vote schemes as they surface, to work on getting blacks to register and vote, and to hope that our efforts will move the next generation beyond our own."

Geneva shook her head sadly. "Must we transform the world to save ourselves? You confuse our freedom campaign with a religious crusade in which you are the proverbial Job of the civil rights movement. You suffer and seek relief in the suffering itself. I don't mean that as a criticism, but your suffering, while real, is on a very different and less harsh level than that endured by the black masses whose numbers are rapidly increasing. I doubt that many of them would subscribe to your stoicism."

"Maybe," I said, "I should ask you the question you posed for me. Short of waving a wand and eliminating racism, how would you exercise the power, for example, to obtain a law that would provide blacks with meaningful voting rights—rights not simply to walk into a booth and vote without harassment, but to get blacks and others supporting their interests into elective offices, from the bottom to the top?"

Geneva smiled. "You must be reading my mind. You've just given a pretty good description of my next Chronicle: the Chronicle of the Ultimate Voting Rights Act. Are you ready?"

"I am ready for at least a good story."

Chapter 3

The Racial Limitation on Black Voting Power

The Chronicle of the Ultimate Voting Rights Act

THE Senator's black Mark VII Lincoln, coming too fast, failed to negotiate the curve and careened, out of control, onto the narrow two-lane bridge, hit the raised median divider, bounced across the opposite lane, and crashed through the bridge's steel railing without slowing down. The motor roared as the car plunged into the water. A spectacular splash and the car quickly sank from sight.

In one of those coincidences that confound fiction, a local news team was stationed above the bridge to film the Senator's triumphant return from a statewide speaking tour. The most powerful politician in this Southern state's history, and by all accounts the most racist, the Senator was a key sponsor of a controversial bill intended to reapportion the state's legislative districts. The redistricting scheme, while meeting legal standards, would make it virtually impossible for blacks to gain election to the state legislature or any statewide office. In fact, at the time of his auto accident, the Senator was rushing back to the state capital where he was to address the legislature on the eve of their vote on his measure.

Just as the Senator's car sank, the television cameras turned from the widening circles in the otherwise lazy river to the bridge's edge, to the break in the railing made by the Senator's car, to—surprisingly—the figure of a tall black woman. As the

75

cameras focused on her, she raised her arms and dived in a long, graceful arch that experts later asserted would have rated 8 or 9 in competition. She disappeared for almost thirty heart-stopping seconds. When at last she surfaced, first the few eyewitnesses and later the whole nation thrilled to see that she had a very water-logged Senator in tow, heading for the shore.

I, Geneva Crenshaw, was the soon-to-be heroine. Explaining why I did it would be more difficult than the rescue itself. I had been driving to an NAACP meeting in a rural town and had had no intention of saving anyone, particularly not a politician who had built his career by tormenting black people. But when I was a young girl, I often daydreamed about rescuing from grave danger a person who would lift up the black race. When that big sedan swerved across the road in front of me and went through the rail, those dreams all flooded back, totally captured my thinking, and literally shouted at me: "This is your chance! This is your chance! This is your chance!"

It was hypnotic. Before I knew what I was doing, I had stopped and was out of my car and sprinting to the break in the bridge railing. Kicking off my shoes, I gauged the distance from the bridge to the river below. Then I jumped.

Actually, I only thought I jumped; the video cameras showed me pushing off from the bridge into what became a swan dive. I do not remember the dive, but the cold water was a shock. Fortunately, the car was right side up and only about ten feet or so below the surface. The doors had come open on impact. Somehow, I hit the water, found the car, and dragged the one occupant to the surface almost automatically. I remember realizing that I was not strong enough to haul him to shore, but then others who saw the accident were scrambling down the riverbank and swimming out to help me.

At first I was too disoriented to understand the significance of the person I had rescued. As I stood, in my sopping dress, shivering from cold and shock, everyone's attention was focused on efforts to revive the Senator. Finally, one of the paramedics handed me a blanket and hot coffee, and told me to sit down. Accepting the blanket and drink, I ignored the advice and tried to make my way back up the riverbank to my car. By then, though, the news people were everywhere and were not about to permit a Lone Ranger tactic to rob them of a good story. When they learned who I was, their main question couched in various guises was, as one reporter bluntly put it: "Would you have gone in and saved him if you had known who he was?"

I gave the reporter the hardest look I could muster, and said, "A human life is a terrible thing to waste." I refused to make any other comment and steadfastly turned down all subsequent invitations to be interviewed by the national television news programs. It made little difference. What they could not get firsthand, they manufactured by means of that wonderful journalistic tool—conjecture.

Within twenty-four hours, most of the country's television viewers had seen the dramatic rescue sequences countless times in close-ups and in slow motion. Tabloid editors, denied the visual drama of the films, tried to compensate with lurid headlines:

BLACK WOMAN SAVES A LIFE, DOOMS HER RACE

BLACK WOMAN WINS THANKS OF WHITE RACISTS

LAWYER LEAPS TO AID OF FALLEN FOE

Media columnists and editorial writers stretched reality to the breaking point to find connections between the always-salable news of an exciting rescue and the growing national interest in the heightened racial tensions in the state as civil rights groups resisted conservative efforts to neutralize the increasingly influential black vote.

The national sympathy and support blacks had generated in the voting rights campaigns of the 1960s had evaporated, and beyond the civil rights community's opposition, there was little public protest against the state's increasingly blatant efforts to dilute black voting power. Even so, the media seemed to feel some need to transform my action into a symbolic statement about the faithful black people who return good for even the most vicious racial evils. Forgotten was the fact that, at the time, I had had no idea whom I was saving. I was a model of behavior that one editorial writer and commentator after another suggested, not very subtly, might well be emulated by all black people "during this tense time of transition." I was helpless to counteract this updated version of the loyal slave/servant routine and determined not to make matters worse by accepting any of the rewards offered me for "doing the right thing."

Why, I wondered, do whites so readily visit on blacks the worst possible motives for actions that may have been well intended despite what whites may have deserved? The fact that I had saved a man committed to emulating the worst characteristics of every race-baiting politician of the last century did not make me less grateful that I had been able to rescue a human being from almost certain death by drowning.

And while, as expected, I had to grin and bear a range of sarcastic comments, that is how the black community viewed it.

"Come on, Sister Geneva," a woman said the day after the accident, at the beauty parlor where I had taken refuge from the constant phone calls. "That sure was quite a dive you made to save that S.O.B!"

"Well," I said, as women in the other booths joined in the friendly chiding, "I did not want the Senator to get out of paying for all his sins by drowning himself. The Lord probably has an appropriate reward waiting for him."

"Right!" the woman said, still smiling. "And the Lord might have been putting His plan into effect when you butted in."

Everyone laughed, including my friend Faith Ann Courage, who stays so involved in her race work, as she calls it, that she seldom sees the humor in anything even remotely touching on the subject. Actually, I had come to the state in response to Faith Ann's urgent call. For years, the Senator had been her major antagonist as she worked to make black voters a meaningful political force in the state.

"You know," Faith Ann said thoughtfully, "the Senator is probably more than a little ambivalent about Geneva saving him from drowning. On the one hand, he's still alive, but on the other, he's going to have a hard time preaching the inherent worthlessness of a people one of whom the whole country watched save his life at the risk of her own."

"Maybe," I replied, "but the media is pitching the rescue as a morality play whose message is that black people should protect and save whites no matter how vicious they are."

"What else would you expect?" Faith Ann said with disdain. "But that antebellum propaganda doesn't fool anyone nowadays. Had the Senator died in the crash, his legislation would have passed overwhelmingly as a memorial to him. But as things stand, he may have difficulty holding his racist support. So, when you saved the Senator, you may have rescued us after all. The question is what should we do now?"

"Watch out, white folks!" one of the beauticians said, unwilling to see the mirth go out of the conversation. "Sister Faith Ann is plotting again."

Faith Ann did not crack a smile. "We will beat them," she said, "if we're not too afraid to be serious at least some of the time."

The hush that followed her comment was not caused by it. Faith Ann's total seriousness was viewed as an acceptable fault by those who knew her. Rather, a young, well-dressed white man had entered, and all turned suspiciously on the intruder, who had arrived in a black limousine now visible in the shop's big front window.

"Yes?" the shop owner asked the visitor, who looked as though he feared he would be devoured on the spot.

"I work," he stammered, "in the Senator's office. He is very anxious to see Lawyer Crenshaw and asked me to bring her to the hospital."

I hesitated. Faith Ann did not. "You better go and see what he wants. And," she said only half in jest, "tell him if he feels the need to express his thanks, we would be much obliged if he would support our ultimate voting rights proposal."

That suggestion broke the tension, and everyone in the beauty shop burst into laughter. Even the Senator's aide managed a wan grin. For years, Faith Ann had been advocating a plan that would guarantee blacks a percentage of elective offices in the state equal to their percentage of the population. No one took her seriously. As one community comic had told her, "Forget it, Faith Ann. Seeking proportional representation in this state where black folk are barely able to vote is like asking the leader of a lynch mob to let you sleep with his mama. It ain't goin' to happen."

As I was soon to learn, the Senator did not agree. When I was ushered into his palatial hospital room, he went pale. Then with a nervous gesture, he dismissed nurses, secretaries, and hangers-on, but never took his eyes off me. Dressed in pajamas and an expensive robe, his head wrapped in bandages, he was reclining on a large chaise lounge. He did not look at all well.

Only after the room was empty did he ease himself to his feet and extend his hand and mutter, "Thank you." Then he motioned at a chair and rather painfully returned to his seat. I sat down, and we both looked at one another. He had barely spoken, and I certainly was not going to say anything. This was *his* meeting.

"Who are you and what do you want from me?" he asked. The plaintiveness in his voice was completely foreign to his character.

"You know who I am, Senator," I responded quietly.

My calm seemed to agitate him. "Please," he pleaded, for likely the first time in his life to anyone, white or black, "I know your name, but who the hell are you really?"

I stared at him, puzzled. Perhaps the concussion he suffered was more serious than the media had been told.

The Senator shook his head. Still watching me, he said slowly, "I have driven that road a thousand times at high speed and never even came close to missing that bridge turn. Know it like my own driveway. Yesterday, suddenly," he pointed at me accusingly, "I couldn't see the road because your face filled my window."

I looked at him, amazed. "Are you feeling well, Senator?"

He ignored my question. "And as my car sank to the bottom, I could see you dressed in a radiant gold gown and repeating over and over in a voice that I could hear even under water, 'This is your chance! This is your chance! This is your chance!' "

I tried not to allow my shock to show. There were powers at work in this incident beyond the control of either of us. For a long time, the Senator said nothing. Then he almost whispered, "Lawyer Crenshaw, I'm a politician. It's my business to know how people will react in any given situation. My accident was not an accident, and your rescue was not a normal reaction either. Nothing in the Good Samaritan rule requires a passing motorist—and a woman at that!—to jump off a damn bridge to save someone she's never seen before."

"Senator," I replied, "what happened just happened. Why don't we both just forget it? Soon the media and your constituents will tire of the subject and go on to something else."

"I wish it was that easy, girl," the Senator's manners had deserted him, "but I don't think whatever caused me to run off the road'll let me just forget it. All last night, and even as I talk, a voice that sounds like yours is pounding in my head repeating over and over, 'This is your chance! This is your chance!' Meantime, every dirty trick I've ever played on black people keeps coming back. When you spoke just now, the voice in my head stopped for the first time since the crash. I'm convinced you folks have mastered some new technology that's causing my harassment, and I'm ready to make a deal. Just tell me what you want."

If ever a man was speaking honestly, he was. But his reputation made sympathy hard, trust impossible. "There is no technology, Senator. Surely, you did not bring me here to rescue you from voices."

Whatever scheme he had in mind, the look of desperation on his face seemed genuine. "Lawyer Crenshaw," he began again, his manners returning, "Mamie, the black lady who raised me, often used to warn me that 'the Lord don't like ugly.' The public thinks my losing control of my automobile was an accident, and your rescue is seen as a heroic act. Only you and I know what really happened. If all of this is not some electronic trickery, is the Lord trying to tell me old Mamie was right?"

"Well, Senator," I replied, mustering all my courtesy and control, "I can't speak for your Mamie, but the black people in this state would say that you waited a long time to get sensitive to what the Lord does and does not like."

It was likely the most direct statement anyone had made to him since he left Mamie. It was clear he did not like it. His face got some color in it for the first time, and he leaned forward, saying, "I don't need a lecture about my political career. I did what thousands of other politicians, North as well as South, have done to get ahead. White people are the majority in this country, and they basically distrust blacks, always have, likely always will. All I've done, like governors George Wallace of Alabama and Orval Faubus of Arkansas, and Mississippi senators James Eastland and Theodore Bilbo, is build on how white people feel about your race."

He caught himself, took a deep breath, and continued more calmly. "It's nothing personal against your people. Fact is, I developed my speaking style listening to records of black preachers. Figured if the Beatles and all those white groups could get rich singing like they was black, I could do the same with my stump speeches. Worked pretty well if I do say so myself."

"Senator," I interrupted, "I am fully aware of the secrets of your political success. I came to North Carolina to try and stop your latest anti–voting rights scheme, and should be out working on it right now unless you have something else you want to say."

"Lawyer," he said angrily, "I told you why I brought you here. Your damned voice is blasting through my head. I want it to stop, and I believe you know what I must do to get some quiet."

It was then that I remembered Faith Ann's perception of my rescue as an opportunity rather than another burden for black people.

He noticed the hint of a smile on my face. "I'm not surprised that you take pleasure in seeing me like this, but your people will get scant benefit from my downfall. There's a long line of others ready to take my place using the same 'nigger-baiting' techniques."

"I am sure you are right, Senator. I was thinking about a black-vote organizer, Faith Ann Courage, who predicted my saving you would create a serious obstacle to your political aims."

"That woman is one helluva fighter. If even one-tenth of your people fought as hard as she does, we whites couldn't get away with what we do to you, that's for sure."

"Perhaps, but you don't know Faith Ann. If one-tenth of blacks were like her, most of us might have been killed by whites who could not stand the threat of even that many truly militant black folks. As a matter of fact, Faith Ann urged me to ask you to switch political gears and support what she calls an 'ultimate voting rights' bill, actually a racial proportional-representation plan that would guarantee blacks a percentage of legislators equal to their percentage of the population."

"Does she want me to join the NAACP, too?" the Senator asked sarcastically.

"I doubt Faith Ann would accept your membership application, and I am certainly not here to help you save a career that has brought so much misery to black people, but if you think about it, Senator, you may discover that the measure Faith Ann believes will help blacks will help your constituency as well."

"Sort of a racial version of the view that what's good for General Motors is good for the nation?"

"A lot of whites have benefited from laws supposedly enacted to help blacks," I reminded him. "By the way, how are the voices?"

"You probably already know. When you started talking about that proportional representation nonsense, your voice booming in my head stopped entirely. What does it mean, Lawyer Crenshaw?"

"Well, Senator, Faith Ann would say it means that if you want permanent relief, you should give her plan some serious thought." I turned to leave.

"I hope, Lawyer Crenshaw," he said hastily, "I can count on you not to mention our talk."

"All I can say is, Senator," I replied, opening the door, "I try not to tell folks things they will not believe."

A week later, the Senator left the hospital and was driven directly to the delayed joint session of the state legislature. The circumstances of his accident and rescue seem not to have affected his hold on that body's members, most of whom were beholden to him for long lists of political favors rendered. So for reasons of either fraternal fidelity or political allegiance, they greeted him with a prolonged standing ovation.

"Damn!" Faith Ann said as we watched the televised proceedings. "You go and save the S.O.B.'s life, and the media, and all those hacks who need him to raise money for their campaigns, save his reputation. He's now so popular he can recommend we be returned to slavery, and those fools would have us back in chains before we could catch our breath."

For once, though, Faith Ann's political foresight was wrong. The Senator began his speech with a melodramatic account of how he had lost control of his car after it was filled with a heavenly light. The steering wheel was yanked from his hands by an "invisible force," and when the car went through the bridge rail, a booming voice told him that he must alter the course of his life as radically as his car's direction had been altered.

"I felt like Paul on the road to Damascus," the Senator intoned in a not-half-bad facsimile of the sermon styles of black preachers he had been copying for so many years. "As my car went under for the last time, the Lord showed me the light for the first time. My body sank with the car, but my soul was lifted up. Everyone watching feared I was dead—but I was being born again. My sins were forgiven and a heavenly voice spoke to me, repeating over and over, 'This is your chance! This is your chance!'

"Tonight, I begin my new career committed to helping white people gain an equal opportunity for heavenly salvation."

Shifting oratorical gears, the Senator spoke confidentially to his thoroughly stunned audience. "Now, my friends, you know where I've always stood on the race question. I don't hate black folks, but I have devoted my life to protecting the good white people of this great state by ensuring they got the priority on whatever was up for grabs. But in that great moment of underwater revelation, I realized it was the white people I was keeping down, while the blacks in their persecution were able to enjoy the heaven-on-earth satisfaction of suffering that comes to all those who labor under the lash of their fellow men."

I looked at Faith Ann. She seemed dazed, a condition she likely shared with the legislature and most of the national television audience. "Watch out!" she warned. "He's leading up to something." Here, she was clearly right.

"Sure," the Senator continued, "we can keep them from the polls today, just as our great grandparents did after Lincoln freed them over a century ago. They used the three Cs: the black codes to take away their citizenship rights, chicanery to take their lands and their labor, and coercion to take their lives if they complained too loud about the first two. We can do the same. But now as then, the blacks will keep strivin' to get up, and we will spend our days and nights schemin' how to keep them down.

"Read your history! Oppressors are always overcome by those they oppress. Eventually, the brutality of the oppression becomes the measure of the oppressor's destruction. We must not condemn our children to playin' keeper in the prison of racism where they will, like we do, spend their lives in spiritual chains of fear, guilt, and hate.

"Because I have seen the light," the Senator proclaimed, "I am withdrawing my reapportionment bill which would have made it almost impossible for black voters to elect one of their own. This act would have been challenged in the courts, and if its validity was upheld, black voters would continue to push for their right to vote and elect representatives of their choice. The racial turmoil in our great state would continue, our difficulties in attracting new business and investments would increase, and we would remain the whipping boy on racial matters for sections of this country with worse race relations than ours.

"As the voice told me, my friends, I am telling you that this is your chance to change, to bring peace and prosperity to all the citizens of this great state and avoid a fate that might send any of you spinnin' off the road of justice to drown in a river of racial bitterness."

"Well! Do tell!" Faith Ann exclaimed. "Diving off that bridge to save that fool may have done more good than I thought."

Usually at this point in one of the Senator's sermon-speeches, the audience would have been on its feet cheering, and the hall filled with applause—and the Senator paused, stepped back, and waited for the familiar sound. It did not come. The legislature seemed in collective shock, as though Ronald Reagan had joined the Communist party or the Pope had renounced the Church's celibacy strictures for the priesthood.

Ignoring the silence, the Senator pushed on. "Tomorrow morning, I will introduce what I consider the ultimate voting rights act, my No Taxation Without Representation Voter Bill. I have intentionally named my plan after the earliest battlecry of red-blooded Americans committed to fairness at all costs. My bill has two indivisible sections that will guarantee that the hope of our first patriots will live and thrive in every hamlet in our great state.

"First, I want to make sure that all our citizens, black and white, will be able to afford to get out on election day and cast their ballots for the candidates of their choice. But in the good ol' American way, I want to encourage the vote, not coerce it. So, under part I of my bill, every voter who casts a ballot in a primary or general election will receive a hundred-dollar state tax rebate to cover travel and other expenses. Those voters who pay no taxes will receive their voter travel costs in cash."

This time when the Senator paused, there was sustained, if tentative, applause. It was probably just as well that he made no mention of the provisions in his bill requiring candidates for public office to contribute one-half of their campaign contributions to a special Voter Travel Fund out of which voter rebates would be paid.

"Second," the Senator continued, "my No Taxation Without Representation Voter Bill ensures that all our citizens will have a fair chance to elect representatives of their choice. Let me explain part II of my bill by asking you a question: Why do people take the time and go to the effort to vote? The answer, of course, is to elect a candidate to represent their interests. Now, my friends"— and his voice fell to a conspiratorial whisper—"how has that process promoted the vote in this great southern state of ours? I'll tell you how: by encouraging the white majority to vote to keep whites in office and discouraging the black minority from even trying because they know they're outnumbered from the start.

"That, my friends"—his voice rising and arms outstretched "— may be majoritarian democracy, but it ain't fair and therefore it ain't American. It's nothing less than what our forefathers deplored: taxation without representation."

The audience was stunned into quiet. But Faith Ann was on her feet, clapping her hands. "That sure is the truth! Praise the Lord! He knows how to make even a devil tell the truth." She turned to me, laughing with joy, "Sister Geneva, what did you do to that so-and-so while you had him under the water?"

I shushed her. "He is not finished yet."

"Follow me now, friends," the Senator was admonishing his stunned audience. "Follow me! If the reason for voting is to elect representatives who will support your interests, how do you ensure a large minority does not get locked out and discouraged? Again, the answer is simple. You amend the voting laws so that the minority race is *guaranteed* to elect representatives of their choice in numbers equal to their portion of the population eligible to vote.

"So part II of my plan is called the Racial Proportionate Representation Bill. I intend it as my proudest legislative achievement, and it is my hope that it will win the support of our great citizenry for it will guarantee our black citizens their fair share of all elective legislative seats and provide the means for a fair rotation of executive positions up to and including the governorship of this state."

"Geneva!" Faith Ann cried out. "That damn man has stolen my plan for an ultimate voting rights act! Do you hear him? That's the same remedy I tried to get our civil rights lawyers to push for over the years. They always tell me it's too radical and would never be approved by the legislature or the courts."

"Our great state," the Senator was winding up, "is facing chaos and great economic loss, perhaps even bloodshed over the electoral processes that serve now, and have always served, either to keep our black citizens away from the polls or to frustrate their desire to elect their people to participate in the governance of this country. They are twenty-three percent of our population. They deserve that percentage of our elective offices. They may find that number insufficient, but we will have done that which by rights we should do. We can do no more. But, by God, we must do no less! Think on it, my white friends. This is *your* chance. Thank you and good night."

The smattering of applause, much of it from the few black and liberal white representatives, did not worry the Senator. He knew he controlled enough votes to gain passage of virtually any legislation he supported. He also knew that he would work hard to implement his No Taxation Without Representation Voter Bill. His conversion was real. White people, too, must be saved. The fact that he no longer heard my voice reverberating in his head was simply a welcome bonus.

UNCERTAIN what Geneva wanted of me, I observed that, while the Chronicle of the Ultimate Voting Rights Act had some interesting characters, its conclusion left something to be desired—a remark on which Geneva pounced.

"It is your legal and not your literary expertise I want," she said coolly. "I want your opinion on whether, if the Senator were to get the state legislature to enact his voting rights bill, it could survive a court challenge; and whether, if it passed constitutional scrutiny, it would serve as the ultimate voting rights act we were discussing—one that might motivate blacks to really participate in expectation of actually electing representatives of their choice."

"Well, Geneva, if you put at my disposal the supernatural powers on display in your Chronicle, then I can straighten out this country without a No Taxation Without Representation Voting Act."

"You could have fooled me!" she replied. "Your every comment since arriving here ascribes supernatural authority to the Constitution and your precious rule of law. I would not think you needed more power than that."

"You needn't be sarcastic, Geneva. The fact is that I would need supernatural help to force the established political powers to enact part I of the Senator's bill providing a hundred-dollar tax rebate or payment to every voter who casts a ballot. Constitutionally, however, it wouldn't be a problem; and practically, it would help get to the polls thousands of poor voters for whom registration and voting can be expensive, time consuming, and often traumatic."

"A good point!" Geneva agreed. "We in the middle class tend to forget that registration and voting for the poor or the working class often means a long trip to the courthouse—still an alien place for many—and perhaps the loss of two days' wages: first to get registered, and later to vote. Many voters are intimidated by voting procedures and hostile officials. And if the percentages of voters who actually vote are disappointing among the middle class because of apathy and the sense that voting is a worthless exercise, how much more deeply ingrained such feelings must be among those for whom putting food on the table and keeping a roof overhead is an ongoing, lifelong ordeal."

"Actually," I said, "the tax rebate might overcome the apathy of the large numbers of middle-class citizens who haven't darkened a voting booth for years. Of course, that's just supposition. What is virtually assured is the fierce opposition to such a measure by many politicians who fear they might not be able to control these new voters. Paradoxically, resistance would come even from legislators whose campaigns regularly spend the equivalent of one hundred dollars a vote to get them elected."

"But no constitutional problems?" Geneva asked again.

"As you know, in 1966, the Court struck down state poll taxes under a Fourteenth Amendment–based principle denying the state the right to dilute a citizen's vote on account of economic status and ability to pay a fee or failure to pay a fee.[1] Were a state to encourage voting by paying voters to compensate for expenses and inconvenience, that measure would be sustained."

"Bravo!" Geneva cheered. "May I count on your similarly enthusiastic support for part II of the Senator's bill, the Racial Proportional Representation Plan, guaranteeing blacks a proportion of the elective seats equal to their percentage of the population?"

"Well, while I welcome the chance to come in out of the cold of your criticism and bask in the unfamiliar warmth of your praise, part II of the Senator's plan poses both political and constitutional problems that may require powers of advocacy beyond either my ability——"

"Or your inclination." Geneva saw I was hedging.

"Before you return to your critical mode, Geneva, let's set the record straight. The use of designated seats to ensure minority-group representation is not an idea the Senator had to steal from Faith Ann Courage. But many civil rights advocates agree with the late Justice William O. Douglas that such schemes 'have no place in a society that honors the Lincoln tradition . . . [where] the individual is important, not his race, his creed, or his color.' "[2]

"You are ever the idealist," Geneva said, shaking her head in frustration. "Though you know the sorry history of black people and the ballot as well as I do, you persist in your fairy-tale beliefs so removed from reality they make the Chronicle I just told sound like a presentation of hard, verifiable fact.' "

As she talked, I reached up and pulled down the Supreme Court Reports volume with Justice Douglas's warning that separate racial constituencies, like those the British established along religious lines in colonial India, would be a divisive force in our country, and would emphasize differences between candidates and voters which are irrelevant in the constitutional sense. Finding the passage, I reminded Geneva that Justice Douglas conceded that race, like religion, plays an important role in the choices voters make at the polls; and warned that 'government has no business designing electoral districts along racial or religious lines.' "And listen to this," I said:

When racial or religious lines are drawn by the State, the multiracial, multireligious communities that our Constitution seeks to weld together as one become separatist; antagonisms that relate to race or to religion rather than to political issues are generated; communities seek not the best representative but the best racial or religious partisan. Since that system is at war with the democratic ideal, it should find no footing here.[3]

"If Justice Douglas is correct," I said, closing the volume, "then the proportional-representation remedy may increase the sense of racial difference and threat that underlie the historic resistance of white society to black voting and political power."

"That is hardly a criticism, friend. Many whites have seen as a threat every remedy intended to protect blacks against American racism from the Emancipation Proclamation on. Moreover, it is past time for us to stop basing our strategies on an assumption that whites will be fair. The whole history of black suffrage efforts belies any such faith. Consider the policy patterns from the beginning to the present day and then tell me we do not need proportional representation in this country:

• "In the periods before and after the Revolutionary War, 93 percent of the Northern free black population lived in states that excluded them completely or practically from the right to vote.[4] Only states with relatively few blacks—Massachusetts, New Hampshire, Vermont, and Maine—extended the franchise to blacks.

• "And during campaigns to eliminate voting qualifications to extend the ballot to all males, the loss of black voting rights was often the *quid pro quo* exacted by those opposed to universal suffrage before they would support unrestricted voting for white males.[5]

• "The Fourteenth Amendment was an insufficient mandate for most states that had barred blacks from voting. And despite the fact that ensuring the right of blacks to vote would guarantee Republican majorities for years to come, the idea of black suffrage was so unpopular that the Fifteenth Amendment was approved only because its ratification was demanded as a condition of readmittance for those few Southern states still out of the Union. New York rescinded its adoption of the amendment, and it was rejected outright by California, Delaware, Kentucky, Maryland, Oregon, and Tennessee.[6] Blacks were thus put on notice that when the political advantage to whites that was the amendment's real motivation came to an end, the amendment would not be enforced.

• "Legal scholars point to *Dred Scott* (1857) as the Supreme Court's most shameful decision, but Chief Justice Roger Taney's opinion finding that blacks were not included in the Constitution's definition of citizen, and striking down the politically wrought Missouri Compromise on the extension of slavery, was written without a clearly contrary mandate in the Constitution's text. But in terms of sheer outrageousness, *Dred Scott* pales beside the series of post-Reconstruction decisions in which the Court ignored the clear intentions of the Civil War amendments and condoned every practice including murder, all of which were openly used by Southerners to disfranchise blacks.[7] Regrettably, these cases are not much taught in law schools even though they offer a clear lesson in how Supreme Court decisions are influenced by the political environment.

• "Justice Oliver Wendell Holmes's opinion in a seldom-mentioned 1903 voting-rights case provided definitive proof that the Fifteenth Amendment was moribund. In denying relief to five thousand blacks who had sought to vote in Alabama, Holmes candidly acknowledged that if 'the great mass of the white population intends to keep the blacks from voting,' ordering them to be registered, as the petition requested, would be pointless because the order would be ignored at the local level. Holmes then proceeded to lecture the blacks that 'relief from a great political wrong, if done, as alleged, by the people of a State and the State itself, must be given by them or by the legislative and political department of the government of the United States.'[8]

• "And as for the hard-fought litigation beginning in the 1930s and culminating in the Voting Rights Act of 1965, one can credit the courage of blacks determined to vote, aided by the dedicated work of civil rights lawyers, for their persistence in invalidating every imaginable anti-black voting scheme from 'grandfather clauses' (exempting whites from stringent literacy tests if their forebears were voters at a time when blacks were slaves) to a myriad of white primary plans. Nevertheless we can conclude that the long campaign did little more than put whites to the task of designing newer, more subtle, but no less effective means of barring blacks from the polls or ensuring that their votes, once cast, would not much alter outcomes favoring the maintenance of white power in the political structure."

Geneva paused, out of breath, letting me get a word in. "I share your disappointment that our hopes of the 1960s have not all been realized, but it's a mistake not to place in the balance the millions of blacks who now are registered and do vote, and the presence of more than six thousand black elected officials. These real gains represent monumental progress when compared with the bleak and totally hostile era of the late nineteenth and early twentieth centuries. Problems remain, of course, but like the old black lady said, 'We ain't what we want to be, but thank God, we ain't what we was.' "

"I do not expect old black ladies to recognize that the so-called changes you boast of are more cosmetic than real, that increased black voting has not much increased political influence or provided representation even close to the percentage of our population. And most of the six thousand–odd black elected officials are mayors and city council members of small, mainly black communities. Those officeholders are welcome, God knows, but they hardly represent black power in politics.

"And spare me a recital of all the major cities that have elected black mayors. Even mayors of major cities are hardly in a position to do more than preside over, rather than relieve, the increasingly serious economic plight of the black masses in urban areas whose eroded economic bases have placed them on the verge of bankruptcy."

"Granting all that you've said, Geneva, I still see reason for a hopeful future. At the least, you must concede that our condition would be worse than it is without the black participation in politics that now exists. And Jesse Jackson's run for the presidency in 1984 proved that a charismatic candidate can both harness the black vote and win a surprising percentage of votes from whites able to see beyond the difference in a candidate's race to the similarity of their views and his on the important issues."

Ignoring my comment, Geneva asked: "Are you so opposed to the concept of proportional representation for blacks that you are willing to see black political power limited to electing blacks in mainly black areas and making a difference in the election of whites, most of whom then ignore black needs until the next election?"

"Don't be both melodramatic and unrealistic! The fact is, no one knows that continued effort won't result in our slow but eventual integration into the political system. We have already discussed and, I assume, agreed that civil rights efforts in the voting field have broadened constitutional coverage for all citizens."

"But what I am proposing now," Geneva insisted, "is a plan that might enable blacks to improve political coverage for themselves. More to the point, I think we should be able to do via legislation what the courts have done fairly frequently in granting relief for proven voting violations."

"They certainly don't call them proportional-representation remedies!" I countered.

"Come on, friend, would you turn down a Brooks Brothers suit because the label had been removed? Several courts have fashioned a proportional-representation remedy for proven violations of the Voting Rights Act, albeit without explicitly stating they were doing so.[9] And one of these courts was all but explicit, stating (as it remanded a court-approved redistricting plan because it provided inadequate assurances of minority political representation): 'There is simply no point in providing minorities with a "remedy" for the illegal deprivation of their representational rights in a form which will not in fact provide them with a realistic opportunity to elect a representative of their choice.' "[10]

I thought of the possible barrier to Geneva's hopes in a section which has come to be called the "Dole Compromise" in the 1982 amendments to the Voting Rights Act, and which provides "that nothing in this section establishes a right to have members of a protected class elected in numbers equal to their proportion in the population."[11] I was about to mention this obstacle, but Geneva anticipated me.

"Of course, I am aware of the Dole Compromise—but, in addition to not labeling their proportional-representation relief as such, courts have not specifically ordered this relief and have avoided potential roadblocks by requiring governmental entities found liable under the act to propose a remedy that will cure the statutory violation. Compliance with that direction usually leads officials to adopt on their own a proportional-representation plan."[12]

"A result," I interjected, "about which the Court's four most conservative members—Chief Justice Burger and Justices Powell, Rehnquist, and O'Connor—complained in 1986 while agreeing that the state of North Carolina had violated the Voting Rights Act by drafting legislative district lines so as to dilute the black vote.[13] A part of their concern was that a judicial direction to the state to create districts that maximize the black vote does not always guarantee that blacks will be able to elect representatives of their choice. Such districting also submerges the interests of black voters not residing in the majority black districts. Moreover, even the election of candidates responsive to black interests at best will have only a moderate impact in local elections and will usually be even less than that at the state legislative level."

"You forget," Geneva replied, "that the Senator's measure does not rely on the uncertainties of districting, but rather guarantees blacks a percentage of elective seats equal to their population percentage."

"I'm not at all sure that will avoid the problem. Consider a city with a three-member city council and a one-third black voting population. Under a multimember or at-large districting plan where all city residents vote for three candidates, there is little chance, particularly in the South, for a black to gain a seat. If, perhaps after a successful Voting Rights Act suit, a city is ordered to create single-member districts, it may comply by creating one mainly black district—although this arrangement may be resisted by blacks who prefer that their influence be spread more broadly.[14] But assuming the adoption of a 'safe black district,' the influence of the blacks' representative will be minimal, particularly about the many issues where the interests of voters diverge along racial lines. And that," I warned, "would also be the case under the Senator's Racial Proportional Representation Plan."

"Are you, then, suggesting that even if blacks were to overcome the many legal and political objections to the open adoption of proportional-representation plans, the improvements they would make in the ability of blacks to participate in the political process would be minimal?"

"Let me simply say that they would be far from an ultimate voting rights act. The reason, as you've been reminding me almost every minute since I arrived, is the caste-like status of blacks in the society: that is, the conditions in fact and in strongly held belief that together convince many whites that blacks as a class are somehow irreparably different from and less worthy than whites. This American mindset renders it impossible for blacks to participate in the political give-and-take with any real expectation that their basic goals can prevail."

"Are you saying that blacks can never profit from political participation?"

"Of course not. It's simply that their gains are almost always the gratuitous dividends of policies favored by a controlling white interest or group. When no such fortuitous arrangements are possible, blacks have found political participation quite difficult and unrewarding."

"Well, I'm pleasantly surprised to hear you take a more radical stance and lead me away from an optimistic posture influenced, I fear, by my friend Faith Ann Courage's enthusiasm for proportional-representation schemes."

"I certainly don't object to their use as relief mechanisms, Geneva, but they're not the representational millennium for black people who remain a minority in a still-hostile majoritarian society."

"Would you see more potential for black voting power if a state restructured all of its electoral districts along racial lines and in accordance with proportional-representation principles?"

"That brings us back to Justice Douglas's objection," I warned. "It would, I fear, worsen racial tensions because it distorts the political process in order to create targeted entities less likely to engage in the coalition building that is the hallmark of American politics. In 1977, Justice William Brennan, another liberal, expressed the same concern while approving the creation of a mainly black congressional district in Brooklyn."[15]

"Now, you are contradicting yourself," Geneva pointed out with ill-concealed irritation. "You just said that dominant white factions can and do ignore discrete and insular minorities."

"And that's true," I answered sharply, "but it is also a truth your irritation will not dissolve that guaranteeing some black representation through the creation of safe black districts constitutes a facsimile of a discrimination-free polity at a considerable cost to the fairness and integrity of the political process as it is viewed by those whose political power is diluted in this process."

"You seem caught up in theory," Geneva accused, "but *representation* as we define the term in this country is a distinctly practical notion. And, even on a theoretical plane, some scholars maintain that if 'one emphasizes political entitlements to vote as derived directly from notions of rights, whether individual or group, proportional representation becomes attractive, for it may well be the most rights-sensitive system of legislative selection available to us.' "[16]

"In theory, yes," I agreed, "but, as I see it at work in countries like Israel, proportioning political representation gives power to small splinter groups able to supply marginally essential votes far out of proportion to their numbers. It offers representation to lunatic fringe and hate groups of which, as you know, this country has more than its fair share. So, Geneva, while it sounds attractive and may have value in remedying the effects of past racial discrimination, as a solution or, as the Senator put it, as an ultimate voting rights act, I fear it would create a political structure that would make the maintenance of other central constitutional values difficult and perhaps impossible."

"As I recall," Geneva mused, "the Framers were afraid of majoritarian government; and in the *Federalist Papers*, James Madison urged a large, diverse electorate composed of many factions as the best defense against majority tyranny[17]—a persuasive approach if coalition building occurs freely across racial lines, but when blacks are consistently excluded from the coalition-building process, 'the ostensible protection against majority tyranny provided by Madison's theory becomes strained.'[18] So—if the coalition-building aspect of the current electoral system doesn't work for blacks and if, as you maintain, proportional representation would not be a better scheme—what kind of voting rights law would you recommend?"

"All things considered, I think blacks should keep up their pressures for enforcement of the existing Voting Rights Act; and, despite all the disadvantages, we should work harder to get our folks registered and out to vote on election day. Again, it'll be difficult, but there are no shortcuts in the struggle to overcome resistance to blacks voting and exercising political power."

"I swear, friend," Geneva said, more as diagnosis than as criticism, "given the dimension of those disadvantages, your refusal to face the facts borders on the idiotic."

"It's a matter of perspective. To those Africans who jumped from the slave ships to death in the shark-filled seas, those who failed to join them must have seemed idiotic. And yet, but for their idiotic 'refusal to face the facts,' we would not be here now."

"Now who is melodramatic? The facts are that the reapportionment cases tie the constitutional standard for review to the traditional American idea of representation by geographic location—an idea acquired at a time when real property was the basis of power, and governmental councils had to be responsive to landed interests.[19] But, contrary to Justice Douglas's assumption, geographic apportionment is not a prerequisite of representative government. John Stuart Mill once complained:

> I cannot see why the feelings and interests which arrange mankind according to localities should be the only ones thought worthy of being represented; or why people who have other feelings and interests, which they value more than they do their geographical ones, should be restricted to these as the sole principle of their political classification."[20]

"Well," I responded, "there's no indication in that quotation that Mill was thinking about districts based on race. So—even if through savvy political leadership and the chance to make one hundred bucks for voting as in the Senator's plan, a racial proportionate plan was enacted—it would hardly survive a judicial challenge given all the language in civil rights decisions speaking of the Court's abhorrence of racial classifications in the voting area."

"I am familiar with many of those cases, and each addressed an effort by whites to bar or limit black voting. The decisions and their language would seem distinguishable on that basis. Why would not the Senator's plan constitute a voluntary affirmative-action policy, voluntarily adopted by the state to address the effects of long years of discrimination against blacks in the electoral process?"

"Designating it an affirmative-action plan in the current racial climate, Geneva, isn't likely to help you win either political acceptance or judicial approval."

"You keep telling me why it cannot be placed in effect and I am more interested in whether, if implemented, it would work as Faith Ann Courage thinks it would."

"I see no reason to speculate about the impossible."

Noting my growing irritation, Geneva suggested we take a break. She went to the kitchen and returned a few minutes later with a tray that reminded me—not wholly with pleasure—that she had been a devotee of natural foods long before they were fashionable. But, having skipped breakfast that morning, I was ready to eat almost anything I could identify on the tray—which was not much.

Suddenly my tolerance began to slip and, despite my past fondness for Geneva, I began to regret my decision to come.

Turning off my tape recorder, I said, "Instructive as it always is, Geneva, to discuss racial issues with you, it's clear that our views differ a great deal, and I doubt my comments on your Chronicles are of help. So, unless you tell me what absolutely requires my presence, I really should start back."

"You misunderstand," Geneva said seriously. "I asked you to trust me, but I never said that I would not tell you why I invited you here. The question is whether you really want to know. The decision is yours. If you want to know, I will tell you."

Geneva stopped eating, pushed her chair back from the table, and looked at me with great kindness and even greater intensity. I felt a sense of foreboding, but could hardly back out now. With as much vigor as I could muster, I said, "Having come this far, I'm quite ready to share whatever trouble you're facing."

"Very well," and Geneva relaxed for the first time since I arrived. "I was never very good at secrets anyhow, and they did not order me not to tell you."

Suddenly, on what had been a beautiful fall day, the room felt warm and stuffy. I swallowed uneasily. "Who are *they*?"

"The members of the Curia, of course. I did not tell you the end of the Chronicle. After completing their agenda, the two Curia Sisters requested me to stay after the audience departed. They told me that they had proposed the Conservative Crusader role simply so that I could get to know them, and so the audience—the Curia Sisters called them the Chorus—could become acquainted with me. They said that the empty chair between them was reserved for me, and they felt that, upon taking it, I would resolve the long-standing dispute on reform strategies that divide them and dilute their powers.

"Right then, I understood the strange nature of the illness that had befuddled my doctors. During my effort to recover, I felt myself fighting, like the Senator, a great pressure to surrender to some strong force. Intermittently the pressure would diminish, and I would experience one of the Chronicles I am sharing with you. Fighting the pressure and living through the stories required all my strength, leaving me unable to communicate with anyone—a state the doctors interpreted as either coma or brain damage.

"The Curia members chided me for being neither a revolutionary ready to commit violence for my beliefs nor a traditional civil rights lawyer committed to legal outcomes no matter what. As one of them, they promised I would have real power to effect racial reform. Finally, I admitted that their offer was challenging, and agreed to accept on condition that I could return here and discuss the Chronicles with someone able to help me puzzle out their significance and perhaps evolve a new vision for achieving racial justice—one that would not rely on violent revolution nor require a black exodus.

"I thought of all the civil rights lawyers I had known and worked with, and came up with you."

"And now," I suggested, "you must regret your choice."

"Not at all," she said quickly. "Of course, when I selected you, I did not know that you had left civil rights work and become a law teacher. Your interpretations clearly are different from mine, but discussing those differences helps me clarify my views and also provides a firmer basis for the policy I hope to evolve as an alternative to those urged by the Curia members."

Whatever my doubts, it was clear that she was deadly serious about all she was telling me. I wondered whether I was being helpful by simply going along with her delusions. "Geneva, this is all quite——" I caught myself, feeling the awkwardness that comes when I am in the presence of a person who is detached from the reality I know. It pained me that this could happen to Geneva. I tried to speak firmly. "You're talking as though all of this really happened. It didn't. It was something you envisioned during your illness."

"The Curia was right," she said, "in warning me that Western peoples simply reject anything not explicable in scientific terms. But, for me, friend"—Geneva spoke slowly, emphasizing every syllable—"it was neither vision nor dream, and no more fantasy than some of the beliefs that you have said you hold."

When I offered no response, she continued. "In our years together at the Legal Defense Fund, I remember you were more committed to our cause than to any dogma regarding how we might best achieve our goals. Now I hope you will stay and hear the other Chronicles. I am sorry to be so argumentative, but I honestly believe the fate of our people may depend on what comes out of our discussions."

Leaving now was unthinkable. I unpacked my papers and turned my tape recorder back on. "Why don't we get started with the next Chronicle?" I reached over and touched her hand. "I'll do what I can," I promised.

Chapter 4

Neither Separate Schools Nor Mixed Schools

The Chronicle of the Sacrificed Black Schoolchildren

ALL THE BLACK school-age children were gone. They had simply disappeared.

No one in authority could tell the frantic parents more than they already knew. It had been one of those early September days that retain the warmth of summer after shedding that season's oppressive humidity. Prodded perhaps by the moderate weather, the pall of hateful racial invective that had enveloped the long desegregation battle lifted on what was to be the first day of a new school year. It was as well implementation day for the new desegregation plan, the result of prolonged, court-supervised negotiations. Plaintiffs' lawyers had insisted on what one called a "full measure" of racial balance, while the school board and the white community resisted, often bitterly, every departure from the previous school structure.

Now it seemed all for nothing. The black students, every one of them, had vanished on the way to school. Children who had left home on foot never appeared. Buses that had pulled away from their last stop loaded with black children had arrived at schools empty, as had the cars driven by parents or car pools. Even parents taking young children by the hand for their first day in kindergarten, or in pre-school, had looked down and found their hands empty, the children suddenly gone.

You can imagine the response. The media barrage, the parents' anger and grief, the suspects arrested and released, politicians' demands for action, analysts' assessments, and then the inevitably receding hullabaloo. Predictable statements were made, predictable actions taken, but there were no answers, no leads, no black children.

Give them credit. At first, the white people, both in town and around the country, were generous in their support and sincere in the sympathy they extended to the black parents. It was some time before there was any public mention of what, early on, many had whispered privately: that while the loss was tragic, perhaps it was all for the best. Except in scruffy white neighborhoods, these "all for the best" rationales were never downgraded to "good riddance."

Eventually they might have been. After all, statistics showed the life chances for most of the poor children were not bright. School dropouts at an early age; no skills; no jobs; too early parenthood; too much exposure to crime, alcohol, drugs. And the city had resisted meaningful school desegregation for so long that it was now possible to learn from the experience of other districts that integrating the schools would not automatically insulate poor black children from the risks of ghetto life.

Even after delaying school desegregation for several years, the decision to proceed this fall with the now-unneeded plan had been bitterly opposed by many white parents who feared that "their schools" would have to have a 50 percent enrollment of black children to enable the school system to achieve an equal racial balance, the primary goal of the desegregation plan and its civil rights sponsors. So high a percentage of black children, these parents claimed, would destroy academic standards, generate discipline problems, and place white children in physical danger. But under all the specifics lay the resentment and sense of lost status. Their schools would no longer be mainly white—a racial status whites equated with school quality, even when the schools were far from academically impressive.

Black parents had differed about the value of sending their children to what had been considered white schools. Few of these parents were happy that their children were scheduled, under the desegregation plan, to do most of the bus riding—often to schools located substantial distances from their homes. Some parents felt that it was the only way to secure a quality education because whites would never give black schools a fair share of school funds, and as some black parents observed: "Green follows white."

Other black parents, particularly those whose children were enrolled in the W. E. B. DuBois School—an all-black, outstanding educational facility with a national reputation—were unhappy. DuBois's parents had intervened in the suit to oppose the desegregation plan as it applied to their school. Their petition read:

> This school is the fruit of our frustration. It is as well a monument of love for our children. Our persistence built the DuBois School over the system's opposition. It is a harbor of learning for our children, and a model of black excellence for the nation. We urge that our school be emulated and not emasculated. The admission of whites will alter and undermine the fragile balance that enables the effective schooling black children need to survive societal hostility.
>
> We want our children to attend the DuBois School. Coercing their attendance at so-called desegregated schools will deny, not ensure, their right to an equal educational opportunity. The board cannot remedy the wrongs done in the past by an assignment policy that is a constitutional evil no less harmful than requiring black children to attend segregated schools. The remedy for inferior black schools sought by others from the courts we have achieved for ourselves. Do not take away our educational victory and leave us "rights" we neither need nor want.

The DuBois School's petition was opposed by the school board and plaintiffs' civil rights lawyers, and denied by the district court. Under the desegregation plan, two-thirds of the DuBois students were to be transferred to white schools located at the end of long bus rides, to be replaced by white children whose parents volunteered to enroll them in an outstanding school.

In fact, DuBois School patrons were more fortunate than many parents whose children were enrolled in black schools that were slowly improving but lacked the DuBois School's showy academic performance. Most of these schools were slated for closure or conversion into warehouses or other administrative use. Under a variety of rationales, the board failed to reassign any of the principals of the closed black schools to similar positions in integrated schools.

Schools in white areas that would have been closed because of declining enrollment gained a reprieve under the school-desegregation plan. The older schools were extensively rehabilitated, and the school board obtained approval for several new schools, all to be built in mainly white areas—the board said—the better to ensure that they would remain academically stable and racially integrated.

Then, in the wake of the black students' disappearance, came a new shock. The public school superintendent called a special press conference to make the announcement. More than 55 percent of the public school population had been black students, and because state funding of the schools was based on average daily attendance figures, the school system faced a serious deficit during the current year.

There were, the superintendent explained, several additional components to the system's financial crisis:

Teacher Salaries. Insisting that desegregation would bring special stresses and strains, the teacher's union had won substantial pay raises, as well as expensive in-service training programs. A whole corps of teacher aides had been hired and trained to assist school faculties with their administrative chores. Many newly hired teachers and all the aides would have to be released.

School Buses. To enable transportation of students required by the desegregation plan, the board had ordered one hundred buses and hired an equal number of new drivers. The buses, the superintendent reported, could be returned. Many had made only one trip; but the new drivers, mechanics, service personnel, and many of the existing drivers would have to be laid off.

School Construction.   Contracts for rehabilitation of old schools and for planning and building new schools had placed the board millions of dollars in debt. The superintendent said that hundreds of otherwise idle construction workers were to have been employed, as well as architectural firms and landscape designers. Additional millions had been earmarked for equipment and furniture suppliers, book publishers, and curriculum specialists. Some of these contracts could be canceled but not without substantial damage to the local economy.

Lost Federal Funds.   After desegregation had been ordered by the courts, the board applied for and received commitments for several million dollars in federal desegregation funds. These grants were now canceled.

Lost State Funds.   Under the court order, the state was obligated to subsidize costs of desegregation; and, the superintendent admitted, these appropriations, as well as the federal grants, had been designated to do "double duty": that is, while furthering school-desegregation efforts, the money would also improve the quality of education throughout the system by hiring both sufficient new teachers to lower the teacher-pupil ratio, and guidance counselors and other advisory personnel.

Tax Rates.   Conceding that the board had won several increases in local tax rates during the desegregation process, the superintendent warned that, unless approval was obtained for a doubling of the current rate, the public schools would not survive.

Annexations.   Over the last several years, the city had annexed several unincorporated areas in order to bring hundreds of additional white students into the public school system and slow the steady increase in the percentage of black students. Now the costs of serving these students added greatly to the financially strapped system.

Attorney Fees.   Civil rights attorneys had come under heavy criticism after it was announced that the court had awarded them $300,000 in attorney fees for their handling of the case, stretching back over the prior five years. Now the superintendent conceded that the board had paid a local law firm over $2,000,000 for defending the board in court for the same period.

Following the school superintendent's sobering statement, the mayor met with city officials and prepared an equally lengthy list of economic gains that would have taken place had the school-desegregation order gone into effect. The president of the local chamber of commerce did the same. The message was clear. While the desegregation debate had focused on whether black children would benefit from busing and attendance at racially balanced schools, the figures put beyond dispute the fact that virtually every white person in the city would benefit directly or indirectly from the desegregation plan that most had opposed.

Armed with this information, a large sum was appropriated to conduct a massive search for the missing black children. For a time, hopes were raised, but eventually the search was abandoned. The children were never found, their abductors never apprehended. Gradually, all in the community came to realize the tragedy's lamentable lesson. In the monumental school desegregation struggle, the intended beneficiaries had been forgotten long before they were lost.

A MOST disturbing story, Geneva! Symbolically, the sacrificed black children in the Chronicle represent literally thousands like themselves who are the casualties of desegregation, their schooling irreparably damaged even though they themselves did not dramatically disappear. It certainly calls into question the real beneficiaries in the thousands of school-desegregation cases that the former Legal Defense Fund director, Jack Greenberg, aptly called the 'trench warfare' of the civil rights movement."

"Why are you taking it so hard?" Geneva asked. "In our discussion following the Chronicle of the Celestial Curia, you cited both Lewis Steel, the civil rights lawyer, and Professor Arthur S. Miller for arguing that the Supreme Court's decision in *Brown* v. *Board of Education* should be seen as furthering the nation's foreign and domestic interests far more than it helped black people gain the critically important citizenship right to equal educational opportunity. In fact, you noted that both the NAACP and the federal government briefs argued the value of ending constitutionally supported racial segregation in our competition with communist governments" (see pages 60–62).

"That's true," I admitted, "but——"

"But what?" Geneva interrupted. "If your self-interest approach is a valid explanation for the change in constitutional interpretation—as you and others insist on viewing the *Brown* decision—then why wouldn't the same self-interest have to be present before that decision could be implemented?"

"I'm not sure many people lacking the intellectual insight of a W. E. B. DuBois recognized the factor of self-interest in the first several years after the *Brown* decision," I replied. "Moreover, the early problem, as I remember it, was that resistance to desegregation was so fierce and came from so many directions that any progress we made in overcoming it was simply accepted as a victory without much thought of *how* we—always the understaffed, underfinanced underdogs—had prevailed. We knew we were in the right, that God was on our side, and all of that, but while we spoke and thought in an atmosphere of 'rights and justice,' our opponents had their eyes on the economic benefits and power relationships all the time. And that difference in priorities meant that the price of black progress was benefits to the other side, benefits that tokenized our gains and sometimes strengthened the relative advantages whites held over us."

"And that," said Geneva, "is precisely the Chronicle's message."

"Indeed," I said, "the Chronicle portrays in dramatic terms the thesis of Daniel Monti's *A Semblance of Justice*, which reviews the long history of school desegregation in St. Louis. Professor Monti reports that St. Louis school officials staunchly resisted any liability for segregation in their schools. Then, after court orders were finally entered, the same individuals utilized school-desegregation mandates to achieve educational reforms, including magnet schools, increased funding for training, teacher salaries, research and development, and new school construction."[1]

"Amazing! And probably at the same time, they were calling the civil rights people everything but a child of God."

"Probably," I agreed, "but according to Monti, school officials accomplished all of these gains for the system without giving more than secondary priority to redressing the grievances of blacks. This did not seem to bother the officials who candidly told him that the only sensible way to deliver educational resources to the metropolitan area of St. Louis was through a metropolitan school system, and they also used desegregation to accomplish that end."

"Would Professor Monti be able to build a similar case of school-desegregation benefit for the system rather than for the blacks in other school districts?" Geneva asked.

"I'm afraid he could. Moreover, Monti's book explains how school officials used the school-desegregation controversy to increase their legitimacy as the proper policy-making location for public education—an accomplishment furthered by the fact that civil rights lawyers did not call for the abandonment of the school board, even though it and its predecessors in office were responsible for the discriminatory policies attacked in the courts."

"That is certainly an accurate statement, but I doubt that it is fair," Geneva said. "School boards do not make policy as much as reflect in their policies the wishes of those in their constituencies whom they really represent. The society was willing, albeit reluctantly, to drop school-segregation policies after *Brown*. But that decision did not require nor did the public want to dismantle the structure of public school systems. Even when courts placed absolutely recalcitrant school systems into a form of judicial receivership,[2] there was criticism that the courts had gone too far."

"A real catch-22 that made every step painful," I recalled. "When districts finally admitted more than a token number of black students to previously white schools, the action usually resulted in closing black schools, dismissing black teachers, and demoting (and often degrading) black principals. There was some effort to stem this practice via litigation,[3] but our main emphasis was on desegregating the schools. Black faculty, in all too many cases, became victims of that desegregation."

"I gather," Geneva commented, "that the desegregated schools did not provide educational compensation to black children for the involuntary loss of their former teachers and schools."

"It was tough, though for a long time we kept pointing to the strong kids who made it rather than to all those who did poorly or dropped out of school. But in the early days, the experience, even when there was little overt hostility, was much as reported in Ray Rist's *The Invisible Children* (1978). Rist, a social scientist, followed every day for a full school year a group of young black children bused to an upper-class, mainly white school.[4] The principal's policy was to 'treat all the kids just alike.' This evenhanded policy meant—in practice—that the handful of black children from the ghetto were expected to perform and behave no differently than did the white children from comfortable suburbs in this mainly white school where the curriculum, texts, and teaching approaches were designed for the middle-class white kids. As you can imagine, the results of this evenhanded integration were disastrous."

"Do you think," Geneva asked, "that we could have avoided some of the tragedy if educators had been more involved in planning the litigation that led to *Brown*?"

"That's what our former associate Robert L. Carter, who played a major role in planning school-desegregation strategy, seems to think. I'm happy to report that, unlike many of our old colleagues who read any criticism of desegregation strategy as a personal attack, Bob Carter, now a federal judge, has remained objective about his role. In a thoughtful article, he wrote that, if he were preparing *Brown* today, 'instead of looking principally to the social scientists to demonstrate the adverse consequences of segregation, [he] would seek to recruit educators to formulate a concrete definition of the meaning of equality in education.' "[5]

"Interesting—but how did he intend to use the definition effectively?"

"Carter said that he would have based his argument on that definition, and tried 'to persuade the Court that equal education in its constitutional dimensions must, at the very least, conform to the contours of equal education as defined by the educators.' "[6]

"Perhaps," Geneva said, "Carter's approach would have enabled us to avoid some of the pitfalls, but it is lawyer's conceit to think that one tactical approach rather than another will over-come society's strong resistance to a particular racial reform as opposed to gaining a favorable outcome in a case."

I smiled. "Knowing Bob Carter as well as we both do, I'd love to hear his response to your observation."

"Don't misunderstand me. Judge Carter's point is well taken. We civil rights lawyers attacked segregation in the public schools because it was the weak link in the 'separate but equal' chain. Our attack worked. But to equate integration with the effective education black children need—well, that was a mistake."

"Again, Geneva," I said, with some annoyance, "that's easy for you to say—but remember how many devices school boards and their lawyers worked out to convey the sense of compliance with *Brown*, while in fact the schools remained segregated. 'Pupil as-signment plans' (requiring black parents to run an administrative gauntlet of forms and requirements),[7] 'grade-a-year' plans (which maintained the pace of desegregation at a glacial rate),[8] 'freedom-of-choice' plans (which relied on community pressures and coer-cion to limit the number of blacks who dared choose white schools),[9] and on and on. Unraveling the seemingly neutral proce-dures contained in these plans to get at their segregation-maintaining intent proved a challenge for both civil rights lawyers and for many federal judges who were ostracized and abused for carrying out the *Brown* mandate."[10]

"I remember how difficult it was," Geneva acknowledged, "but, for the life of me, I can't understand how you allowed school-board resistance to trap you into relying on racial balance as the only acceptable remedy for segregated schools. If you ask me, it was the civil rights' lawyers' personal commitment to racial integration that trapped them into a strategy that could not succeed."

"Criticism based on hindsight is easy," I said heatedly, "but what would you, Geneva, had you been around, have recom-mended as an alternative strategy?"

"I see that, unlike your friend and mentor, Judge Carter, you are a bit sensitive about criticism of your legal tactics. Or," she added, with a wry smile, "is your apparent anger really advocacy at work?"

"I'll ignore that, Ms. Know-it-all," I sputtered. "But let's assume that, instead of refusing to clarify its mandate to desegregate the public schools 'with all deliberate speed'[11]—a refusal that, in effect, gave the South ten years of delay—the Supreme Court in 1955, in addition to sensing the strong opposition to desegregation, had recognized that the separation of students by race was actually not an end in itself but a convenient means of perpetuating the primary aim: the dominance of whites over blacks in every important aspect of life."

"Fine!" Geneva said, "but where would they have gained that insight? Probably not from most of you who were convinced that, once we got the damned Jim Crow signs removed, the racial-integration millennium would roll in with the next tide."

"Please stop rubbing it in! We did what we felt was right at the time, and I haven't heard of an alternative that had a better chance of success, given the hostility of the climate."

"Well, I don't agree that a better desegregation policy was beyond the reach of intelligent people whose minds were not clogged with integrationist dreams. For example—if we recognize that the real motivation for segregation was white domination of public education—suppose the Court had issued the following orders:

"1. Even though we encourage voluntary desegregation, we will not order racially integrated assignments of students or staff for ten years.

"2. Even though 'separate but equal' no longer meets the constitutional equal-protection standard, we will require immediate equalization of all facilities and resources.

"3. Blacks must be represented on school boards and other policy-making bodies in proportions equal to those of black students in each school district.

"The third point would have been intended to give blacks meaningful access to decision making—a prerequisite to full equality still unattained in many predominantly black school systems. For example, an 'equal representation' rule might have helped protect the thousands of black teachers and principals who were dismissed by school systems during the desegregation process."

"In other words," I asked, "under this 'educational policy' approach, the courts would have given priority to desegregating not the students but the money and the control?"

"Exactly. And rather than beat our heads against the wall seeking pupil-desegregation orders the courts were unwilling to enter or enforce, we could have organized parents and communities to ensure effective implementation for the equal-funding and equal-representation mandates."

"How can you be sure that black parents—as well as some of their integration-crazed lawyers—would not have become demoralized by the ten-year delay and simply done nothing until the courts were willing to take direct action on pupil desegregation?"

"The proof," Geneva answered quickly, "is in the number of black schools like DuBois in the Chronicle where neither personnel nor parents have accepted the argument that black schools must be inferior. Even in the pre-*Brown* era, some black educators, without equal resources and with whites controlling school-board policy, managed to create learning environments that encouraged excellence, motivated ambition, and taught the skills and self-assurance that have produced scores of successful blacks in business and the professions.[12] The educational sociologist Professor Sara Lightfoot, in her *The Good High School*, provides an impressive report of an all-black high school in Atlanta, Georgia— George Washington Carver—and the policies that enabled it to gain a reputation for academic quality."[13]

"It does happen," I conceded, "but good schools in a hostile environment are always fragile, subject to constant stress and continuing challenge. Look what happened to the DuBois School in the Chronicle. Despite the fact that it was effective and the pride of the black community, and that blacks wanted to send their children to its schools, it was sacrificed to school desegregation."

"By the way," Geneva asked, somewhat sarcastically, "had you been the judge in the Sacrificed Black Schoolchildren Chronicle, how would you have ruled on the DuBois School parents' petition?"

"It was a moving petition, I will admit, but——"

Geneva was on her feet. "Oh no you don't! You are not going to sit there and tell me that you would have denied their petition, disavowed the justice of their cause, and dismissed their claim?"

"The problem," I observed in my most measured tones, "is that you black women get so emotionally involved in tactical matters that you fail to see that some must pay a price so that all may advance"—and then I ducked as Geneva rose with a vase in her hand.

But then she smiled and placed it back on the table. "Thought you would taunt me into forgetting my question, did you? *Black woman, emotional*—my foot! Now, Mr. Professor, I am waiting for your answer. What about the black parents' petition to save the DuBois School?"

"I'm shocked," I said in mock horror, "that you'd ever resort to violence over a simple jest and even think I'd resort to trickery to evade an answer on so important a question. A question of that magnitude would require a court, particularly a district court, to check the case law carefully for binding precedents. And, in fact, the DuBois School situation is much like the facts in a case brought by black parents in Chicago whose children had been assigned by lottery away from their integrated neighborhood schools because the percentage of nonwhites in those schools exceeded 60 percent, a figure the board feared would trigger white flight."[14]

"Surely, the district court told the board to amend its plan to reflect better the wishes of the black parents?"

"I'm afraid not. The court did insist that the schools to which the black children were assigned be integrated, and then approved the amended plan. And let me hasten to add that other courts facing similar issues have reached similar results.[15] So, you see, if the issues in the Chronicle suit are viewed primarily from a doctrinal viewpoint, it is a difficult case."

Geneva sighed. "It sounds like you want to play law professor rather than judge. Can you justify the Chicago decision in the next few minutes?"

"It shouldn't be hard. The board's lottery scheme involves an obvious racial classification. That is, when the percentage of non-whites reaches 60 percent, the number of students—selected by race—exceeding that percentage will be selected by lottery for assignment to other integrated schools farther from their homes. Ordinarily, racial classifications of that type are deemed by courts inherently 'suspect' and can survive judicial scrutiny only if justified by a 'compelling state interest' and if there's a close connection or 'fit' between the classification and the compelling interest to be served."

"And," Geneva anticipated me, "the Chicago school board maintained that stable racial integration is the compelling state interest and that the lottery plan is closely tailored to achieve that interest with the least possible harm."

"Well, they will use that argument if their primary argument is rejected. Basically, they'll contend that their lottery plan involves a benign racial classification. Since race is being used to further an appropriate goal—integrated schools—only an intermediate level of scrutiny is required."

"What is benign about excluding students from the schools they want to attend solely on the basis of their race?"

"The board might respond, 'Look, Miss, you civil rights types got us into this school-desegregation business. Now we've looked at the "white flight" studies, and if we do nothing to change the balance of these schools, they'll soon be all black, and you folks will be back in court screaming that the board allowed the schools to become all black. We don't want that to happen, but we can't force whites to go to the public schools. So, as the percentage of nonwhites increases, we must reassign some of the black kids. Do you have a better plan?' "

"I doubt," said Geneva, "that any court would base its approval on grounds that the society's racism required them to withhold a group's rights."

"I wouldn't bet any serious money on that doubt. One court wrote: 'Although white fears about the admission of minority students are ugly, those fears cannot be disregarded without imperiling integration across the entire system. . . . The exodus of white children from the public schools would disadvantage the entire minority community and nullify this voluntary desegregation effort.' "[16]

"And would you feel bound by these decisions?"

"Given your likely reaction, I hesitate to say this, but I think both courts reached the only decision they could for the reason pointed out in the decision I just quoted. While my sympathies are with the black parents, the school board plans are the only way to maintain racial balance."

"That, of course," Geneva chided, "is precisely the problem with equating the 'equal educational opportunity' right established in the *Brown* decision with racial balance. The racial-balance goal can be met only in schools where whites are in a majority and retain control. The quality of schooling black children receive is determined by what whites (they of the group who caused the harm in the first place) are willing to provide—which, as we should not be surprised to learn, is not very much."

"And you, Geneva? Let's just suppose that you were on the bench, sitting there without the vaunted power of your Curia friends, and with all the restraints of legal doctrine that bind a judge. How would you rule on the DuBois School parents' petition?"

Geneva's eyes flashed. "I cannot imagine anyone offering me or my accepting a judgeship, but were I somehow to find myself up there in a black robe instead of a Curia gold one, I sure as hell would not dismiss their petition out of hand, either because there was precedent for such action or because both the plaintiffs and the defendants urged me to do it. In fact, a petition like that filed by both a sizable and an articulate portion of the plaintiff class should put any judge on notice that the plaintiffs' class-action suit does not represent all the plaintiffs."

"In defense of the judge," I interjected, "these petitions by portions of the class do not come to light until long after the suit is filed and at a time when formal intervention would be both difficult and unfair to the parties."

"If I were the judge, I would hope to employ either judicial imagination or some good old mother wit in the situation."

"Such as?"

"Such as calling for testimony from the petitioners and perhaps holding a nonbinding referendum in the affected community regarding the plan."

"I fear you'd expose yourself to criticism for turning the judicial process into a popularity contest."

"I would not be afraid of criticism, and I think black parents—and likely some white parents as well—would welcome an opportunity to engage in a discussion that has been taken over by the lawyers weighing inappropriate legal standards to reach unjust results."

"You're a tough woman!"

"I assume that *tough* is intended as a grudging compliment and not as a synonym for *evil*, which I would take as an affront. Howsomever," she continued, smiling at her "down home" expression, "my action would not be a precedent. As you know—but likely do not approve—several courts have become more sensitive over time to the fact that the plaintiffs' class in school desegregation is not a monolith, particularly on the issue of relief. Moreover, a few courts have come to recognize both the importance of the educational potential in desegregation remedies, and the fact that racial balance is not synonymous with, and may be antithetical to, effective education for black children. As a result of their tardy but still welcome awakening, a few courts have responded to black parents' preference for relief intended to make the schools more educationally effective rather than simply more racially balanced."[17]

"It's unwise," I cautioned, "to read those decisions for more than they're worth."

"Spoken like the law teacher you are!" Geneva replied, in friendly disdain. "You tell me how I should 'read' the 1981 *Dallas* school-case decision rejecting a civil rights request that a mainly black subdivision of the district be broken up in order to maximize desegregation with neighboring subdistricts that were mainly white.[18] The black subdistrict, like the DuBois School parents, intervened in the case and put on testimony that convinced the district court of the wide difference of opinion within the minority community on the issue of relief.[19] Based on that testimony, the court observed: 'Minorities have begun to question whether busing is "educationally advantageous, irrelevant, or even disadvantageous." ' To illustrate his concern, the judge's lengthy opinion referred to what I consider a classic statement by the school-board president, one of three minorities on the board, who had said:

117

I don't think that additional busing is even the issue. . . . It has never been the issue. . . . The issue is whether we are going to educate the children and youth. . . . I think that the whole question around the whole busing issue just loses sight of why we are here and what the schools are about now. I think it was a noble idea in 1954 . . . but what I envisioned and I'm sure what other black parents envisioned in 1954 just never happened.[20]

"The witness could extend that comment to cover virtually every aspect of civil rights," Geneva added. "Now, given our general agreement that the Chronicle's message is tragic, how can we use its insight to formulate more effective civil rights strategies in the future?"

"Well, Geneva, my feeling is that while whites continue to use their power to allocate to themselves the best educational resources, and to honor our pleas for justice only when there is further profit for the system, it will be difficult to gain more than limited benefits—whether in racial balance or in improved resources."

"Of course," Geneva said, "neither strategy will be easy! But if the issue and the goal are as the Dallas witness suggested—'whether or not we are going to educate the children and the youth'—then you simply have to agree, first, that racial balance and integration—what the witness called 'a noble idea in 1954'—is of very limited value today; and, second, that our priority must be to gain educationally effective schools for our children."

Geneva's eyes were bright, her black skin had a warm glow, and perspiration was trickling down her forehead. She caught me staring as she looked for her handkerchief. We both laughed.

"Friend," she asked, "if white folks ever decided to straighten up and do right, what would we black folks have to talk about?"

"Lord only knows," I answered. "Take our debate over school policy. It has been going on for two hundred years. In 1787, Prince Hall, the black Revolutionary War veteran and community leader, urged the Massachusetts legislature to provide funds for an 'African' school because, in his words, 'we . . . must fear for our rising offspring to see them in ignorance in a land of gospel light.'[21] That petition was urging separate schools for black children who, while admitted to the public schools in Boston, were treated so poorly that their parents withdrew them."

"I bet your forebears were critical of Hall's action and urged black parents to return their children for more insults and mistreatment."

"Listen, Geneva, I'm not going to swell the ranks of the multitudes of black folks in Boston who claim their forebears were never slaves. Suffice it to say that I'd be proud to be a descendant of such a prophetic critic for, after the black community built a school for themselves which later the school committee assumed responsibility for, parents were soon complaining that the schoolmaster was an incompetent teacher and guilty of 'improper familiarities' with female students—all of which charges the school committee ignored. The result was a suit to desegregate the schools—which the black parents lost in 1850."[22]

"Yes," Geneva agreed, "but the legislature came to the rescue of that nineteenth-century school-integration movement and, a few years later, voted to desegregate the Boston schools. The blacks were likely overjoyed, but they should have listened to one Thomas P. Smith, whom I would like to adopt as an ancestor. On Christmas Eve in 1849, Brother Smith spoke to the 'Colored Citizens of Boston' urging them not to abolish the colored schools. He warned that if the schools were desegregated, black children would have to be assigned to white schools, where the space would be inadequate, necessitating the construction of new schools which would again be all black. Sure enough, within a dozen years, the Boston public schools were totally segregated."[23]

"Despite the Boston setbacks, though, black people continued over the succeeding decades to file dozens of suits either to desegregate the schools or to gain equal facilities in the black schools."[24]

"All that proves," Geneva responded, "is that some truths come hard. In his 1849 speech, Thomas Smith argued that the black school was in good condition, and added that 'the order and discipline of the scholars, their cheerfulness and spirit, are unsurpassed by any school in the city.' Smith said further that if the black school was abolished at the request of blacks, the inference would be drawn that 'when equally taught and equally comfortable, we are ashamed of ourselves, and feel disgraced by being together; but the proverb says, "Respect yourself ere others respect you." ' "[25]

"Well, Geneva, I don't think Mr. Smith really understood how the segregation he supported undermined the self-respect he espoused."

"You sound like one of the civil rights stalwarts who castigated W. E. B. DuBois when he said much the same thing in the 1930s. He had serious misgivings about the massive school-desegregation litigation campaign the NAACP was contemplating. In urging a more flexible strategy, Dr. DuBois advised that blacks need neither segregated schools nor mixed schools. What they need is education."[26]

"With all due respect to Dr. DuBois who, as you know, is one of my heroes, I think he was begging the question. We agree our children need education. The issue debated over two centuries is how blacks can best obtain it in a still-resistive society."

"Like too many black folks," Geneva scolded, "you spend more time doing homage to his memory than reading his words. DuBois argued that the priority for blacks should be the educational goal rather than the means of achieving that goal. He also suggested that effective schooling for black children might be possible even though the socializing aspects of integrated classrooms were not available."

"Geneva, we've heard it all before, but the NAACP did proceed with its school-desegregation campaign. After years of trying, they won, and the *Brown* decision settled the matter of our approach to quality schooling for black children—desegregated schools."

"You sound as though the schools were *in fact* desegregated, as though you are still committed to 'the noble idea of 1954.' You need to start paying tardy heed to your hero. What Dr. DuBois said over half a century ago is still pertinent to all the black parents in this damned country who care more about their children's schooling than about their long-lost noble dreams. Listen!

A mixed school with poor and unsympathetic teachers, with hostile public opinion, and no teaching of truth concerning black folk, is bad. A segregated school with ignorant placeholders, inadequate equipment, poor salaries, and wretched housing, is equally bad. Other things being equal, the mixed school is the broader, more natural basis for the education of all youth. It gives wider contacts; it inspires greater self-confidence; and suppresses the inferiority complex. But other things seldom are equal, and in that case, Sympathy, Knowledge, and Truth, outweigh all that the mixed school can offer."[27]

"The man was a powerful writer," I acknowledged. "Black kids with his ability would make it whatever the school they attended."

"True, but no group produces more than a few persons of Dr. DuBois's caliber. Most children will benefit from good schooling and will suffer if their educations are poor. They are the real subjects of our debate, the real victims of our mistakes, the innocent sacrifices to our continued refusal to face up to our real problem as black people in a white land."

"I thought our real problem was education, Geneva."

"Nonsense. If that were so, you and I would not encounter the discrimination we and even the best educated of us continue to experience. And statistics would not continue to report that, on average, white high school dropouts earn more than blacks who have finished high school, white high school grads earn more than blacks who have finished college, and so on, and on."[28]

"Are you suggesting that the attainment of 'equal educational opportunity' must await a time when we are at least moving in the direction of 'equal economic opportunity'?"

"In a country where individual rights were created to protect wealth, we simply must find a means to prime the economic pump for black people, particularly those of us living at the poverty level."

"That statement," I warned, "will win you several awards from conservative groups who oppose further 'benefits' for blacks and urge that they roll up their sleeves and make it the way immigrants from Europe did several generations ago—and the way some Hispanic and Asian groups seem to be doing today."[29]

"I don't care who agrees with me," Geneva said militantly. "Those conservatives are right about the need for blacks to get into jobs and off welfare. And, whatever their handicaps, Hispanics and Asians are not burdened with the legacy of slavery and segregation in a land of freedom that, over time, has undermined the sense of self-worth for many black people. Nor will these immigrants face, at least initially, obstacles based on the deeply held belief that blacks *should* be on the bottom. Furthermore, white ethnics were helped up the socio-economic ladder by several rungs that have seldom, if ever, been available to blacks."

"A point Professor Martin Kilson made quite well," I said, "reminding us that the white ethnics' experience with upward mobility required no special individualism as far as obtaining government assistance:

Jews, Italians, Irish, Slavs, Greeks, and other white ethnic groups exploited every conceivable opportunity, including extensive corruption, to bring government—the public purse and public authority—into the balance, providing capital for construction firms and new technological industries, city and state colleges and technical institutes, educational grants and loans, among other government benefits."[30]

Geneva clapped her hands. "Well stated! But it leaves open the question of how those blacks for whom civil rights statutes are mostly meaningless will get a start at a time when unskilled jobs hardly pay a living wage, and manufacturing is leaving the country for so-called off-shore sites where employees can be hired for very low wages."

"You ask the question as though you have an answer."

"Not an answer—but a way of testing the viability of such an economic answer. Bear with me, friend, for the next Chronicle."

Chapter 5

The Racial Barrier
to Reparations

The Chronicle of the Black Reparations Foundation

AFTER MONTHS of excitement, the big day had arrived. The news conference was packed and hot. Television spots, like tiny orbitless suns, bathed the big stage where two dozen civil rights luminaries sat on folding chairs in a blinding glare of hot light. None of them seemed uncomfortable or even slightly put out that all eyes at this media event were on the large, balding white man who walked purposefully to the podium bristling with microphones, shuffled through a stack of notes, and then, in a deep, firm voice, began to give details of what had been rumored for months.

Given his status as one of the world's richest men, Ben Goldrich was accustomed to attention. To paraphrase a popular television commercial, "when Ben Goldrich spoke, people *really* listened"—but not always. Goldrich was here now, he told the televised news conference, because so few had heeded his warnings that the growing black underclass represented both a disgrace to the nation and a potential danger far more serious than any foreign enemy.

The son of an immigrant Jewish tailor, Goldrich said that the familiar statistics regarding the ever-worsening plight of roughly ten million black people living at or below the official poverty level provided a poignant proof that "for those whose ruined lives are reflected in these statistics, the oft-heralded Supreme Court decisions and civil rights laws protecting against overt discrimination had come too late." He quoted a famous economist's conclusion that the "pattern of racial oppression in the past created the huge black underclass, as the accumulation of disadvantages were passed on from generation to generation, and the technological and economic revolution of advanced industrial society combined to insure it a permanent status."[1]

"I credit my success to hard work, faith in my ability, and the opportunity this country provided me when I was young. But," Goldrich asserted, "were I both poor and black, starting out in today's economy, I would fail: my hard work exploited by dead-end service jobs, my faith exploded by the society's still-virulent racism, my promised opportunity exposed as an unobtainable myth for all but a few people of color.

Whatever the benefits of affirmative action for blacks with educational skills and potential, Goldrich warned, again quoting the economist, these programs "are not designed to deal with the problem of the disproportionate concentration of blacks in the low-wage labor market. Their major impact has been in the higher-paying jobs of the expanding service-producing industries in both the corporate and government sectors." As a result, there is indeed, Goldrich feared, a "deepening economic schism . . . developing in the black community, with the black poor falling further and further behind middle- and upper-income blacks."[2]

As Goldrich spoke, the black leaders on the platform nodded, more out of courtesy than surprise. For years Goldrich had been making similar statements, to which few beyond the civil rights community had listened very closely. No government or industry leader believed that anything more was needed than the existing social welfare programs. While expressing concern about the growing black underclass, their main commitment remained with their personal and corporate "bottom lines"—their *sine qua non* for success and achievement and worth. It was, his critics pointed out, easy enough for Ben Goldrich to play humanitarian, but he was speaking as a man whose wealth was reputed to exceed five billion dollars. "Let him put *his* money on the poverty firing line. Then, perhaps, we'll take him seriously."

Frustrated by this response and convinced of the reality of the dangers he warned against, Goldrich had withdrawn from active involvement in his many business holdings to dedicate his life to righting what he believed was the nation's crucial sin. "I have been mightily disappointed in those liberals who, in the 1960s—when it was fashionable—joined blacks in their churches to sing 'We Shall Overcome,' but refuse to make way for them in the workplaces of the 1980s. All of Jewish history," he said, "counsels my commitment to defend any group designated as society's scapegoat, and condemns those long the victims of oppression who now feel so accepted in America that they can join in—even lead—the hypocrisy that urges blacks to forgo government help and pull themselves up on rungs of the economic ladder that no longer exist."

"Today," he said, "with the active participation of those sitting behind me, I am responding to the righteous need of blacks and the sorry hypocrisy of whites by establishing the Black Reparations Foundation, whose simple purpose is to bring economic justice today to the least fortunate of those black people whose forebears were refused such justice after the Civil War. It is with great humility and a strong sense of purpose that I stand here to carry on the work of the greatest abolitionist of them all, the nineteenth-century Radical Republican Thaddeus Stevens of Pennsylvania.[3] You all remember"—Goldrich gave most of his listeners undue credit for a knowledge of American history—"how, in and out of Congress, Congressman Stevens, known as the 'Great Commoner,' urged the nation to break up all the Confederate-owned plantations and, under what was called the 'Forty Acres and a Mule' plan, distribute the land to the freedmen in forty-acre lots. The great Massachusetts senator Charles Sumner made a similar fight in the Senate. But neither of these men were able to persuade the Congress or the country to act. Land that the Freedman's Bureau, the federal agency set up to administer the emancipation process, had distributed to the former slaves was reclaimed and given back to the original Confederate owners.

"The historian Lerone Bennett has written that, when Thaddeus Stevens was seventy-four years old and gnarled as an oak tree, he rose in the House and, always a realist, admitted that his dream of providing reparations to the former slaves was stillborn. In pronouncing the eulogy for his plan, Stevens said:

> In my youth, in my manhood, in my old age, I had fondly dreamed that when any fortunate chance should have broken up [the institution of slavery, we would have] so remodeled all our institutions as to have freed them from every vestige of human oppression, of inequality of rights.... This bright dream has vanished like the baseless fabric of a vision.[4]

"Here," said Goldrich, with a dramatic flourish, "I pause to allow you to consider the enormous price this country has paid over the last century because the pleas for economic justice so eloquently voiced by Stevens and Sumner and other ardent abolitionists were not heeded. Though I, too, have tasted the bitter defeat on the issue of black reparations which these men knew so well, I am convinced that their goal was right, but their vehicle, government, was wrong."

Goldrich quickly went on to explain his reason for rejecting federal funding—the twentieth-century version of the rejected nineteenth-century reparations plan the reporters had anticipated. "First," he said, "for better or worse, we live in an era when there is great public support for spending billions for military defense to protect against foreign threats, and equally great opposition to any spending for social programs to guard against domestic disruption."

As he deplored this attitude, he acknowledged its existence and strength. "Moreover," he said, "even if our sensitivities to justice for blacks and real security for us all were greater, my second reason for eschewing government in a reparations plan would retain its validity." Referring to the motivations and the performance of Germany in paying $820 million in reparations to Israel for the resettlement of five hundred thousand Jews, Goldrich referred to the warning of a scholar who had studied the Jewish experience: "Moral commitment to redress of historic wrongs against humanness can be badly compromised in the political and legislative process by which moral commitment is translated into programs and financial support."[5] "This means," Goldrich explained, "that politics and moral rhetoric tend to become confused in the legislative process. We talk about the 'good' reason, while that reason is contradicted by the 'real' reason for political action reflected in the legislation. As a result, 'we are caught off guard, and the legislative actions supposedly designed to correct social and political injustice actually result in greater injustice.' "[6]

Looking up from his text, Goldrich noted that the reporters were getting nervous, looking at their watches, feverishly dashing off to phone their editors and program directors. This, after all, was not simply news; it was racial drama—a subject, more likely than any, save perhaps sex, to hold the attention of readers and viewers.

Goldrich sensed that it was time for specifics. "For the reasons I have just described, I have decided that this program must be privately funded. I'm pleased to report that several wealthy individuals who wish to remain anonymous have contributed to this effort, and it's my fervent hope that many others will join in it. But whether or not such assistance is forthcoming, I am prepared to proceed and have transferred virtually all of my resources—the total assets will exceed twenty-five billion dollars—to the Black Reparations Foundation."

Although Goldrich announced his gift without any special emphasis, the enormous sum shocked even seasoned reporters, who spontaneously joined the blacks on the platform in applause. Not waiting for the applause to die down, Goldrich continued. "With the help of experts in several fields, the Black Reparations Foundation has prepared a complex reparations formula that will move blacks at the poverty level and below up to the economic levels they likely would have held but for the impediments of historic slavery and the continuing disadvantages of racism.

"As should now be clear, while I earnestly believe that black people are entitled to racial reparations, I am concerned about the corrupting effect of any windfall wealth, such as raffles and lotteries. Experience shows that the sudden acquisition of large sums can be destructive to the recipients and endangers relationships with family and friends. For this reason, entitlement to reparations grants will be based on free-enterprise models in which monthly payments are a percentage of currently earned income.

"The grant formula is carefully calibrated to reward enterprise and discourage sloth. Minimum-wage workers will receive grants supplementing their pay by an amount representing what they would have been paid had they been unionized and their wages set through collective bargaining rather than the disadvantageous economies of an overcrowded market of unskilled workers. And as to unemployed blacks or those unable to work, the grants will raise above poverty level the income of each such individual in the underclass. Additional sums will be provided to enable grantees to obtain remedial schooling, job training, job placement, and child care."

Pointing to Black Reparations Foundation associates who were now distributing informational reports to the media members, Goldrich explained that the brochures contained program details as well as answers to their questions. "You will find that the complicated computer algorithms used in the grant formula will not turn the poor into fat cats, but will produce some satisfying results. For example, sharecroppers, exploited over the generations by their landowners, may come into sufficient sums to gain real independence in bargaining, and some may be able to buy the land on which they have labored so long for little return.

"As another example, little-known rhythm and blues singers and jazz musicians, whose work has been systematically copied and presented by whites over the years, may suddenly become wealthy. As they invest earnings to get exposure once denied them, they may also achieve the recognition their talents and skills justify. On the other hand, some well-known white singers and musicians, whose work is simply derivative, may be rejected and fall swiftly not only in fame but in income. The same phenomenon may occur," he predicted, "in other areas where the social vulnerability of black people has made them ready targets of exploitation by whites and, sometimes, by other blacks."

Some in the audience laughed nervously, but Goldrich did not smile. "I want to make clear that the purpose of the Black Reparations Foundation is to do justice to blacks and not cause mischief or sow misery among whites. We must expect readjustments in our social status and in our expectations. It isn't possible to do justice to a long-exploited minority without cost to the majority, all of whom have benefited directly or indirectly. With the understanding and cooperation of all, the dislocations will prove minimal and will soon be forgotten as all our citizens prosper in an environment not involuntarily subsidized by some based on their race. I thank you."

Blacks at all economic levels were overjoyed by the announcement that the Black Reparations Foundation was scheduled to begin functioning in one year. One observer noted that, in black communities across the country, "optimism is up and blood pressure levels are down." "Thanks to the Black Reparations Foundation," a black construction worker said, "I feel now I can make it in America." "The racism remains," a civil rights leader cautioned, while acknowledging that "the economic component of that racism has been neutralized for the black poor."

Predictably, the reaction of much of white America was far less positive. Indeed, there was growing opposition to the scheme. The government launched an official investigation of Ben Goldrich's holdings and scrutinized his reparations plan for legal flaws. None were found. Still, there was concern and growing resentment despite the foundation's expensive, low-key advertising campaign designed to broaden awareness of blacks' historic disadvantages.

The implications and threat to the socio-economic status quo was not lost on the nation's policy makers, who tried to dissuade Goldrich with arguments that his reparations program would disrupt the economy and increase racial hostility as white workers saw their black counterparts doing the same work but in effect earning more money through reparations grants.

Opponents were planning several legal attacks. One challenge would assert that the Black Reparations Foundation was practicing racial discrimination and thus was not entitled to its charitable status under the tax laws. These opponents also contended that, while the foundation was not a government entity bound by the Fifth and the Fourteenth amendments, the scale of the Goldrich holdings was so large, its potential impact on people's lives so mammoth, that it was both appropriate and necessary to bring the foundation under governmental control. In addition, several state legislatures were studying anti-reparations bills which, while racially neutral on their face, would prohibit foundations from distributing assets according to the race of the recipient. Both approaches were characterized by their supporters as upholding integration.

Concerned black groups met with Black Reparations Foundation officials about the opposition. Some representatives recommended canceling the program and agreed with its opponents that it would do more harm than good. Others urged broadening it to include all economically disadvantaged Americans, even though this change would substantially dilute the benefits slated now for poor blacks. Most urged the foundation to go forward with its plans.

Ben Goldrich, now condemned by many people as both a traitor to his class and an enemy of his race, determined even more vigorously to proceed with the implementation of his reparations plans. As he put it, "only an act of Congress sustained by a definitive U.S. Supreme Court decision will bring the program to a halt."

A FTER several minutes, I decided to break the silence. "Did the Black Reparations Foundation survive the legal attacks?"

Looking a bit embarrassed, Geneva shrugged. "I am afraid there is no ending to this Chronicle—or at least none that I now remember."

"That's strange," I said, somewhat annoyed. "There must be more to the story. Reparations claims as compensation for both slavery and discrimination have often been discussed as a remedy for the victims of racism. Proponents have pointed to the abortive post–Civil War effort to give blacks land discussed by Ben Goldrich in the Chronicle, and have also used the precedent of reparations paid by this country to American Indians[7] as well as

German relocation costs of Jews seeking to emigrate to Israel after the Second World War."[8]

"Not only that," said Geneva, "but, in 1948, a federal law, the Japanese American Evacuation Claims Act, was enacted that paid $38,000,000 in claims made against the government by Japanese-Americans evacuated from the West Coast in the early years of the war. Of course, that sum represented less than ten cents for every dollar claimed lost by Japanese-American evacuees,[9] but it does provide a precedent."

"For a time, it appeared that their story might have a more just ending," I remarked. "As you know, the government forcibly removed 120,000 citizens of Japanese descent from their homes and placed them in internment camps, where they remained as long as four years. In 1944, the Supreme Court determined that the internment policy was valid as a proper exercise of federal war powers.[10] But, on the basis of information in newly uncovered documents, Japanese-American citizens interned during the Second World War, or their representatives, brought suit in federal court charging that the U.S. Government fraudulently concealed the fact that there was no military necessity for the internment program, and thereby violated several of these citizens' rights. The court of appeals—in an opinion written in 1986 by that old civil rights warrior J. Skelly Wright[11]—found that, despite the passage of forty years, plaintiffs may still maintain an action for damages."[12]

"Any idea how the Supreme Court will rule?" Geneva asked.

"It will certainly be divided, as was the court of appeals; but the issue for the Japanese-Americans will be, as it has been for blacks, less whether injustice was done than whether serious procedural—that is, political—difficulties can be removed. The dissenting judge in the Japanese-American case admitted, for example, that the 'internment of fellow Americans on the basis of race, and out of what now appear to have been an excessive enshrinement of military necessity, sets a scenario for retributive justice.'[13]

"Also, the reparations concept was given a good deal of attention when, during the late 1960s, James Forman, then president of the Student Non-Violent Coordinating Committee (SNCC), disrupted the Sunday-morning service at New York's liberal Riverside Church and read a 'black manifesto' statement condemning racism in the church and the country and demanding five hundred million dollars from the 'Christian white churches and the Jewish synagogues.' ' "[14]

"How were Forman's claims handled?" Geneva asked.

"It was a wonderful publicity ploy. One writer reported that 'Forman's violation of the most sacred hour of the week and his violent anti-American rhetoric against America, capitalism and the church touched millions of nerve ends like a multi-pronged cattle prod.'[15] Although the disruption was universally condemned, and other black militant groups who tried similar tactics won little support from the courts,[16] during the next year or so, various churches and denominational groups gave several million dollars to black churches for social-reform programs."

"I will bet," Geneva interrupted, laughing, "that the gifts all carried provisions that the funds not go to Forman or the group he represented."

"You're exactly right. This predictable reaction to black demands that are other than gentle would be funny if it weren't so sad. But the historic evidence on the willingness of those in power to provide a reparations remedy for past injustice is mixed. Are you sure," I asked again, "that you don't remember the conclusion to this Chronicle?"

"Not so far," Geneva confessed. "My mind simply went blank—but the many attractive components in the Ben Goldrich proposal would seem to give it a far better chance than Forman's threatening demands."

"I'm surprised, Geneva. Are you, the arch racial pessimist of all time, actually suggesting that the Black Reparations Foundation wasn't doomed to fail from the start?"

"I am," said Geneva. "Look, my pessimism reflects my current assessment of our racial condition. It will shift to enthusiastic optimism when I discover a strategy with promise that justifies my faith. That is why I am studying these Chronicles with such care. You would be of more help if you were more objective about the continuing worth of those obsolete litigation approaches to which you remain so devoted."

"Just a minute, Geneva, it's you, not I, who forgot the Chronicle's ending. And without an ending, how can we really know what message the Chronicle intends to convey?"

"I apologize, but the alternative outcomes are apparent. Either opponents of the reparations plan would prevail and no foundation grants would be made, or Ben Goldrich would put his plan into operation on schedule and millions of blacks would begin to receive carefully calculated compensation for discrimination suffered by them and their forebears. As a prerequisite to the latter possibility, the foundation would have to obtain some pretty good lawyering to ward off the hostile lawsuits suggested by the Chronicle. Do you think you could handle those cases, Professor?"

"Taking the cases wouldn't be difficult, Geneva, but winning them in the atmosphere of public resentment and fear generated by the mere announcement of the plan—that might be a formidable task. The public was outraged by Forman's disruption of a church service, but the Chronicle reports an uproar when the public learns that perhaps the nation's richest man has donated his whole fortune to help remedy wrongs the society has ignored for years."

Geneva interrupted. "Please stop bemoaning the usual resistance to any program promising gains for blacks, particularly if—as Goldrich admits—they might involve dislocations for whites. Simply tell me how you would represent the Black Reparations Foundation."

"Assuming its officers would have more faith in my legal acumen than present company does," I replied, "I'd counsel the following:

"First, as to the charge that the grants reflect a policy of racial discrimination, we must argue that the foundation grants do not represent an invidious discrimination against whites barred by civil rights laws. Rather, eligibility is based on previous condition of servitude because of race. Since only blacks were held in slavery and only blacks have suffered the injustice of racial discrimination, it would be appropriate and not invidious to target grants intended to remedy the continuing harm done on the basis of race.

"I would argue vigorously against the judicial tendency to

use—in order to forestall effective remediation of discrimination already suffered—standards established by blacks to end discrimination. The Supreme Court's 1978 decision in the *Bakke* case is an unhappy example of this practice.[17] Similarly, I would distinguish the situation of only blacks being eligible for Black Reparations Foundation grants from cases like *Bob Jones University* (1983),[18] where the Court found it appropriate for the government to deny charitable tax status to a private church school that bars students or staff involved in or advocating interracial marriage."

"And would you expect to win on at least that aspect of the legal challenge?" Geneva asked.

"I would hope so, but there would be some difficulty. Remember that *Bob Jones University* became a major case even though the legal issues it raised had apparently been settled a dozen years earlier.[19] To take seriously the church school's claim that its opposition to intermarriage—based on the inferiority of blacks—is a part of its religious belief, one must assume, as much of the country does, that the deity is white. Given that assumption, we must not be surprised that 'racial discrimination' prohibitions are applied to obviously remedial programs even as the prohibitions themselves are evaded to perpetuate discrimination against blacks.

"Even so," I continued with more confidence than I felt, "the Black Reparations Foundation should survive this test. And if Congress or state legislatures were to carry out plans suggested in the Chronicle to enact laws barring such grants, a similar argument responding to the alleged racially discriminatory character of those grants could be raised. Foundation giving has traditionally been allowed broad discretion. There must be thousands of programs whose mission was to aid blacks in one way or another. To prohibit Black Reparations Foundation grants as discriminatory while acquiescing in many similar programs would raise serious due-process questions that I think courts would be unable to ignore."

"None of those programs," Geneva pointed out, "has the coverage and potential impact of the Black Reparations Foundation's twenty-five billion dollars."

"But the size of a program shouldn't determine its validity."

"Not logically, but politically it would make a major difference out of which a legal distinction could be carved."

It still did not seem to me to pose a problem. "Not too long ago, a New York businessman told students finishing the sixth grade at a Harlem school that, if they remained in school and graduated, he would pay for their college educations.[20] The promise received wide and positive media coverage, and the businessman was almost canonized as a living saint. Other businessmen made similar promises,[21] I would imagine to similar acclaim."

"That's a very different thing," Geneva interrupted. "The scope of the New York businessman's beneficence on behalf of blacks is limited and takes the form of scholarships to students that improve their potential. Goldrich planned to raise the actual status of blacks as compared with their white counterparts, and that is why in the Chronicle he was more condemned than canonized. Suppose for a moment, though, that the grants did not have a racial character and, as some advised, were made on the basis of poverty. Would there then be any basis for legal attack or motivation for legislative prohibition?"

"I'd think not, but spreading the resources so broadly as to dilute dissent means that the basic racial remediation is lost. After all, if everyone moves up one notch on the ladder, blacks will remain below their white counterparts, vulnerable to all the disadvantages of their subordinate status."

"But there might," Geneva suggested, "be opposition other than racial. In a competitive society, all are threatened by any aid to those deemed lower on the economic scale that exceeds bare minimum subsistence—as in the resentment to the food-stamp program when a recipient is seen purchasing a steak or other luxury food."

"That's a social phenomenon," I said. "Many social reformers find that any improvement in the status of the poor requires a bigger improvement in the status of the middle and the upper classes. Take the Tax Reform Act of 1986, where long-sought reform was gained when six million poor taxpayers were dropped from the rolls—but the price was a major reduction in tax rates for higher-income taxpayers."[22]

Geneva glanced at the big wall clock, as she had been doing every few minutes. "To get back to the point, let me ask you this. We know that today there would be broad opposition to any modern reparations plan like the 'forty acres and a mule' of the 1860s. Considering all the components of this opposition, do you see a theme or point around which to center an argument that the plan is unconstitutional?"

"I'd like a week in the library to prepare a response to your question, curbstone opinions being worth no more when they come from law professors than from lawyers in practice."

"Some of us would maintain that they are worth less," Geneva said, smiling, "but I will consider your status with your answer."

"Your generosity is overwhelming," I murmured, trying to organize my thoughts. "It seems to me that, even without a major legal theory, the Black Reparations Foundation program could be seriously undermined by petty harassments."

"For example?"

"Suppose employers, concerned that the presence of reparations grantees among their employees would create dissension in the workplace, intensify racial divisions, and thus threaten productivity and profits. Acting on those fears, employers might refuse to employ blacks receiving grants, rejecting them not on the basis of race, but because of their disruptive potential. An anti-foundation employment policy would likely spread swiftly and might even be incorporated into state and federal laws."

"Such a policy would seem to violate fair-employment laws," Geneva said indignantly.

I looked at her with amusement. "Shall we prepare a list of all the policies like those requiring teacher applicants to gain a certain level on standardized tests—policies that are held valid even though they seriously disadvantage black applicants?"[23]

"I get the point. At the least, foundation funds and energies would be sidetracked into fighting legal battles, and more than a few blacks would conclude that the grants, helpful as they might be, were not worth risking a job—even a low-paying job."

"Exactly. But I doubt the country would be satisfied with coercion on an employer-by-employer basis. Ben Goldrich's proposal makes him, as his critics claim, a traitor to his class. This is not philanthropy, but a major redistribution of the wealth, a danger even if carried out according to class alone. Limiting the redistribution to the black poor would upset or at least threaten the long-standing arrangement, no less fixed because it is unspoken, that whites are to be taken care of first in this society—on the ongoing assumption that they, not blacks, are America's chosen ones."

"But is that motivation and belief so strong that the nation would accept all the dangers of black poverty, crime, and degradation? Until now, such dangers have been tolerated, as was slavery, because no one has offered to pay the price of remedying the evil. But if the government or someone like Ben Goldrich were to come forward and accept the bill, wouldn't that make a big difference?"

"Paying the financial cost is only one component of opposition. Protecting the vested interest of superior status is of equal importance."

"You sound convincing, but somehow I do not agree, perhaps because I do not . . ." Her voice trailed off, as a perplexed look came over her face.

"What is it?" I asked. "Are you OK?"

Geneva put her head in her hands. "Just give me a few minutes. I think the end of the Chronicle is coming back to me."

Five minutes passed. Ten. Geneva sat motionless, almost in a trance. When I mentioned the time, she did not respond and seemed not to hear me. In fact, I felt I was in the room alone. It was more than a little unnerving. What, I wondered, had all the years done to this brilliant woman? She was not, I thought, insane, but she was far from normal, whatever that is. I sighed in resignation. She was one of my best friends. She had been ill for a very long time and now viewed herself in some sort of serious trouble, which seemed to me—I hesitated to raise the word even to myself—*crazy.*

At that point she recovered herself, her expression far from happy. "You are right," she said, shaking her head, "and I have been foolish.

"It must have been two years after Goldrich announced his plan. The Black Reparations Foundation had been undermined by lawsuits, and recipients had been harassed as un-American and worse. I recall seeing Goldrich, now old and beaten down, in court standing before a judge. Apparently, in the Chronicle, Congress has enacted a statute barring from interstate commerce the distribution of any funds, from public or private sources, that have the effect of providing a financial advantage to recipients based on race—programs providing such assistance to fewer than one thousand persons not being covered, I assume, to save traditional aid programs."

"And the Supreme Court has approved this law?"

"According to the Chronicle, yes. I remember many references to the broad power of Congress under the Commerce clause to regulate commerce between the states: that this power had been utilized by Congress to eliminate racial discrimination in privately owned businesses under Title II of the Civil Rights Act of 1964;[24] and that programs prohibited by the act have a potential for racial disruption and injustice no less than had the Jim Crow laws."

"That's ridiculous!" I spluttered.

"Save your anger," Geneva warned, "until you hear this. In the Chronicle, the Supreme Court's opinion spends some time with the Black Reparations Foundation argument that, while the grants have been targeted to blacks, that is the only means of remedying the disadvantage of slavery and the badges of servitude. The Court responds that not only are the origins of the slavery standard of eligibility too remote in time to justify their continued validity at a period when nondiscrimination is the acknowledged legal standard, but the fact that the ancestors of blacks were black is no more justifiable as a criterion for receiving grants than was the right to vote without taking any tests justified in the 1915 grandfather-clause cases (see page 92)[25] because a white applicant's grandparents had voted at a time when blacks were barred from voting."

"Well," I said with resignation, "legal critics who claim that doctrinal rules are indeterminate and can be used to reach any result the courts choose, would have a field day with this decision. But," I asked, "you spoke of Ben Goldrich as being before a court himself on some matter related to the Black Reparations Foundation?"

"Apparently, a flaw has been found in the structure he created in giving his wealth to the foundation and reserving a few million for his personal needs. He now has to choose between giving everything he has to the foundation or dissolving it."

"A demand, I assume, that he make the supreme economic sacrifice to atone for his sin of showing up the rest of society. What is his decision?"

"I'm not sure. I remember black people, many of them crying, crowding into the court to offer Goldrich support. He himself insisted on prefacing his choice by reading the speech Thaddeus Stevens gave in the House when he acknowledged defeat of the original 'forty acres and a mule' idea. Then I recall a lot of commotion, the judge furiously pounding his gavel, and—at the last—all of the other blacks drowning him out and raising their voices in a spiritual: 'Nobody Knows the Trouble I've Seen.' "

Chapter 6

The Unspoken Limit on Affirmative Action

The Chronicle of the DeVine Gift

IT WAS a major law school, one of the best, but I do not remember how I came to be teaching there rather than at Howard, my alma mater. My offer, the first ever made to a black, was the culmination of years of agitation by students and a few faculty members. It was the spring of my second year. I liked teaching and writing, but I was exhausted and considering resigning.

I had become the personal counselor and confidante of virtually all the black students and a goodly number of the whites. The black students clearly needed someone with whom to share their many problems, and white students, finding a faculty member actually willing to take time with them, were not reluctant to help keep my appointments book full. I liked the students, but it was hard to give them as much time as they needed. I also had to prepare for classes—where I was expected to give an award-winning performance each day—and serve on every committee at the law school and the university where minority representation was desired. In addition, every emergency involving a racial issue was deemed my problem. I admit I wanted to be involved in these problems, but they all required time and energy. Only another black law teacher would believe what I had to do to make time for research and writing.

So, when someone knocked on my door late one warm spring

afternoon as I was frantically trying to finish writing final exam questions, I was tempted to tell the caller to go away. But I did not. The tall, distinguished man who introduced himself as DeVine Taylor was neither a student nor one of the black students' parents who often dropped by, when in town, just to meet their child's only black teacher.

Mr. Taylor, unlike many parents and students, came quickly to the point. He apologized for not having made an appointment, but explained that his visit involved a matter requiring confidentiality. He showed me a card and other papers identifying him as president of the DeVine Hair Products Company, a familiar name in many black homes and one of the country's most successful black businesses. By that time, I recognized Mr. Taylor's face and assured him I knew of his business even if I did not use his products.

"You may also know," Mr. Taylor said, "that my company and I haven't been much involved in this integration business. It seems to me that civil rights organizations are ready to throw out the positive aspects of segregation with the bad. I think we need to wake up to the built-in limits on all the 'equal opportunity' they're preaching. Much of it may prove a snare that will cost us what we have built up over the years without giving us anything better to take its place. Personally, I'm afraid they will integrate me into bankruptcy. Even now, white companies are undercutting me in every imaginable way.

"But," he interrupted himself with a deep sigh, "that is not why I'm here. You have heard of foundations that make awards to individuals based on their performance rather than on their proposals. Well, for some time my company has been searching for blacks who are truly committed to helping other blacks move up. We have located and helped several individuals over the years with what we call the 'DeVine Gift.' We know of your work and believe your efforts merit our support. We want to help you help other blacks, and we can spend a large amount of money to fund your endeavors. For tax and other business reasons, we can't provide our help in cash. And we don't wish anyone to know that we're providing the help."

He was clearly serious, and I tried to respond appropriately.

"Well, Mr. Taylor, I appreciate the compliment, but it is not clear how a black hair products company can be of assistance to a law teacher. Unless"—the idea struck me suddenly—"unless you can help locate more blacks and other minorities with the qualifications needed for membership on the faculty of this law school."

Mr. Taylor understood at once. "I was a token black in a large business before I left in frustration to start my own company," he said. "With our nationwide network of sales staff, I think we can help."

When I had been hired, the faculty promised that although I was their first black teacher, I would not be their last. This was not to be a token hire, they assured me, but the first step toward achieving a fully integrated faculty. But subsequent applicants, including a few with better academic credentials than my own, were all found wanting in one or another respect. Frustration regarding this matter, no less than fatigue, had brought me to the point of resignation before Mr. Taylor's visit.

With the behind-the-scenes help from the DeVine Gift, the law school hired its second black teacher during the summer—a young man with good credentials and with some teaching experience at another law school. He was able to fill holes in the curriculum caused by two unexpected faculty resignations. The following year, we "discovered," again with the assistance of Mr. Taylor's network, three more minority teachers—a Hispanic man, an Asian woman, and another black woman. In addition, one of our black graduates, a law-review editor, was promised a position when he completed a judicial clerkship.

We now had six minority faculty members, far more than any other major white law school. I was ecstatic, a sentiment that I soon learned was not shared by many of my white colleagues. While I am usually sensitive about such things, I so enjoyed the presence of the other minority faculty members, who eased the burdens on my time and gave me a sense of belonging to a "critical mass," that I failed to realize the growing unrest among some white faculty members.

Had we stopped at six, perhaps nothing would have been said. But the following year, Mr. Taylor's company, with growing expertise, recruited an exceptionally able black lawyer. The aca-

142

demic credentials of this, the Seventh Candidate, were impeccable. The top student at our competitor school, he had edited the law review and written a superb student note. After clerking for a federal court of appeals judge and a U.S. Supreme Court Justice, he had joined a major New York City law firm where, after three years of work they rated "splendid," he was in line for early election to partnership. Now, though, the DeVine people had inspired him to teach.

When the dean came to see me, he talked aimlessly for some time before he reached the problem troubling him and, I later gathered, much of the faculty. The problem was that our faculty would soon be 25 percent minority. "You know, Geneva, we promised you we would become an integrated faculty, and we've kept that promise—admittedly with a lot of help from you. But I don't think we can hire anyone else for a while. I thought we might 'share the wealth' a bit by recommending your candidate to some of our sister schools whose minority-hiring records are far less impressive than our own."

"Dean," I said, as calmly and coldly as I could, "I am not interested in recruiting black teachers for other law schools. Each of the people we have hired is good, as you have boasted many times, publicly and privately. And I can assure you that the Seventh Candidate will be better than anyone now on the faculty without regard to race."

"You could be right, Geneva, but let's be realistic. This is one of the oldest and finest law schools in the country. It simply would not be the same school for our students and the alumni with a predominantly minority faculty—as I thought you, an advocate of affirmative action, would understand."

"I am no mathematician," I said, "but 25 percent is far from a majority. Still, it is more racial integration than you want, even though none of the minorities, excluding perhaps myself, has needed any affirmative-action help to qualify for the job. I also understand, tardily I admit, that you folks never expected that I would find more than a few minorities who could meet your academic qualifications. You never expected that you would have to reveal what has always been your chief qualification—a white face, preferably from an upper-class background."

To his credit, the dean remained fairly calm throughout my tirade. "I've heard you argue that black law schools, like Howard,
should retain mainly black faculties and student bodies, even if to
do so they have to turn away whites with better qualifications. We
have a similar situation in that we want to retain our image as a
white school just as you want Howard to retain its image as a
black school."

"That's a specious argument, Dean, and you know it! Black
schools have a remediation responsibility for the victims of this
country's long-standing and, from what I am hearing, continuing
racism—a responsibility different from schools like this one,
which should be grateful for the chance to change its all-white
image. And," I added, "if you're not grateful, I'm certain the
courts will give you ample reason to reconsider when my seventh
candidate sues you for the job he earned and is entitled to get."

The dean was not surprised by my unprofessional threat to sue.
"I have discussed this at length with some faculty members, and
we realize that you may wish to test this matter in the courts. We
think, however, that there are few precedents on the issues such
a suit will raise. I don't want to be unkind. We do appreciate your
recruitment efforts, Geneva, but a law school of our caliber and
tradition simply cannot look like a professional basketball team."

He left my office after that parting shot, and my first reaction
was rage. Then, as I slowly realized the real significance of all that
had happened since I received the DeVine Gift, the tears came,
and kept coming. Through those tears, over the next few days, I
completed grading my final exams. Then I announced my resignation as well as the reasons for it.

When I told the Seventh Candidate that the school would not
offer him a position and why, he was strangely silent, only thanking me for my support. About a week later, I received a letter from
him—mailed not from his law firm but, according to the post-
mark, from a small, all-black town in Oklahoma.

Dear Professor Crenshaw:

   Until now, when black people employed race to explain
failure, I, like the black neoconservative scholars, wondered

how they might have fared had they made less noise and done more work. Embracing self-confidence and eschewing self-pity seemed the right formula for success. One had to show more heart and shed fewer tears. Commitment to personal resources rather than reliance on public charity, it seemed to me, is the American way to reach goals—for blacks as well as for whites. Racial bias is not, I thought, a barrier but a stimulant toward showing *them* what *we* can do in the workplace as well as on the ball field, in the classroom as well as on the dance floor.

Now no rationale will save what was my philosophy for achievement, my justification for work. My profession, the law, is not a bulwark against this destruction. It is instead a stage prop illuminated with colored lights to mask the ongoing drama of human desolation we all suffer, regardless of skills and work and personal creed.

You had suggested I challenge my rejection in the courts, but even if I won the case and in that way gained the position to which my abilities entitled me, I would not want to join a group whose oft-stated moral commitment to the meritocracy has been revealed as no more than a hypocritical conceit, a means of elevating those like themselves to an elite whose qualifications for their superior positions can never be tested because they do not exist.

Your law school faculty may not realize that the cost of rejecting me is exposing themselves. They are, as Professor Roberto Unger has said in another context, like a "priesthood that had lost their faith and kept their jobs."[1]

But if I condemn hypocrisy in the law school, I must not condone it in myself. What the law school did when its status as a mainly white institution was threatened is precisely what even elite colleges faced with a growing number of highly qualified Asian students are doing: changing the definition of merit.[2] My law firm and virtually every major institution in this country would do the same thing in a similar crisis of identity. I have thus concluded that I can no longer play a role in the tragic farce in which the talents and worth of a few of us who happen to get there first is dangled like bait before the masses who are led to believe that what can never be is a real possibility. When next you hear from me, it will be in a new role as avenger rather than apologist. This system must be forced to recognize what it is doing to you and me and to itself. By the time you read this, it will be too late for you to reason with me. I am on my way.

Yours,
The Seventh Candidate

This decision, while a shock, hardly prepared me for the disturbing letter that arrived a few days later from DeVine Taylor, who evidently had read of my well-publicized resignation.

Dear Geneva,

Before you received the DeVine Gift, your very presence at the law school posed a major barrier to your efforts to hire additional minority faculty. Having appointed you, the school relaxed. Its duty was done. Its liberal image was assured. When you suggested the names of other minorities with skills and backgrounds like your own, your success was ignored and those you named were rejected for lack of qualifications. When the DeVine Gift forced your school to reveal the hidden but no less substantive basis for dragging their feet after you were hired, the truth became clear.

As a token minority law teacher, Geneva, you provided an alien institution with a facade of respectability of far more value to them than any aid you gave to either minority students or the cause of black people. You explained your resignation as a protest. But you should realize that removing yourself from that prestigious place was a necessary penance for the inadvertent harm you have done to the race you are sincerely committed to save.

I am happy to see that the DeVine Gift has served its intended purpose. I wish you success in your future work.

DeVine Taylor

A DEVASTATING NOTE," I murmured, imagining how it must have shocked Geneva, as I watched her pacing the room in agitation, oblivious of me. She said something about the foolishness of accepting a teaching position at a school where she would be so vulnerable.

I tried to reassure her. "I think that most black people, faculty as well as students, feel exposed and vulnerable at predominantly white law schools. And I know that most black teachers run into faculty resistance when they seek to recruit a second nonwhite faculty member."

"Why black law teachers more than blacks in any other occupation?" Geneva asked, finally taking notice of me.

"It is true," I said, trying to organize my thoughts, "that there are few black workers who do not experience some sense of exclusion because of race. For example, there's plenty of discrimination in professional sports where ability can be measured accurately by performance.[3] The sense of unease to which I refer, though, is blacks' experience in positions where it's difficult to objectify job performance. In elite, academic settings, an applicant without outstanding grades, earned preferably at a major educational institution, is usually given little consideration. Law schools adhere to this fixation on grades even for applicants who have done extremely well in law practice."

"Well do I know it," said Geneva. "My faculty colleagues insisted that, in the hiring of law teachers, grades are a better indicator of intellectual ability and predictor of scholarly potential than is success in law practice."

"A response that simultaneously insults law practitioners—in-

cluding those trained at the law schools where the policy is followed—and raises questions about the real value of legal scholarship which could be the subject of a separate discussion. But the
unease I want to focus on is that experienced by the black faculty
member who did not earn the highest grades or graduate from a
top school. Reports from minority law teachers who are 'firsts' at
their schools parallel your experience in the Chronicle. When they
suggest the names of other blacks and Hispanics, often with
grades as good as, even better than, their own, the usual response
is: 'We want more minorities, but those you recommend just don't
seem to have the intellectual background we need at this
school.' "[4]

"Tell me about it," Geneva said.

"Even with all the problems, law teaching has many wonderful
advantages whether you're black or white—but for blacks, it's
also the perfect environment in which to develop paranoia. Your
black friends who want to get into teaching wonder why you're
never able to follow through on your promises to help. And you
know that the black applicant your faculty rejects out of hand
today would be hired tomorrow if you suddenly suffered a fatal
heart attack."

"Before I gained the questionable advantage of the DeVine
Gift," Geneva confessed, "rejection of the minorities I recommended would send me into a depression. What were they trying
to tell me? Was it that I was doing such a great job that they saw
no need to hire others like myself? Or was it, rather, that my performance was so poor that they refused to hire anyone else for
fear of making another serious mistake?"

"Happily," I said, trying to steer the discussion back to the
Chronicle, "our question is whether the Supreme Court would
view the law school's rejection of a seventh eminently qualified
candidate as impermissible racial discrimination. I would guess
from the Chronicle that the law school's action was not challenged in court."

Geneva thought for a moment. "That part is fuzzy. I probably
knew all along, but repressed, what the school really thought
about its minority faculty members. I guess I was naïve, but even
with all the problems about who was qualified, and who was re-

ally smart—I had discovered that those questions bedevil even those whites on the faculty who have flawless academic credentials—I had come to feel a part of the school. The Seventh Candidate, according to his letter, was in no mood to challenge his rejection in the courts. But all I remember is resigning and that most troubling note from Mr. Taylor."

"That's too bad because, at first glance, I don't think the dean's justified in his confidence that the law would support the school's rejection of the Seventh Candidate. Although the courts have withdrawn from their initial expansive reading of the federal fair-employment laws,[5] I would think that even a conservative court might find for your seventh minority candidate, owing to his superior credentials and the hard-to-deny fact that his race was the major factor in his rejection."[6]

"Remember," Geneva cautioned, "that, despite what the dean told me, the law school would claim first that its preference for whites seeking the opening is based on their superior qualifications. I gather that the cases indicate that an employer's subjective evaluation can play a major role in decisions involving highly qualified candidates who seek professional positions."

"That's true. Courts are reluctant to interfere with upper-level hiring decisions in the absence of strong proof that those decisions have been based on an intent to discriminate. Judicial deference is particularly pronounced when the employment decision at issue affects the health or safety of large numbers of people. The courts, for example, have hesitated to interfere with decisions regarding the hiring of airline pilots.[7] But, more generally, courts have shown an unwillingness to interfere with upper-level hiring decisions in the 'elite' professions,[8] including university teaching.[9] Under current law, if there are few objective hiring criteria and legitimate subjective considerations, plaintiffs will only rarely obtain a searching judicial inquiry into their allegation of discrimination in hiring."[10]

"In other words," Geneva said, with a hint of sarcasm, "despite your optimistic opening, what you are now saying is that this would not be an easy case even if the plaintiff were the first rather than the seventh candidate."

"I never said it would be an easy case. I do think the Court could surprise the law-school dean if the school's action were challenged and the litigation record showed the Seventh Candidate's qualifications to be clearly superior to those of other candidates. It might be an attractive situation for the Court. The discrimination is clear, and the situation isn't likely to arise very often. The Court just might use the case to reach a 'contradiction-closing' decision: that is, one that narrows the gap between the country's equality precepts and its often blatantly discriminatory practices. In predictable fashion, minorities and liberal whites would hail a decision for the black applicant as proof that racial justice is still available through the courts."

Geneva gave me a look best described as stunned pity. "Having painted that scenario filled with rosy 'just mights,' are you now ready to tell me what the Court would be *most* likely to do in this case?"

Like most law teachers, I am ready to predict judicial outcomes even without being asked, but knowing how important this discussion was to Geneva, I thought it wise to review the situation realistically. "Well, weighing all the factors in the cold light of the current Court's conservative drift, the dean's belief that his law school would prevail in court may be justified after all."

"Well," Geneva slumped in mock exhaustion, "getting that out of you was like pulling teeth. And we have not yet considered the possibility that, even if the Court found that our candidate had the best paper credentials, the law school might have an alternative defense."

"I'm afraid that's also correct. The law school might argue that, even if its rejection of the Seventh Candidate was based on race, the decision was justified. The school might aver that its reputation and financial well-being were based on its status as a 'majority institution.' The maintenance of a predominantly white faculty, the school would say, is essential to the preservation of an appropriate image, to the recruitment of faculty and students, and to the financial support of alumni. With heartfelt expressions of regret that 'the world is not a better place,' the law school would urge the Court to find that neither federal fair-employment laws nor the Constitution would prohibit it from discriminating against minority candidates when the percentage of minorities on the faculty exceeds the percentage of minorities within the population. At the least, the school would contend that no such prohibition should apply while most of the country's law schools continue to maintain nearly all-white faculties."

"That," Geneva observed with a raised eyebrow, "was an effective summary, counselor. Are you sure you do not harbor a secret urge to represent the other side?"

"If that's supposed to be a joke, its humor is lost on me. What I am suggesting is less what a school would actually argue, but what most of them, in fact, believe—and what the courts believe as well."

"Well, then, how do you think the Court would respond to such an argument?"

"Given the outstanding quality of the minority faculty, courts might discount the law school's fear that it would lose status and support if one-fourth of its teaching staff were other than white."

Geneva did not look convinced. "I don't know. I think a part of the dean's concern was that, if I could find seven outstanding minority candidates, then I could find more—so many more that the school would eventually face the possibility of having a 50 percent minority faculty. And the courts would be concerned about that precedent. What, they might think, if other schools later developed similar surfeits of superqualified minority job applicants?"

"Well, the courts have hardly been overwhelmed with cases demanding that upper-level employers have a 25 to 50 percent minority work force, particularly in the college and university teaching areas. But perhaps you're right. A Supreme Court case involving skilled construction workers suggests that an employer may introduce evidence of its hiring of blacks in the past to show that an otherwise unexplained action was not racially motivated.[11] Perhaps, then, an employer who has hired many blacks in the past may at some point decide to cease considering them. Even if the Court didn't explicitly recognize this argument, it might take the law school's situation into account. In fact, the Court might draw an analogy to housing cases in which courts have recognized that whites usually prefer to live in predominantly white housing developments."

"I am unfamiliar with those cases," Geneva said. "Have courts approved ceilings on the number of minorities who may live in a residential area?"

"They have, indeed. Acting on the request of housing managers trying to maintain integrated developments, courts have tailored tenant racial balance to levels consistent with the refusal of whites to live in predominantly black residential districts. A federal court, for example, has allowed the New York City Housing Authority to limit the number of apartments it made available to minority persons whenever 'such action is essential to promote a racially balanced community and to avoid concentrated racial pockets that will result in a segregated community.'[12] The court feared that unless it allowed the housing authority to impose limits on minority occupancy, a number of housing developments would reach the 'tipping point'—the point at which the percentage of minorities living in an area becomes sufficiently large that virtually all white residents move out and other whites refuse to take their places.[13]

"You know, civil rights groups developed 'benign' housing quotas before most fair-housing laws were enacted. But the technique has always been controversial. Professor Boris Bittker examined the legal issues in a 1962 article written in the form of three hypothetical judicial opinions reviewing the constitutionality of an ordinance designed to promote residential integration by limiting the number of blacks and whites who would reside in a planned community.[14] The majority opinion struck down the ordinance on the rationale that the Constitution is 'colorblind.' The opinion relied on prior cases invalidating housing-segregation schemes,[15] and refused to examine the town's contention that this ordinance differed from invalid schemes because it was intended to promote racial integration. A dissenting opinion maintained that the Constitution 'may be color-blind, but it is not short-sighted.'[16] Distinguishing the cases that the majority cited, the dissent viewed the ordinance as a reasonable approach intended to remedy a vexing problem. Although the ordinance involved a racial classification, the dissent argued, it was not hostile toward blacks and should not be struck down. Finally, a concurring opinion noted that blacks are likely to resent the restrictions imposed by invidious segregation schemes. Emphasizing the odiousness of racial classifications, the concurring judge urged the town to seek integration through education and other voluntary means. The concurrence also expressed concern about the precedential potential of a decision approving the 'proportional representation' of blacks in housing, jobs, and elective offices.[17]

"The analogy is not perfect, but the 'tipping point' phenomenon in housing plans may differ little from the faculty's reaction to your seventh candidate. Both reflect a desire by whites to dominate their residential and nonresidential environments. If this is true, the arguments used to support benign racial quotas in housing could be enlisted to support the law school's employment decision."

"But," argued Geneva, "I do not view as in any way benign the law school's refusal to hire the Seventh Candidate. The school's decision was unlike the adoption of a housing quota intended to establish or protect a stable integrated community before most private discrimination in the housing area was barred by law. The law school did not respond to a 'tipping point' resulting from the individual decisions of numerous parties beyond the authorities' ability to control, but instead imposed a 'stopping point' for hiring blacks and other minorities, regardless of their qualifications. School officials, whose actions are covered by federal civil rights statutes, arbitrarily determined a cutoff point."

"Don't get trapped in semantics, Geneva! A so-called benign housing quota seems invidious to the blacks excluded by its operation. They are no less victims of housing bias than are those excluded from neighborhoods by restrictive covenants. Yet at least in some courts, those excluded by benign quotas have no remedy. In our case, the law school could argue that the Seventh Candidate should likewise have no remedy: he has made—albeit involuntarily—a sacrifice for the long-run integration goals that are often persuasive in the housing sphere.

"In any event, the Court would likely apply a rule that incorporates a desire for white dominance without, of course, admitting as much. Perhaps someone would resurrect and revamp Professor Herbert Wechsler's view that the legal issue in state-imposed segregation cases is not discrimination but rather associational rights.

Assuming, he said, that segregation denies blacks freedom of association with whites, then 'integration forces an association upon those for whom it is unpleasant and repugnant.' The task, according to Professor Wechsler, was to consider and balance these associational rights in accord with neutral principles of law.[18] Of course, courts originally ignored Professor Wechsler's call for a neutrally principled formulation of the antisegregation decisions, but they might now take up and distort his views in order to establish limits on the *level* of desegregation required by law. Specifically, courts might hold that once employers have achieved a certain compliance with civil rights laws, they may consider openly how hiring more minorities will affect the conditions and atmosphere of their workplaces. I don't believe Professor Wechsler would be pleased with this development, but his emphasis on associational rights in desegregation cases may be used to support just such a result."

"In other words," Geneva said, "if and when the number of blacks qualified for upper-level jobs exceeds the token representation envisioned by most affirmative-action programs, opposition of the character exhibited by my law school could provide the impetus for a judicial ruling that employers have done their 'fair share' of minority hiring. This rule, while imposing limits on constitutionally required racial fairness for a black elite, would devastate civil rights enforcement for all minorities. In effect, the Court would formalize and legitimize the subordinate status that is already a *de facto* reality."

"Indeed, affirmative-action remedies have flourished because they offer more benefit to the institutions that adopt them than they do to the minorities whom they're nominally intended to serve. Initially, at least in higher education, affirmative-action policies represented the response of school officials to the considerable pressures placed on them to hire minority faculty members and to enroll minority students. Rather than overhaul admissions criteria that provided easy access to offspring of the upper class and presented difficult barriers to all other applicants, officials claimed they were setting lower admissions standards for minority candidates. This act of self-interested beneficence had unfortunate results. Affirmative action now 'connotes the undertaking of remedial activity beyond what normally would be required. It sounds in *noblesse oblige*, not legal duty, and suggests the giving of charity rather than the granting of relief.'[19] At the same time, the affirmative-action overlay on the overall admissions standards admits only a trickle of minorities. These measures are, at best, 'a modest mechanism for increasing the number of minority professionals, adopted as much to further the self-interest of the white majority as to aid the designated beneficiaries.'[20]

"And one last point. Some courts have been reluctant to review academic appointments, because 'to infer discrimination from a comparison among candidates is to risk a serious infringement of first amendment values.' "[21]

"In other words," said Geneva, "the selection of faculty members ascends to the level of a First Amendment right of academic freedom."

"I'm afraid so, and the law school's lawyers would certainly not ignore Justice Lewis F. Powell's perhaps unintended support for this position given in his 1978 *Bakke* opinion, in which he discussed admissions standards in the context of a university's constitutional right of academic freedom.[22] He acknowledged that ethnic diversity was 'only one element in a range of factors a university properly may consider in attaining the goal of a heterogeneous student body.'[23] Given the importance of faculty selection in maintaining similar aspects of this form of academic freedom, it would seem only a short step to a policy of judicial deference to a school's determination that the requirement to surpass an already successful minority hiring policy would unbalance the ethnic diversity of its faculty."

"You assume," Geneva said, "that any faculty would react as mine did to an apparently endless flow of outstanding minority faculty prospects. But I would wager that if the Chronicle of the DeVine Gift were presented to white law teachers in the form of a hypothetical case, most would insist that their faculties would snap up the Seventh Candidate in an instant."

"What you're seeking," I replied, "is some proof that a faculty *would* respond as yours did, and then some explanation *why*. The record of minority recruitment is so poor as to constitute a *prima facie* case that most faculties *would* reject the Seventh Candidate.

And most black law teachers would support this view. Their universal complaint is that, after hiring one or two minority teachers, predominantly white faculties lose interest in recruiting minorities and indicate that they are waiting for a minority candidate with truly outstanding credentials. Indeed, as long as a faculty has one minority person, the pressure is off, and the recruitment priority disappears."

"No one, of course, can prove *whether* a given faculty would react as mine did," Geneva said, "but for our purposes, the more interesting question is *why* a faculty would if it did. You would think that whites would be secure in their status-laden positions as tenured members of a prestigious law school faculty. Why, then, would they insist on a predominantly white living and working environment? Why reject the Seventh Candidate?"

"Initially, it's important to acknowledge that white law teachers aren't bigots in the redneck, sheet-wearing sense. Certainly, no law teacher I know consciously shares Ben Franklin's dream of an ideal white society[24] or accepts the slave owner's propaganda that blacks are an inferior species who, to use Chief Justice Roger Taney's prescription in the 1857 *Dred Scott* decision, 'might justly and lawfully be reduced to slavery for his benefit.'[25] Neither perception flourishes today, but the long history of belief in both undergirds a cultural sense of what Professor Manning Marable has identified as the 'ideological hegemony' of white racism.[26] Marable asserts that all of our institutions of education and information—political and civic, religious and creative—either knowingly or unknowingly 'provide the public rationale to justify, explain, legitimize, or tolerate racism.' In his view, a collective consensus within the social order of the United States gives rise to the result that

> the media play down potentially disruptive information on the race question; inferior schooling for black children denies them necessary information and skills; cultural and social history is rewritten so that racial conflict and class struggle are glossed over and the melting pot ideal stressed; religious dogmas such as those espoused by fundamentalist Christians

divert political protest and reaffirm the conservative values on which the white middle class's traditional illusions of superiority are grounded.[27]

"You'll notice, Geneva, that Professor Marable doesn't charge that ideological hegemony is the result of a conspiracy, plotted and executed with diabolical cunning. Rather, it's sustained by a culturally ingrained response by whites to any situation in which whites aren't in a clearly dominant role. It explains, for example, the 'first black' phenomenon in which each new position or role gained by a black for the first time creates concern and controversy about whether 'they' are ready for this position, or whether whites are ready to accept a black in this position."[28]

"Putting it that way," said Geneva, "helps me understand why the school's rejection of my seventh candidate hurt without really surprising me. I had already experienced a similar rejection on a personal level.[29] When I arrived, the white faculty members were friendly and supportive. They smiled at me a lot and offered help and advice. When they saw how much time I spent helping minority students and how I struggled with my first writing, they seemed pleased. It was patronizing, but the general opinion seemed to be that they had done well to hire me. They felt good about having lifted up one of the downtrodden. And they congratulated themselves for their affirmative-action policies.

"Then after I became acclimated to academic life, I began receiving invitations to publish in the top law reviews, to serve on important commissions, and to lecture at other schools. At this point, I noticed that some of my once-smiling colleagues now greeted me with frowns. For them, nothing I did was right: my articles were flashy but not deep, rhetorical rather than scholarly. Even when I published an article in a major review, my colleagues gave me little credit; after all, students had selected the piece, and what did they know anyway? My popularity with students was attributed to the likelihood that I was an easy grader. The more successful I appeared, the harsher became the collective judgment of my former friends."

"I'm glad," I replied, "I haven't experienced that reaction, but

I know many minority teachers who have. It is a familiar phenomenon. One of its forms is condescension thinly veiled as collegiality. Professor Regina Austin's experience is an example. Shortly after publishing two articles for which she was granted tenure, one faculty member—the school's affirmative-action officer—came into her office and draped himself on her couch ready for conversation. He proceeded to inform me," she reports, "that he was glad that it had been unnecessary for him to write a memorandum in support of my promotion because he really did not know what he would have written about my articles.

"Professor Richard Delgado thinks that something like 'cognitive dissonance' may explain this reaction:

> At first, the white professor feels good about hiring the minority. It shows how liberal the white is, and the minority is assumed to want nothing more than to scrape by in the rarefied world they both inhabit. But the minority does not just scrape by, is not eternally grateful, and indeed starts to surpass the white professor. This is disturbing; things weren't meant to go that way. The strain between former belief and current reality is reduced by reinterpreting the current reality. The minority has a fatal flaw. Pass it on.[30]

"The value of your Chronicle, Geneva, is that it enables us to gauge the real intent and nature of affirmative-action plans. Here, the stated basis for the plan's adoption—'to provide a more representative faculty and student body'—was pushed to a level its authors never expected to reach. The influx of qualified minority candidates threatened, at some deep level, the white faculty members' sense of ideological hegemony and caused them to reject the Seventh Candidate. Even the first black or the second or the third no doubt threatens a white faculty to some extent. But it is only when we reach the seventh, or the tenth, that we are truly able to see the fear for what it is. Get my point?"

"I do," said Geneva. "But the question is whether the Supreme Court would get it and, if they understood, whether that understanding would help my case. I suppose we have already agreed that it would not. We have both noted the judicial reluctance to interpret Title VII requirements strictly in academic settings. And we have agreed that the courts might view my law school's hiring efforts as a voluntary affirmative-action plan so impressively successful that it moved the school beyond the ambit of antidiscrimination law."

"That's all true, but I would still recommend that the seventh candidate take his case to court. We civil rights advocates don't give up so easily, Geneva. Assuming that the case could survive a motion to dismiss, the trial court would require the law school to *explain* its rejection of a highly qualified black man—a process that would educate the public, embarrass the law school, and at least provide a liberal judge with the factual support necessary to decide in our favor."

"Does your strategy," Geneva asked sarcastically, "for going ahead with litigation include an offer of representation on a contingent-fee basis?"

"Why not? I'd be willing to take the risk."

Geneva shook her head. "God help our people!" she said, lifting her eyes toward the ceiling in mock prayer. "You concede that consideration of 'The Chronicle of the DeVine Gift' is a helpful exercise for civil rights proponents. The Chronicle is a sharp reminder that *progress* in American race relations is largely a mirage, obscuring the fact that whites continue, consciously or unconsciously, to do all in their power to ensure their dominion and maintain their control. But what good is the lesson, if you evade the very points that the exercise is designed to teach?

"Let me try once more to reach you. Now we know that the disadvantages wrought by generations of racial discrimination cannot be remedied simply by enjoining discriminatory practices. In adopting affirmative-action plans, many institutions and governments have attempted to address this problem. But the controversy over whether and to what degree affirmative action is wise, legal, and moral has obscured the inherent limitations on the affirmative-action approach in particular and on the integration ideology in general. Perhaps because of my long absence, I see more clearly that racial integration is this era's idealistic equivalent of abolition in the pre–Civil War years. Each represented in its time a polestar by which those seeking reform could guide their course during a desperately hard journey—away from slavery in the last century and away from segregation in ours. While pointing the way, these beacons fail to provide us with a detailed blueprint of what to do upon arrival. They do not tell us how to ensure that those who have been long exploited by the evil now removed shall be recompensed for their losses in pocket, psyche, and public regard. Confusion arises from the failure to recognize the difference between the beacon we have and the blueprint we need. We inevitably lose our way and wander back to the situations of subordination from which we worked so hard to escape."

Finally, Geneva, who had been pacing back and forth again, sat down. "The DeVine Gift Chronicle illumines the reasons why affirmative-action remedies advance our frustration as much as our cause, and yet I sense a more viable blueprint hidden somewhere in its bleak message."

"While you were speaking," I said, "I thought of an observation that the Protestant theologian Reinhold Niebuhr made more than fifty years ago. He wrote that black people could not expect 'complete emancipation from the menial social and economic position into which the white man has forced him [the black man], merely by trusting in the moral sense of the white race.' He suggested that, although large numbers of white people would identify with our cause, the white race in America will not admit the Negro to equal rights if it is not forced to do so. Upon that point, Niebuhr said, 'one may speak with a dogmatism which all history justifies.' "[31]

"I know the passage," Geneva said, "and its note of deep despair, which rings as clear and true now as then, challenges even you to give it a positive twist."

"I'm not so sure. Remember, Niebuhr spoke at a time when progress would have been defined as a reduction in the number of blacks lynched each year.[32] You are right, Geneva, that the statement has meaning for our time—but a meaning suggestive rather than fatalistic. Even in his pessimism, Niebuhr assumed that, if whites perceive that substantive rather than symbolic racial reform is necessary, meaningful reform will take place—an assumption validated by history. What we need is some common crisis: war is the best example. Whenever the country has been engaged in armed conflict, beginning with the Revolutionary War, the need for manpower has enabled blacks to gain opportunities in the military as well as in domestic positions formerly closed to them. Other kinds of national crisis can have the same result. I am thinking of an event that captures the nation's imagination and makes clear how much our future depends on mutual effort—on our relating as equals, rather than as superiors and subordinates. In other words, I envision a common crisis that will serve as a catalyst to move us out of the traditional *we/they* racial thinking."

"Well," Geneva said, "I guess you're entitled to your modern-day equivalent of the slaves' Old Testament hopes that a Moses would come and rescue them—hopes that certainly helped them survive. But if your prayers were answered, a common crisis of the type you envision would be self-effecting. There would be no need for civil rights lawyers to go into court and seek the creation of new rights."

"I don't expect a common crisis to bring on the millennium. The post–Second World War conditions that prepared the way for an end to racial segregation were not self-effecting. We still needed years of litigation to gain any benefit from the *Brown* decision. I would expect a common crisis to do no more than to impress on policy makers on the Court and in government the necessity for further racial reform."

Geneva looked at me with both sympathy and sadness in her eyes. "The best response to your common crisis strategy is contained in my next Chronicle—which, I warn you, may strain your faith in this approach beyond the breaking point."

Chapter 7

The Declining Importance of the Equal-Protection Clause

The Chronicle of the Amber Cloud

At midnight the Lord smote all the first-born in the land of Egypt, from the first-born of Pharaoh who sat on his throne to the first-born of the captive who was in the dungeon, and all the first-born of the cattle. And Pharaoh rose up in the night, he, and all his servants, and all the Egyptians; and there was a great cry in Egypt, for there was not a house where one was not dead.

—Exodus 12:29–30

THE AMBER CLOUD descended upon the land without warning, its heavy, chilling mist clearly visible throughout the long night it rolled across the nation. By morning, it was gone, leaving disaster in its wake. The most fortunate young people in the land—white adolescents with wealthy parents—were stricken with a debilitating affliction, unknown to medical science, but whose symptoms were all too familiar to parents whose children are both poor and black.

The media called it Ghetto Disease, a term that made up in accuracy what it lacked in elegance. Within days, the teen-age offspring of the nation's most prosperous families changed drastically in both appearance and behavior. Their skins turned a dull amber color. Those afflicted by the disease could not hide it. Because its cause and contagious potential were unknown, its victims, after an initial wave of sympathy, were shunned by everyone not so afflicted.

Perhaps the victims' bizarre personality changes were a direct result of the Amber Cloud itself; perhaps they simply reflected the youths' reaction to being treated as lepers, both in public and in all but the most loving of homes. Whatever the cause, the personality changes were obvious and profound. Youngsters who had been alert, personable, and confident became lethargic, suspicious, withdrawn, and hopelessly insecure, their behavior like that of many children in the most disadvantaged and poverty-ridden ghettos, barrios, and reservations.

The calamity dominated all discussion. The wealthy felt the effects directly and were distraught. Before the crisis ended, more than one parent had publicly expressed envy for their ancient Egyptian counterparts whose first-born were singled out and slain during the night of the Passover. Attendance and achievement in the finest schools plummeted. Antisocial behavior rose sharply as parents whose child-rearing credo had been "privileged permissiveness" lost the status-based foundation of their control. Apathy was the principal symptom of the afflicted; but in many cases, undisciplined behavior in the home escalated to gang warfare in suburban streets. Police had difficulty coping with serious crimes committed by those who earlier had committed only minor misdemeanors. Upper-income enclaves, which had long excluded blacks and the poor, now were devastated from within.

Working-class whites, although not directly affected by the cloud, sympathized deeply with the plight of the wealthy. Long accustomed to living the lives of the well-to-do vicariously through television and tabloids, they reacted with an outpouring of concern and support for the distressed upper class.

Private efforts raised large sums of money to further Ghetto Disease research. At the same time, governmental welfare programs extended their operations from the inner-city poor to the suburban rich. No one questioned the role of government in the emergency. Even those far to the political right sounded themes of the necessity of state involvement. The proffered public aid was not "welfare," they said, for the nation's future—now in danger—must of necessity be secured.

The young victims did not blame their plight on blacks. But many of their well-to-do and powerful parents claimed that subversive black elements were responsible for the disaster—an accusation they supported by noting that no children of color were affected and by recalling that some civil rights leaders recently had expressed bitterness at the government's failure to improve the conditions in which ghetto children were raised and educated. Police officials soon responded to political pressures to "do something" about the crisis by rounding up civil rights leaders on a variety of charges. During the next few months, a growing number of whites urged even greater retaliatory measures against black leaders and those whom they represented.

Racial hostility did not extend to a group of black social scientists, all experts on the destructive behavior of black ghetto life, who worked with government experts to develop an effective treatment plan. During the search for a cure, hundreds of blacks volunteered for extensive psychiatric testing designed to determine the precise nature of Ghetto Disease.

After a year of strenuous effort, the president announced the development of a psychological-conditioning process and a special synthesis of mind-altering chemicals that appeared capable of curing Amber Cloud victims. Both the treatment and the new medicine were very expensive; together they would cost up to $100,000 per person. But a nation that had prayed for a cure "at any cost" proved willing to assume the burden.

Civil rights leaders hailed the discovery and urged that the treatment be made available to nonwhite youths whose identical behavior symptoms were caused by poverty, disadvantage, and racial prejudice. They cited scientific appraisals predicting that the treatment would prove as effective in curing minority youths as Amber Cloud victims. They also argued that society owed minorities access to the cure, both because blacks had been instrumental in developing the cure and because the nation was responsible for ghetto pathology afflicting poor minorities.

The public responded negatively to this initiative, criticizing the attempt to "piggyback" onto the Amber Cloud crisis the long-standing problems of minority youth. Moderate critics felt that minority leaders were moving too fast; the vehement openly charged that the problem with ghetto youths was not disease but inherent sloth, inferior IQ, and a life-long commitment to the "black lifestyle."

A presidential task force recommended legislative action authorizing the billions needed to effectuate the cure. Congress budgeted the costs largely by cutting appropriations for defense systems. "Defense," it was argued, "must begin at home." The Amber Cloud Cure bill included a "targeting" provision that specifically limited treatment to the victims of the Amber Cloud. Over the furious objections of minority-group legislators, the Amber Cloud Cure bill was quickly enacted.

Civil rights litigants prepared and filed lawsuits challenging the exclusion of minority youths from coverage under the Amber Cloud Cure Act. The lower courts, however, dismissed the suits on a variety of procedural grounds. The treatment program was carried out with maximum efficiency and patriotic pride, as the nation faced and overcame yet another emergency. Following the cure of the last Amber Cloud victim, a national day of prayer and thanksgiving was proclaimed, and the nation and its privileged youth returned to normality. The supply of the cure was exhausted.

I t was all too clear that The Chronicle of the Amber Cloud undermined my theory that progress for blacks might evolve out of a national crisis endangering whites as well as blacks; and, reluctant to accept all the Chronicle's implications, I confined myself to murmuring that it would make an interesting question for my constitutional law course.

"I surely hope I have not gone to all this trouble just to provide you with teaching aids," Geneva said angrily. "And I hope that asinine comment does not reflect any lingering illusion that this country would not respond any differently than in the Chronicle. Or have you forgotten the discriminatory way in which government benefits were distributed during the Great Depression? As the historian John Hope Franklin reports, 'Even in starvation there was discrimination, for in few places was relief administered on a basis of equality. . . . In many of the communities where relief work was offered, Negroes were discriminated against, while in the early programs of public assistance there was, in some places, as much as a six-dollar differential in the monthly aid given to white and Negro families.'[1] In that, the country's most serious economic crisis, there was widespread suffering and an unprecedented amount of government intervention to relieve it—but the usual racial priorities were scarcely altered. Furthermore, have you forgotten that, even during the Second World War, the meager gains made by blacks were not achieved in an atmosphere free of racial hostility and discrimination?"[2]

"No, I haven't," I assured her, my mind jumping ahead. "It's not easy to accept but there does seem to be more historical support for the Chronicle's conclusion than for a happier outcome. Even more recently, the nation's frantic response to the recession of 1980–81, when unemployment rose to double-digit figures for both whites and blacks, compares poorly with the lack of concern during the last few years when only the black unemployment rate has remained high."

"Given that evidence"—Geneva was pushing me—"what possible basis sustains your theory?"

"If any possibility remains of making progress during a common crisis, it's no more than an opportunity that fate may provide. It is not a promise around which blacks can plan a strategy. Still, I wonder what significance the Chronicle has as a predictor of how the Supreme Court would address issues like those the civil rights groups tried vainly to raise in the lower courts."

"Well, I am encouraged that you seem to have abandoned your idea that a common crisis would miraculously accelerate the pace of racial reform. But," Geneva continued, the sarcastic edge returning to her voice, "is your continued hope of success in the Supreme Court based on some major decisions that I have overlooked in my reading?"

"No, but I think that the Court might view as a racial classification the provision that effectively 'targets' the Amber Cloud Cure for whites. The Court must review with great care laws that burden a racial minority.[3] And to justify such discrimination, which otherwise could constitute a violation of the Fourteenth Amendment's equal-protection clause, the government must show a compelling state interest."

"Perhaps you know better than I," Geneva interrupted, "but it has always seemed to me that the application of the so-called strict-scrutiny test to determine the validity of racial classifications is more rhetoric than reality. When minorities most need the Fourteenth Amendment's shield, the Court does not seem to respond."

"I'm not sure I understand your problem, Geneva. You certainly remember the language in the Japanese internment case *Korematsu* v. *United States* (1944): 'all legal restrictions which curtail the civil rights of a single racial group are immediately suspect. . . . Courts must subject them to the most rigid scrutiny. . . . Although pressing public necessity may sometimes justify the existence of such restrictions, racial antagonism never can.' "[4]

"I remember it," Geneva acknowledged, "and its rhetoric is reassuring—but not, to my mind, as telling as the Court's application of its test. For example, I find it hard to forget the actual decision in the *Korematsu* case. The governmental rules excluded Japanese-Americans from their home areas solely on the basis of race, assuming 'that all persons of Japanese ancestry may have a dangerous tendency to commit sabotage and espionage and to aid our Japanese enemy in other ways.'[5] And yet while the Court claimed to review the regulations with super suspiciousness or strict scrutiny, that standard, as applied in *Korematsu*, did not prevent a majority of the Court from approving orders excluding Japanese-Americans from areas where they lived and worked and, in a companion case of the same time, from subjecting them to a curfew."[6]

"Well, the strict-scrutiny standard did have a rather shaky birth, but obtaining judicial protection of individual rights during a wartime crisis is always problematic."

"Problematic, hell! It was predictable racism. Justice Frank Murphy called it by its right name when he stated in dissent that whatever deference should be given to the military's judgment in its own sphere, the judgment here was premised on 'questionable racial and sociological,' rather than military, considerations."[7]

"Perhaps so, Geneva, but you must concede that reliance on the military's judgment in wartime, when the nation's very future is at stake, is a tendency the courts are likely to follow rather then defy. Remember Justice Felix Frankfurter's concurring opinion in the *Korematsu* decision: that the challenged rules were justified by the constitutional provisions authorizing the president and the Congress to wage war. In his view, 'to find that the Constitution does not forbid the military measures now complained of does not carry with it approval of that which Congress and the Executive did. That is their business and not ours.' "[8]

"It seems to me," said Geneva, "that blacks have always been treated like an alien force in this country, and that you are all too ready to rationalize judicial tentativeness on civil rights issues on just those occasions when courageous certainty has been most needed. You seem to forget, my friend, that blacks seeking to enforce their rights are always 'special situations' that courts must handle sensitively. 'Political sensitivity'—like 'wartime necessity'—acts as an unacknowledged barrier when we ask the Court to apply the strict-scrutiny standard. So much of the Court's sensitivity is reserved for white concerns that there seems to be little left for black needs. Have you forgotten *Brown II*'s 'all *deliberate* speed' formula of 1955[9] for implementing *Brown I*'s ringing mandate the previous year to save the 'hearts and minds' of black children?"[10]

"Geneva," I cautioned, "you're being too harsh. Long before the 'strict scrutiny of racial classifications' approach was formally announced, the Court struck down some racial classifications that prevented blacks from voting and living in white neighborhoods, barred Chinese from operating laundries, and limited jury service to white males."[11]

"I have not forgotten those decisions," Geneva said, "but I also recall that the same Court upheld segregation schemes that resulted in separate and equal facilities for blacks.[12] Not until 1954 did the Court recognize that separate facilities are 'inherently unequal.'[13] And since then, far too little has changed. Every law student is familiar with 'suspect classification' decisions such as *Loving* v. *Virginia* (1967)[14] in which the Court applied the standard to a statute barring interracial marriage. By the mid-1960s, a full decade after *Brown*, these rulings were generally accepted and, outside the deep South, even applauded. But I will bet that few law students know, and even fewer law scholars remember, that only a few months after *Brown*, the Court refused to review the conviction, under an Alabama antisegregation law, of a black man who had married a white woman.[15] Many of us do remember, of course—and remember, too, the procedural contortions that the Court used one year after *Brown* to avoid deciding another challenge to a state law barring interracial marriages."[16]

"You're a hard woman, Geneva. But you must agree with Professor Gerald Gunther, who, although not happy about the procedural process in the decision you speak of, conceded that 'there [were] strong considerations of expediency against considering the constitutionality of anti-miscegenation statutes in 1956.'[17] Moreover, I'm not sure how much light these old cases can shed on how the Court would handle equal-protection issues today."

"A strange statement," Geneva shot back, "for someone whose racial theories rely as much on history as yours do! And it becomes even stranger when we consider that modern cases have continued the pattern."

I was confused. "What is this pattern in the strict-scrutiny cases that you see as limiting the protection provided to blacks under the equal-protection clause?"

"It seems to me that the Court strikes down laws that contain racial classifications only if they (1) overtly discriminate on the basis of race, (2) cannot be justified by crisis needs or the protection of socioeconomic stability, and (3) can be invalidated without creating too much opposition either to the decision or to the Court."[18]

Geneva sat back, pleased with her summary, but I wanted to

put her three-part formula into perspective. "After 1937, when the Court abandoned its half-century of effort to protect economic rights,[19] it adopted a very relaxed standard of equal-protection review of social and economic legislation.[20] On the other hand, in 1938, the Court unofficially suggested that 'discrete and insular minorities' would receive a special measure of judicial protection[21]—a suggestion later spelled out in the language, although not in the outcome, of the Japanese-American exclusion cases. As a result, there were two standards for judicial review of claims that state laws violated the Fourteenth Amendment's equal-protection test.

"My point is that some legal commentators concluded that, under the Court's equal-protection test, the standard that was 'strict in theory' ended up being 'fatal in fact.'[22] That is, every challenge to a law containing a racial classification led the Court to strike down that law. Now you seem to be saying that racial classifications survived strict scrutiny unless they met your three-part test. Most people will want more evidence of the accuracy of your assessment than you have provided."

"At this point," Geneva said, "my first concern is not in convincing most people but in converting you. Keep in mind that, by the end of the 1960s, most states had abandoned enforcement of blatant segregation statutes—those requiring 'white' and 'colored' signs in rest rooms, and so on. It was the Court's record of invalidating these 'Jim Crow' statutes that gave rise to Professor Gunther's observation that, in practice, the strict-scrutiny standard was 'strict in theory, fatal in fact.'[23] Later cases tended to involve laws or policies that adversely affected blacks but did not explicitly mention race. Obviously troubled by such cases, the Court, after some uncertainty, shifted the focus of its review away from a measure's 'suspectness,' as determined by the harm a law caused blacks, and toward the 'intentions' and 'purposes' of those who enacted the measure.[24] The Court assures us that the harm to blacks, its 'disproportionate impact, is not irrelevant, but . . . is not the sole touchstone of an invidious racial discrimination forbidden by the Constitution.' "[25]

"What you're saying," I suggested, "is that in most contemporary cases, the Court, while perhaps mouthing the standard, actually applies strict scrutiny only after the plaintiffs have overcome the heavy burden of proving that an official action, ostensibly serving a legitimate end, was really intended to discriminate against blacks."

"Exactly," Geneva said, "and the burden of proving discriminatory intent in most of these cases is so great that blacks gain no benefit from the suspect-classification standard—and, without overwhelming proof that the challenged policy is an act of outright bigotry, will not prevail. Some decisions indicate that even evidence of obvious racial hostility may not be enough."

"Can you cite particular decisions that support your point?" I asked.

"Please," Geneva urged, "do not treat me like one of your law students. You know the cases as well as I do, though I imagine you would rather forget *City of Memphis* v. *Greene* (1981). There, the city of Memphis, at the request of a white neighborhood association, closed a street at the border between a white and a black neighborhood, forcing residents of the black neighborhood to take an alternate route to the city center. Blacks claimed the barrier's creation of racially separate neighborhoods was barred by the Thirteenth Amendment's prohibition of 'badges of slavery' that in this instance reduced property values in the black community for the benefit of the white neighborhood. The Court held that legitimate motives of safety and residential tranquillity justified the closure, and that the blacks had not suffered a significant property injury by the action.[26]

"The *Memphis* street-closing measure was challenged, under a civil rights statute based on the Thirteenth Amendment rather than the Fourteenth,[27] in an effort to avoid the tough-to-meet intent standard the Court was certain to apply under the Fourteenth Amendment. As it turned out, the Court applied the hard-to-meet standard by claiming there was not sufficient evidence of harm to reach the intent issue. Justice Thurgood Marshall, joined by Justices William Brennan and Harry Blackmun, filed a vigorous dissent, asserting that the Court's majority ignored evidence of historic segregation in Memphis, that there was evidence of discriminatory intent in this situation, and that the erection of a barrier to carve out racial enclaves within the city is precisely the kind of injury that the Thirteenth Amendment–based civil rights statute was enacted to prevent.

"And, if you want an example involving the Fourteenth Amendment, take *Palmer* v. *Thompson* (1971), where the Court by a five-to-four vote refused to find unconstitutional the decision of Jackson, Mississippi, to close its public swimming pool rather than comply with a court order requiring desegregation of all public facilities. In response to claims that the city officials' motivation for closing the pool was a desire to avoid integration, the majority acknowledged evidence of some ideological opposition to pool integration but, contending that legislative motivation was difficult for a court to ascertain, concluded that 'no case in this Court has been held that a legislative act may violate equal protection solely because of the motivations of the men who voted for it.' "[28]

"Perhaps," I suggested, "this and the Memphis street-closing decisions reflect the Court's reluctance to antagonize large numbers of whites over minor matters, which do not involve crucial rights like voting, jobs, and schools."

"The Court is applying the same tough-to-meet intent standard in critical as well as in less important cases. Moreover," Geneva said sadly, "it is the 'minor matters,' as you call them, that I fear convey unintended signals to blacks and whites about how the Court weighs the relative interests of the two races. The Court's inclination to avoid upsetting whites any more than is necessary, combined with its use of a standard of review that encourages government officials to create 'neutral' rules that everyone knows will disadvantage blacks, in effect creates a property right in whiteness and the consequent loss of some cases that we should by all rights win."

"Proving discriminatory intent can be tough, Geneva, but on occasion, civil rights lawyers have enlisted historians to help them to prove that a challenged law is discriminatory despite its racially neutral text and arguably legitimate purpose. This technique was successful after remand in *City of Mobile* v. *Bolden* (1980),[29] where the Supreme Court approved an at-large districting plan even though it prevented blacks from electing representatives to the city commission. The city argued that its at-large method of electing city commissioners, adopted in 1909, could not have been motivated by racial discrimination because at that time blacks were barred from voting by a 1901 state constitutional amendment. Historical evidence, however, showed that the at-large system was adopted to dilute the vote of blacks in the event the federal government were to order their re-enfranchisement. The district court invalidated the city's at-large elections."[30]

"We should applaud the civil rights lawyers' resourcefulness," said Geneva, "but we should also question more closely why the Court's majority was willing to accept the city's argument that a blatantly unconstitutional state provision—the Alabama constitutional amendment—should serve to insulate from close scrutiny an at-large scheme that had prevented any black from gaining election to a city commissioner's seat, despite the fact that blacks constituted 35.4 percent of the voting population.

"But before I let you further apologize for the Court, I would like to hear your response to my conclusion that, under the Court's interpretation of the equal-protection clause, the targeting provision of the Amber Cloud Cure Act would easily withstand legal challenge."

"Why are you so certain litigation would fail?" I asked.

"Because, the Court might find that the targeting provision was a racial classification and that strict scrutiny should be applied, but nevertheless conclude that, in light of the crisis created by the Amber Cloud, the government had shown a compelling state interest justifying the limiting of the cure to victims of the Cloud—to the exclusion of minority children. The opinion would read much like the one in the wartime Japanese-American exclusion cases.

"Alternatively, the Court might conclude that the act did not constitute a racial classification, but rather provided a remedy for one distinct form of a widespread ill. In arriving at this conclusion, the Court would focus on the different *sources* of the ailments—the Amber Cloud and the sociological conditions of life in the ghetto—and conclude that the racial differentiation of the act was entirely fortuitous, rather than invidiously intended. With no need to apply the strict-scrutiny test, the Court would find that under its more relaxed equal-protection review standard, Congress was justified in deciding to address one ill at a time.[31] Finally, at least one justice would not be able to resist the observation that if any racial discrimination was practiced in this case, it was by the unknown forces responsible for the Amber Cloud. The government, he or she would say, was simply aiding in a race-neutral way those who were the victims of that discrimination."

"Geneva," I said, as she paused, "I think your assessment of the equal-protection clause's value in contemporary civil rights cases has some validity. The current Court's interpretation of the clause, while certainly more helpful to civil rights litigants than was the interpretation in effect when we began the long struggle to overturn the 'separate but equal' doctrine, provides ample leeway for an adverse ruling in the Amber Cloud litigation. On the other hand, the facts are enough to shock the conscience of even the most conservative jurist, and might, reviewed against the backdrop of the black experience in this country, induce the Court to rule in our favor. Could a society burdened with the guilt of two centuries of slavery and another century of formal segregation survive the moral onus of withholding from the black community a tested cure for its devastating social ills? And if a concern for the image we as a nation presented to Third World peoples after the Second World War influenced the decisions to abandon racial segregation, then wouldn't the nation's policy makers be concerned about the message projected by the denial of medical treatment to poor black children?"

"You remind me," Geneva snorted, "of that typical response to nineteenth-century abolitionists: 'Certainly slavery is wrong, but who will pay to free the slaves?' Cost would be no less a barrier today."

"Well, Geneva, perhaps we might argue that the government's provision of health benefits to whites and its denial of the same benefits to blacks with precisely the same needs infringes on a fundamental personal right to a minimum level of health, triggering strict scrutiny review. Certainly health benefits are crucial to an individual's well-being—no less critical than the educational benefits to which Justice William Brennan referred when he wrote that we 'cannot ignore the significant social costs borne upon our

Nation when select groups are denied the means to absorb the values and skills upon which our social order rests.' "[32]

"Interesting," Geneva conceded, "but in recent years the Supreme Court seems to have closed the ranks of fundamental rights in equal-protection review.[33] Do you have reason to believe that the Court will return to a more expansive approach?"

"Look, Geneva, we might lose the case for all the reasons you've mentioned. Suspect-classification doctrine has helped relatively powerless minorities, but only when the classification under review is so blatantly and arbitrarily discriminatory that the Court could strike it down under a much less exacting standard of review. Strict scrutiny under the equal-protection clause has not served to protect minorities against the operating laws and governmental policies that are racially neutral on their face but very burdensome in effect.

"The Court rightly sought to maintain heightened equal-protection review for minorities after its post-1937 adoption of a lenient 'reasonableness' standard of review for most governmental actions. What it perhaps could not have foreseen was that overt exploitation and subordination are not the only forms of racial discrimination, and that facially neutral social and economic legislation may wreak havoc on blacks because of their past deprivation. Thus, as it is with so many civil rights principles, the symbolic value of the suspect-classification standard, while reassuring, in practice provides no protection at all.

"I admit the prospects aren't good, but perhaps we could convince the Court to undertake a full-scale review of equal-protection jurisprudence and its usefulness in contemporary racial cases. Such a review, conducted in the dynamic and volatile context presented in the Amber Cloud Chronicle, could prove enlightening to everyone. Even in defeat, as we learned in *Korematsu*, the Court may yet gain new insight into the problems of modern racism and devise an improved method of addressing those problems in future cases."

Geneva smiled. "My friend," she said, "I remember when I shared your never-say-die enthusiasm. But now I am no longer certain that such earnest commitment is a help to our people in the absence of a still-to-be-discovered new approach to our age-old problem. In fact, I fear that your efforts to effect change through unthinking trust in the law and the courts place you not on the side of black people, but rather in their way."

I looked at her soberly. "We blacks have enough problems without charging one another with obstructionism simply for doing the best we can."

"You're right, friend, and I am sorry. I guess I am tired. It's been a long day and we must both be ready for a break. I do hope you have planned to stay over. That couch you're sitting on converts into a fairly comfortable bed."

"No, Geneva, I think not. Since you have no phone, I want to get back to town and call my wife, so she won't worry about me tramping around in the wilds of Virginia."

"Is it the wilds she minds—or the wild woman in the wilds?" Geneva inquired, raising an eyebrow.

"Oh," I said, smiling, guarding against her sudden irritation, "if she knew you the way I do, she'd know she has nothing to fear."

"If she knows me only as well as you do," Geneva said, her voice as flat as a large lake at high noon on a hot day, "then she knows nothing at all."

"What do you mean by that?" I, too, now defensive.

"Only that some things seem never to change. White folks want to run everything. And you want to act stupid about women."

"I wonder," I said, packing up my papers and tape recorder, "whether you and I are doomed by fate not to be able to talk more than two minutes about anything without an argument."

"Fate?" she asked, relentless. "Mother Nature may not like your blaming on fate your inability to function with women on other than a serious basis."

I stood up. "I always try to be a gentleman, Geneva. I am sorry if my efforts to treat you as a valuable human being entitled to respect seem cold and uncaring."

"Well," she said, her eyes flashing, "I resent your holier-than-thou posture of being interested only in my mind as much as I would were you one of those men who can't see me beyond my——"

"The problem with you strong, black women," I interrupted,

"is that there's no pleasing you. It's impossible to survive in this racist society and live up to your images of what you want us to be. You, above all, should know that the dilemma of black males from slavery until now is the same: we must either accommodate to white domination and live, or challenge it as males should, unceasingly and without compromise, and be ground down to dust."

"Have you forgotten, Mr. Male Ego, that black women live in this society, too, and must face the same racism as black men?"

"True enough, but, out of a combination of fears and guilt, it is black men who are deemed the threat, as indicated by any number of measures: lynching, arrest and sentencing disparities, prison populations, employment bias, and on and on."

"You know, friend, black men and women face interpersonal problems caused by this country's racism that are every bit as important as the law-related issues we have been discussing. I think we must explore them fully."

"Not tonight, Geneva, please."

"Not tonight—but it should be at the top of our agenda tomorrow. Do come early—nine at the latest."

Then we hugged, and I went down the steps and out to my car. Glancing back, I saw her standing in the doorway. She was still there as I drove off.

PART II

The Social Affliction of Racism

Prologue to Part II

EVEN HAD I not been preoccupied with thoughts of that last exchange with Geneva, my chances of finding my way back to town would have been no better than fifty-fifty. But I was somewhat groggy with the long day of talk, and the bright moon cast just enough light to enable me to see side roads not mentioned in Geneva's original directions. All of them looked promising, and none was marked by a sign that meant anything to me. I was totally lost in about twenty minutes.

Finally I came upon a paved road wide enough to seem likely to lead me back to town. Just as I stepped on the gas, I was passed by an old car that must have been doing at least eighty. One of those "good ole Southern boys," I thought, practicing the skills that produce so many champion stock-car drivers—and for a moment considered giving chase, on the chance he'd lead me to some outpost of civilization. But before I could act on the idea, I glanced in the car mirror and saw the revolving blue lights that every driver both recognizes and dreads. I pulled over immediately, braced for trouble, but the police cruiser sped by me and soon disappeared in the distance. I sighed with relief and tried to relax.

It was not easy. No driver welcomes being stopped by the police, but for blacks such incidents contain a potential for harm and abuse seldom experienced by whites save those who are actually wanted by the law. Few blacks ever feel so secure as to be free of such trepidation.

I thought back to another dark road many years before. I had graduated from college with a B.A. degree and a commission in the air force. Driving to my duty station in Louisiana, my new uniform in the back seat, I missed a turn and found myself on a dark country road where my worst fear became fact in the presence of a state policeman, huge and hostile, who stopped my car, refused to accept "lost" as the reason I was so far off the main highway, and threatened to hold me responsible for various thefts in the area reportedly made by, as he put it, "some damned nigger." It was only by showing him my uniform with its gold lieutenant's bars and my military orders that I managed to calm him. Finally, after a long look at the orders, comparing the name with that on my driver's license, he handed them back to me and, scowling still, told me how to get on the right road. Then he stamped back to his cruiser and roared away.

The lesson of that exchange was not lost on me. While air force officers were entitled to wear civilian clothes while off duty, I wore my full-dress uniform every time I left the base. Northern-born and raised, and insulated by my parents from the meanest manifestations of discrimination, my first trip South was traumatic. I felt clearly, and was convinced accurately, that my life and well-being lay totally at the whim of any white person I encountered. Even when they were not hostile, as many were not, I knew that the choice of courtesy or rudeness was theirs to make, mine to accept—or face the consequences. Gaining a measure of protection for my person through my officer's uniform was the first of many techniques I have adopted in my life as supplement— more accurately, substitute—for the respect racism denied me as a person.

Even now, a respected lawyer and law professor, I was fearful of being stopped and hassled because of my race—even now, with the many civil rights statutes protecting me against police violation of my right to due process of law. On that dark country road, any legal rights I had seemed remote and irrelevant.

Suddenly, topping a rise in the road, I could see far ahead the flashing blue light of a patrol car. Coming closer, I saw it was parked behind another car like the one that had flashed by me so fast. Two figures were standing in the light of the police cruiser's headlights. Thank God, it's not me! I thought, and prepared to drive past.

By then, I was close enough to make out the two figures. While one was, of course, a police officer, the other was not the "good ole Southern boy" I had imagined, but a black woman wearing what appeared to be a choir robe of some shade of gold. As my headlights picked up the scene, I saw the woman was crying, obviously in distress and, from the way the policeman was brandishing his flashlight at her, in some little danger as well. I had to stop, however little I wanted to. I eased the car to the side of the road, turned on the emergency flashers, fished the rental-car contract out of the glove compartment, and, getting slowly out, walked back to the two vehicles.

The policeman challenged me at once. "Mister, I ain't got time to give no directions. You want to go to town, you headed in the wrong direction."

Before I could say anything, the woman broke in, "Sir, he forced me off the road, claims I was speeding, and look what he made me do to my tire!" I had by this time noticed that her car, a vintage Pontiac, had a flat tire. "Now he's trying to turn me into a criminal, which he knows full well I am not."

"What is she charged with, officer?" I asked him, but it was the woman who answered.

"So far, he wants to charge me with speeding, driving a defective vehicle, and assaulting an officer."

"And," the officer interrupted, turning to me, "unless you move on right this minute, I'll charge you with interfering with a policeman in the performance of his duty. Now move!"

"But, officer, I'd like to help if I can. This lady is mighty upset."

Slowly and ominously he removed his service revolver from its holster and pointed it directly at me. "Look, mister, I don't know who you are, but you're not going to rescue this suspect. She's none of your business. Interfering with a police officer in the performance of duty is a violation of state law. Now I am ordering you to leave the area."

I was scared. Not for a long time—not since the early civil rights struggles—had anyone pointed a gun at me, and that empty feeling in my stomach didn't feel any better now than it did then. But the woman offered me an opening. Putting her hand on my arm, she said quietly, "I needs a lawyer, sir. Could you go and call someone for me?"

"Officer," I said, making an effort to keep my voice from shaking, "I am a lawyer, though not admitted to practice in Virginia. I want to represent the lady until she obtains local counsel."

"I don't care who you are, mister. This woman is my suspect. You're interfering with my questioning, and I'm warning you one last time to clear the area."

I began to have second thoughts. After all, I didn't know the woman or what she might have done. A married man with children in college, I felt my attempt to be a knight errant fade. Still, I could give it one more try.

"Officer, however easy it may be to put me down, I don't think you'll find it quite so easy to dismiss my friends in this area." I dropped the names of a prominent politician, the federal judge in the area, and the president of the local university. "I've known each of them for years, and I am sure they would state, on the witness stand if necessary, that I would never have threatened you so as to justify you in using your gun."

The news of my high-placed connections would not have deterred a policeman making a legitimate arrest. It clearly disconcerted the officer standing in front of me.

"Who the hell are you anyway?" he demanded, slipping his gun back in its holster.

I reached in my pocket for my wallet and handed him a card. "That shows I am a law professor, and I'm sure my faculty colleagues would support the president and the dean here in Virginia."

In that moment of silence, some of the tension went out of the scene. The officer said to no one in particular, "How the hell this country ever get in such a fix?" I was thinking the same thing, though I had come at it by a very different route.

"This lady got a heavy foot and a big mouth," he said, taking out his book and writing a ticket for speeding. After handing it to the woman, he stalked back to his patrol cruiser without another word and sped off.

"Thank you," the woman said. "He was real ugly, knowin' I belong to the church up the road, where we been petitionin' to stop police harassments around here, and he takin' his anger out on me."

After my scare, I was disgusted with myself, and the woman's thanks made me feel no less embarrassed. She had assumed me to be powerless—an assumption she'd seen verified when I hesitated and almost started back for my car until I thought to invoke the names of important white men.

"Don't thank me," I said. "You owe your thanks to my friends in high places."

"Those people not here tonight. You were, and it's you I'm thankin'—especially since you a friend of Geneva Crenshaw's."

"How do you know that?" I asked, taken entirely by surprise.

The woman giggled slyly. "Well," she said, "in this small Southern town, don't no one keep nothin' quiet, especially a big-time law professor payin' a call on our own Lawyer Geneva, who only got home herself a short time back. When you see her next, you can thank her from me for havin' a man with courage 'round when I needed him."

"I think you mean a man with contacts rather than courage."

"Far as I'm concerned, it amounts to the same thing. And most of our mens ain't got neither one."

Though I was anxious to leave, her comment demanded a response. "That's not fair. I'd bet that any black man driving by and seeing you stranded, with a state patrolman hassling you, would have stopped and tried to help."

"Now *you* mixin' up courage and contact," she said. "The only courage the black mens around here show is when they making contact with some white womens."

"I doubt that, too. But as a civil rights lawyer, I helped get rid of laws that barred marriage across racial lines. Black men have a constitutional right to marry whomever they please, white as well as black—a change in the law effected, in fact, by a 1967 Supreme Court decision in a case from this very state."[1]

"Not talkin' about marryin' no white womens—though that's bad enough. I'm mad at those who go pantin' 'round after them, ignorin' us women who black just because we ain't droppin' our drawers soon as they look our way. It just makes me sick. We black womens got the name of loose and lusty, and the white womens got the game."

"I think you exaggerate. The sexual revolution has affected all

185

races. But this is no place to discuss either law or morality. I need to get back to town and with that flat tire, you need a ride, Miss ——?"

"My name is Delia Jones, but just call me Delia. Now I could fix the tire, but I think I'll ride with you and come back for my car tomorrow."

After we got into the car and I'd started it up, Delia turned on me with all Geneva's intensity. "You married?" she asked.

"Yes."

"Your wife white?"

"What difference does that make given my rights under the laws I just told you about?"

Delia winced as though I had slapped her, and then was silent.

"Well?" I asked finally.

"Question like that," she said with some sadness, "take far more time than we have between here and town to answer. Why don't you take me on home and we talk it over there?"

"Well, I'll take you home, but likely your husband won't care for a stranger dropping in so late."

Delia laughed. "But I ain't got husband or boyfriend. I tried both but have about given up on you black mens ever gettin' your damn selves together in this country."

Delia was an ample woman built on the classic mold, and not at all unattractive. But I thought of my wife and said, "Thanks, Delia, but I can't." To change the subject, I asked whether the robe she was wearing meant she had been singing earlier in the evening—a question that left Delia tongue-tied. "It's a beautiful robe," I went on. "I'll bet it's for a gospel choir."

"It is, but I don't get out here to sing with them very often. My work keeps me busy."

"What do you do?" I was glad to have eased the conversation to neutral grounds.

"You bein' a friend to Geneva, you won't think much of my work. She don't."

"I don't understand."

"Well, I do a little cleanin', I work in the black school helpin' the teachers sometime, and do a little preachin' when the spirit moves me, but mostly I agitate for emigration."

"You do what?"

"You ever hear of Bishop Henry McNeil Turner, Martin Delany, Henry Bibb, or Marcus Garvey?"[2]

"Of course," I responded. "Each of them advocated black exodus from this country. I've read particularly about Garvey, the charismatic black nationalist from Jamaica who founded the Universal Negro Improvement Association and pushed his 'back to Africa' movement through his Black Star Line steamship company during the 1920s."[3]

"You know what happened to him then?"

"He raised millions of dollars and gained broad support among the black masses, but he was convicted—about 1925, I think—of mail fraud and later deported back to Jamaica."[4]

Garvey, Delia told me with obvious pride, was a distant relative, and she in her own way was committed to continuing his work. "That must be pretty hard to do in the rural South," I remarked. "Blacks are a conservative people, and the notion of leaving the country and starting over in a place foreign to them is a very radical idea."

"Life ain't suppose to be no crystal stair, professor," she said, "but white folks so mean, they do most of my work for me. I get to those blacks who tired of takin' low and do what I can to move them in the right direction. You know," she added, "Marcus Garvey said that racial prejudice was buried deep in the white man's nature, and that it's useless to talk to him about justice and all that high-soundin' jazz that nobody believes. Our only hope is to leave this place and start over."

"And even after all the progress made by blacks since Garvey's time, you still believe that?" I asked.

"All that progress, as you call it, didn't keep that white redneck cop from calling me outta my name and pointin' his gun at you when you try to help."

"Well, Delia, that could have happened to anyone interfering like I did."

"Not to your big-shot white friends. Mentionin' their names got that gun right back where it'd never have left if any of them had stopped to inquire why I was upset."

"Your point is well taken, Delia, but America is our home. We were born here."

She laughed. "You remember what Malcolm X said about blacks who boasted they was born here? He would tell them that 'because a cat has kittens in an oven, it don't make them biscuits.' "[5]

"Maybe not," I replied, "but humorous analogies don't alter the fact that we've invested a great deal in this country and gained some rights, and many of us are determined to continue the struggle of those who came before until we or our children have all the rights to which we're entitled by law and simple justice."

"Justice!" Delia mouthed the word in disdain. "Let me ask you something," she said. " 'If you believe that black people will gain their freedom in this racist land, *why* do you believe it? What is the source of your belief, your faith, your hope?' "

I recognized the questions as ones the abolitionist orator H. Ford Douglass asked of black folks who opposed emigration at a conference in 1854,[6] and told Delia so, while conceding their pertinence today. "You really know this subject, Delia."

"And I've got reason to!" she replied. "Livin' with the upper classes like you do, you may not have noticed, but things not gettin' better for the black masses, they's gettin' worse—fast. Unless you got two degrees, the right connections, and a lot of luck, jobs are just not to be had. Our schools about back to black after all that mess to integrate them. Only difference is whites now holdin' down teaching jobs that black folks would've had back in the old segregation days. We votin', but not electin' any of us to anything that counts. And the harassments by police is gettin' worse all the time, as you saw firsthand out here tonight."

Again she reminded me of Geneva, but was more extreme. "Are you advocating separate areas in the country where black people can settle and live?" I asked.

"It just ain't workable. Separatist groups, Black Muslims, New Republic of Africa, others too—they all tried that. It's too threatenin' to whatever white folks was around. No, sir, we got to get out of this America altogether."

"Have you stopped to think that the racism that moves you to leave might bar your departure?"

"Break that down, professor, so a poor home girl can understand."

"Think about it, Delia. When blacks in great numbers began migrating north during the First World War, white southerners, who had maintained that blacks were a liability rather than an asset to the region's economy, resorted to coercive tactics—including arrests, threats, and violence—in an effort to slow the exodus.[7] This country denied a passport to Paul Robeson in the 1950s because 'during his concert tours abroad, Robeson repeatedly criticized the conditions of Negroes in the United States.'[8] Federal law requires a passport for those leaving the country for any purpose, and a passport may be denied to any person whose activities abroad are considered to interfere with foreign relations or otherwise be prejudicial to the interests of the United States."[9]

"Are you tellin' me if I recruited a boatload of black folks who wanted to leave this country for good, the government could stop us?"

"I don't know of any precedents, Delia, but a country that feared what Robeson might do to its image would not waive any available restrictions if a boatload of blacks tried to depart, claiming they were forced to emigrate because racial discrimination in the nation of their birth rendered their lives unbearable.

"And another thing, Delia, assuming the country decided to let all the blacks leave who wished to go, where would we go? How would we get there? Who would finance this emigration movement and stake our claims in some new place?"

She had obviously heard all these questions many times. Her answer was quick and confident. "First, we decide to go. Once we make that decision, answers to your other questions will come to us."

"That sounds like another of your prepared responses, Delia. What specific plans do you have if and when you recruit blacks who are ready to join your emigration movement?"

Without hesitation, Delia launched into a surprisingly detailed outline of how she hoped to carry out a dream she had held for a long time. Viewing the establishment of a new nation as a long-term goal, for the present she advocated an emigration equivalent of the Peace Corps. Blacks with skills useful in African or Caribbean countries would commit themselves to live and work in those countries for a period of years, their work subsidized by funding from an emigration organization that would solicit money from across the country. After a corps of persons had found homes in their new countries, they would make it possible for others to follow. Both Africa and the Caribbean islands offered, she argued, great variety in life style, political and social organization, and economic opportunity. It was, she insisted, possible to go there and help rather than exploit, to contribute and not simply add to the immense burdens of countries still struggling in the postcolonial phases of their development. Every well-publicized departure, she assured me, would throw the country into a quandary of ambivalence and uncertainty that could not fail to benefit those blacks who remained.

"You're really committed to a black exodus," I observed as we drew up in front of her house in the black area of town.

"It's either exodus or extinction," she replied. "Not much of a choice. I just hope we not too late."

"As a gospel singer, you must know that old song with the refrain 'Please be patient with me, God is not through with me yet.' Think about that song when you think of me, Delia, and all those men who look like me—and you. If we're not worth saving here, we won't be worth taking any place else. Good night."

The motel sign, for all its neon garishness, looked like fine art. After calling my wife, I went to bed. It was very late, after midnight, but I couldn't clear my mind of thoughts about the incident with the policeman. It was just one more reminder of my inability to defend myself or another black against the racial hostility that any black person, but particularly men, can encounter at any moment, regardless of who we are. That knowledge of my powerlessness affects my relationships, and all relationships between black men and women, in ways no less hurtful because they are impossible to prove—or even discuss. Despite all my legal arguments, Delia might be right about the need to make a new start "any place but here."

Unable to sleep, I turned the options over and over in my mind: physical emigration, or accommodation of a kind most costly to self-worth. It is a dilemma as difficult to explain as it is painful to face. I recalled the lectures over the years in which I had attempted to explain to mostly unbelieving white audiences how vulnerable to the smallest aggressions of racial fear and hostility even the most successful black person remains. Income, professional achievements, and prestige, none of these is a certain defense.

And now I had another experience that would be hard to get my audiences to comprehend. To save one black woman from a white cop's verbal abuse and possibly worse, I had surrendered a bit more of my self-esteem. Using the names of well-known white men as a shield against the cop's anger was but a contemporary form of the shuffling my forebears had had to do, a form of the "scratchin' when it don't itch and laughin' when it ain't funny" tactic that generations of blacks have used to show subservience when whites have threatened their well-being or their lives. While what I had done was no worse, it surely was no better, than the stereotype of the beloved obsequious black so popular in this country.[10]

I remembered my early days at the NAACP Legal Defense Fund when the then general counsel Thurgood Marshall would regale the staff with stories about going to the South in the 1940s to represent some black man charged with rape or another crime against a white that had turned the community into a racial tinderbox. On such trips, the defendant's attorney from up North was the target of local scorn and risked being attacked. I was saddened more than amused when Thurgood, asked how he handled those situations, in mock humor gravely explained that when he got to town, he would take out his civil rights and fold them very carefully, and then put them down deep in his back pocket, and—pausing for effect—he would leave them there where they and their owner would be safe until he got out of that damned town.

It was hardly a comfort to realize many years later that Thurgood's self-deprecatory anecdote illustrated a survival formula used, in one form or another, by all of us. Of course, the law prohibits intimidating conduct by state officials, including police, but the sanctions always seem inadequate or, at the most, remote. Even today, for blacks as well as whites, the traditions of racial subordination are deeper than the legal sanctions. Such statutes, making racial harassment by law-enforcement officials a criminal offense, had been enacted after the Civil War and, after a long period of neglect, had received judicial rejuvenation in the 1960s;[11] while, in the 1970s, civil remedies also received more liberal interpretations enabling at least victims of particularly heinous police abuse to recover damages.[12] Geneva and I must surely discuss all of this tomorrow.

I awoke with a start, jarred back to consciousness by the bright sunlight that filled the room. Geneva would be furious. I dressed and after a quick breakfast at the motel to spare my stomach any more of her health food than was necessary, I set off for her cottage. As I feared, she was waiting at the door, frowning. She stood aside as I entered, but said nothing, nor did her frown soften.

"I ran into some trouble finding my way back to town last night," I apologized, "and overslept. But I had a dream associated with your Chronicles."

"Association based on one day?" Geneva interrupted. "Sounds more like guilt to me. I offer you a perfectly good couch to spend the night here—but, oh no! You have to rush off into the night like some male Cinderella about to turn back into a pumpkin. It was hardly a compliment to me. I certainly wasn't going to attack you, and I am equally certainly able to resist any untoward overtures of yours—though any such action on your part would have been quite a switch from our NAACP days."

"And what's that last comment supposed to mean?" I asked warily. "I thought we were friends, two lawyers committed to bringing our people out of the wilderness of racial segregation."

"You may not have noticed, but in the old days"—her sarcasm revealing some old resentment I had never suspected—"some of our colleagues found time, on occasion—how shall I put it?—to 'socialize.' " Her sarcasm slurred *socialize* into a paragraph of suggestive meaning.

"Of course, I noticed, Geneva—that whenever there was time for anything other than work, you were always surrounded by a panting pack of amorous males. And I wasn't going to be a part of that macho horde."

"You're simply brimming over with compliments this morning. Why in God's name do you think that you would have been 'part of that macho horde' had you expressed at least a tiny interest in anything other than my lawyerly skills?"

"I cannot be hearing Geneva Crenshaw talking—that woman of the fierce, feminine independence and stickler for gender equality. Are you saying you were waiting for me to make the first move, exhibit male dominance, assume a posture of patrimony in a patrimonial world?"

She looked me in the eye and said simply, "I am Geneva. And it would have been no crime had you at least once discussed something other than the cases, the clients, and the civil rights cause."

The Geneva I remembered had never seemed likely to make such a concession about her interest in anyone.

"But Geneva, at the risk of prolonging this less-than-joyous reminiscence, I would like to know why you of all people didn't at least suggest that I join the crowd of your male admirers?"

"Lord!" Geneva said, shaking her head slowly. "Why must black women be doubly cursed: victimized by white racism and black sexism?"

"I don't follow you."

She spoke cautiously. "Let me start with the suggestion that you may not have wanted to join those men chasing after me in New York because you saw in their stud type of behavior a not very praiseworthy compensation for all the other expressions of male power denied them as black men in a white world.

"And," she added before I could comment, "you have spent your life in self-assertion of one form or another, proving that a black man can challenge his subordinate place and survive. However praiseworthy the results, much of your life is spent teaching white folks a lesson about their racial stereotypes—namely, that those racist myths do not apply to you. At bottom, though, yours is just another form of compensation, little different—and certainly no less sexist—than the compensation affected by those New York characters you so despised."

Geneva's tone softened, though her words continued to sting. "You see," she explained, "neither approach is a compliment to women however much you and the macho men, each for your own reasons, think it is. And both approaches are manifestations of frustration at a society that refuses to acknowledge your personhood even though you accept its assumptions about male domination by behaving like sex-starved dogs or the most chivalrous of men."

"Must I feel privileged then that you saw sufficient difference in the compensatory mechanisms to invite me here rather than one of those New York characters?"

"Don't be peevish! The fact is that your claim that you wanted to treat me simply as a working associate is self-serving, a typical response from men unable to understand that professional women can be respected and loved simultaneously. For them, we must be aggressive 'bitches' to make it professionally, but servile or at least docile to be loved, and perhaps eventually married."

"You're entitled to your opinion," I told her, determined not to oppose the expression of that entitlement, as irrational as I found it. "But my question remains. If you identified what you thought was my misguided sense of male chivalry while we were working together, and were interested, why didn't you simply tell me so?"

She laughed. "It seemed to me that you were fond of me but were afraid to admit it lest you'd have to compete with those smooth-talking New York dudes. But had I said anything intended to encourage your interest, you would have concluded that I was another overly assertive woman, and fled in panic.

"You may not have realized it yourself but, unwilling to compete in the usual way, you tried harder to be a good friend—which, of course, I could appreciate at the professional level. You worked hard at your job, were serious about using your life well, showed real courage in the courtroom, and seemed always worried about principle rather than self in your decisions. I was impressed, but——"

"It seems," I interjected, "that with all your militant insistence on equality for women—an area you felt strongly about long before the national movement got started—your social standards resemble those of the Victorian era. And I have seen that lingering insistence on traditional courting in many of my black women law students."

"Precisely how most black women in what were considered middle-class families were brought up back then. And," she conceded, "I gather, some of that background lingers today in black women's desire for traditional courtship rituals. But my problem with you, friend, was not my upbringing but your well-intentioned but no less demeaning confusion of sex and sexuality with sexism. In an effort not to be sexist in a Don Juan way, you effectively denied that it was possible to respect my professionalism and love me as a person.

"Now let's move on. But before you tell me your dream, I would like to hear about the trouble you had on your way back to town last night."

"A state patrolman was harassing a black woman whose car had a flat tire. I stopped to help, and I got him to leave her alone—though not in a manner I want to boast about. Actually, the woman is an acquaintance of yours who knows you're here and that I'm visiting you."

"Impossible!" exclaimed Geneva. "I am absolutely certain no one knows I am here."

"Well, Delia Jones indicated that she grew up around here and that you know her."

Geneva looked blank. "I don't remember anyone by that name, but she may have been much younger than I. What did she look like?"

"Brown skin and solidly built, you might say on the heavy side. The heaviness, though, was all in the right places."

Geneva frowned. "Sexism does live in your heart unaccompanied, as far as I can see, by any compensatory characteristics. What else can you tell me?"

"She's probably in her forties, but looks younger. When I first saw her, she was crying and being harassed by a local cop. While I was driving her back to town, she told me she was a distant relative of Marcus Garvey and was trying to form a back-to-Africa movement in this area. But she's also a gospel singer and was wearing a beautiful gold robe."

"Oh, my God! Oh, my God!" Geneva sank down on the couch and put her head in her hands.

"Then you do know Delia?" I asked.

Geneva shook her head slowly. "My friend," she said, staring into my eyes, "I do not know Delia Jones, because there is no Delia Jones. You saw a woman who must have looked quite real as well as quite good, to judge by the gleam in your eye as you were describing her. But Delia Jones is, in fact, one of the Celestial Curia Sisters. Did she try to convince you that her black-exodus project was the only option left to our people?"

"That she did."

"Those women are not trustworthy," Geneva said furiously. "I am trying as hard as I can to decide what I believe we blacks should do to overcome racism, and they damn well know I chose you to help me in my evaluation. How dare they interfere and try to influence you to influence me?"

"It makes sense to me," I said, trying to remain calm in the light of this revelation. "You know that each of the Curia members are urging very different strategies, and you, in conflict, are looking for a third approach militant enough to meet the reality of our condition and yet humane enough to equate with the religious faith that helped sustain us through so many bad times."

"Well, if this Sister felt you might be able to win me to support a black-exodus strategy, she was mighty mistaken. With your commitment to legal reform, you're hardly the ideal recruit for an emigration scheme."

"I don't know about that. Delia's plans sounded pretty good. And you have such a poor opinion of my militancy that, had I returned here espousing a black exodus, the shock might have won you over."

Geneva laughed. "You may be right—but unless we get back to work, I may have to choose emigration by default."

"How about the other Curia Sister who advocates disruption and possibly violence?" I asked. "Is she likely to appear and try to influence your decision through me?"

"I doubt seriously that the other Curia Sister really cares whether or not I adopt her strategy. As far as she is concerned, increasing violence and eventual armed racial struggle is inevitable. It may be a long time, but she is willing to wait."

"That's frightening."

"What is really frightening is the apparent certainty of many conservatives that they can dismantle the few social welfare programs, and the civil rights agencies now providing inadequate protection against poverty and racism, without blacks reacting violently here as oppressed peoples have reacted elsewhere in the world—as, indeed, over two centuries ago, white Americans reacted to an oppressive government."

"We likely encourage that certainty," I said soberly, remembering last night's exchange with the policeman and Delia's diatribe against black men. "Given our history, it's understandable but no less deplorable that our automatic reaction—of both black men and black women—to white hostility is to accommodate, accommodate, accommodate. And then we let off our frustration by violence against one another and often unspeakable treatment of our women whom we can't respect because their very presence is a constant reminder of our inability to protect them against the racism that constantly challenges us either to accommodate or to pay the price. Indeed, the dream I spoke of bears on the society's racial pressures and their impact on black male-female relationships."

"If it were a Chronicle, what would you call it?"

"Well, it's influenced by your Chronicle of the Amber Cloud, but takes a quite different direction. Let's call it the Chronicle of the Twenty-Seventh-Year Syndrome."

Chapter 8

The Race-Charged Relationship of Black Men and Black Women

The Chronicle of the Twenty-Seventh-Year Syndrome

IT WAS NOT LONG after the terrible phenomenon of the Amber Cloud, when the nation had been totally preoccupied with saving its upper-class, white, adolescent youth from the devastating effects of Ghetto Disease, that it was discovered that the Amber Cloud had, after all, affected at least one category of the black population: able black women, many of them with excellent positions in government, industry, or the professions. Gathering the data was difficult, but it appeared that each month twenty-seven black women in this socio-economic group were falling ill without apparent reason, about three months after their twenty-eighth birthday.

The illness itself was bizarre in the extreme. Without any warning, women who had contracted the malady went to sleep and did not wake up. They did not die nor go into a coma. Their bodies functioned but at less than 2 percent of normal. Nothing known to medical science could awaken the women, save one natural remedy—time. After four to six weeks, the illness seemed to run its course, the women awakened, and, after a brief recovery period, all their physical functions returned to normal.

That was the good news. The tragedy was that, in a special form of amnesia, the women lost their professional skills and were forced to return to school or otherwise retrain themselves in order to continue their careers. In some cases, this meant several years of work and sacrifice that some of the victims were unable or unwilling to make. After some time, medical researchers were able to delineate more specifically the characteristics of the black women at risk. They had: (1) held at least one degree beyond the bachelor's and had earned an average of thirty-five thousand dollars per year over the three years prior to their twenty-seventh year; (2) completed their twenty-seventh year of life; and (3) had neither ever been married or entertained a *bona fide* offer of marriage to a black man.

Women who were or had been married to, or who had received a serious offer of marriage from, a black man, seemed immune to the strange malady. But not sexual activity, or a relationship outside of marriage, or even out-of-wedlock motherhood served to protect the victims. Marriages of convenience did not provide immunity, nor did a sexual preference for other women. Strangely, black women married to white men also contracted the disease. Public-health officials called the sickness the "Twenty-Seventh-Year Syndrome," while the tabloids referred to it, with an editorial snicker, as "Snow White's Disease."

For a time, the media followed the story eagerly. But gradually—because there were no fatalities, and the victims of the malady were spread across the country—the ailment slipped into the category of illnesses like sickle-cell anemia that strike mainly blacks and thus are of only passing interest to whites.

The nation's refusal to make the Ghetto Disease cure available to black young people barred all hope that a national mobilization would be undertaken to find a remedy for the Twenty-Seventh-Year Syndrome. And, as one high-placed government health official explained, there was little interest in searching for a medical remedy when a social remedy was at hand: these women should each find a black man who would offer to marry them. "It was," he said, "as simple as that."

But as virtually everyone in the black community knew,

the simple remedy was, in fact, extremely difficult. The Twenty-Seventh-Year Syndrome had added a dire dimension to what had long been a cause of deep concern to black leaders and a source of great pain and frustration to able black women. For many years before the strange disease made its appearance, the most successful black women had had a very hard time locating eligible black men with whom to have social relationships that might blossom into love, marriage, and family.

Social scientists have isolated several components of the social problem confronting all professional women, but exacerbated for blacks by the fact that the black population includes over one million more women than men, and by the high proportion of black men in prisons and among drug addicts compared with the very few who attend college and graduate school. In addition, those black men who survive, and achieve success comparable to that attained by black women professionals, have many more social choices. They may not marry at all, or can marry very young women without advanced degrees or professional skills. Some few of the otherwise eligible men are gay; and much to the chagrin of black women, a goodly number are married to white women.

For all of these reasons and more, many of the most talented, successful, and impressive black women remain single or do not marry until well into their thirties. As a result, at the very time when the black community is racking its wits about how to address the problem of teen-age black girls becoming pregnant and bearing children by young males unable to support them, many of those black women most qualified to raise the next generation of black children remain unmarried and childless.

The unhappy paradox produces disunity in the black middle-class community, where women tend to condemn the inadequacies of black men; and the men, resentful at being further burdened with society's faults, lash out at black women as being unsupportive and hard-hearted. With the onset of the Twenty-Seventh-Year Syndrome, this debate intensified as speakers claiming to represent the interests of men or of women demanded that the other "do something."

Federal health officials, still smarting from the attacks by blacks outraged at the government's failure to extend the Amber Cloud Cure to black youths, determined to act aggressively on the Twenty-Seventh-Year Syndrome. Lacking funds to search for a cure, they decided, with little or no consultation, to issue compulsory Syndrome Control regulations which would, as they said, "serve as a quasi cure by making known to the 'cure carriers' (black men) the identities of those persons at risk." In summary, single black women between twenty-four and twenty-seven years of age and deemed vulnerable because of their marital and socio-economic status were required to register with the government. If they had not established stable marriages with black men by the middle of their twenty-seventh year, the law required broad public disclosure of this fact along with detailed biographical information.

The populace in general and black people in particular were appalled and angered by the new regulations. The charges of "cruel and heartless" were not much reduced by amendments to the law providing that the records of a woman married to, or in a stable relationship with, someone other than a black man would not be made public. It was pointed out that while the Syndrome was disabling, it struck only 27 women each month, and 324 women each year—a serious matter, to be sure, but hardly justifying subjecting literally thousands of black women to a humiliating public display of their personal lives. Civil liberties lawyers seeking to challenge the constitutionality of the regulations as being in violation of First Amendment rights of privacy were stymied by procedural provisions that rendered it difficult for any woman to gain standing to challenge the rules until after she had been subjected to the compulsory publicity in the regulations.

As it turned out, the first woman whose name was selected in a special drawing to receive the publicity expressed little interest in challenging the regulations. Amy Whitfield, a well-known writer, said the law represented a particularly pernicious form of male chauvinism, one more indignity heaped on black women. Given the legacy of rape and degradation that her sisters had endured down through history, she assumed she should be thankful that a male-dominated society had not designed some still more odious process to harass those women already enduring the frightful knowledge that they might soon become a Twenty-Seventh-Year-Syndrome victim.

Ms. Whitfield explained that marriage was not the sole goal of her life, that she and her educated sisters had made contributions and lived full lives without the need to seek rescue from men who were not interested in them. "I am not opposed to marriage," she said. "There are men I would have married and men who would have married me—but they have never been the same person.

"Conjugal convergence," she went on, "requires more men than are available, particularly for black women, all of whom, owing to the horrors of American racial history, find it difficult to contemplate marrying a white man, while some consider it out of the question. Basically," she concluded, "if the public disclosure required by the statute serves to spotlight some of the dual burdens of racism and sexism black women carry, the humiliation may be bearable. But at this stage of my life, I am not interested in becoming any man's damned damsel in distress."

Most black men agreed. The frustrated anger they felt upon learning that the Twenty-Seventh-Year Syndrome attacked only black women turned to rage when government health officials announced their Syndrome Control regulations. Urged by a group of black ministers to vent their fury in positive ways, black men across the country organized "Together at Last" clubs to raise money for the medical research the government refused to fund, set up "sleep-care" facilities to nurse Syndrome victims, and established scholarships to assist recovered women in regaining their skills.

What black men did not do was rush out and propose to black women simply to save them from contracting the Syndrome. As one young black professional put it, "Black women have suffered enough because we have emulated the society's sexism. Now, in their time of need, we should not add to their Syndrome-caused despair by patronizing marriage proposals that are little more than romantic vaccinations."

But the Syndrome experience did cause many black men who had—"as one option"—taken black women for granted to begin recognizing them for the remarkable individuals they are: survivors in a tough, hostile world, who have overcome difficult barriers and seek men able to share their success and not be threatened by the strengths without which that success would not have been possible.

The change in black male attitudes was slow, halting, and produced no miracles of sex-role reformation. The Syndrome continued to claim its predictable number of victims, and there remained far more black women than eligible black men. But out of tragedy came a new awareness and understanding. And while the "black male versus black female" debate continued, the bitterness disappeared from discussions that looked toward reform and away from recrimination.

W ELL, I was wrong," Geneva began, "and you were right in predicting that I would not like your Chronicle. Despite some camouflage, it just brims with patriarchy and sexism. Sure, the society's racism is a substantial cause of the shortage of eligible black men. I rather doubt, though, that black women or the race will be much advanced if the only cure for racism's impact on black families is male domination of the sort implicit in the so-called cure for the Twenty-Seventh-Year Syndrome."

I raised both hands in defense against her harsh words. "It was only a dream, Geneva. I'm not personally invested in it. Still, it can serve as a vehicle for discussing the degree to which racism has exacerbated for blacks the always-difficult social relationships between men and women. The focus was narrow: namely, on those black women who, having overcome society's hurdles, find that their professional achievements present barriers to their hopes for personal happiness through marriage and family.[1]

"The Chronicle of the Twenty-Seventh-Year Syndrome does not disparage the fact that many, many women, regardless of race, live meaningful and entirely happy lives without either marriage or children. The simple point is that, in today's world, many white women and black women must choose the single road. And black women in particular are denied free choice on that important matter precisely because of society's erosion of the role of black men."

"And your Chronicle," Geneva burst out, "provides these societally disabled black men with their long-awaited chance to come riding to our rescue just as their white chauvinist prototypes do. Perhaps we should retitle it the 'Chronicle of the Black Male Castration Cure.'"

"You shouldn't condemn what you obviously don't understand," I cautioned. "Black men do feel castrated by the society and can be male chauvinists in some of the worst ways imaginable, as a whole cadre of black women writers have been reporting to the world for years.[2] I certainly don't want to condone wife cheating, wife beating, and all the other forms of abuse—even though one needn't be a psychologist to recognize that much of this conduct is the manifestation of frustration with racism."

"There are some acts we cannot blame on white people," Geneva said firmly, plucking a book out of a huge pile beside her chair and opening it to a page marked with a slip of yellow paper. "I agree with Grange Copeland, the character in Alice Walker's first novel who warns his son of the trap of blaming others for making a mess out of your life. Listen to this:

> I'm bound to believe that that's the way white folks can corrupt you even when you done held up before. 'Cause when they got you thinking that they're to blame for *every*thing they have you thinking they's some kind of gods! You can't do nothing wrong without them being behind it. You gits just as weak as water, no feeling of doing *nothing* yourself. Then you begins to think up evil and begins to destroy everybody around you, and you blames it on the crackers. *Shit!* Nobody's as powerful as we make them out to be. We got our own *souls* don't we?"[3]

"That's a powerful statement," I said, "and it reflects a wisdom

Grange Copeland has to travel a bitter road to gain. But that's my point. There's a history here that cannot be ignored. A major component of slavery was the sexual exploitation of black women and the sexual domination of black men. The earliest slavery statutes devoted substantial attention to prohibitions on interracial sex and marriage.[4] The clear intent of these laws was to delineate the inferior status of blacks as much as to discourage interracial sexual activity, a goal furthered by the double standards generally followed in their enforcement.[5] And while slavery is over, a racist society continues to exert dominion over black men and their maleness in ways more subtle but hardly less castrating than during slavery, when male-female relationships generally weren't formalized and, even when a marriage was recognized, the black man's sexual access to his wife was determined by when the master or his sons or his overseer did not want her.[6]

"As Professor Oliver Cox observed," I continued, " 'If a Negro could become governor of Georgia, it would be of no particular social significance whether his wife is white or colored; or, at any rate, there would be no political power presuming to limit the color of his wife.' On the other hand, as Professor Cox has also said, if in what is supposedly a democracy, the state can insist that a black man have a black wife, it is then possible to have a structure in which not only can the black not become governor, but he can be required to do the dirtiest work at the most menial wages."[7]

Geneva was not impressed. "That is digging rather deep into history for racial injustices to explain current failures by black males. You seem to forget that black women as well as black men suffered the pains of slavery. The black activist Lucy Parsons said it all when she wrote that 'we are the slaves of slaves; we are exploited more ruthlessly than men.' "[8]

"I've not forgotten, Geneva. But I am suggesting that, while the racial injustice was shared, the sexual harm differed. Black women were exploited, abused, and demeaned, and that harm was serious. Forced to submit to the sexual desires of their masters or of slaves selected by their masters, these women then suffered the agony of watching helplessly as their children were sold off. But black men were also dealt a double blow. They were forced to stand by powerless and unable to protect black women from being sexually available to white men, and were denied access to white women as a further symbol of their subordinate status. The harm done black men by this dual assault has never been fully assessed. Moreover, the assault continues in less blatant but still potent forms."

"True, it was a serious problem," said Geneva, "but the wounds in present relationships caused by the nonfunctioning of black men seem self-inflicted, as Alice Walker and scores of less articulate but no less wronged black women have testified."

My patience was exhausted. "Ms. Crenshaw, I am not a sociologist. I agree that historically 'black women have carried the greatest burden in the battle for democracy in this country.'[9] If you and your black sisters achieve a perverse pleasure out of castigating black men, I can't stop you. I think, though, that there is value in trying to find an explanation other than the condemnation 'no good' to explain our admitted shortcomings."

"I am listening," Geneva replied, "but I hope you do not expect me to maintain a respectful silence during your effort to justify with words what is often unjustifiable behavior."

"Having your sympathetic and impartial ear will make my task easier," I said, teasingly. "Let me say again that unconscionable behavior by black men makes my point. For the physical restraints of slavery that rendered the black male powerless have been perpetuated in the present, with economic restraints, joblessness, and discrimination in all its forms today rendering many black men powerless to protect wives and family. Shame and frustration drive them from their homes and lead them to behavior that can be as damaging to black women as any actions by whites in this racist society.

"While you and many proponents of women's rights feel that it is sexist for a man to feel some special responsibility to protect his woman, in this society such feelings go with the territory. And by making it so damned difficult to fulfill that protective urge, the society has turned many black men into modern instruments of their own oppression, mistreating black women and disrupting the struggle for a semblance of family life. This is not our intent, but it is, in fact, the result of conduct growing out of our unconscious realization that we, as much as our slave forebears, are powerless to protect whatever or whomever whites decide they want."

"It all sounds rather melodramatic," Geneva observed, "particularly now that laws barring racial discrimination, including interracial marriage, have been struck down by the courts."

"Again," I explained, "we have to look at history. It's important to remember that economic exploitation, rather than an abhorrence of interracial sex, was the real basis for all the so-called antimiscegenation laws that were contained in the first slavery statutes and remained on the books of twenty-nine states as late as 1951.[10] Professor Cox argued that these laws were motivated by the cultural advantage they secured for whites. By asserting that they were protecting the 'honor and sanctity of white womanhood,' white elites provided themselves with both a moving war cry and an excellent smokescreen for furthering and shielding their basic purpose: refusing blacks the opportunity to become the economic peers of whites."[11]

"In effect, then, white women became tools of white male oppression?"

"That at least is how one student of the problem, Calvin Hernton, characterizes it," I responded. "Hernton, who rejects Cox's 'economic' explanation as 'too mechanical,' believes that both white women and black men are in a 'semi-oppressed' class in terms of jobs, political power, money, property, and access to opportunities for higher status.[12] And as a predictable result, any number of black spokesmen—including Frantz Fanon, Malcolm X, and Eldridge Cleaver—have acknowledged the political implication in the black man's attraction for white women."[13]

"I wonder," Geneva interrupted, "whether you are not making too much of the economic and political functions of antimiscegenation laws. Is not the main view that these sanctions were motivated by whites' basic fear and abhorrence of interracial sex?"[14]

"One need not deny that view," I said, "to agree with Frantz Fanon that it is reasonable to assume that attitudes about sex are embedded in a given cultural and historical context; and that even if sexuality is basically biological, its form of expression is influenced by variables including economics, status, and access to power.[15] And Cox, on this point, notes that whenever whites are in a ruling-class situation, there is a very strong urge among black men to marry or have sex with white women."[16]

"It is this seemingly ungovernable urge that many white men fear and a great many black women detest," Geneva observed.

"Don't I know it! But Professor Cox is, I think, on target with his comment that 'it must not be supposed that it is the white woman as a mere sexual object which is the preoccupation of colored men, it is rather her importance to him as a vehicle in his struggle for economic and cultural position.' "[17]

"Does all that sociological theory explain the vastly greater number of black men who marry white women than black women who marry white men?" asked Geneva.

"Well, I gathered the census data a few years ago, and the disparity you speak of does exist. As I recall, of 125,000 black-white couples in 1977, three-fourths involved a black husband and a white wife. And by 1981, the percentage of black husband–white wife couples had increased to almost 80 percent. I should add that interracial marriages of all types are on the rise, having jumped, between 1960 and 1970, by 108 percent (from 148,000 to 310,000). They increased 36 percent from 1970 to 1977, and even more from 1977 to 1981."[18]

"Those figures must put you in something of a quandary," Geneva remarked. "Wearing the sociologist hat you've been sporting for the last few minutes, you must view those interracial marriages as psychologically explainable but no less regrettable in the ammunition they provide for accusations and recriminations among black people. On the other hand, as an integrationist, I assume you applaud these figures as a happy fruit of civil rights victories in cases like *Loving* v. *Virginia* (1967) that struck down anti-miscegenation laws?"[19]

"I do feel some ambivalence," I admitted, "but I'm also aware that, as with other racial reforms, the removal of barriers against interracial marriage serves the needs of the whole society but not necessarily those of the blacks as a people within that society. Chief Justice Warren, speaking for a unanimous Court in the *Loving* case, dismissed the state's arguments for retaining the laws as 'obviously an endorsement of the doctrine of white supremacy.'[20] Of course, he was correct, but the remedy—opening the way for marriage across racial lines—cured only one evil while doing little to reconstruct the deeply damaged sense of what we might call 'black male wholeness.' "

"Evidently," Geneva said sarcastically, "it is sufficient cure for those black men who choose white women as wives or sexual partners."

"I'm not sure you're being fair," I responded. "White women must also choose black men. It is possible for a black man and a white woman to mate and marry for the old-fashioned reason: love. But my point is that, for whatever reason black men are drawn to choose white women, that attraction, and the Court's decision that made it legal, simply decreases the already inadequate number of potential mates for black women. And, as our discussion on this subject illustrates, the decision exacerbated tensions between black men and black women, particularly on the issue of black male responsibility to black women."

"A responsibility," Geneva observed, "that, according to your theory, they're too damaged by what happened in slavery even to recognize, much less assume."

I nodded. "But it's more complicated than that. The continuing powerlessness of black men affects black women as well, particularly strong black women. A strong woman doesn't achieve that status by accident. She knows her strength, has developed it over the years, appreciates it, perhaps even revels in it. It's her basis of survival. Her strength makes her intolerant of weakness, particularly in those whose weakness threatens her survival. Thus, even though she may love a man, her contempt for weakness will come out. And if her man is black, you can believe that in this society there will be many opportunities for that weakness to be all too obvious—no matter how successful he is and how strong he tries to be. No matter how hard she tries to accept him as he is, her true estimate of his strength comes out in ways that her man reads as a lack of respect—and resents precisely because he knows damn well that because of this society's racism he can never earn the respect his woman wants to give, and cannot."

I took a deep breath. "I haven't wanted to confess it, but I had one such reminder of my powerlessness last night when I stopped to help Delia Jones as she was being harassed by that policeman. He pulled his gun and threatened me in a way he would not have threatened a white man similarly dressed and behaving as I did— a lesson I reinforced in effect by shielding my race-based inadequacy and warning him that well-connected white men I knew would cause him grief if he didn't leave me alone. It worked, but it was a further proof, in my mind, of who is strong in this country and who is weak."

"That wasn't weakness," Geneva said. "That was using your head to keep from losing it. We have always been able to outsmart white folks. It was a key part of our survival technique. You're foolish to confuse it with a stupid macho image of how a 'real man' would have handled the situation. For the most part, real men of that type are either myth or dead."

"It's easy for you, Geneva, to dismiss the protective male urge as patriarchal in origin and suicidal when emulated by black men. But didn't you just admit that you accepted—*acquiesced* was your word—in male-dominant modes of courtship because, given the current patriarchal structure of our society, it was likely the only romantic approach I could handle?"

Geneva blushed. "Please don't confuse the subject of the male urge to protect his woman with your inability to deal with me as lawyer and lover. My problem with your Chronicle of the Twenty-Seventh-Year Syndrome is that it ignores all the black males with problems like yours, and elevates to the level of indisputable truth the sexist ideal of men as the natural protectors of women. So, while recognizing that society is patriarchal, your Chronicle does not analyze the harm that priority does to the black community's struggle against racist oppression. Rather, it encourages black men to assume a role equal to the white man within the patriarchal order. It does not even hint at—much less espouse—a more desirable option: that is, for black men to reject the whole 'protective role' concept and become one with black women in order effectively to confront the common enemy—racism."

"My Chronicle is based on the world as it is," I tried to explain, "not as some of us would like it to be. Within that context, it provides a dramatic situation intended to show black men that black women, even those who have demonstrated outstanding ability and survival strengths, cannot themselves create black mates with abilities and strengths equal to their own. To the extent this is a problem—and at the risk of being labeled sexist—I consider it damn serious, and a problem that only black men can cure."

"And are you saying that, before the crisis caused by the Twenty-Seventh-Year Syndrome, black men were unable to function in what you call a 'manly' way regarding these single black women?"

"Why do you find that so hard to believe?" I asked. "There have been many such transcendent events in black history—in fact, in all history. Consider the reaction of black people to the Emancipation Proclamation and the *Brown* decision. Both sparked waves of activity far beyond anything justified by the words of the documents. Perhaps a closer example, because more tragic, was the assassination of Martin Luther King, Jr., in 1968. His death led to tremendous change. Losing him was a tragedy and certainly not a 'fair trade,' but it's clear that the civil rights reforms and progress of the following few years resulted from the transcendent event of his death."

"What do you think about Amy Whitfield, and likely many other women in her situation, who do not want to become any man's 'damn damsel in distress'?"

"I think such women miss the point, Geneva. No one should devise any sort of Twenty-Seventh-Year Syndrome as a means of getting black men to function. That would be evil, just as killing Dr. King was evil. The Chronicle simply replicates this type of evil. Even without the federal health regulations, the disease puts the spotlight on black men: they have the opportunity and the obligation. If the television pictures of afflicted black women lying asleep in the hospitals don't provide the necessary incentive, nothing will. Black women are in danger. Only black men can save more of them from a pretty awful fate.

"And keep in mind that the women are not forced to marry in order to gain protection from the Twenty-Seventh-Year Syndrome. Men have only to provide black women with the *choice* whether to have a black home. That's all. Black women are entitled to that, as I think even you will agree. I can understand why women who have spent their lives developing and defending their individual identities do not want to change them, especially not to demean them for anyone. As Amy Whitfield makes clear in the Chronicle, she does not want her life to read like a dime-store medieval romance. But I don't think Amy or—in light of our conversation of last evening—even you are opposed to men expressing their interest in such a way as to provide black women with choice."

"In other words," Geneva said, "it's a matter not of whether women want to be saved, but of giving them a choice and thereby saving yourselves. I don't see why, even in your dreams, you men can envision only chauvinistic solutions that perpetuate sexist stereotypes.

"Amy Whitfield was kind. What she is trying to say tactfully is that most black professional women have 'choices.' But because of the quality of those choices, many reluctantly opt to remain single. If the black men in your Chronicle have not engaged in any self-reflection, if they have not determined and continue to fail to appreciate that black women face real and significant racial problems that equal and, yes, surpass those that men face, they will not provide a 'meaningful choice' to black women.

"More blatantly, unless black men can pause for one minute, can stop feeling sorry for themselves—that is, free themselves of their castration complex—and *try* to understand and empathize with the condition of black women, that condition—as hellish as the Twenty-Seventh-Year Syndrome—will not change. Black professional women will continue to opt to be alone or to compromise themselves for their wounded black warriors, providing their men with support while the men bemoan their inability to offer their women a form of protection that the women neither need nor would want save for their understanding that the men have a misguided need to provide it."

"Someday," I replied, "the society will evolve beyond its present rigid views of sex roles, but that time has not come. And black men won't be ready for the era of complete sex equity until they have gained that confidence and sense of themselves essential to male-female relationships based on mutuality and sharing."

"True enough, friend. I am simply saying that black men cannot hope to attain their independence through the subordination of their women. The black man needs to direct his attention outward—as I gather your Chronicle suggests some black men are doing through the 'Together at Last' clubs—and recognize that, even historically, as his sexual access to his wife was determined by the white man, the wife was similarly restricted from him. When she was raped, something that was hers—not his—was being robbed.

"Once black men realize that racial oppression equally afflicts black women, perhaps our mutual problems will be easier to address. The powerlessness about which black men so bitterly complain is no less severe in the black woman. These feelings emanate from what we expect of ourselves vis-à-vis our loved ones as opposed to what society expects from us. But until black men critically assess the sexist expectations of society and define their own expectations, they will not be compatible mates for black women who have expectations of their own for themselves. The problem with the Chronicle is that it perpetuates this black male focus instead of viewing the plight of the black woman through her eyes and, in the process, honestly assessing the problems black men have independently caused owing to their intransigent adherence to sexism."

"The issues involved here, Geneva, are as complex as any we have discussed. Your perspectives are valid although not necessarily the primary concern of the Chronicle as I dreamed it."

"I have one last concern about your Chronicle."

"Yes?"

"If it was intended, as you claim, to reveal to black men their opportunity to give black women a choice, why does the Twenty-

Seventh-Year Syndrome afflict successful black women who are involved in nonmarital relationships or have children out of wedlock, and especially why are black women married to white men not exempted? Women in these categories obviously had choices and exercised them, and yet all are subject to the illness. Why?"

I thought about the question for a full minute, and finally admitted, "I'm not sure. It may be that the supernatural powers responsible for the illness were influenced by that Victorian mindset on sex you mentioned earlier. Furthermore, the vulnerability of black women married to white men may reflect the strong negative feelings in some portions of the black community—as well as among whites—about interracial marriage, particularly when black men marry white women."[21]

"Your response is not convincing," Geneva observed. "And it maintains attention on the quantitative aspects of black women's choices, ignoring in the process the key qualitative issue for black professional women. I honestly do not believe any of us are personally—as distinguished from politically—distraught over the black men who are married to white women. They are simply not an issue. They are not 'eligibles' in our personal lives. Our distress is caused by the quality of the limited choices we do have. So, even if black men stopped marrying white women, were released en masse from prisons, rejected homosexuality, and so forth, the quality of our choices would not necessarily change."

"Well, Geneva, this is a subject we could discuss for the remainder of your time without coming any closer to agreement than we are right now. I think we'd better move on to what I'm afraid will be the last Chronicle I have time for."

Chapter 9

The Right to Decolonize Black Minds

The Chronicle of the Slave Scrolls

From my cabin window I look out on the full moon, and the ghosts of my forefathers rise and fall with the undulating waves. Across these same waters how many years ago they came! What were the inchoate mutterings locked tight within the circle of their hearts? In the deep, heavy darkness of the foul-smelling hold of the ship, where they could not see the sky, nor hear the night noises, nor feel the warm compassion of the tribe, they held their breath against the agony! . . .

O my fathers, what was it like to be stripped of all supports of life save the beating of the heart and the ebb and flow of fetid air in the lungs? In a strange moment, when you suddenly caught your breath, did some intimation from the future give to your spirits a hint of promise? In the darkness did you hear the silent feet of your children beating a melody of freedom to words which you would never know, in a land in which your bones would be warmed again in the depths of the cold earth in which you will sleep unknown, unrealized and alone.

—HOWARD THURMAN

THE MUSINGS of the black theologian Dr. Howard Thurman[1] give eloquent voice to questions that led me, in frustration and growing despair, to abandon my civil rights law practice and seek refuge in religion. After several years of study and missionary endeavor, I became the minister of an urban black church. A short time later, I decided to make a pilgrimage to Ghana. As Christians of old sought the Holy Grail as proof of the miraculous in Christ's death and our redemption, so I was drawn to Africa seeking secrets of the slaves' survival that might offer their descendants sustenance and possible salvation. And, amazingly, on my last evening there, I found the revelation for which I had come—and for which, indeed, I have been searching all of my life.

On that evening I walked along a wide desolate beach; and as the sun fell slowly beyond the waves, it cast a fan of gold and salmon and rose across the sky. Even the gray sand was transformed into a palette of rich pastels. As I marveled, I saw the ship. It was not some far-off sail etching an invisible line between brilliant sky and darkening sea, but rather lay at my feet, a model ship perhaps two feet long. By its worn appearance, I could tell that until the sands shifted, it had lain submerged for a very long time.

I picked up the ship and studied it in fading light. I knew from my studies of slave history that I was holding a likeness of the ships the slave traders had used to transport African captives to the Americas, and I felt renewed sympathy for those whose first contact with Western civilization had brought generations of despair and misery. For, as Dr. Thurman had written:

Nothing anywhere in all the myths, in all the stories, in all the ancient memory of the race had given hint of this tortuous convulsion. There were no gods to hear, no magic spell of witch doctor to summon; even one's companion in chains muttered his quivering misery in a tongue unknown and a sound unfamiliar.[2]

Examining the vessel more closely, I found it to be hollow, and it had a corklike plug stuck deep into its stern. Later that evening in my hotel room, I managed with some difficulty to withdraw the cork and found in the ship's hold three tight-rolled parchment scrolls. Unrolling the scrolls, I found them to be covered with thin, fine writing in antiquated English. I read them through at once. They were a testament from the slaves themselves.

Dr. Thurman has asked: "How does the human spirit accommodate itself to desolation? How did they? What tools of the spirit were in their hands with which to cut a path through the wilderness of their despair."[3] The answers were in the scrolls. The identity of those who recorded the secrets of survival, like that of the composers of the spirituals, would likely never be known. But the miracle of their being far outweighed the importance of their origins. And just as the spirituals had enabled slaves to survive, so the scrolls would enable their descendants to overcome.

Returning home to my church, I began to teach the message of the Slave Scrolls. The members of my congregation were profoundly affected. After a few weeks of intense study conducted as the scrolls prescribed in "healing groups" of twenty-five people, the myriad marks of racial oppression began to fall away. There were no "magic" potions to take, no charms to wear, no special religious creed to adopt, and no political philosophy to espouse. Mainly, the scrolls taught the readily available but seldom-read history of slavery in America—a history gory, brutal, filled with more murder, mutilation, rape, and brutality than most of us can imagine or easily comprehend.[4]

But the humanity of our ancestors survived, as the spirituals prove. In the healing-group sessions, black people discovered this proud survival and experienced the secular equivalent of being "born again." Those who completed the healing process began to wear wide metal bands on their right wrists to help them remember what their forebears had endured and survived. Blacks left the healing groups fired with a determination to achieve in ways that would forever justify the faith of the slaves who hoped when there was no reason for hope. If revenge was a component of their drive, it was not the retaliatory "we will get them" but the competitive "we will *show* them."

In this spirit, the healing groups demonstrated a deep desire, precursor to the soon-to-be-gained ability, to accomplish all that white people have long claimed blacks must do to win full acceptance by American society. Blacks who were good workers before learning of the Slave Scrolls became whirlwinds of purposeful activity. Even previously shiftless and lazy black people became models of industry.

Word spread quickly, and soon the congregation grew beyond the confines of our small church. At first, we held healing sessions in public auditoriums but then determined to share the teachings with other ministers and community leaders. The members of my congregation became missionaries traveling across the country teaching black people what we had learned. Excitement in black communities grew; but with the exception of a few black newspapers, the media initially ignored what they viewed as just another charlatan scheme preying on the superstitions of ignorant and gullible black folk.

Within a year, though, neither the media nor the nation could ignore the rapid transformation in the black community. After a time, blacks who heard about, but had not actually gone through, the healing sessions began reading slave histories on their own and later were able to experience the change within themselves simply by seeing its powers working in other black people.[5] All the "Marks of Oppression"[6]—crime, addiction, self-hate—disappeared; and every black became obsessed by a fierce desire to compete, excel, and—as Booker T. Washington used to admonish—"prove thyself worthy."[7]

Unemployed blacks who could find work did so. Those who could not joined together to work for those who did. All manner of community enterprises were started and flourished. Black churches became social-aid centers, and blacks who had been receiving public assistance took themselves off the rolls and soon began sending small repayment checks to welfare agencies. Black family life strengthened as divorce and out-of-wedlock births disappeared. Black children excelled in the public schools, and attended newly opened community classes held in converted taverns and pool halls. They learned the truth about their slave history while preparing themselves to be future leaders.

In a word, black people became in fact what white people

boasted their own immigrant forebears had been. Even the storied Saturday-night party disappeared, and was replaced in many areas by organizations working to eliminate poverty and unemployment among whites. Blacks began outachieving whites in every area save sports and entertainment—activities that black people no longer believed could compare with the challenge of getting ahead through business and industry. Blacks not only voted together but spent their money for only those products that they made or, if white-owned, had been given a vote of approval by the black community.

Understandably, a great many white people, after an initial rather patronizing surprise, became alarmed. They deemed it strange, abnormal, when large numbers of blacks—as opposed to the token one or two—began surpassing whites in business, industry, and education. It was, some whites felt, neither right nor fair—even un-American—for a minority group to gain so much advantage over the majority in a majoritarian society. Spurred by this unease, both government and media investigators searched frantically, without success, for wrongdoing or evidence of subversive elements. For many whites, lack of proved wrongdoing did not deter retaliation. Employers and educational institutions disbanded their affirmative-action programs, replacing them instead with explicit ceilings on the number of black candidates they would hire or admit.

Working-class whites, severely threatened by the increasingly widespread pattern of black economic and political gains, carried out violent attacks against adherents of the healing movement. At several public healing sessions, groups of whites pelted blacks with insults and missiles; in one notorious incident, white attacks resulted in a violent melee in which several persons were killed. In other incidents, several blacks who wore the metal wristbands in public were brutally beaten.

Finally, a popular television minister found in "American morality" what no one had yet discovered in law: an answer to what was now openly referred to as the "black success" problem. In a rousing sermon, the minister told his fundamentalist audience: "Success that is the result of self-help is the will of God"—but the preaching of racial hatred is subversive. The Slave Scrolls, he asserted, created hostility between the races by teaching blacks about the evils of a system wiped out more than a century ago. The minister warned that, unless the scrolls were banished, their teachings would prove as pernicious as those of Nazism and the Ku Klux Klan. Ideologies based on racial hatred, he reiterated, should have no place in a country committed to brotherhood across racial boundaries.

The minister's sermon provided the key to action. Despite the opposition of blacks and civil libertarians, virtually every state enacted what were called Racial Toleration Laws, which severely restricted—and, in some states, banned outright—public teaching that promoted racial hatred by focusing on the past strife between blacks and whites. Penalties were severe for leading or participating in unauthorized public healing sessions, or for publicly wearing what the law termed "symbols of racial hatred." State officials enforced these laws with vigor, severely hampering the ability of blacks to carry out their healing campaign. Whites whose fears were not allayed by the government's actions organized volunteer citizens' groups to help rid their communities of those whose teachings would destroy the moral fabric of American society.

The rest is almost too painful to tell. Whites perverted the law; many still resorted to violence. Like their forebears in the Reconstruction era, blacks tried to hold on. For longer than was perhaps wise, black people resisted, but the campaign to suppress those who wore the distinctive bracelets proved too strong. Black enterprise was no match for the true basis of majoritarian democracy: white economic and military power. Nor were the courts of much help. Our best lawyers' challenges to the Racial Toleration Laws were to no avail.

For the black community, the Slave Scrolls experience served as a bitter reminder that sheer survival rather than inherent sloth has prompted the shiftless habits that, continued over time, led many to forget that whites are threatened by black initiative and comforted by black indolence. If blacks were to survive, they had to make overtures to peace—a prelude to a return to the past. My church, which had become the symbol of what by then was called the "Slave Scrolls movement," undertook "negotiations" with the white community. In fact, we had no choice but to surrender all. We returned the scrolls to the hallowed model ship. Then, at a massive service held in accordance with the surrender terms, thousands of black people renounced the lessons of the healing groups. Having removed and destroyed our bracelets, we watched, and wept, in silence, as both ship and Slave Scrolls were burned.

F OR A LONG TIME, neither Geneva nor I said anything. I was overcome with the ultimate defeat of the Chronicle.

"That's quite a story," I finally ventured, "but one I imagine many whites and more than a few blacks will dismiss as highly implausible."

"Are you suggesting," Geneva asked apprehensively, "that you find yourself in the disbelieving group?"

"Well," I hedged, "it's hard to predict how the public would react to so dramatic a transformation in black conduct and competitiveness. One would have hoped that most whites would hail the black achievements as proof that any group can make it in America by pulling themselves up by their own bootstraps."

"Your hopes, friend, are not supported by Reconstruction history. In that brief period after the Civil War, the newly freed blacks, despite the failure of the national government to provide meaningful reparations, made impressive educational and political gains.[8] But their very success served to deepen and intensify the hostility of southern whites."

"Nineteenth-century history certainly supports your pessimism," I conceded. "And before you remind me, it is true that white society has often persecuted black leaders and groups who have placed a high priority on ridding blacks of their slave mentality. There is the fate of Delia Jones's hero Marcus Garvey, and the more recent experiences of the Black Muslims, Paul Robeson, W. E. B. DuBois, Martin Luther King, Jr., and Malcolm X[9]—whose calls for black communities to organize for mutual protection and benefit gained them many black followers but engendered crushing enmity among whites.

"Malcolm X was a good example of what might be called the black leadership dilemma. That is, during the early 1960s, his trenchant and highly articulate condemnation of white racism gained him tremendous support among poor blacks but harsh hostility from most of white society. He didn't want, as many whites feared, to lead a revolution, but was trying through his angry tirades to show blacks that racism, not inherent inferiority, was the source of their self-hate and self-destructive behavior. What Malcolm X hoped to bring about was the 'decolonization of the black mind—the awakening of a proud, bold, impolite new consciousness of color and everything that color means in white America.'"[10]

"And," Geneva interjected, "it is precisely that threshold task of decolonization through condemnation of white racism that—when espoused by black leaders, whether a Malcolm X or a Martin Luther King—arouses such hostility as to lead enemies of these leaders to believe that society will see killing them as a great public favor. This has been the fate of our leaders who have merely espoused the cure of decolonization of the black mind. What makes you think that whites would be more receptive to the actual achievement of this goal, as in the Chronicle of the Slave Scrolls?"

"Perhaps it is less black achievement than fear of the Slave Scrolls' almost supernatural powers that leads whites to strike back and eradicate the Scrolls and the ship they deem the sources of that strange and threatening power.

"What bothers me, though, is how could blacks ever return to a colonized mindset even with the destruction of the Scrolls and the model ship? After all, they must have known by then that their achievements had been the result of their efforts and not some magic of the Slave Scrolls."

"Think about it," said Geneva. "The Chronicle is not suggesting that black people need to be taught how to succeed, but reminds us that they have learned very early that too much success in competition with whites for things that really matter like money and power threatens black survival. In a society where success is a supreme virtue, a deliberate decision not to succeed creates a spiritual vacuum. Just as some poor whites relieve their frustration by feeding on the myth of their superiority, many blacks engage in self-destructive and antisocial behavior as an outlet for their despair. The teachings in the Slave Scrolls cause black people to forget their basic lesson of survival through self-subordination, but their resulting success leads to a life-threatening reaction by whites that makes it necessary for blacks to relearn that lesson the hard way. The public ceremony where they are forced to renounce the truth they know about their history and themselves is a symbolic action, a surrender of the rediscovered knowledge, and the end of expectations that black people can gain acceptance in America by becoming superachievers in business and displacing white people, or at least those whites who blacks believe have been getting by owing to their color rather than their competence."

"Well," I admitted, "it has certainly been the experience of blacks that life's playing field is tilted toward whites—a belief beautifully portrayed in the 1979 film *Being There*, in which the late Peter Sellers plays a middle-aged, mentally retarded character who has lived his entire life in a house owned by a well-to-do but eccentric old man who provides a black maid to care for him and a television as his sole connection with the outside world. When the old man dies, and estate lawyers, unaware that he was the deceased's ward, order him to leave, Sellers walks through the streets of Washington, D.C., well dressed but totally bewildered. Through a series of hilarious chances, he finds himself the houseguest of a wealthy and powerful family and is introduced to the President of the United States, who interprets his idle comments about gardening, the only work he knows, as sound economic advice. Within a few days, he becomes a celebrity, respected by power brokers and even considered as a presidential candidate. The black maid who raised him is astounded to see him lionized on television, and views his sudden rise as typical of what any white, regardless of competence, can achieve with a little luck. For her, Sellers's rise is not a minor miracle but a totally predictable event. In the film's best lines, the former maid points to Sellers on the screen and laments to her friends:

> For sure, it's a white man's world in America.
>
> Hell, I raised that boy since he was the size of a pittance. But I'll say right now he never learned to read and write. No sir! Had no brains a'tall. Stuffed with rice pudding between the ears. Shortchanged by the Lord, and dumb as a jack-ass.
>
> Look at him now! Yes sir, all you got to be is white in America to get whatever you want."[11]

"A conclusion," said Geneva, smiling, "I can remember my parents and their friends coming to again and again. It provided a fatalistic humor to a set of rules that seemed to reward whites with cake regardless of their worth, and parceled out crumbs to blacks no matter how hard they tried."

"The sense that whites have numerous opportunities, and blacks have none, is one of the most debilitating of all the 'badges of servitude,' "[12] I observed. "It leads to resignation and despair and makes blacks less likely to succeed. But the question for us to address, Geneva, is whether there is a new legal theory that will persuade courts to provide protection for blacks who are attempting to rescue their people from these unhappy attributes of racism."

"Why a *new* legal theory?" Geneva demanded. "The Chronicle tells us that civil rights lawyers argued that the Racial Toleration Laws violated First Amendment rights of speech,[13] religion,[14] and association,[15] all of which were recognized in cases litigated by black people. But in the Chronicle's atmosphere of racial antipathy, the courts refuse to come to their defense."

"That's somewhat surprising," I responded. "Whatever the general racial unfairness, I'd have thought that lawyers would have little difficulty getting the courts to strike down the Racial Toleration Laws as an obvious violation of the blacks' First Amendment rights."

Geneva looked at me in disbelief. "You surely did not base that thought on history," she said. "Why do you expect the law to provide any more protection during the crisis described in the Slave Scrolls than it did during the Reconstruction period when the law failed even to defend black lives and certainly did nothing to protect black rights?"

"The likely determinative factor here was the sense of crisis," I surmised. "We discussed earlier the Court's reluctance to protect individual rights when the country is involved in a war or other crisis (see pages 131 and 167–68). Free-speech rights under the First Amendment are no different—broad in theory but far more limited in fact, particularly in crisis times. The tortuous history of the 'clear and present danger' standard is proof of the varying levels of protection the Court provides to politically threatening speech.[16] And the long Cold War has eroded First Amendment rights as the government and the courts have blurred the distinction between military secrets required for national security and information kept secret to preserve and enhance the government's reputation."[17]

"You forget," Geneva interrupted, "that the Slave Scrolls do not advocate either war against or subversion of the government. They simply enable blacks to discard their oppression mentality and compete in the good old American way."

"Now, who isn't learning from the Chronicles?" I said. "In the Chronicle of the DeVine Gift, you suggested how whites would react if you introduced more than a few token minority teachers into an elite law school faculty. And we discussed the concern caused by the high test scores achieved by Asian students. Imagine the crisis that would occur if millions upon millions of competent and confident blacks started challenging whites at every rung of the societal ladder. And don't forget that, in the Slave Scrolls Chronicle, the sense of crisis is heightened by the outbreak of civil violence. None of the many precedents in which advocacy of racial justice has gained free-speech protection would be applied in a situation where the audience hostile to the activity includes much of the nation's white population. I haven't forgotten how the Court's strong support for blacks during the sit-in era of the early 1960s quickly waned along with public sympathy."[18]

"I wonder," asked Geneva, "whether, had you experienced the Slave Scrolls Chronicle, you would be able to rationalize so calmly the courts' flat refusal to come to our aid."

"Ms. Crenshaw, one of us has to be rational and lawyerly—and please don't conclude that, just because the healing sessions prescribed in the Slave Scrolls threaten whites, the blacks wouldn't be entitled to receive full First Amendment protection."

Geneva looked surprised. "I thought you were concluding that, because of the crisis caused by the black achievements, no protection was possible."

"No, the Racial Toleration Laws either ban or restrict the association of blacks and the content of speech that were necessary parts of the healing sessions. Thus, under existing First Amendment standards, those laws should be subjected to a greater-than-usual scrutiny by the courts."[19]

"May I assume that the emphasis you gave the word *should* was inadvertent?"

"Well, the Racial Toleration Laws clearly infringe on the content of the blacks' talk in the healing groups—an activity that should be protected. But several cases indicate the Court may tolerate restrictions on the content of controversial speech by approving state regulations enacted to regulate the time, the place, and the manner of all public speech.

"Take the *Dick Gregory* case (1969), where the Supreme Court reversed the disorderly conduct convictions of civil rights protesters led by Gregory who picketed the mayor of Chicago's residence and incurred the hostility of white hecklers. But the opinions strongly suggested that, had the government enacted a sufficiently specific statute limiting protests in residential neighborhoods, the convictions under that law would have been upheld—despite the suppression of the protesters' free-speech rights. Two liberal justices, Hugo Black and William Douglas, concurred in the *Gregory* case, saying that the Constitution does not bar state regulations designed 'to protect the public from the kind of boisterous and threatening conduct that disturbs the tranquility of spots selected by the people . . . for homes, wherein they can escape the hurly-burly of the outside business and political world.' "[20]

"They seem to have forgotten that the disorder was caused by the white hecklers," observed Geneva.

I nodded in agreement. "They noted that the best-trained police cannot maintain tranquillity and order 'when groups with diametrically opposed, deep-seated views are permitted to air their emotional grievances, side by side, on city streets.' Their opinion predicted that even laws 'regulating conduct, even though connected with speech, press, assembly, and petition would be approved if such laws specifically bar only the conduct deemed obnoxious and are carefully and narrowly aimed at that forbidden conduct.' "[21]

"Correct me if I miss the point," Geneva said, "but the preservation of 'tranquillity and order,' even when disturbed by a violent white response to peaceful civil rights protests, causes you to doubt the Court's commitment to protect the free-speech and associational interests of blacks in tumultuous times, such as those presented in the Chronicle of the Slave Scrolls."

"You haven't missed the point," I conceded, "but——"

"But my point," Geneva said emphatically, "is the futility of civil rights litigation to protect even basic free speech and associational rights when those activities, while perfectly peaceful, evoke a hostile response from whites."

"You may not be prepared for this," I warned, "but civil rights lawyers in the Slave Scrolls Chronicle might gain the relief they seek if they recognize the crisis-time shortcomings of First Amendment protection and urge the Court to find a substantive due-process right of privacy that bars government interference with the racial healing sessions, especially those requiring a public forum."

"Tell me you're not serious!"

"Why not?" I replied. "Surely, this is a right different in subject, but similar in character, to the rights of privacy that, in 1965, the Court recognized and protected in the use of contraceptives, whether or not one is married.[22] The right was extended in *Roe* v.

Wade (1973) to provide women the right to determine whether or not to sustain a pregnancy."[23]

Geneva sighed and rolled her eyes toward the ceiling. I waited for her to speak, but she shook her head. "Oh, no! I would not dream of interrupting before you explain the connection you see between the right to an abortion and the racial harassment suffered by black people in the Slave Scrolls Chronicle."

"Woman," I said, exasperated, "your skepticism will be your undoing. Were I to represent the harassed blacks in that Chronicle, I would urge the Court to recognize that, after two centuries of racial exploitation and subordination, we need the psychological exhilaration gained from the discovery of what we can achieve— the actual cure contained in the 'racial healing' process. I would compare that need with the treatment war veterans receive after long periods of combat. My goal would be a judicial finding that what they deemed the right of privacy under the due-process clause of the Fourteenth Amendment which protects rights to contraception and abortion, should also encompass the freedom to meet, preach, teach, and engage in all activities that serve to effect racial healing.

"Actually, blacks have a stronger constitutional case than the Court made in protecting contraception and abortion rights. In addition to what the Court identified as the 'penumbra' of First and Fourteenth Amendment rights supporting the privacy rights in the sexual and reproduction areas, we can cite the guarantee in the Thirteenth Amendment protecting blacks against the 'badges and incidents of slavery.' If you think about it, the motivation for the hostility of whites toward the healing sessions is quite like that which prompted slave states to pass laws prohibiting anyone from teaching slaves to read and write.[24] The real concern, then and now, was less what blacks would learn than what they would do with that learning. And given that all too familiar motivation, blacks should be entitled to protection under the Thirteenth Amendment.

"Furthermore, social science experts can help us prove what should be obvious: namely, that blacks cannot purge self-hate without nurturing black pride through teaching designed to show that the racism of whites, rather than the deficiencies of blacks, causes our lowly position in this society—a dangerous truth that indicts the nation's leaders, institutions, and long-hallowed beliefs.[25] And yet the teaching of that truth is essential if black people—not just those in the underclass, but *all* black people—are ever to view themselves as fully capable human beings."

The look on Geneva's face indicated that my argument had won her pity rather than her support. "I realize that the cases I'm relying on—particularly the abortion case of *Roe* v. *Wade*—have been controversial, and also that the critics who doubt the existence of constitutional authority for the Court's action on the abortion issue can make an impressive argument for their position.[26] But there are two points that would support my argument.

"First, some commentators who support the decision caution those seeking to extend its coverage to homosexuals. In striking down state laws barring contraceptives and abortion, the Court is endorsing not sexual freedom of consenting adults, 'but the stability-centered concerns of moderate conservative family and population policy.'[27] This view gained validity when, in 1986, the Court refused, albeit by a close 5-to-4 vote, to strike down the state of Georgia's sodomy law on right of privacy grounds.[28] Professor Thomas Grey predicts, though, that future Supreme Court decisions in the area of sexual preference 'will respond to the same demands of order and social stability that have produced the contraception and abortion decisions.'[29] And I predict that as the cost to society of ignoring the plight of the black underclass rises, an argument that racial healing is entitled to constitutional protection based on similar 'demands of order and social stability' may well win favor with the Court.

"Second, the Supreme Court's decision in the abortion cases aided women who were either poor or under the domination of their parents, husbands, or communities. Wealthy women, even before these decisions, had little difficulty in obtaining relatively safe, albeit expensive, abortions. But poor and dominated women who wished to have abortions were forced to undergo risk-filled and exploitative nightmares. Because the political climate prevented politicians from protecting these people, the Court felt a need to step in. In much the same way, the Court might feel compelled to act in the racial-healing area; there, too, the nation's stability may be gravely threatened."

"Have you anything else to say before I respond?" Though listening quietly to my argument, Geneva obviously had not been shaken in her view that no approach would save her precious Slave Scrolls.

"There is one thing. The greatest danger to our society's order and social stability is not Communists attacking our shores, but the socio-economic discrimination already endemic across our land.[30] While the Court, as we have said, is reluctant to raise such issues directly to constitutional status, some progress may be possible through the 'penumbra of rights' rhetoric of the contraception and abortion cases—depending, of course, on the willingness of the different members of the Court to go forward."

"Well!" said Geneva, "I am amazed. Little did I dream when I asked you to come here that your legal assessments of the Chronicles would contain more fantasy than the Chronicles themselves. I do not want to be unkind, but your basis for belief that the Court may move, even indirectly, in what you call the socio-economic area is the stuff of which dreams are made. For example, while you claim the plight of poor women seeking abortions helped motivate the Court to grant constitutional protection for such operations, this concern was not able to muster a majority of the Court in the cases holding that neither the Constitution nor federal legislation compels states to use federal funds to pay for nontherapeutic abortions for indigent women—the very group you claim *Roe* v. *Wade* was intended to aid.[31] And the Court reached this conclusion despite Justice Blackmun's objections to the state statutes because through them 'the Government punitively impresses upon a needy minority its own concepts of the socially desirable, the publicly acceptable and the morally sound.'[32]

"And, Counselor, you will not be surprised when the states' lawyers take the high ground and claim that they, rather than you, are the guardians of racial tolerance and harmony. In the old days, states would defend policies of segregation by claiming they were necessary to 'preserve order and keep down racial strife.'[33]

In the Chronicle, the states contend that the Racial Tolerance Laws are intended to further harmony within an integrated society. To support their argument that even sincere religious beliefs must be exposed to constitutional scrutiny in order to preserve racial harmony, the states will rely on the litany of cases won by civil rights lawyers like *Bob Jones University* v. *United States* (1983).[34]

"Finally," she concluded, looking suddenly tired, "I fear that the claimed disruption will serve as justification for the real concern: the threat posed by black diligence to the vested expectations of those currently enjoying wealth, power, and status. Finding that blacks were entitled to constitutional protection for the healing sessions would affirm the reordering of society that black successes have brought about. Such an affirmation would be contrary to the concerns about stability that seem to animate the Court's substantive due-process holdings. Now while I admit that your substantive due-process argument is innovative, it rests on the same infirmity as the First Amendment case: the Court could still find that the states have a compelling interest in restricting or removing the Scrolls—those inflammatory and provocative materials[35] so like political pornography,[36] and so likely to bring racial tensions to the boiling point that the states have a compelling state interest in acting to remove these materials from public circulation."

"Obviously, Geneva," I said, weary myself, "the result you suggest is possible, even likely, but we discussed earlier that the *Brown* decision was handed down in 1954—rather than in all the earlier years when blacks were complaining about segregated schools—because in 1954, finally, whites in policy-making positions realized that it was in their interest to eliminate segregated schools. Well, why wouldn't it be beneficial to whites—particularly to elite whites—for blacks to throw off their ghetto mentality and begin contributing to the society? Surely the society would be better if all blacks became truly productive members rather than burdening the nation with the exorbitant costs of crime, poverty, illiteracy, and poor health."

"It would be a benefit," Geneva acknowledged, "and the 'equal opportunity' ideology of *Brown I* is evidence of some recognition that change should come. Nevertheless, this ideology has not altered the traditional measure of racial progress—the *Brown II* standard that change should come only with 'all deliberate speed.'[37] Even liberals, on the Court and elsewhere, have realized that truly substantive remedies for blacks would necessarily disrupt settled economic arrangements: 'The more that civil rights law threatened the "system" of equality or opportunity, which threat was essential to the production of victim-perspective results, the more it threatened to expose and delegitimize the relative situation of lower-class whites.' "

"But, Geneva, the powerful in our society no longer need to rely on the subordination of blacks to help secure their own superior situation or to prevent lower-class whites from recognizing that there is, after all, a class structure and realizing their position on it."

"Very few black working-class people would agree with you," Geneva responded, "but the ideology of consumerism, fundamental religion, and, in recent years, a form of media-packaged nationality that integrates patriotism with religion, have served to mask the fact that domestic policy has increased the gap between rich and poor for whites as well as for blacks."

"Even so," I countered, "if *Brown* teaches us anything, it is that blacks must push the law in the direction of full equality. The NAACP worked for twenty-five years for a change that, although proving inadequate in the end, seemed at one time impossible to achieve. If we begin to work toward another landmark decision— perhaps one recognizing a right to racial healing—our legal theory will be ready for judicial adoption at some future point when the potential benefits of a whole, healthy, and productive black America are more obvious than they are today."

"It is hard to imagine when those benefits will be more obvious," Geneva said, "unless, of course, after thousands of young blacks turn to terrorism, as oppressed people have done in many parts of the world. No," she added, "our goals must be redirected. Otherwise, we are destined to keep losing—even when we think we have won."

"But, Geneva," I protested, "isn't that the end? If the law has failed, and all our efforts to attain full citizenship are simply turned into new policy devices to maintain our subordinate position, isn't self-help our last chance?"

Geneva winced. "I wish," she said sadly, "that your question were not rhetorical. The Slave Scrolls Chronicle's message seems to be that even a monumental effort to pull ourselves up, sufficient to make even Booker T. Washington proud, will not move us out of our traditional place in this society. I really do not want to face the next conclusion."

"You mean," I said, with something less than seriousness, "the options the Curia members are urging on you?"

"I can tell from the tone of your voice that you are taking the Curia challenge much less seriously than I am."

"I didn't mean it that way. You shouldn't confuse my concern for you, which is genuine, with my inability to view the plight of American blacks as pessimistically as you do."

My attempt at reassurance seemed to ease Geneva's distress. "I have not given up. I sense something more positive in the Chronicles that I can't explain, but I need more time. You have been honest, and, despite my bickering, you have helped me. It is just that I am a long way from formulating a response that I can live with—or, if it comes to that, die for. And, speaking of time, it's late. When must you leave for your plane?"

"Given the distance and my unerring ability to take the wrong roads, I should have left an hour ago."

Geneva smiled. "Well, friend, take care that you don't lose your way again. The Lord only knows what wiles the next woman you stop to help will employ to lure you away from your praiseworthy, if predictable, conventionality."

I arrived at the airport in good time, only to discover my flight was first delayed and finally canceled. The next available flight would not leave until the next day. I decided to drive back to Geneva's cottage, bear her sharp sarcasm, and accept her earlier offer of a bed for the night.

The small house seemed far more drab than it had a few hours ago; but in anticipation of seeing her and perhaps of hearing one more Chronicle, I barely noticed its condition until I knocked and got no response. Thinking she might have left the house to do some chore in the garden, I walked to the rear. The yard was over-grown, and the back door was boarded up. Running back to the front door, I knocked again and then looked in the front window.

I couldn't believe it. Except for the mute evidence of an undis-turbed layer of dust on the floor, the house was empty. Neighbors up and down the road confirmed what my eyes had seen. It was some time since tenants had lived in the house, they told me, and no member of the Crenshaw family had lived there for years. One elderly black man remembered Geneva, but was sure she had not been home for many years. He boasted that he knew every black person for miles around. With some hesitancy, I inquired, "Have you ever heard of a woman named Delia Jones, who sings in a local church choir, and is working to organize a back-to-Africa movement in this community?"

The old man thought for a moment. "There sure is a church by that name. Been a member for fifty years. But I never heard of no back-to-Africa movement 'round here, and I know ain't no woman named Delia Jones livin' in these parts."

I shouldn't have asked. I suddenly wanted a mirror to assure myself of my identity. I tried to be logical. Could I be in the wrong area? I checked nearby roads, postponing in the process the neces-sity of even considering what my senses told me was true. Though I had accepted what Geneva said about her arrangement with the Celestial Curia, I had not really believed it.

I drove into town and, from a phone booth, called the West Coast sanatorium where Geneva had spent many years. When I asked for her, I was told that she had been released three months ago and had gone home. So, I thought, Geneva must have come back here at some point.

I checked my airline ticket and hotel receipt. Yes, I had arrived two evenings ago—and had, I swear, spent the last two days at a cottage with Geneva. Then I remembered my tape recorder—and how Geneva had smiled when I dug it out of my briefcase and plugged it in before our conversations started. Still, she had not objected, and I had filled nine cassettes.

My hands were shaking as I put new batteries into the recorder, inserted the first cassette, and pushed the "play" button. Then I relaxed when I heard my voice—until I realized that mine was the only voice recorded. Where Geneva's voice should have been, there was not so much silence as a sound like the murmur of the sea on a calm evening.

And from that evening until I opened the book containing a complete set of Geneva's Chronicles at the Black Bicentennial Convention, I had no further word from her.

PART III

*Divining a
Nation's
Salvation*

Prologue to Part III

NOW the Black Bicentennial Convention was entering its third and final day. In the morning, the delegates divided into nine groups, each of which studied one of the Chronicles and then gathered, after lunch, for a final coordination and summing up of their several messages. This gathering was to be the prelude to the final session, in the evening, when we hoped to choose a workable strategy for achieving racial justice on which we could all agree.

Most of the delegates agreed that the Chronicle of the Constitutional Contradiction had persuaded them that even an adversarial confrontation about the contradiction the Framers were creating would not have led them to change their minds. Moreover, the concept of individual rights, unconnected to property rights, was totally foreign to these men of property; and thus, despite two decades of civil rights gains, most blacks remain disadvantaged and deprived because of their race. The delegates saw as all too likely the possibility presented by the Chronicle of the Celestial Curia: that, unless mitigated by social reform, racial conditions could so deteriorate that blacks would have to choose between emigration to another country and violent protests intended to disrupt the United States. That this situation is not easily addressed by black political power was the clear message of the Chronicle of the Ultimate Voting Rights Act and is borne out by statistics: thus, while 10.8 percent of the voting age population is black, only 1.2 percent of elected officials were black in 1985.[1]

Delegates who had worked in school desegregation were distressed by the Chronicle of the Sacrificed Black Schoolchildren. "A serious indictment of our work," one attorney concluded, "it suggests that we failed to protect black children who integrated the schools from all manner of tragedies, and allowed people who opposed implementation of the *Brown* decision to profit both from their opposition and from the actual provisions in the school desegregation plan." Chastened as well by the Chronicle of the Black Reparations Foundation were the militant delegates who had urged massive demonstrations to support demands for reparations programs that might close the economic gap between blacks and whites. Even so, these delegates saw potential in a privately funded plan, particularly if it could be funded and implemented with little fanfare.

Affirmative action had caused heated discussions at the Convention even before the delegates read the Chronicle of the DeVine Gift. And while most in the Convention viewed the benefits of such action as worth its disabling aspects, few needed to be reminded that employment-discrimination law offers blacks little protection against job bias that is not overt, particularly when the motivations for that bias include the desire to maintain a workplace in which whites are not simply dominant but are comfortably so.

The delegates were clearly most moved by the Chronicle of the Amber Cloud, which tests and finds wanting the long-held belief that a common crisis would break down the "we" and "they" basis of racial policy making. Even the most diehard integrationists were unwilling to challenge the whites' refusal in the Chronicle to sacrifice for blacks as they have done for disabled whites— or to contest the likely inability of legal doctrine to provide a remedy for a clear denial of equal protection, clear at least to the victims.

As for the most controversial story, that was easily the Chronicle of the Twenty-Seventh-Year Syndrome, with the delegates sharply divided along sex lines. "It is," one woman conceded, "a good vehicle for exploring our differing perspectives on a painful subject that white racism caused but only black togetherness can resolve." Finally, while some delegates doubted the hostile response of white society to black superachievers, as related in the Chronicle of the Slave Scrolls, other delegates countered with facts on recent changes in college admissions policies intended to limit the number of high-achieving Asian students.[2]

For many delegates, the real message of the Chronicles was stark: white society would never grant blacks a fair share of the nation's benefits, and would continue as Professor Kenneth Karst has said "to identify blacks as 'them,' and set us apart as a separate—and less worthy—category of beings."[3] The challenge that had led Geneva to call for my help now obsessed us all. What should we do now that in our distress we cry out with Jeremiah: "The Harvest is past, the summer is ended, and we are not saved"?

Our dinner before the final session was frugal compared with earlier meals, as befitted the Convention's commitment to those blacks whose lives bring them too few banquets and too many burdens. Afterward, we moved in a formal procession to the final plenary session in the Great Hall. Each delegate was wearing a simple black robe connoting the judicial decisions that would determine a new civil rights strategy. Finding my seat and gazing about, it struck me why the impressive room seemed familiar: it was quite like Geneva's description of the hall where she had first met the Celestial Curia. As the delegates filed in and took their places, I thought, with a combination of admiration and despair, of the many times black people had come together in conventions and conferences to debate, orate, plan, plead, and pray about their subservient status in the "land of the free." I wondered in the words of the old hymn, "Oh Lord, how long, how long?"

As the presentations began, the spirit of fellowship and unity so intense at the beginning of the session, started to wane. One impassioned speaker followed another, each advocating his or her, or a particular group's, solution for achieving the common goal of an effective strategy against racism.

To my surprise, an advocate for a back-to-Africa emigration scheme received a positive response to her impassioned appeal. This speaker, using arguments similar to those made by Delia Jones, contended that an exodus by a substantial group of American blacks, though difficult and fraught with peril, would be the salvation of those who went and would provide a basis for pride and organized support for those who remained behind.

A culture-based internal development program, intended to develop pride and self-confidence and presented by a Black Muslim lawyer-teacher, sounded to me like the techniques the blacks adopt in the "Chronicle of the Slave Scrolls," but without the Scrolls' magical properties. The delegates questioned whether many blacks would make the sacrifices and accept the discipline the Muslims would impose on participants in their program.

Pragmatism, aided by insight gained from the Chronicles, served to dilute enthusiasm for a national voting registration campaign urged by representatives of a major civil rights organization long active in the voting-rights field. Critics acknowledged the group's dedicated work, but suggested the need for an approach that might transform voting rights into something other than "ritualistic altar play in a power selection process in which blacks play no real role."

Among other proposals, a really good program would update the 1920s strategy of James Weldon Johnson, the black poet, teacher, diplomat, and NAACP executive secretary, who urged "creative disruption,"[4] a form of passive resistance to protest discriminatory policies. Despite my good intentions, my mind wandered and I missed the balance of the presentation as well as the opening of the next speaker who offered litigation strategies that he claimed were new. Although many delegates were enthusiastic, I fear they were responding more or less automatically to the familiar use of the courts as the forum for racial grievances rather than to any innovative means of avoiding the traditional shortcomings of civil rights litigation.

The tolerance shown to litigation advocates was not, however, extended to the spokesperson from the neoconservative black movement, whose espousal of "bootstraps" philosophy as the only sensible means of black advancement in a free enterprise society, and whose frequent comparisons of how Jews, Asians, and West Indians have "made it," worsened the already strained relationships in the audience. Opposing delegates challenged almost every aspect of the black neoconservative position. Some of the attacks turned personal. Voices were raised, and order as well as the ambitious hopes for the Convention were soon in jeopardy.

I looked toward the dais to see how the Chair would handle the disturbance—but he was no longer there. In his place, standing quietly, a woman waited. Though at the rear of the hall, I recognized her at once. Not the Geneva of an old cottage in rural Virginia, or of that earlier time when we had been civil rights attorneys in the South. Now, in a flowing gold robe, she exuded a radiance that touched not only me, who knew her, but all the fiercely arguing men and women in that hall, and calmed them in a few moments. When the bedlam had given way to an uneasy peace, Geneva spoke.

"Hosts and delegates to this convention," she said quietly but with authority, "I am Geneva Crenshaw. You have read my Chronicles. Now I have come to relate one final Chronicle and help you rise above this dissension—dissension that springs from frustration not from any difference in goals. It is my hope that together we can discover the true road to our salvation."

Along with everyone in the Great Hall, I stood and applauded. But the keenest advocates of the various strategic programs, while joining in the welcome, viewed Geneva's appearance as ceremonial. Many were concerned that the interruption might consume valuable time from the final session's main purpose: a decisive vote on the primary strategy and then, no doubt, the election of one of the delegates to direct an implementing program.

In spite of the protracted and vigorous applause, there were gathering murmurs of dissent, and people began to raise their hands and shout to be recognized. As the clapping died down, the Chair returned to the podium and raised his hands for attention. "It is because of Geneva and her Chronicles," he said, "that we have had this fruitful meeting. I rule therefore that we let her speak before we decide on a final strategy."

The ruling was not popular. Several delegates moved toward the platform to register strong objections to it and to demand that it be voted on. Voices were raised for and against this suggestion, and the Chair pounded his gavel, to no avail. Within moments the session was in an uproar. Then I saw a group of delegates advancing purposefully toward the podium, while others were trying to push them back. Fearing for Geneva's safety, I jumped up and looked for a way to get to her.

But suddenly before I or anyone else could move further, there was a mighty fanfare from the huge pipe organ to the left of the podium. At the same time, the curtains at the front of the hall parted and rolled away to reveal a choir whose white-robed ranks stretched back as far as the eye could see, into a beautiful cloud-filled vista. Awed, the delegates subsided into their seats. Throughout the turmoil, Geneva had stood quietly by the podium, listening, watching. I wondered whether this was how she had faced the angry Framers at the Constitutional Convention of her Chronicle.

It was she whom I—and, indeed, everyone—watched while, following the initial organ fanfare, the choir sang two spirituals. First, the overwhelming jubilation of "The Lord Will Make a Way Somehow," and then "There Is a Balm in Gilead," the latter bringing tears to my eyes. By now, whether as a result of the tears or of my imagination, Geneva had become a transcendent presence, otherworldly, radiant. When the last chords died away, the choir sat row by row in a human wave.

Now, throughout the Great Hall, reverent silence prevailed—a silence it had taken a miracle to accomplish. But now the delegates were ready to heed a voice other than their own or some particular group's. Looking out over the upturned faces, Geneva allowed that period of silent transition between music and sermon familiar to men and women steeped in the drama of black church worship. Her voice, when at last she spoke, needed no amplification; it resonated through the hall in harmony with the organ playing softly in the background.

Chapter 10

Salvation for All: The Ultimate Civil Rights Strategy

The Chronicle of the Black Crime Cure

AFTER CENTURIES of slavery and then decades of unremitting struggle to gain recognition of their rights, black people, both those who had achieved success and those still mired in poverty, felt that future progress was barred by the many criminals in their midst. For years, the crime problem had endangered blacks living in poor black areas, and had increasingly been cited by whites as a prime reason for their reluctance to end discrimination in jobs, housing, schools, and places of public accommodation. The crime statistics more than supported white fears about black people; and—despite vigorous crime-control programs and prosecutions, more police, longer sentences, and new prison facilities—the black crime problem grew worse. Vigilantes who took the law into their own hands were hailed as heroes.[1] Social scientists and civil rights proponents who tried to explain black crime as a predictable output of black oppression were not simply not believed: they were ignored.

And then the Black Crime Cure was discovered. Deep in a cave used to hide illegal narcotics, a black gang from a big-city ghetto found a stream whose bed was covered with small ruby-red stones about the size of peas. It is not clear how the gang leader came to swallow one of the small stones, perhaps by accident, but the effect was immediate and acute.

The converted drug dealer himself not only immediately lost all inclination to wrongdoing but was possessed with an overpowering desire to fight black crime wherever it existed. Somehow associating his changed outlook with the stone, he managed to feed one to each of his band. Instantly, they, too, were changed from criminals to crime fighters. After considering how they might further their newly adopted crusade, they dumped all their narcotics and filled the containers with what they were already calling the "crime cure stones."

Time does not permit a full recounting of how the Black Crime Cure was distributed across the country. While the stones seemed to give indigestion to whites who took them, they worked as they had in the cave for anyone with a substantial amount of African blood. Black people were overjoyed and looked forward to life without fear of attack in even the poorest neighborhoods. Whites also lost their fear of muggings, burglary, and rape.

But, now that blacks had forsaken crime and begun fighting it, the doors of opportunity, long closed to them because of their "criminal tendencies," were not opened more than a crack. All-white neighborhoods continued to resist the entry of blacks, save perhaps for a few professionals. Employers did not hasten to make jobs available for those who once made their living preying on individuals and robbing stores. Nor did black schools, now models of disciplined decorum, much improve the quality of their teaching. Teachers who believed blacks too dangerous to teach continued their lackadaisical ways, rationalized now because blacks, they said, were too dumb to learn.

And so it went. Although the crime excuse was gone, the barriers to racial equality—Jim Crow signs in one era, black crime in another—that had from time to time given way to black pressure, were in the end unable to prevail against the apparently implacable determination of whites to dominate blacks by one means or another.

Moreover, the Black Crime Cure drastically undermined the crime industry. Thousands of people lost jobs as police forces were reduced, court schedules cut back, and prisons closed. Manufacturers who provided weapons, uniforms, and equipment of all forms to law enforcement agencies were brought to the brink of bankruptcy. Estimates of the dollar losses ran into the hundreds of millions.

And most threatening of all, police—free of the constant menace of black crime and prodded by the citizenry—began to direct attention to the pervasive, long-neglected problem of "white-collar" crime and the noxious activities of politicians and their business supporters. Those in power, and the many more who always fear that any change will worsen their status, came to an unspoken but no less firm conclusion: fear of black crime has an important stabilizing effect on the nation. By causing whites with otherwise conflicting economic and political interests to suspect all blacks as potential attackers, the threat persuades many whites that they must unite against their common danger. The phenomenon is not new. In the pre–Civil War era, slave owners used the threat of violent slave revolts as the "common danger" to gain support for slavery among whites, including those who opposed the institution on moral grounds and those in the working class whose economic interests were harmed by the existence of slave labor. Black crime serves a similar contemporary function.

Those in power soon recognized how the lack of black crime threatened their comfortable status. Many committees of government officials studied the problem, at great cost to the taxpayer—but in the end, it was decided to do . . . nothing. If, as the liberal social scientists claimed, lack of opportunity rather than inherent immorality had led many blacks into criminal pursuits, a similar outcome would follow society's failure to provide meaningful opportunity for schooling and jobs to blacks who had taken the Cure. And so it worked out.

How, exactly, was never clear. Perhaps the crime cure stones' effect wore off. But certain it is that the cave that was their sole source was mysteriously blown up, and the area where it was located became a landfill. Certain it is, too, that the era free of black crime came to an end.

Happily, not many blacks who had taken the Cure ever returned to lives of crime. But their example and urging had little influence on younger blacks growing up with prospects so bleak that stealing and worse seemed the only available route to survival and, if one were lucky, to success.

F OR several moments, Geneva stood quietly at the podium and allowed her Chronicle to have its intended effect: we sat in stunned silence. None of her stories had been models of optimism, but the Chronicle of the Black Crime Cure touched the very nadir of our despair. It stimulated no discussion. Rather, a pall of resignation fell over the gathering. What could Geneva possibly hope to achieve by this ultimate depiction of futility and defeat?

Evidently viewing our dejection as an advantage, she challenged us: "Does any group among you advocating an end to black crime as the means of our people's salvation wish to take issue with the outcome of my Chronicle?"

The stillness was intense as Geneva confronted the delegates. "I come here today to determine whether any of your strategies has the potential claimed for it." Again she paused, then continued with her challenge. "Come, sisters and brothers, which of you will pledge your lives to those in this Great Hall—and to all the multitudes of men, women, and children whom you here represent—that a particular civil rights strategy, even if it is successfully implemented, indeed, particularly if adopted by all and successfully implemented, will not lead society to circumvent your goals as they were circumvented in the Chronicle I have just related?

Another pause, during which no one stirred or spoke.

"Your silence tells me," she went on, "that you have found the consensus that has eluded you in your discussions today. Each of you, in advocating one program over another, has lost sight of a basic truth: while the central motivating theme of black struggle is faith, the common thread in all civil rights strategies is eventual failure. Like the drowning person who grasps for straws, you contend for your positions here with the fervor of desperation. Have you learned nothing from experience?"

Her question echoed across the utterly silent hall. Then, in a quiet voice, she told us, "I understand and share your despair. The Chronicle of the Black Crime Cure is, unlike many of the others, entirely without any hope of redemption. It affects me as it clearly has affected you. Of what value, I wonder, is my militancy against the monstrous message of the Chronicle? Since I have come to understand that I cannot alone answer this painful question, it is my hope that the Celestial Curia will see fit to join us here to help me—and all of you—find a strong and fruitful answer to it."

At her words, there was a low rumble from the bass section of the great choir. In sequence, first the tenors, then the contraltos, and finally the sopranos joined in, each group of voices one-third of a scale higher than the one before, to conclude in a chord of enthralling beauty. At some moment, while it was building to a crescendo, the Celestial Curia appeared on a raised dais overlooking the podium where Geneva was standing. I recognized the two women at once from her description of them all those weeks ago in her Virginia cottage. Now they sat straight and proud as queens in two chairs as ornately carved as ancient thrones. Between them stood another, equally elaborate chair, empty and—it seemed to me—waiting.

"We have come, Sister Geneva," the Curia announced in a rhythmic chant. "We are here to provide you and those gathered here with the guidance you seek."

Geneva turned to face the Curia. "You must know that I am angry," she said. "Why have you required me both to experience and to recount your Chronicles if their only message is that our civil rights programs are worthless opiates offering no more than delusions of hope to a people whose color has foredoomed them to lives of tokenism, subservience, and exclusion? Neither I nor any man or woman here needs your supernatural gifts to recognize the weaknesses of these strategies. They are only too plain. If the Chronicles are intended to help us, you must provide a key to their interpretation more positive than the bleakness of racial barriers they portray."

The Curia's initial response was obscure and unenlightening: "There are no new truths. There are only new perspectives for seeing what you already know."

As usual, Geneva wanted specifics. "Surely," she protested, "the Chronicles are more than tales of racial distress."

"Indeed they are," the Curia acknowledged. "The Chronicles are intended to serve as dramatic diagrams pointing away from your earthbound yearning for equal opportunity and acceptance"—a response Geneva refused to accept. "Sisters," she challenged, "explain, if you will, why it is unreasonable for black people to seek their share of what this system offers whites along with, when needed, appropriate compensation for the myriad harms caused by past discrimination."

"Amen, sister!" a delegate shouted. "You sure are speaking for me and mine!"

Scattered murmurs of approval spurred Geneva on. "Our people helped build this country. We have fought and died in its wars. We have sweated in its factories and fields. Out of the anguish of our lives, we have given the nation a language and a music that have vitalized its culture. And always we have been exploited, underpaid, and overworked. We deserve, we want, and we are determined to have a share of America's dividends—dividends equal to the burdens we have borne, and adequate to compensate us for our gifts."

The Curia Sisters regarded Geneva sternly for a long moment, then asked, "Had you been alive before the Civil War, would it have been in keeping with your goal to transform blacks from slaves to slave owners?"

"Of course not! Blacks wanted freedom for themselves, not the enslavement of whites."

"If that is so, Sister Geneva, why do you state a goal for blacks today that would, if achieved, simply make them the exploiting rich rather than the exploited poor, the politically powerful rather than the pitifully powerless, the influential and prestigious rather than the ignored and the forgotten?"

"That is not what we seek," Geneva replied. "Neither I nor any of the delegates here would have us integrate into a white society simply to share in the moral corruption of which we have been the unwilling victims."

The Curia came back with yet another question. "In that case, why do you and the others here seek a fair share in the country *as it is*? Would it not be more accurate as well as more praiseworthy to choose either to rebel against your oppressors or simply to depart from them?"

"As you well know, I have scrutinized the Chronicles with great care in search of some further option. We have invested too much in this country simply to give up and move on to Lord knows what. Moreover, the resort to violence and bloodshed would betray the morality of our cause—even in the unlikely possibility that our rebellion succeeded. As despairing as they are, the Chronicles suggest that there is a Third Way."

"You have truly studied the Chronicles, Sister Geneva. There is indeed such an option. An awesome option, one that rests on the vision of this country as a truly democratic society of liberated men and women, all of whom are endowed with dignity and self-respect, and all of whom enjoy equal opportunity unhindered by race, religion, or class discrimination."

"Can I be hearing rightly?" Geneva asked, her voice trembling with indignation. "Are you asking us to fall back on the rhetoric— so noble on great national occasions, so empty in our daily lives— of 'America the Beautiful'? Are you truly saying that we must be condemned forever to labor for the salvation of our oppressors, perpetually forgiving them for our suffering, for which they are responsible? Is it not clear that our civil rights efforts have resulted in laws and legal precedents that broaden the rights of white Americans more than of ourselves? I see our work and their gain as one more manifestation of white domination."

"And so have we seen it as well," the Curia replied. "And it is because of this ultimate exploitation of your freedom efforts that we have urged the radical measures of revolution or emigration— measures that you reject. If you insist on a Third Way, you must recognize the restrictions you yourselves impose on your goal when you seek justice for blacks within a society where only the most powerful or wealthy whites are able either to insist on or to pay for lives free of exploitation. Now, one of the privileges of these whites is the freedom, both subtly and not so subtly, to practice and profit from racism—a privilege we, of course, despise. You must be careful, in setting goals for blacks, to discriminate among white privileges and not seek to adopt their belief in racial superiority. You must, that is, not seek status advantages like those that have held you and others down.

"Moreover, while it is certainly rhetorically neat to claim that you want for blacks only those constitutional rights whites take for granted, that formula offers neither political success nor the moral satisfaction you so highly value."

"But we did not write the Constitution," Geneva said. "All we can do is to try to gain the protection that its provisions guarantee to all."

"Nor," the Curia Sisters reminded her, "did the slaves write the Bible. White men handed your forebears their most sacred book as a pacifier, intending it to lull them into contentment with their lowly lot.[2] They found, instead, within its text both a comfort for their pain and the confirmation of our humanity. The Bible provided a vision of life for the slaves unlike anything their masters could ever know. It inspired them both to survive and to leave as their legacy the spirituals—literally, a theology in song."

"I am beginning to understand," answered Geneva. "You are saying that if our slave ancestors could accomplish so much with the Bible, we should be able to do no less with the Constitution. For it, too, as it referred to us, sought to sanction our servitude, to ratify our downtrodden condition—even though the amendments proclaiming us free and citizens were used to further the interests of the liberators rather than to deliver us from the canons of racism."

"Furthermore, Sister Geneva—and this you must never forget—it was the determination of black men and women to be truly free that transformed the Constitution from a document speaking of rights as the main means of protecting property and privilege into an instrument in which the concept of rights has gained a humane purpose and significance for even those who lack property, and for whites as well as blacks. Viewed from this perspective, blacks have used the Constitution to accomplish miracles!"

"An inspiring statement," Geneva conceded, "but you have to admit that those miracles did not obviate the conditions that prompted this Convention nor, with all due respect, our need for guidance and direction."

"Nor, Sister Geneva, did the Bible deliver the Promised Land on a platter to your slave ancestors—and would not have served them as well had it done so. As for guidance, look to the Chronicles. Of course, some of you"—and the Curia Sisters nodded solemnly at the audience assembled—"will view them as merely metaphorical essays on the plight of blacks—and will leave here seeking theories of liberation from white legal philosophers, who are not oppressed, who do not perceive themselves as oppressors, and who thus must use their impressive intellectual talent to imagine what you experience daily. Black people, on the other hand, come to their task of liberation from the battleground of experience, not from the rarefied atmosphere of the imagination. Do you understand?"

"It is true," Geneva acknowledged. "We have real-life stories to tell—stories on which we have built our movements. For Harriet Tubman in the nineteenth century and Rosa Parks just a few decades ago are not mere names but heroines whose courage is as life affirming today as in their own time. Their stories teach us, and inspire us, and lift us up when we and our plans fall short. Just as the Bible is filled with stories of men and women who, like Moses, succeeded ultimately even as they failed in their immediate goals, so the history of the Constitution is filled with stories of humanizing reforms sought and sometimes gained by blacks and others of the dispossessed.

"I see then, Sisters, that you view the Chronicles as parables of our efforts to achieve what whites possess rather than what we, and they, might become. But is it not understandable that we should seek to emulate those able by virtue of race to take for granted rights our Constitution promises equally to all?"

"A slave," the Curia explained, "laboring in a field under a broiling hot sun and lifting her sweat-drenched eyes toward her mistress sipping mint juleps on a cool veranda must have envied and longed to emulate that white woman at least as much as we do today. And yet we now know that, in reality, many white women on the plantation, though pampered, led a no less servile existence. Such is the real status of many whites today whose skin color is not sufficient to protect them from economic disaster. Just as many blacks are losing their jobs to automation, factory closings, and farm bankruptcies, so are white families suffering similar affliction. The stark truth is that whites as well as blacks are being exploited, deceived, and betrayed by those in power."

"Nor," interjected Geneva, "is this a new phenomenon. Even back in 1892, Tom Watson, then a staunch advocate of the Populist party, which favored a union between Negro and white farmers, warned both blacks and whites:

> You are kept apart that you may be separately fleeced of your earnings. You are made to hate each other because upon that hatred is rested the keystone of the arch of financial despotism which enslaves you both. You are deceived and blinded that you may not see how this race antagonism perpetuates a monetary system which beggars both.[3]

"The Populist movement failed," Geneva went on, "because whites were unable to resist the superior status promised them, and thus rejected the potentially powerful coalition they could have formed with black workers. To win white support this time, must we limit our strategies to those in which whites will join?"

"Of course not!" the Curia Sisters snapped. "But you should not foreclose the possibility of coalition with those who, except for the disadvantages imposed on blacks because of color, are in the same economic and political boat."

"I assume," Geneva probed, "that you mean: first, that the option of the Third Way will require that we seek justice for all through a systematic campaign of attacking poverty as well as racial discrimination; and second, that our traditional civil rights strategies will not be of any help in this enterprise?"

"Any strategy that leads toward the goal of a more just and humane society can be effective. Traditional civil rights programs, aggressively pursued, will exert continuing pressure on the legal process—no matter whether the courts grant the specific request for relief.[4] Lawyers have placed too much weight on whether they win a case, and too little on the impact of the litigation. Has it served to educate the community, to facilitate the organization of the poor, or has it conveyed to government officials the dissatisfaction of constituents who intend to insist on reform?"

"My Curia Sisters," Geneva said, "I think I speak for the delegates in confessing confusion. You warn us that our legal programs are foredoomed to failure, and yet you urge us to continue those very programs because they will create an atmosphere of protest. I must reiterate my fear that this approach will simply perpetuate the pattern of benefit to whites of legal reforms achieved by civil rights litigation intended to help blacks."

"The benefit they bring to all is proof of how potent a weapon your civil rights programs can be in seeking a restructured society. Future campaigns, while seeking relief in traditional forms, should emphasize the chasm between the existing social order and the nation's ideals. Thus, Sister Geneva, litigation as well as protests and political efforts would pursue reform directly as well as create a continuing tension between what you are and what you might become. Out of this tension may come the insight and imagination necessary to recast the nation's guiding principles closer to the ideal—for all Americans."

"*May?*" Geneva echoed. "You are not sure?"

"The Third Way is no less risky than the more pragmatic tactics of emigration or than truly disruptive, even violent, struggle. You are opting for a utopian reformation of government, difficult even to envision, and urging such reform through the existing legal and legislative structures."

"But you, Sisters, have made it clear," Geneva said, "that the Third Way has a chance for success."

"A fact in your favor," the Curia responded, "is that the structure of your country's government, as well as the interpretation of the basic law of the Constitution and its few dozen amendments, are in constant flux—a fluidity you must take advantage of to make the laws reflect the needs of both blacks and whites. Only in that way can you all experience democracy, not simply pay verbal homage to it on ceremonial occasions. Even so, there is no guarantee of success."

"As to the risks," Geneva responded, "you have commented on the many contributions blacks have made to this society despite the tremendous obstacles they faced. Those achievements stand as proof that the Constitution and the law generally—as flawed as they are—can be vehicles of reform. Of course," she added, "reliance on existing legal structures involves enormous risk, but is there not risk in any significant human enterprise? Consider the odds against a successful marriage, and yet most people keep trying. And the perils of parenthood seem to grow exponentially in our complex world, without noticeable lessening of the desire to have children. Even our survival against a host of daily dangers becomes ever more problematic, and yet most of us willingly face each new day with renewed hope as our main defense against our all too justified fears. Surely, the risk involved in our continuing civil rights campaigns is no greater than those each of us faces inevitably in our personal lives."

"We hear you, Geneva, and agree," the Curia intoned, "but beware lest your people's enemies construe your desire to change the structure of government as some form of subversion—a risk that, in the past, civil rights organizations have taken pains to avoid."

"I have not forgotten," Geneva said, and her voice rang out to the farthest corner of the Great Hall, "but this is no time to become conservative or to draw back from controversy. We must commit ourselves to salvation for all through means that are peaceful and ethical. And," she added, "let me warn those critics who would brand us as advocates of revolution. If our efforts fail, we are likely to be replaced by actual, and active, subversives who will earn the apprehensions undeservedly aimed at us."

Then Geneva turned to face the delegates. "I am now convinced that the goal of a just society for all is morally correct, strategically necessary, and tactically sound. The barriers we face, though high, are not insuperable, and the powers that brought me these Chronicles are no greater than the forces available to you—and within you. Use them to the fullest in the difficult times that lie ahead. And be of good cheer. As our forebears survived the most virulent slavery the world has ever known, we will survive contemporary conservatism. Already our faith and perseverance have rewarded us. We know that life is to be lived, and not always simply enjoyed; that, in struggle, there is joy as well as pain. And—even in a society corrupted by wealth and endless material comforts, forgetful of its noble precepts, and cursed by the conviction that the mainstays of existence are money rather than morality and cunning rather than compassion—we find courage in the knowledge that we are not the oppressors and that we have committed our lives to fighting the oppression of ourselves as well as of others.

"Finally, let us find solace and strength in the recognition that black people are neither the first nor the only group whose age-old struggle for freedom both still continues and is worth engaging in even if it never results in total liberty and opportunity. Both history and experience tell us that each new victory over injustice both removes a barrier to racial equality and reveals another obstacle that we must, in turn, grapple with and—eventually—overcome. For emancipation did not really free the slaves; and Lincoln's order was but a prerequisite, the necessary first step in a process that will likely continue as long as there are among us human beings who, for whatever reason, choose to hold other human beings in their power.

"Let us, then, rejoice in the memory of the 'many thousands gone,' those men and women before us who have brought us this far along the way. Let us be worthy of their courage and endurance, as of our own hopes, our own efforts. And, finally, let us take up their legacy of faith and carry it forward into the future for the sake not alone of ourselves and our children but of all human beings of whatever race or color or creed."

As Geneva neared the end of her talk, the chords of the organ intensified; and the celestial choir, if that is what it was, stood and began to sing. The sound swelled; and as she finished a last word of encouragement, she joined in the singing, gesturing to the delegates to do the same. As they stood, their faces were no longer angry or confused. They looked hopeful, exhilarated, as they joined wholeheartedly in an old and stirring spiritual.

Geneva's task was done. As I strained to see her over the heads of the delegates, the two Curia Sisters came down from the dais, took her by the hand, and escorted her to the seat between their own. For a moment they sat there, hands clasped, and gazed out over the hall. Then someone moved in front of me, cutting off the dais from view. When I could see it again, it was empty of chairs, of the Curia Sisters, of Geneva. We were on our own once again.

Joining hands with the delegates on either side of me, I sang with them, with everyone in that great hall, filled so recently with dissension but now with hope and exhilaration. In the music, in our joined voices, all our differences were for the moment harmonized into a single powerful sense of dedication—a dedication renewed and echoed in the spiritual's soaring refrain:

> Done made my vow to the Lord,
> and I never will turn back.
> Oh, I will go. I shall go.
> To see what the end will be.

Classroom Appendix

Thoughts for Discussion

This classroom appendix contains chapter-by-chapter suggestions for discussion. Many of them originated in reviews, letters, and student comments on the issues presented in *And We Are Not Saved*. Stories are, of course, valuable teaching tools. Subject matter in story form can gain and hold students' attention, and the very telling of a story evokes ideas and images about the subject matter that broaden and deepen the issues for discussion. Often the story-sparked portraits take the form of new stories. Teachers assigning readings from *And We Are Not Saved* can utilize their students' involvement in the Chronicles by encouraging them to prepare short papers of reflection about the material. These should not be summaries, but impressions felt or conclusions reached as a result of their reading. The discussion based on these written reflections will have special value because the issues are framed by the students themselves. That discussion may be introduced by requesting a few students—either chosen at random or preselected—to read their reflections to the class.

Chapter 1 The Current Role of Slavery in Racial Debate

Beyond its guilt-evoking potential, does slavery have any value in analyzing contemporary racial policies and civil rights doctrine? Those who respond in the negative maintain that the Constitution's recognition of slavery is a historical anomaly because: (1) most whites in the late eighteenth century (including the framers of the Constitution) believed themselves to be superior to blacks and thus "racists" as we define the term; and (2) the dire need for a strong central government committed to protecting property pushed the framers to accept protection of slave property despite impassioned arguments that slavery was morally wrong.

Opponents of this view point out that slavery was an important unifying factor for whites whose interests differed because of economic status and geographic location. Indeed, the slavery provisions in the original Constitution reflected pragmatic, political compromises by the framers. Policy makers today emulate the framers' use of race as a unifying factor based on a continuing sense that America is a white nation—a belief that survives and even flourishes in our late-twentieth-century world. Thus, slavery in the U.S. Constitution is a prototype for American racial policy, now as well as then.

The conclusions you reach in this debate might well influence your response to the question of whether the great percentage of blacks at the bottom of income and wealth statistics serves to lessen the political significance of the income gap between rich and poor that each year widens steadily.

Chapter 2 The Effect of Unpredictable
Events on Racial Policies

Even without supernatural intervention, there is a good chance that the Supreme Court in the next decade will become quite conservative on social-reform issues. While far from a certainty, it is possible that in response the black disinherited will " 'be stirred by this stimulus toward revolt or reasoned Emigration' " (p. 54). There are arguments that serious movement in either direction would: (a) move the country and the Court toward racial reform; (b) strengthen the position of those opposed to civil rights; or (c) make no appreciable difference in racial policy making. Choose your position and make arguments supporting it.

One of the difficulties of emigration as an alternative to direct-action revolts is the absence of a new land to colonize. But suppose the long-lost continent of Atlantis is discovered, recovered from the depths at enormous expense by a coalition of large, multinational corporations, and dubbed "Atlantis, Inc." Disappointed that the land, though fertile, contains no rich mineral deposits, the multinationals put the continent up for sale to the highest bidder. Roughly one million blacks, convinced that America will never grant them equal rights, petition the government to make good on its post–Civil War reparations promises and purchase Atlantis for all blacks who wish to go there. As a black, would you go? As a white, what position would you take regarding black emigration? If you were counsel to the black groups wishing to emigrate, what arguments would you make in their behalf? And, as counsel for groups formed to oppose the necessary legislation and funding, what arguments would you make in opposition to the plan?

Chapter 3   Is the Proportional
Representation by Race a Workable Ideal?

Geneva and her law professor friend did not resolve their dispute about the potential value of restructuring voting districts to provide for proportional representation by race. Even if enacted, the Ultimate Voting Rights Act might not be politically desirable. Whites would remain the majority in most legislatures, and since their representatives would not need to be responsive to black voters, could easily outvote the black representatives on every issue in which black-white interests diverged. In short, might this remedy for political powerlessness become the electoral equivalent of school integration for unequal educational opportunity?

On the other hand, a modicum of black political power might be better than none. Representation based on population would substantially increase the number of blacks in Congress and in most state legislatures. The enhanced representation would be better able to influence key votes on a range of issues and, for this reason, would earn respect as well as bargaining chips from differing groups of the white majority.

Chapter 4   Might an All-Black School
System Provide an Educational Answer
as Well as Pose a Constitutional Problem?

In 1987, a group of black parents in Milwaukee, Wisconsin, petitioned the state legislature to create an independent and largely black school system that would encompass nine schools serving 6,000 children (97 percent black) located in the heart of Milwaukee's black community. The parents denied the plan was either unconstitutional or a return to "separate but equal" schools. Rather, they viewed their plan as a chance to rescue black children from schools that remained mainly black and educationally ineffective after two decades of school desegregation litigation. Their goal: to gain control over the schools their children attend and install administrators and teachers who are both accountable to the community and dedicated to improving the quality of their schools and the academic performance of their children.

It is not difficult to imagine the opposition the black parents encountered from school officials, the media, and even from certain segments of the black community. After a prolonged public debate, the legislature rejected the separate school district proposal. How would you have voted on this measure given the Chronicle of the Sacrificed Black Schoolchildren?

For those who would oppose the separate school system, consider Yale psychiatrist James Comer's observation that schools serving disadvantaged children must give priority attention to solving problems of relationship between schools structured along middle-class lines and children coming from severely troubled homes (James Comer, "The Social Factor," *New York Times*, 7 August 1988, p. 26). Black schools that are effective—such as those in New Haven, Connecticut, operated under a program developed by Dr. Comer—give high priority to solving child-development and relationship problems. It is difficult to obtain the necessary attention for these issues in racially desegregated (read, mainly white) schools. For example, how many mainly white schools would undertake willingly the character of change urged by Harvard professor Sara Lightfoot, who, after a survey of educationally effective black schools, concludes:

Schools will only become comfortable and productive environments for learning when the cultural and historical presence of black families and communities are infused in the daily interactions and educational processes of children. When children see a piece of themselves and their experience in the adults that teach them and feel a sense of constancy between home and school, then they are likely to make a much smoother and productive transition from one to the other. Black familial and cultural participation will require profound changes in the structural and organizational character of schools, in the dynamic relationship between school and community, in the daily, ritualistic interactions between teachers and children, and finally in the consciousness and articulation of values, attitudes, and behaviors of the people involved in the educational process. (Sara Lightfoot, *Worlds Apart: Relationships Between Families and Schools* [1978], p. 175)

Chapter 5   The Realism of Racial Reparations

In 1988, Congress enacted legislation providing compensation for the Japanese-American survivors of the World War II evacuation policy approved by the Supreme Court in *Koramatsu* v. *United States*. Should this action encourage black reparations proponents? Keep in mind that barriers of cost, identification of recipients, method of payment, and political opposition would not be eased by the Japanese-American precedent, although the precedent might forestall legal attacks claiming that a black reparations policy is a racial classification that violates the equal-protection clause.

White hostility to even a privately funded black reparations program is inevitable in a society where order and stability seem based to a substantial degree on the presence of blacks at the bottom of the socio-economic ladder. But would Ben Goldrich's Black Reparations Foundation have fared better if his announcement focused on its indirect benefits to whites, including lowered taxes because of less welfare and crime and the millions of unproductive blacks who would become wage earners and taxpayers, thereby increasing the market for consumer goods and the nation's productivity?

Chapter 6   The Advantages of
Socio-Economic Class:
The Accepted Affirmative Action

A white student at a suburban law school serving those who will become their families' first generation of professionals was unimpressed by The Chronicle of the DeVine Gift. He acknowledged that blacks were disadvantaged by past and present racial discrimination but insisted that jobs should be filled strictly on the basis of merit as determined by traditional measures: grades and test scores. In response, I noted that he seemed as able as most students attending nationally known law schools like Harvard and Yale, but predicted that if after graduation he sought employment in the large New York law firms, he would be rejected in favor of students whose social-class advantages had enabled them to graduate from nationally known schools.

"That's the breaks," he said softly after a pause.

I jumped on him. "What kind of answer is that? You seem ready to die rather than see a job you seek go to a black hired under an affirmative-action program if you have the higher grades and test scores, but you are ready to stand by passively if someone uses upper-class status to get a position you want that would advance your career and provide for your family."

The student was silent for a long time. Obviously, he had not considered class-based bias as a threat to his ambitions far more likely to limit his chances than the workings of an affirmative-action program. Finally he said, "Well, one day, perhaps, I will be able to send my children to Harvard or Yale."

Chapter 7   The Amber Cloud Insight

Following the reading of The Chronicle of the Amber Cloud, audiences are asked to assure the author that in the real world the
outcome would be very different; that after experiencing the devastation of their children, upper-class whites, the major policy
makers and policy shapers, would identify with the plight of black
parents and push successfully for the additional funds needed to
cure cases of Ghetto Disease caused by racism and poverty. The
response is always a discomforting silence. Without a more positive response, is there any chance that Geneva's friend is correct
about the chances of using the Fourteenth Amendment's equal-
protection clause to gain court-ordered treatment for blacks
suffering from the disease?

The Chronicle posed a troubling question for one reviewer:

> Why is it that his fictional civil rights leaders call for the treat-
> ment of only *minority* low-income youths? What about poor
> white youths, who are excluded by Congress? By casting the
> unequal treatment of low and middle-income youths solely as
> an issue of race, and not of class, Bell seems to succumb to the
> fallacy that poor equals black. While it is true that the poverty
> rate among blacks is more than double that for whites, more
> than two-thirds of all Americans living below the poverty line
> are white. Racism is indeed pervasive in the United States to-
> day, but focusing on race may at times prove more distracting
> than useful. Poverty and dependency, intractable problems in
> their own right, are best not treated solely as symptoms of racial
> injustice. (Peter M. Yu, review, *Harvard Civil Rights and Civil
> Liberties Law Review* 23 [1988]: 287)

Compare this comment with economist Robert Heilbroner's observation that race is one reason the United States lags behind
countries like Norway, Denmark, England, and Canada in addressing social needs. In those countries,

there is no parallel to the corrosive and pervasive role played by race in the problem of social neglect in the United States. It is the obvious fact that the persons who suffer most from the kinds of neglect (mentioned above) are disproportionately Negro. This merging of the racial issue with that of neglect serves as a rationalization for the policies of inaction that have characterized so much of the American response to need. Programs to improve slums are seen by many as programs to "subsidize" Negroes; proposals to improve conditions of prisons are seen as measures to coddle black criminals; and so on. In such cases, the fear and resentment of the Negro takes precedence over the social problem itself. The result, unfortunately, is that the entire society suffers from the results of a failure to correct social evils whose ill effects refuse to obey the rules of segregation. (Robert Heilbroner, "The Roots of Social Neglect in the United States," in E. Rostow, ed., *Is Law Dead?* [1971], pp. 288, 296)

The Chronicle is intended to raise the question of the continued vitality of the equal-protection clause to protect blacks against government-sponsored racial discrimination, but would Congress and the country be more willing to bear the infinitely greater cost of curing Ghetto Disease symptoms in poverty-level whites? Indeed, given the nagging threat black poverty poses for the nation, there is some chance that society might be willing to cure Ghetto Disease in blacks except for the realization that the same treatment would be demanded for all disadvantaged youths. Isn't that the concern that underlies the judicial difficulty with the rights of "innocent whites" in affirmative-action cases? And, finally, is the Third Way set out in chapter 10 more or less convincing as a result of this discussion?

Chapter 8   Can Patriarchal Solutions Correct Patriarchal Problems?

The Chronicle of the Twenty-Seventh-Year Syndrome, easily the most controversial section of the book, prompted serious criticism from some young black women. One law student wrote:

> I am a black woman, soon to be professional, twenty-nine years of age and facing a shrinking pool of eligible black males. I can't help but be distressed by this, but what also distresses me is the increasing difficulty that we, black men and women, face in communicating our respective needs and concerns. . . .
>
> I never thought you intended to be sexist or patriarchal . . . however I think that because men and women think differently, some of what is presented in [your Chronicle] has the *effect* of being somewhat offensive. . . .
>
> The problem that I and many other women see, in using . . . [a devastating ailment] to make a point or to stimulate discussion, is that you may begin on the wrong foot by disenabling one group, namely women. We, as women, have been struggling for a long time, and we recognize the need to do something about the legions of black men that are lost for a variety of reasons, but why must we be weakened in the process? Are we responsible? Is that the only way men will wake up and start relating to each other more positively?

There are several possible responses to this student's question, including a suggestion that the student go back and read the Chronicle again . . . all of it this time. Many will not find that response adequate. They may prefer Professor Regina Austin's observations contained in a letter to the author pointing out that blacks control neither their material conditions nor the production of the dominant ideology that by and large gives legitimacy to their disproportionate share of hardship. In her view: "It behooves us to be as critical of sexual and class oppression as we are of racial oppression. Black feminist notions of strength cannot be equated with white feminist notions of 'liberation' and black masculine notions of sustenance cannot be equated with white masculine notions of breadwinning." An impressive statement, but one wonders whether this advice can be translated into patterns of behavior that will relieve the woes black men—and women—suffer in this society.

On the other hand, perhaps this Chronicle has further confused an already complex problem by juxtaposing two rather different problems: (1) the special sense of threat posed by the black male's very existence in this society, and the stresses resulting from the continuing danger they and the black women associated with them must face; and (2) the acute shortage of black males, particularly at the level of black women who have achieved professional status and success? Problem one is the direct cause of problem two. And the friction between black men and women is caused by their inability to do much about either problem. Assuming this is so, it may be that the government's "public notice" approach in the Chronicle, while hardhearted, is both reasonable and the means of making a modicum of difference—albeit at the cost of black women's privacy rights.

Chapter 9   Real-World Lawyers Might Successfully Challenge the Racial Toleration Laws

Geneva's friend concludes their discussion of The Chronicle of the Slave Scrolls by asking whether the society's unwillingness to support black self-help efforts does not doom their hopes to attain full citizenship. Geneva views the question as "rhetorical" (p. 233), but Clarence Thomas, chair of the Equal Employment Opportunity Commission, would not agree. Civil rights thinking, he believes, has been crippled by confusing a "colorblind Constitution" and a "colorblind society." We are entitled to the first, but the second is impossible, and the effort to achieve it, he writes, "would destroy limited government and liberal democracy to confuse the private, societal realm (including the body and skin color) and the public, political realm (including rights and laws)."

Thomas fears that obscuring the difference between public and private allows private passions (including racial ones) "to be given full vent in public life and overwhelm reason." Reason, as urged by James Madison, should alone control and regulate government so that government can control and regulate passions. He acknowledges that keeping "race out of public life in no way implies it will disappear from private or social life. But justice must focus on the rational defense of individual freedoms, including the property rights Mr. Bell is so contemptuous of. It is difficult to see how his characters' ultimate faith that the Constitution can offer 'salvation for all' could be otherwise affirmed." Thomas urges blacks not to fear to express their diversity as individual citizens and as members of society, suggesting that the goal of " 'decolonizing black minds' would require an emancipation from reliance on government and overemphasis on race and class. In my mind," Thomas concludes, "uniting black Americans means giving them the security to be diverse" (Clarence Thomas, "The Black Experience: Rage and Reality," *Wall Street Journal*, 12 October 1987, p. 10).

Chapter 10   Searching for the Ultimate Civil Rights Strategy

The principal weakness in Bell's book is that when he approaches the question of what we do next, his literary-pedagogical device gets in the way. His supernatural expositions, including celestial choirs, stand where I would have preferred to see hard analysis about strategy, organization and politics. Bell urges blacks to continue the struggle and suggests that by doing so, we may contribute a higher morality to the nation. (Roger Wilkins, "Talking Past History," *The Nation*, 19 March 1988, p. 383)

Wilkins urges specific actions, particularly by those blacks who have benefited from civil rights laws. He would begin in "the inner city schools, which undeniably need help and which have student populations desperately in need of black role models." An invasion of black middle-class volunteers into the schools of poor

black children would surely lead to a new politics, as the black rejection of segregation in Montgomery did a generation ago. Changes would occur.... But that can only happen if black people struggle together to save themselves. (Wilkins, p. 385)

But how realistic is such an invasion given the barriers of time, distance, and dangers involved in the black, middle-class volunteer program? Or does the book's experience-based prescription ring hollow to Mr. Wilkins, as another reviewer suggests, because he was a reader who became too "deeply engaged in the theoretical critique of the book's first part...." She explains:

Having spent much of the book arguing that litigation has done little to alter the face of racism, in the end he suggests an approach that seems merely to urge blacks to go back for more of the same and to continue bearing the burden imposed by whites' lack of commitment to civil rights. This interpretation, however, would miss Bell's more profound message. The impossibility of formulating an ultimate strategy reflects not Bell's own shortcomings but rather the shortcomings of a "process that will likely continue as long as there are among us human beings who, for whatever reason, choose to hold other human beings in their power" (p. 257). His final chapter, in which he argues that blacks should forsake their myths of liberation and their hopes of achieving through law an "ultimate civil rights strategy," is therefore not a disappointing denouement but rather the central insight of his work. (Preeta Bansal, "The Battleground of Experience," *Harvard Law Review* 101 [1988]: 849–53)

Ms. Bansal's assessment captures Geneva's closing admonition as she urges her civil rights colleagues to " 'find solace and strength in the recognition that black people are neither the first nor the only group whose age-old struggle for freedom both still continues and is worth engaging in even if it never results in total liberty and opportunity. Both history and experience tell us,' " she reminds them, " 'that each new victory over injustice both removes a barrier to racial equality and reveals another obstacle that we must, in turn, grapple with and—eventually—overcome' " (p. 257).

NOTES

Introduction

1. Charles Lawrence, "The Id, the Ego and Equal Protection: Reckoning with Unconscious Racism," *Stanford Law Review* 39 (1987): 317, 330.

2. Robert Darnton, *The Great Cat Massacre and Other Episodes in French Cultural History* (1984), p. 33.

3. See Derrick Bell, "An American Fairy Tale: The Income-Related Neutralization of Race Law Precedent," *Suffolk University Law Review* 18 (1984): 331.

4. Linda Greene, "A Short Commentary on the Chronicles," Harvard *Blackletter Journal* 60 (Spring 1986).

5. See generally *The Dialogues of Plato*, B. Jowett, trans., reprinted in Robert Hutchins, ed., *Great Books of the Western World* (1952).

6. See, for example, Henry Hart, "The Power of the Congress to Limit the Jurisdiction of Federal Courts: An Exercise in Dialectic," *Harvard Law Review* 66 (1953): 1362.

7. Lon Fuller, "The Case of the Speluncian Explorer," *Harvard Law Review* 62 (1949): 616. In a fictional story, cave explorers, trapped by landslides and facing death by starvation, select by lot and kill an unwilling victim whose flesh provides the nourishment that enables them to survive and stand trial for murder. Professor Fuller then uses a series of hypothetical appellate opinions to explore several jurisprudential themes concerning the appropriateness of even settled legal principles to do justice to situations beyond anything the lawmakers envisioned.

8. Alison Anderson, "Lawyering in the Classroom: An Address to First Year Students," *Nova Law Review* 10 (1986): 271, 274. See also Gerald Lopez, "Lay Lawyering," *UCLA Law Review* 32 (1984): 1.

9. Kim Crenshaw, "From Celebration to Tribulation: The Constitution Goes to Trial," *Harvard Law Review* 101 (1988).

10. Manning Marable, "Beyond the Race-Class Dilemma," *The Nation*, 11 April 1981, pp. 428, 431.

Prologue to Part I

1. See, for example, G. Fredrickson, *The Black Image in the White Mind* (1981).

2. See, for example, Charles Murray, *Losing Ground* (1984), who argues that programs financed by government have brought about social ills, including increases in crime, teenage unemployment, teenage pregnancies, abortions, poverty, households headed by single mothers.

3. See, for example, Thomas Sowell, *Civil Rights: Rhetoric or Reality?* (1984).

4. E. Frazier, *Black Bourgeoisie* (1962 ed.).

5. See, for example, *Hamilton v. Alabama*, 376 U.S. 650 (1964) (per curiam), reversing contempt conviction, 156 S. 2d 926 (1963).

6. Among the very few blacks who held full-time teaching positions at white law schools in the 1950s and 1960s were William Robert Ming, Jr., associate professor and professor at the University of Chicago School Law School from 1947 to 1953; Charles W. Quick, professor at Wayne State Law School from 1958 to 1967, and at the University of Illinois College of Law from 1967 to 1979; John R. Wilkens, acting professor, professor, and professor emeritus at the University of California at Berkeley School of Law from 1964 to 1976; and Harry E. Groves, professor at the University of Cincinnati College of Law from 1968 to 1970. Ming was the first black to hold a full-time faculty position at a predomi-

nantly white law school. See Kellis Parker and Betty Stebman, "Legal Education for Blacks," *Annals* 407 (1973): 144, 152.

7. The careers of these black scholars and civil rights lawyers are documented in R. Bland, *Private Pressure on Public Law: The Legal Career of Justice Thurgood Marshall* (1973); Richard Kluger, *Simple Justice* (1976) (documenting the civil rights careers of Justice Marshall and Judge Carter); Genna Rae McNeil, *Groundwork: Charles Hamilton Houston and the Struggle for Civil Rights* (1983); and Gilbert Ware, *William Hastie: Grace under Pressure* (1984).

8. W. E. B. DuBois, "The Talented Tenth," in J. Lester, ed., *I The Seventh Son: The Thought and Writings of W. E. B. DuBois* (1971), p. 385.

9. John Gwaltney, *Drylongso: A Self-Portrait of Black America* (1980).

10. Peter Bergman, *The Chronological History of the Negro in America* (1969), pp. 586–87.

11. See, for example, Bergman, *Chronological History*, pp. 583, 584.

12. See Harold Schonberg, "A Bravo for Opera's Black Voices," *New York Times*, 17 January 1982, sec. 6, pp. 24, 82–90.

13. *Brown v. Board of Education*, 347 U.S. 483 (1954).

Chapter 1

1. Samuel Eliot Morison, *The Oxford History of the American People* (1965), p. 305.

2. See J. Miller, *The Wolf By the Ears* (1977), p. 31.

3. Donald Robinson, *Slavery in the Structure of American Politics: 1765–1820* (1971), p. 92, quoting from Thomas Jefferson, *Notes on the State of Virginia*, T. Abernethy, ed. (1964).

4. Ibid.

5. Staughton Lynd, *Class Conflict, Slavery, and the United States Constitution* (1967), pp. 181–82 (quoting Max Farrand, ed., *The Records of the Federal Convention of 1787* [1911], vol. I, p. 533).

6. See, for example, Lynd, *Class Conflict*, p. 182.

7. Robinson, *Slavery in the Structure of American Politics*, p. 185.

8. Farrand, *Records*, vol. I, p. xvi.

9. William Wiecek, *The Sources of Antislavery Constitutionalism in America: 1760–1848* (1977), pp. 63–64.

10. Robinson, *Slavery in the Structure of American Politics*, p. 210.

11. Ibid., pp. 55–57.

12. Charles Beard, *An Economic Interpretation of the Constitution of the United States* (1913), pp. 64–151. See also Pope McCorkle, "The Historian as Intellectual: Charles Beard and the Constitution Reconsidered," *American Journal of Legal History* 38 (1984): 314, reviewing the criticism of Beard's work and finding validity in his thesis that the Framers primarily sought to advance the property interests of the wealthy.

13. Morison, *Oxford History*, p. 304.

14. Dumas Malone, *Jefferson and the Rights of Man* (1951), p. 172 (letter from Washington to Thomas Jefferson, 31 August 1788).

15. W. Mazyck, *George Washington and the Negro* (1932), p. 112.

16. Ibid.

17. Derrick Bell, *Race, Racism and American Law* (2d ed. 1980), pp. 29–30.

18. James Madison, quoted in Farrand, *Records*, vol. I, p. xvi.

19. Malone, *Jefferson*, p. 167 (letter written in 1788 from James Madison to Philip Mazzei).

20. *The Records of the Federal Convention of 1787* (rev. ed. 1937), vol. II, p. 222.

21. Gouverneur Morris, quoted in Robinson, *Slavery in the Structure of American Politics*, p. 200.

22. *The Records of the Federal Convention of 1787*, p. 222.

23. See Edmund Morgan, "Slavery and Freedom: The American Paradox," *Journal of American History* 59 (1972): 1, 6.

24. See Wiecek, *Sources of Antislavery Constitutionalism*, pp. 62–63.

25. A. Leon Higginbotham, *In the Matter of Color, Race and the American Legal Process: The Colonial Period* (1978), p. 380.

26. Wiecek, *Sources of Antislavery Constitutionalism*, p. 42.

27. Luther Martin, quoted in David Brion Davis, *The Problem of Slavery in the Age of Revolution, 1770–1823* (1975), p. 323.

28. In the Northern states, slavery was abolished by constitutional provision in Vermont (1777), Ohio (1802), Illinois (1818), and Indiana (1816); by a judicial decision in Massachusetts (1783); by constitutional interpretation in New Hampshire (1857); and by gradual abolition acts in Pennsylvania (1780), Rhode Island (1784), Connecticut (1784 and 1797), New York (1799 and 1817), and New Jersey (1804). See L. Litwack, *North of Slavery* (1961), pp. 3–20.

29. Broadus Mitchell and Louise Mitchell, *A Biography of the Constitution of the United States* (1964), pp. 100–101.

30. Morgan, "Slavery and Freedom." The position taken by the Colonel is based on the motivation for American slavery set out in Professor Morgan's paper; he developed the thesis at greater length in his *American Slavery, American Freedom* (1975).

31. Morgan, "Slavery and Freedom," p. 22.

32. Morgan, *American Slavery, American Freedom*, pp. 380–81.

33. Morgan, "Slavery and Freedom," p. 24.

34. Morgan, *American Slavery, American Freedom*, p. 381.

35. *Brown* v. *Board of Education*, 347 U.S. 483 (1954).

36. James 2: 17.

37. Center on Budget and Policy Priorities, *Falling Behind: A Report on How Blacks Have Fared Under the Reagan Policies* (October 1984).

38. John E. Jacob, in National Urban League, *The State of Black America* (1985), pp. i–ii.

39. Bureau of the Census, *Household Wealth and Asset Ownership: 1984* (July 1986), pp. 4–5.

40. Alphonso Pinkney, *The Myth of Black Progress* (1984).

41. Joint Center for Political Studies, *A Policy Framework for Racial Justice* (1983), p. 10.

42. James McGhee, "The Black Family Today and Tomorrow," in National Urban League, *The State of Black America* (1985), pp. 1–2.

43. Center For the Study of Social Policy, *The "Flip-Side" of Black Families Headed by Women: The Economic Status of Black Men* (1984), p. 1.

44. Ibid., p. 6. See also William J. Wilson and Kathryn Neckerman, "Poverty and Family Structure: The Widening Gap Between Evidence and Public Policy issues," in *Fighting Poverty: What Works and What Doesn't*, ed. S. Danziger and D. Weinberg (1986), pp. 232–59.

45. Center on Budget and Policy Priorities, *A Report on How Blacks Have Fared Under the Reagan Policies*, 3 (1984).

46. Ibid., pp. 3–4.

47. William J. Wilson, *The Declining Significance of Race* (1978), p. 120.

48. Ibid., pp. 110, 152.

Chapter 2

1. David Shapiro, "Mr. Justice Rehnquist: A Preliminary View," *Harvard Law Review* 90 (1976): 293. Professor Shapiro found that, in Justice Rehnquist's first four and one-half years on the bench, his judicial product had been adversely affected by "the unyielding character of his ideology" which made possible a tripartite characterization of his votes. Whenever possible, Justice Rehnquist (1) resolved conflicts between an individual and the government, against the individual; (2) resolved conflicts between state and federal authority—whether on an executive, a legislative, or a judicial level—in favor of the states; and (3) resolved questions of the exercise of federal jurisdiction—whether on the district, the appellate, or the Supreme Court level—against such exercise (p. 294). See also John Jenkins, "Partisan: A Talk with Justice Rehnquist," *New York Times Magazine*, 3 March 1985, p. 28, where Justice Rehnquist candidly discusses his view of the Court's role in American government.

2. See, for example, Laurence Tribe, "Unraveling National League of Cities: The New

Federalism and Affirmative Rights to Essential Government Services," *Harvard Law Review* 90 (1977): 1065. In this article, Professor Tribe departs from those commentators who read the decision in *National League of Cities* v. *Usery*, 426 U.S. 833 (1976), as a judicial capitulation under the banner of "federalism" from the Court's earlier staunch protection of individual rights. Rather, he argues that Justice William Rehnquist's majority opinion reflects a perhaps unconscious recognition of affirmative rights owed by the state to its citizens. Later, Professor Tribe reports that when they met at a conference, Justice Rehnquist said that he had read the article, and laughingly chided Tribe for trying to turn him into a closet socialist.

For a later, somewhat more generous, but ultimately no less critical view of Justice Rehnquist's judicial philosophy, see Powell, "The Compleat Jeffersonian: Justice Rehnquist and Federalism," *Yale Law Journal* 91 (1982): 1317, arguing that "Justice Rehnquist's work is consistent with the Jeffersonian theory of federalism" (p. 1320), even when it leads him to ends inconsistent with conservative politics. "If the Court had followed Justice Rehnquist's analysis in First National Bank v. Bellotti, 435 U.S. 765 (1978), Massachusetts would have been allowed to take a very reasonable step to ensure that big business and its money would not drown out other voices in a political controversy" (p. 1363). But the author concludes, "Rehnquist's attempt to transform this federalism into an objective constitutional first principle must fail because it cannot be established that the Framers intended to embody the theory in the Constitution" (p. 1320).

3. Frances Fox Piven and Richard Cloward, *Poor People's Movements: Why They Succeed, How They Fail* (1977), pp. xx–xxi, 6.

4. *Cooper* v. *Aaron*, 358 U.S. 1, 26 (1958) (Justice Frankfurter concurring).

5. See, for example, *Dred Scott* v. *Sandford*, 60 U.S. (19 How.) 393 (1857).

6. See Bruce Ackerman, "Beyond Carolene Products," *Harvard Law Review* 98 (1985): 713, who suggests the institution-preserving function of both the *Lochner* era and the *Carolene Products* doctrine.

7. See Steel, "Nine Men in Black Who Think White," *New York Times Magazine*, 13 October 1968, p. 56.

8. *Brown* v. *Board of Education*, 349 U.S. 294 (1955). Often referred to as *Brown II*, this decision set a standard of compliance so vague that school boards were able to evade real school desegregation for more than a decade.

9. Steel, "Nine Men in Black Who Think White," p. 112.

10. See *New York Times*, 15 October 1968, p. 53, col. 2.

11. *New York Times*, 29 October 1968, p. 43, col. 3.

12. See NAACP, "The Issues in the Lewis M. Steel Case," January 1969, pp. 6–7.

13. Arthur S. Miller, "Social Justice and the Warren Court: A Preliminary Examination," *Pepperdine Law Review* 11 (1984): 473, 489.

14. See Derrick Bell, "Brown v. Board of Education and the Interest-Convergence Dilemma," *Harvard Law Review* 93 (1980): 518, 524–25.

15. See Brief for Appellant at 28, *Morgan* v. *Virginia*, 328 U.S. 373 (1946) (no. 704).

16. W. DuBois, *The Autobiography of W. E. B. Du Bois* (1968), p. 333.

17. See, generally, Norman Amaker, "De Facto Leadership and the Civil Rights Movement: Perspective on the Problems and the Role of Activists and Lawyers in Legal and Social Change," *Southern University Law Review* 6 (1980): 225, who discusses the representation of civil rights protestors during the 1960s.

18. See, for example, N. Jones, Correspondence, *Yale Law Journal* 86 (1976): 378. Responding to charges that NAACP lawyers were pressing for racial-balance remedies contrary to the wishes and interests of black parents, Mr. Jones, then NAACP General Counsel, said that "lawyers are reaching judgments of feasibility and effectiveness based upon established judicial precedents. . . . This they do without breaching their ethical responsibilities to their clients . . . and the Constitution" (p. 382).

19. Speech of Justice Thurgood Marshall (18 November 1978), reprinted in *The Barrister*, 15 January 1979, p. 1.

20. Boris Bittker, "The Case of the Checker-Board Ordinance: An Experiment in Race Relations," *Yale Law Journal* 71 (1962): 1387, 1393.

21. Professor Paul Freund, "The Civil Rights Movement and the Frontiers of Law," in T. Parsons and K. Clark, eds., *The American Negro* (1967), pp. 363, 364. See also Arthur

Kinoy, "The Constitutional Right of Negro Freedom," *Rutgers Law Review* 21 (1967): 387, 389–90.

22. *New York Times* v. *Sullivan*, 376 U.S. 254 (1964).

23. *NAACP* v. *Button*, 371 U.S. 415 (1963). The decision, Professor Freund said, in "The Civil Rights Movement," provided a precedent for later group representation efforts. He cited *Brotherhood of Railroad Trainmen* v. *Virginia*, 377 U.S. 1 (1964). See also *United Mine Workers* v. *Illinois Bar Association*, 389 U.S. 217 (1967) (union's hiring of attorney to assist members with workmen's compensation claims is not unauthorized practice of law by the union); and *United Transportation Union* v. *State Bar of Michigan*, 401 U.S. 576 (1971) (union protected in setting up group representation plan intended to protect union members from excessive fees by incompetent lawyers in Federal Employers Liability Act [FELA] actions).

24. *Shelley* v. *Kraemer*, 334 U.S. 1 (1948).

25. *Dixon* v. *Alabama State Board of Education*, 294 F.2d 150 (5th Circuit 1961). See also *Tinker* v. *Des Moines Independent Community School District*, 393 U.S. 503 (1969).

26. *Smith* v. *Allwright*, 321 U.S. 649 (1944).

27. See *United States* v. *Classic*, 313 U.S. 299 (1941) (alleged fraudulent vote count in a Louisiana primary, led to finding that primary elections are "elections" under Article I, Section 4, of the Constitution, the provision empowering Congress to regulate the manner, times, and places of elections).

28. See, for example, *Peters* v. *Kiff*, 407 U.S. 493 (1972) (white defendants are denied their rights to due process of law by the systematic exclusion of minorities from their juries). The authorities extend back more than a century: *Strauder* v. *West Virginia*, 100 U.S. 303 (1880) (sustaining the validity under the Fourteenth Amendment of federal statutes prohibiting the exclusion of blacks from state juries).

29. See *Batson* v. *Kentucky*, 106 S. Ct. 1712 (1986) (the equal-protection clause bars a prosecutor from challenging potential jurors "solely on account of their race or on the assumption that black jurors as a group will be unable impartially to consider the state's case against a black defendant"). The *Batson* decision overruled the portion of *Swain* v. *Alabama*, 380 U.S. 202 (1965), that had precluded a criminal defendant from making out an equal-protection violation based on the exclusion by peremptory challenges of black jurors in the defendant's particular case. The seriousness of racial prejudice in the jury box is reviewed in Sheri Johnson, "Black Innocence and the White Jury," *Michigan Law Review* 83 (1985): 1611.

30. *NAACP* v. *Alabama*, 357 U.S. 449 (1958).

31. *Gomillion* v. *Lightfoot*, 364 U.S. 339 (1960).

32. *Moore* v. *Dempsey*, 261 U.S. 86 (1923).

33. *Powell* v. *Alabama*, 287 U.S. 45 (1932).

34. *Brown* v. *Mississippi*, 297 U.S. 278 (1936).

35. Robert Cover, "The Origins of Judicial Activism in the Protection of Minorities," *Yale Law Journal* 91 (1982): 1287, 1305–6. See also Professor Harry Kalvin's published lectures reviewing the 1960s' civil rights movement's contributions to free-speech theory (H. Kalvin, *The Negro and the First Amendment* [1965]). Hailing the NAACP's strategy of systematic litigation as a "brilliant use of democratic *legal* process" (p. 67; emphasis in the original), Professor Kalvin discusses how *New York Times* v. *Sullivan*, 376 U.S. 254 (1964), extended First Amendment protection to bar seditious libel; developed rights of association and privacy as a result of successful efforts to halt harassment of NAACP and its members by southern states (see, for example, *NAACP* v. *Button* [1963]); and made real, if indirect, First Amendment inroads on traditional notions of trespass while defending the sit-in cases (see, for example, *Bell* v. *Maryland*, 378 U.S. 226 [1964]).

36. *Gomillion* v. *Lightfoot* (1960), p. 341.

37. Frankfurter warned against the promulgation of jurisdiction in the abstract, "for it conveys no intimation what relief, if any, a District Court is capable of affording that would not invite legislatures to play ducks and drakes with the judiciary" (*Baker* v. *Carr*, 369 U.S. 186, 268 (1962) (Frankfurter, J., dissenting). Fourteen years before the *Tuskegee* case, the Supreme Court in *Colegrove* v. *Green*, 328 U.S. 549 (1946), dismissed as nonjusticiable a challenge that state law prescribing congressional districts was unconstitutional because districts were not approximately equal in population. Justice Frankfurter, speaking for only himself and Justices Stanley Reed and Harold Burton, felt courts "ought not to enter this

political thicket." Frankfurter viewed such questions of party and the people as beyond judicial competence, and an infringement of power conferred by the Constitution on Congress (p. 556). See also *South* v. *Peters*, 339 U.S. 276 (1950).

38. *Baker* v. *Carr*, 369 U.S. 186 (1962). See James Blacksher and Larry Menefee, "From Reynolds v. Sims to City of Mobile v. Bolden: Have the White Suburbs Commandeered the Fifteenth Amendment?" *Hastings Law Journal* 34 (1982): 1, 6, who state that reliance on *Gomillion* and earlier Fifteenth Amendment black voting cases was a "significant feature" of *Baker*'s majority opinion.

39. *Reynolds* v. *Sims*, 377 U.S. 533, 535 (1964).

40. *Baker* v. *Carr* (1962), pp. 254, 259.

41. See *Gray* v. *Sanders*, 372 U.S. 368 (1963); and *Wesberry* v. *Sanders*, 376 U.S. 1 (1964).

42. *Reynolds* v. *Sims*, 377 U.S. 533, 566 (1964).

43. Compare the very close scrutiny of congressional districting plans in *Karcher* v. *Daggett*, 462 U.S. 725 (1983) (invalidating New Jersey's plan that deviated from pure equality by an average of 0.1384 percent, because the legislature had both rejected other plans with smaller variations between the largest and the smallest districts, and had not borne the burden of showing that the variances in its plan were intended to achieve some legitimate goal), with the far more relaxed scrutiny given state legislative-apportionment schemes as in *Brown* v. *Thompson*, 463 U.S. 835 (1983) (upheld Wyoming's apportionment plan for its House of Representatives even though average percentage deviation was 16 percent with a maximum of 89 percent, held permissible to preserve state's long-standing policy of providing at least one representative to even the least populated counties).

44. *Davis* v. *Bandemer*, 106 S. Ct. 2797 (1986) (political gerrymandering cases are justiciable, and such gerrymandering may violate the equal-protection clause). See also Justice John Paul Stevens's concurrence in *Karcher* v. *Daggett*, 462 U.S. 725, 754 (1983).

45. See *Avery* v. *Midland County*, 390 U.S. 474, 484–85 (1968).

46. James Blacksher, "Drawing Single-Member Districts to Comply with the Voting Rights Amendments of 1982," *Urban Lawyer* 17 (1985): 347, 349–50.

47. *Fortson* v. *Dorsey*, 379 U.S. 433, 439 (1965).

48. See Emma Jordan, "Taking Voting Rights Seriously: Rediscovering the Fifteenth Amendment," *Nebraska Law Review* 64 (1985): 389.

49. See *City of Mobile* v. *Bolden*, 446 U.S. 55 (1980); see also *Whitcomb* v. *Chavis*, 403 U.S. 124, 149 (1971) (rejecting charges that an apportionment plan diluted black votes in the absence of proof that multimember districts in the plan "were conceived or operated as purposeful devices to further racial or economic discrimination").

50. See, for example, *Wright* v. *Rockefeller*, 376 U.S. 52, 53 (1964) (noting that some black political leaders opposed a civil rights challenge to a congressional districting plan that excluded nonwhite voters from mainly white districts, because the districting protected the political power of black and Hispanic voters in other districts).

51. See *United Jewish Organization of Williamsburgh, Inc.* v. *Carey*, 430 U.S. 144 (1977) (rejecting charge of vote dilution made by Hasidic Jews whose district was divided to ensure black and Hispanic voting representation).

52. See *Rogers* v. *Lodge*, 458 U.S. 613 (1982); *White* v. *Regester*, 412 U.S. 755 (1973).

53. *City of Mobile* v. *Bolden*, 446 U.S. 55 (1980).

54. Public Law No. 97–205, 96 Stat. 131 (1982) (codified at 42 U.S.C. §1973 [1982]).

55. See H. R. Rep. No. 227, 97th Cong., 1st Sess. 29–30 (1982); S. Rep. No. 417, 97th Cong., 2d Sess. 27–30 (1982), reprinted in 1982 *U.S. Code Congressional and Administration News*, 177, 192–93.

56. See *Washington Post*, 31 August 1985, p. A1, col. 5, reporting on Justice Department's brief submitted on appeal of *Gingles* v. *Edmisten*, 590 F. Supplement 345 (Eastern District of North Carolina 1984). In response to the Justice Department's position, the Senate majority leader, Robert Dole, and nine other members of Congress filed an amicus brief stating that the Justice Department's position was expressly rejected by Congress when it amended the Voting Rights Act in 1982.

57. *Thornburg* v. *Gingles*, 106 S. Ct. 2752 (1986).

58. See, for example, *Hunter* v. *Underwood*, 471 U.S. 222 (1985), in which the Court invalidated an Alabama constitutional provision disenfranchising persons convicted of "crimes of moral turpitude." The Court found that the 1902 state constitutional convention had enacted the provision with racially discriminating intent.

59. See Arthur Waskow, *From Race Riot to Sit-In, 1919 and the 1960s* (1967), p. 203 (describing Johnson's disavowal of violent tactics in favor of tactics such as work stoppages and other peaceful protests).

60. See James W. Johnson, *Negro Americans, What Now?* (1934).

61. James Blacksher and Larry Menefee, *From Reynolds v. Sims to City of Mobile v. Bolden: Have the White Suburbs Commandeered the Fifteenth Amendment?*, 34 Hastings 1, 62, L. J. 62 (1982).

62. Ibid., p. 63.

63. See, for example, *Washington* v. *Davis*, 426 U.S. 229, 248 (1976).

64. David Brion Davis, *The Problem of Slavery in the Age of Revolution: 1770–1820* (1975), p. 260, quoting Edmund S. Morgan; Davis stated further that whites' "rhetoric of freedom was functionally related to the existence—and in many areas to the continuation—of Negro Slavery" (p. 262).

Chapter 3

1. *Harper* v. *Virginia Board of Elections*, 383 U.S. 663 (1966). The Twenty-Fourth Amendment prohibits the use of poll taxes as a prerequisite to voting in federal elections (U.S. Constitution Amendment XXIV, §1, 1964).

2. *Wright* v. *Rockefeller*, 376 U.S. 52, p. 66 (1964) (Justice Douglas dissenting).

3. Ibid., p. 67.

4. L. Litwack, *North of Slavery* (1961), pp. 74, 79.

5. Ibid., p. 79.

6. Arthur Blaustein and Robert Zangrando, *Civil Rights and the American Negro* (1968), p. 423.

7. In *United States* v. *Reese*, 92 U.S. 214 (1876)—a prosecution of Kentucky voting officials who refused to count the votes of blacks—the Court held provisions of the Civil Rights Act to be unconstitutional, interpreting them as barring all interference with the right to vote, and thus finding them beyond the scope of the Fifteenth Amendment, which prohibits only interference based on race, color, or previous condition of servitude.

And in *United States* v. *Cruikshank*, 92 U.S. 542 (1876), the Court held that deprivation of life, liberty, or property without due process does not cover deprivations that are the result of private acts. The *Cruikshank* case grew out of the famous 1873 Colfax Massacre in Louisiana where, in an election dispute, a large number of blacks were killed by whites. The convictions of nine whites, who were found guilty of violating the rights of the blacks, were reversed by the Supreme Court's decision.

The Supreme Court did affirm convictions in *Ex parte Yarbrough*, 110 U.S. 651 (1884), and ruled that a Ku Klux Klansman who had forcefully prevented a black from voting in a congressional election in Georgia, had violated a Civil Rights Act section providing criminal penalties. The section (the predecessor of the current law, 18 U.S.C. §241) was found a valid exercise of the federal power to control elections.

8. *Giles* v. *Harris*, 189 U.S. 475, 488 (1903).

9. See, for example, *Ketchum* v. *Byrne*, 740 F.2d 1398, 1413 (7th Circuit 1984) (requiring redrawing of boundaries to ensure "effective" majorities of 65 percent in nineteen black and four Hispanic wards); *Jones* v. *City of Lubbock*, 727 F.2d 365, 386–87 (5th Circuit 1984) (affirming district court plan creating two minority districts in six-district council where minority population was 26.1 percent).

The cases are collected in Note, "Vote Dilution, Discriminatory Results, and What Proportional Representation: What Is the Appropriate Remedy for a Violation of Section 2 of the Voting Rights Act?" *UCLA Law Review* 32 (1985): 1203, 1205–8.

10. *Ketchum* v. *Byrne*, 740 F.2d 1398, 1413 (7th Circuit 1984).

11. 1982 Amendments to the Voting Rights Act, section 2, 96 Stat. at 134; 42 U.S.C. § 1973 (b) (1982).

12. *Thornburg* v. *Gingles*, 106 S. Ct. 2752 (1986).

13. Ibid., pp. 2784–85. Justice Sandra Day O'Connor—with whom Chief Justice Warren Burger and Justices Powell and Rehnquist joined, concurring in the judgment—wrote: "Al-

though the Court does not acknowledge it expressly, the combination of the Court's definition of minority voting strength and its test for vote dilution results in the creation of a right to a form of proportional representation in favor of all geographically and politically cohesive minority groups that are large enough to constitute majorities if concentrated within one or more single-member districts."

14. See *Wright* v. *Rockefeller*, 376 U.S. 52, 57–58 (1964) (minority plaintiffs and black intervenors disagreed over desirability of concentrating minority voters in a few districts).

15. See *United Jewish Organization of Williamsburgh, Inc.* v. *Carey*, 430 U.S. 144 (1977). In concurring, Justice Brennan said, "An effort to achieve proportional representation, for example, might be aimed at aiding a group's participation in the political process by guaranteeing safe political offices, or, on the other hand, might be a 'contrivance to segregate' the group . . . thereby frustrating its potentially successful efforts at coalition building across racial lines" (pp. 172–73).

16. Sanford Levinson, "Gerrymandering and the Brooding Omnipresence of Proportional Representation: Why Won't It Go Away?," *UCLA Law Review* 33 (1985): 257.

17. James Madison, in B. Wright, ed., *The Federalist* (1961), no. 10, p. 135 (the more factions required for a majority, the less likely it is that the majority will have a common motive to invade the rights of other citizens).

18. See Note, "Vote Dilution," p. 1249.

19. Eric Van Loon, "Representative Government and Equal Protection," *Harvard Civil Rights–Civil Liberties Law Review* 5 (1970): 472.

20. J. S. Mill, *Representative Government* (1861), p. 373.

Chapter 4

1. Daniel Monti, *A Semblance of Justice: St. Louis School Desegregation and Order in Urban America* (1985).

2. See, for example, *Morgan* v. *Kerrigan*, 409 F. Supp. 1141, 1151 (D. Mass. 1976) (placing the South Boston High School in receivership to insure compliance with desegregation orders); *Turner* v. *Goolsby*, 255 F. Supp. 724, 730–35 (S.D. Ga. 1966).

3. See, for example, *Chambers* v. *Hendersonville City Bd. of Educ.*, 364 F.2d 189 (4th Circuit 1966); *McCurdy* v. *Bd. of Public Instruction*, 509 F.2d 540 (5th Circuit 1975); *Williams* v. *Albemarle City Bd. of Educ.*, 508 F.2d 1242 (4th Circuit 1974). But despite dozens of suits in which black teachers won reinstatement and back pay after being terminated during the desegregation process, literally thousands of black teachers and administrators lost their jobs as Southern school boards complied with desegregation orders. See amicus curiae brief prepared by the *National Educational Association for United States* v. *Georgia*, No. 30,338 (5th Circuit 1971).

4. Ray Rist, *The Invisible Children: School Integration in American Society* (1978).

5. Robert L. Carter, "A Reassessment of Brown v. Board," in D. Bell, ed., *Shades of Brown: New Perspectives on School Desegregation* (1980), pp. 21–27.

6. Ibid., p. 27.

7. See, for example, *Covington* v. *Edwards*, 264 F.2d 780 (4th Circuit 1959), *cert. denied*, 361 U.S. 840 (1959) (pupil-placement law validated and procedures established required to be followed).

8. *Kelley* v. *Board of Educ.*, 270 F.2d 209 (6th Circuit 1959), *cert. denied*, 361 U.S. 924 (1959).

9. *Green* v. *County School Bd of New Kent Co.*, 391 U.S. 430 (1968) (after several years of approving such plans, they were held not valid unless they work to effectuate a desegregated school system).

10. See, for example, A. Miller, *A "Capacity for Outrage": The Judicial Odyssey of J. Skelly Wright* (1984), pp. 48–88; J. Bass, *Civil Rights Lawyers on the Bench* (1981); J. Peltason, *Fifty Eight Lonely Men* (1961).

11. *Brown* v. *Board of Education*, 349 U.S. 294, 301 (1955).

12. See Faustine C. Jones-Wilson, *A Traditional Model of Educational Excellence: Dunbar High School of Little Rock, Arkansas* (1981); Thomas Sowell, "Black Excellence—The Case

of Dunbar High School," *Public Interest* 35 (1974): 3; Thomas Sowell, "Patterns of Black Excellence," *Public Interest* 43 (1976): 26.

13. Sara Lightfoot, *The Good High School* (1983), pp. 29–55.

14. *Johnson* v. *Chicago Board of Educ.*, 604 F.2d 504 (7th Circuit 1979).

15. See, for example, *Parent Ass'n of Andrew Jackson High School* v. *Ambach*, 598 F.2d 705 (2d Circuit 1979) (approving a limit, inspired by "white flight," on the number of black students permitted to transfer from an all-black school to neighboring, less-segregated schools).

16. Ibid., p. 720.

17. See, for example, *Milliken* v. *Bradley II*, 433 U.S. 267 (1977) (federal courts can order remedial educational programs as a part of a school-desegregation decree where such relief is in response to the constitutional violation, is designed to as nearly as possible restore victims of the discriminatory conduct to the position they would have occupied in the absence of such conduct, and takes into account the interests of state and local authorities in managing their own affairs, consistent with the Constitution).

18. *Tasby* v. *Wright*, 520 F. Supp. 683 (Northern District of Texas 1981).

19. Ibid., p. 689. The court described the intervenors as a "broad-based minority community group composed of parents, patrons and taxpayers with children in the [schools], as well as representatives from a number of civic, political and ecumenical associations in the black community" (p. 689).

20. Ibid., pp. 732–33.

21. Prince Hall, "Negroes Ask for Equal Educational Facilities" (1787), in H. Aptheker, ed., *A Documentary History of the Negro People in the United States* (1951), p. 19.

22. *Roberts* v. *City of Boston*, 59 Mass. (5 Cush.) 198 (1850) (the school committee's segregation policy was deemed reasonable; and as to plaintiff's charge that segregated schools breed racial prejudice, the court observed that feelings of prejudice by whites were rooted deep in community opinion and feelings, and would influence white actions as effectually in an integrated as in a separate school).

23. Arthur White, "The Black Leadership Class and Education in Antebellum Boston," *Journal of Negro Education* 42 (1973): 504, 513, 514.

24. For a collection of the cases, see Derrick Bell, *Race, Racism and American Law* (2d ed. 1980), pp. 368–74.

25. White, "Black Leadership Class," p. 514.

26. W. E. B. DuBois, "Does the Negro Need Separate Schools?" *Journal of Negro Education* 4 (1935): 328. The essay is reprinted in J. Lester, ed., *The Seventh Son: The Thought and Writings of W. E. B. DuBois* (1971), vol. II, p. 408.

27. Ibid., p. 335.

28. See, for example, Olsen, "Employment Discrimination Litigation: New Priorities in the Struggle for Black Equality," *Harvard Civil Rights–Civil Liberties Law Review* 6 (1970): 20, 24–25.

29. See, for example, Charles Murray, *Losing Ground* (1984). Such views have been challenged vigorously: see, for example, Bernard Anderson, "The Case for Social Policy," in National Urban League, *The State of Black America* (1986), p. 153.

30. Martin Kilson, "Whither Integration," *American Scholar* 45 (1976): 360, 372.

Chapter 5

1. William J. Wilson, *The Declining Significance of Race* (1978), p. 120.

2. Ibid., pp. 110, 152.

3. See Ralph Korngold, *Thaddeus Stevens* (1955).

4. Lerone Bennett, *Before the Mayflower* (1961), p. 189.

5. Arnold Schuchter, *Reparations* (1970), p. 244.

6. Ibid.

7. Reynold Strickland, ed., *Felix S. Cohen's Handbook of Federal Indian Law* (1982 ed.).

8. Arnold Schuchter, *Reparations* (1970), pp. 240–44. The legal arguments for and against the provision of reparations to blacks are reviewed in Boris Bittker, *The Case for Black Reparations* (1973).

9. See W. Hosokawa, *Nisei: The Quiet American* (1969), pp. 445–47.

10. *Korematsu* v. *United States*, 323 U.S. 214 (1944). See also *Hirbayashi* v. *United States*, 320 U.S. 81 (1943) (sustaining a conviction for violation of a curfew order imposed against Japanese-Americans as an exercise of the power to take steps necessary to prevent espionage and sabotage in an area threatened by Japanese attack).

11. A. Miller, *A "Capacity for Outrage": The Judicial Odyssey of J. Skelly Wright* (1984).

12. *Hohri* v. *United States*, 782 F.2d 227 (D.C. Circuit 1986), *rehearing en banc denied*, 793 F.2d 304 (1986), *cert. granted*, 107 S. Ct. 454 (1986).

13. Ibid., p. 256.

14. The incident is discussed in substantial detail in Schuchter, *Reparations*. See also, R. Lecky and H. Wright, eds., *Black Manifesto* (1969).

15. Schuchter, *Reparations*, p. 5.

16. See, for example, *Gannon* v. *Action*, 303 F. Supp. 1240 (Eastern District of Missouri 1969), *aff'd* 450 F.2d 1227 (8th Circuit 1971) (a broad injunction was issued to a Catholic church where services over several weeks were disrupted by black militants). Similar relief was granted barring similar protests in *Central Presbyterian Church* v. *Black Liberation Front*, 303 F. Supp. 894 (Eastern District of Missouri 1969).

17. See, for example, *Regents of the Univ. of California* v. *Bakke*, 438 U.S. 265 (1978). The issues are discussed in Rodney Smolla, "In Pursuit of Racial Utopias: Fair Housing, Quotas, and Goals in the 1980's," *Southern California Law Review* 58 (1985): 947.

18. *Bob Jones University* v. *United States*, 461 U.S. 574 (1983).

19. See *Green* v. *Connally*, 330 F. Supp. 1150 (District, District of Columbia 1971), *aff'd sub nom. Coit* v. *Green*, 404 U.S. 997 (1971) (barring federal-tax-exempt status unless the schools demonstrate a publicized nondiscriminatory admissions policy).

20. See *New York Times*, 8 September 1986, p. 20, and 13 September 1986, p. 26; and "Eugene Lang Makes a Long Bet on Young Learners," *Time*, 25 November 1985, p. 86.

21. Several corporations in Boston established a fund to assist graduates of Boston's public schools in obtaining a college education. See *The Boston Globe*, 10 September 1986, p. 1, and 11 September 1986, pp. 29, 32.

22. P. L. 99–514 (1986).

23. See, for example, *United States* v. *South Carolina*, 445 F. Supp. 1094 (D.S.C. 1977), *aff'd mem. sub nom. National Educ. Assn.* v. *South Carolina*, 434 U.S. 1026 (1978).

24. 78 stat. 243, 42 U.S.C. §§2000a et seg.

25. *Guinn* v. *United States*, 238 U.S. 347 (1915).

Chapter 6

1. Roberto Unger, "The Critical Legal Studies Movement," *Harvard Law Review* 96 (1983): 563, 675.

2. See "Do Colleges Set Asian Quotas?" *Newsweek*, 9 February 1987, p. 60. In the face of rising applications from Asian-American students who are proud of their high grades and test scores, critics charge that Ivy League schools are imposing unwritten quotas making it more and more difficult for Asians to get into selective schools. For example, at Yale, the "admit" rate for Asian-Americans fell from 39 percent to 17 percent in the last decade.

3. Harry Edwards, *The Revolt of the Black Athlete* (1969), pp. 21–29; Jack Olsen, "The Anguish of a Team Divided," *Sports Illustrated*, 29 July 1968, pp. 20–35; Frank Deford, "40 Christmases Later: What Began with Jackie Robinson Is Not Yet Done," *Sports Illustrated*, 22 December 1986, p. 172.

4. See, for example, David Kaplan, "Hard Times for Minority Profs," *National Law Journal*, 10 December 1984, p. 1, col. 1. The story reviews a report, written by Charles Lawrence, on minority faculty hiring sponsored by the Society of American Law Teachers (SALT). After surveying the still-minuscule percentage of minority law teachers on faculties of predominantly white schools, Professor Lawrence called on such schools to adopt "voluntary quotas" for minority hiring, because: "We are persuaded that, despite our best intentions, law school faculties will remain virtually all white unless we impose clear, unalterable obligations upon ourselves by holding designated positions open until they are

filled by high-caliber minority faculty" (p. 28). The white administrators interviewed in the story reported several reasons for their opposition to the SALT recommendation, the most frequently cited being the paucity of minorities with the necessary credentials.

For a report on the experiences of blacks in the corporate world, see Edward Jones, "Black Managers: The Dream Deferred," *Harvard Business Review* (1986): 84.

5. Compare *Griggs* v. *Duke Power Co.*, 401 U.S. 424, 431 (1973) (finding that Title VII was directed at the consequences of employment practice, rather than at the motivation of employers, and holding that "if an employment practice which operates to exclude Negroes cannot be shown to be related to job performance, the practice is prohibited"), with *Firefighters Local Union No. 1784* v. *Stotts*, 467 U.S. 561 (1984) (holding that only proven victims of discrimination are entitled to protection against being laid off, and suggesting that Title VII is intended "to provide make-whole relief only to those who have been actual victims of illegal discrimination").

6. *McDonnell Douglas Corp.* v. *Green*, 427 U.S. 273 (1976) (when plaintiff makes out a *prima facie* case, the employer must articulate a legitimate nondiscriminatory reason for the refusal to hire). Compare *Hishon* v. *King & Spaulding*, 467 U.S. 69 (1984) (a law firm partnership is a benefit of employment within the coverage of Title VII, application of which does not infringe the partners' constitutionally protected rights of expression or association).

7. See, for example, *Spurlock* v. *United Airlines*, 475 F.2d 215 (10th Circuit 1972) (upholding airline requirements of college degree and minimum of five hundred flight hours for flight officer applicants, even though minority applicants were excluded thereby, the court proposing a sliding-scale standard under which validation requirements would be relaxed in relation to the importance of the job); and *Boyd* v. *Ozark Air Lines, Inc.*, 568 F.2d 50 (8th Circuit 1977) (upholding height qualifications for pilots).

8. See Elisabeth Bartholet, "Application of Title VII to Jobs in High Places," *Harvard Law Review* 95 (1982): 947, 960-64, 978-80 (arguing that courts distinguish between selection systems primarily on the basis of social and economic status of the jobs involved, and both maintain a hands-off attitude with regard to high-status jobs and intervene freely in low-status jobs, even when poor performance in these jobs might threaten significant economic and safety interests).

9. See ibid., p. 961; see also *Zahorik* v. *Cornell Univ.*, 729 F.2d85m 94 (2d Circuit 1984) (expressing reluctance to disturb a long-standing faculty hiring process and stating that "absent evidence sufficient to support a finding that . . . forbidden considerations such as sex or race [influenced hiring or tenure decisions] universities are free to set their own required levels of academic potential and achievement and to act upon the good faith judgments of their departmental faculties or reviewing authorities"); *Powell* v. *Syracuse Univ.*, 580 F2d 1150, 1153 (2d Circuit) (characterizing the hands-off approach as an "anti-interventionist policy [that] has rendered colleges and universities virtually immune to charges of employment bias, at least when the bias is not expressed overtly," but holding that because an independent legitimate reason had been shown for termination, no violation had occurred), *cert. denied*, 439 U.S. 984 (1078).

10. Ironically, judges are more likely to defer to upper-level selection processes with which they are personally familiar than to unfamiliar processes: "They know these decisionmakers; they sympathize and identify with their concerns and their use of traditional selection methods." (Bartholet, "Application of Title VII," p. 980.)

11. See *Furnco Construction Corporation* v. *Waters*, 438 U.S. 567, 579-80 (1980). But compare cf. *Connecticut* v. *Teal*, 457 U.S. 440, 442 (1982) (rejecting an employer's argument that promotion practices with an adverse impact on minority applicants should nevertheless be insulated from the Title VII review if the "bottom line" of the practices resulted in an appropriate racial balance). In *Teal*, the employer in effect sought to conform Title VII with the administrative rule of thumb used by the Equal Employment Opportunity Commission to separate worthy from unworthy cases for agency action. Some civil rights lawyers favor acceptance of the "bottom line" compromise (see Alfred Blumrosen, "Employment Opportunity after a Reagan Victory in 1984," *Suffolk University Law Review* 18 [1984]: 581, 586-87; others oppose it (see Linda Greene, "Equal Employment Opportunity Law Twenty Years after the Civil Rights Act of 1964: Prospects for the Realization of Equality in Employment," *Suffolk University Law Review* 18 [1984]: 593, 595-97).

12. *Otero* v. *New York City Housing Authority*, 484 F.2d 1122, 1140 (2d Circuit 1973)

(holding that a housing authority can limit the influx of nonwhites into a public housing community that is racially balanced in order to prevent the community from becoming predominately nonwhite); specifically, "the Authority is obligated to take affirmative steps to promote racial integration even though this may in some instance not operate to the immediate advantage of some nonwhite persons" [p. 1125]).

The *Otero* case was cited with approval in *Parent Ass'n of Andrew Jackson High School* v. *Ambach*, 598 F.2d 705 (2d Circuit 1979), where the court of appeal reversed a district court order striking down a "white flight"–inspired limit on the number of black students permitted to transfer from all-black schools to neighboring less-segregated schools. The court wrote: "Although white fears about the admission of minority students are ugly, those fears cannot be disregarded without imperiling integration across the entire system. . . . The exodus of white children from the public schools would disadvantage the *entire* minority community and nullify this voluntary desegregation effort" (p. 720).

See also *Stipulation of Settlement and Consent Decree, Arthur* v. *Starrett City Assocs.*, 79 Civ. 3096 (ERN), (Eastern District of New York 2 April 1985), where minority apartment seekers challenged the defendant's quota policies limiting to 36 percent minority occupancy of a 5,881-unit, 46-building rental project; the settlement agreement calls for defendants to provide an additional 175 apartments for minorities over five years. The Justice Department, unhappy with the settlement, challenged the racial-quota system: see *United States* v. *Starrett City Assoc.*, 605 F. Supp. 262 (E.D.N.Y. 1985) (denying defendant's motion to dismiss on grounds of judicial estoppel).

13. For explanation and examinations of the "tipping point" phenomenon, see Anthony Downs, *Opening Up the Suburbs* (1973), pp. 68–73; Bruce Ackerman, "Integration for Subsidized Housing and the Question of Racial Occupancy Controls," *Stanford Law Review* 26 (1974): 245, 251–66; and Note, "Tipping the Scales of Justice: A Race-Conscious Remedy for Neighborhood Transition," *Yale Law Journal* 90 (1980): 377, 379–82.

14. Boris Bittker, "The Case of the Checker-Board Ordinance: An Experiment in Race Relations," *Yale Law Journal* 71 (1962): 1387.

15. See *Shelley* v. *Kraemer*, 334 U.S. 1 (1948) (finding unlawful "state action" in privately made, racially restrictive land covenants); *Buchanan* v. *Warley*, 245 U.S. 60 (1917) (voiding a residential segregation ordinance).

16. Bittker, "Checker-Board Ordinance," p. 1394.

17. See ibid., pp. 1412–13. For appraisals of Bittker's article and extended discussions of remedial plans with "benign" discrimination characteristics, see Rodney Smolla, "In Pursuit of Racial Utopias: Fair Housing, Quotas, and Goals in the 1980's," *Southern California Law Review* 58 (1985): 947; Mark Tushnet, "The Utopian Technician," *Yale Law Journal* 93 (1983): 208.

18. Herbert Wechsler, "Toward Neutral Principles of Law," *Harvard Law Review* 73 (1959): 1.

19. Derrick Bell, "Bakke, Minority Admissions and the Usual Price of Racial Remedies," *California Law Review* 67 (1979): 3, 8.

20. Ibid., p. 17.

21. *Leiberman* v. *Gant*, 630 F.2d 60, 67 (2d Circuit 1980).

22. See *Regents of the Univ. of California* v. *Bakke*, 438 U.S. 265, 311–12 (1978).

23. Ibid., p. 314.

24. In 1751, Benjamin Franklin complained that the proportion of the world's "purely white People" was too small, and expressed the wish that "their Numbers were increased." By clearing America of woods, Franklin hoped to "reflect a brighter Light to the Eyes of Inhabitants in Mars or Venus," and questioned "why should we in the Sight of Superior Beings, darken its People? why increase the Sons of Africa, by Planting them in America, where we have so fair an Opportunity, by excluding all Blacks and Tawneys, of increasing the lovely White and Red" (*Observations Concerning the Increase of Mankind* reprinted in 4 *Papers of Benjamin Franklin*, L. Labaree, ed. [1959], pp. 227, 234).

25. *Dred Scott* v. *Sandford*, 60 U.S. (19 How.) 393, 407 (1857).

26. Manning Marable, "Beyond the Race Dilemma," *Nation*, 11 April 1981, pp. 428, 431. See also Charles Lawrence, "The Id, the Ego and Equal Protection: Reckoning with Unconscious Racism," *Stanford Law Review* 39 (1987): 317, 330.

27. See Manning Marable, "Race Dilemma," p. 431.

28. Regina Austin, "Resistance Tactics for Tokens," *The Harvard Blackletter Journal* 46 (Spring 1986).

29. Letter from Richard Delgado to Linda Greene (24 April 1985) (copy on file with the author).

30. Ibid.

31. R. Niebuhr, *Moral Man and Immoral Society* (1932), pp. 252–53.

32. See Peter Bergman, *The Chronological History of the Negro in America* (1969), pp. 450, 456, 458 (reporting that twenty blacks were lynched in 1930, twelve in 1931, and six in 1932).

Chapter 7

1. John Hope Franklin, *From Slavery to Freedom* (3d ed. 1967), pp. 496–97. See also John Salmond, "The Civilian Conservation Corps and the Negro," in B. Sternsher, ed., *The Negro in Depression and War* (1969), p. 78, who reviews the administration's failure to prevent discrimination in the Civilian Conservation Corps, despite an anti-bias provision in the statute.

2. See, for example, Dan Lacy, *The White Use of Blacks in America* (1972), pp. 175–81, who describes the discriminatory treatment of blacks in the military and in civilian defense plants; Richard Dalfiume, "The 'Forgotten Years' of the Negro Revolution," in Bernard Sternsher, *The Negro in Depression and War*, pp. 298, 301, who reports that flagrant discrimination undermined blacks' morale in the war effort but "heightened [their] race consciousness and determination to fight for a better position in American society" (p. 301).

3. See, for example, *Loving v. Virginia*, 388 U.S. 1 (1967). Invalidating a state law that prohibited marriage across racial lines, the Court summarized as follows what is generally called the "strict scrutiny" standard: "Over the years, this Court has consistently repudiated 'distinctions between citizens solely because of their ancestry' as being 'odious to a free people whose institutions are founded upon the doctrine of equality,' *Hirabayashi v. United States*, 320 U.S. 81, 100 (1943). At the very least, the Equal Protection Clause demands that racial classifications, especially suspect in criminal statutes, be subjected to the 'most rigid scrutiny,' *Korematsu v. United States*, 323 U.S. 214, 216 (1944), and, if they are ever to be upheld, they must be shown to be necessary to the accomplishment of some permissible state objective, independent of the racial discrimination which it was the object of the Fourteenth Amendment to eliminate. 388 U.S. at 11."

4. *Korematsu v. United States*, 323 U.S. 214, 216 (1944).

5. Ibid., p. 235 (Justice Murphy dissenting).

6. See *Hirabayashi v. United States*, 320 U.S. 81 (1943).

7. *Korematsu v. United States*, p. 236.

8. Ibid., p. 225.

9. *Brown v. Board of Education*, 349 U.S. 294, 301 (1955) (emphasis added).

10. *Brown v. Board of Education*, 347 U.S. 483, 494 (1954).

11. See, for example, *Nixon v. Herndon*, 273 U.S. 536 (1927) (invalidating a state law barring blacks from voting in primary elections); *Buchanan v. Warley*, 245 U.S. 60 (1917) (voiding a residential segregation ordinance); *Yick Wo v. Hopkins*, 118 U.S. 356 (1886) (striking down a facially neutral ordinance that was administered to bar only Chinese-run laundries); *Strauder v. West Virginia*, 100 U.S. 303 (1880) (invalidating a statute limiting jury service to white males).

12. See, for example, *Plessy v. Ferguson*, 163 U.S. 537 (1896) (upholding a state statute requiring segregated railway coaches); *Cumming v. Richmond County Bd. of Educ.*, 175 U.S. 528 (1899) (upholding the closing of the only black high school by a county continuing to maintain a high school for whites); *Berea College v. Kentucky*, 211 U.S. 45 (1908) (upholding a state statute imposing a heavy fine on a private college admitting both white and black students).

13. See *Brown v. Board of Education* (1954), p. 495.

14. *Loving v. Virginia*, 388 U.S. 1 (1967); see also *McLaughlin v. Florida*, 379 U.S. 1984

(1964) (invalidating a state statute providing higher penalties for interracial cohabitation than for the same offense committed by couples of the same race).

15. See *Jackson* v. *State*, 37 Ala. App. 519, 72 So. 2d 114, cert. denied, 348 U.S. 888 (1954).

16. In *Naim* v. *Naim*, 197 Va. 80, 87 S.E. 2d 749, remanded, 350 U.S. 891 (1955), *aff'd*, 197 Va. 734, 90 S.E. 2d 819, *appeal dismissed*, 350 U.S. 985 (1956), the Supreme Court remanded the case after oral argument for development of the record regarding the parties' domicile. After the state court refused to comply with the mandate, claiming that no state procedure existed for reopening the case, the Supreme Court dismissed the appeal, finding that the state court ruling left the case devoid of substantial federal question. Professor Wechsler remarked that this dismissal was "wholly without basis in law" (Herbert Wechsler, foreword, "Toward Neutral Principles of Constitutional Law," *Harvard Law Review* 73 (1954): 1, 34.

17. Gerald Gunther, *Constitutional Law* (1985), 1596.

18. See, for example, *Anderson* v. *Martin*, 375 U.S. 399 (1964) (voiding statute requiring candidate's race to be listed on nomination papers and ballot); *Hunter* v. *Erickson*, 393 U.S. 385 (1969) (voiding amendment to city charter requiring prior referendum approval of any fair housing law); *Palmore* v. *Sidoti*, 466 U.S. 429 (voiding state court divestiture of white mother's custody of infant child after the mother married a black man).

19. Often referred to as the "*Lochner* era," the period stretched from the decision in *Lochner* v. *New York*, 198 U.S. 45 (1905), to that in *West Coast Hotel Co.* v. *Parrish*, 300 U.S. 379 (1937).

20. See, for example, *Williamson* v. *Lee Optical Co.*, 348 U.S. 483 (1955).

21. See *United States* v. *Carolene Prods. Co.*, 304 U.S. 144, 152 n.4 (1938).

22. See Gerald Gunther, "The Supreme Court, 1971 Term—Foreword: In Search of Evolving Doctrine on a Changing Court: A Model for a Newer Equal Protection," *Harvard Law Review* 86 (1972): 1, 8.

23. In a prison desegregation case, however, several justices suggested a scenario in which segregation might be approved: see *Lee* v. *Washington*, 390 U.S. 333, 334 (1968) (Justices Hugo Black, John Marshall Harlan, and Potter Stewart concurring) (stating that segregation "in particularized circumstances," to maintain security during times of racial tension, would not violate the Constitution).

24. See, for example, *Washington* v. *Davis* 426 U.S. 229 (1976) (upholding a test for police-force candidates in which a higher percentage of blacks failed than whites, in the absence of proof that the test was administered with a racially discriminatory purpose); see also *Crawford* v. *Board of Educ.*, 458 U.S. 527 (1982) (upholding a California constitutional amendment that withdrew from state courts the power to order mandatory busing to achieve racial balance in schools except to remedy a federal constitutional violation, where the state court found that no discriminatory animus had motivated the voters' approval of the amendment). But compare *Washington* v. *Seattle School Dist, No. 1*, 458 U.S. 457 (1982) (invalidating by a 5 to 4 vote a state initiative requiring a judicial declaration of a constitutional duty to desegregate before any school board could assign a student to a school other than the student's nearest or next nearest school on the ground that the measure worked an unconstitutional reallocation of political power that impermissibly imposed substantial and unique burdens on racial minorities).

25. *Washington* v. *Davis* (1976), p. 242.

26. *City of Memphis* v. *Greene*, 451 U.S. 100, 123, 126–27 (1981).

27. 42 U.S.C. § 1982. (All citizens of the United States shall have the same right, in every State and Territory, as is enjoyed by white citizens thereof to inherit, purchase, lease, sell, hold, and convey real and personal property.)

28. *Palmer* v. *Thompson*, 403 U.S. 217, 224 (1971).

29. *City of Mobile* v. *Bolden*, 446 U.S. 55 (1980).

30. See *Bolden* v. *City of Mobile*, 542 F. Supp. 1050 (Southern District of Alabama 1982).

31. Compare *City of New Orleans* v. *Dukes*, 427 U.S. 297, 303 (1976) (per curiam) (stating that in economic regulation "legislatures may implement their program step by step, . . . adopting regulations that only partially ameliorate a received evil and deferring complete elimination of the evil to future regulation") (citation omitted).

32. *Plyer* v. *Doe*, 457 U.S. 202, 221 (1982) (striking down, on equal-protection grounds,

a state regulation denying education to undocumented school-age children).

33. See, for example, *San Antonio Independent School District* v. *Rodriguez*, 411 U.S. 1, 29–39 (1973).

Prologue to Part II

1. *Loving* v. *Virginia*, 388 U.S. 1 (1967) (anti-miscegenation laws barring marriages across racial lines were designed to maintain white supremacy, and invalidated as denial of equal protection of the laws).

2. Bishop Henry McNeil Turner (1834–1915), deemed the most prominent and outspoken American advocate of black emigration in the years between the Civil War and the First World War; see Edwin Redkey, *Black Exodus* (1969). Martin Delaney, newspaper publisher and radical abolitionist; see Vincent Harding, *There Is a River: The Black Struggle for Freedom in America* (1983), pp. 127–29, 149–50. Henry Bibb, an escaped slave who organized black emigration movement from Canada; see Harding, *There Is a River*, p. 168.

3. See E. Fax, *Garvey* (1972); E. Cronon, *Black Moses: The Story of Marcus Garvey and the Universal Negro Improvement Association* (1969); M. Garvey, *Philosophy and Opinions of Marcus Garvey*, ed. A. Garvey (2d ed. 1968).

4. John Hope Franklin, *From Slavery to Freedom* (3rd ed. 1969), pp. 489–93.

5. Harding, *There Is a River*, p. 189.

6. Ibid., p. 188.

7. Arna Bontemps and Jack Conroy, *Anyplace But Here* (1966), pp. 160–64.

8. Paul Robeson, *Here I Stand* (1958), p. 73.

9. *Haig* v. *Agee*, 453 U.S. 279, 299 (1981) (upholding passport denial to former CIA employee who threatened "to expose CIA officers and agents and to take the measures necessary to drive them out of the countries where they are operating").

10. Joseph Boskin, "Sambo: The National Jester in the Popular Culture," in *The Great Fear: Race in the Mind of America*, ed. Gary Nash and Richard Weiss (1970), pp. 165–85.

11. See, for example, *United States* v. *Price*, 383 U.S. 787 (1966); *United States* v. *Guest*, 383 U.S. 745 (1966).

12. See, for example, *Monell* v. *New York City Dept. of Social Services*, 436 U.S. 658 (1978); *Griffin* v. *Breckenridge*, 403 U.S. 88 (1971).

Chapter 8

1. See, for example, Paula Giddings, *When and Where I Enter* (1984), p. 149, who reports that, when there is a scarcity of women, men tend to have a protective, monogamous attitude toward them; while during a scarcity of men, protectiveness dissolves and men become reluctant to make permanent commitments. See also "How Black Women Can Deal with the Black Male Shortage," *Ebony*, May 1986, p. 29; "Too Late for Prince Charming," *Newsweek*, 2 June 1986, pp. 54, 55.

2. See, for example, Alice Walker, *The Color Purple* (1982); Gayl Jones, *Eva's Man* (1976); Ntozake Shange, *For Colored Girls Who Have Considered Suicide When the Rainbow Is Enuf* (1976); and Toni Morrison, *The Bluest Eye* (1969).

3. Alice Walker, *The Third Life of Grange Copeland* (1970), p. 207.

4. See, for example, Alpert, "The Origin of Slavery in the United States—the Maryland Precedent," *American Journal of Legal History* 14 (1970): 189.

5. E. Genovese, *Roll, Jordan, Roll: The World the Slaves Made* (1974), pp. 413–31.

6. According to B. Day, *Sexual Life Between Blacks and Whites* (1972), "In the South, . . . black women . . . were lynched, murdered, and beaten by whites as well as sexually exploited on a mass scale. And their men had no means of protecting them" (p. 122); while Angela Davis, *Women, Race and Class* (1981), has said, "One of racism's salient historical features has always been the assumption that white men—especially those who wield economic power—possess an incontestable right of access to Black women's bodies. . . .

Slavery relied as much on routine sexual abuse as it relied on the whip and the lash" (p. 175).

7. Oliver Cox, *Caste, Class, and Race* (1948), pp. 526–27.

8. Lucy Parsons, quoted in M. Marable, *How Capitalism Underdeveloped Black America* (1983), p. 69.

9. Marable, *How Capitalism*, p. 103. See also, Judith Jones, *Labor of Love, Labor of Sorrow* (1985).

10. H. Applebaum, "Miscegenation Statutes: A Constitutional and Social Problem," *Georgia Law Journal* 53 (1964): 49, 50–51.

11. Cox, *Caste, Class and Race*, p. 387.

12. Calvin Hernton, *Sex and Racism in America* (1965), pp. 32–33.

13. C. Stember, *Sexual Racism: The Emotional Barrier to an Integrated Society* (1965). Stember points out that the phenomenon is not limited to black men, and quotes Philip Roth in his 1969 novel *Portnoy's Complaint*, in which the main character discusses his fascination with gentile girls (pp. 114–18).

14. Gunnar Myrdal, *An American Dilemma*, vol. I (1964), p. 60.

15. Frantz Fanon, *The Wretched of the Earth* (1963), p. 39.

16. Cox, *Caste, Class and Race*, p. 386.

17. Ibid.

18. Figures for 1970 and 1977 from U.S. Bureau of the Census, Current Population Reports, series P–23, no. 77, *Perspectives on American Husbands and Wives*, U.S. Government Printing Office, Washington, D.C., 1978 (pp. 7–10). Figures for 1981 from U.S. Bureau of the Census, Current Population Reports, series P–20, no. 371, *Household and Family Characteristics*, March 1981, U.S. Government Printing Office, Washington, D.C., 1982 (pp. 163–64).

19. *Loving* v. *Virginia*, 388 U.S. 1 (1967).

20. Ibid., p. 7.

21. Stember, *Sexual Racism*, p. 8. See also polls indicating that resistance to interracial sex, though weakened, still exists, particularly among close relatives or family members of the people involved. One survey of these polls found that, between 1968 and 1972, the proportion of whites who disapproved of marriages between blacks and whites declined from 76 percent to 65 percent, but the proportion who would be "concerned" if one's own teen-age child dated a black dropped only from 90 percent to 83 percent. And in a 1975 survey, fully 85 percent expressed disapproval, in varying degrees of intensity, to the idea of marriage of one's daughter to someone of another race.

Chapter 9

1. Howard Thurman, "On Viewing the Coast of Africa," in A. Thurman, ed., *For the Inward Journey: The Writings of Howard Thurman* (1984), p. 199.

2. Ibid., pp. 199–200.

3. Ibid.

4. See, for example, E. Genovese, *Roll, Jordan, Roll: The World the Slaves Made* (1974); L. Higginbotham, *In the Matter of Color: Race and the American Legal Process* (1978).

5. See K. Keyes, Jr., *The Hundredth Monkey* (1982), who suggests, on the basis of animal behavior studies, that "when a certain critical number achieves an awareness, this new awareness may be communicated from mind to mind" (p. 17).

6. Kardiner and Ovesey, *The Mark of Oppression* (1962).

7. L. Harlan, *Booker T. Washington: The Making of a Black Leader, 1856–1901* (1972). Washington's life and policies are summarized in J. Franklin, *From Slavery to Freedom* (3d ed.,

8. See, for example, James McPherson, "Comparing the Two Reconstructions," *Princeton Alumni Weekly*, 26 February 1979, pp. 16, 18–19. McPherson reports that between 1860 and 1880 the proportion of blacks who were literate climbed from 10 percent to 30 percent, and of black children who attended public schools, from 2 percent to 34 percent; that by 1870, 15 percent of all southern public officials were black; and that by 1880, 20 percent of blacks owned land, whereas none had owned land in 1865.

9. See E. Cronon, *Black Moses: The Story of Marcus Garvey and the Universal Negro Improvement Association* (1955); C. E. Lincoln, *The Black Muslims in America* (1961); Paul Robeson, *Here I Stand* (1958); E. Hoyt, *Paul Robeson: The American Othello* (1967); A. Rampersad, *The Art and Imagination of W. E. B. Du Bois* (1976); D. Garrow, *The FBI and Martin Luther King, Jr.* (1981); P. Goldman, *The Death and Life of Malcolm X* (1973); *The Autobiography of Malcolm X*, A. Haley, ed. (1964).

10. Goldman, *Malcolm X*, p. 396.

11. *Being There*, 1979. Lorimar Film-Und Fernschproduktion GmbH.

12. In an early interpretation, the Supreme Court both regarded the Thirteenth Amendment as "nullifying all State laws which establish or uphold slavery" and empowered Congress "to pass all laws necessary and proper for abolishing all badges and incidents of slavery," The Civil Rights Cases, 109 U.S. 3, 19 (1883). The Court did not find that state-sanctioned racial segregation was a badge of slavery until it did so by implication in *Brown* v. *Board of Education*, 347 U.S. 483 (1954), and specifically so found in *Jones* v. *Alfred H. Mayer Co.*, 392 U.S. 409 (1968).

13. *Edwards* v. *South Carolina*, 372 U.S. 229 (1963) (arrests of black college students peacefully protesting segregation on statehouse grounds interfered with First Amendment rights). Compare *New York Times* v. *Sullivan*, 376 U.S. 254 (1964).

14. Compare *Clay* [Muhammad Ali] v. *United States*, 403 U.S. 698 (1971) (conviction based on improper denial of defendant Black Muslim's conscientious objector claim overturned).

15. Compare *NAACP* v. *Alabama*, 357 U.S. 449 (1958) (protecting civil rights group's membership lists against disclosure to state so as to avoid reprisals). See also *Bates* v. *Little Rock*, 361 U.S. 516 (1960); and *NAACP* v. *Button*, 371 U.S. 415 (1963).

16. The Court provided scant protection of free speech during the "Red scares" following the First World War: see *Schenck* v. *United States*, 249 U.S. 47 (1919) (upholding Espionage Act convictions of defendants who published and distributed antiwar leaflets).

Following the Second World War, see *Dennis* v. *United States*, 341 U.S. 494 (1951) (upholding Smith Act convictions for Communist party activities found to constitute the advocacy of unlawful action). The vague provisions of the Smith Act were read more strictly to distinguish between advocacy of unlawful action and advocacy of abstract doctrine. See *Yates* v. *United States*, 354 U.S. 298 [1957], and *Scales* v. *United States*, 367 U.S. 203 [1961].

In peacetime, when antigovernment speech is less threatening, the Court has provided greater protection of free speech: see *Brandenburg* v. *Ohio*, 395 U.S. 444 (1969) (per curiam) (reversing the conviction of a Ku Klux Klan leader, under Ohio's Criminal Syndicalism statute, for his advocacy of the use of force and illegal actions to accomplish political reform); *Bond* v. *Floyd*, 385 U.S. 116 (1966) (holding that a black state senator's advocacy of draft alternatives was protected by the First Amendment); *Herndon* v. *Lowry*, 301 U.S. 242 (1937) (reversing the conviction of a black communist for attempting to incite insurrection and uging war on racism); *Stromberg* v. *California*, 283 U.S. 359 (1931) (reversing conviction for displaying a red flag as a symbol of opposition to government).

17. See, for example, *Haig* v. *Agee*, 453 U.S. 280 (1981) (upholding revocation of passport of a former Central Intelligence Agency agent whose disclosure of information threatened the safety of CIA undercover agents); *Snepp* v. *United States*, 444 U.S. 507 (1980) (imposing a constructive trust on profits from a book about the CIA's last days in Vietnam, which was written by a former CIA agent in violation of a contract requiring prepublication approval by the CIA, even though no classified information was revealed); *United States* v. *The Progressive, Inc.*, 467 F. Supp. 990 (Western District of Wisconsin) (barring journalist from publishing details about the design of the hydrogen bomb); appeal dismissed, 610 F.2d 819 (7th Cir. 1979). These and similar cases are discussed in J. Koffler and B. Gershman, "The New Seditious Libel," *Cornell Law Review* 69 (1984): 816.

18. Compare *Edwards* v. *South Carolina*, 372 U.S. 229 (1963) (protecting right of black students to protest on statehouse grounds), with *Adderley* v. *Florida*, 385 U.S. 39 (1966) (affirming conviction of college students for protesting on jail property).

19. See, for example, *Linmark Assocs., Inc.* v. *Willingboro*, 431 U.S. 85 (1977) (invalidating ordinance banning "for sale" and "sold" signs to prevent the flight of white homeowners from a racially integrated town as a content-based restriction on speech).

20. *Gregory* v. *City of Chicago*, 394 U.S. 111, 118 (1969).

21. Ibid., pp. 117–18. See also *Carey* v. *Brown*, 447 U.S. 455, 470 (1980) (reversing on

equal-protection grounds the convictions of civil rights protesters who were arrested while picketing the mayor of Chicago's residence, but noting, "We [the Supreme Court] are not to be understood to imply . . . that residential picketing is beyond the reach of uniform and nondiscriminatory regulation"). Compare *Hudgens* v. *NLRB*, 4324 U.S. 507 (1976) (rejecting the argument that labor pickets had First Amendment rights in shopping center); *Lloyd Corp.* v. *Tanner*, 407 U.S. 551 (1972) (barring distribution of anti-Vietnam War leaflets in shopping center where protest was not aimed at activities in shopping mall and protesters had alternative means of reaching the public).

22. *Griswold* v. *Connecticut*, 381 U.S., 479 (1965) (recognizing the right of married couples to use contraceptives); and *Eisenstadt* v. *Baird*, 405 U.S. 438 (1972) (extending *Griswold's* right of privacy to unmarried individuals).

23. *Roe* v. *Wade*, 410 U.S. 113 (1973) (recognizing a woman's right to decide to have an abortion).

24. See, for example, Genovese, *Roll, Jordan, Roll*, pp. 561–63.

25. For the classic study of racism's adverse impact on the personality and functioning of blacks, see Kenneth Clark, *Dark Ghetto* (1965). For a series of essays describing the problem and suggesting approaches to treatment, see C. Willie, B. Kramer, and B. Brown, eds., *Racism and Mental Health* (1973).

26. See, for example, John Ely, "The Wages of Crying Wolf: A Comment on Roe v. Wade," *Yale Law Journal* 82 (1973): 920.

27. T. Grey, "Eros, Civilization, and the Burger Court," *Law and Contemporary Problems* 43 (1980): 83, 90.

28. *Bowers* v. *Hardwick*, 106 S. Ct. 2841 (1986) (the constitutional right of privacy does not prohibit states from proscribing private, consensual sexual conduct between homosexuals).

29. Ibid., p. 97.

30. Center on Budget and Policy Priorities, *A Report on How Blacks Have Fared Under the Reagan Policies* (1984), pp. 3–4.

31. *Beal* v. *Doe*, 432 U.S. 438 (1977); *Maher* v. *Roe*, 432 U.S. 464 (1977); *Poelker* v. *Doe*, 432 U.S. 519 (1977).

32. *Beal* v. *Doe* (1977), pp. 463–64.

33. See, for example, *Buchanan* v. *Warley*, 245 U.S. 60 (1917) (housing segregation ordinance intended to maintain public peace and keep down racial disorders violated Fourteenth Amendment).

34. *Bob Jones University* v. *United States*, 461 U.S. 574 (1983) (approving loss of tax-exempt status to private religious school that engages in racial discrimination based on religious belief). Compare *Roberts* v. *United States Jaycees*, 468 U.S. 609 (1984) (application of state "public accommodations law" to national civic organization that limited membership to males, ages eighteen and thirty-five, not an interference with members' freedom of association).

35. Compare *Cox* v. *Louisiana* (No. 49), 379 U.S. 559 (1965).

36. Compare *Cohen* v. *California*, 403 U.S. 15 (1971).

37. *Brown* v. *Board of Education*, 349 U.S. 294, 300 (1955).

Prologue to Part III

1. Joint Center for Political Studies, *Black Elected Officials* 11 (1985).

2. "Do Colleges Set Asian Quotas?" *Newsweek*, 9 February 1987, p. 60.

3. Kenneth Karst, "Why Equality Matters," *Georgia Law Review* 17 (1983): 245, 269.

4. See Arthur Waskow, *From Race Riot to Sit-In, 1919 and the 1960s* (1967), p. 203 (describing Johnson's disavowal of violent tactics in favor of tactics such as work stoppages and other peaceful protests).

Chapter 10

1. Lillian Rubin, *Quiet Rage* (1986), the story of Bernard Goetz, the white, middle-class man who in 1984 shot four black teen-agers on a New York City subway car and became, for some, a folk hero.

2. See John Hope Franklin, *From Slavery to Freedom* (3d ed. 1969), pp. 199–201. "Once the planters were convinced that conversion did not have the effect of setting their slaves free, they sought to use the church as an agency for maintaining the institution of slavery" (p. 200).

3. Tom Watson, "The Negro Question in the South," in *Black Power: The Politics of Liberation in America*, ed. Stokely Carmichael and Charles Hamilton (1967).

4. R. Unger, "The Critical Legal Studies Movement," *Harvard Law Review* 96 (1983): 563.

INDEX

305.896

10/212